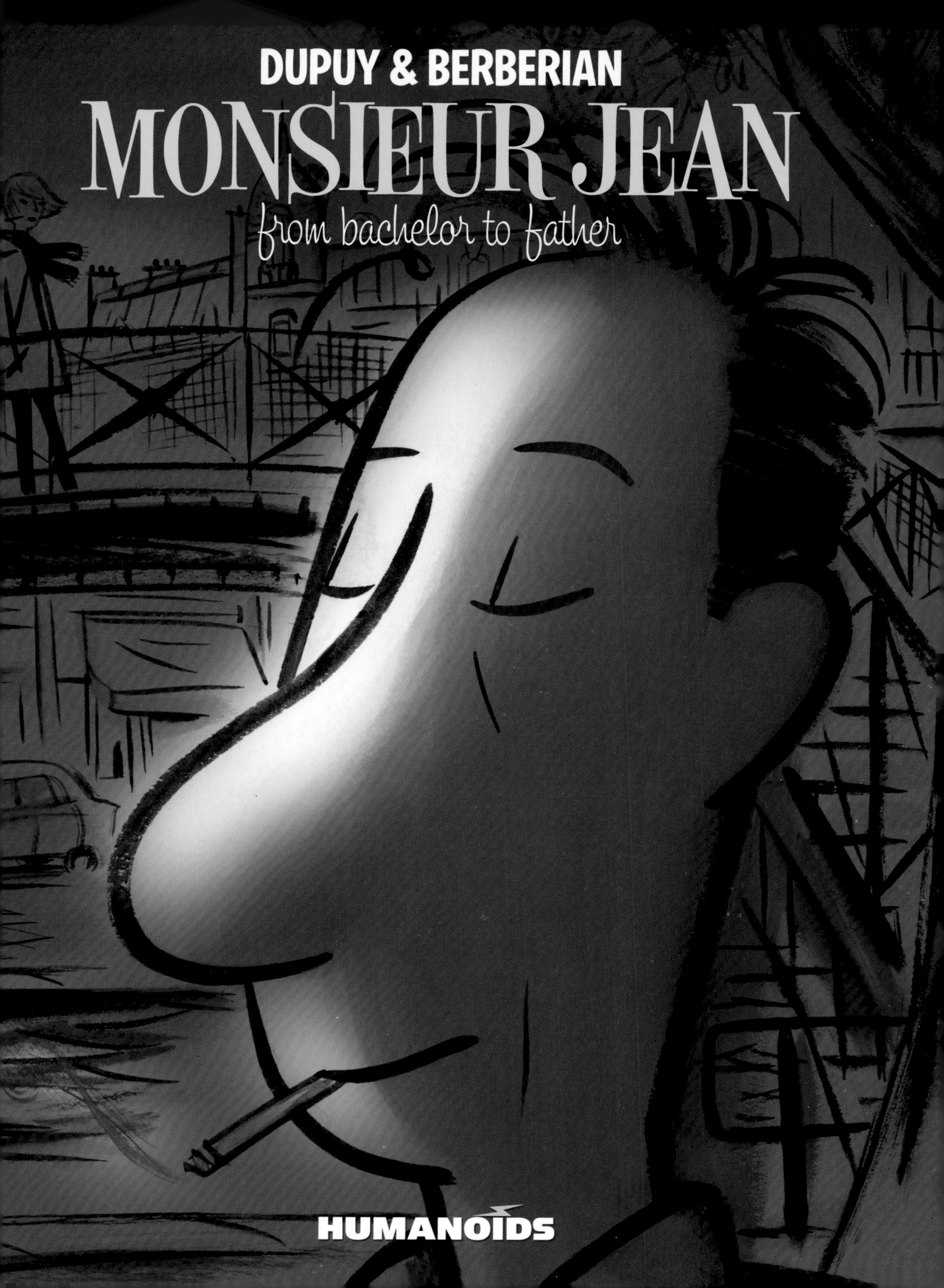
DUPUY & BERBERIAN
MONSIEUR JEAN
from bachelor to father
HUMANOIDS

PHILIPPE DUPUY & CHARLES BERBERIAN
TEXT AND ART

CLAUDE LEGRIS, DUPUY & BERBERIAN **(PAGES 7 TO 50);**
CLAUDE LEGRIS **(PAGES 53 TO 97);**
DUPUY & BERBERIAN, CLAUDE LEGRIS
AND ISABELLE BUSSCHAERT **(PAGES 101 TO 146);**
ISABELLE BUSSCHAERT **(PAGES 149 TO 202 AND 205 TO 258)**
COLORISTS

HELGE DASCHER
TRANSLATOR

ALEX DONOGHUE, U.S. EDITION EDITOR - JERRY FRISSEN, BOOK DESIGNER - FABRICE GIGER, PUBLISHER

RIGHTS & LICENSING - LICENSING@HUMANOIDS.COM
PRESS AND SOCIAL MEDIA - PR@HUMANOIDS.COM

Page 218, Felix's monologue is an excerpt from the sketch "Heureux"
by French stand-up comic star Fernand Raynaud, translated from the French.

MONSIEUR JEAN: FROM BACHELOR TO FATHER.
This title is a publication of Humanoids, Inc. 8033 Sunset Blvd. #628, Los Angeles, CA 90046.
Copyright © 2014 Humanoids, Inc., Los Angeles (USA).
All rights reserved. Humanoids and its logos are ® and ©2014 Humanoids, Inc.

MONSIEUR JEAN

LOVE AND THE CONCIERGE

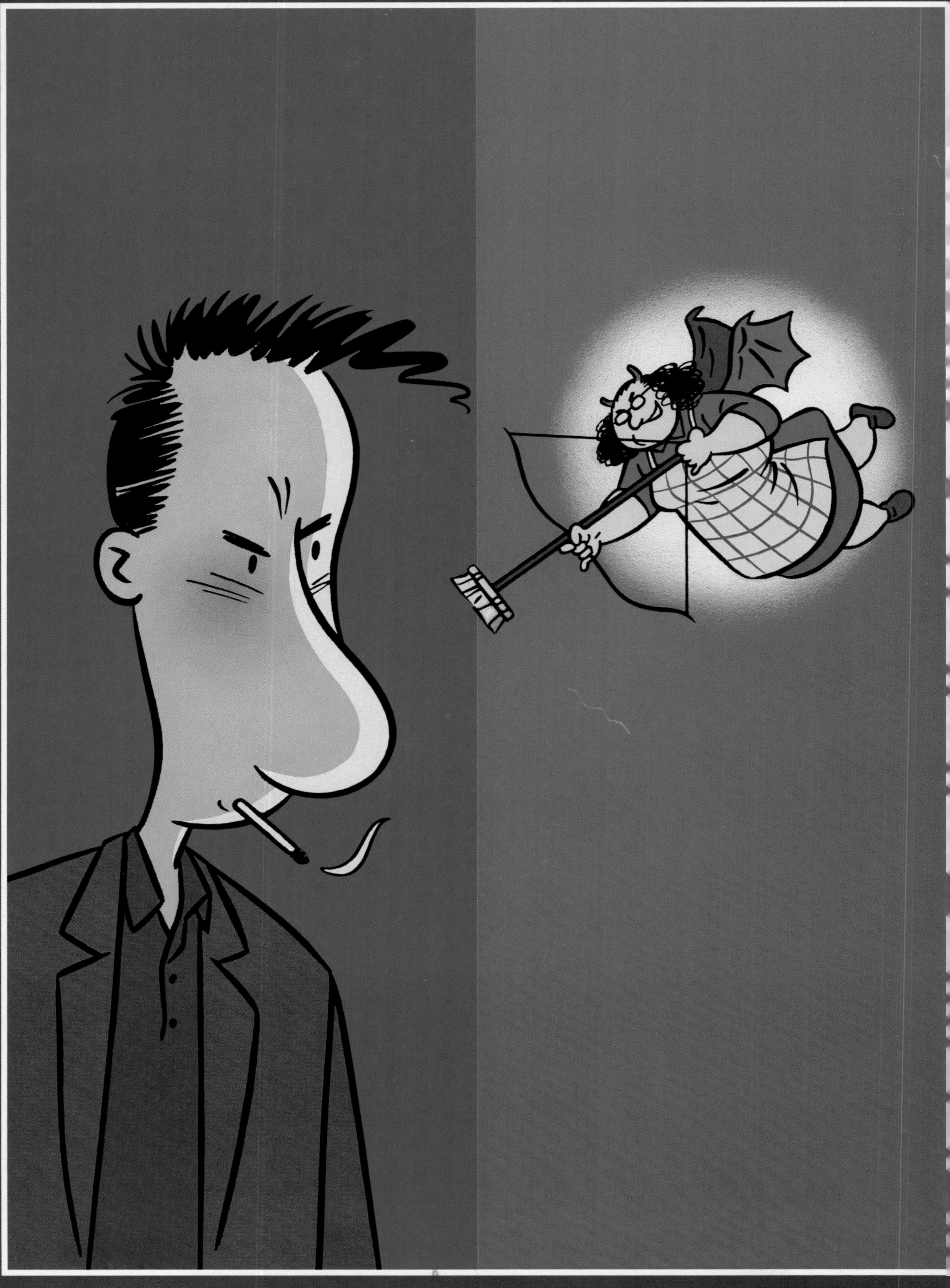

Love and the Concierge

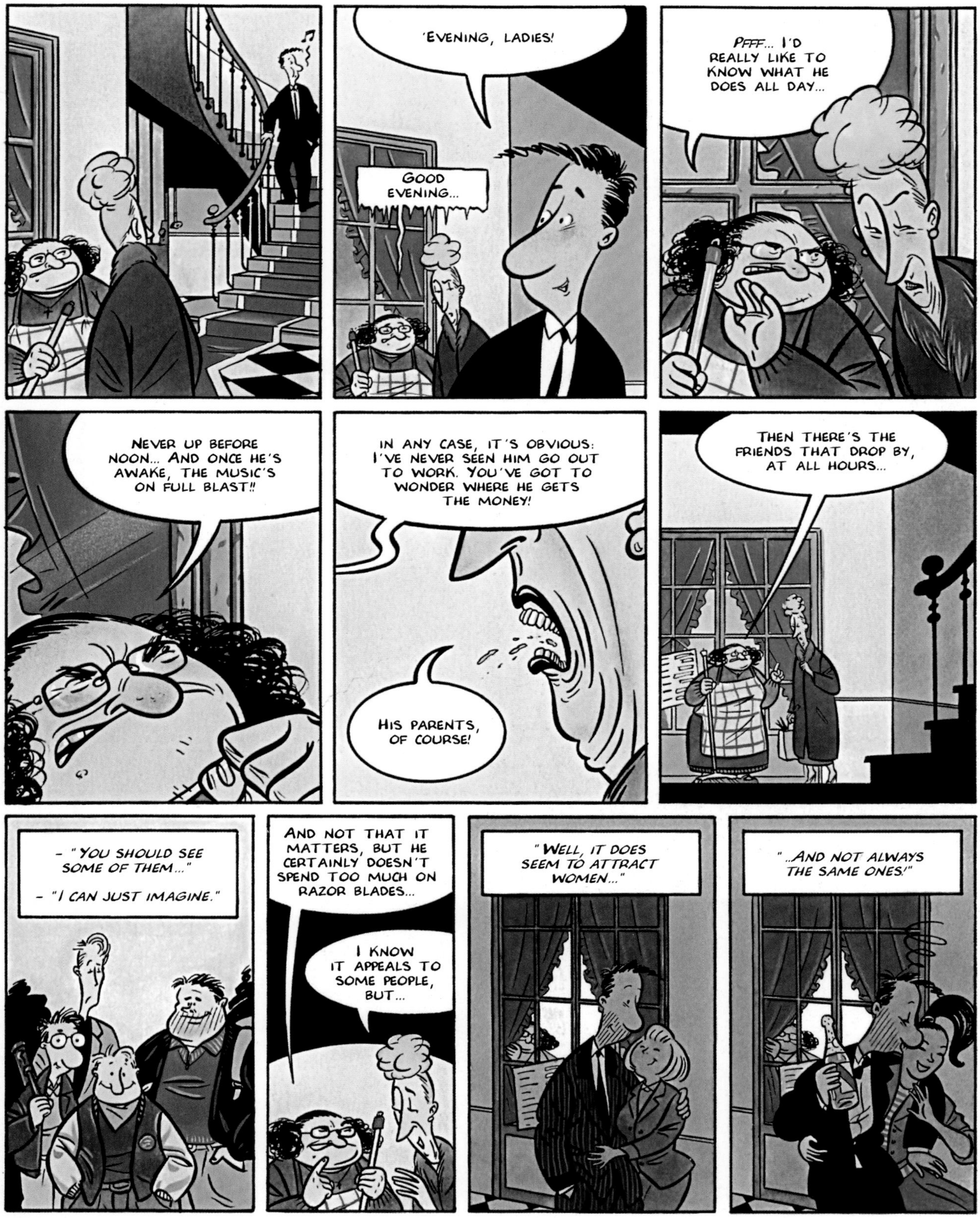
'Evening, ladies!
Good evening...
Pfff... I'd really like to know what he does all day...
Never up before noon... And once he's awake, the music's on full blast!!
In any case, it's obvious: I've never seen him go out to work. You've got to wonder where he gets the money!
His parents, of course!
Then there's the friends that drop by, at all hours...
- "You should see some of them..."
- "I can just imagine."
And not that it matters, but he certainly doesn't spend too much on razor blades...
I know it appeals to some people, but...
"Well, it does seem to attract women..."
"...And not always the same ones!"

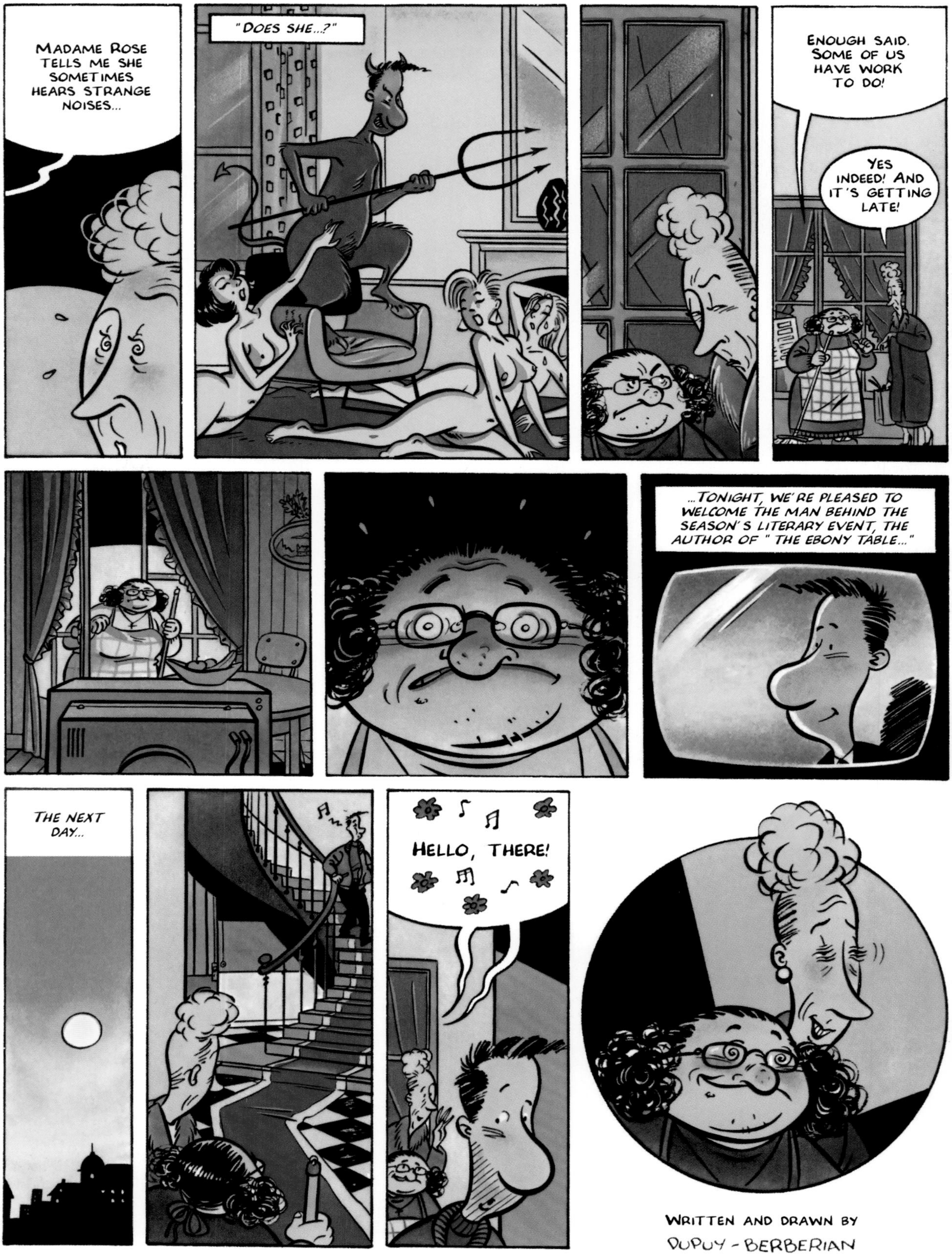

MADAME ROSE TELLS ME SHE SOMETIMES HEARS STRANGE NOISES...
"DOES SHE...?"
ENOUGH SAID. SOME OF US HAVE WORK TO DO!
YES INDEED! AND IT'S GETTING LATE!
...TONIGHT, WE'RE PLEASED TO WELCOME THE MAN BEHIND THE SEASON'S LITERARY EVENT, THE AUTHOR OF "THE EBONY TABLE..."
THE NEXT DAY...
HELLO, THERE!
WRITTEN AND DRAWN BY
DUPUY - BERBERIAN

CHANTAL

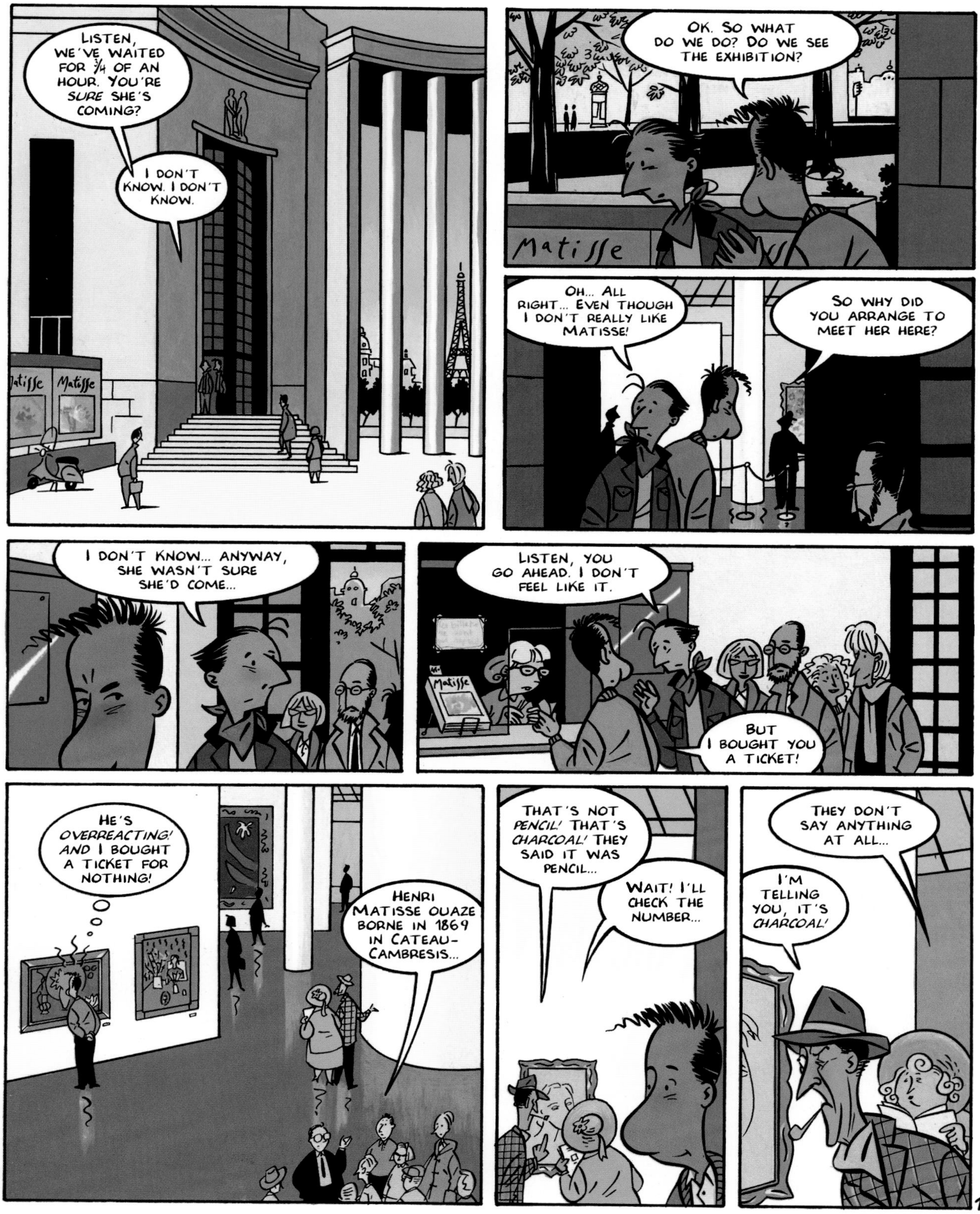
LISTEN, WE'VE WAITED FOR 3/4 OF AN HOUR. YOU'RE *SURE* SHE'S COMING?
I DON'T KNOW. I DON'T KNOW.
OK. SO WHAT DO WE DO? DO WE SEE THE EXHIBITION?
Matisse
OH... ALL RIGHT... EVEN THOUGH I DON'T REALLY LIKE MATISSE!
SO WHY DID YOU ARRANGE TO MEET HER HERE?
I DON'T KNOW... ANYWAY, SHE WASN'T SURE SHE'D COME...
LISTEN, YOU GO AHEAD. I DON'T FEEL LIKE IT.
Matisse
BUT I BOUGHT YOU A TICKET!
HE'S *OVERREACTING!* AND I BOUGHT A TICKET FOR NOTHING!
HENRI MATISSE OUAZE BORNE IN 1869 IN CATEAU-CAMBRESIS...
THAT'S NOT *PENCIL!* THAT'S *CHARCOAL!* THEY SAID IT WAS PENCIL...
WAIT! I'LL CHECK THE NUMBER...
THEY DON'T SAY ANYTHING AT ALL...
I'M TELLING YOU, IT'S *CHARCOAL!*

1

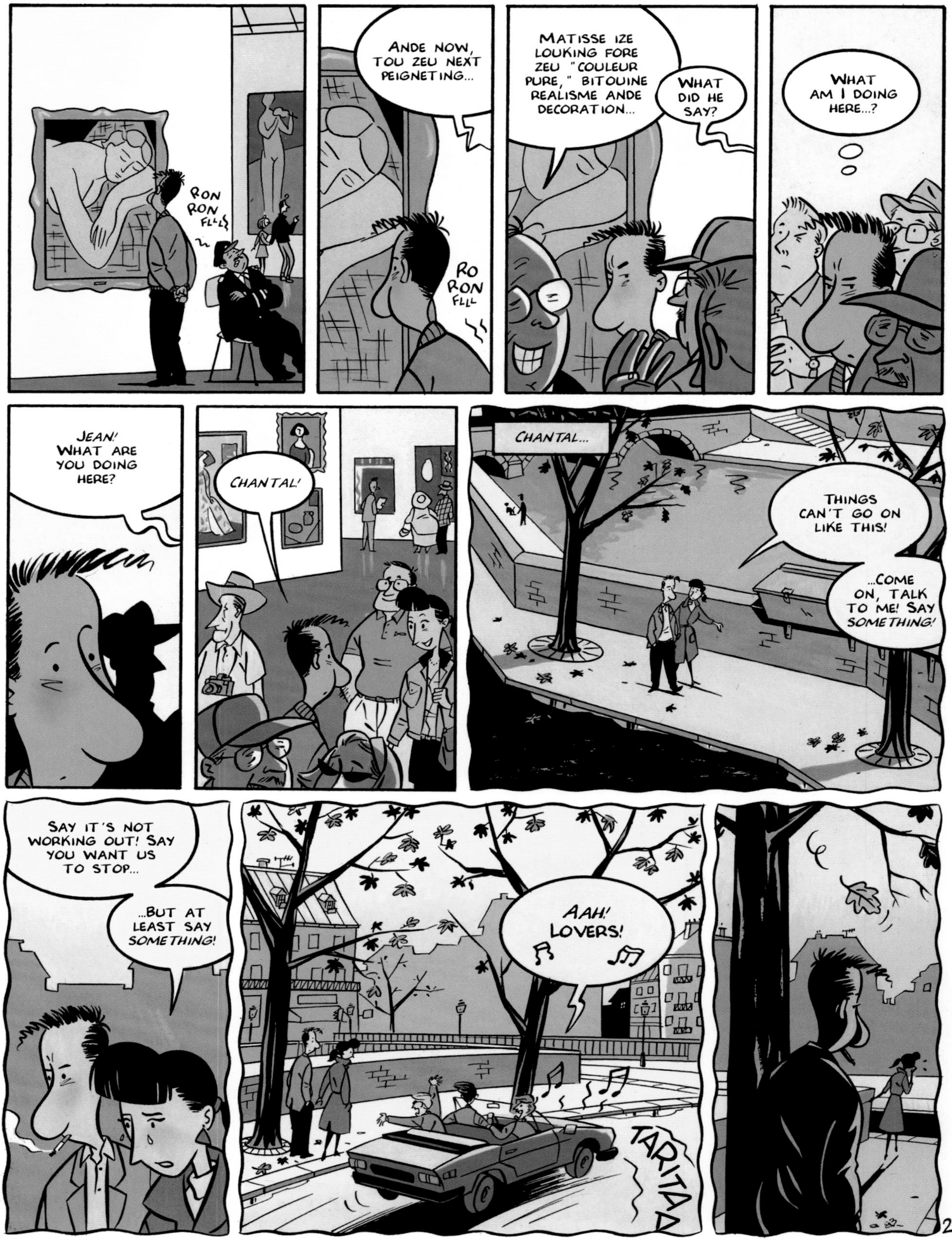
RON RON FLLL
ANDE NOW, TOU ZEU NEXT PEIGNETING...
RO RON FLLL
MATISSE IZE LOUKING FORE ZEU "COULEUR PURE," BITOUINE REALISME ANDE DECORATION...
WHAT DID HE SAY?
WHAT AM I DOING HERE...?
JEAN! WHAT ARE YOU DOING HERE?
CHANTAL!
CHANTAL...
THINGS CAN'T GO ON LIKE THIS!
...COME ON, TALK TO ME! SAY SOMETHING!
SAY IT'S NOT WORKING OUT! SAY YOU WANT US TO STOP...
...BUT AT LEAST SAY SOMETHING!
AAH! LOVERS!
TARITA
2

JEAN, THIS IS MICHEL...

MICHEL... JEAN.

DELIGHTED!

NO. 124: PEN AND INK!

YES IT IS!

DO YOU THINK WE'LL EVER FALL OUT OF LOVE?

I CAN'T PICTURE MYSELF WITH SOMEBODY ELSE. IN ANY CASE, HE WOULD HAVE TO BE DIFFERENT. I WOULD CHOOSE SOMEONE TALL, BLOND, WITH BLUE EYES.

WHAT DO YOU THINK?

COME ON, ANSWER ME! WHY DON'T YOU EVER TALK TO ME?

ARE YOU SLEEPING?

DO YOU LOVE ME?

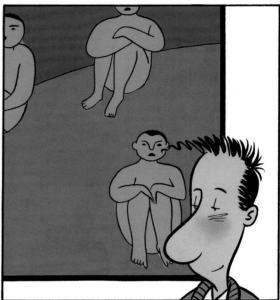

I FEEL TIRED. I'M GOING TO SIT DOWN FOR A MOMENT...

OF COURSE, MY LOVE! YOU REALLY SHOULDN'T OVERDO THINGS!

THERE YOU GO! YOU'LL BE FINE HERE...

I'LL LEAVE YOU TWO ALONE. YOU MUST HAVE A LOT TO TALK ABOUT.

SEE YOU LATER!

3

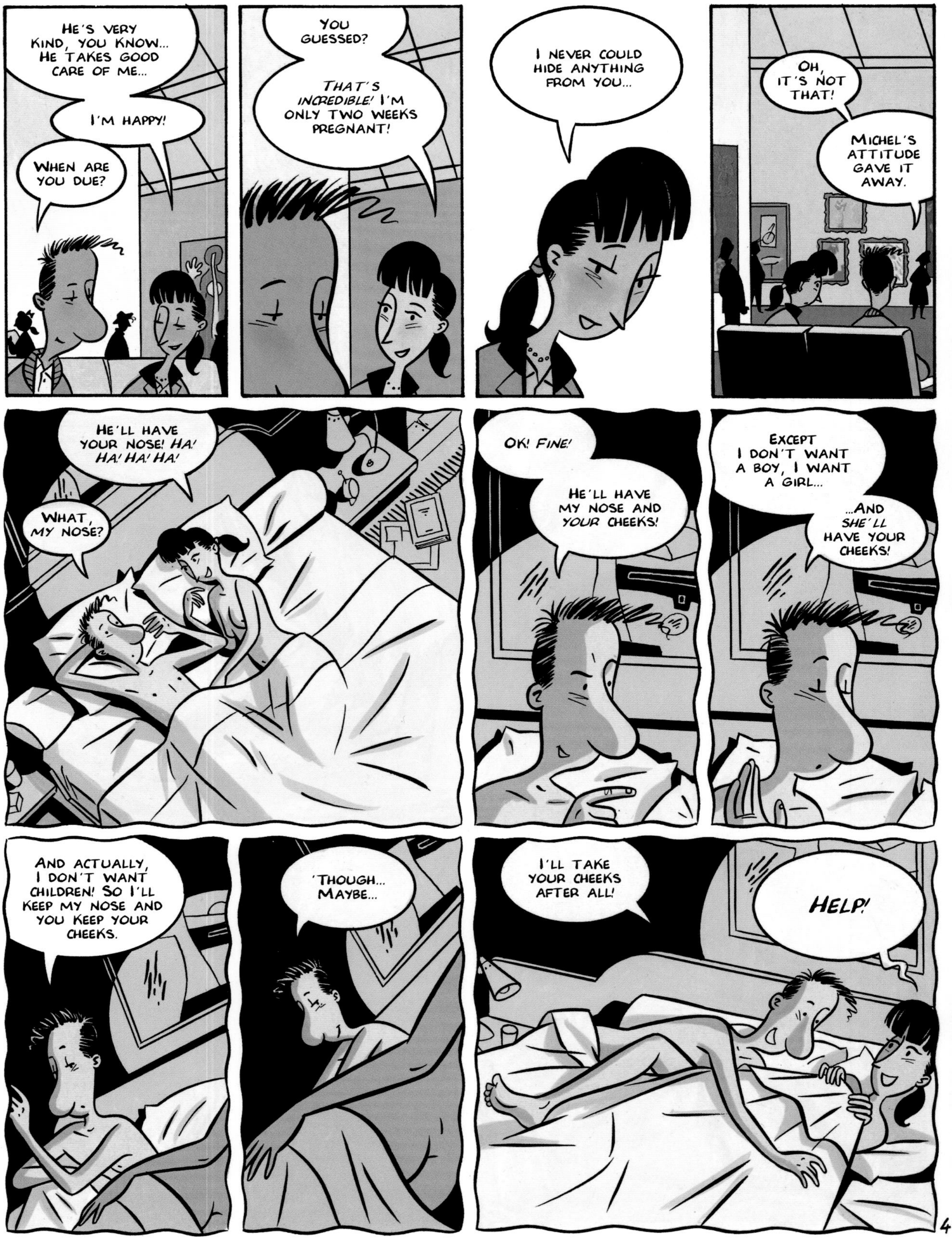
HE'S VERY KIND, YOU KNOW... HE TAKES GOOD CARE OF ME...
I'M HAPPY!
WHEN ARE YOU DUE?
YOU GUESSED?
THAT'S INCREDIBLE! I'M ONLY TWO WEEKS PREGNANT!
I NEVER COULD HIDE ANYTHING FROM YOU...
OH, IT'S NOT THAT!
MICHEL'S ATTITUDE GAVE IT AWAY.
HE'LL HAVE YOUR NOSE! HA! HA! HA! HA!
WHAT, MY NOSE?
OK! FINE!
HE'LL HAVE MY NOSE AND YOUR CHEEKS!
EXCEPT I DON'T WANT A BOY, I WANT A GIRL...
...AND SHE'LL HAVE YOUR CHEEKS!
AND ACTUALLY, I DON'T WANT CHILDREN! SO I'LL KEEP MY NOSE AND YOU KEEP YOUR CHEEKS.
'THOUGH... MAYBE...
I'LL TAKE YOUR CHEEKS AFTER ALL!
HELP!
4

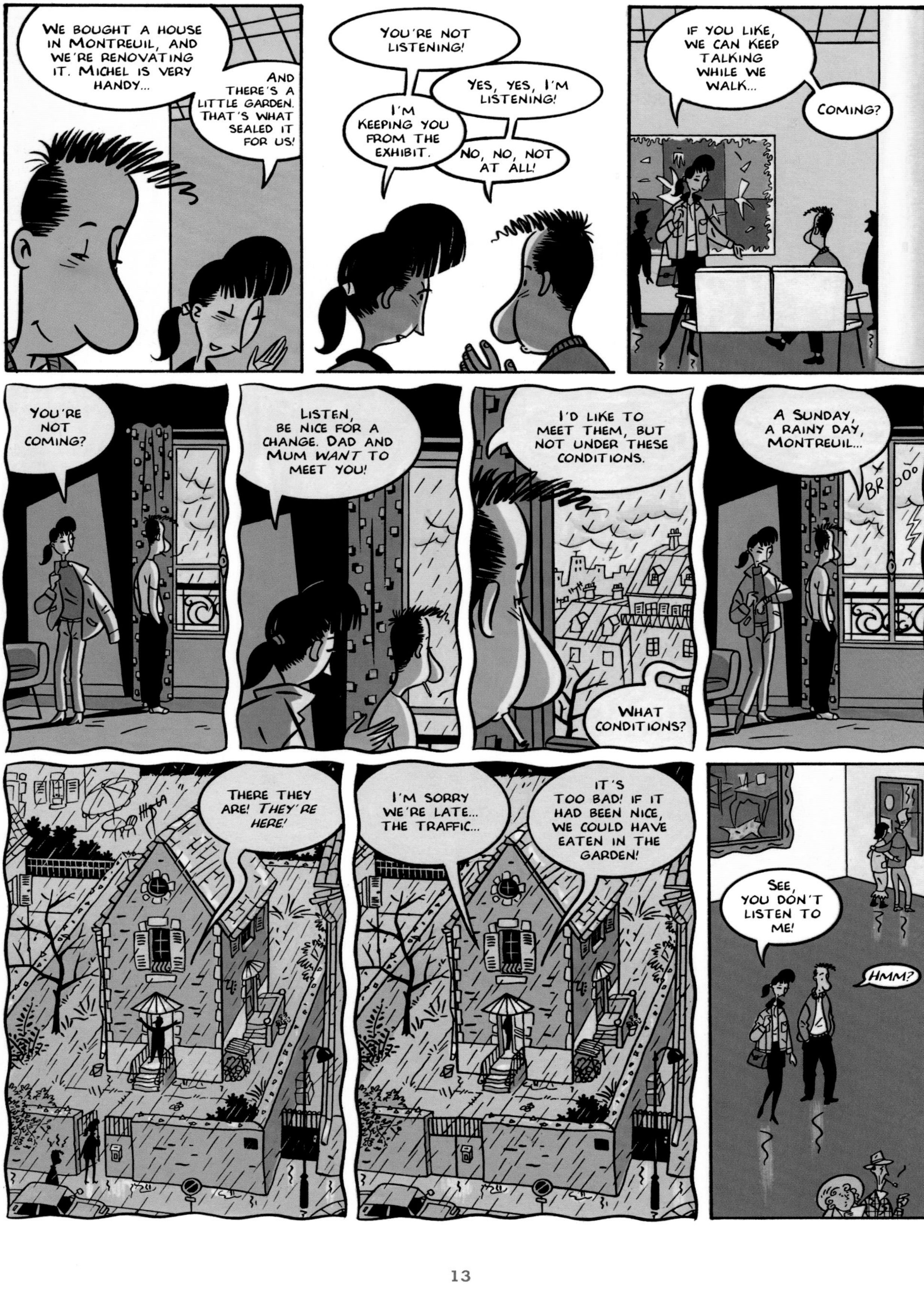
We bought a house in Montreuil, and we're renovating it. Michel is very handy...
And there's a little garden. That's what sealed it for us!
You're not listening!
Yes, yes, I'm listening!
I'm keeping you from the exhibit.
No, no, not at all!
If you like, we can keep talking while we walk...
Coming?
You're not coming?
Listen, be nice for a change. Dad and Mum *want* to meet you!
I'd like to meet them, but not under these conditions.
What conditions?
A Sunday, a rainy day, Montreuil...
BRooo
There they are! *They're here!*
I'm sorry we're late... the traffic...
It's too bad! If it had been nice, we could have eaten in the garden!
See, you don't listen to me!
Hmm?

5

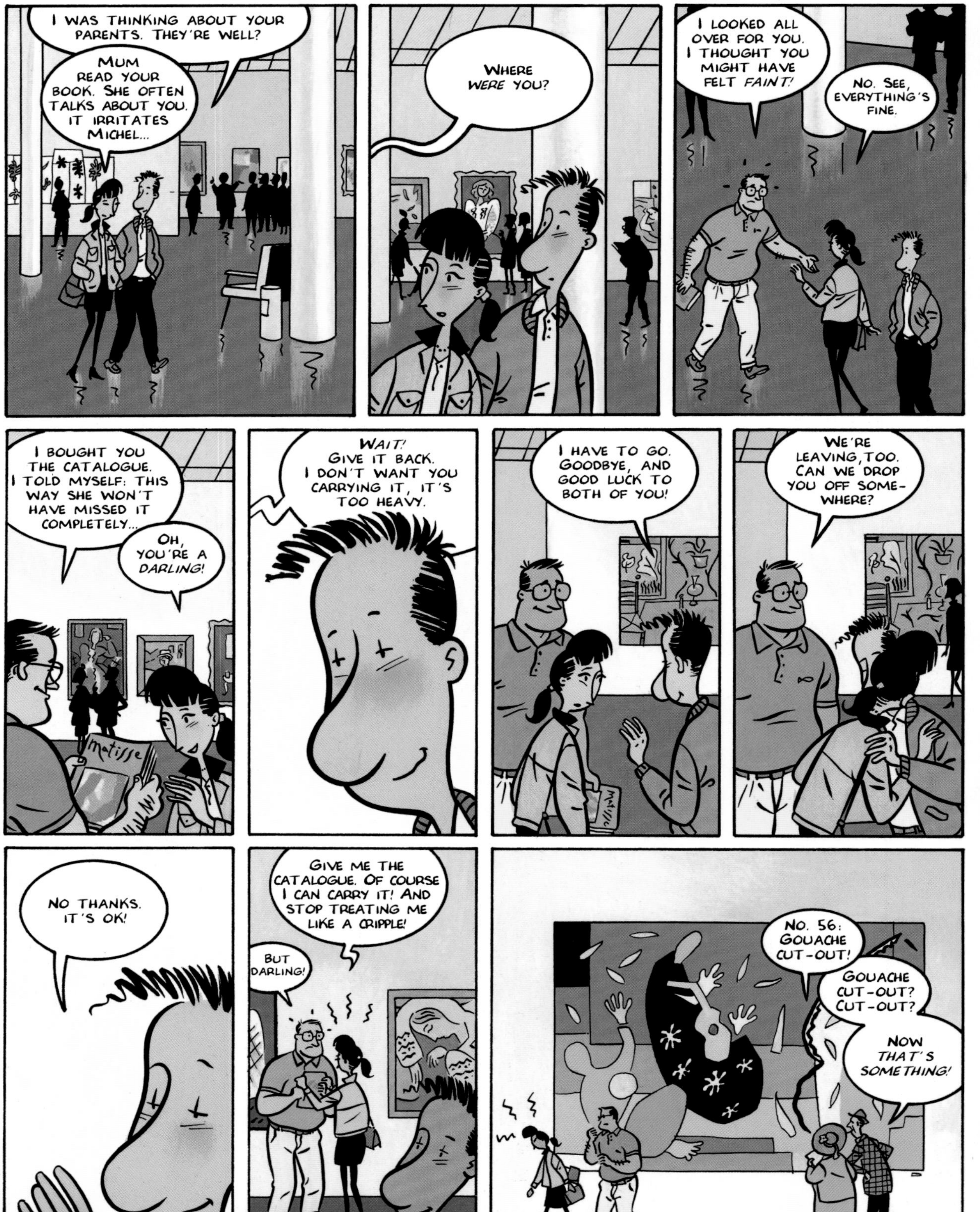

I WAS THINKING ABOUT YOUR PARENTS. THEY'RE WELL?
MUM READ YOUR BOOK. SHE OFTEN TALKS ABOUT YOU. IT IRRITATES MICHEL...
WHERE WERE YOU?
I LOOKED ALL OVER FOR YOU. I THOUGHT YOU MIGHT HAVE FELT *FAINT!*
NO. SEE, EVERYTHING'S FINE.
I BOUGHT YOU THE CATALOGUE. I TOLD MYSELF: THIS WAY SHE WON'T HAVE MISSED IT COMPLETELY...
OH, YOU'RE A *DARLING!*
matisse
WAIT! GIVE IT BACK. I DON'T WANT YOU CARRYING IT, IT'S TOO HEAVY.
I HAVE TO GO. GOODBYE, AND GOOD LUCK TO BOTH OF YOU!
WE'RE LEAVING, TOO. CAN WE DROP YOU OFF SOMEWHERE?
NO THANKS. IT'S OK!
GIVE ME THE CATALOGUE. OF COURSE I CAN CARRY IT! AND STOP TREATING ME LIKE A CRIPPLE!
BUT DARLING!
NO. 56: GOUACHE CUT-OUT!
GOUACHE CUT-OUT? CUT-OUT?
NOW *THAT'S* SOMETHING!
6

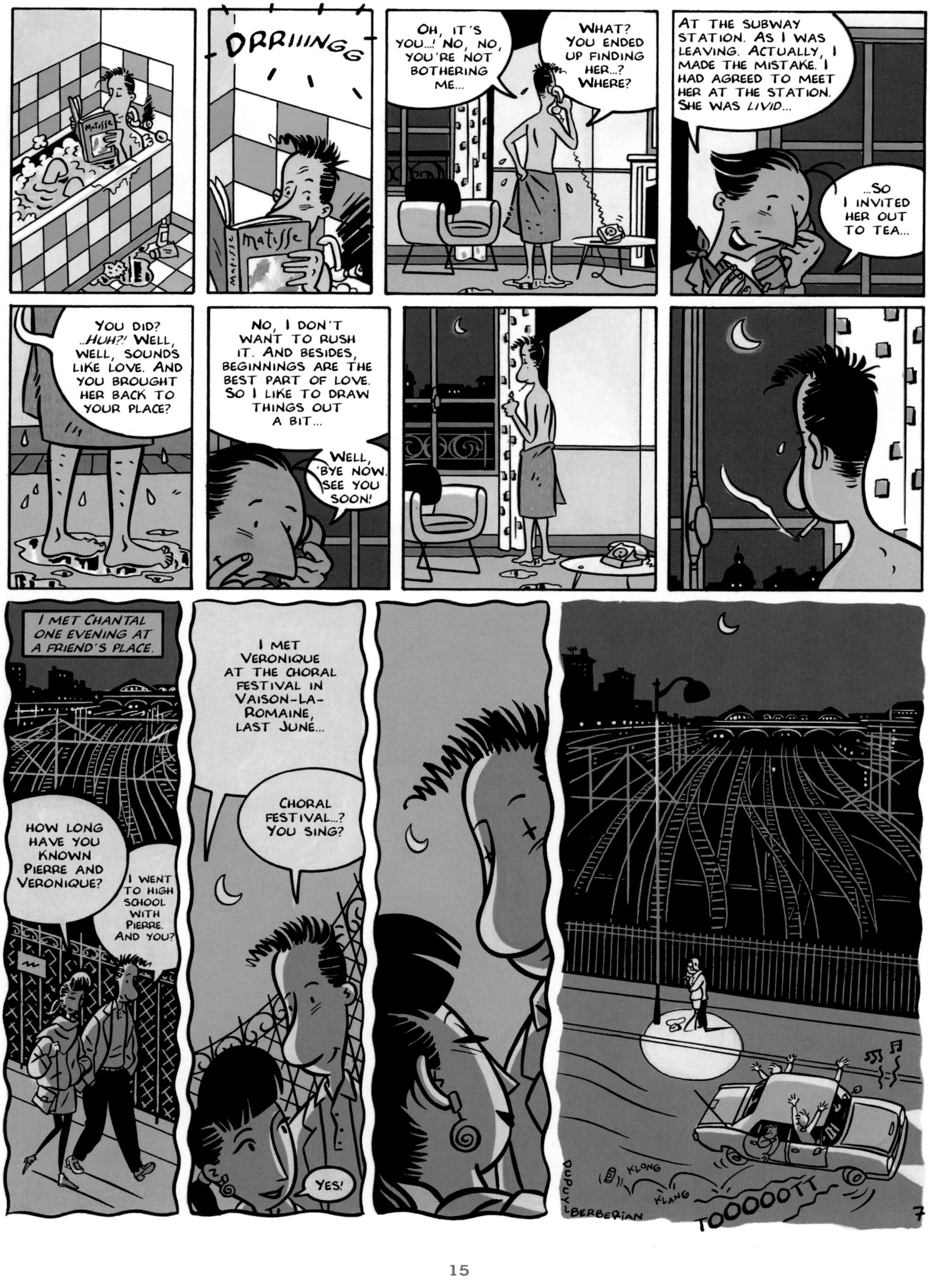

DRRIIINGG
OH, IT'S YOU...! NO, NO, YOU'RE NOT BOTHERING ME...
WHAT? YOU ENDED UP FINDING HER...? WHERE?
AT THE SUBWAY STATION. AS I WAS LEAVING. ACTUALLY, I MADE THE MISTAKE. I HAD AGREED TO MEET HER AT THE STATION. SHE WAS *LIVID*...
...SO I INVITED HER OUT TO TEA...
YOU DID? ..*HUH?!* WELL, WELL, SOUNDS LIKE LOVE. AND YOU BROUGHT HER BACK TO YOUR PLACE?
NO, I DON'T WANT TO RUSH IT. AND BESIDES, BEGINNINGS ARE THE BEST PART OF LOVE. SO I LIKE TO DRAW THINGS OUT A BIT...
WELL, 'BYE NOW. SEE YOU SOON!
I MET CHANTAL ONE EVENING AT A FRIEND'S PLACE.
HOW LONG HAVE YOU KNOWN PIERRE AND VERONIQUE?
I WENT TO HIGH SCHOOL WITH PIERRE. AND YOU?
I MET VERONIQUE AT THE CHORAL FESTIVAL IN VAISON-LA-ROMAINE, LAST JUNE...
CHORAL FESTIVAL...? YOU SING?
YES!
KLONG
KLANG
TOOOOOTT
DUPUY BERBERIAN
7

A NICE SURPRISE

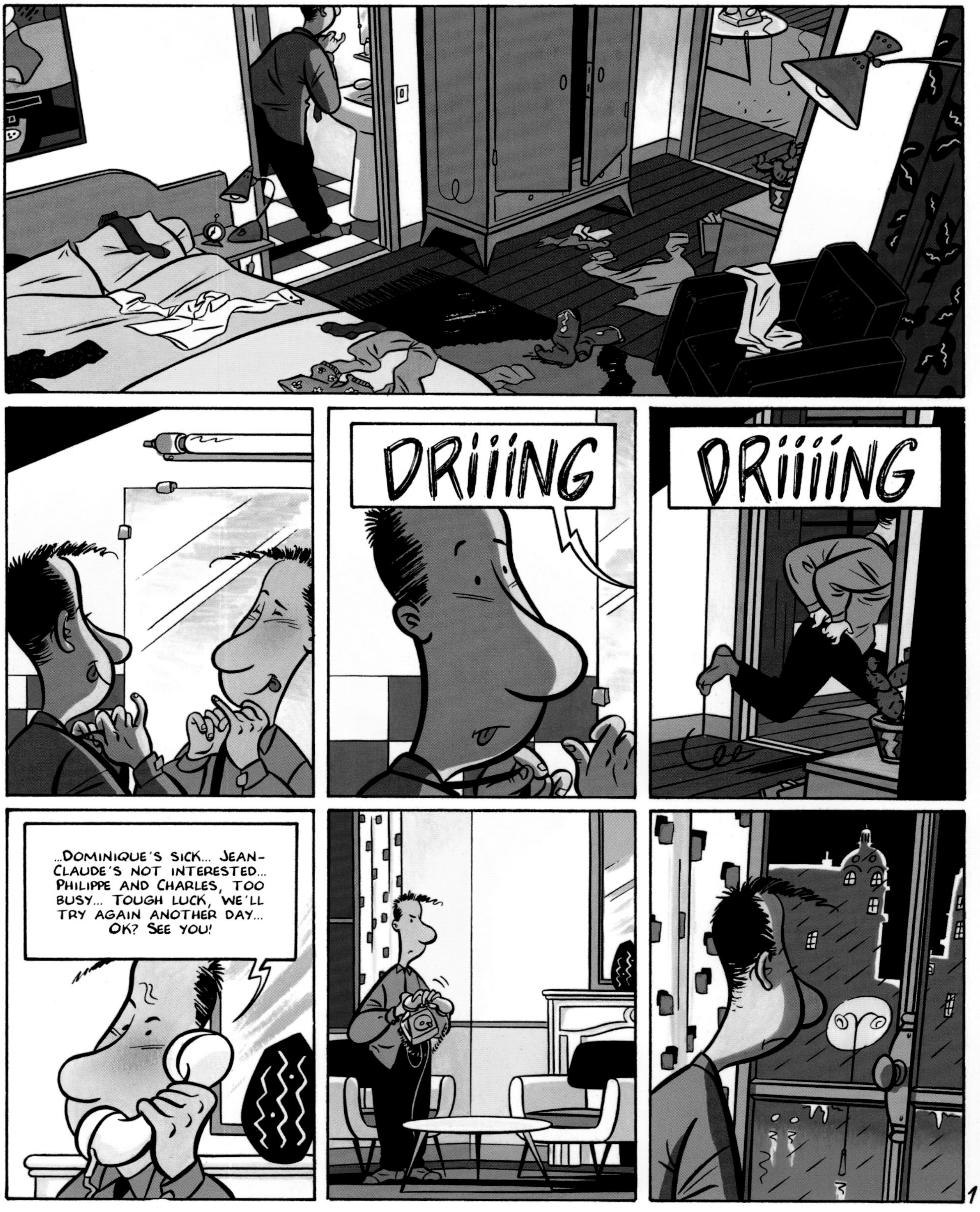
DRiiiNG
DRiiiiNG
...DOMINIQUE'S SICK... JEAN-CLAUDE'S NOT INTERESTED... PHILIPPE AND CHARLES, TOO BUSY... TOUGH LUCK, WE'LL TRY AGAIN ANOTHER DAY... OK? SEE YOU!
1

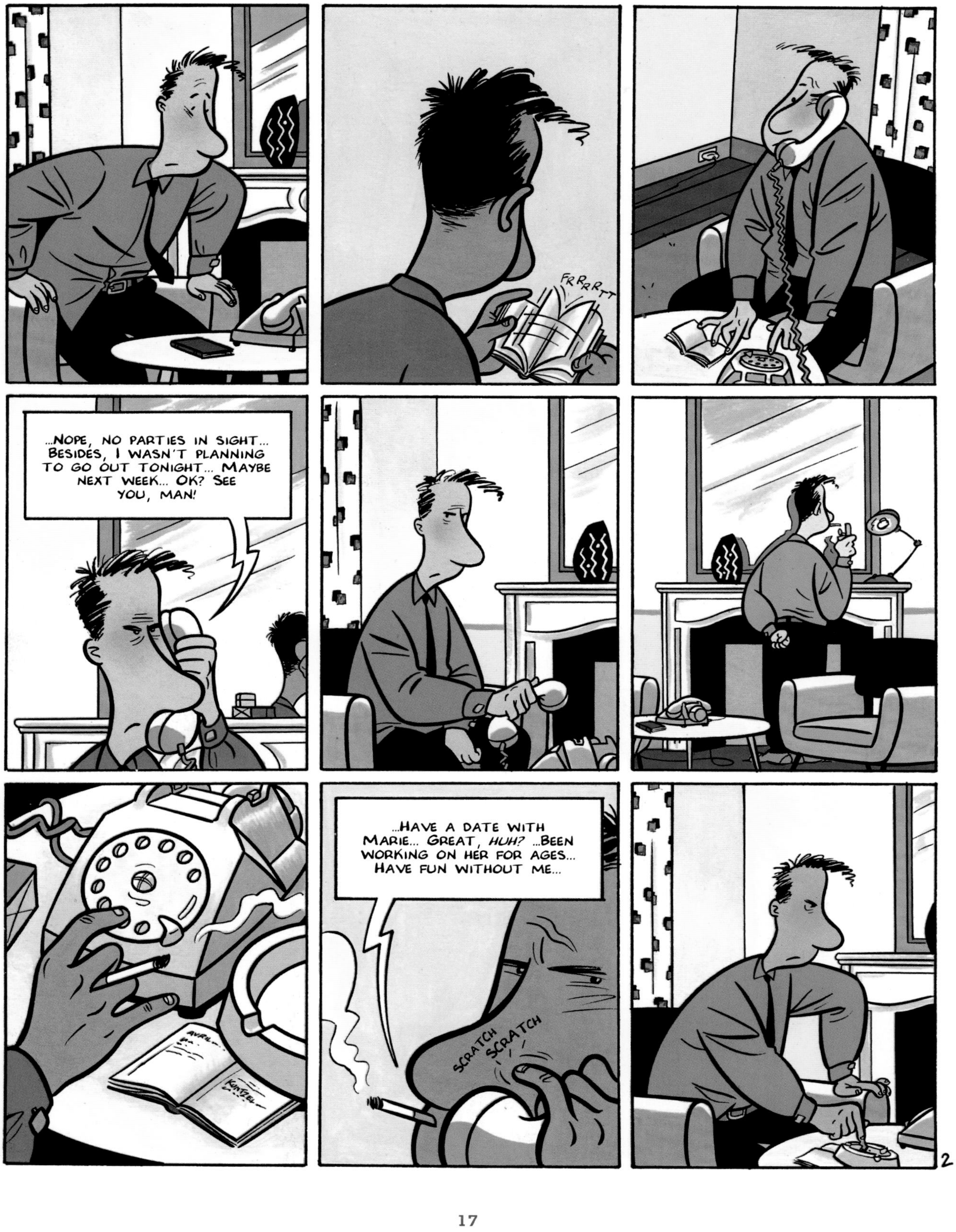
FRRRRTT
...NOPE, NO PARTIES IN SIGHT... BESIDES, I WASN'T PLANNING TO GO OUT TONIGHT... MAYBE NEXT WEEK... OK? SEE YOU, MAN!
...HAVE A DATE WITH MARIE... GREAT, *HUH?* ...BEEN WORKING ON HER FOR AGES... HAVE FUN WITHOUT ME...
SCRATCH SCRATCH

...TOOOT...TOOOT...TOOOT...
TOOOT...TOOOT...TOOOT...
TOOOT...TOOOT...TOOOT...

...ALREADY GOING OUT TONIGHT... CAN'T SHAKE THIS GUY... DELICATE SITUATION...

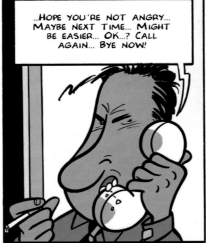

...HOPE YOU'RE NOT ANGRY... MAYBE NEXT TIME... MIGHT BE EASIER... OK...? CALL AGAIN... BYE NOW!

CLICK

...SOCCER GAME ON TV TONIGHT... BEER... CHIPS... WELCOME TO COME OVER... SURE, WHATEVER...

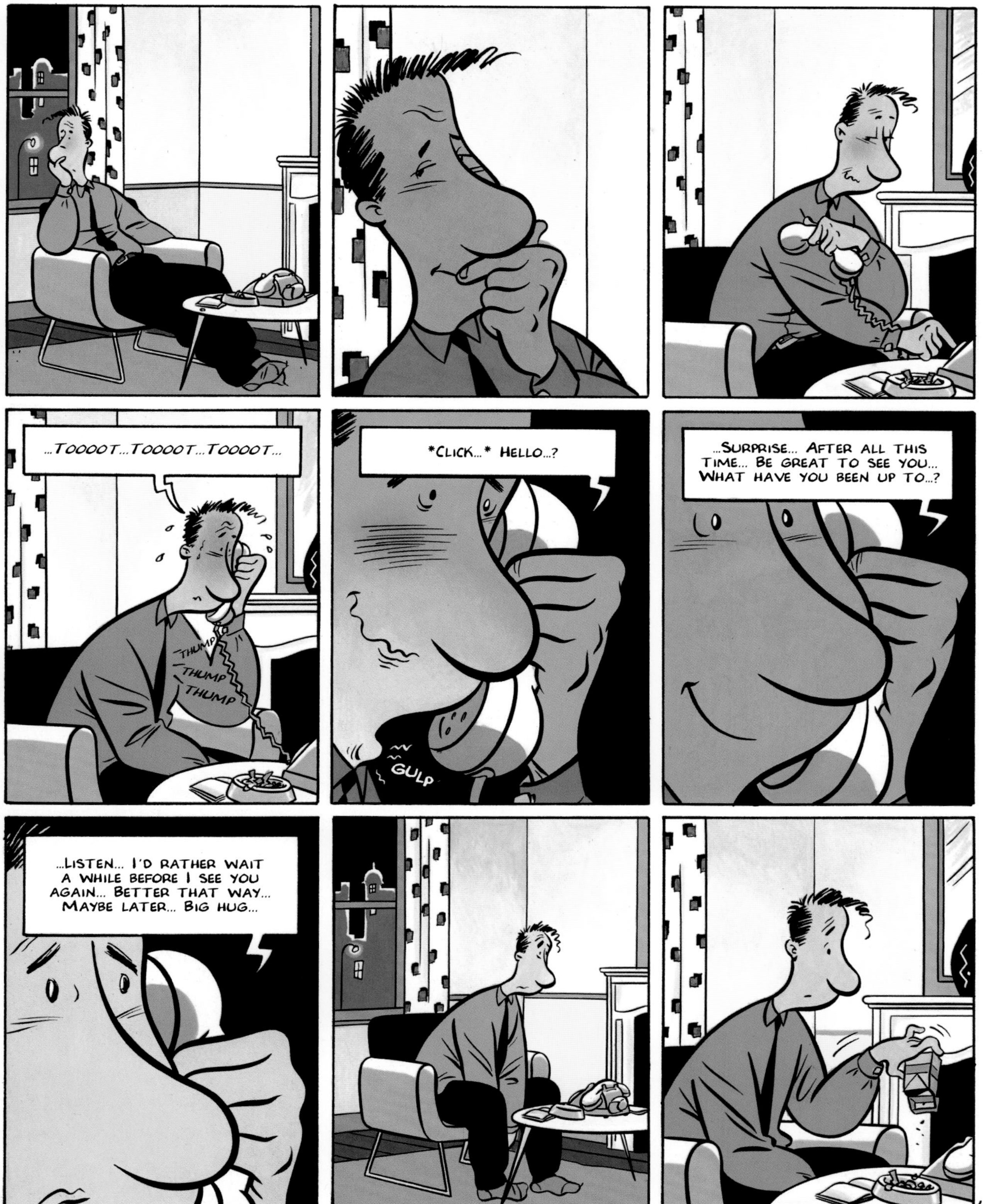

...TOOOOT...TOOOOT...TOOOOT...
THUMP
THUMP
THUMP
CLICK... HELLO...?
GULP
...SURPRISE... AFTER ALL THIS TIME... BE GREAT TO SEE YOU... WHAT HAVE YOU BEEN UP TO...?
...LISTEN... I'D RATHER WAIT A WHILE BEFORE I SEE YOU AGAIN... BETTER THAT WAY... MAYBE LATER... BIG HUG...
4

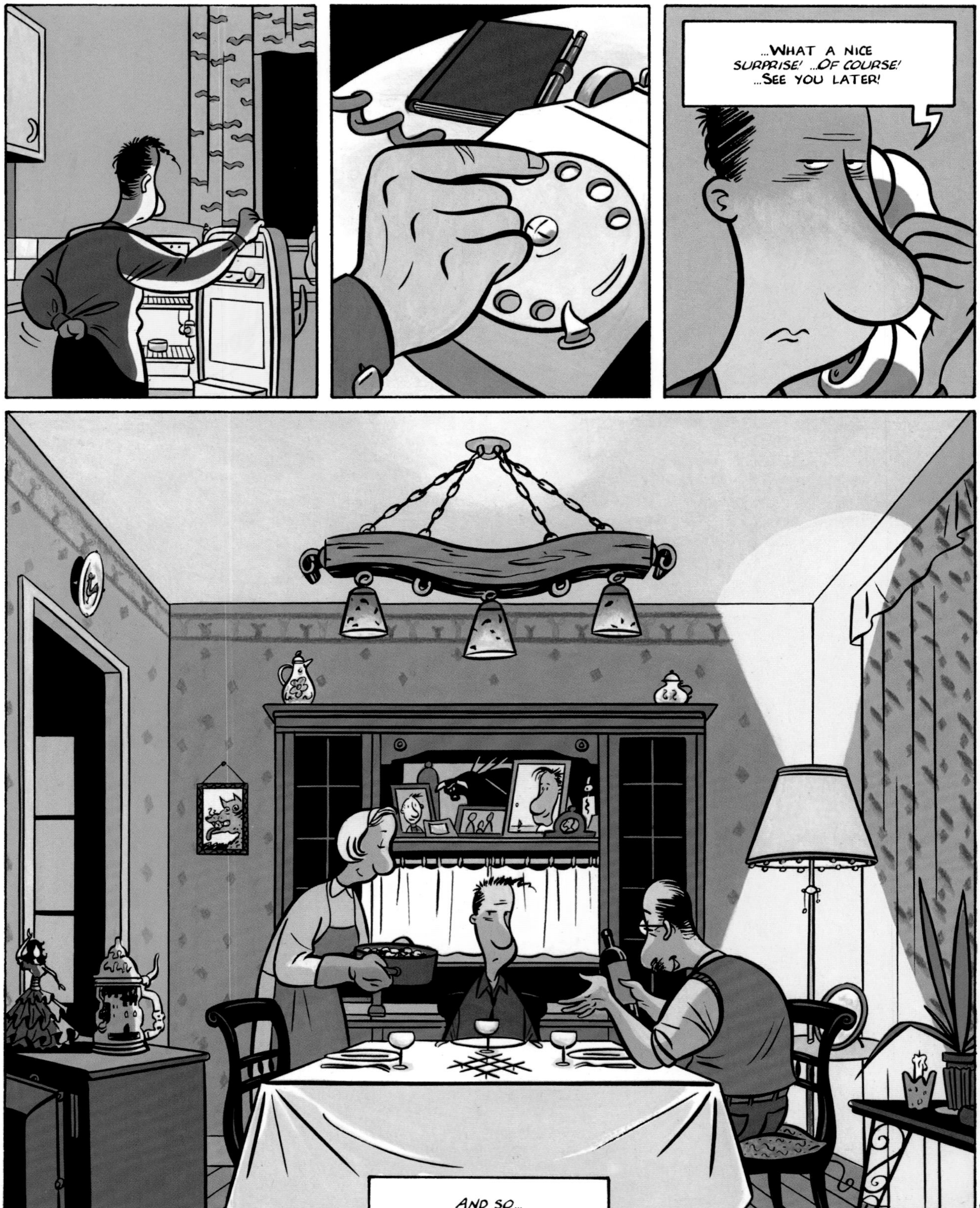
...WHAT A NICE SURPRISE! ...OF COURSE! ...SEE YOU LATER!
AND SO...

MY BELOVED CONCIERGE PART 1

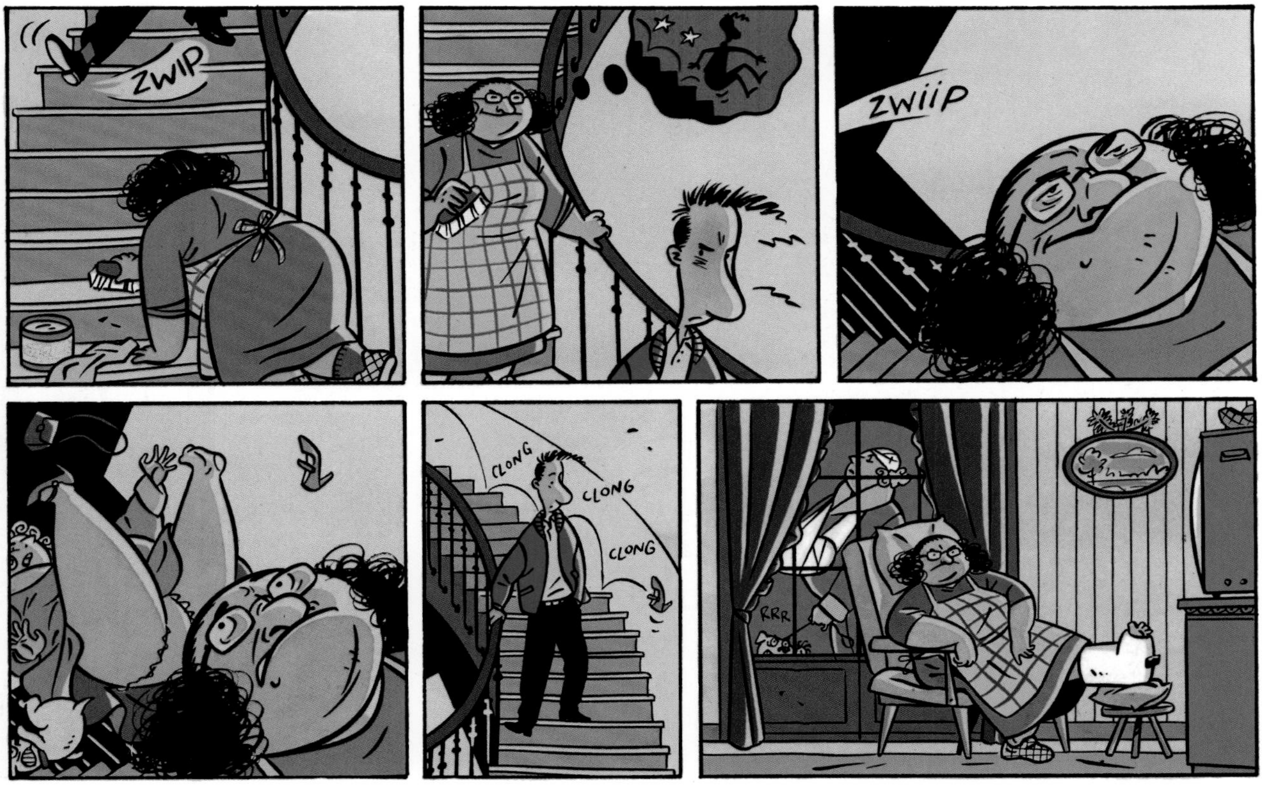

ZWIP
ZWIIP
CLONG
CLONG
CLONG
RRR

MONSIEUR JEAN GOES SHOPPING

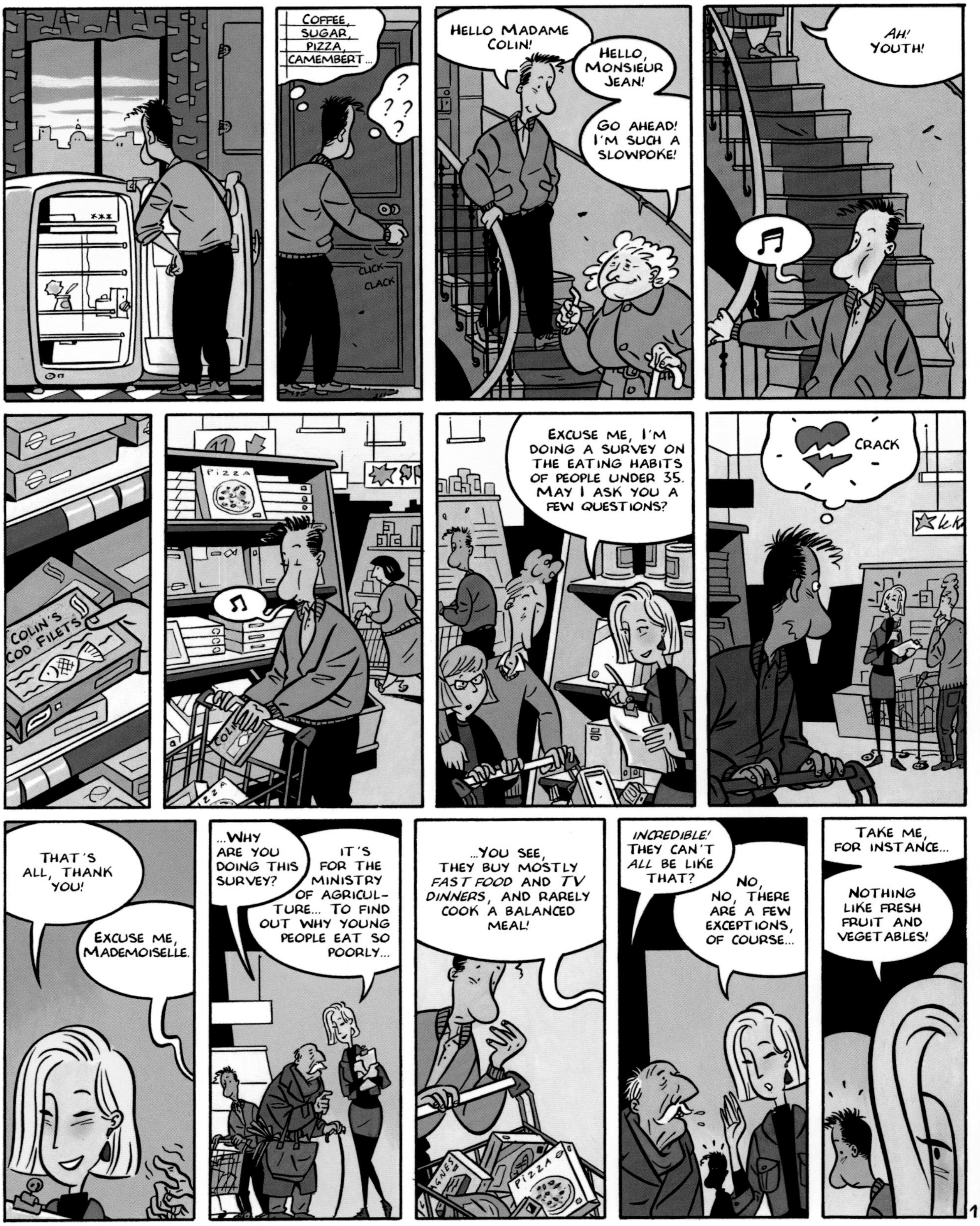
COFFEE, SUGAR, PIZZA, CAMEMBERT...
? ? ? ?
CLICK CLACK
HELLO MADAME COLIN!
HELLO, MONSIEUR JEAN!
GO AHEAD! I'M SUCH A SLOWPOKE!
AH! YOUTH!
COLIN'S COD FILETS
PIZZA
EXCUSE ME, I'M DOING A SURVEY ON THE EATING HABITS OF PEOPLE UNDER 35. MAY I ASK YOU A FEW QUESTIONS?
CRACK
THAT'S ALL, THANK YOU!
EXCUSE ME, MADEMOISELLE.
...WHY ARE YOU DOING THIS SURVEY?
IT'S FOR THE MINISTRY OF AGRICULTURE... TO FIND OUT WHY YOUNG PEOPLE EAT SO POORLY...
...YOU SEE, THEY BUY MOSTLY FAST FOOD AND TV DINNERS, AND RARELY COOK A BALANCED MEAL!
PIZZA
INCREDIBLE! THEY CAN'T ALL BE LIKE THAT?
NO, NO, THERE ARE A FEW EXCEPTIONS, OF COURSE...
TAKE ME, FOR INSTANCE...
NOTHING LIKE FRESH FRUIT AND VEGETABLES!
1

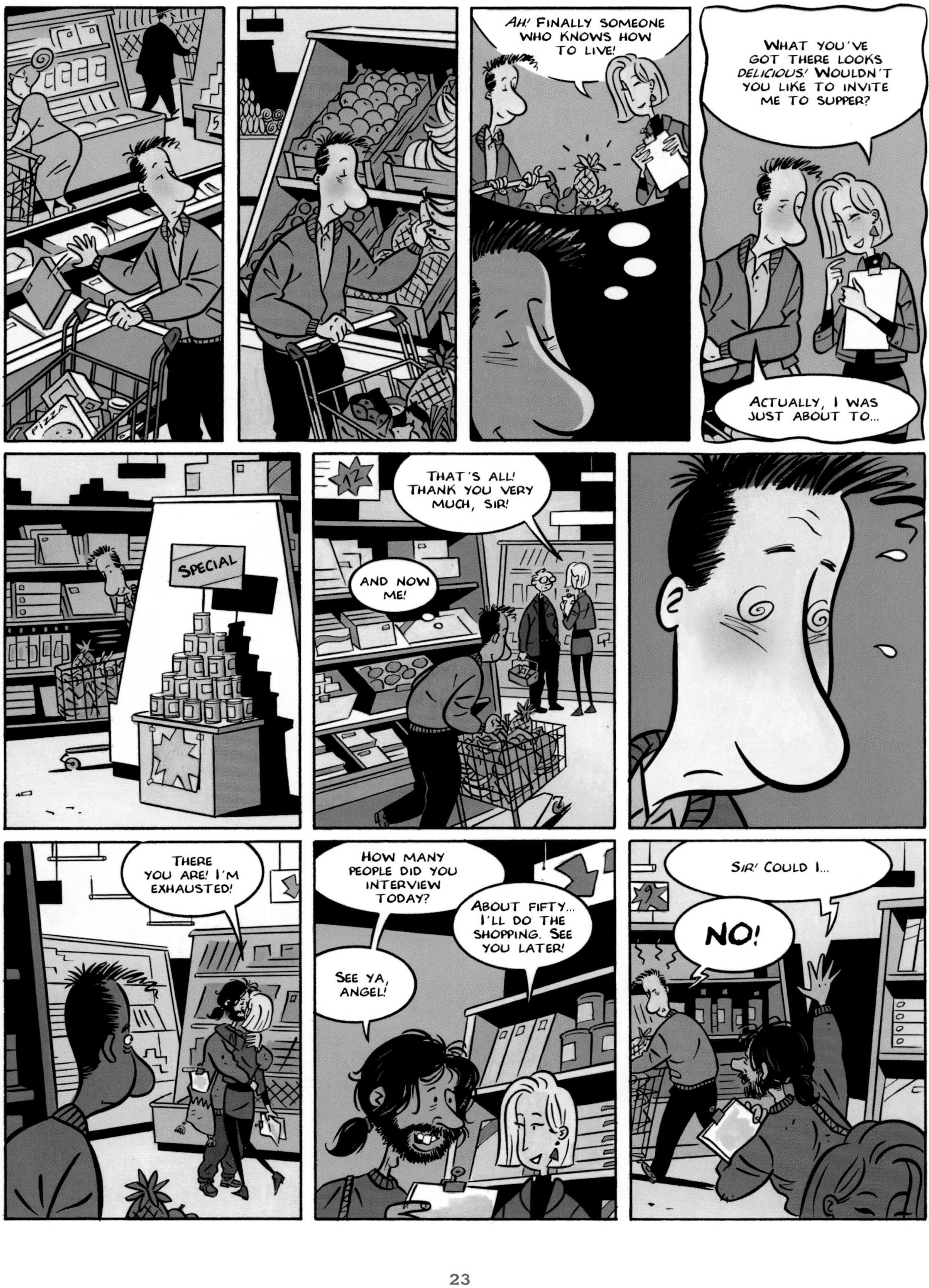
AH! FINALLY SOMEONE WHO KNOWS HOW TO LIVE!
WHAT YOU'VE GOT THERE LOOKS DELICIOUS! WOULDN'T YOU LIKE TO INVITE ME TO SUPPER?
ACTUALLY, I WAS JUST ABOUT TO...
SPECIAL
THAT'S ALL! THANK YOU VERY MUCH, SIR!
AND NOW ME!
THERE YOU ARE! I'M EXHAUSTED!
HOW MANY PEOPLE DID YOU INTERVIEW TODAY?
ABOUT FIFTY... I'LL DO THE SHOPPING. SEE YOU LATER!
SEE YA, ANGEL!
SIR! COULD I...
NO!

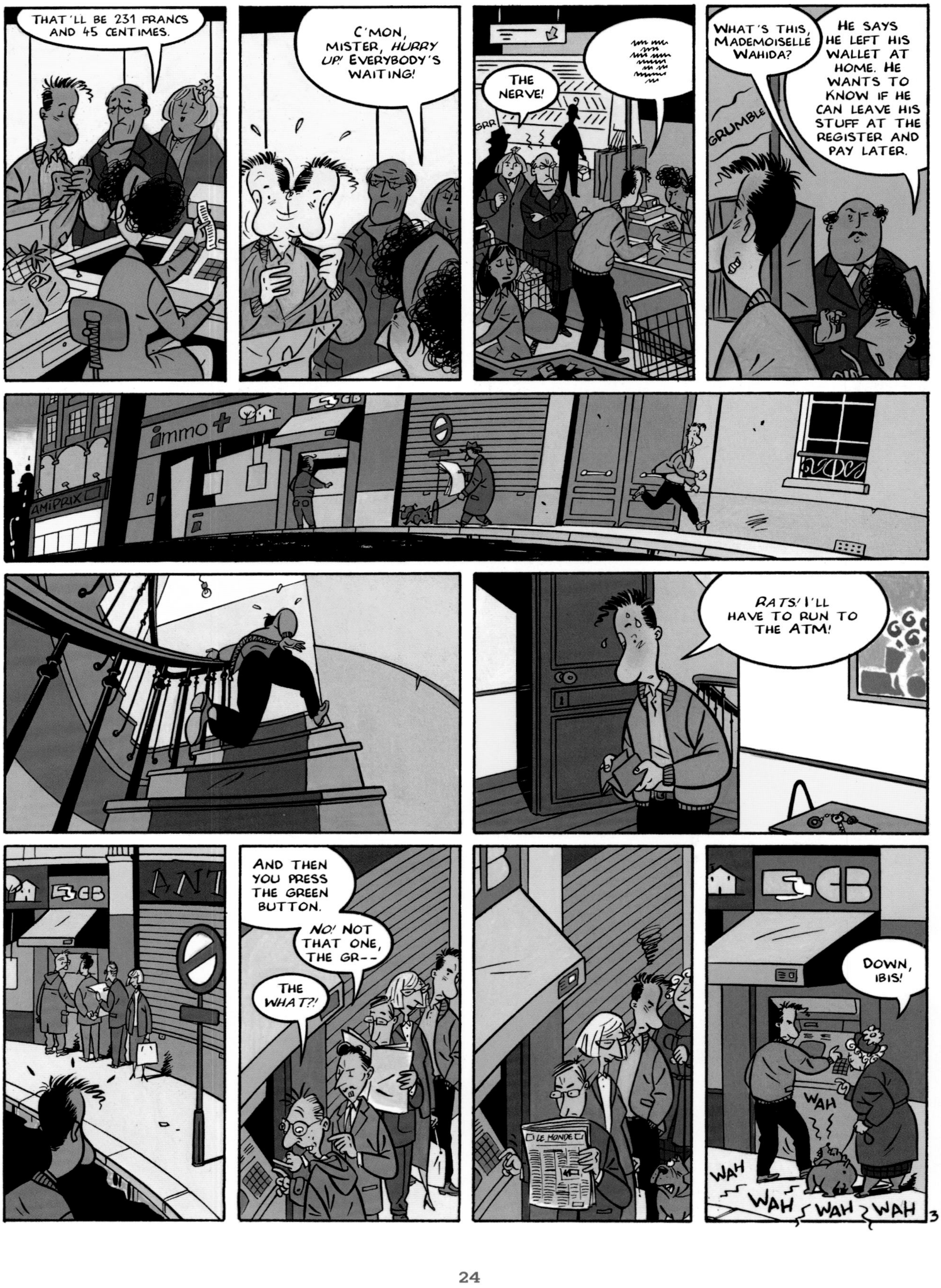
THAT'LL BE 231 FRANCS AND 45 CENTIMES.
C'MON, MISTER, HURRY UP! EVERYBODY'S WAITING!
THE NERVE!
GRR
WHAT'S THIS, MADEMOISELLE WAHIDA?
GRUMBLE
HE SAYS HE LEFT HIS WALLET AT HOME. HE WANTS TO KNOW IF HE CAN LEAVE HIS STUFF AT THE REGISTER AND PAY LATER.
AMIPRIX
immo
RATS! I'LL HAVE TO RUN TO THE ATM!
CB
AND THEN YOU PRESS THE GREEN BUTTON.
NO! NOT THAT ONE, THE GR--
THE WHAT?!
LE MONDE
DOWN, IBIS!
WAH
WAH
WAH
WAH
WAH

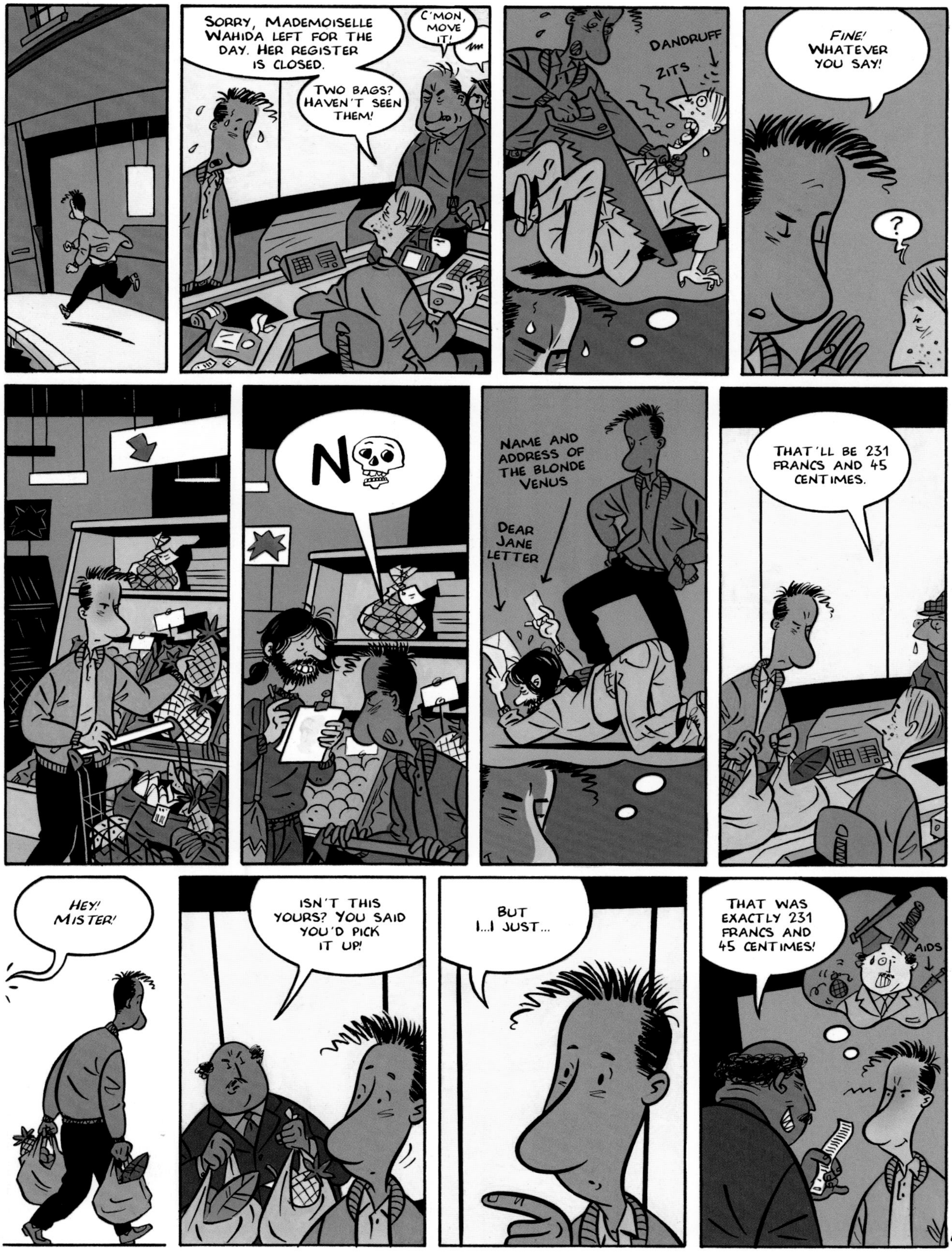

Sorry, Mademoiselle Wahida left for the day. Her register is closed.
C'mon, move it!
Two bags? Haven't seen them!
Dandruff
Zits
Fine! Whatever you say!
?
N
Name and address of the blonde Venus
Dear Jane letter
That'll be 231 francs and 45 centimes.
Hey! Mister!
Isn't this yours? You said you'd pick it up!
But I...I just...
That was exactly 231 francs and 45 centimes!
AIDS
4

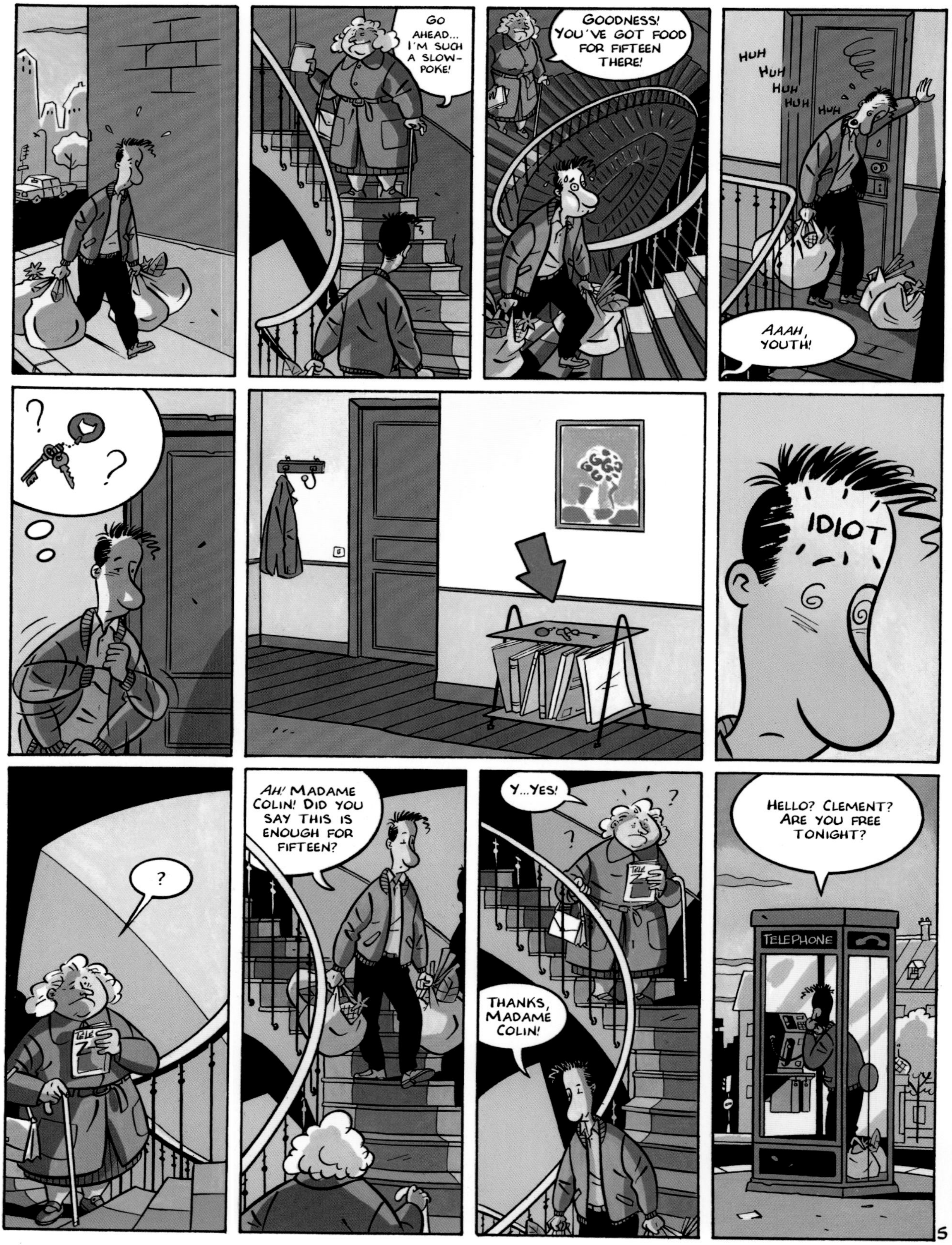
GO AHEAD... I'M SUCH A SLOW-POKE!
GOODNESS! YOU'VE GOT FOOD FOR FIFTEEN THERE!
HUH HUH HUH HUH HUH
AAAH, YOUTH!
IDIOT
?
AH! MADAME COLIN! DID YOU SAY THIS IS ENOUGH FOR FIFTEEN?
Y...YES!
THANKS, MADAME COLIN!
HELLO? CLEMENT? ARE YOU FREE TONIGHT?
TELEPHONE
5

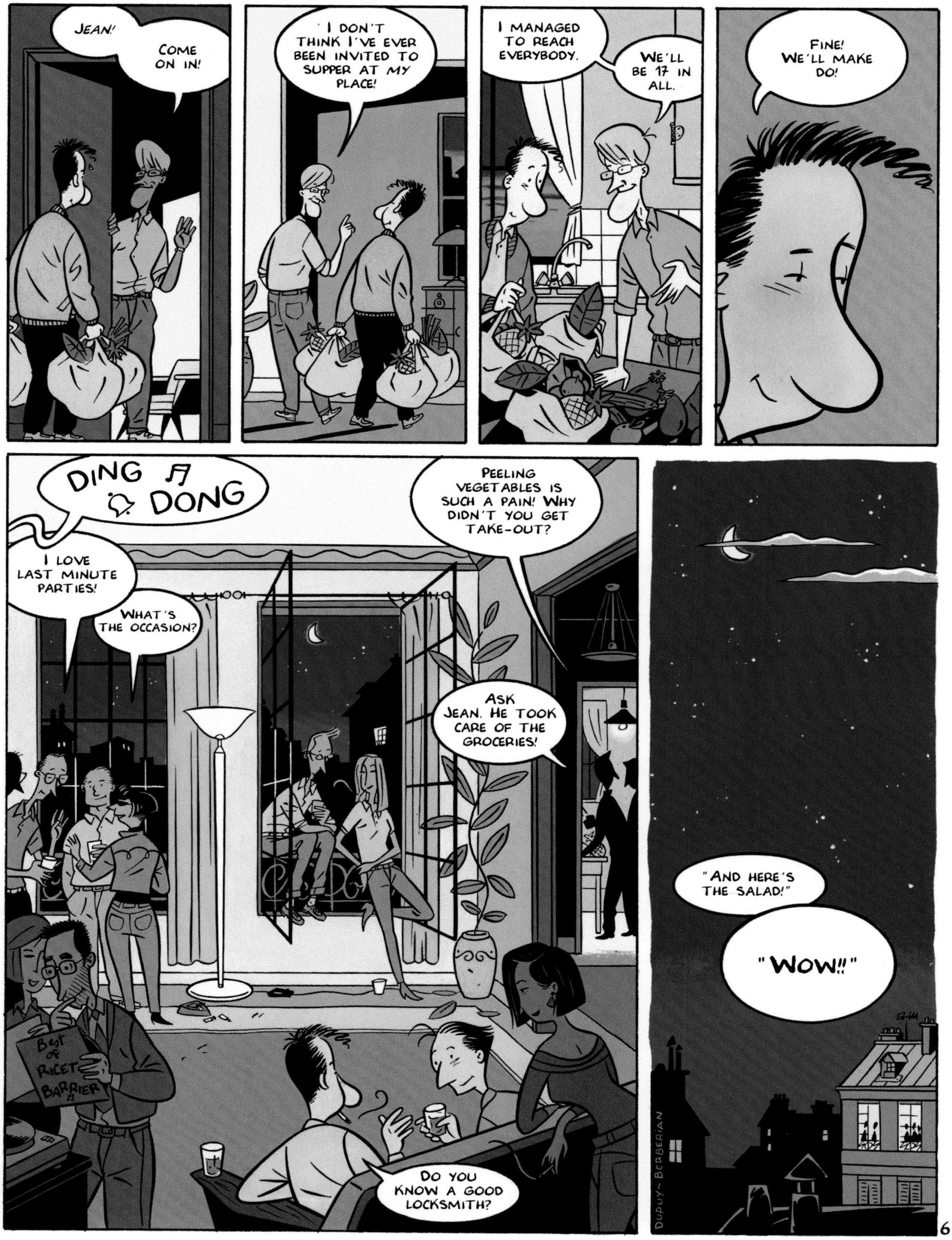
JEAN!
COME ON IN!
I DON'T THINK I'VE EVER BEEN INVITED TO SUPPER AT MY PLACE!
I MANAGED TO REACH EVERYBODY.
WE'LL BE 17 IN ALL.
FINE! WE'LL MAKE DO!
DING DONG
I LOVE LAST MINUTE PARTIES!
WHAT'S THE OCCASION?
PEELING VEGETABLES IS SUCH A PAIN! WHY DIDN'T YOU GET TAKE-OUT?
ASK JEAN. HE TOOK CARE OF THE GROCERIES!
Best of RICET BARRIER
DO YOU KNOW A GOOD LOCKSMITH?
"AND HERE'S THE SALAD!"
"WOW!!"
DUPUY-BERBERIAN
6

MY BELOVED CONCIERGE PART 2

WAF
RF
WAF
I WON'T ALLOW YOU TO D
YOU'R NOTHIN BUT A BIG
I'M
COM
TO T
WOOF! WOOF! WOOF!
STUPI
UTT B
ICK UP
MESS
LADIES...!
RR
RRRRR
THAT'S THE FIFTH FLOOR TENANT... YOU KNOW, THE NOISY ONE...

NICE KITTY

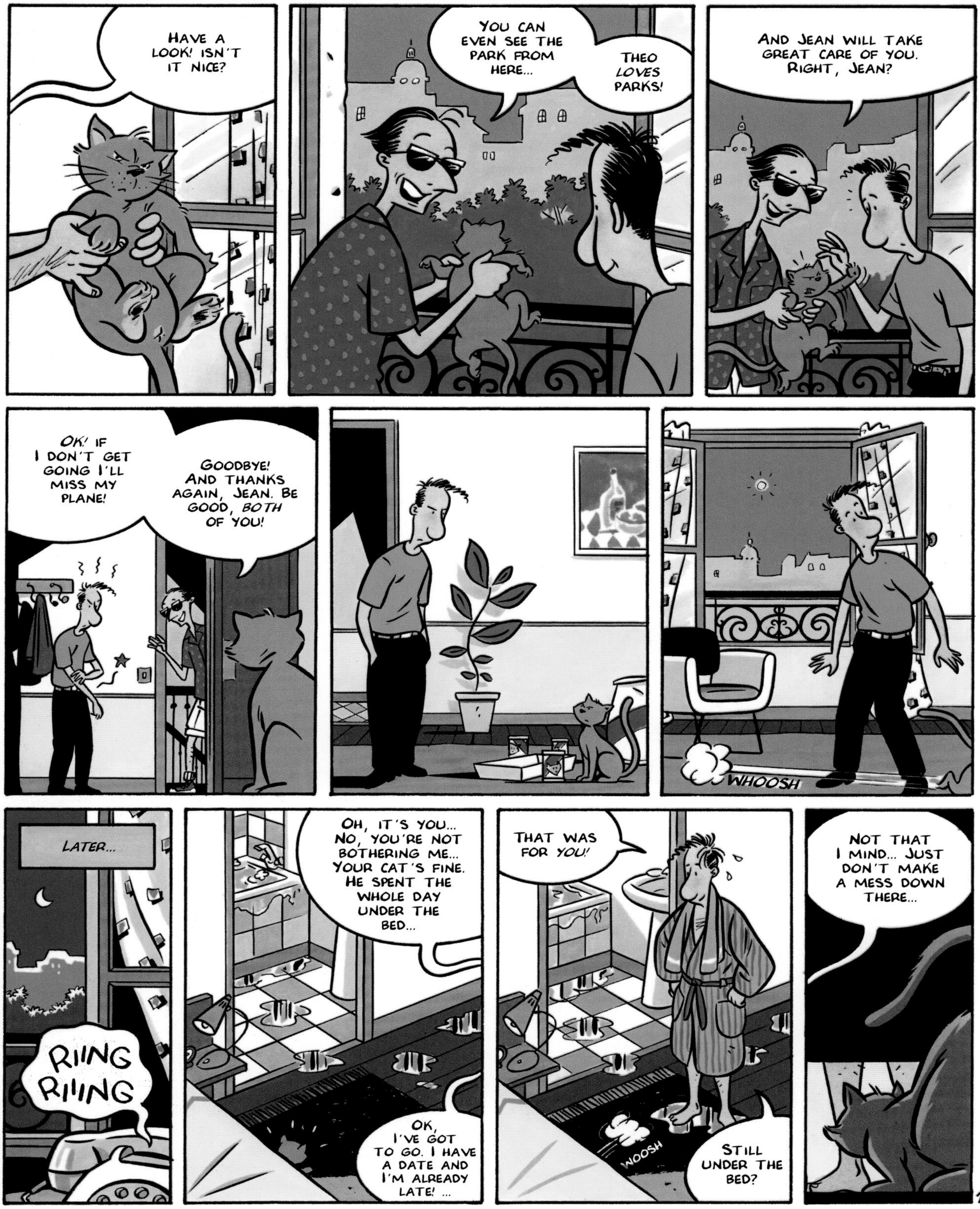

HAVE A LOOK! ISN'T IT NICE?
YOU CAN EVEN SEE THE PARK FROM HERE...
THEO LOVES PARKS!
AND JEAN WILL TAKE GREAT CARE OF YOU. RIGHT, JEAN?
OK! IF I DON'T GET GOING I'LL MISS MY PLANE!
GOODBYE! AND THANKS AGAIN, JEAN. BE GOOD, BOTH OF YOU!
WHOOSH
LATER...
RIIING RIIING
OH, IT'S YOU... NO, YOU'RE NOT BOTHERING ME... YOUR CAT'S FINE. HE SPENT THE WHOLE DAY UNDER THE BED...
OK, I'VE GOT TO GO. I HAVE A DATE AND I'M ALREADY LATE! ...
THAT WAS FOR YOU!
WOOSH
STILL UNDER THE BED?
NOT THAT I MIND... JUST DON'T MAKE A MESS DOWN THERE...
1

SO? HOW DO YOU LIKE MY NEW APARTMENT? YOU'VE MET SUZANNE, HAVEN'T YOU?

SHE'S A STYLIST AT BABYGROOVE...!

"MONSIEUR" JEAN IS AN AUTHOR. I HELPED HIM FINISH HIS LAST NOVEL, "THE EBONY TABLE..."

...BY NOT CALLING FOR THREE MONTHS!

I HEAR THEO IS STAYING AT YOUR PLACE...

THEO?

A CAT!

POOR JEAN! YOU'RE A BRAVE MAN, MY FRIEND...

I TOOK CARE OF HIM LAST TIME. THAT CAT IS A PEST...!

YOU'LL SEE! WHEN THEO'S ANGRY, HE'LL LET YOU KNOW...

WELL, I'LL LEAVE YOU TWO. SO LONG!

I... UH... YOU KNOW, I READ YOUR BOOK, IT'S GREAT!

I REALLY LIKED YOUR DESCRIPTION OF LENINGRAD...

LENINGRAD IS REALLY FAST... LIKE A NE... I'VE THEN... EN AN... DE THE... RLS I'LL... GOING

LENINGRAD...

KSSSSS

CRIPES...!

I FORGOT TO FEED THE CAT!

2

30

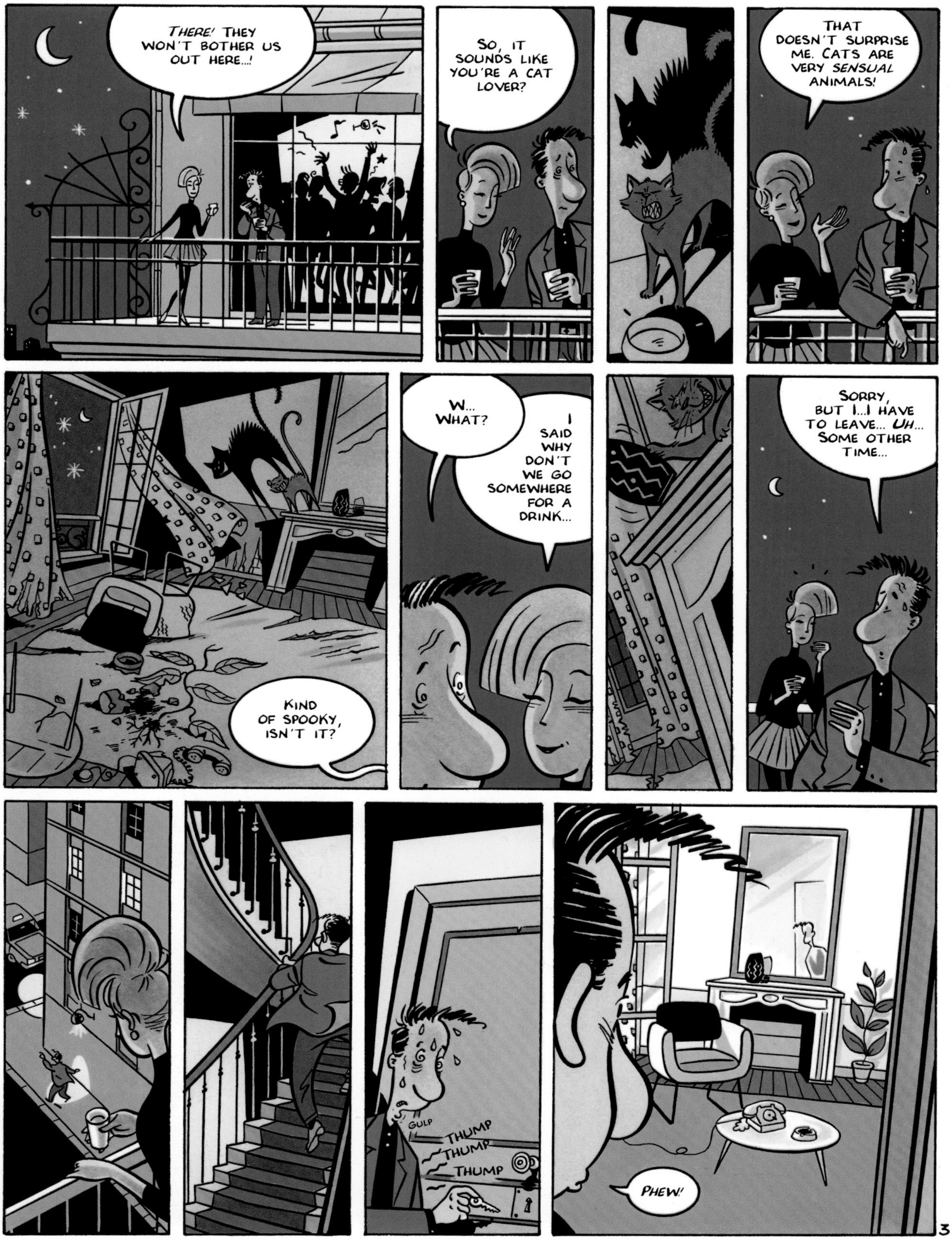
THERE! THEY WON'T BOTHER US OUT HERE...!
SO, IT SOUNDS LIKE YOU'RE A CAT LOVER?
THAT DOESN'T SURPRISE ME. CATS ARE VERY SENSUAL ANIMALS!
KIND OF SPOOKY, ISN'T IT?
W... WHAT?
I SAID WHY DON'T WE GO SOMEWHERE FOR A DRINK...
SORRY, BUT I...I HAVE TO LEAVE... UH... SOME OTHER TIME...
GULP
THUMP
THUMP
THUMP
PHEW!
3

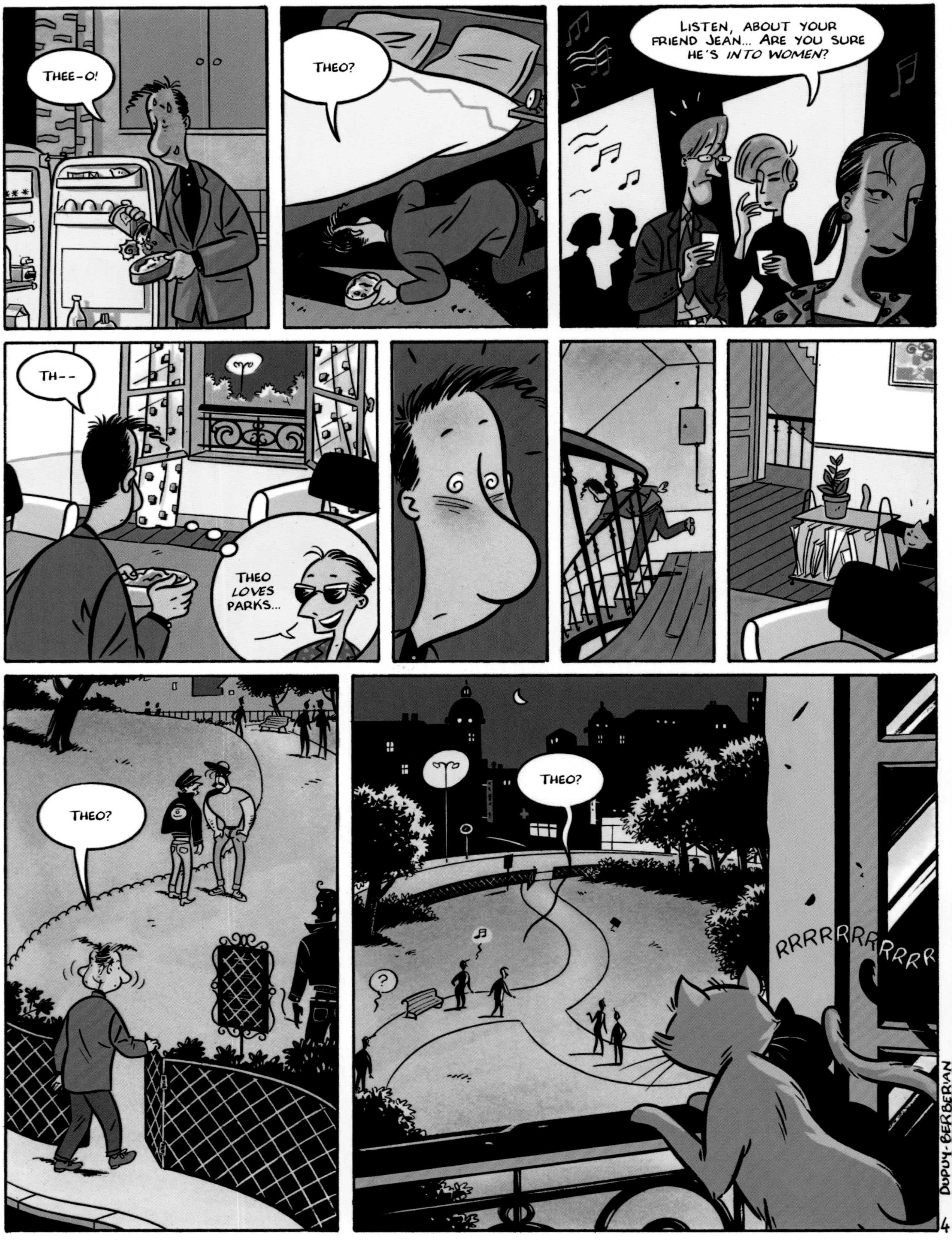
THEE-O!
THEO?
LISTEN, ABOUT YOUR FRIEND JEAN... ARE YOU SURE HE'S INTO WOMEN?
TH--
THEO LOVES PARKS...
THEO?
THEO?
RRRRRRRRRRR
DUPUY-BERBERIAN
4

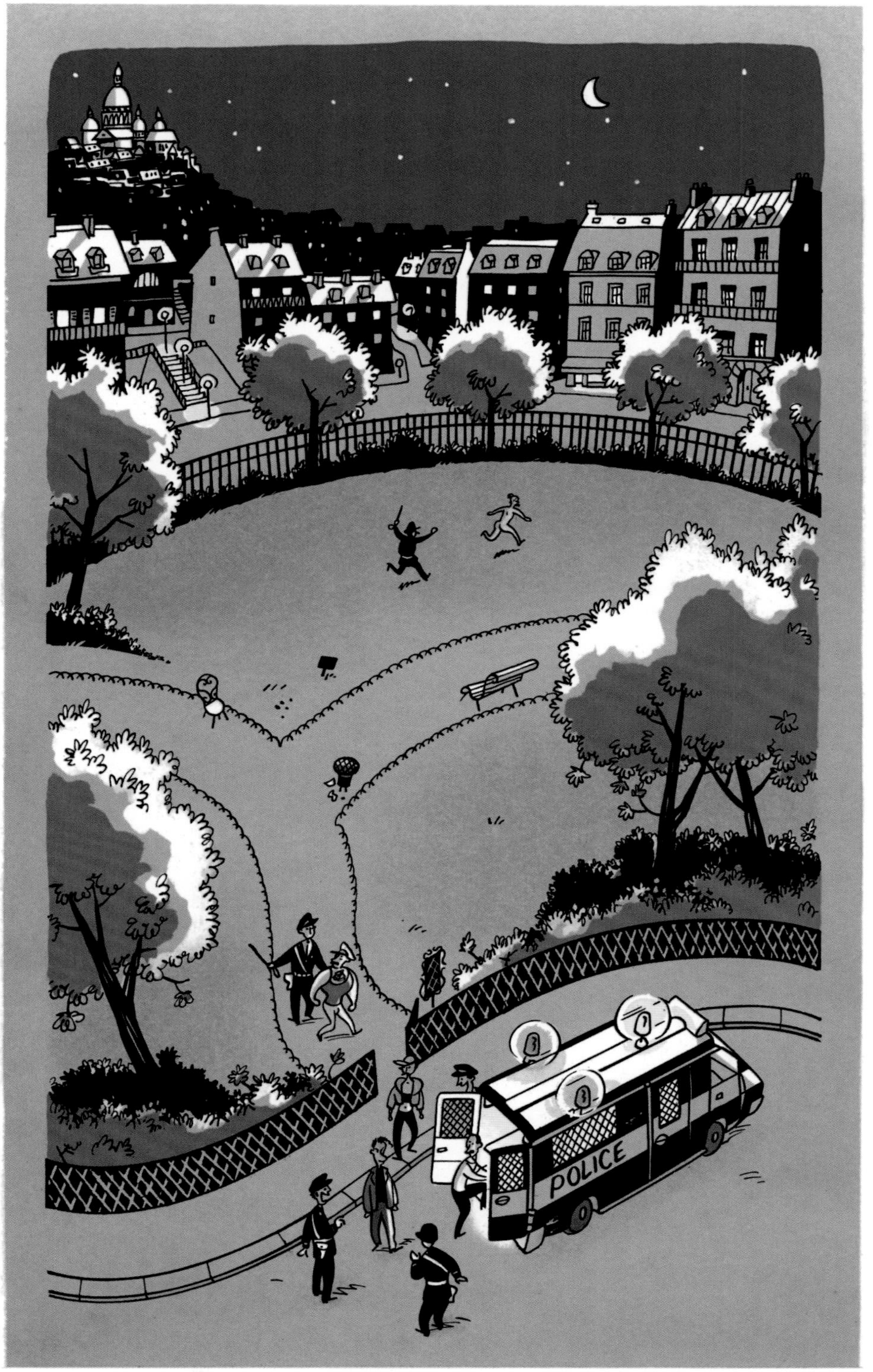
POLICE

"HEY, CHIEF! ONE OF 'EM SAYS SHE LOST HER CAT!"

ICE CUBE IN FORMALDEHYDE

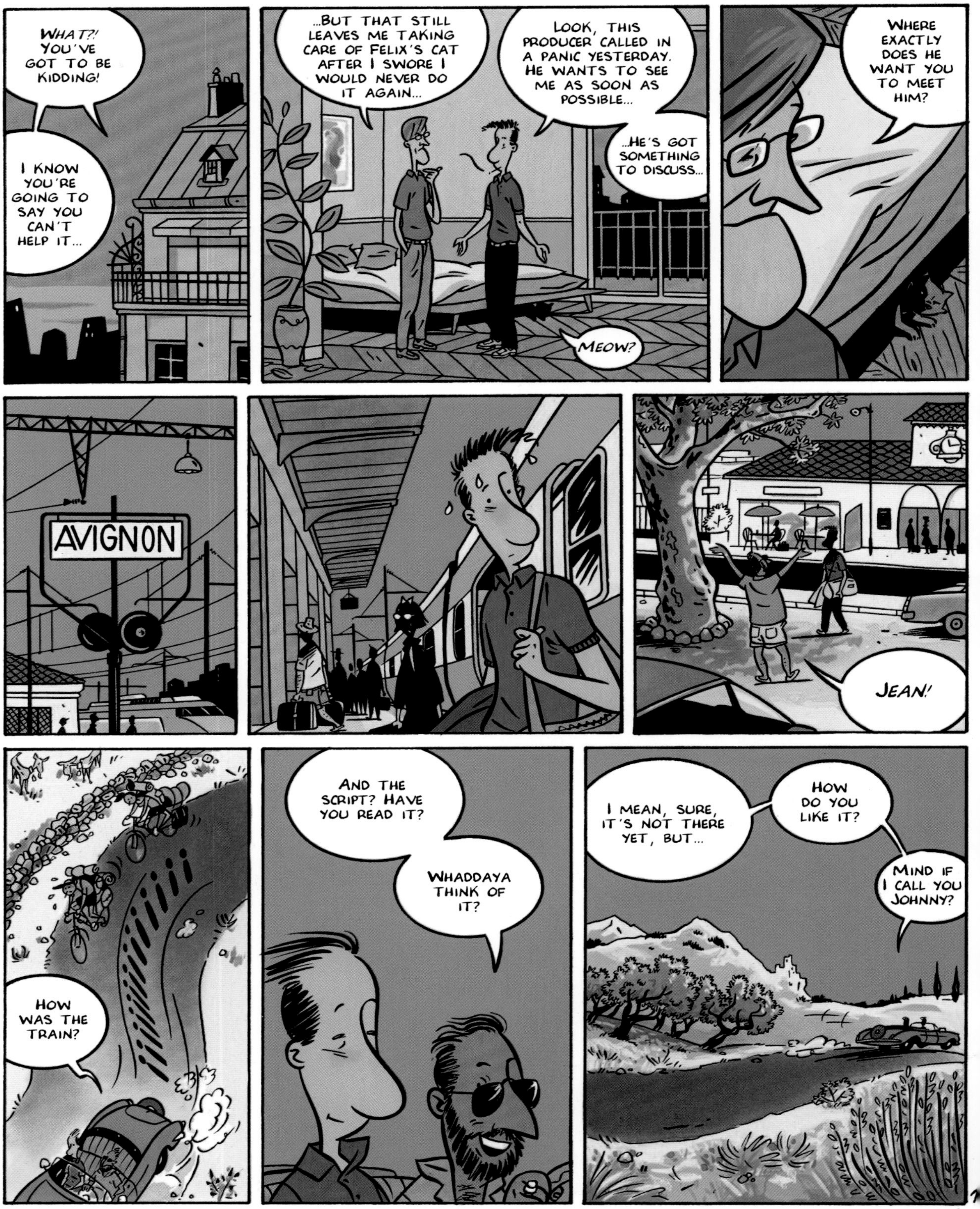
WHAT?! YOU'VE GOT TO BE KIDDING!
I KNOW YOU'RE GOING TO SAY YOU CAN'T HELP IT...
...BUT THAT STILL LEAVES ME TAKING CARE OF FELIX'S CAT AFTER I SWORE I WOULD NEVER DO IT AGAIN...
LOOK, THIS PRODUCER CALLED IN A PANIC YESTERDAY. HE WANTS TO SEE ME AS SOON AS POSSIBLE...
...HE'S GOT SOMETHING TO DISCUSS...
MEOW?
WHERE EXACTLY DOES HE WANT YOU TO MEET HIM?
AVIGNON
JEAN!
HOW WAS THE TRAIN?
AND THE SCRIPT? HAVE YOU READ IT?
WHADDAYA THINK OF IT?
I MEAN, SURE, IT'S NOT THERE YET, BUT...
HOW DO YOU LIKE IT?
MIND IF I CALL YOU JOHNNY?

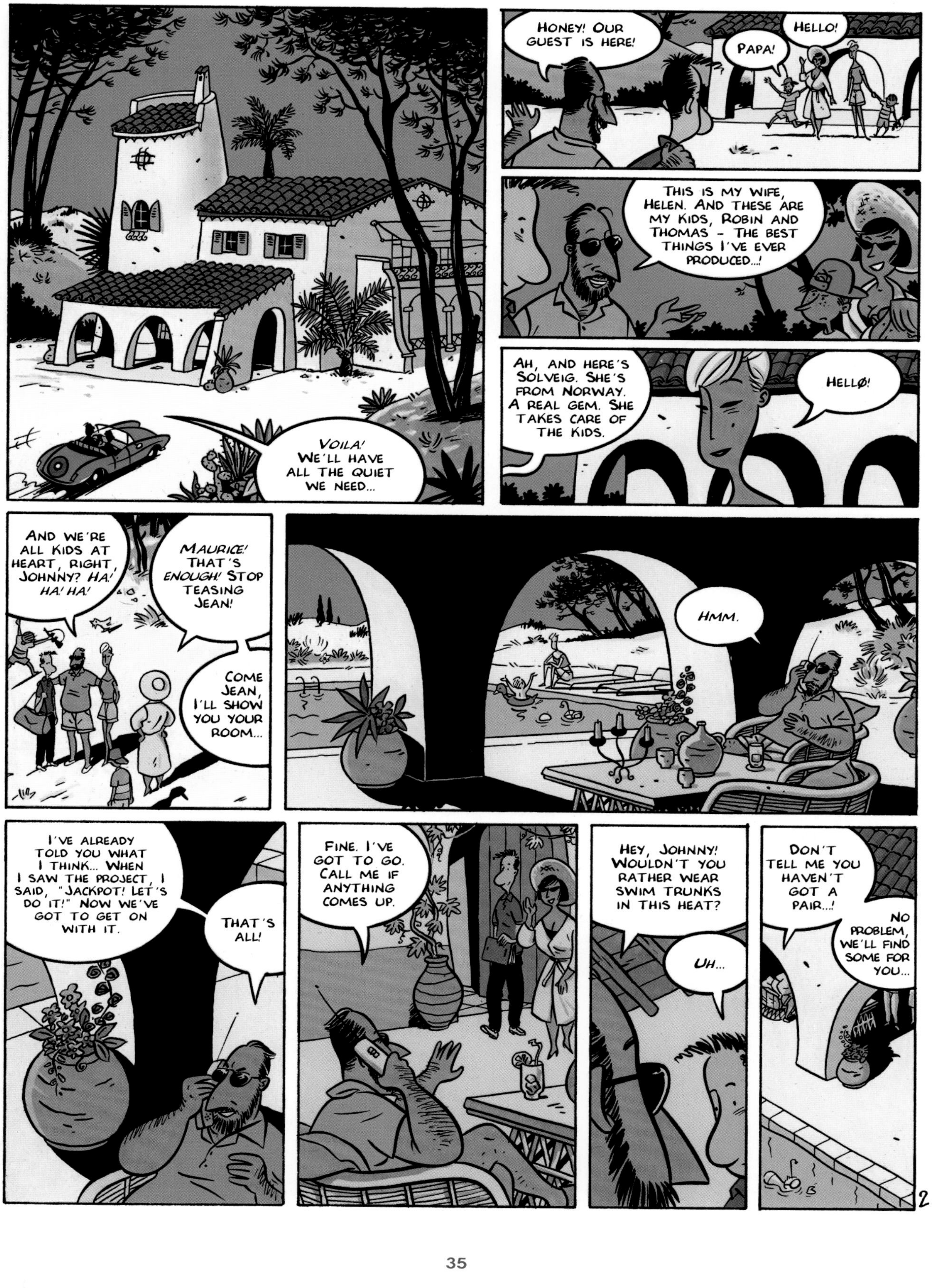

VOILA! WE'LL HAVE ALL THE QUIET WE NEED...
HONEY! OUR GUEST IS HERE!
PAPA!
HELLO!
THIS IS MY WIFE, HELEN. AND THESE ARE MY KIDS, ROBIN AND THOMAS - THE BEST THINGS I'VE EVER PRODUCED...!
AH, AND HERE'S SOLVEIG. SHE'S FROM NORWAY. A REAL GEM. SHE TAKES CARE OF THE KIDS.
HELLØ!
AND WE'RE ALL KIDS AT HEART, RIGHT, JOHNNY? HA! HA! HA!
MAURICE! THAT'S ENOUGH! STOP TEASING JEAN!
COME JEAN, I'LL SHOW YOU YOUR ROOM...
HMM.
I'VE ALREADY TOLD YOU WHAT I THINK... WHEN I SAW THE PROJECT, I SAID, "JACKPOT! LET'S DO IT!" NOW WE'VE GOT TO GET ON WITH IT.
THAT'S ALL!
FINE. I'VE GOT TO GO. CALL ME IF ANYTHING COMES UP.
HEY, JOHNNY! WOULDN'T YOU RATHER WEAR SWIM TRUNKS IN THIS HEAT?
UH...
DON'T TELL ME YOU HAVEN'T GOT A PAIR...!
NO PROBLEM, WE'LL FIND SOME FOR YOU...
2

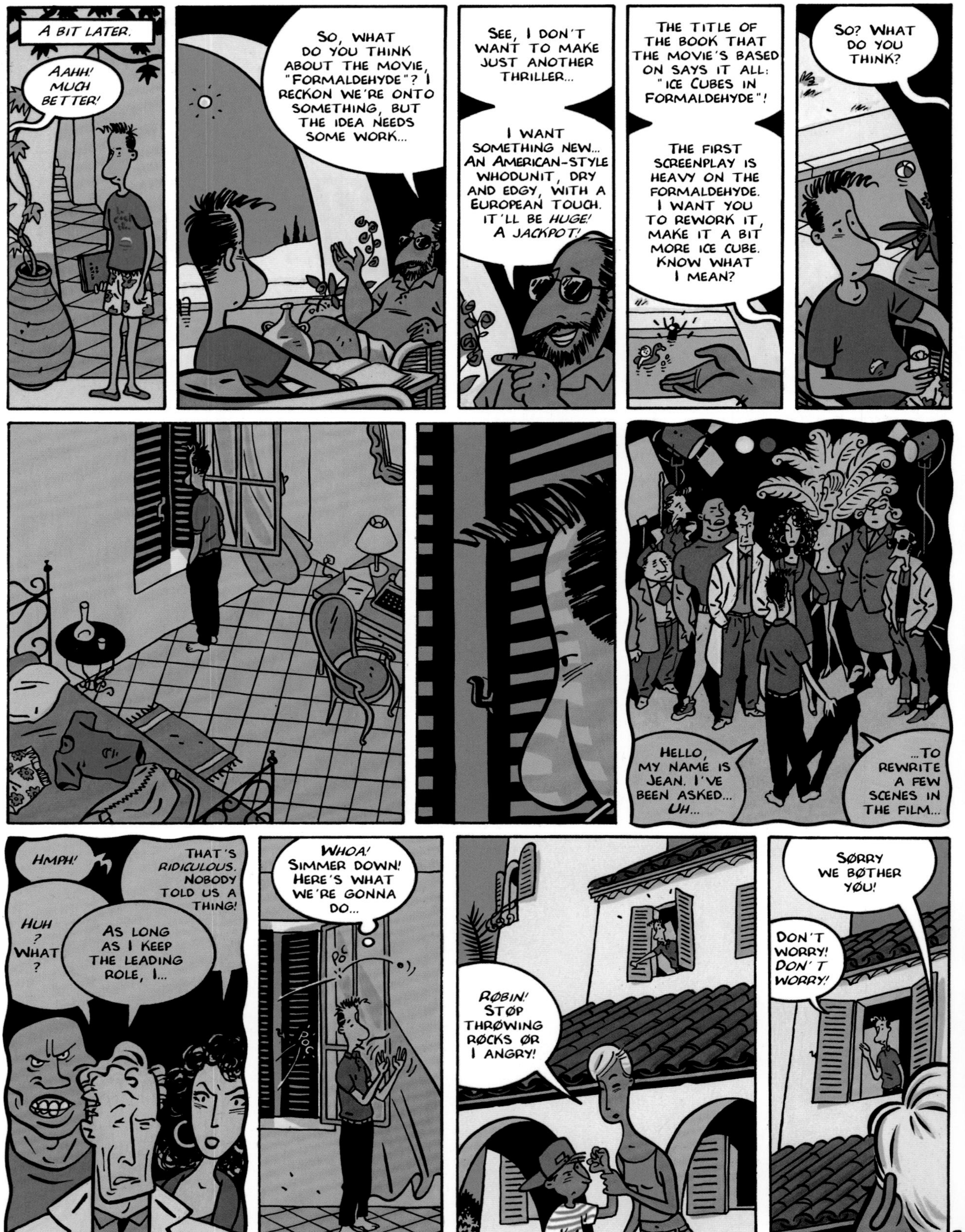
A BIT LATER.
AAHH! MUCH BETTER!
SO, WHAT DO YOU THINK ABOUT THE MOVIE, "FORMALDEHYDE"? I RECKON WE'RE ONTO SOMETHING, BUT THE IDEA NEEDS SOME WORK...
SEE, I DON'T WANT TO MAKE JUST ANOTHER THRILLER...
I WANT SOMETHING NEW... AN AMERICAN-STYLE WHODUNIT, DRY AND EDGY, WITH A EUROPEAN TOUCH. IT'LL BE HUGE! A JACKPOT!
THE TITLE OF THE BOOK THAT THE MOVIE'S BASED ON SAYS IT ALL: "ICE CUBES IN FORMALDEHYDE"!
THE FIRST SCREENPLAY IS HEAVY ON THE FORMALDEHYDE. I WANT YOU TO REWORK IT, MAKE IT A BIT MORE ICE CUBE. KNOW WHAT I MEAN?
SO? WHAT DO YOU THINK?
HELLO, MY NAME IS JEAN. I'VE BEEN ASKED... UH...
...TO REWRITE A FEW SCENES IN THE FILM...
HMPH!
THAT'S RIDICULOUS. NOBODY TOLD US A THING!
HUH? WHAT?
AS LONG AS I KEEP THE LEADING ROLE, I...
WHOA! SIMMER DOWN! HERE'S WHAT WE'RE GONNA DO...
RØBIN! STØP THRØWING RØCKS ØR I ANGRY!
SØRRY WE BØTHER YØU!
DON'T WORRY! DON'T WORRY!
3

POC
POC
POC

WHAT YOU HAVE TO DO IS CHOOSE YOUR ANGLE OF ATTACK...

SURE, YOU'VE GOT A LITTLE WRITER'S BLOCK. IT ISN'T EASY TO COME INTO A SCREEN-PLAY COLD...

POC

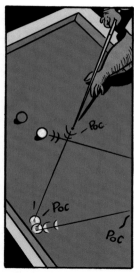

MAURICE! TELEPHØNE!

POC

HELLO? OH, IT'S YOU...

WHAT?! FORGET IT! WE'RE STARTING PRODUCTION IN 3 WEEKS!

YØU SMØKE VERY MUCH?

ALWAYS WRITERS SMØKE VERY MUCH: SARTRE, GIDE, GAINSBØURG...

GAINSBOURG? BUT GAINSBOURG ISN'T A WRITER...

YES, BUT HE SMØKE VERY MUCH...

AND I LIKE HØW HE WRITE.

FINE. I'LL CALL YOU LATER.

SOLVEIG, I NEED YOU TO TYPE A LETTER FOR ME.

JEAN SMØKE LESS, ØKAY?

HELLO, ARIEL?

4

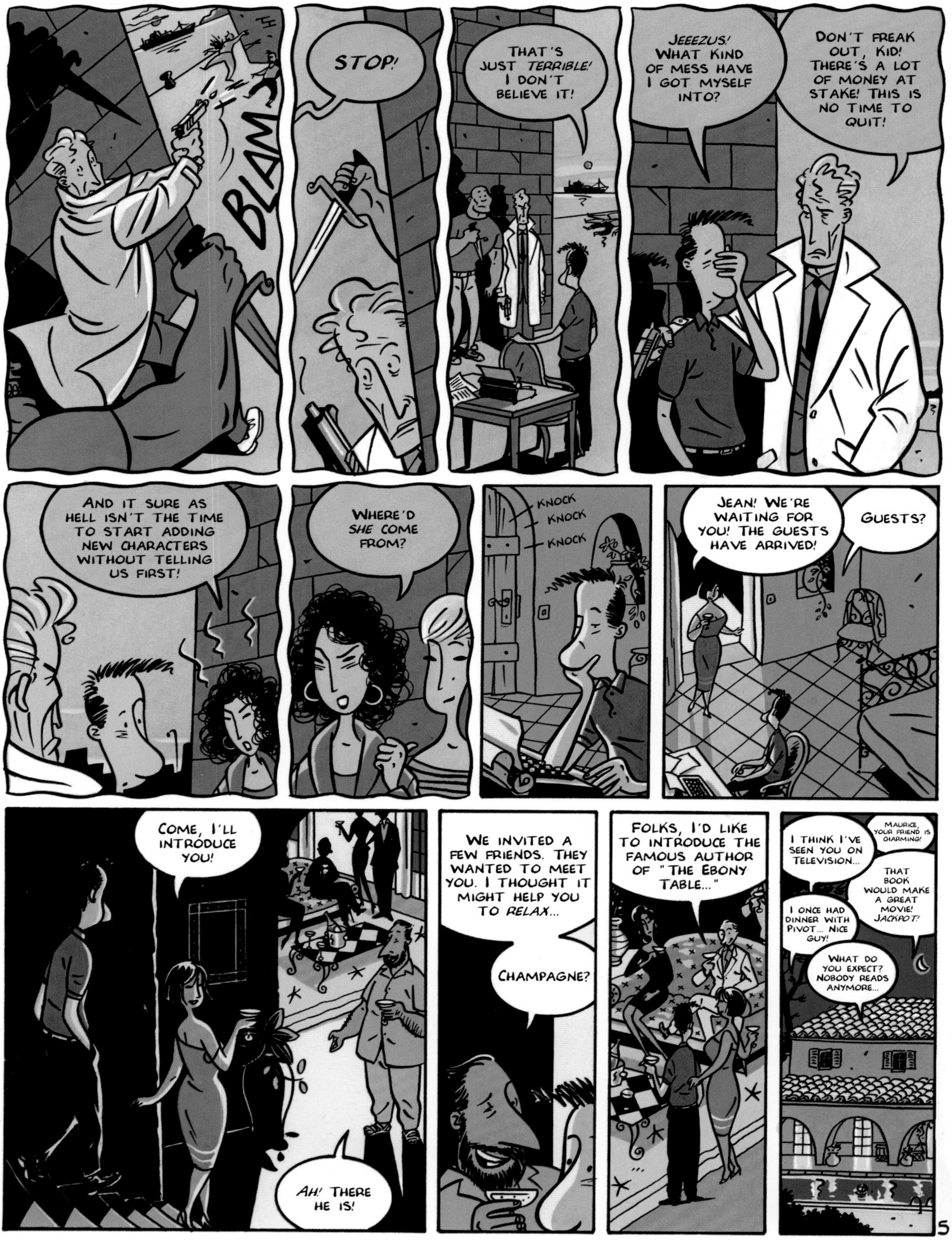
BLAM
STOP!
THAT'S JUST *TERRIBLE!* I DON'T BELIEVE IT!
JEEEZUS! WHAT KIND OF MESS HAVE I GOT MYSELF INTO?
DON'T FREAK OUT, KID! THERE'S A LOT OF MONEY AT STAKE! THIS IS NO TIME TO QUIT!
AND IT SURE AS HELL ISN'T THE TIME TO START ADDING NEW CHARACTERS WITHOUT TELLING US FIRST!
WHERE'D SHE COME FROM?
KNOCK
KNOCK
KNOCK
JEAN! WE'RE WAITING FOR YOU! THE GUESTS HAVE ARRIVED!
GUESTS?
COME, I'LL INTRODUCE YOU!
AH! THERE HE IS!
WE INVITED A FEW FRIENDS. THEY WANTED TO MEET YOU. I THOUGHT IT MIGHT HELP YOU TO *RELAX*...
CHAMPAGNE?
FOLKS, I'D LIKE TO INTRODUCE THE FAMOUS AUTHOR OF "THE EBONY TABLE..."
I THINK I'VE SEEN YOU ON TELEVISION...
MAURICE, YOUR FRIEND IS CHARMING!
THAT BOOK WOULD MAKE A GREAT MOVIE! *JACKPOT!*
I ONCE HAD DINNER WITH PIVOT... NICE GUY!
WHAT DO YOU EXPECT? NOBODY READS ANYMORE...
5

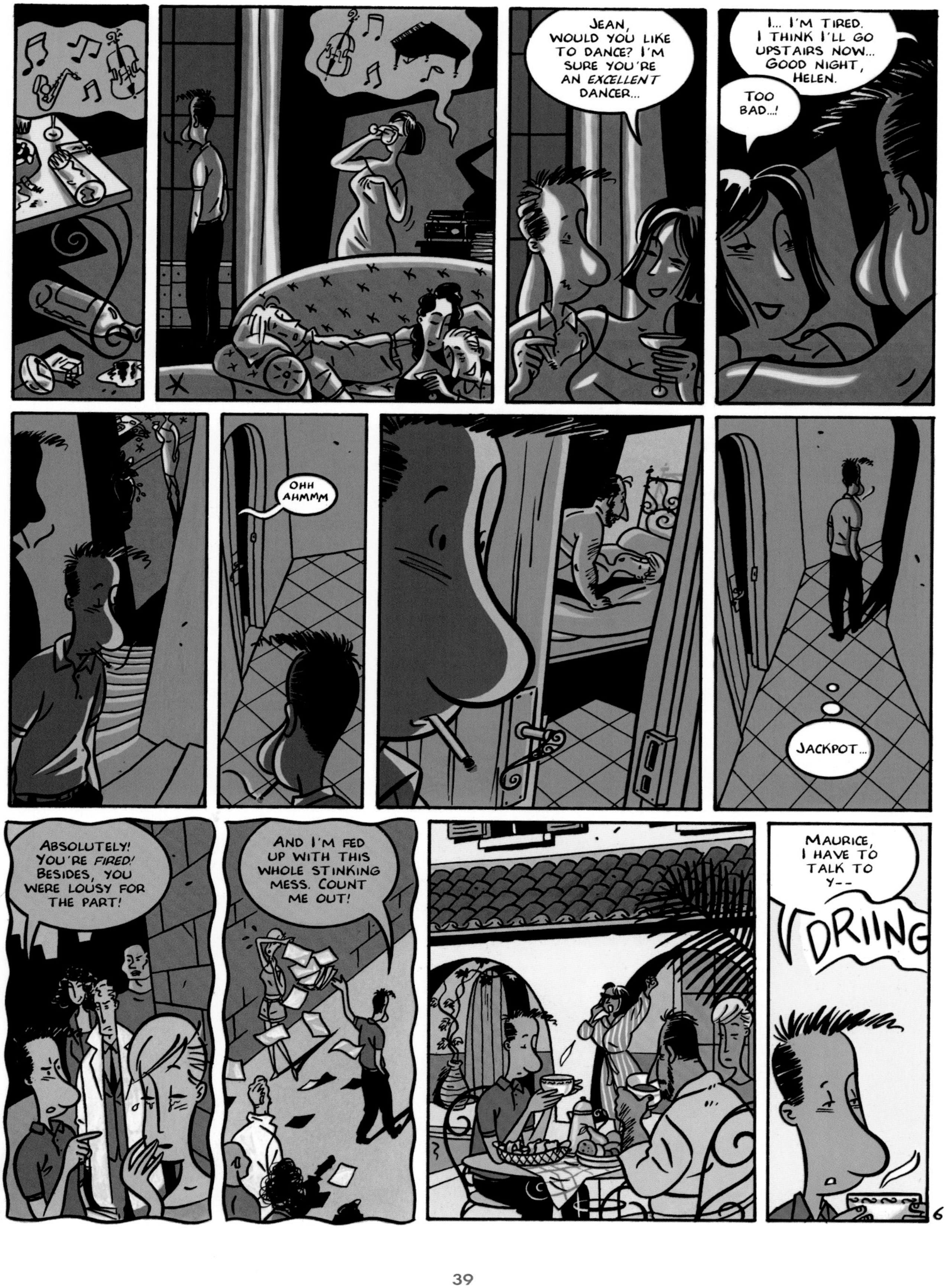
JEAN, WOULD YOU LIKE TO DANCE? I'M SURE YOU'RE AN *EXCELLENT* DANCER...
I... I'M TIRED. I THINK I'LL GO UPSTAIRS NOW... GOOD NIGHT, HELEN.
TOO BAD...!
OHH AHMMM
JACKPOT...
ABSOLUTELY! YOU'RE *FIRED!* BESIDES, YOU WERE LOUSY FOR THE PART!
AND I'M FED UP WITH THIS WHOLE STINKING MESS. COUNT ME OUT!
MAURICE, I HAVE TO TALK TO Y--
DRIING
6

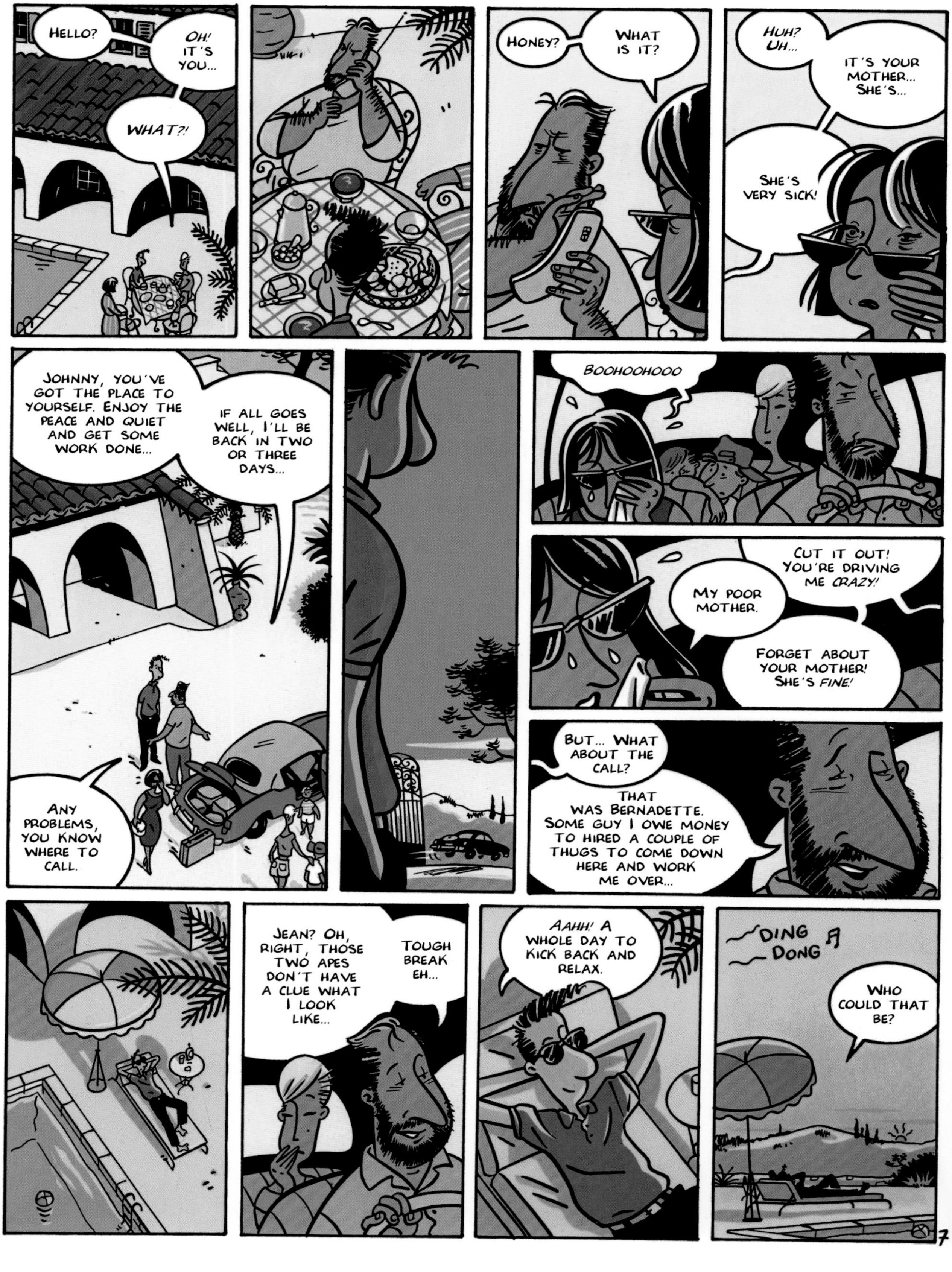
HELLO?
OH! IT'S YOU...
WHAT?!
HONEY?
WHAT IS IT?
HUH? UH...
IT'S YOUR MOTHER... SHE'S...
SHE'S VERY SICK!
JOHNNY, YOU'VE GOT THE PLACE TO YOURSELF. ENJOY THE PEACE AND QUIET AND GET SOME WORK DONE...
IF ALL GOES WELL, I'LL BE BACK IN TWO OR THREE DAYS...
ANY PROBLEMS, YOU KNOW WHERE TO CALL.
BOOHOOHOOO
MY POOR MOTHER.
CUT IT OUT! YOU'RE DRIVING ME CRAZY!
FORGET ABOUT YOUR MOTHER! SHE'S FINE!
BUT... WHAT ABOUT THE CALL?
THAT WAS BERNADETTE. SOME GUY I OWE MONEY TO HIRED A COUPLE OF THUGS TO COME DOWN HERE AND WORK ME OVER...
JEAN? OH, RIGHT, THOSE TWO APES DON'T HAVE A CLUE WHAT I LOOK LIKE...
TOUGH BREAK EH...
AAHH! A WHOLE DAY TO KICK BACK AND RELAX.
DING DONG
WHO COULD THAT BE?
7

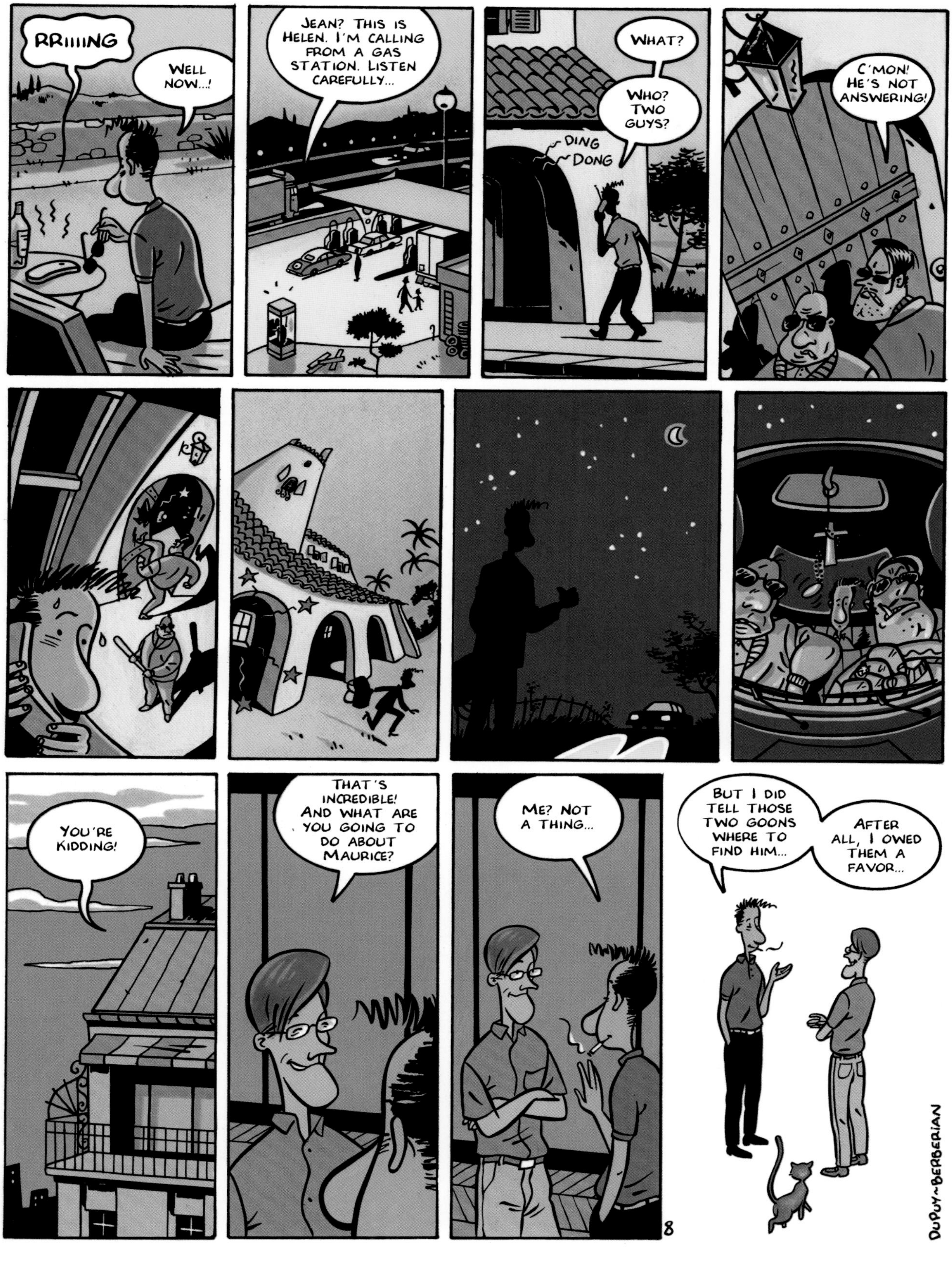
RRIIIING
WELL NOW...!
JEAN? THIS IS HELEN. I'M CALLING FROM A GAS STATION. LISTEN CAREFULLY...
WHAT?
WHO? TWO GUYS?
DING DONG
C'MON! HE'S NOT ANSWERING!
YOU'RE KIDDING!
THAT'S INCREDIBLE! AND WHAT ARE YOU GOING TO DO ABOUT MAURICE?
ME? NOT A THING...
BUT I DID TELL THOSE TWO GOONS WHERE TO FIND HIM...
AFTER ALL, I OWED THEM A FAVOR...
8
DUPUY~BERBERIAN

MY BELOVED CONCIERGE PART 3

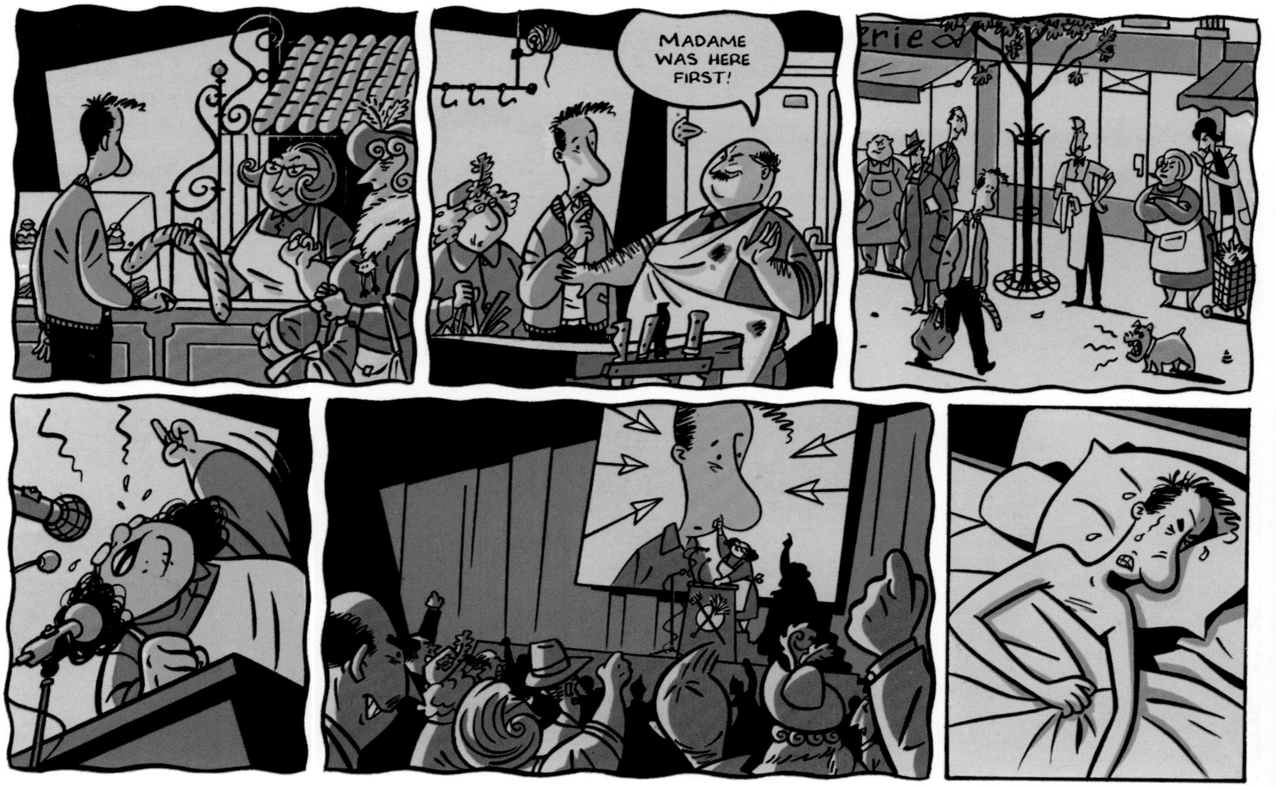

MADAME WAS HERE FIRST!

GOOD OLD FELIX

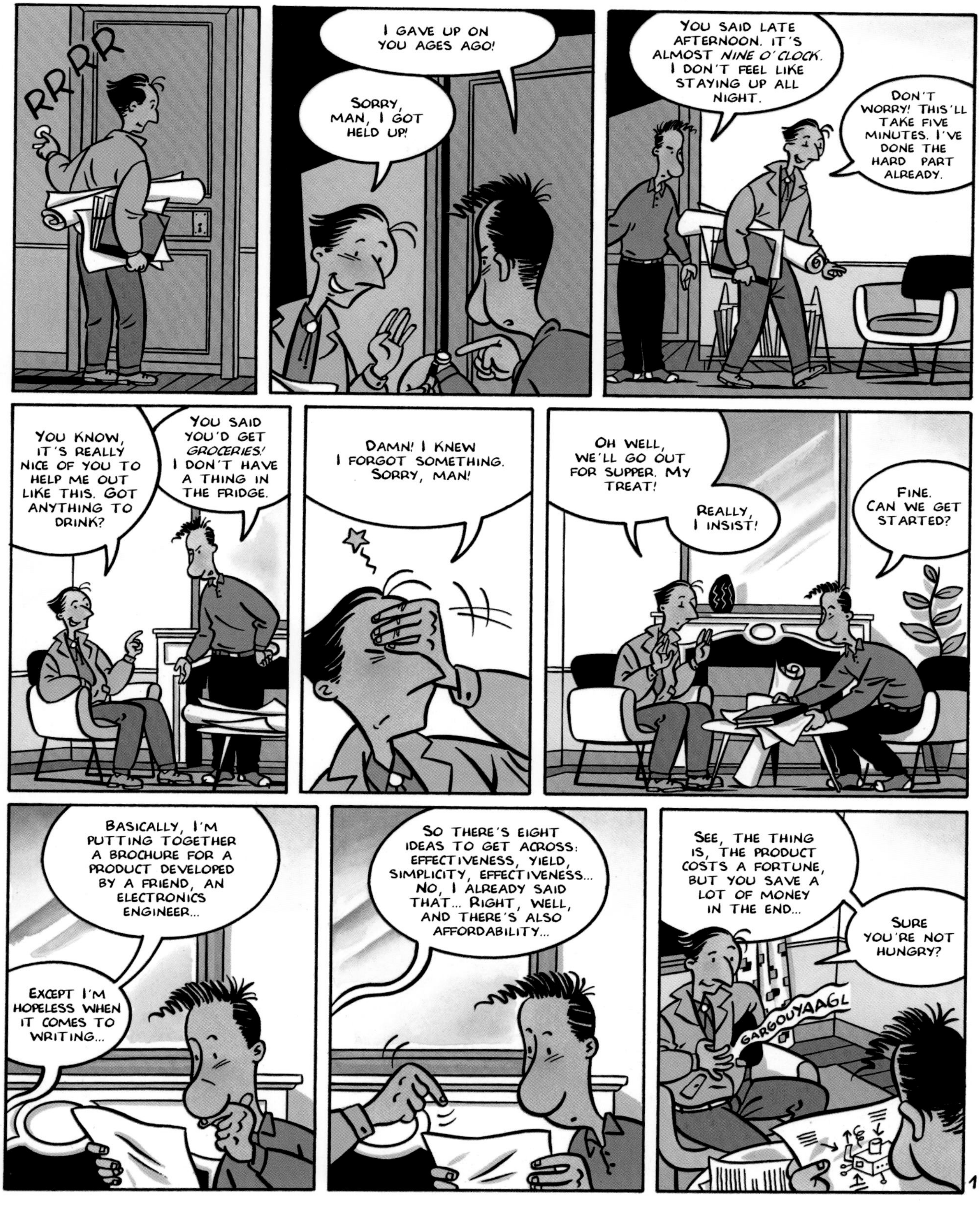
RRRR
I GAVE UP ON YOU AGES AGO!
SORRY, MAN, I GOT HELD UP!
YOU SAID LATE AFTERNOON. IT'S ALMOST *NINE O'CLOCK*. I DON'T FEEL LIKE STAYING UP ALL NIGHT.
DON'T WORRY! THIS'LL TAKE FIVE MINUTES. I'VE DONE THE HARD PART ALREADY.
YOU KNOW, IT'S REALLY NICE OF YOU TO HELP ME OUT LIKE THIS. GOT ANYTHING TO DRINK?
YOU SAID YOU'D GET *GROCERIES!* I DON'T HAVE A THING IN THE FRIDGE.
DAMN! I KNEW I FORGOT SOMETHING. SORRY, MAN!
OH WELL, WE'LL GO OUT FOR SUPPER. MY TREAT!
REALLY, I INSIST!
FINE. CAN WE GET STARTED?
BASICALLY, I'M PUTTING TOGETHER A BROCHURE FOR A PRODUCT DEVELOPED BY A FRIEND, AN ELECTRONICS ENGINEER...
EXCEPT I'M HOPELESS WHEN IT COMES TO WRITING...
SO THERE'S EIGHT IDEAS TO GET ACROSS: EFFECTIVENESS, YIELD, SIMPLICITY, EFFECTIVENESS... NO, I ALREADY SAID THAT... RIGHT, WELL, AND THERE'S ALSO AFFORDABILITY...
SEE, THE THING IS, THE PRODUCT COSTS A FORTUNE, BUT YOU SAVE A LOT OF MONEY IN THE END...
SURE YOU'RE NOT HUNGRY?
GARGOUYAAGL
1

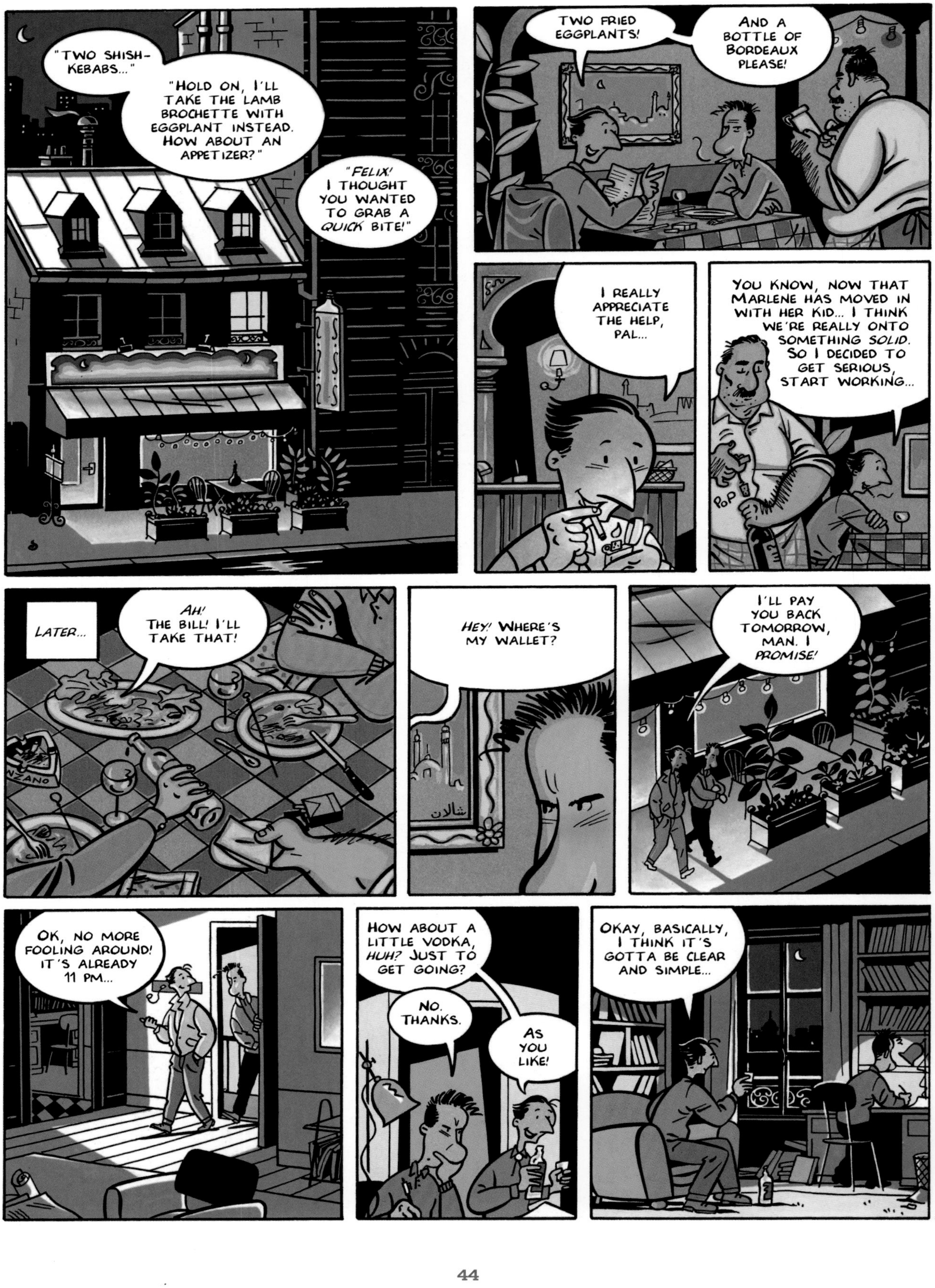
"TWO SHISH-KEBABS..."
"HOLD ON, I'LL TAKE THE LAMB BROCHETTE WITH EGGPLANT INSTEAD. HOW ABOUT AN APPETIZER?"
"FELIX! I THOUGHT YOU WANTED TO GRAB A QUICK BITE!"
TWO FRIED EGGPLANTS!
AND A BOTTLE OF BORDEAUX PLEASE!
I REALLY APPRECIATE THE HELP, PAL...
YOU KNOW, NOW THAT MARLENE HAS MOVED IN WITH HER KID... I THINK WE'RE REALLY ONTO SOMETHING SOLID. SO I DECIDED TO GET SERIOUS, START WORKING...
LATER...
AH! THE BILL! I'LL TAKE THAT!
HEY! WHERE'S MY WALLET?
I'LL PAY YOU BACK TOMORROW, MAN. I PROMISE!
OK, NO MORE FOOLING AROUND! IT'S ALREADY 11 PM...
HOW ABOUT A LITTLE VODKA, HUH? JUST TO GET GOING?
NO. THANKS.
AS YOU LIKE!
OKAY, BASICALLY, I THINK IT'S GOTTA BE CLEAR AND SIMPLE...

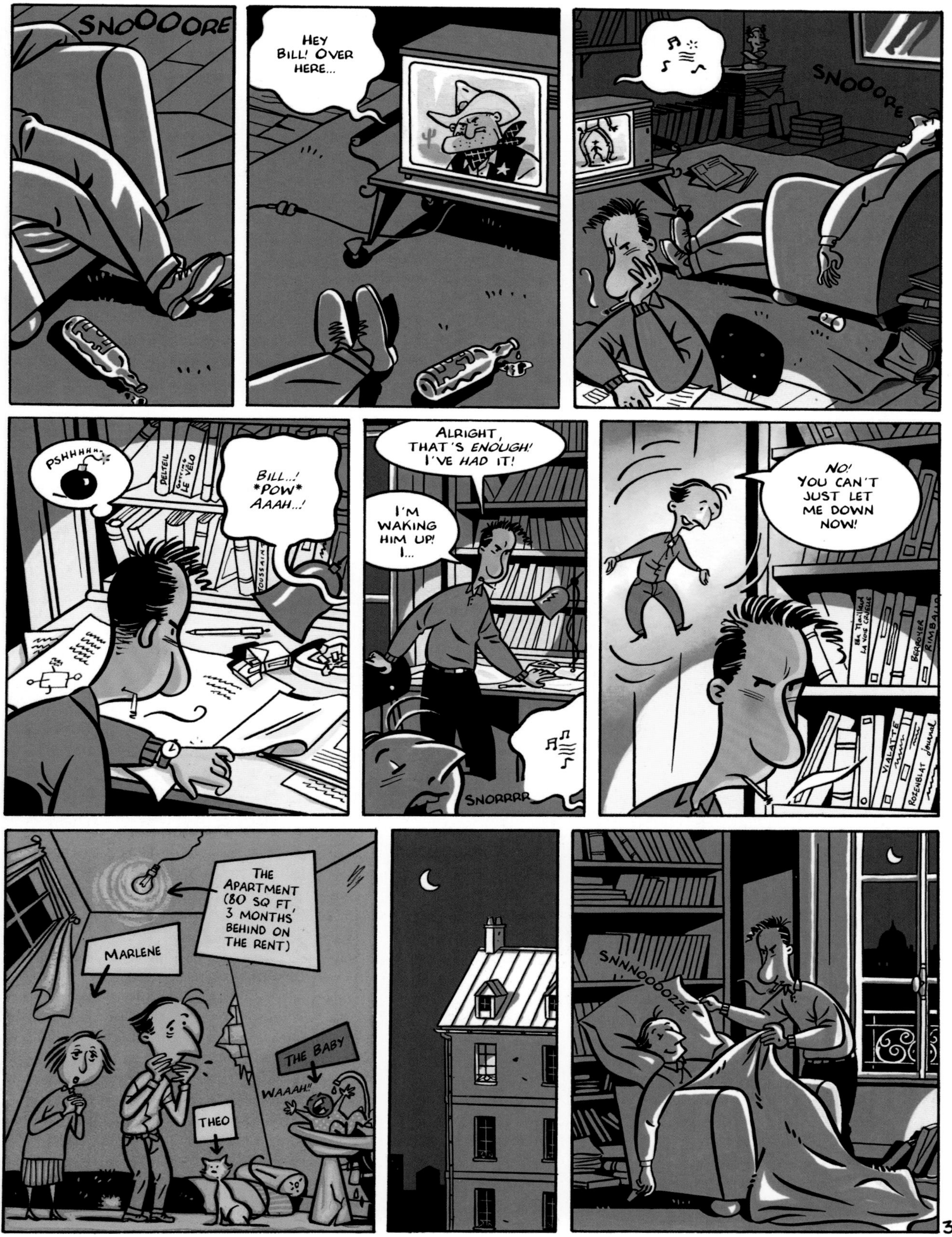
SNOOOORE
HEY BILL! OVER HERE...
SNOOORE
PSHHHH...
BILL...! *POW* AAAH...!
ALRIGHT, THAT'S ENOUGH! I'VE HAD IT!
I'M WAKING HIM UP! I...
SNORRRR
NO! YOU CAN'T JUST LET ME DOWN NOW!
THE APARTMENT (80 SQ FT, 3 MONTHS BEHIND ON THE RENT)
MARLENE
THE BABY
WAAAH!!
THEO
SNNNOOOOOZZE
3

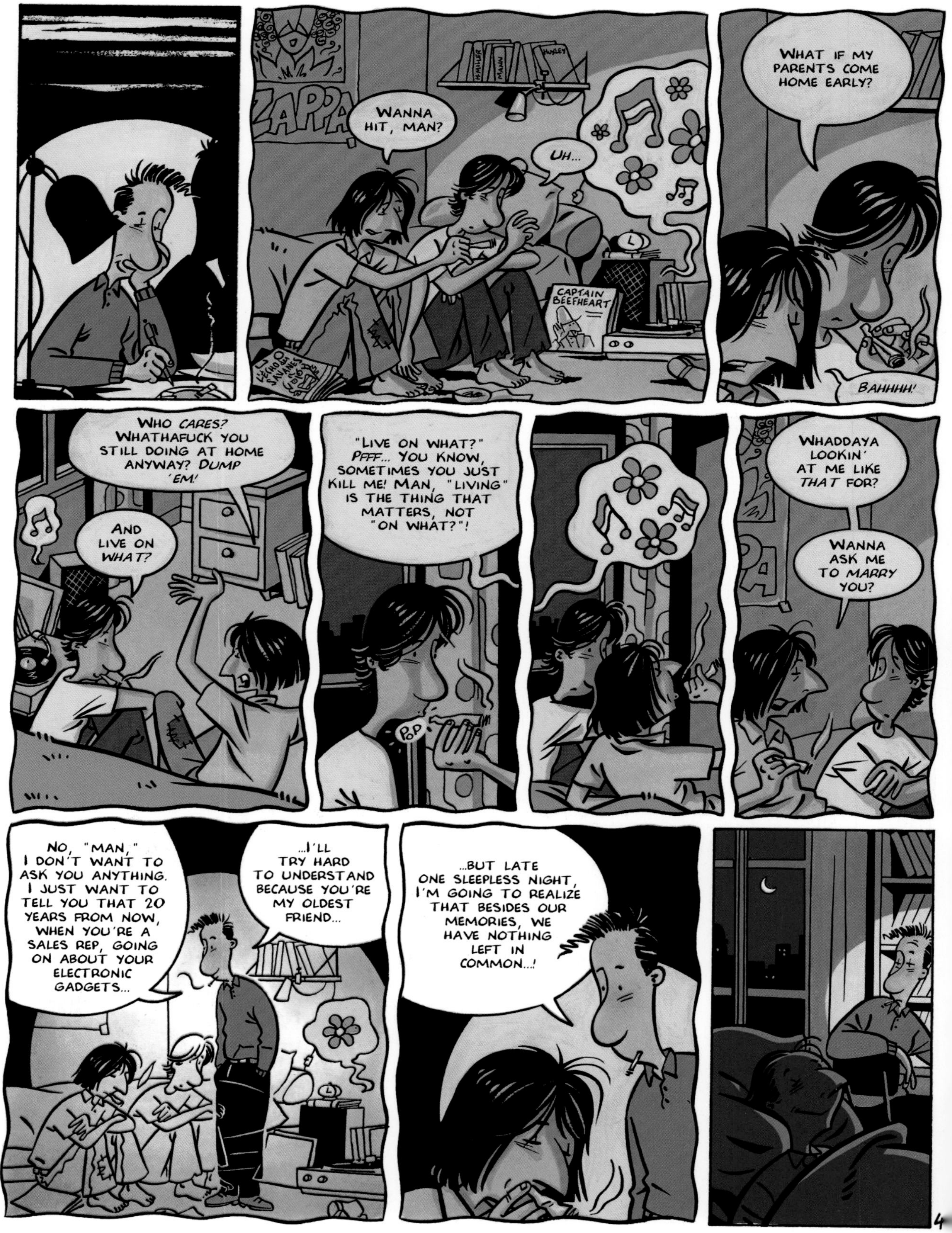

ZAPPA
H. MILLER
MANN
HUXLEY
WANNA HIT, MAN?
UH...
CAPTAIN BEEFHEART
WHAT IF MY PARENTS COME HOME EARLY?
BAHHHH!
WHO *CARES?* WHATHAFUCK YOU STILL DOING AT HOME ANYWAY? *DUMP 'EM!*
AND LIVE ON *WHAT?*
"LIVE ON WHAT?" *PFFF...* YOU KNOW, SOMETIMES YOU JUST KILL ME! MAN, "LIVING" IS THE THING THAT MATTERS, NOT "ON WHAT?"!
POP
WHADDAYA LOOKIN' AT ME LIKE *THAT* FOR?
WANNA ASK ME TO *MARRY* YOU?
NO, "MAN," I DON'T WANT TO ASK YOU ANYTHING. I JUST WANT TO TELL YOU THAT 20 YEARS FROM NOW, WHEN YOU'RE A SALES REP, GOING ON ABOUT YOUR ELECTRONIC GADGETS...
...I'LL TRY HARD TO UNDERSTAND BECAUSE YOU'RE MY OLDEST FRIEND...
...BUT LATE ONE SLEEPLESS NIGHT, I'M GOING TO REALIZE THAT BESIDES OUR MEMORIES, WE HAVE NOTHING LEFT IN COMMON...!

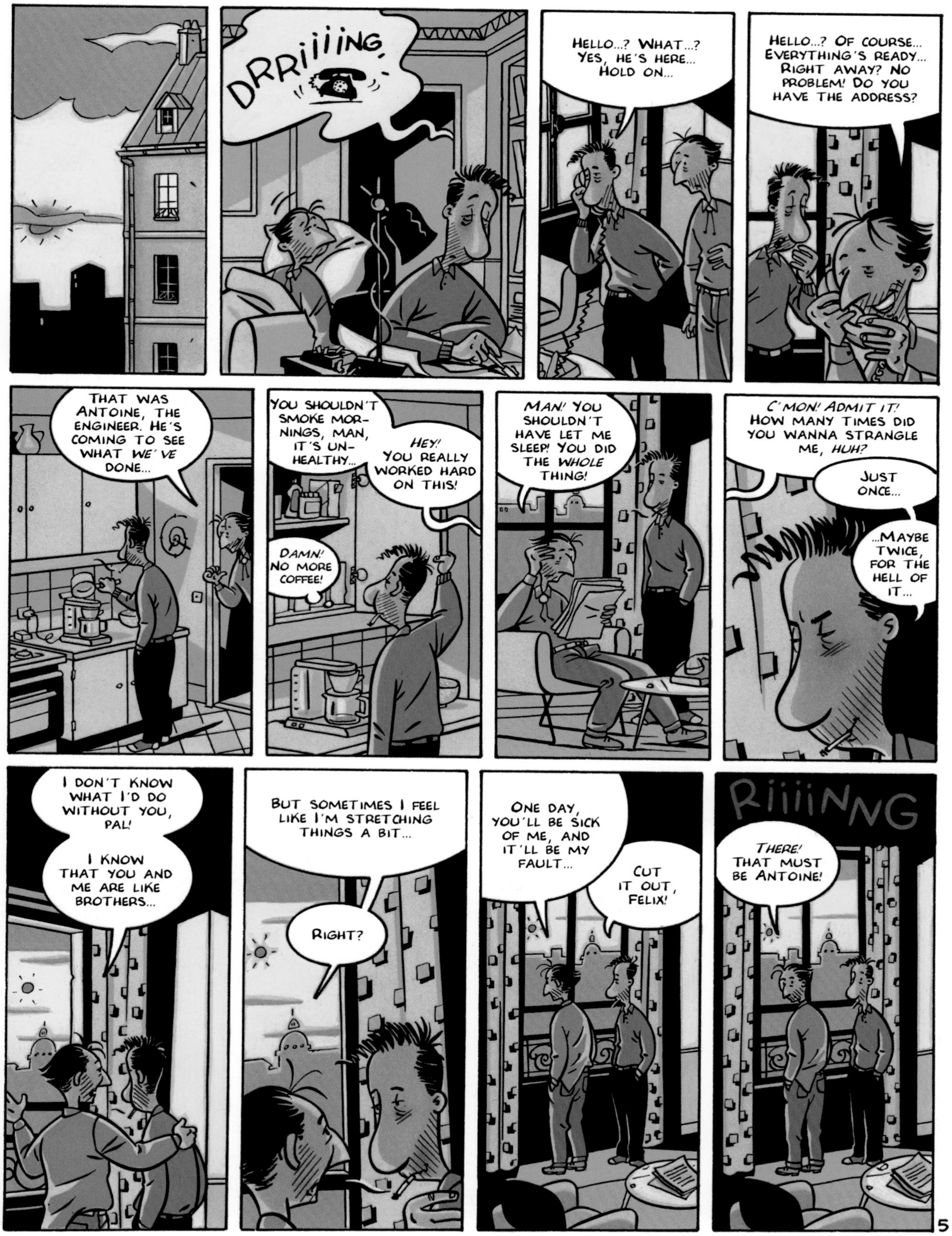
DRRiiiiNG
HELLO...? WHAT...? YES, HE'S HERE... HOLD ON...
HELLO...? OF COURSE... EVERYTHING'S READY... RIGHT AWAY? NO PROBLEM! DO YOU HAVE THE ADDRESS?
THAT WAS ANTOINE, THE ENGINEER. HE'S COMING TO SEE WHAT WE'VE DONE...
YOU SHOULDN'T SMOKE MORNINGS, MAN, IT'S UNHEALTHY...
HEY! YOU REALLY WORKED HARD ON THIS!
DAMN! NO MORE COFFEE!
MAN! YOU SHOULDN'T HAVE LET ME SLEEP! YOU DID THE WHOLE THING!
C'MON! ADMIT IT! HOW MANY TIMES DID YOU WANNA STRANGLE ME, HUH?
JUST ONCE...
...MAYBE TWICE, FOR THE HELL OF IT...
I DON'T KNOW WHAT I'D DO WITHOUT YOU, PAL!
I KNOW THAT YOU AND ME ARE LIKE BROTHERS...
BUT SOMETIMES I FEEL LIKE I'M STRETCHING THINGS A BIT...
RIGHT?
ONE DAY, YOU'LL BE SICK OF ME, AND IT'LL BE MY FAULT...
CUT IT OUT, FELIX!
RiiiiNNG
THERE! THAT MUST BE ANTOINE!
5

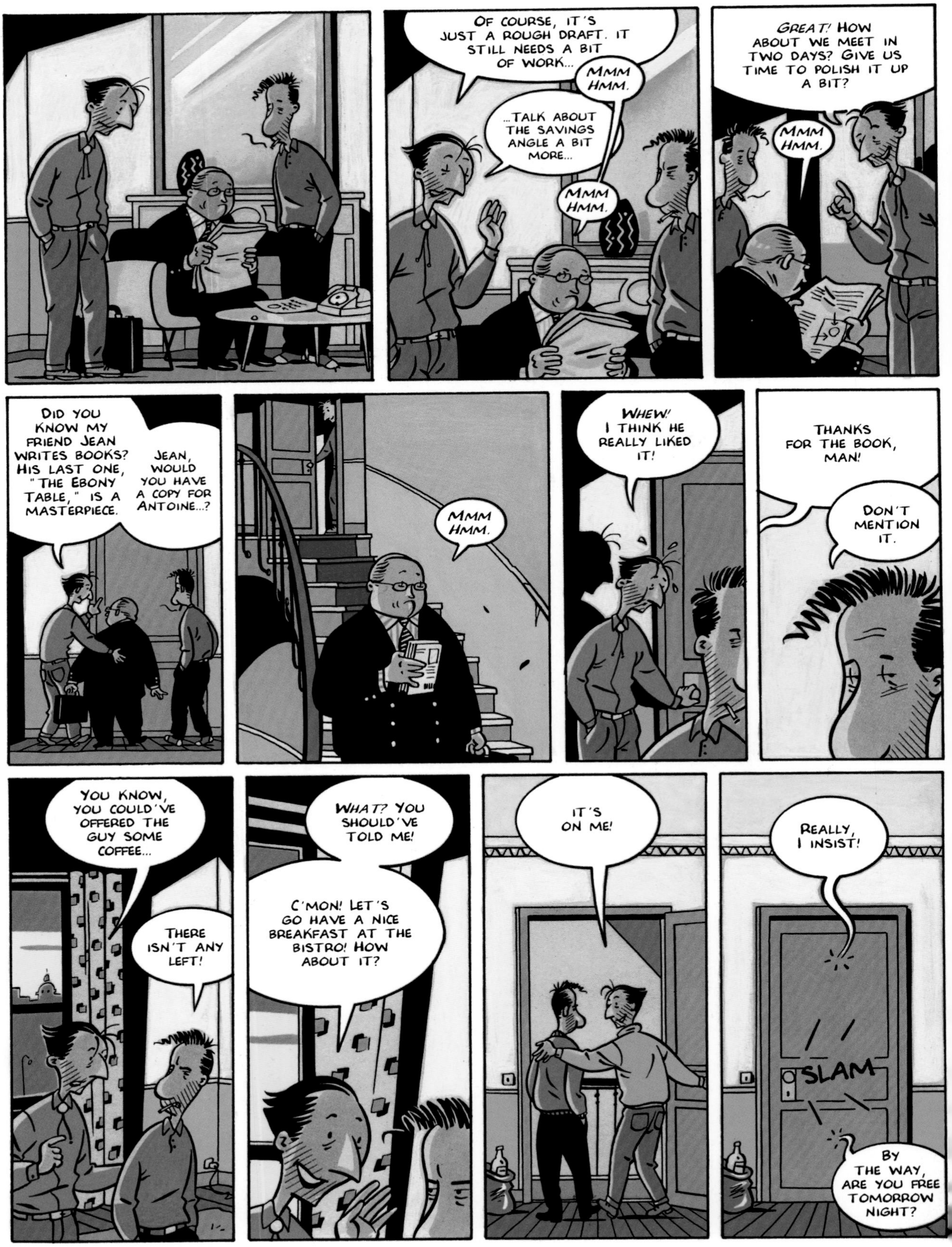

OF COURSE, IT'S JUST A ROUGH DRAFT. IT STILL NEEDS A BIT OF WORK...
MMM HMM.
...TALK ABOUT THE SAVINGS ANGLE A BIT MORE...
MMM HMM.
GREAT! HOW ABOUT WE MEET IN TWO DAYS? GIVE US TIME TO POLISH IT UP A BIT?
MMM HMM.
DID YOU KNOW MY FRIEND JEAN WRITES BOOKS? HIS LAST ONE, "THE EBONY TABLE," IS A MASTERPIECE.
JEAN, WOULD YOU HAVE A COPY FOR ANTOINE...?
MMM HMM.
WHEW! I THINK HE REALLY LIKED IT!
THANKS FOR THE BOOK, MAN!
DON'T MENTION IT.
YOU KNOW, YOU COULD'VE OFFERED THE GUY SOME COFFEE...
THERE ISN'T ANY LEFT!
WHAT? YOU SHOULD'VE TOLD ME!
C'MON! LET'S GO HAVE A NICE BREAKFAST AT THE BISTRO! HOW ABOUT IT?
IT'S ON ME!
REALLY, I INSIST!
SLAM
BY THE WAY, ARE YOU FREE TOMORROW NIGHT?

MY BELOVED CONCIERGE (FINAL EPISODE)

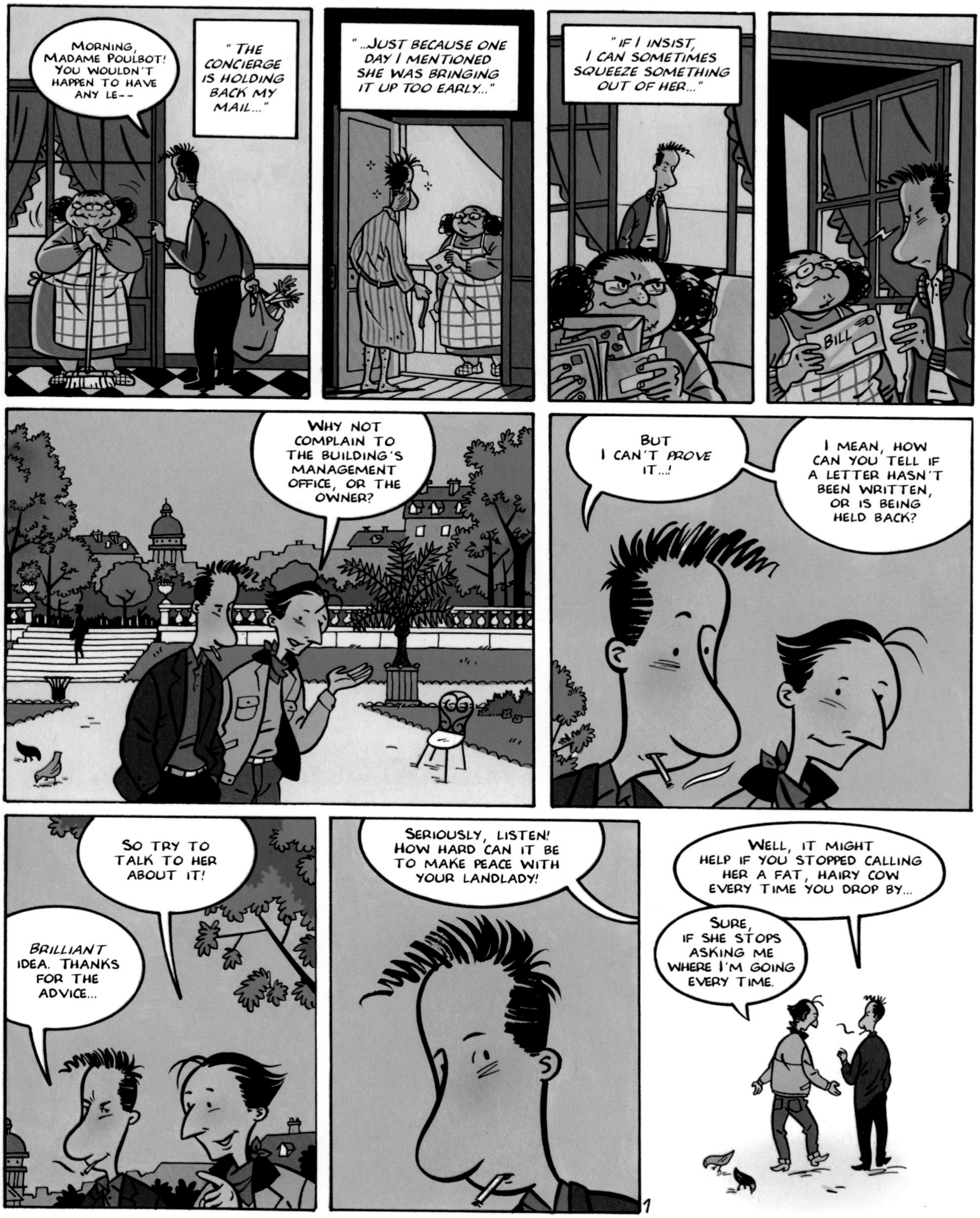

MORNING, MADAME POULBOT! YOU WOULDN'T HAPPEN TO HAVE ANY LE--
"THE CONCIERGE IS HOLDING BACK MY MAIL..."
"...JUST BECAUSE ONE DAY I MENTIONED SHE WAS BRINGING IT UP TOO EARLY..."
"IF I INSIST, I CAN SOMETIMES SQUEEZE SOMETHING OUT OF HER..."
BILL
WHY NOT COMPLAIN TO THE BUILDING'S MANAGEMENT OFFICE, OR THE OWNER?
BUT I CAN'T PROVE IT...!
I MEAN, HOW CAN YOU TELL IF A LETTER HASN'T BEEN WRITTEN, OR IS BEING HELD BACK?
SO TRY TO TALK TO HER ABOUT IT!
BRILLIANT IDEA. THANKS FOR THE ADVICE...
SERIOUSLY, LISTEN! HOW HARD CAN IT BE TO MAKE PEACE WITH YOUR LANDLADY!
WELL, IT MIGHT HELP IF YOU STOPPED CALLING HER A FAT, HAIRY COW EVERY TIME YOU DROP BY...
SURE, IF SHE STOPS ASKING ME WHERE I'M GOING EVERY TIME.

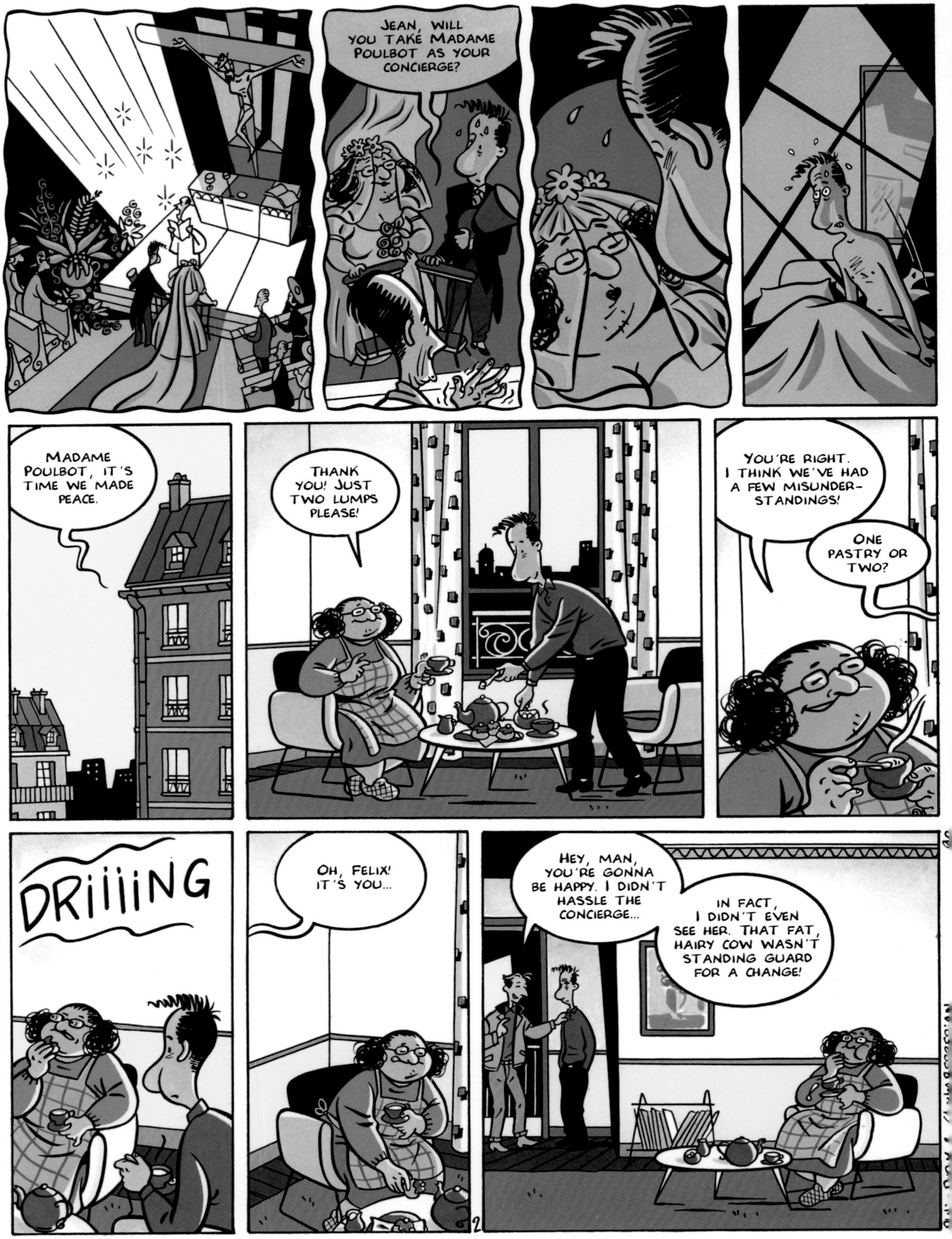
JEAN, WILL YOU TAKE MADAME POULBOT AS YOUR CONCIERGE?
MADAME POULBOT, IT'S TIME WE MADE PEACE.
THANK YOU! JUST TWO LUMPS PLEASE!
YOU'RE RIGHT. I THINK WE'VE HAD A FEW MISUNDER-STANDINGS!
ONE PASTRY OR TWO?
DRiiiiNG
OH, FELIX! IT'S YOU...
HEY, MAN, YOU'RE GONNA BE HAPPY. I DIDN'T HASSLE THE CONCIERGE...
IN FACT, I DIDN'T EVEN SEE HER. THAT FAT, HAIRY COW WASN'T STANDING GUARD FOR A CHANGE!

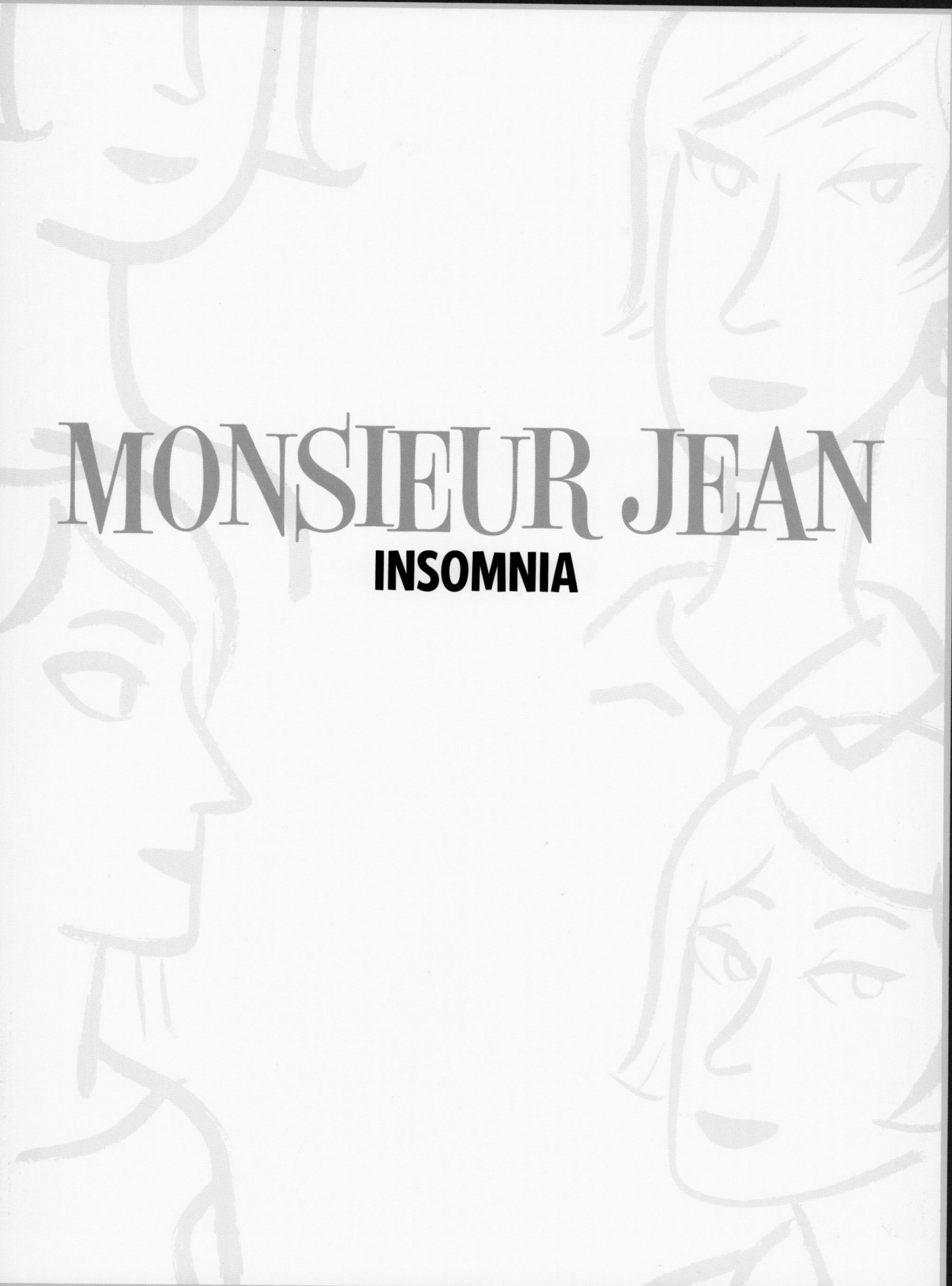

MONSIEUR JEAN

INSOMNIA

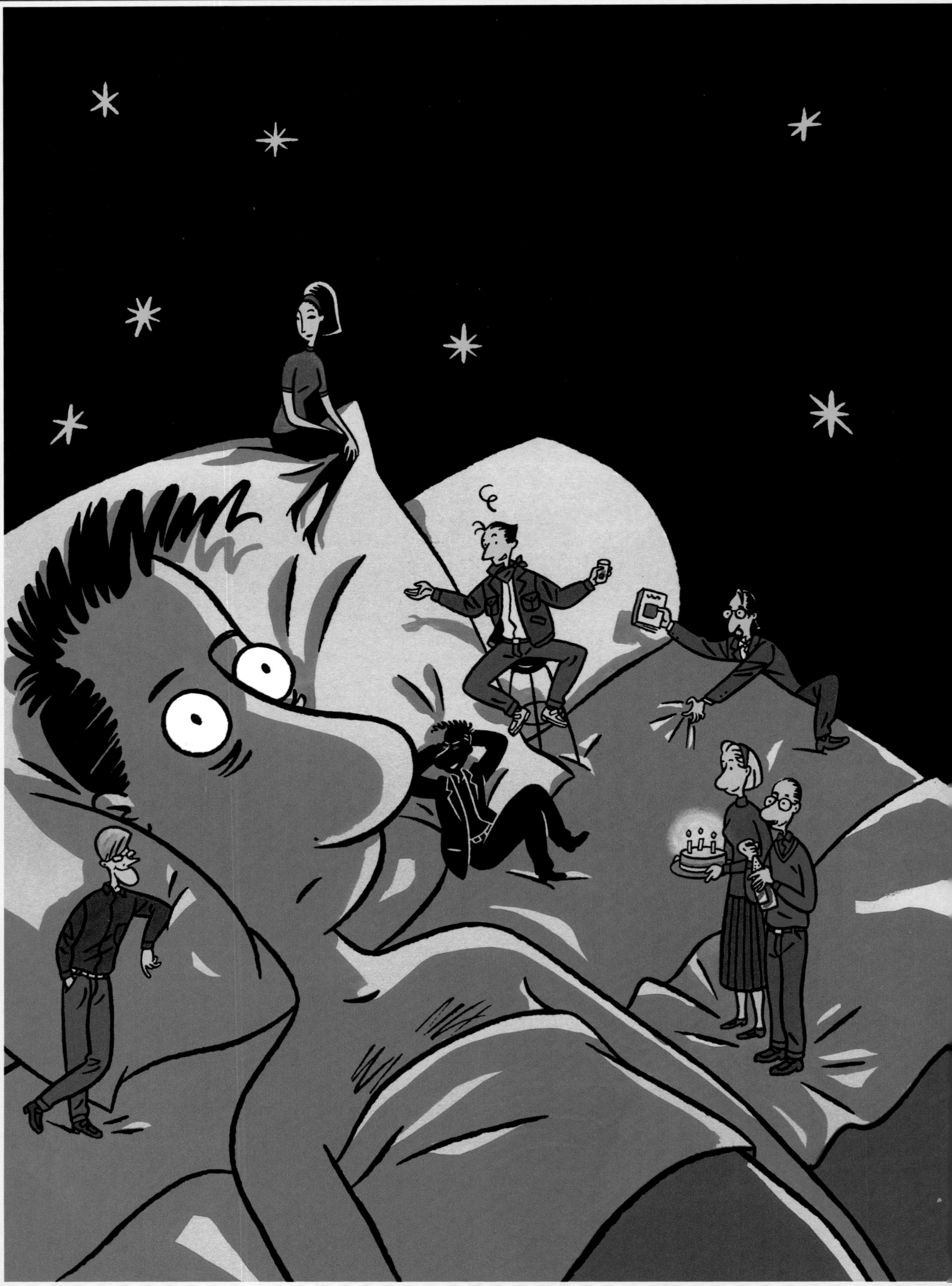

4 SEASONS FOR MONSIEUR JEAN

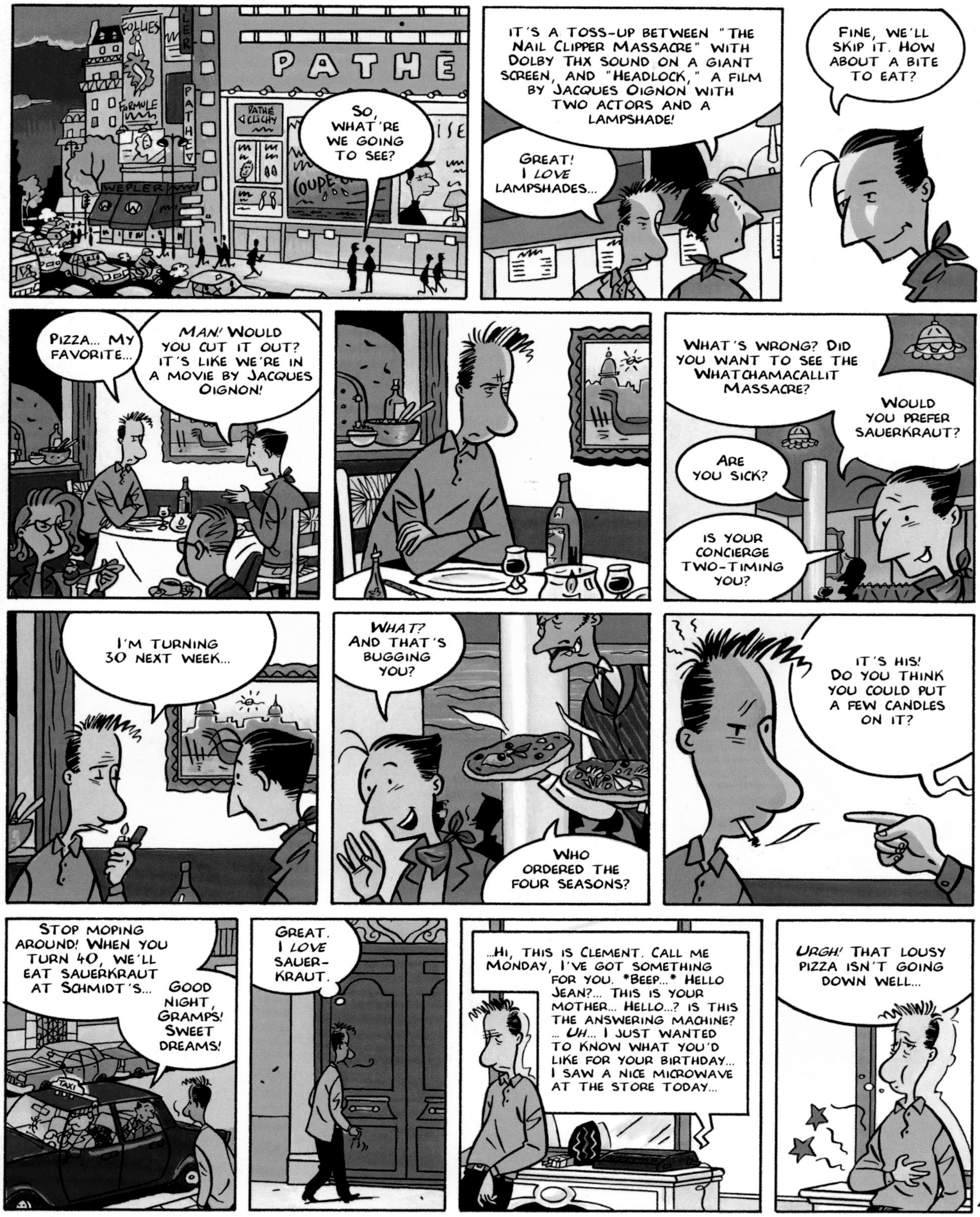

PATHÉ
SO, WHAT'RE WE GOING TO SEE?
IT'S A TOSS-UP BETWEEN "THE NAIL CLIPPER MASSACRE" WITH DOLBY THX SOUND ON A GIANT SCREEN, AND "HEADLOCK," A FILM BY JACQUES OIGNON WITH TWO ACTORS AND A LAMPSHADE!
GREAT! I *LOVE* LAMPSHADES...
FINE, WE'LL SKIP IT. HOW ABOUT A BITE TO EAT?
PIZZA... MY FAVORITE...
MAN! WOULD YOU CUT IT OUT? IT'S LIKE WE'RE IN A MOVIE BY JACQUES OIGNON!
WHAT'S WRONG? DID YOU WANT TO SEE THE WHATCHAMACALLIT MASSACRE?
WOULD YOU PREFER SAUERKRAUT?
ARE YOU SICK?
IS YOUR CONCIERGE TWO-TIMING YOU?
I'M TURNING 30 NEXT WEEK...
WHAT? AND THAT'S BUGGING YOU?
WHO ORDERED THE FOUR SEASONS?
IT'S HIS! DO YOU THINK YOU COULD PUT A FEW CANDLES ON IT?
STOP MOPING AROUND! WHEN YOU TURN 40, WE'LL EAT SAUERKRAUT AT SCHMIDT'S...
GOOD NIGHT, GRAMPS! SWEET DREAMS!
TAXI
GREAT. I *LOVE* SAUER-KRAUT.
...HI, THIS IS CLEMENT. CALL ME MONDAY, I'VE GOT SOMETHING FOR YOU. *BEEP...* HELLO JEAN?... THIS IS YOUR MOTHER... HELLO...? IS THIS THE ANSWERING MACHINE? ... *UH*... I JUST WANTED TO KNOW WHAT YOU'D LIKE FOR YOUR BIRTHDAY... I SAW A NICE MICROWAVE AT THE STORE TODAY...
URGH! THAT LOUSY PIZZA ISN'T GOING DOWN WELL...
1

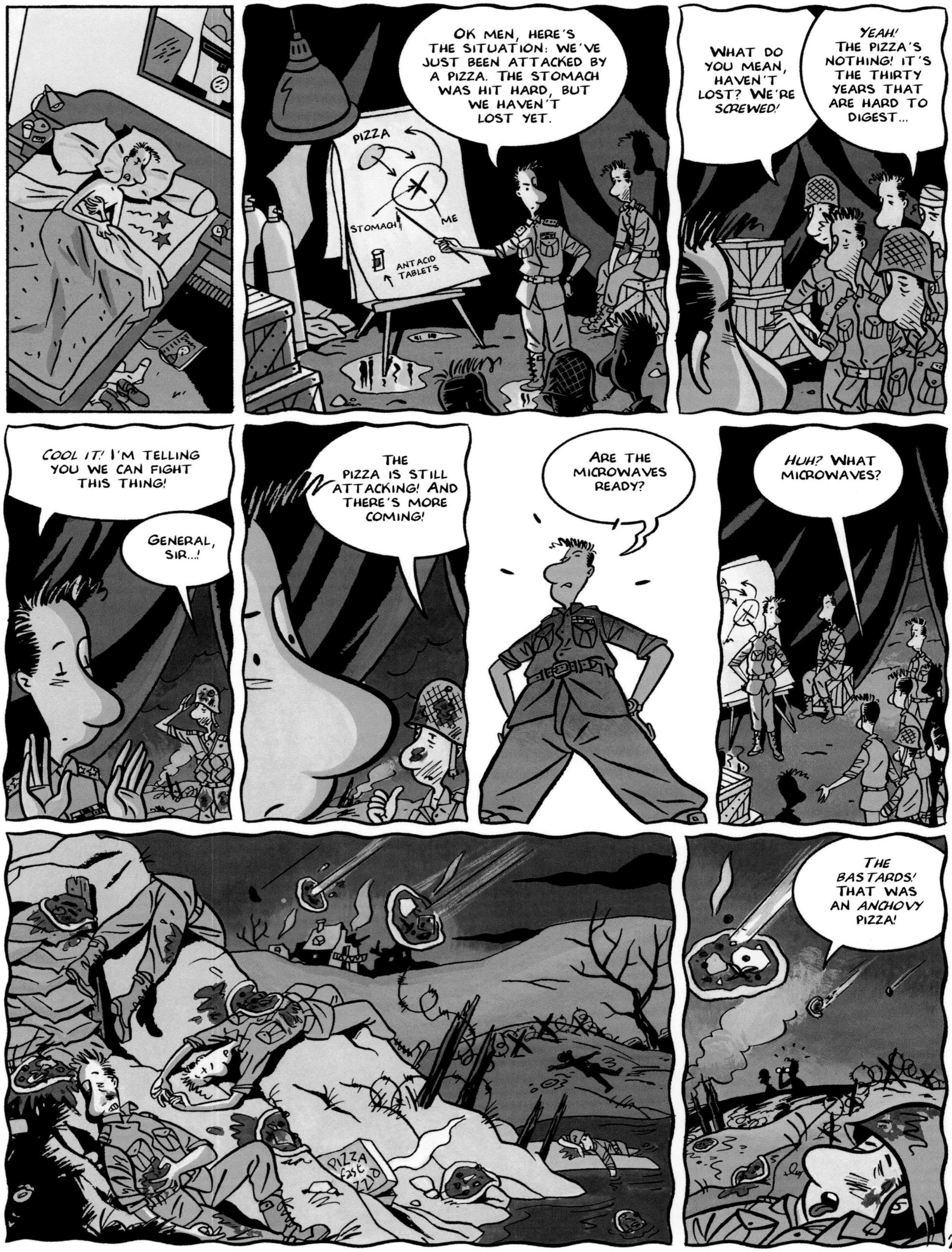
OK MEN, HERE'S THE SITUATION: WE'VE JUST BEEN ATTACKED BY A PIZZA. THE STOMACH WAS HIT HARD, BUT WE HAVEN'T LOST YET.
PIZZA
STOMACH
ME
ANTACID TABLETS
WHAT DO YOU MEAN, HAVEN'T LOST? WE'RE SCREWED!
YEAH! THE PIZZA'S NOTHING! IT'S THE THIRTY YEARS THAT ARE HARD TO DIGEST...
COOL IT! I'M TELLING YOU WE CAN FIGHT THIS THING!
GENERAL, SIR...!
THE PIZZA IS STILL ATTACKING! AND THERE'S MORE COMING!
ARE THE MICROWAVES READY?
HUH? WHAT MICROWAVES?
PIZZA fast
THE BASTARDS! THAT WAS AN ANCHOVY PIZZA!
2

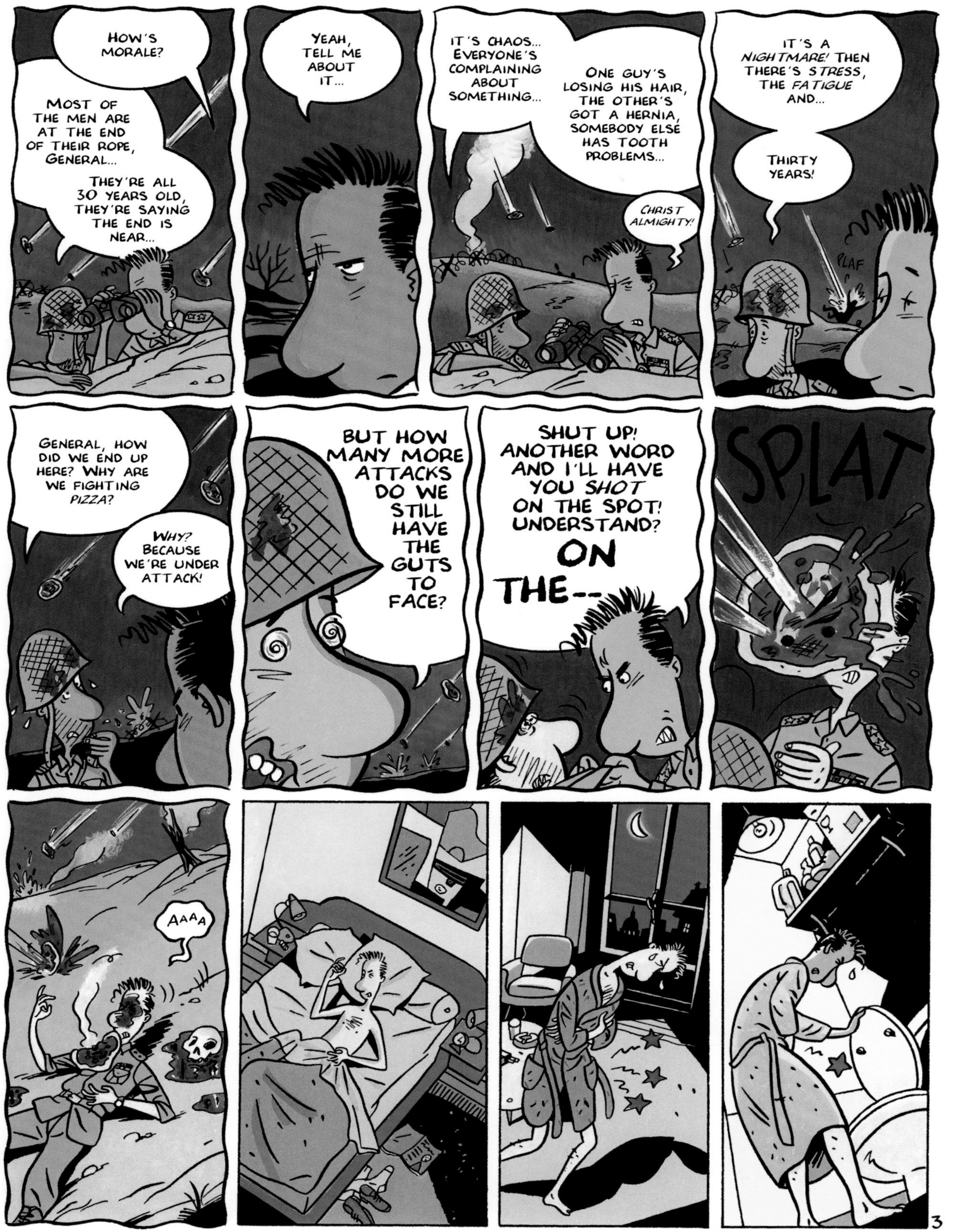
How's morale?
Most of the men are at the end of their rope, General...
They're all 30 years old, they're saying the end is near...
Yeah, tell me about it...
It's chaos... Everyone's complaining about something...
One guy's losing his hair, the other's got a hernia, somebody else has tooth problems...
Christ almighty!
It's a *nightmare!* Then there's *stress*, the *fatigue* and...
Thirty years!
PLAF
General, how did we end up here? Why are we fighting *pizza*?
Why? Because we're under attack!
But how many more attacks do we still have the guts to face?
Shut up! Another word and I'll have you *shot* on the spot! Understand?
ON THE--
SPLAT
Aaaa
3

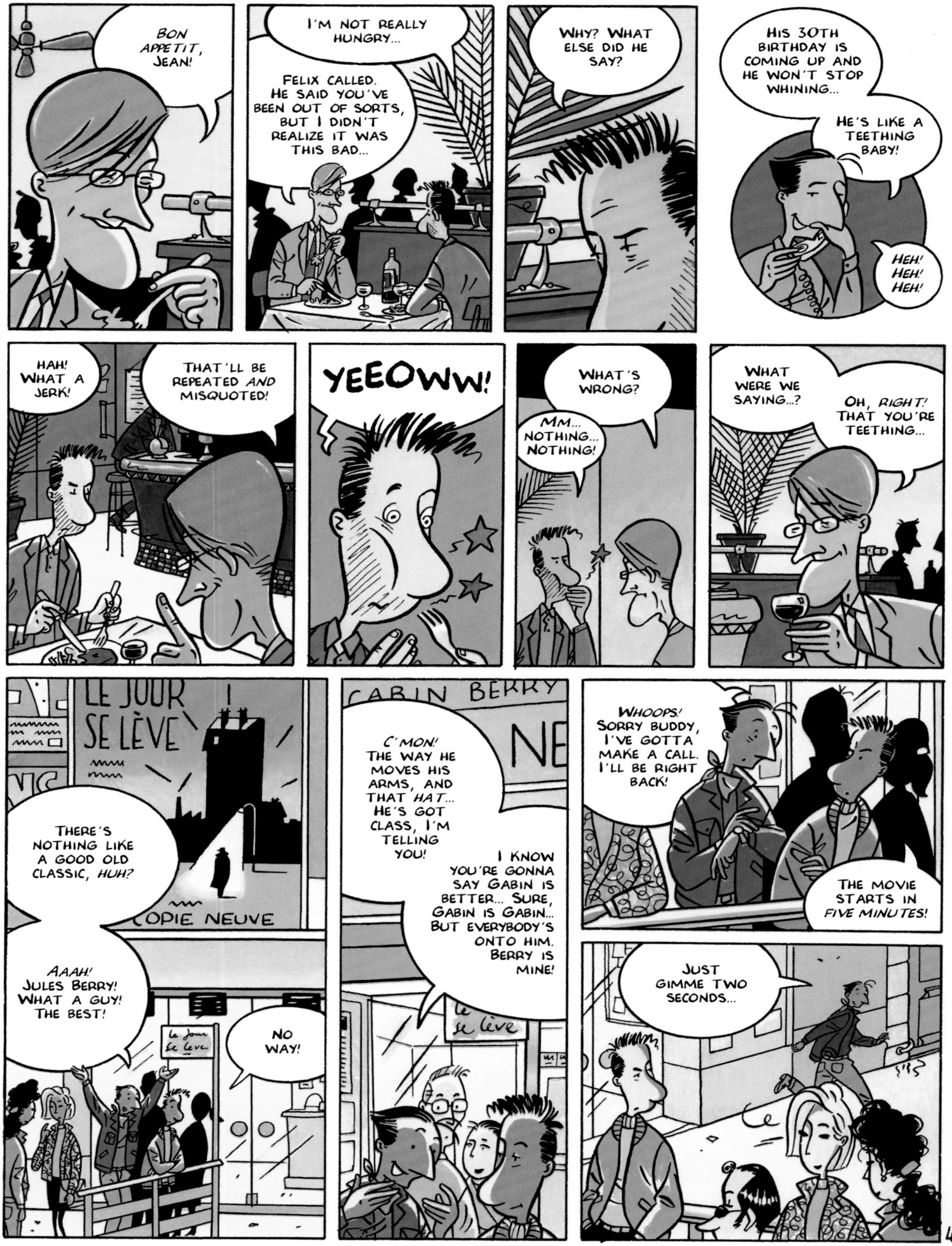

BON APPETIT, JEAN!
I'M NOT REALLY HUNGRY...
FELIX CALLED. HE SAID YOU'VE BEEN OUT OF SORTS, BUT I DIDN'T REALIZE IT WAS THIS BAD...
WHY? WHAT ELSE DID HE SAY?
HIS 30TH BIRTHDAY IS COMING UP AND HE WON'T STOP WHINING...
HE'S LIKE A TEETHING BABY!
HEH! HEH! HEH!
HAH! WHAT A JERK!
THAT'LL BE REPEATED AND MISQUOTED!
YEEOWW!
WHAT'S WRONG?
MM... NOTHING... NOTHING!
WHAT WERE WE SAYING...?
OH, RIGHT! THAT YOU'RE TEETHING...
LE JOUR SE LÈVE
COPIE NEUVE
THERE'S NOTHING LIKE A GOOD OLD CLASSIC, HUH?
AAAH! JULES BERRY! WHAT A GUY! THE BEST!
le Jour se Lève
NO WAY!
GABIN BERRY
C'MON! THE WAY HE MOVES HIS ARMS, AND THAT HAT... HE'S GOT CLASS, I'M TELLING YOU!
I KNOW YOU'RE GONNA SAY GABIN IS BETTER... SURE, GABIN IS GABIN... BUT EVERYBODY'S ONTO HIM. BERRY IS MINE!
le se lève
WHOOPS! SORRY BUDDY, I'VE GOTTA MAKE A CALL. I'LL BE RIGHT BACK!
THE MOVIE STARTS IN FIVE MINUTES!
JUST GIMME TWO SECONDS...

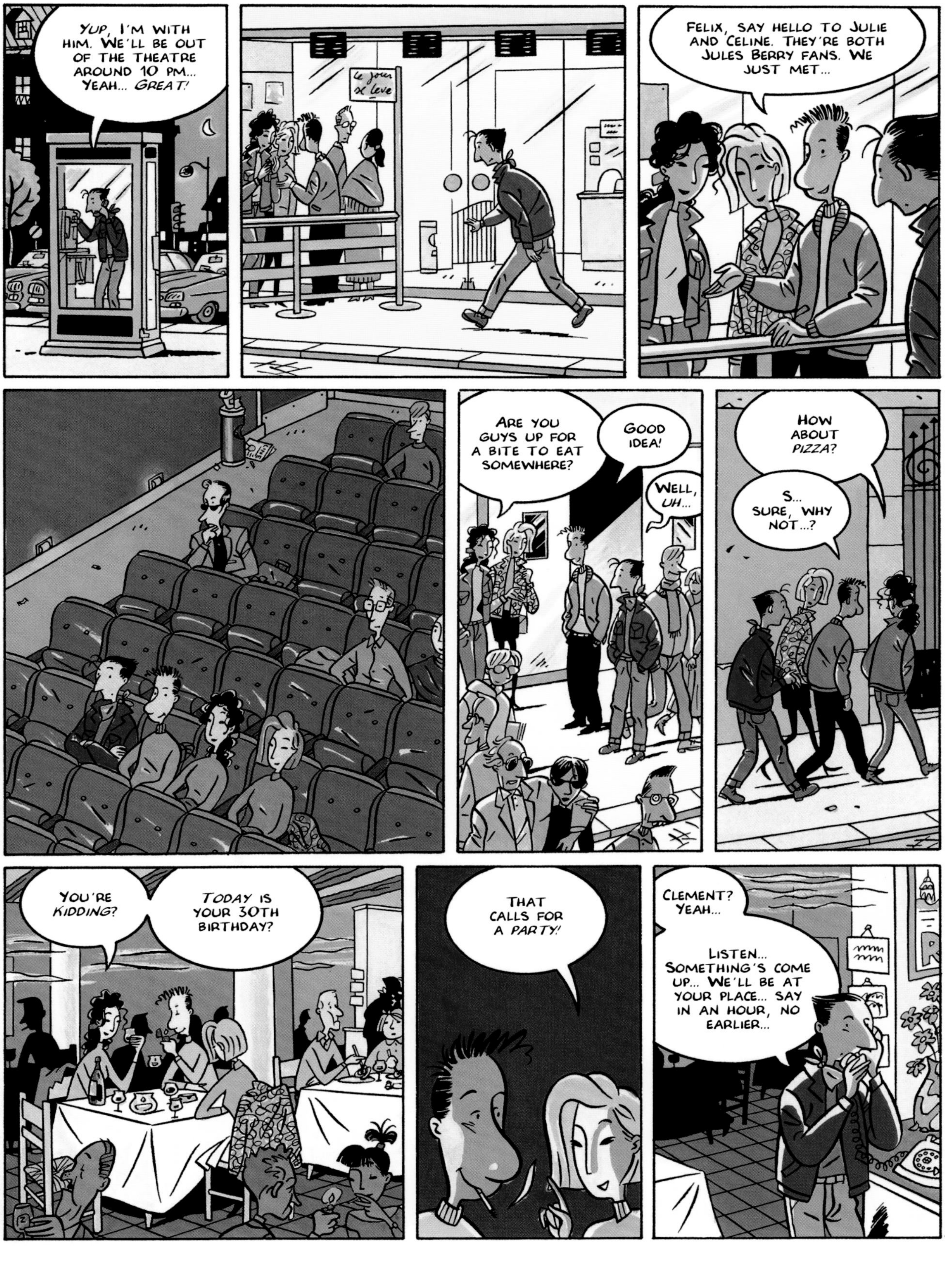

YUP, I'M WITH HIM. WE'LL BE OUT OF THE THEATRE AROUND 10 PM... YEAH... GREAT!
Le jour se lève
FELIX, SAY HELLO TO JULIE AND CELINE. THEY'RE BOTH JULES BERRY FANS. WE JUST MET...
ARE YOU GUYS UP FOR A BITE TO EAT SOMEWHERE?
GOOD IDEA!
WELL, UH...
HOW ABOUT PIZZA?
S... SURE, WHY NOT...?
YOU'RE KIDDING?
TODAY IS YOUR 30TH BIRTHDAY?
THAT CALLS FOR A PARTY!
CLEMENT? YEAH...
LISTEN... SOMETHING'S COME UP... WE'LL BE AT YOUR PLACE... SAY IN AN HOUR, NO EARLIER...

5

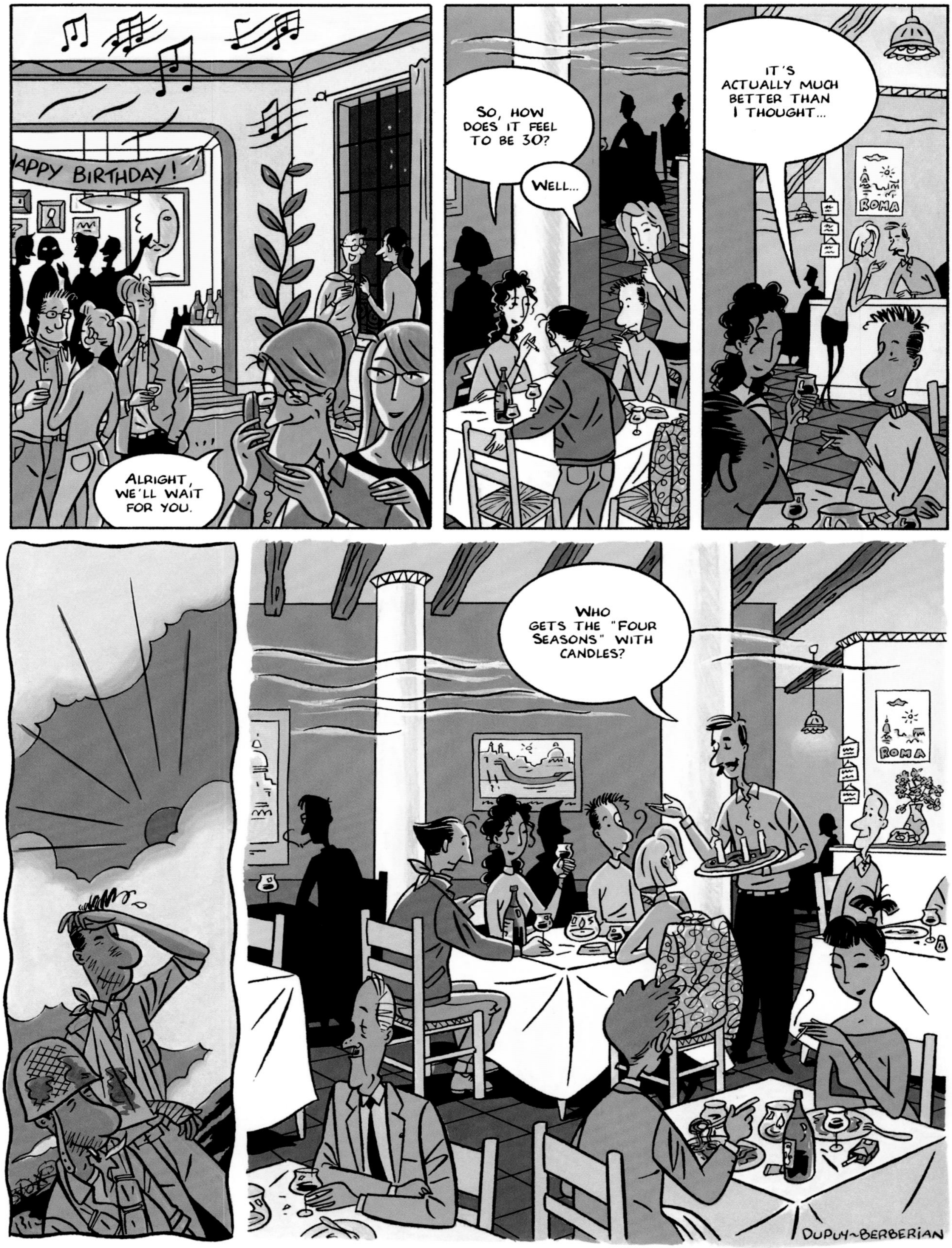

HAPPY BIRTHDAY!
ALRIGHT, WE'LL WAIT FOR YOU.
SO, HOW DOES IT FEEL TO BE 30?
WELL...
IT'S ACTUALLY MUCH BETTER THAN I THOUGHT...
ROMA
WHO GETS THE "FOUR SEASONS" WITH CANDLES?
ROMA
DUPUY~BERBERIAN

INSOMNIA PART 1

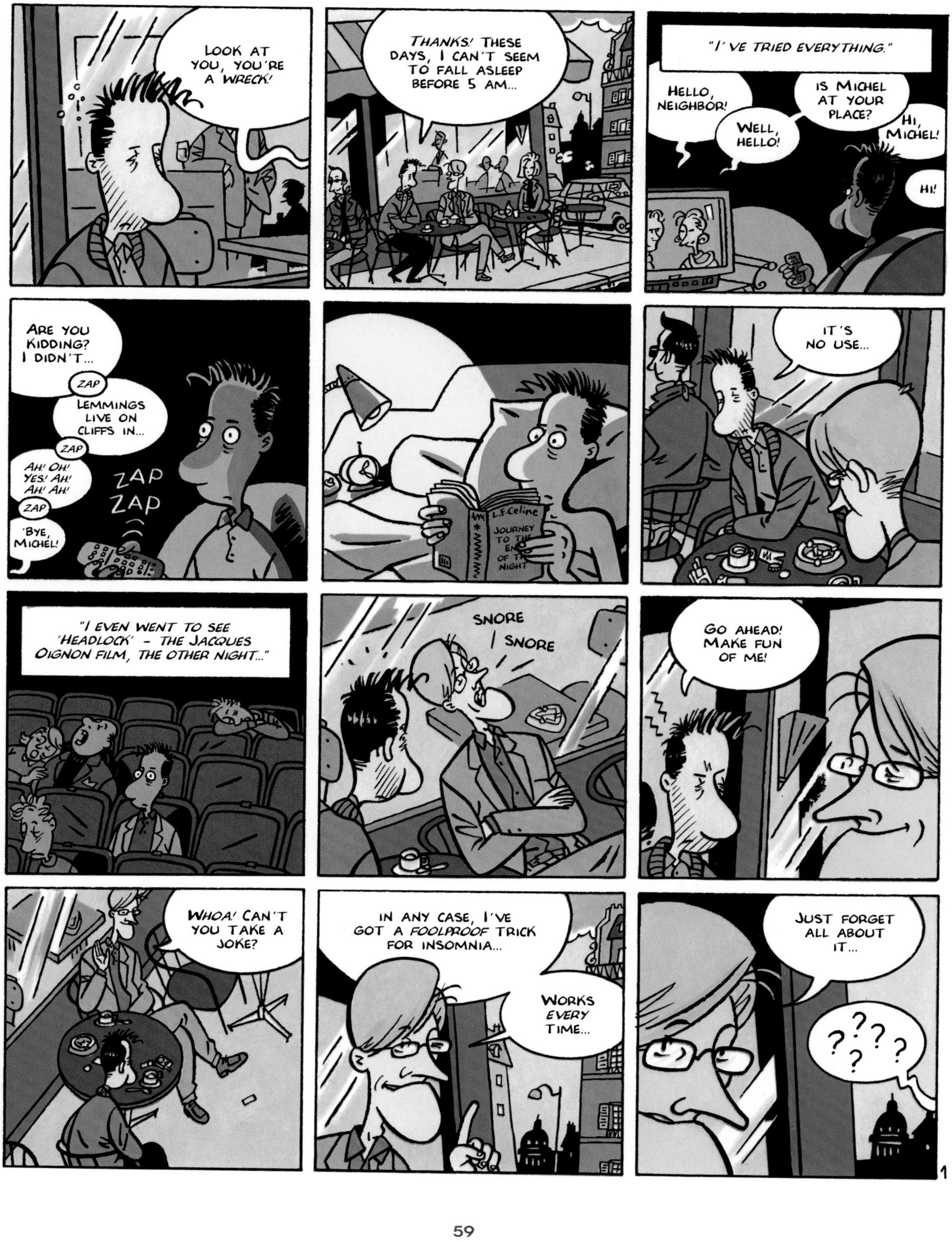

LOOK AT YOU, YOU'RE A WRECK!
THANKS! THESE DAYS, I CAN'T SEEM TO FALL ASLEEP BEFORE 5 AM...
"I'VE TRIED EVERYTHING."
HELLO, NEIGHBOR!
WELL, HELLO!
IS MICHEL AT YOUR PLACE?
HI, MICHEL!
HI!
ARE YOU KIDDING? I DIDN'T...
ZAP
LEMMINGS LIVE ON CLIFFS IN...
ZAP
AH! OH! YES! AH! AH! AH!
ZAP
'BYE, MICHEL!
ZAP ZAP
L.F. Celine
JOURNEY TO THE EN OF T NIGHT
IT'S NO USE...
"I EVEN WENT TO SEE 'HEADLOCK' - THE JACQUES OIGNON FILM, THE OTHER NIGHT..."
SNORE
SNORE
GO AHEAD! MAKE FUN OF ME!
WHOA! CAN'T YOU TAKE A JOKE?
IN ANY CASE, I'VE GOT A FOOLPROOF TRICK FOR INSOMNIA...
WORKS EVERY TIME...
JUST FORGET ALL ABOUT IT...
????
1

YOU HAVE TO *ACCEPT* YOUR INSOMNIA. IF YOU FIGHT IT, IT'LL DRIVE YOU CRAZY, AND THEN YOU REALLY WON'T BE ABLE TO SLEEP.

YOU HAVE TO KEEP YOUR MIND OFF IT...

AND THE WHEN YOU LEAST EXPECT IT, *BANG!* YOU'RE OUT LIKE A HIPPO...

TELL YOURSELF THIS: SLEEP IS LIKE LOVE – THE MORE YOU LOOK FOR IT, THE HARDER IT IS TO FIND...

"SO ACCORDING TO YOUR THEORY, HIPPOS IN LOVE SLEEP BEST OF ALL..."

YOU THINK I'M PULLING YOUR LEG, BUT I'M NOT KIDDING!

WHOA! CAN'T TAKE A JOKE...?

OK, JUST DON'T THINK ABOUT SLEEP...

MAYBE I SHOULD TAKE A BATH?

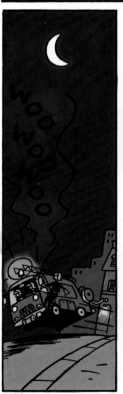

WOO WOO WOO

ZZZ

DUPUY~BERBERIAN

BOOM! BOOM BOOM

2

A TRIP TO LISBON

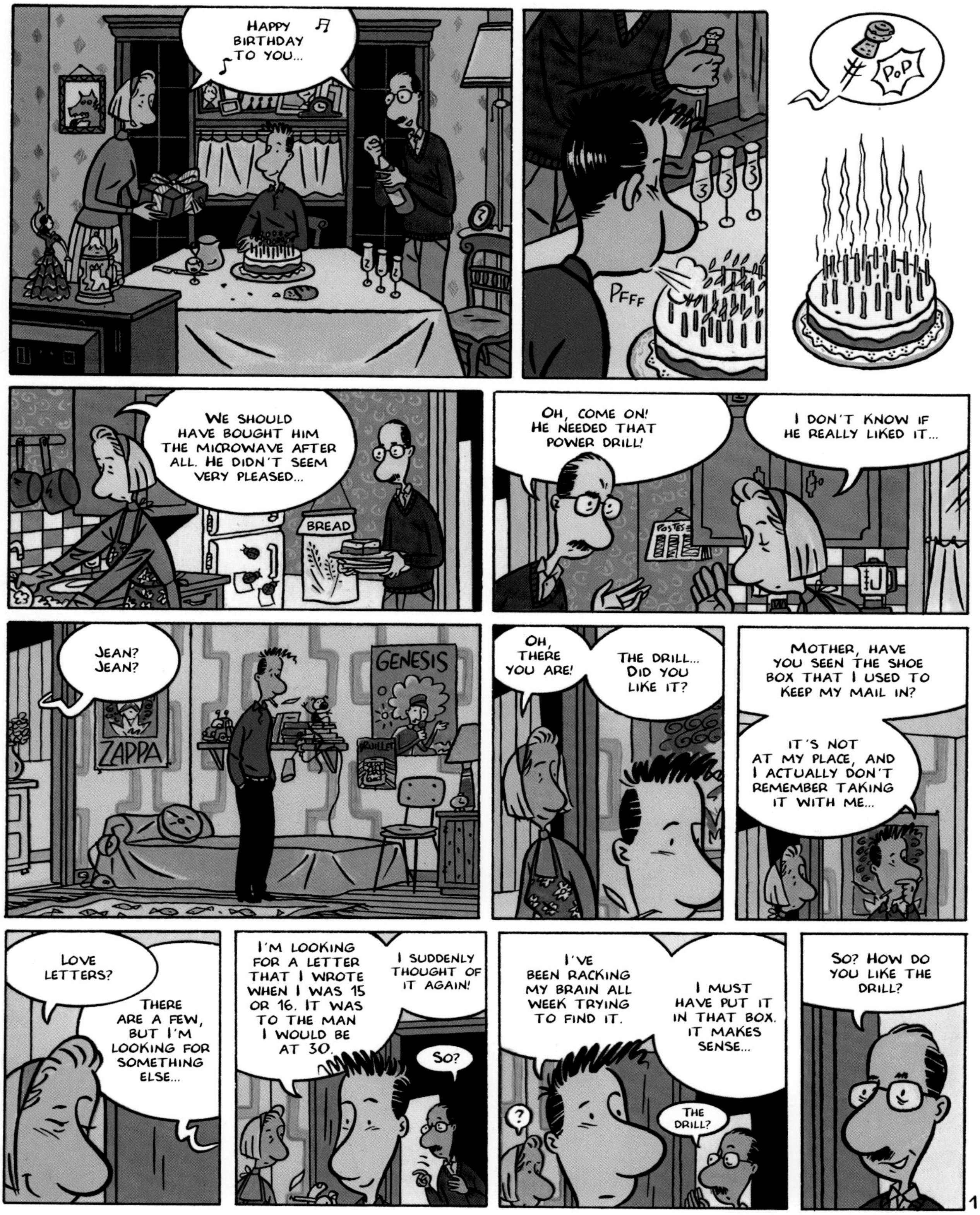
HAPPY BIRTHDAY TO YOU...
POP
PFFF
WE SHOULD HAVE BOUGHT HIM THE MICROWAVE AFTER ALL. HE DIDN'T SEEM VERY PLEASED...
BREAD
OH, COME ON! HE NEEDED THAT POWER DRILL!
I DON'T KNOW IF HE REALLY LIKED IT...
POSTES
JEAN? JEAN?
ZAPPA
GENESIS
DRUILLET
OH, THERE YOU ARE!
THE DRILL... DID YOU LIKE IT?
MOTHER, HAVE YOU SEEN THE SHOE BOX THAT I USED TO KEEP MY MAIL IN?
IT'S NOT AT MY PLACE, AND I ACTUALLY DON'T REMEMBER TAKING IT WITH ME...
LOVE LETTERS?
THERE ARE A FEW, BUT I'M LOOKING FOR SOMETHING ELSE...
I'M LOOKING FOR A LETTER THAT I WROTE WHEN I WAS 15 OR 16. IT WAS TO THE MAN I WOULD BE AT 30.
I SUDDENLY THOUGHT OF IT AGAIN!
SO?
I'VE BEEN RACKING MY BRAIN ALL WEEK TRYING TO FIND IT.
I MUST HAVE PUT IT IN THAT BOX. IT MAKES SENSE...
?
THE DRILL?
SO? HOW DO YOU LIKE THE DRILL?
1

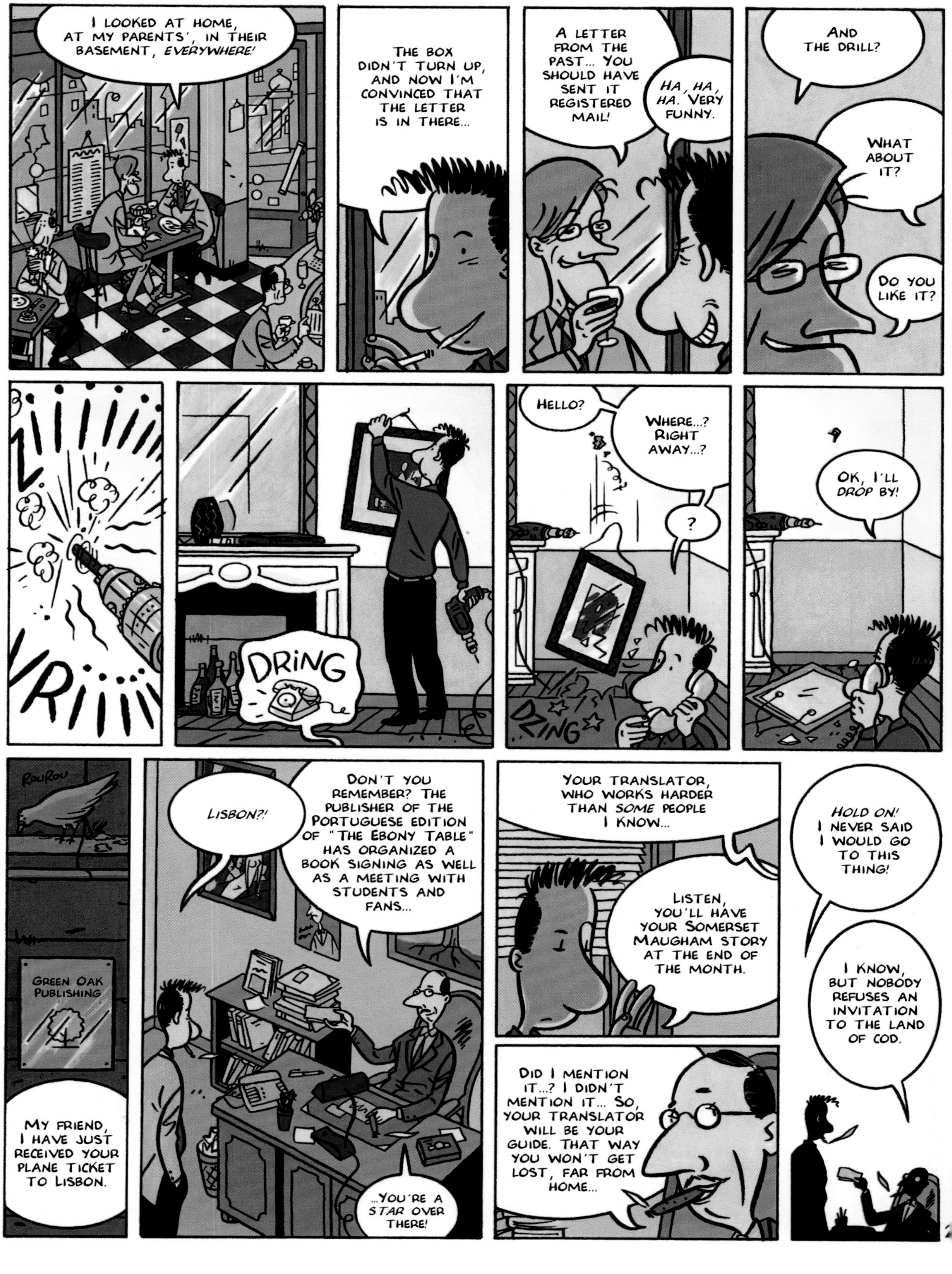
I LOOKED AT HOME, AT MY PARENTS', IN THEIR BASEMENT, *EVERYWHERE!*
THE BOX DIDN'T TURN UP, AND NOW I'M CONVINCED THAT THE LETTER IS IN THERE...
A LETTER FROM THE PAST... YOU SHOULD HAVE SENT IT REGISTERED MAIL!
HA, HA, HA. VERY FUNNY.
AND THE DRILL?
WHAT ABOUT IT?
DO YOU LIKE IT?
ZIIIIII
VRIIIIII
DRING
HELLO?
WHERE...? RIGHT AWAY...?
?
DZING
OK, I'LL *DROP BY!*
ROUROU
GREEN OAK PUBLISHING
MY FRIEND, I HAVE JUST RECEIVED YOUR PLANE TICKET TO LISBON.
LISBON?!
DON'T YOU REMEMBER? THE PUBLISHER OF THE PORTUGUESE EDITION OF "THE EBONY TABLE" HAS ORGANIZED A BOOK SIGNING AS WELL AS A MEETING WITH STUDENTS AND FANS...
...YOU'RE A *STAR* OVER THERE!
YOUR TRANSLATOR, WHO WORKS HARDER THAN *SOME* PEOPLE I KNOW...
LISTEN, YOU'LL HAVE YOUR SOMERSET MAUGHAM STORY AT THE END OF THE MONTH.
DID I MENTION IT...? I DIDN'T MENTION IT... SO, YOUR TRANSLATOR WILL BE YOUR GUIDE. THAT WAY YOU WON'T GET LOST, FAR FROM HOME...
HOLD ON! I NEVER SAID I WOULD GO TO THIS THING!
I KNOW, BUT NOBODY REFUSES AN INVITATION TO THE LAND OF COD.

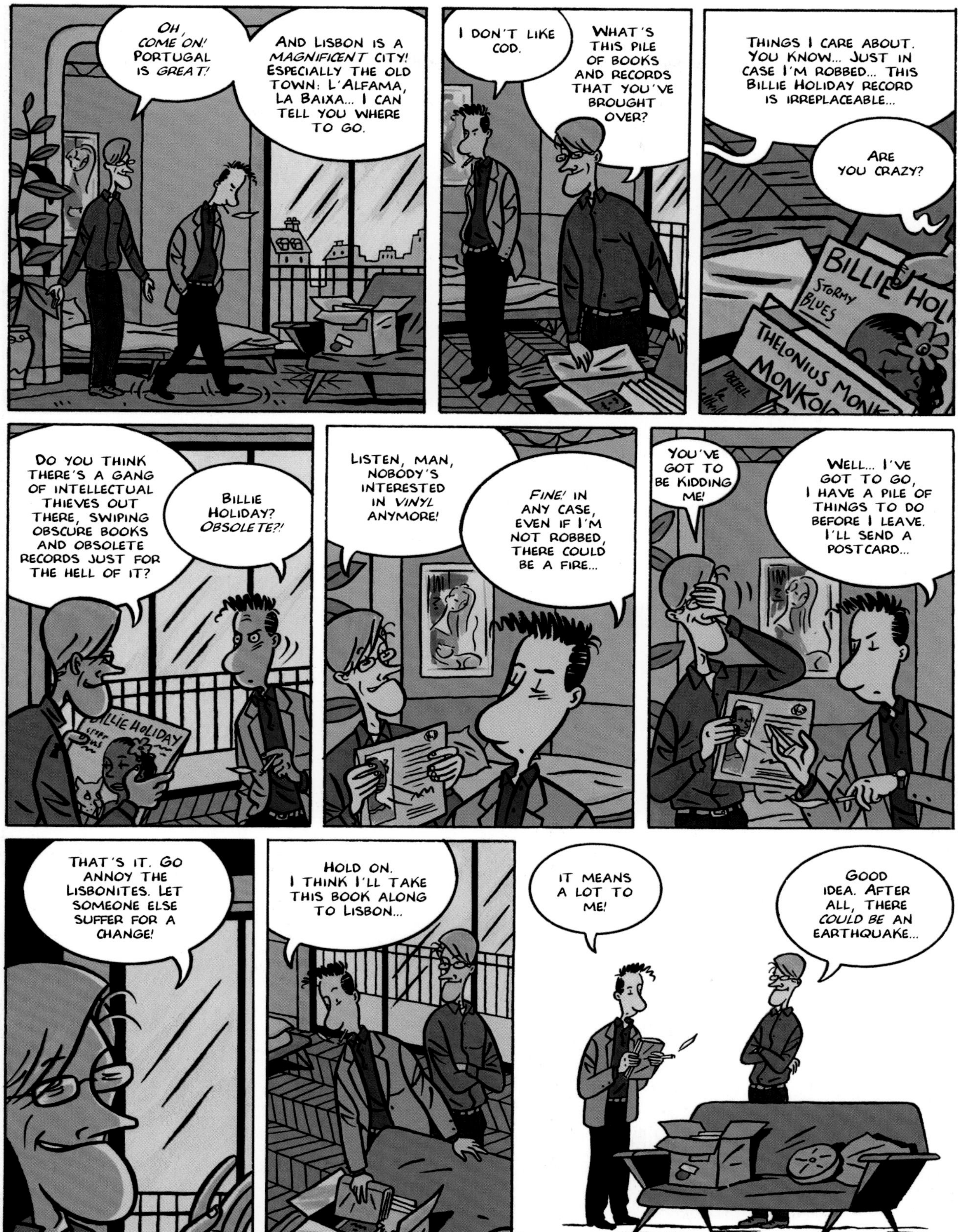
OH, COME ON! PORTUGAL IS GREAT!
AND LISBON IS A MAGNIFICENT CITY! ESPECIALLY THE OLD TOWN: L'ALFAMA, LA BAIXA... I CAN TELL YOU WHERE TO GO.
I DON'T LIKE COD.
WHAT'S THIS PILE OF BOOKS AND RECORDS THAT YOU'VE BROUGHT OVER?
THINGS I CARE ABOUT. YOU KNOW... JUST IN CASE I'M ROBBED... THIS BILLIE HOLIDAY RECORD IS IRREPLACEABLE...
ARE YOU CRAZY?
BILLIE HOLI
STORMY BLUES
THELONIUS MONK
DO YOU THINK THERE'S A GANG OF INTELLECTUAL THIEVES OUT THERE, SWIPING OBSCURE BOOKS AND OBSOLETE RECORDS JUST FOR THE HELL OF IT?
BILLIE HOLIDAY? OBSOLETE?!
BILLIE HOLIDAY
LISTEN, MAN, NOBODY'S INTERESTED IN VINYL ANYMORE!
FINE! IN ANY CASE, EVEN IF I'M NOT ROBBED, THERE COULD BE A FIRE...
YOU'VE GOT TO BE KIDDING ME!
WELL... I'VE GOT TO GO, I HAVE A PILE OF THINGS TO DO BEFORE I LEAVE. I'LL SEND A POSTCARD...
THAT'S IT. GO ANNOY THE LISBONITES. LET SOMEONE ELSE SUFFER FOR A CHANGE!
HOLD ON. I THINK I'LL TAKE THIS BOOK ALONG TO LISBON...
IT MEANS A LOT TO ME!
GOOD IDEA. AFTER ALL, THERE COULD BE AN EARTHQUAKE...

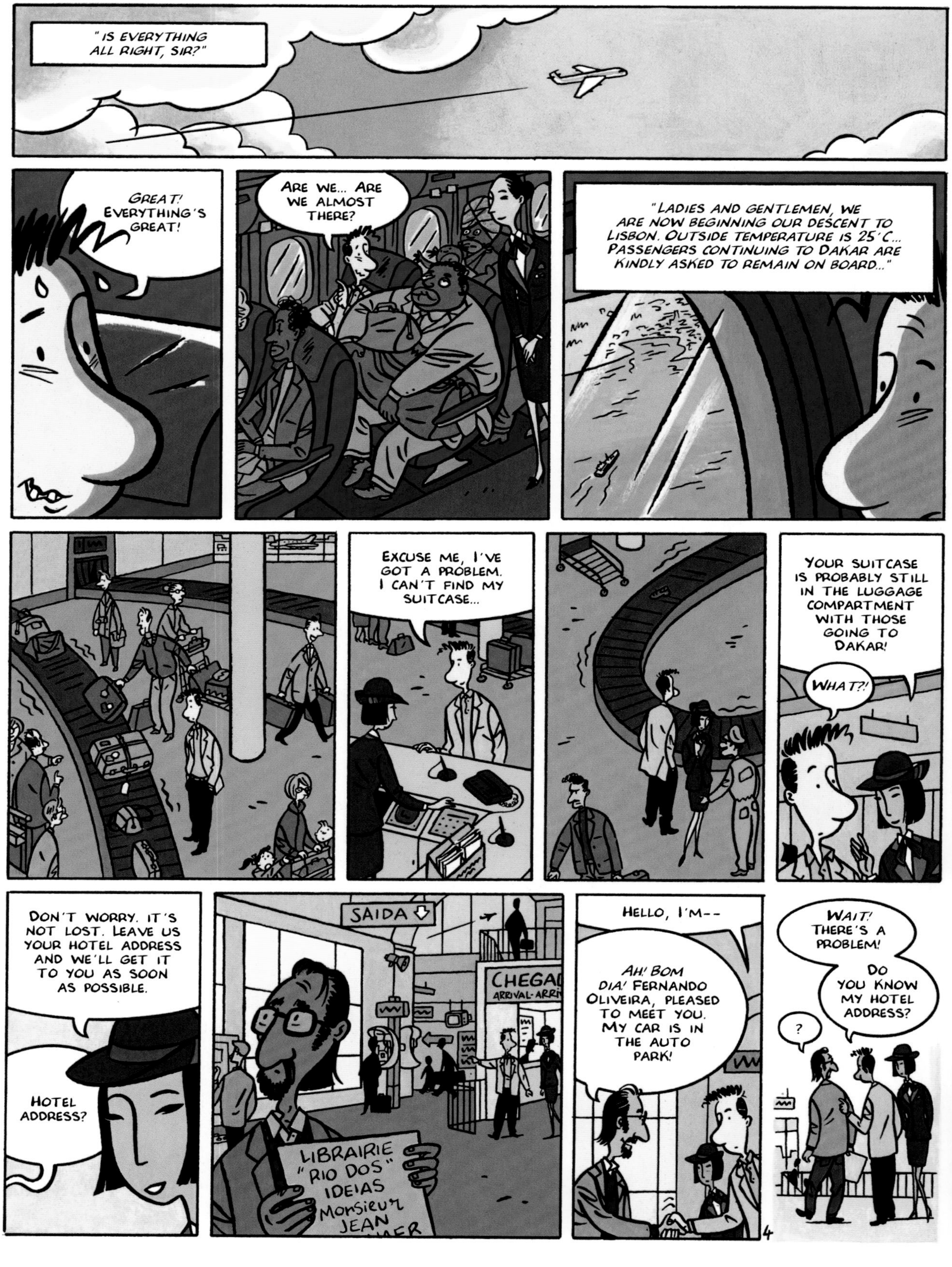
"IS EVERYTHING ALL RIGHT, SIR?"
GREAT! EVERYTHING'S GREAT!
ARE WE... ARE WE ALMOST THERE?
"LADIES AND GENTLEMEN, WE ARE NOW BEGINNING OUR DESCENT TO LISBON. OUTSIDE TEMPERATURE IS 25°C... PASSENGERS CONTINUING TO DAKAR ARE KINDLY ASKED TO REMAIN ON BOARD..."
EXCUSE ME, I'VE GOT A PROBLEM. I CAN'T FIND MY SUITCASE...
YOUR SUITCASE IS PROBABLY STILL IN THE LUGGAGE COMPARTMENT WITH THOSE GOING TO DAKAR!
WHAT?!
DON'T WORRY. IT'S NOT LOST. LEAVE US YOUR HOTEL ADDRESS AND WE'LL GET IT TO YOU AS SOON AS POSSIBLE.
HOTEL ADDRESS?
SAIDA
CHEGAD
ARRIVAL-ARRI
LIBRAIRIE "RIO DOS" IDEIAS Monsieur JEAN
HELLO, I'M--
AH! BOM DIA! FERNANDO OLIVEIRA, PLEASED TO MEET YOU. MY CAR IS IN THE AUTO PARK!
WAIT! THERE'S A PROBLEM!
DO YOU KNOW MY HOTEL ADDRESS?
?
4

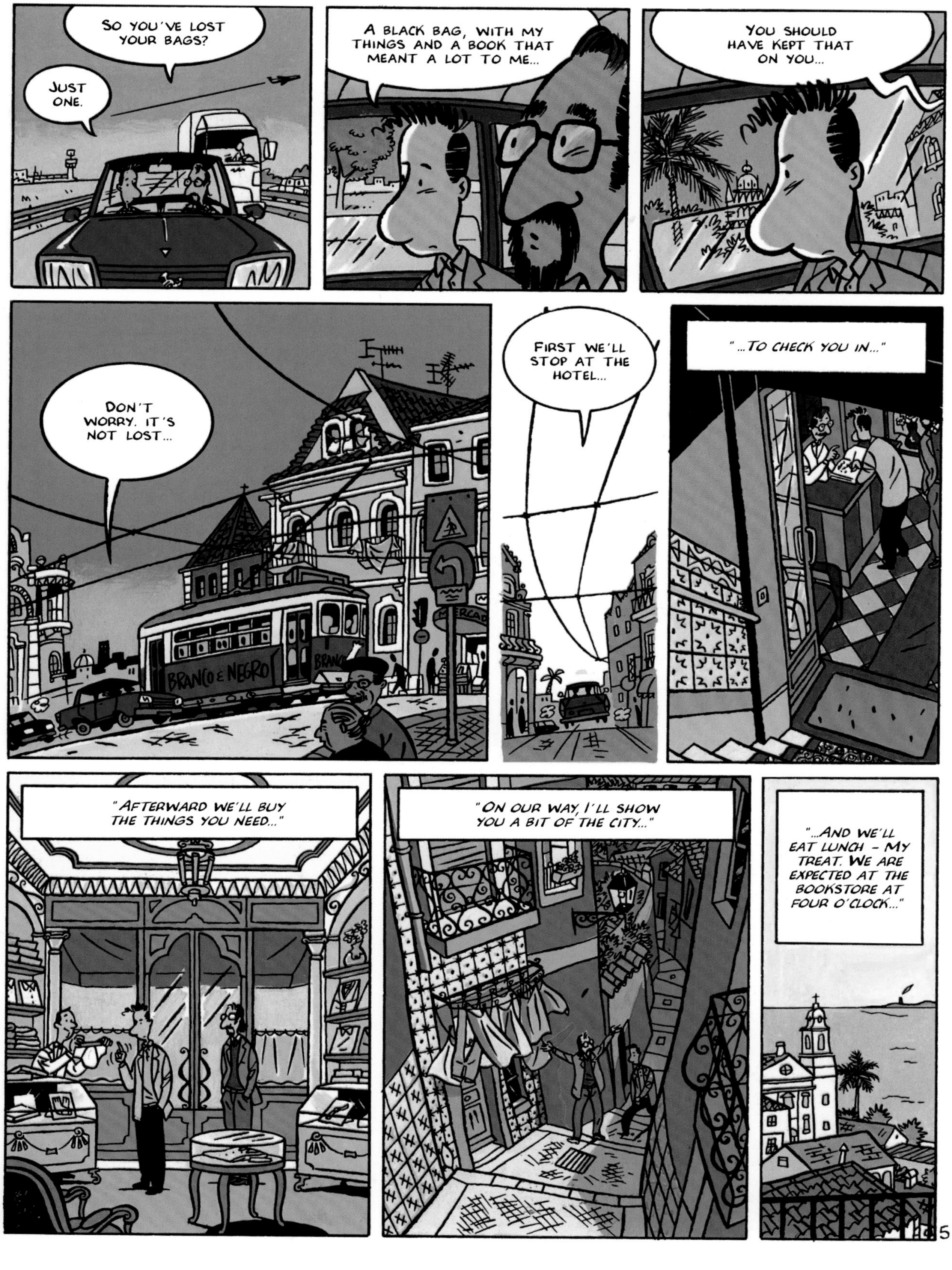
SO YOU'VE LOST YOUR BAGS?
JUST ONE.
A BLACK BAG, WITH MY THINGS AND A BOOK THAT MEANT A LOT TO ME...
YOU SHOULD HAVE KEPT THAT ON YOU...
DON'T WORRY. IT'S NOT LOST...
BRANCO E NEGRO
FIRST WE'LL STOP AT THE HOTEL...
"...TO CHECK YOU IN..."
"AFTERWARD WE'LL BUY THE THINGS YOU NEED..."
"ON OUR WAY, I'LL SHOW YOU A BIT OF THE CITY..."
"...AND WE'LL EAT LUNCH - MY TREAT. WE ARE EXPECTED AT THE BOOKSTORE AT FOUR O'CLOCK..."

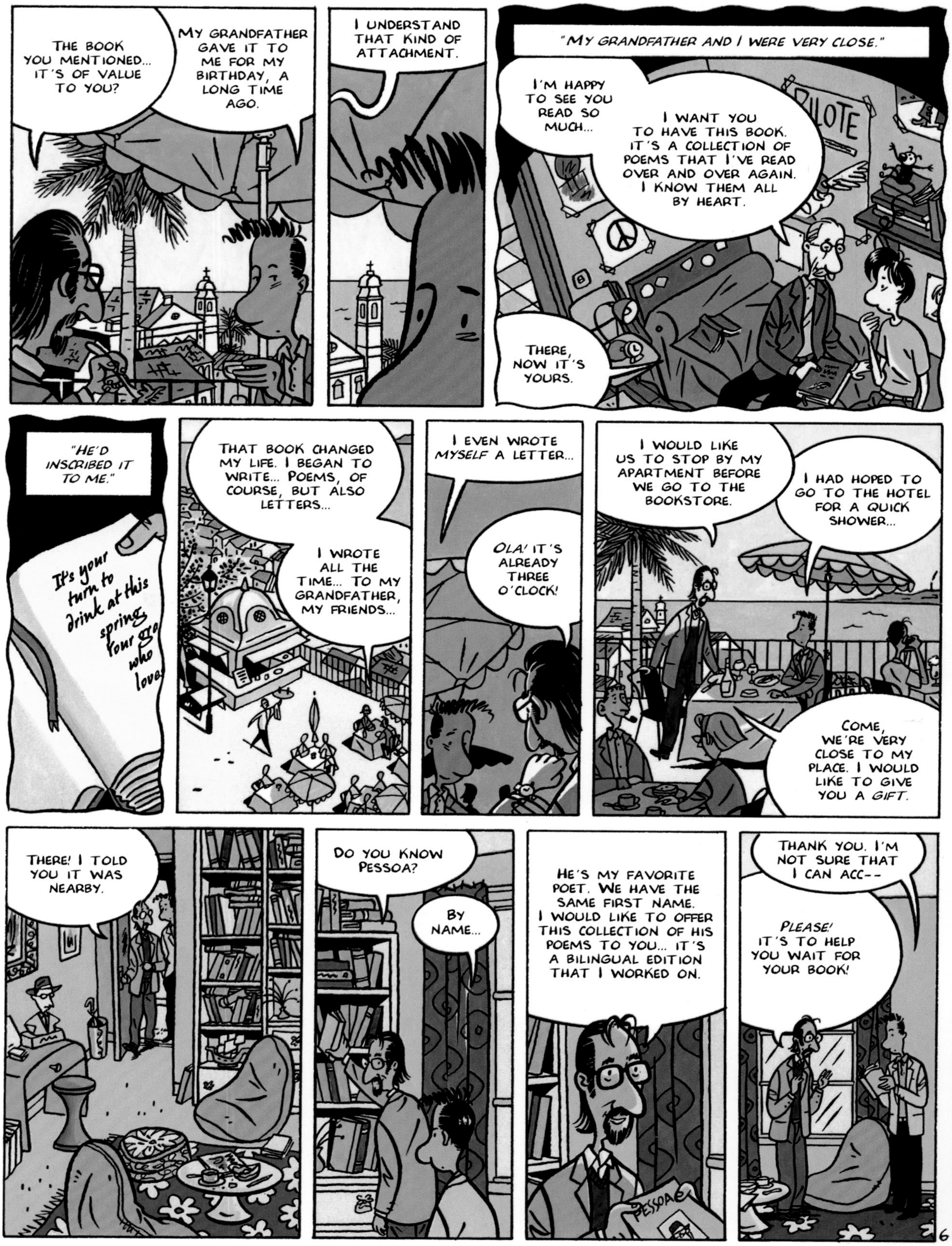
THE BOOK YOU MENTIONED... IT'S OF VALUE TO YOU?
MY GRANDFATHER GAVE IT TO ME FOR MY BIRTHDAY, A LONG TIME AGO.
I UNDERSTAND THAT KIND OF ATTACHMENT.
"MY GRANDFATHER AND I WERE VERY CLOSE."
I'M HAPPY TO SEE YOU READ SO MUCH...
I WANT YOU TO HAVE THIS BOOK. IT'S A COLLECTION OF POEMS THAT I'VE READ OVER AND OVER AGAIN. I KNOW THEM ALL BY HEART.
PILOTE
THERE, NOW IT'S YOURS.
"HE'D INSCRIBED IT TO ME."
It's your turn to drink at this spring. Your gra
who
love
THAT BOOK CHANGED MY LIFE. I BEGAN TO WRITE... POEMS, OF COURSE, BUT ALSO LETTERS...
I WROTE ALL THE TIME... TO MY GRANDFATHER, MY FRIENDS...
I EVEN WROTE MYSELF A LETTER...
OLA! IT'S ALREADY THREE O'CLOCK!
I WOULD LIKE US TO STOP BY MY APARTMENT BEFORE WE GO TO THE BOOKSTORE.
I HAD HOPED TO GO TO THE HOTEL FOR A QUICK SHOWER...
COME, WE'RE VERY CLOSE TO MY PLACE. I WOULD LIKE TO GIVE YOU A GIFT.
THERE! I TOLD YOU IT WAS NEARBY.
DO YOU KNOW PESSOA?
BY NAME...
HE'S MY FAVORITE POET. WE HAVE THE SAME FIRST NAME. I WOULD LIKE TO OFFER THIS COLLECTION OF HIS POEMS TO YOU... IT'S A BILINGUAL EDITION THAT I WORKED ON.
PESSOA
THANK YOU. I'M NOT SURE THAT I CAN ACC--
PLEASE! IT'S TO HELP YOU WAIT FOR YOUR BOOK!
6

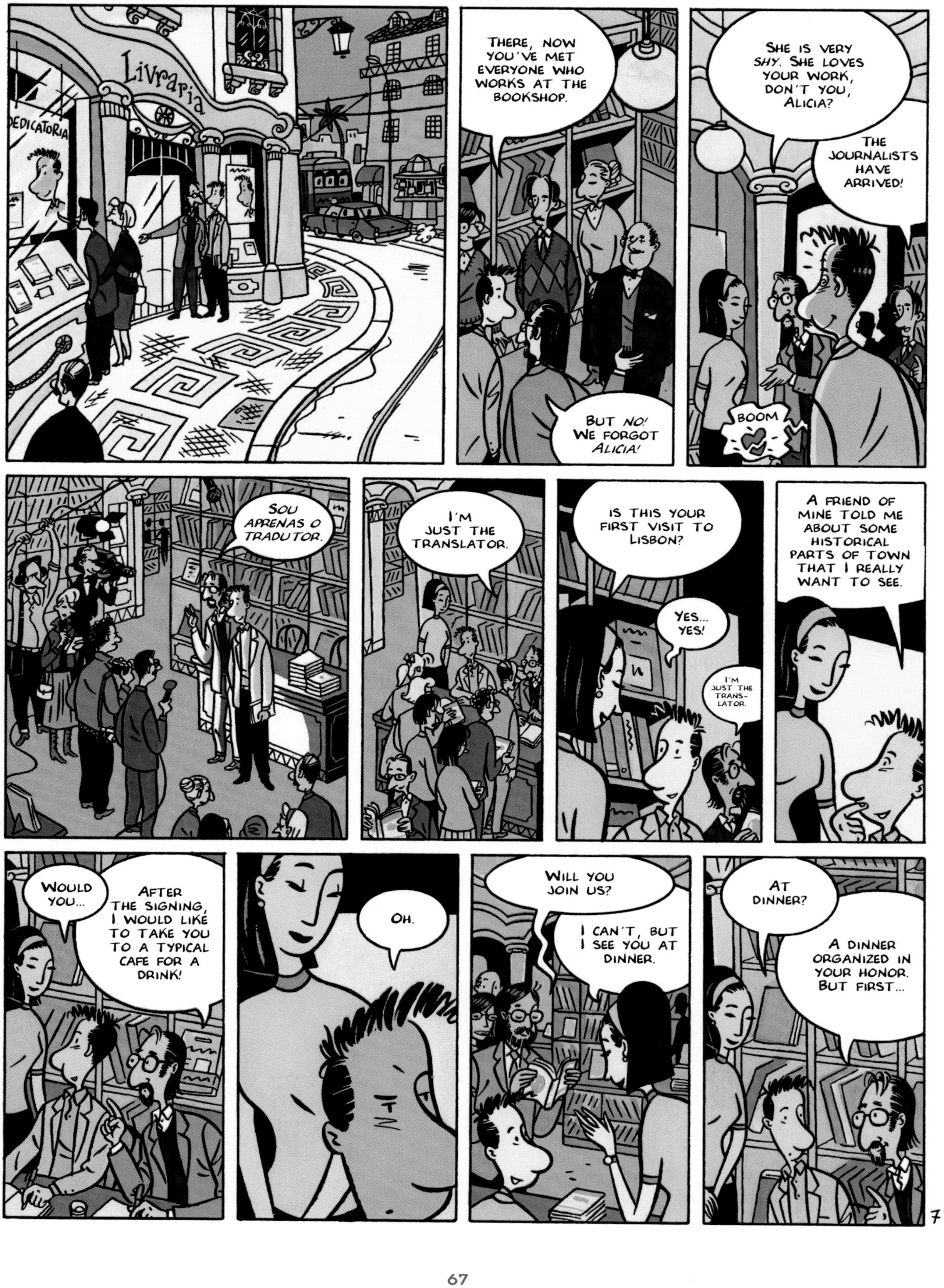
Livraria
DEDICATORIA
THERE, NOW YOU'VE MET EVERYONE WHO WORKS AT THE BOOKSHOP.
BUT *NO!* WE FORGOT *ALICIA!*
SHE IS VERY *SHY*. SHE LOVES YOUR WORK, DON'T YOU, ALICIA?
THE JOURNALISTS HAVE ARRIVED!
BOOM
SOU *APRENAS O TRADUTOR.*
I'M JUST THE TRANSLATOR.
IS THIS YOUR FIRST VISIT TO LISBON?
YES... YES!
I'M JUST THE TRANS-LATOR.
A FRIEND OF MINE TOLD ME ABOUT SOME HISTORICAL PARTS OF TOWN THAT I REALLY WANT TO SEE.
WOULD YOU...
AFTER THE SIGNING, I WOULD LIKE TO TAKE YOU TO A TYPICAL CAFE FOR A DRINK!
OH.
WILL YOU JOIN US?
I CAN'T, BUT I SEE YOU AT DINNER.
AT DINNER?
A DINNER ORGANIZED IN YOUR HONOR. BUT FIRST...
7

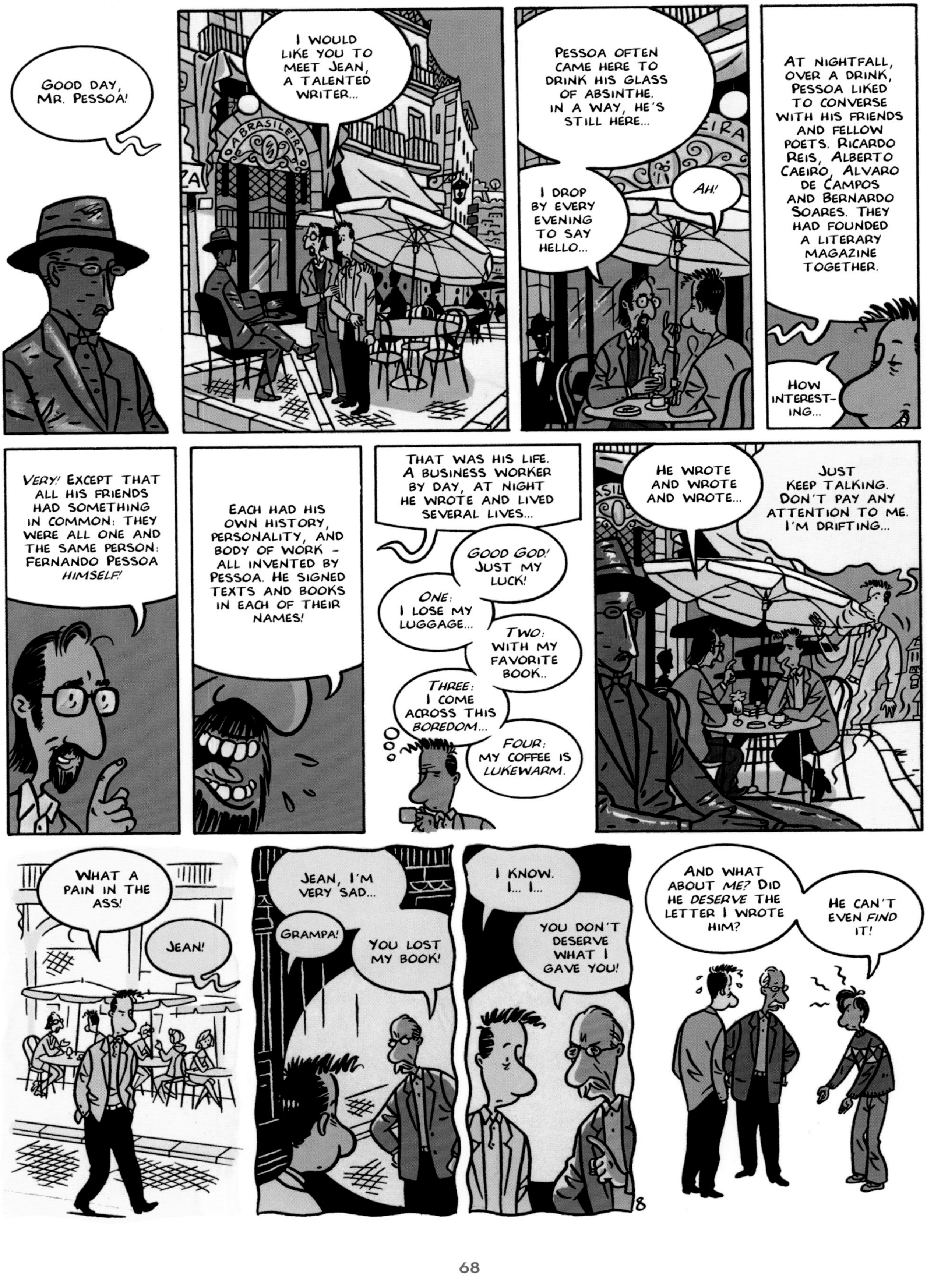
Good day, Mr. Pessoa!
I would like you to meet Jean, a talented writer...
Pessoa often came here to drink his glass of absinthe. In a way, he's still here...
I drop by every evening to say hello...
Ah!
At nightfall, over a drink, Pessoa liked to converse with his friends and fellow poets. Ricardo Reis, Alberto Caeiro, Alvaro de Campos and Bernardo Soares. They had founded a literary magazine together.
How interest-ing...
Very! Except that all his friends had something in common: they were all one and the same person: Fernando Pessoa himself!
Each had his own history, personality, and body of work - all invented by Pessoa. He signed texts and books in each of their names!
That was his life. A business worker by day, at night he wrote and lived several lives...
Good God! Just my luck!
One: I lose my luggage...
Two: with my favorite book..
Three: I come across this boredom...
Four: my coffee is lukewarm.
He wrote and wrote and wrote...
Just keep talking. Don't pay any attention to me. I'm drifting...
What a pain in the ass!
Jean!
Jean, I'm very sad...
Grampa!
You lost my book!
I know. I... I...
You don't deserve what I gave you!
And what about me? Did he deserve the letter I wrote him?
He can't even find it!
8

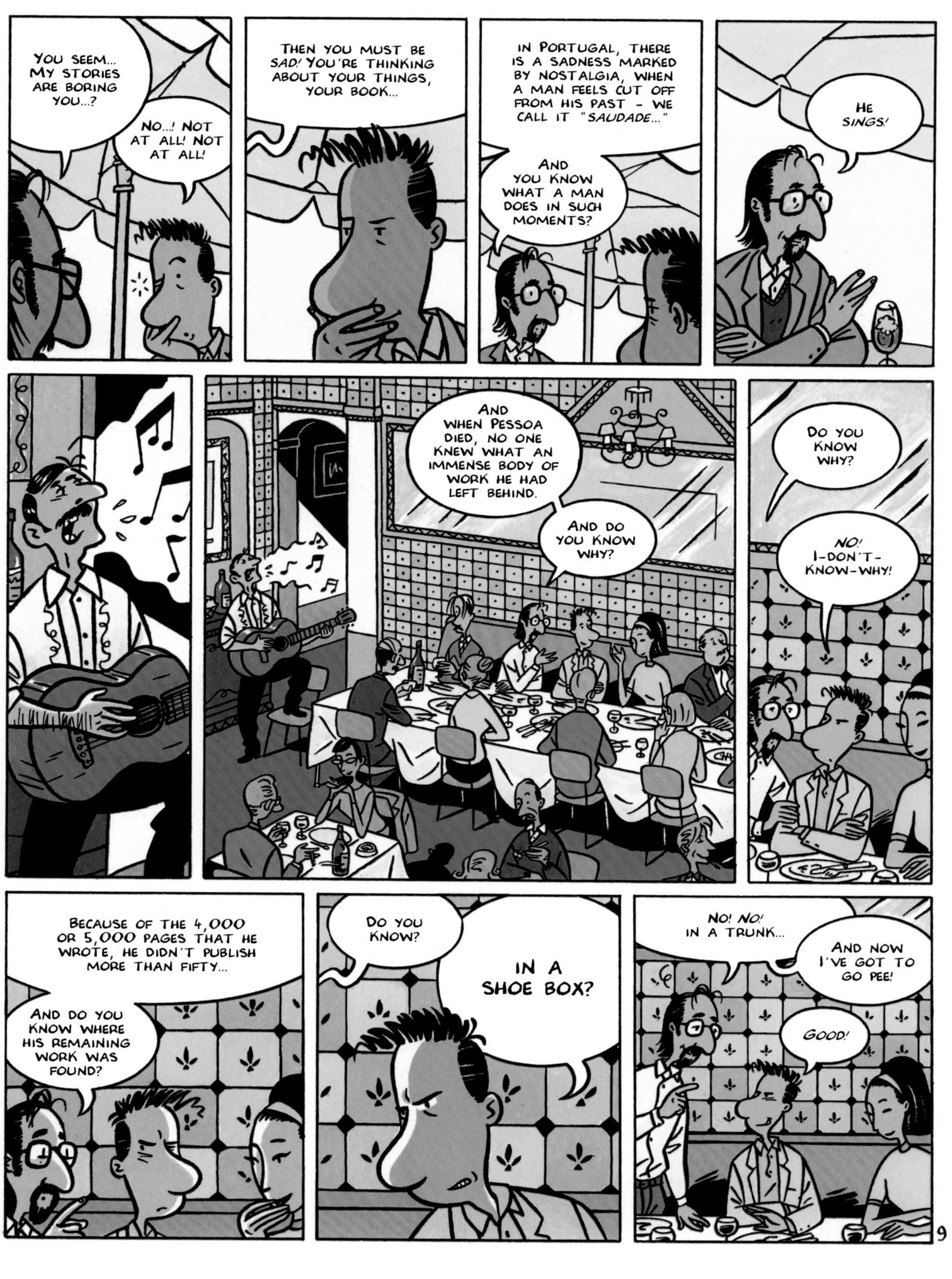
YOU SEEM... MY STORIES ARE BORING YOU...?
NO...! NOT AT ALL! NOT AT ALL!
THEN YOU MUST BE SAD! YOU'RE THINKING ABOUT YOUR THINGS, YOUR BOOK...
IN PORTUGAL, THERE IS A SADNESS MARKED BY NOSTALGIA, WHEN A MAN FEELS CUT OFF FROM HIS PAST - WE CALL IT "SAUDADE..."
AND YOU KNOW WHAT A MAN DOES IN SUCH MOMENTS?
HE SINGS!
AND WHEN PESSOA DIED, NO ONE KNEW WHAT AN IMMENSE BODY OF WORK HE HAD LEFT BEHIND.
AND DO YOU KNOW WHY?
DO YOU KNOW WHY?
NO! I-DON'T-KNOW-WHY!
BECAUSE OF THE 4,000 OR 5,000 PAGES THAT HE WROTE, HE DIDN'T PUBLISH MORE THAN FIFTY...
AND DO YOU KNOW WHERE HIS REMAINING WORK WAS FOUND?
DO YOU KNOW?
IN A SHOE BOX?
NO! NO! IN A TRUNK...
AND NOW I'VE GOT TO GO PEE!
GOOD!
9

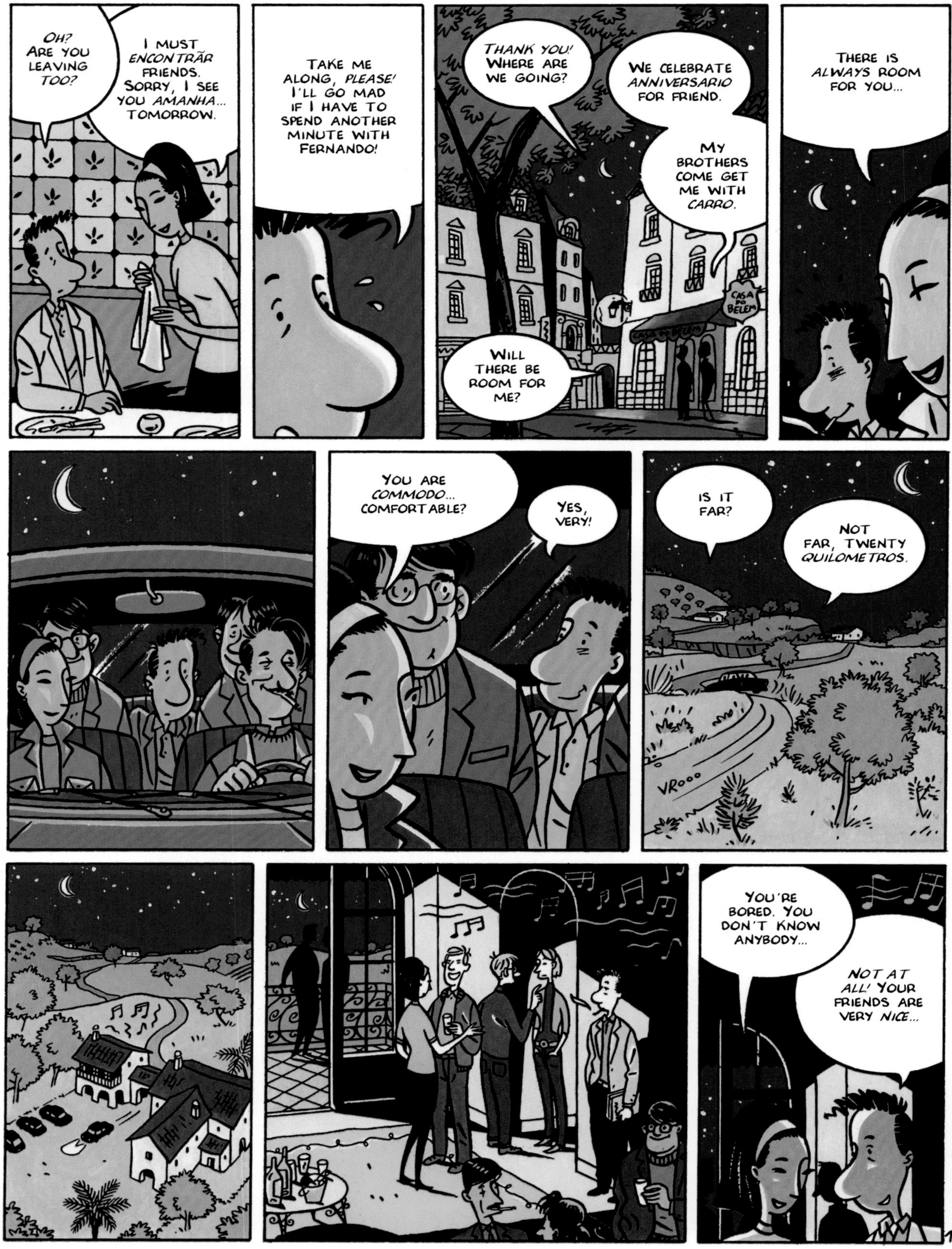

OH? ARE YOU LEAVING TOO?
I MUST ENCONTRÃR FRIENDS. SORRY, I SEE YOU AMANHA... TOMORROW.
TAKE ME ALONG, PLEASE! I'LL GO MAD IF I HAVE TO SPEND ANOTHER MINUTE WITH FERNANDO!
THANK YOU! WHERE ARE WE GOING?
WE CELEBRATE ANNIVERSARIO FOR FRIEND.
MY BROTHERS COME GET ME WITH CARRO.
CASA DO BELEM
WILL THERE BE ROOM FOR ME?
THERE IS ALWAYS ROOM FOR YOU...
YOU ARE COMMODO... COMFORTABLE?
YES, VERY!
IS IT FAR?
NOT FAR, TWENTY QUILOMETROS.
VROOO
YOU'RE BORED. YOU DON'T KNOW ANYBODY...
NOT AT ALL! YOUR FRIENDS ARE VERY NICE...

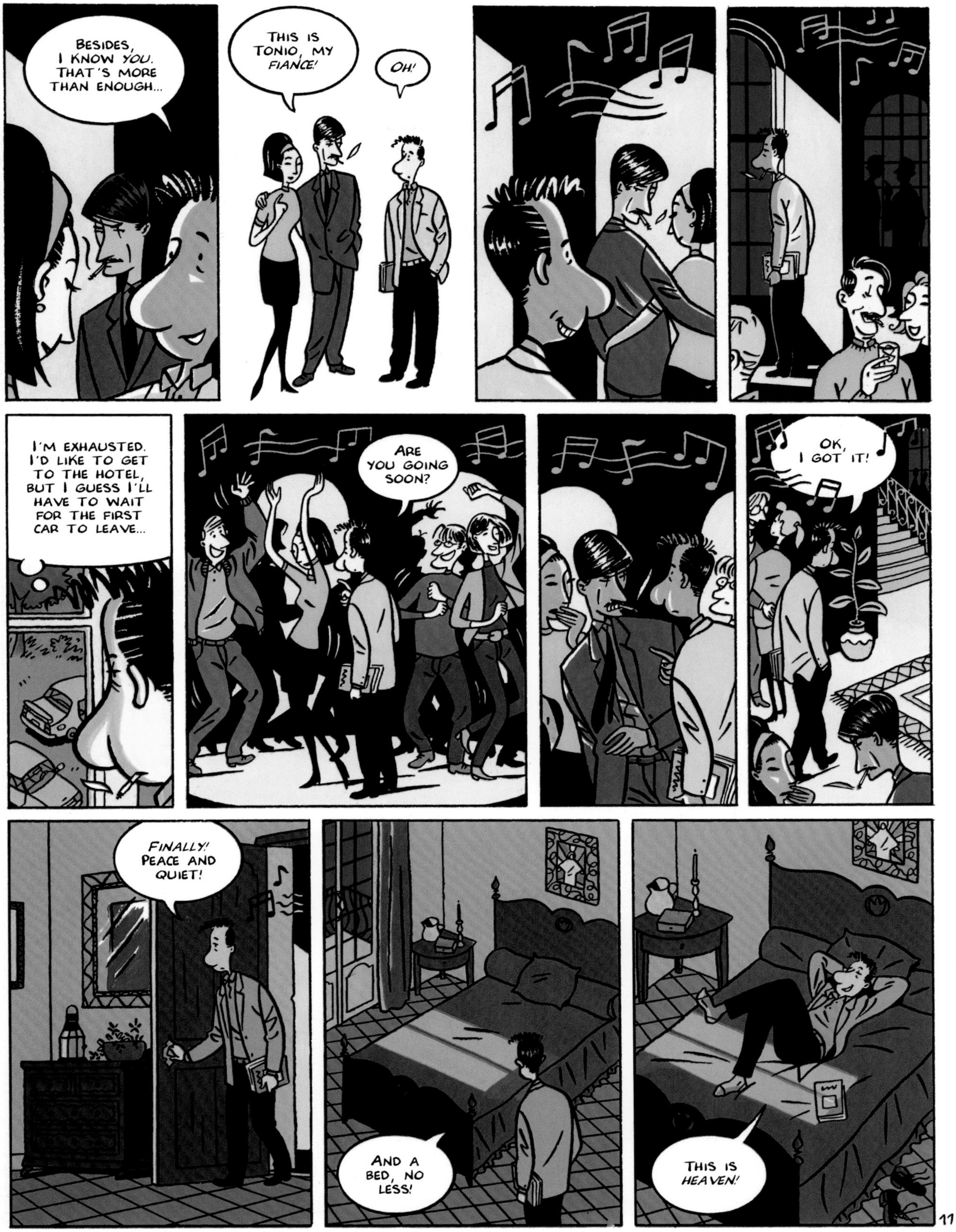
BESIDES, I KNOW YOU. THAT'S MORE THAN ENOUGH...
THIS IS TONIO, MY FIANCE!
OH!
I'M EXHAUSTED. I'D LIKE TO GET TO THE HOTEL, BUT I GUESS I'LL HAVE TO WAIT FOR THE FIRST CAR TO LEAVE...
ARE YOU GOING SOON?
OK, I GOT IT!
FINALLY! PEACE AND QUIET!
AND A BED, NO LESS!
THIS IS HEAVEN!
11

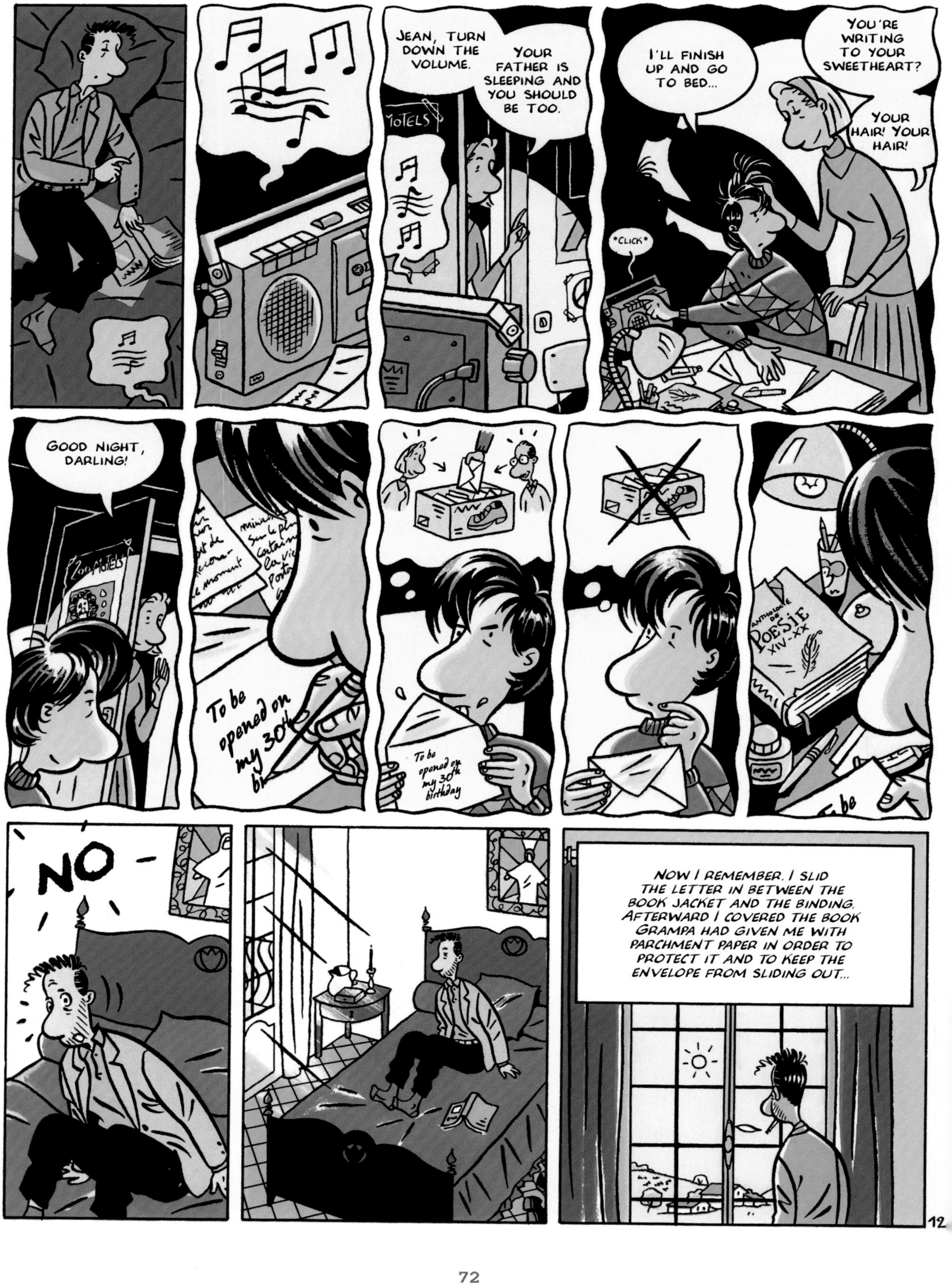

JEAN, TURN DOWN THE VOLUME.
YOUR FATHER IS SLEEPING AND YOU SHOULD BE TOO.
MOTELS
I'LL FINISH UP AND GO TO BED...
YOU'RE WRITING TO YOUR SWEETHEART?
YOUR HAIR! YOUR HAIR!
CLICK
GOOD NIGHT, DARLING!
To be opened on my 30th bi
To be opened on my 30th birthday
ANTHOLOGIE DE POESIE XIV-XX
NO
NOW I REMEMBER. I SLID THE LETTER IN BETWEEN THE BOOK JACKET AND THE BINDING. AFTERWARD I COVERED THE BOOK GRAMPA HAD GIVEN ME WITH PARCHMENT PAPER IN ORDER TO PROTECT IT AND TO KEEP THE ENVELOPE FROM SLIDING OUT...
12

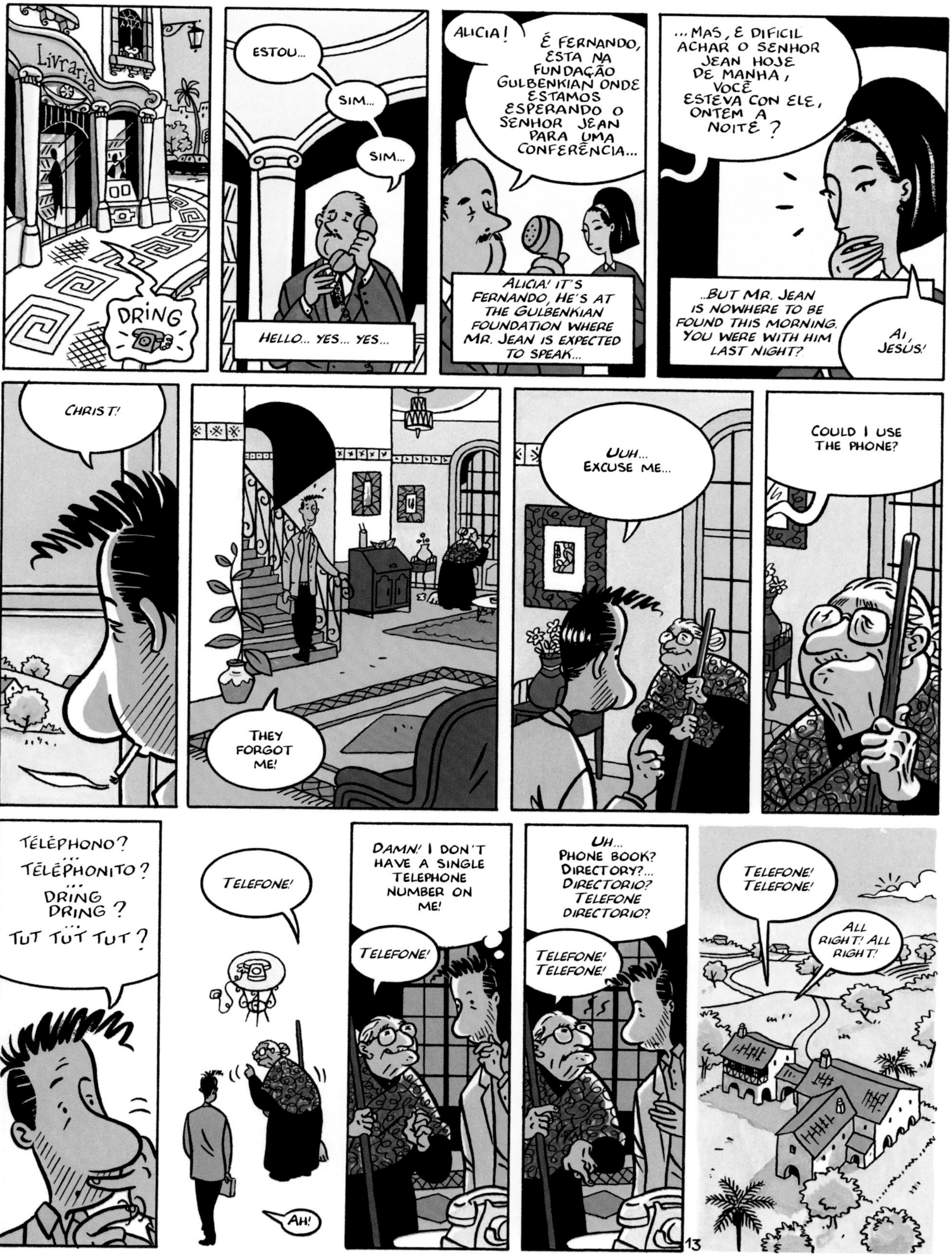
Livraria
DRING
ESTOU...
SIM...
SIM...
HELLO... YES... YES...
ALICIA!
É FERNANDO, ESTA NA FUNDAÇÃO GULBENKIAN ONDE ESTAMOS ESPERANDO O SENHOR JEAN PARA UMA CONFERÊNCIA...
ALICIA! IT'S FERNANDO, HE'S AT THE GULBENKIAN FOUNDATION WHERE MR. JEAN IS EXPECTED TO SPEAK...
...MAS, É DIFICIL ACHAR O SENHOR JEAN HOJE DE MANHA, VOCÊ ESTEVA CON ELE, ONTEM A NOITE?
...BUT MR. JEAN IS NOWHERE TO BE FOUND THIS MORNING. YOU WERE WITH HIM LAST NIGHT?
AI, JESÚS!
CHRIST!
THEY FORGOT ME!
UUH... EXCUSE ME...
COULD I USE THE PHONE?
TÉLÉPHONO? ... TÉLÉPHONITO? ... DRING DRING? ... TUT TUT TUT?
TELEFONE!
AH!
DAMN! I DON'T HAVE A SINGLE TELEPHONE NUMBER ON ME!
TELEFONE!
UH... PHONE BOOK? DIRECTORY?... DIRECTORIO? TELEFONE DIRECTORIO?
TELEFONE! TELEFONE!
TELEFONE! TELEFONE!
ALL RIGHT! ALL RIGHT!
13

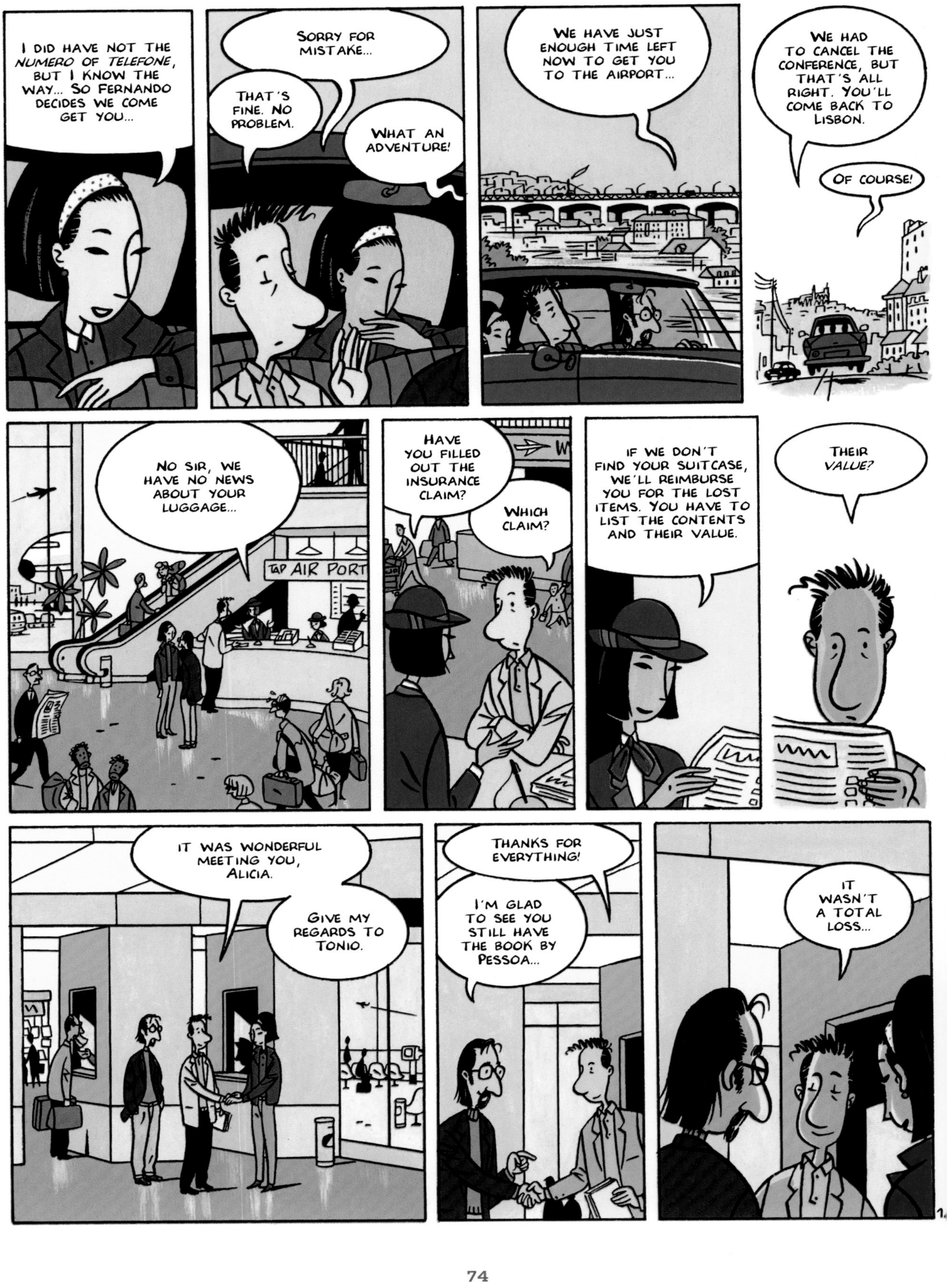
I DID HAVE NOT THE *NUMERO* OF *TELEFONE*, BUT I KNOW THE WAY... SO FERNANDO DECIDES WE COME GET YOU...
SORRY FOR MISTAKE...
THAT'S FINE. NO PROBLEM.
WHAT AN ADVENTURE!
WE HAVE JUST ENOUGH TIME LEFT NOW TO GET YOU TO THE AIRPORT...
WE HAD TO CANCEL THE CONFERENCE, BUT THAT'S ALL RIGHT. YOU'LL COME BACK TO LISBON.
OF COURSE!
NO SIR, WE HAVE NO NEWS ABOUT YOUR LUGGAGE...
TAP AIR PORT
HAVE YOU FILLED OUT THE INSURANCE CLAIM?
WHICH CLAIM?
IF WE DON'T FIND YOUR SUITCASE, WE'LL REIMBURSE YOU FOR THE LOST ITEMS. YOU HAVE TO LIST THE CONTENTS AND THEIR VALUE.
THEIR *VALUE?*
IT WAS WONDERFUL MEETING YOU, ALICIA.
GIVE MY REGARDS TO TONIO.
THANKS FOR EVERYTHING!
I'M GLAD TO SEE YOU STILL HAVE THE BOOK BY PESSOA...
IT WASN'T A TOTAL LOSS...

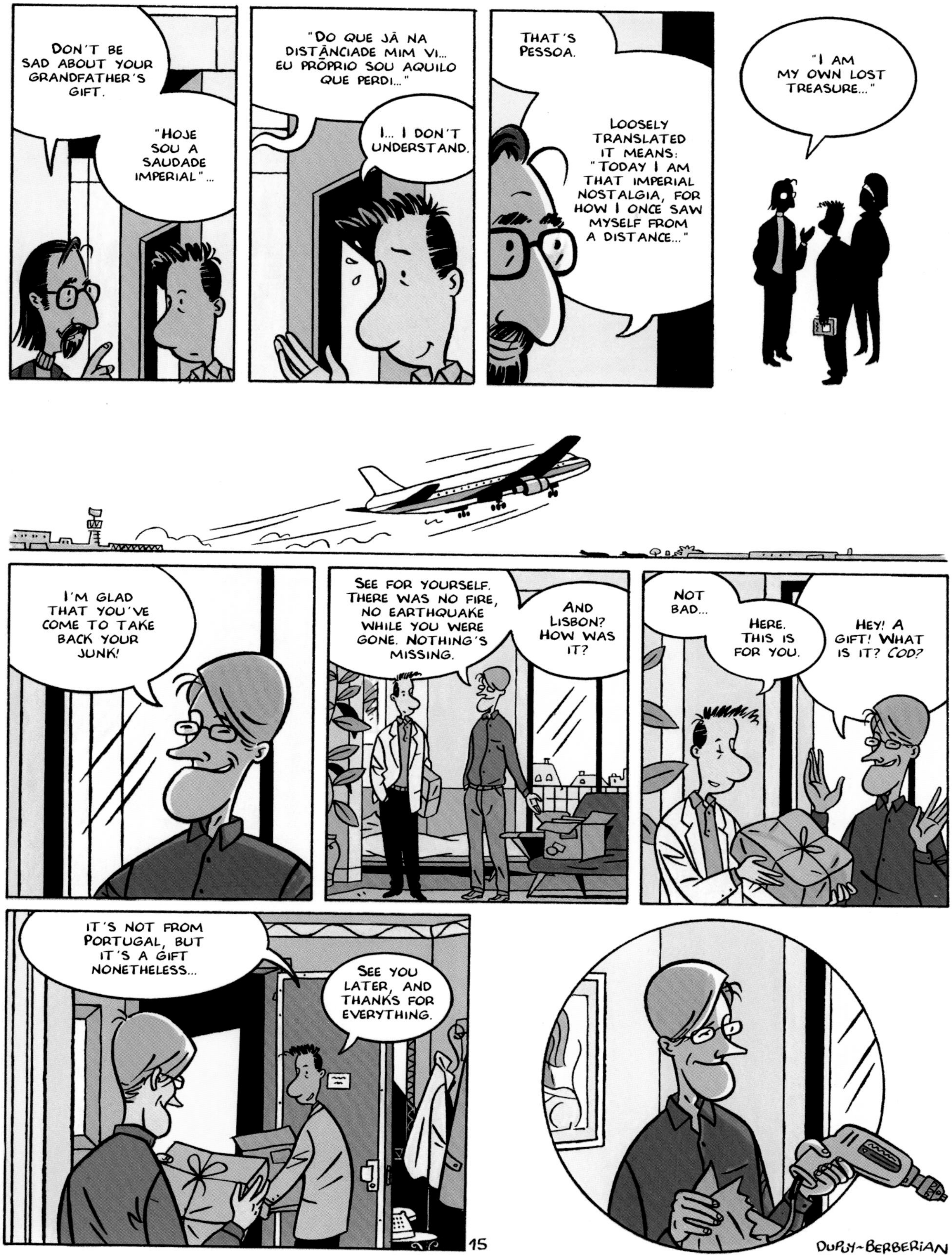
Don't be sad about your grandfather's gift.
"Hoje sou a saudade imperial"...
"Do que já na distânciade mim vi... Eu próprio sou aquilo que perdi..."
I... I don't understand.
That's Pessoa.
Loosely translated it means: "Today I am that imperial nostalgia, for how I once saw myself from a distance..."
"I am my own lost treasure..."
I'm glad that you've come to take back your junk!
See for yourself. There was no fire, no earthquake while you were gone. Nothing's missing.
And Lisbon? How was it?
Not bad...
Here. This is for you.
Hey! A gift! What is it? Cod?
It's not from Portugal, but it's a gift nonetheless...
See you later, and thanks for everything.
15
Dupuy-Berberian

INSOMNIA PART 2

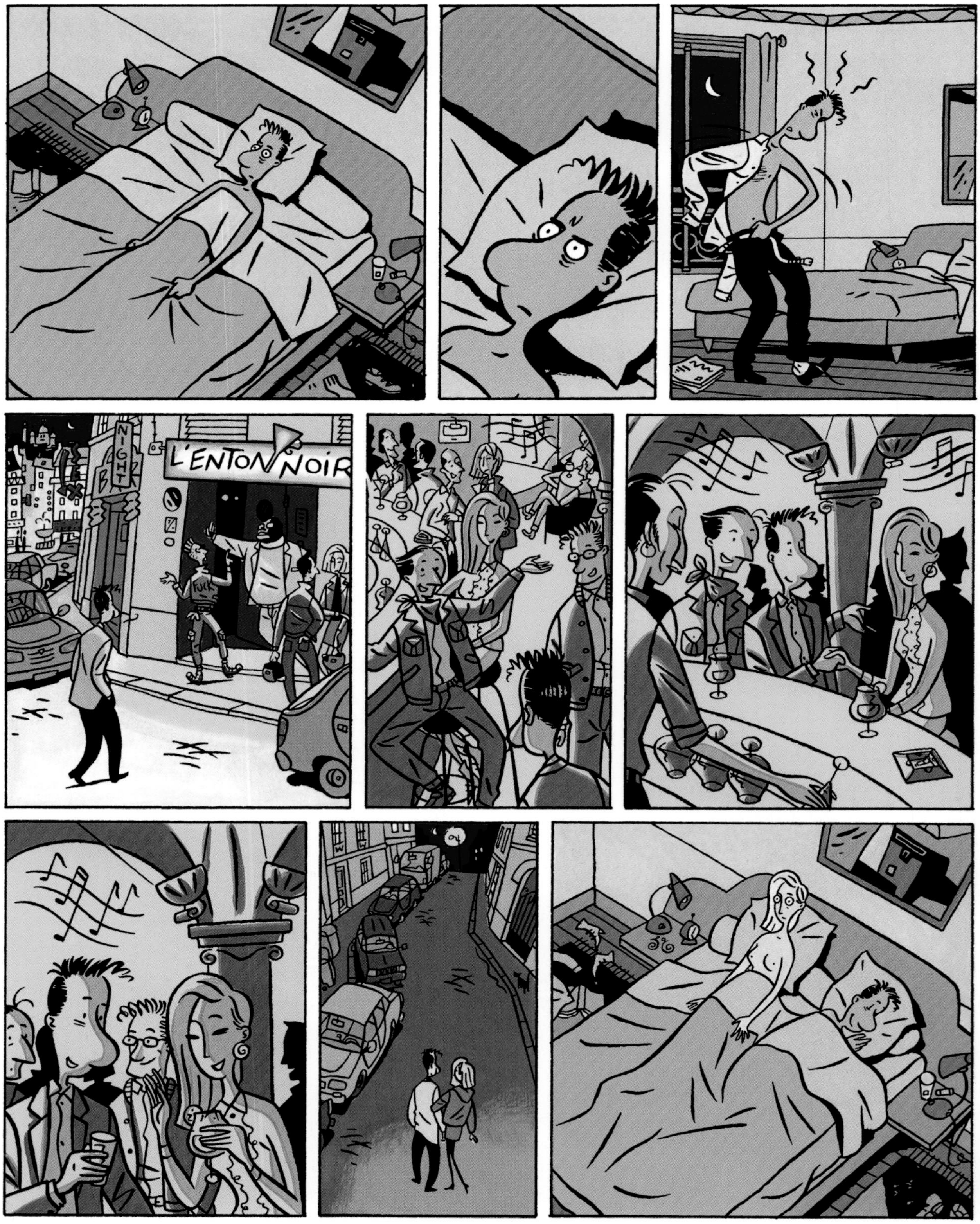
NIGHT
L'ENTONNOIR

BILLIE, SOMERSET, AND THE GARTER BELT

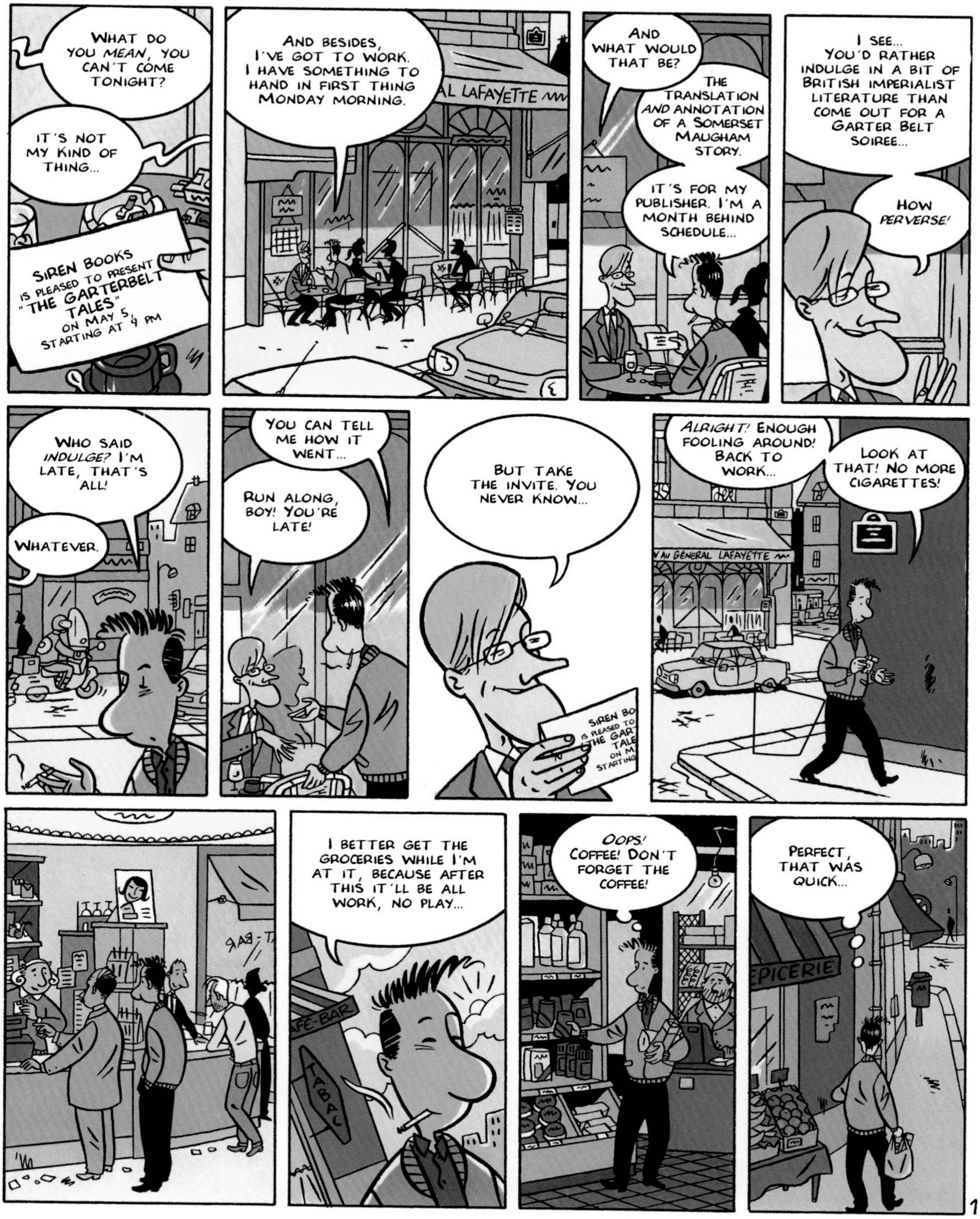
WHAT DO YOU *MEAN*, YOU CAN'T COME TONIGHT?
IT'S NOT MY KIND OF THING...
SIREN BOOKS IS PLEASED TO PRESENT "THE GARTERBELT TALES" ON MAY 5, STARTING AT 9 PM
AND BESIDES, I'VE GOT TO WORK. I HAVE SOMETHING TO HAND IN FIRST THING MONDAY MORNING.
AL LAFAYETTE
AND WHAT WOULD THAT BE?
THE TRANSLATION *AND* ANNOTATION OF A SOMERSET MAUGHAM STORY.
IT'S FOR MY PUBLISHER. I'M A MONTH BEHIND SCHEDULE...
I SEE... YOU'D RATHER INDULGE IN A BIT OF BRITISH IMPERIALIST LITERATURE THAN COME OUT FOR A GARTER BELT SOIREE...
HOW *PERVERSE!*
WHO SAID *INDULGE?* I'M LATE, THAT'S ALL!
WHATEVER.
YOU CAN TELL ME HOW IT WENT...
RUN ALONG, BOY! YOU'RE LATE!
BUT TAKE THE INVITE. YOU NEVER KNOW...
ALRIGHT! ENOUGH FOOLING AROUND! BACK TO WORK...
AU GÉNÉRAL LAFAYETTE
LOOK AT THAT! NO MORE CIGARETTES!
I BETTER GET THE GROCERIES WHILE I'M AT IT, BECAUSE AFTER THIS IT'LL BE ALL WORK, NO PLAY...
CAFÉ-BAR
TABAC
OOPS! COFFEE! DON'T FORGET THE COFFEE!
PERFECT, THAT WAS QUICK...
EPICERIE
1

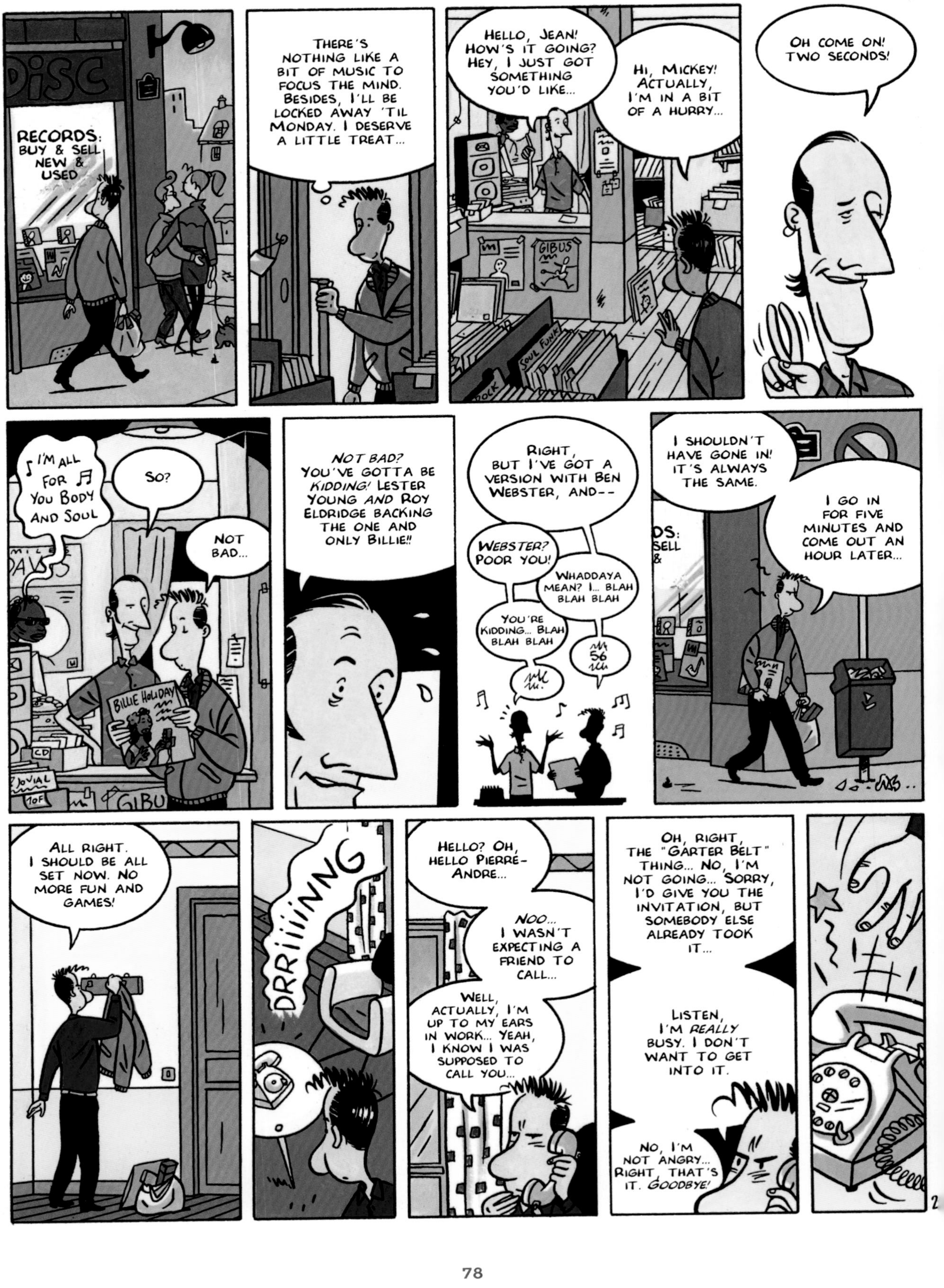
DISC
RECORDS: BUY & SELL NEW & USED
THERE'S NOTHING LIKE A BIT OF MUSIC TO FOCUS THE MIND. BESIDES, I'LL BE LOCKED AWAY 'TIL MONDAY. I DESERVE A LITTLE TREAT...
HELLO, JEAN! HOW'S IT GOING? HEY, I JUST GOT SOMETHING YOU'D LIKE...
HI, MICKEY! ACTUALLY, I'M IN A BIT OF A HURRY...
GIBUS
SOUL FUNK
ROCK
OH COME ON! TWO SECONDS!
I'M ALL FOR YOU BODY AND SOUL
SO?
NOT BAD...
BILLIE HOLIDAY
CD
JOVIAL
10F
GIBU
NOT BAD? YOU'VE GOTTA BE KIDDING! LESTER YOUNG AND ROY ELDRIDGE BACKING THE ONE AND ONLY BILLIE!!
RIGHT, BUT I'VE GOT A VERSION WITH BEN WEBSTER, AND--
WEBSTER? POOR YOU!
WHADDAYA MEAN? I... BLAH BLAH BLAH
YOU'RE KIDDING... BLAH BLAH BLAH
56
I SHOULDN'T HAVE GONE IN! IT'S ALWAYS THE SAME.
I GO IN FOR FIVE MINUTES AND COME OUT AN HOUR LATER...
DS: SELL &
ALL RIGHT. I SHOULD BE ALL SET NOW. NO MORE FUN AND GAMES!
DRRIIIIINNG
HELLO? OH, HELLO PIERRE-ANDRE...
NOO... I WASN'T EXPECTING A FRIEND TO CALL...
WELL, ACTUALLY, I'M UP TO MY EARS IN WORK... YEAH, I KNOW I WAS SUPPOSED TO CALL YOU...
OH, RIGHT, THE "GARTER BELT" THING... NO, I'M NOT GOING... SORRY, I'D GIVE YOU THE INVITATION, BUT SOMEBODY ELSE ALREADY TOOK IT...
LISTEN, I'M REALLY BUSY. I DON'T WANT TO GET INTO IT.
NO, I'M NOT ANGRY... RIGHT, THAT'S IT. GOODBYE!

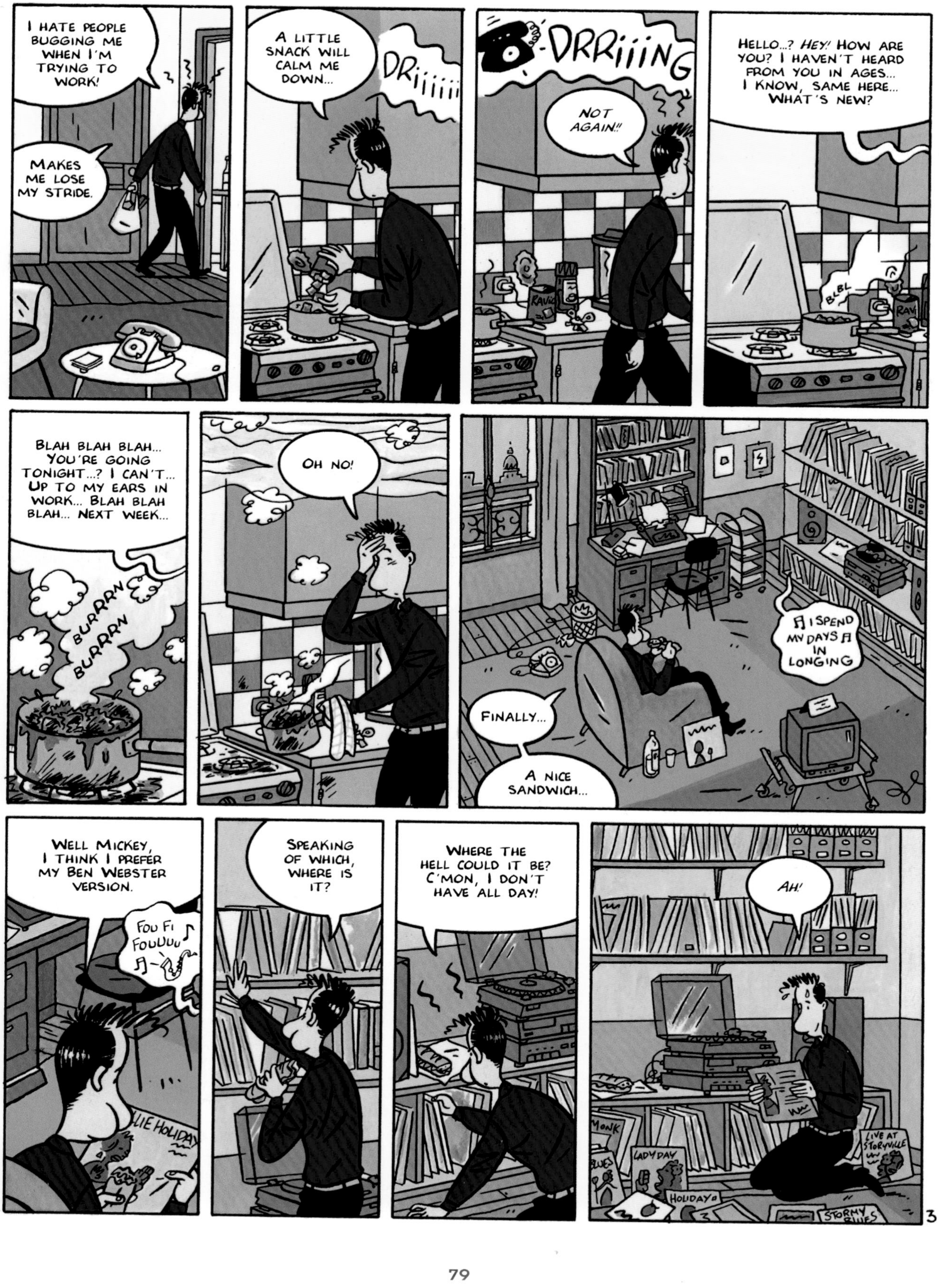

I HATE PEOPLE BUGGING ME WHEN I'M TRYING TO WORK!
MAKES ME LOSE MY STRIDE.
A LITTLE SNACK WILL CALM ME DOWN...
DRiiiiii
DRRiiiNG
NOT AGAIN!!
HELLO...? HEY! HOW ARE YOU? I HAVEN'T HEARD FROM YOU IN AGES... I KNOW, SAME HERE... WHAT'S NEW?
BLBL
BLAH BLAH BLAH... YOU'RE GOING TONIGHT...? I CAN'T... UP TO MY EARS IN WORK... BLAH BLAH BLAH... NEXT WEEK...
BURRRN BURRRN
OH NO!
♫ I SPEND MY DAYS ♫ IN LONGING
FINALLY...
A NICE SANDWICH...
WELL MICKEY, I THINK I PREFER MY BEN WEBSTER VERSION.
FOU FI FOUUUU
SPEAKING OF WHICH, WHERE IS IT?
WHERE THE HELL COULD IT BE? C'MON, I DON'T HAVE ALL DAY!
AH!
MONK
LADY DAY
HOLIDAY
LIVE AT STORYVILLE
STORMY BLUES
3

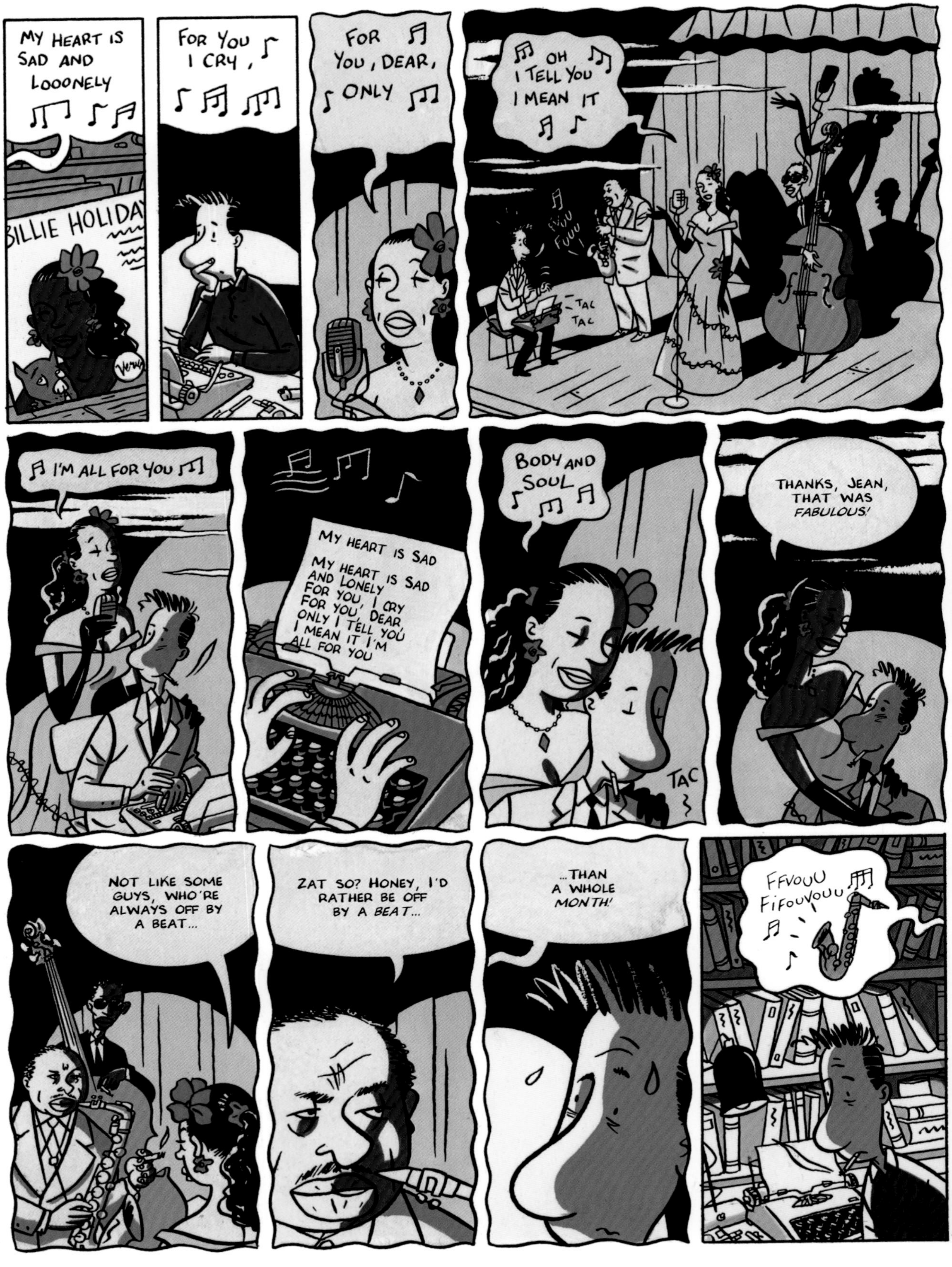
MY HEART IS SAD AND LOOONELY
BILLIE HOLIDAY
FOR YOU I CRY,
FOR YOU, DEAR, ONLY
OH I TELL YOU I MEAN IT
FUUU FUUU!
TAC TAC
I'M ALL FOR YOU
MY HEART IS SAD
MY HEART IS SAD AND LONELY FOR YOU, I CRY FOR YOU, DEAR, ONLY I TELL YOU I MEAN IT I'M ALL FOR YOU
BODY AND SOUL
TAC
THANKS, JEAN, THAT WAS FABULOUS!
NOT LIKE SOME GUYS, WHO'RE ALWAYS OFF BY A BEAT...
ZAT SO? HONEY, I'D RATHER BE OFF BY A BEAT...
...THAN A WHOLE MONTH!
FFVOUU FIFOUVOUU

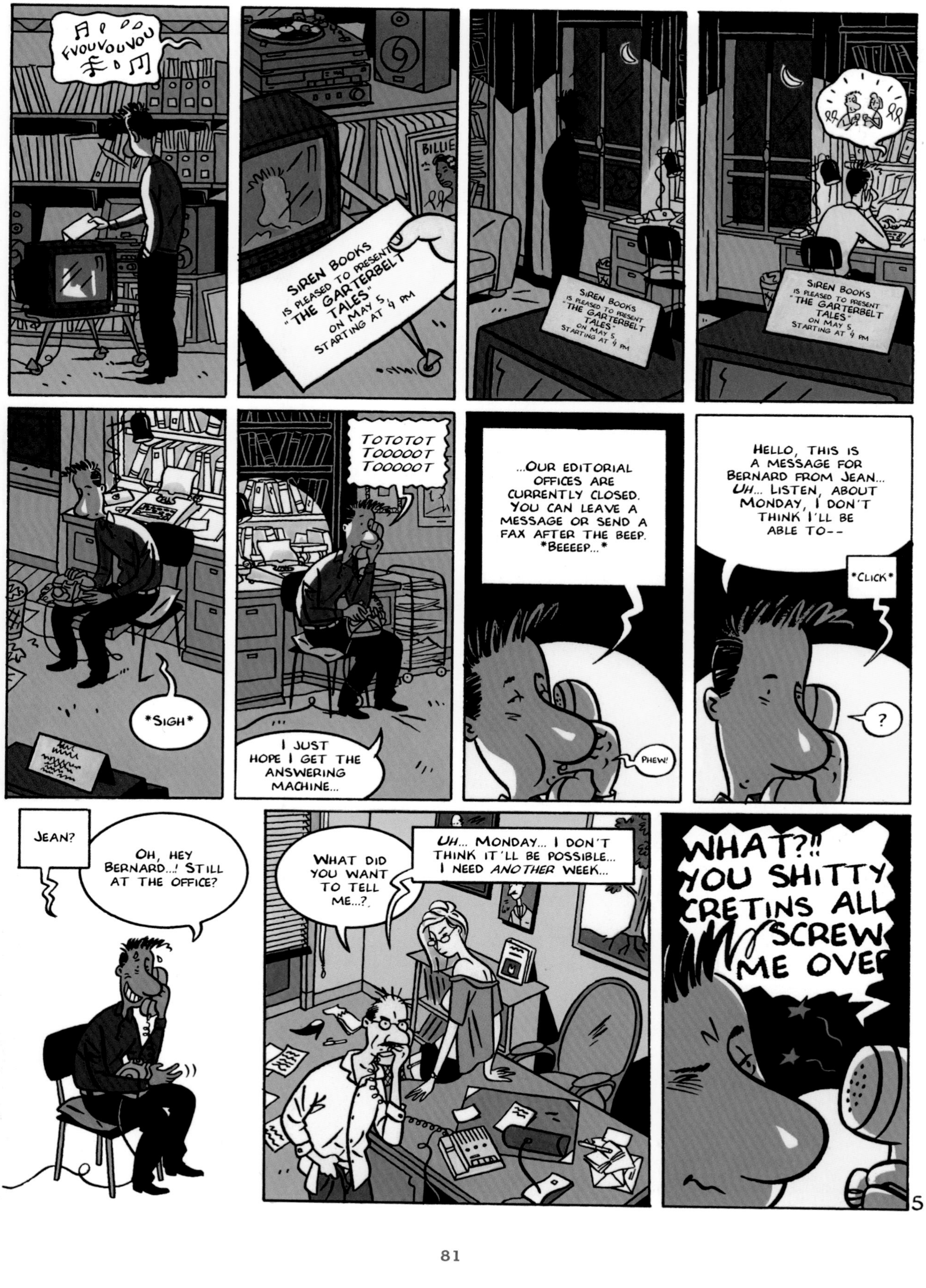

FVOUVOUVOU
SIREN BOOKS IS PLEASED TO PRESENT "THE GARTERBELT TALES" ON MAY 5, STARTING AT 9 PM
SIREN BOOKS IS PLEASED TO PRESENT "THE GARTERBELT TALES" ON MAY 5, STARTING AT 9 PM
SIREN BOOKS IS PLEASED TO PRESENT "THE GARTERBELT TALES" ON MAY 5, STARTING AT 9 PM
SIGH
TOTOTOT TOOOOOT TOOOOOT
I JUST HOPE I GET THE ANSWERING MACHINE...
...OUR EDITORIAL OFFICES ARE CURRENTLY CLOSED. YOU CAN LEAVE A MESSAGE OR SEND A FAX AFTER THE BEEP. *BEEEEP...*
PHEW!
HELLO, THIS IS A MESSAGE FOR BERNARD FROM JEAN... UH... LISTEN, ABOUT MONDAY, I DON'T THINK I'LL BE ABLE TO--
CLICK
?
JEAN?
OH, HEY BERNARD...! STILL AT THE OFFICE?
WHAT DID YOU WANT TO TELL ME...?
UH... MONDAY... I DON'T THINK IT'LL BE POSSIBLE... I NEED ANOTHER WEEK...
WHAT?!! YOU SHITTY CRETINS ALL SCREW ME OVE
5

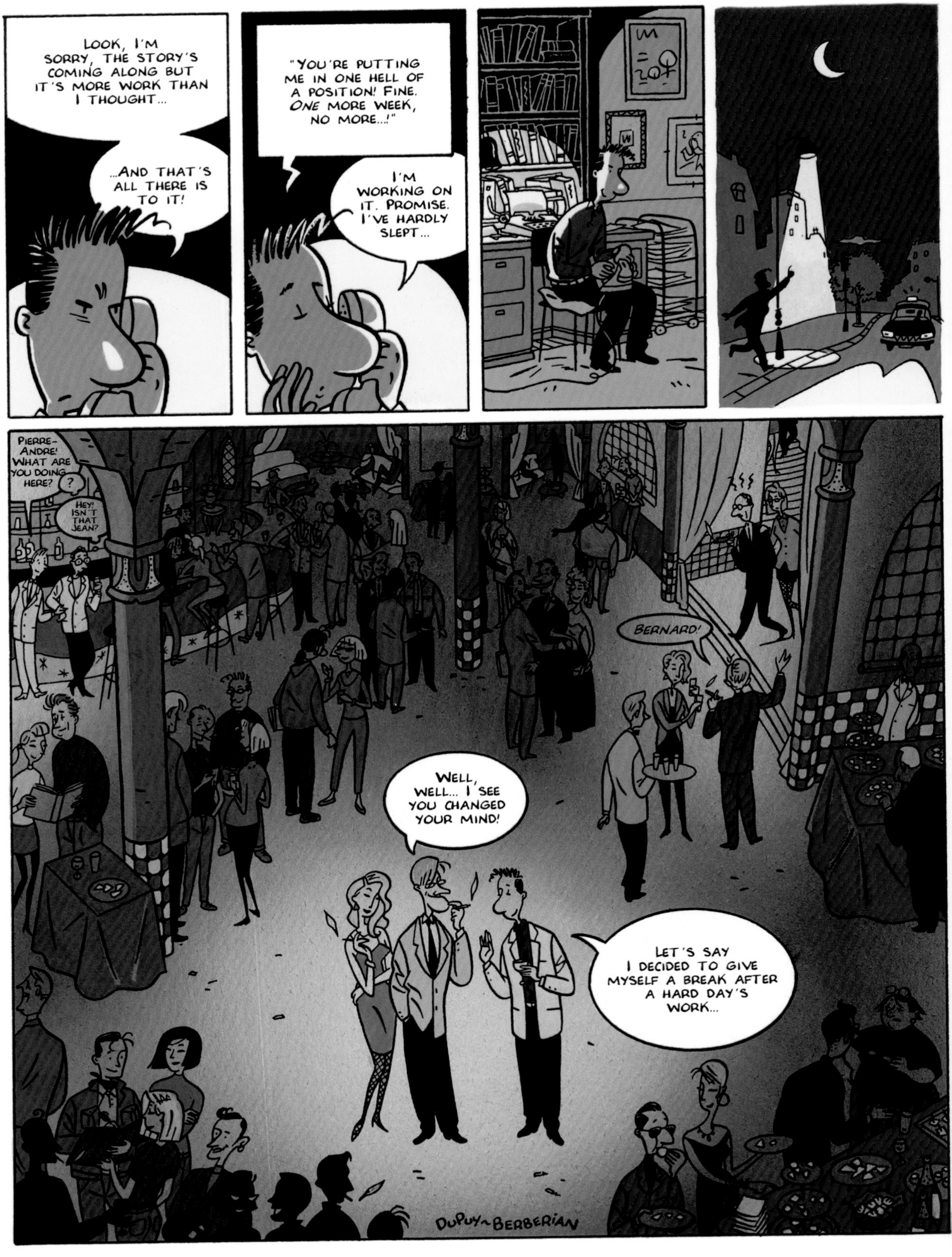
LOOK, I'M SORRY, THE STORY'S COMING ALONG BUT IT'S MORE WORK THAN I THOUGHT...
...AND THAT'S ALL THERE IS TO IT!
"YOU'RE PUTTING ME IN ONE HELL OF A POSITION! FINE. *ONE* MORE WEEK, NO MORE...!"
I'M WORKING ON IT. PROMISE. I'VE HARDLY SLEPT...
PIERRE-ANDRE! WHAT ARE YOU DOING HERE?
?
HEY! ISN'T THAT JEAN?
BERNARD!
WELL, WELL... I SEE YOU CHANGED YOUR MIND!
LET'S SAY I DECIDED TO GIVE MYSELF A BREAK AFTER A HARD DAY'S WORK...
DUPUY~BERBERIAN

INSOMNIA PART 3

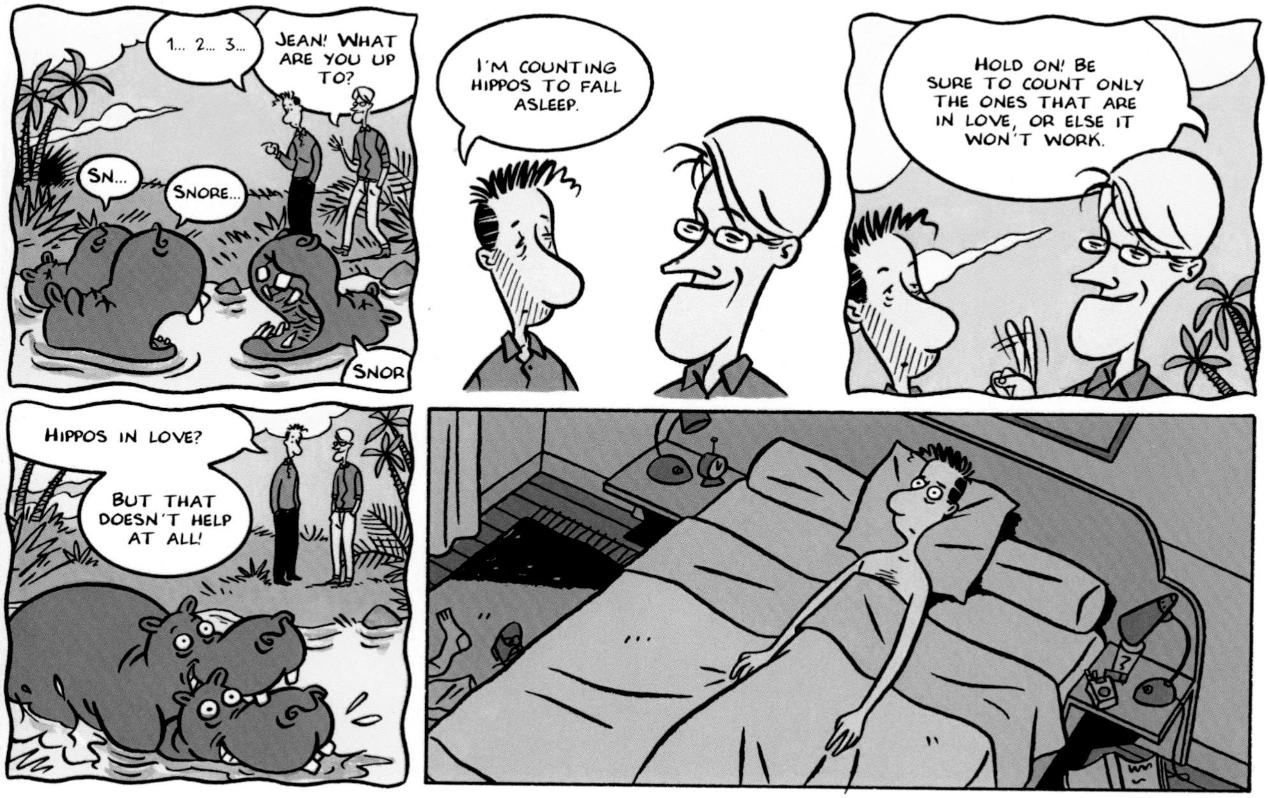
1... 2... 3...
JEAN! WHAT ARE YOU UP TO?
SN...
SNORE...
SNOR
I'M COUNTING HIPPOS TO FALL ASLEEP.
HOLD ON! BE SURE TO COUNT ONLY THE ONES THAT ARE IN LOVE, OR ELSE IT WON'T WORK.
HIPPOS IN LOVE?
BUT THAT DOESN'T HELP AT ALL!
...

Monsieur Gloom

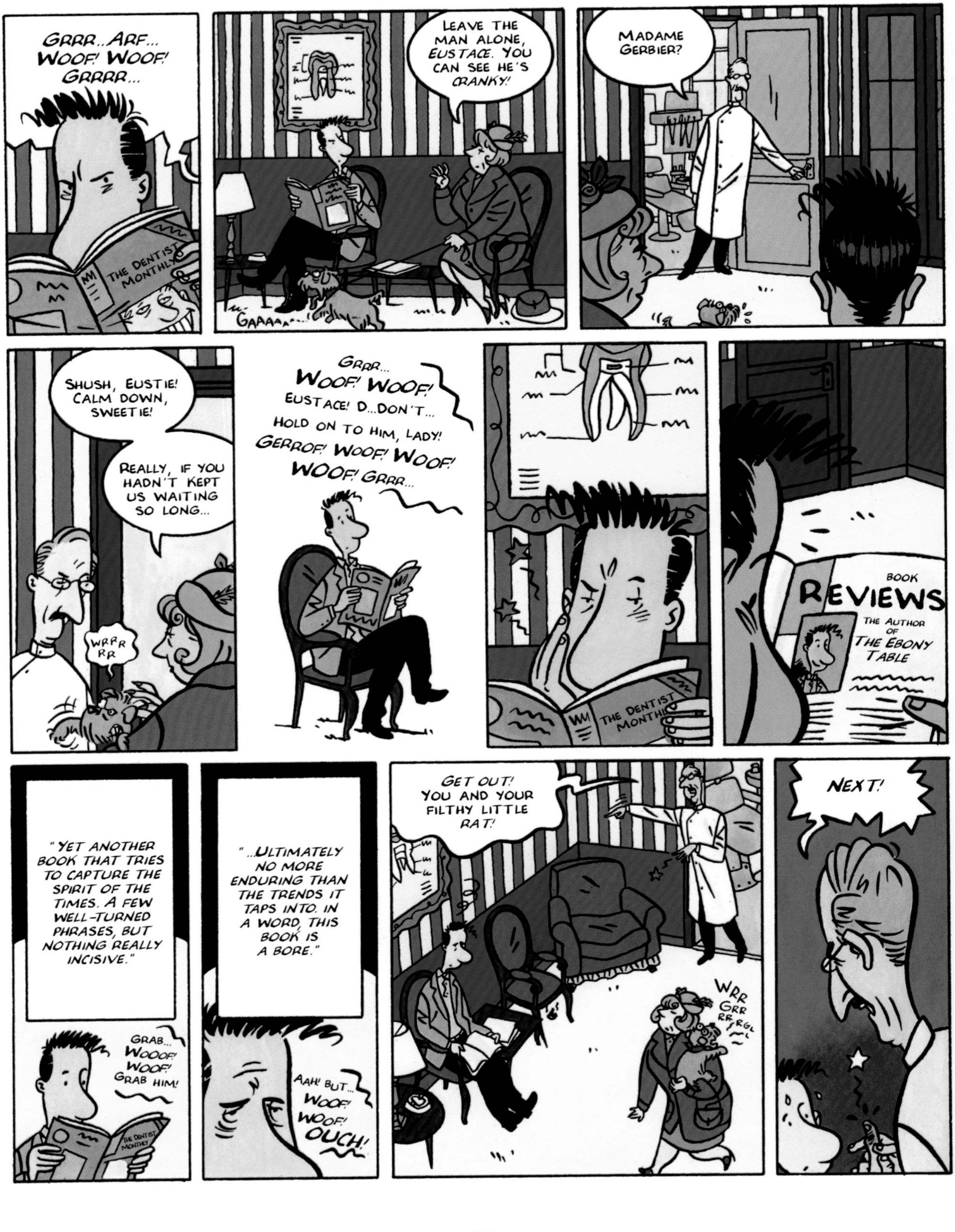

Grrr.. Arf... Woof! Woof! Grrrr...
The Dentist Monthly
Leave the man alone, Eustace. You can see he's cranky!
Gaaaa...
Madame Gerbier?
Shush, Eustie! Calm down, sweetie!
Really, if you hadn't kept us waiting so long...
Wrrr rr
Grrr... Woof! Woof!
Eustace! D...don't...
Hold on to him, lady!
Gerrof! Woof! Woof!
Woof! Grrr...
The Dentist Monthly
Book Reviews
The author of The Ebony Table
"Yet another book that tries to capture the spirit of the times. A few well-turned phrases, but nothing really incisive."
Grab... Wooof! Woof! Grab him!
The Dentist Monthly
"...Ultimately no more enduring than the trends it taps into. In a word, this book is a bore."
Aah! But... Woof! Woof! Ouch!
Get out! You and your filthy little rat!
Wrr Grr rr rrgl
Next!

JERK! I THINK HE HIT A NERVE...

IT HURTS, HUH?

?

UH... YES, IT DOES

BUT...

C'MON, JEAN! DON'T TRY TO FOOL ME! YOU KNOW WHAT I'M TALKING ABOUT!

WHAT? THE ARTICLE?

HMPF... WHO ACTUALLY READS THOSE IDIOTIC MAGAZINES?

HEH! HEH! HEH!

THAT "IDIOTIC MAGAZINE" IS IN EVERY DENTIST'S WAITING ROOM, AND LOTS OF PEOPLE HAVE TOOTHACHES...

ARE YOU TRYING TO MAKE ME DEPRESSED?

PA~~~~IE~JOURNAUX

ACTUALLY, YOU ALREADY ARE, OR I WOULDN'T BE HERE!

COULD YOU RECOMMEND ME A BOOK FOR A GIFT?

OF COURSE! THERE'S "HOUSEPLANT PSYCHOANALYSIS..." OR PERHAPS "HARD CASH," THE LATEST BESTSELLER BY...

WHICH ONE COSTS LESS?

AH! IF IT'S A QUESTION OF PRICE...

PATRICK DUROI TAKE A BITE OUT OF LIFE +1 FREE BADGE

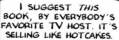

I SUGGEST THIS BOOK, BY EVERYBODY'S FAVORITE TV HOST. IT'S SELLING LIKE HOTCAKES.

I'LL TAKE IT!

2

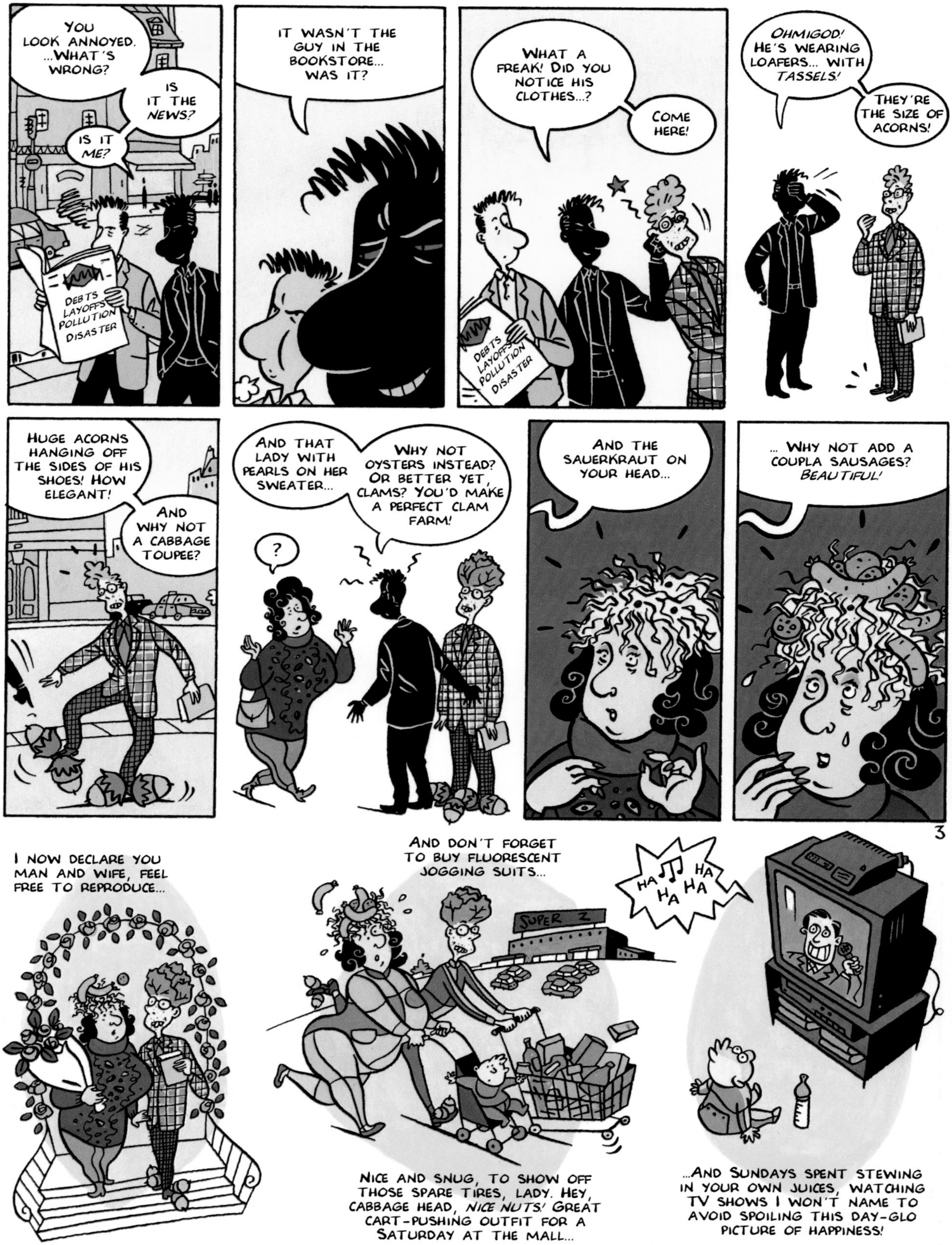
YOU LOOK ANNOYED. ...WHAT'S WRONG?
IS IT THE NEWS?
IS IT ME?
DEBTS LAYOFFS POLLUTION DISASTER
IT WASN'T THE GUY IN THE BOOKSTORE... WAS IT?
WHAT A FREAK! DID YOU NOTICE HIS CLOTHES...?
COME HERE!
DEBTS LAYOFFS POLLUTION DISASTER
OHMIGOD! HE'S WEARING LOAFERS... WITH TASSELS!
THEY'RE THE SIZE OF ACORNS!
HUGE ACORNS HANGING OFF THE SIDES OF HIS SHOES! HOW ELEGANT!
AND WHY NOT A CABBAGE TOUPEE?
AND THAT LADY WITH PEARLS ON HER SWEATER...
WHY NOT OYSTERS INSTEAD? OR BETTER YET, CLAMS? YOU'D MAKE A PERFECT CLAM FARM!
?
AND THE SAUERKRAUT ON YOUR HEAD...
... WHY NOT ADD A COUPLA SAUSAGES? BEAUTIFUL!
3
I NOW DECLARE YOU MAN AND WIFE, FEEL FREE TO REPRODUCE...
AND DON'T FORGET TO BUY FLUORESCENT JOGGING SUITS...
SUPER Z
NICE AND SNUG, TO SHOW OFF THOSE SPARE TIRES, LADY. HEY, CABBAGE HEAD, NICE NUTS! GREAT CART-PUSHING OUTFIT FOR A SATURDAY AT THE MALL...
HA HA HA HA
...AND SUNDAYS SPENT STEWING IN YOUR OWN JUICES, WATCHING TV SHOWS I WON'T NAME TO AVOID SPOILING THIS DAY-GLO PICTURE OF HAPPINESS!

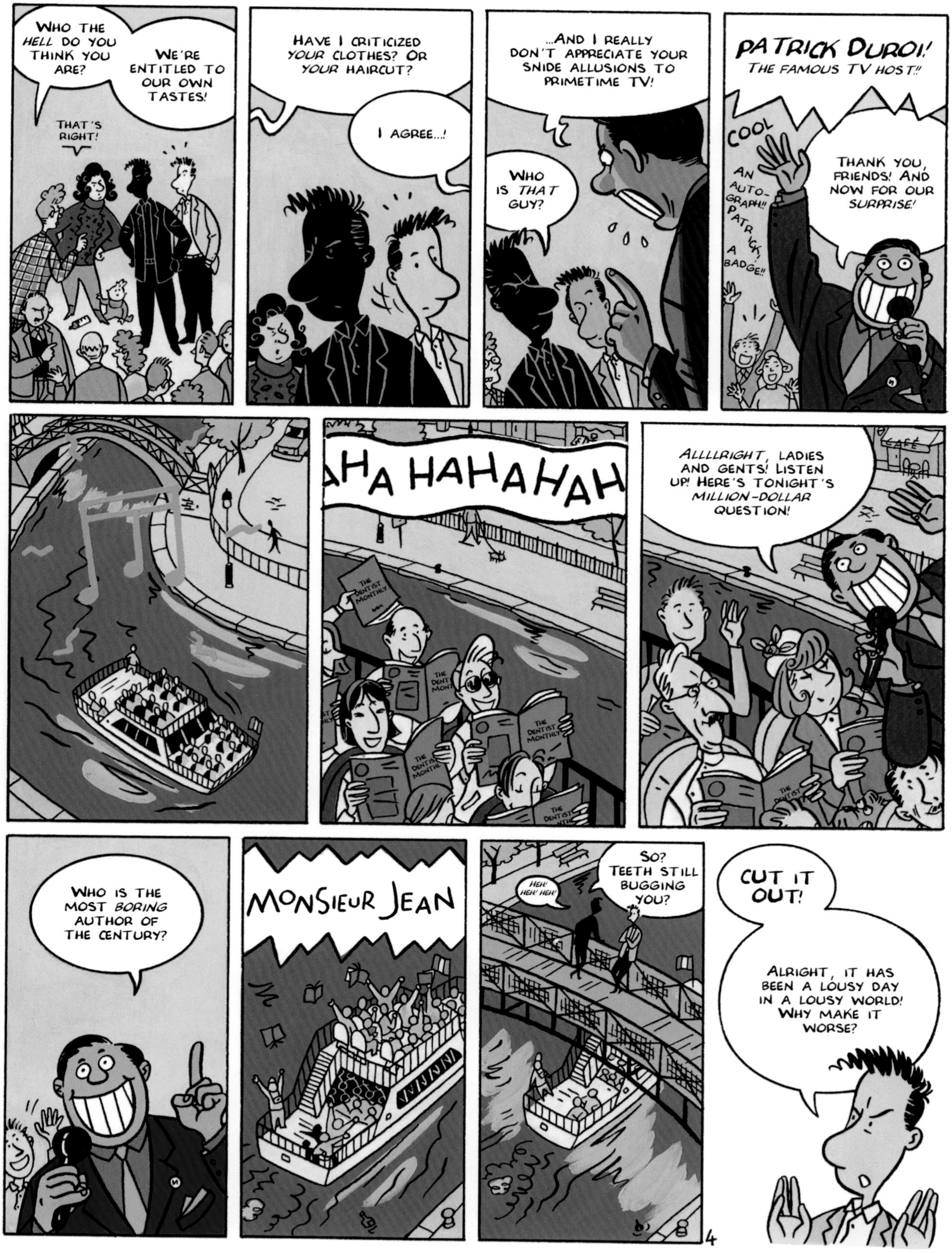
WHO THE HELL DO YOU THINK YOU ARE?
WE'RE ENTITLED TO OUR OWN TASTES!
THAT'S RIGHT!
HAVE I CRITICIZED YOUR CLOTHES? OR YOUR HAIRCUT?
I AGREE...!
...AND I REALLY DON'T APPRECIATE YOUR SNIDE ALLUSIONS TO PRIMETIME TV!
WHO IS THAT GUY?
PATRICK DUROI! THE FAMOUS TV HOST!!
COOL
AN AUTOGRAPH!! PATRICK! A BADGE!!
THANK YOU, FRIENDS! AND NOW FOR OUR SURPRISE!
AHAHAHAHAH
THE DENTIST MONTHLY
ALLLLRIGHT, LADIES AND GENTS! LISTEN UP! HERE'S TONIGHT'S MILLION-DOLLAR QUESTION!
CAFÉ
WHO IS THE MOST BORING AUTHOR OF THE CENTURY?
MONSIEUR JEAN
HEH! HEH! HEH!
SO? TEETH STILL BUGGING YOU?
CUT IT OUT!
ALRIGHT, IT HAS BEEN A LOUSY DAY IN A LOUSY WORLD! WHY MAKE IT WORSE?
4

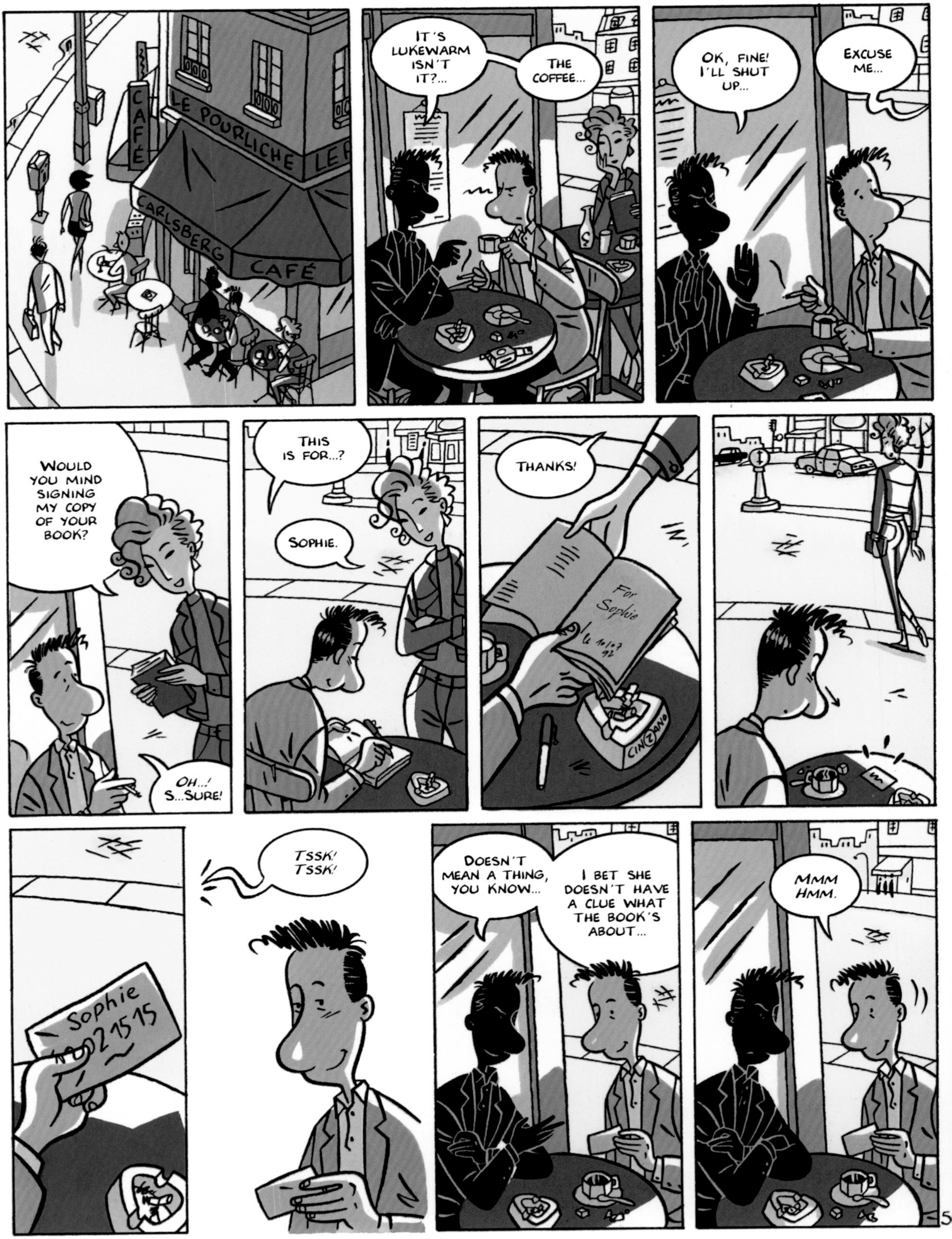
CAFÉ
LE POURLICHE
CARLSBERG
CAFÉ
IT'S LUKEWARM ISN'T IT?...
THE COFFEE...
OK, FINE! I'LL SHUT UP...
EXCUSE ME...
WOULD YOU MIND SIGNING MY COPY OF YOUR BOOK?
OH...! S...SURE!
THIS IS FOR...?
SOPHIE.
THANKS!
For Sophie
CINZANO
Sophie
TSSK! TSSK!
DOESN'T MEAN A THING, YOU KNOW...
I BET SHE DOESN'T HAVE A CLUE WHAT THE BOOK'S ABOUT...
MMM HMM.

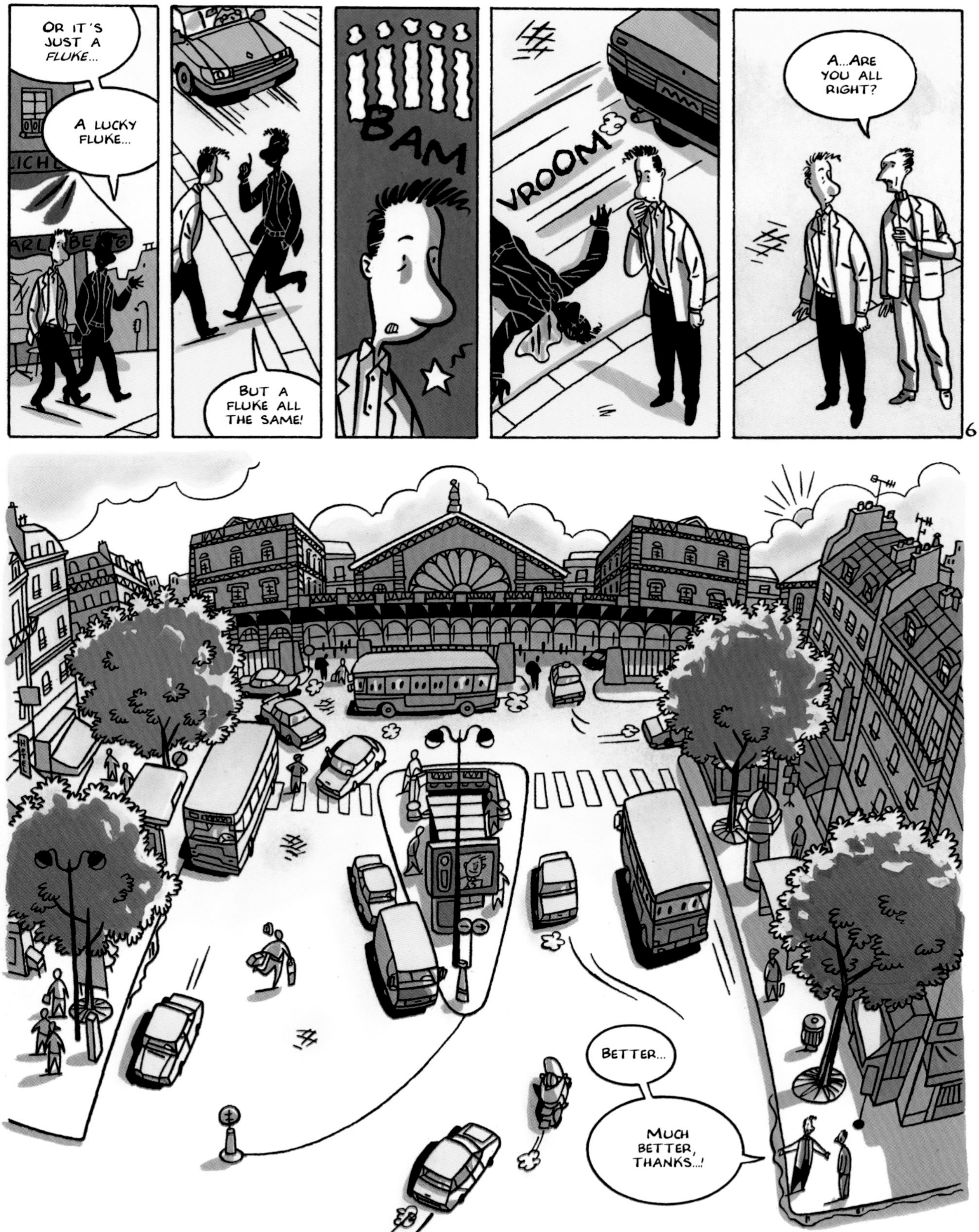
OR IT'S JUST A *FLUKE*...
A LUCKY FLUKE...
BUT A FLUKE ALL THE SAME!
BAM
VROOM
A...ARE YOU ALL RIGHT?
BETTER...
MUCH BETTER, THANKS...!

Philippe Dupuy

Charles Berberian

LISA

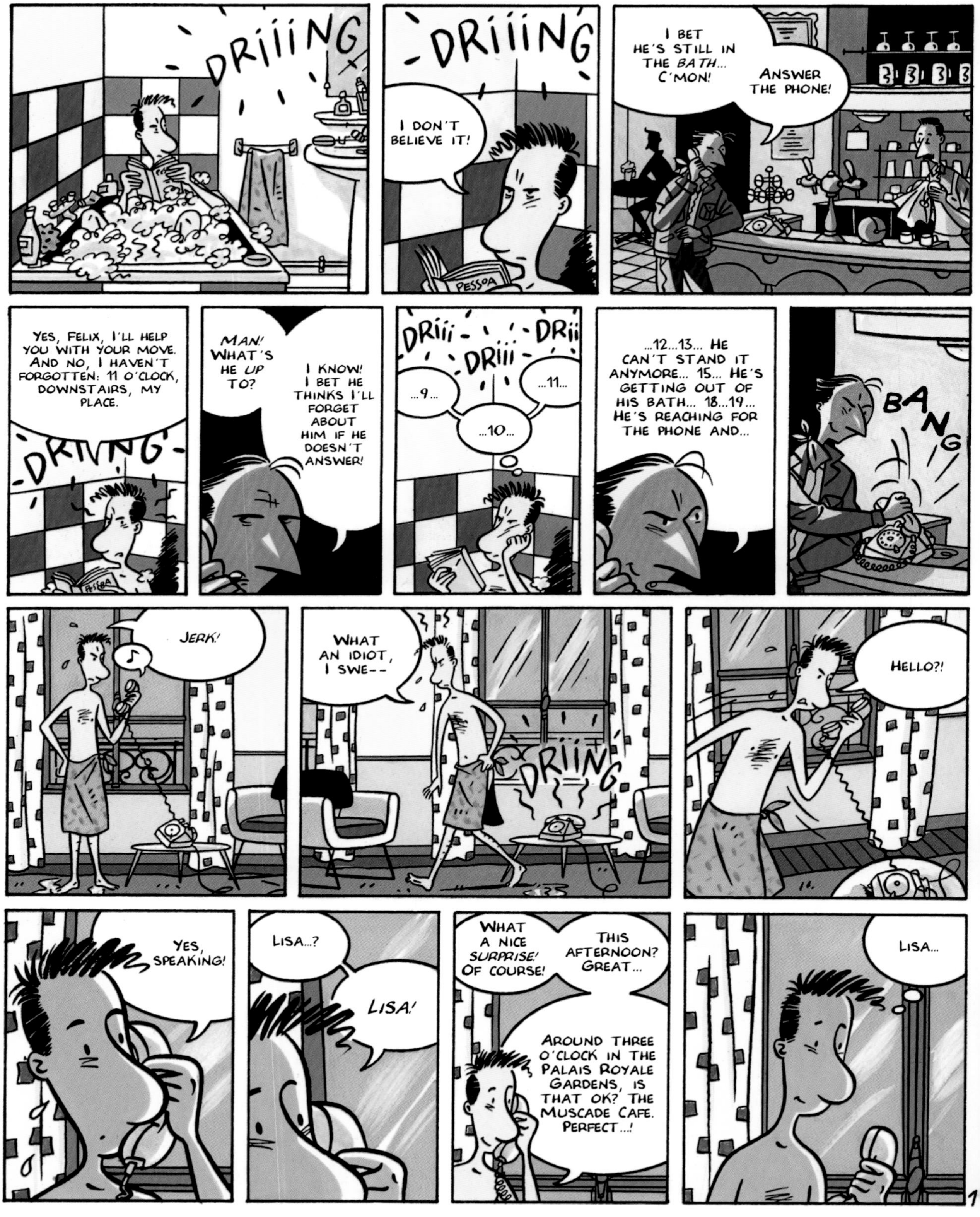
DRIIING
DRIIING
I DON'T BELIEVE IT!
PESSOA
I BET HE'S STILL IN THE *BATH*... C'MON!
ANSWER THE PHONE!
YES, FELIX, I'LL HELP YOU WITH YOUR MOVE. AND NO, I HAVEN'T FORGOTTEN: 11 O'CLOCK, DOWNSTAIRS, MY PLACE.
DRIING
PESSOA
MAN! WHAT'S HE *UP* TO?
I KNOW! I BET HE THINKS I'LL FORGET ABOUT HIM IF HE DOESN'T ANSWER!
DRIII - DRIII - DRII
...9...
...10...
...11...
...12...13... HE CAN'T STAND IT ANYMORE... 15... HE'S GETTING OUT OF HIS BATH... 18...19... HE'S REACHING FOR THE PHONE AND...
BANG
JERK!
WHAT AN IDIOT, I SWE--
DRIING
HELLO?!
YES, SPEAKING!
LISA...?
LISA!
WHAT A NICE *SURPRISE!* OF COURSE!
THIS AFTERNOON? GREAT...
AROUND THREE O'CLOCK IN THE PALAIS ROYALE GARDENS, IS THAT OK? THE MUSCADE CAFE. PERFECT...!
LISA...

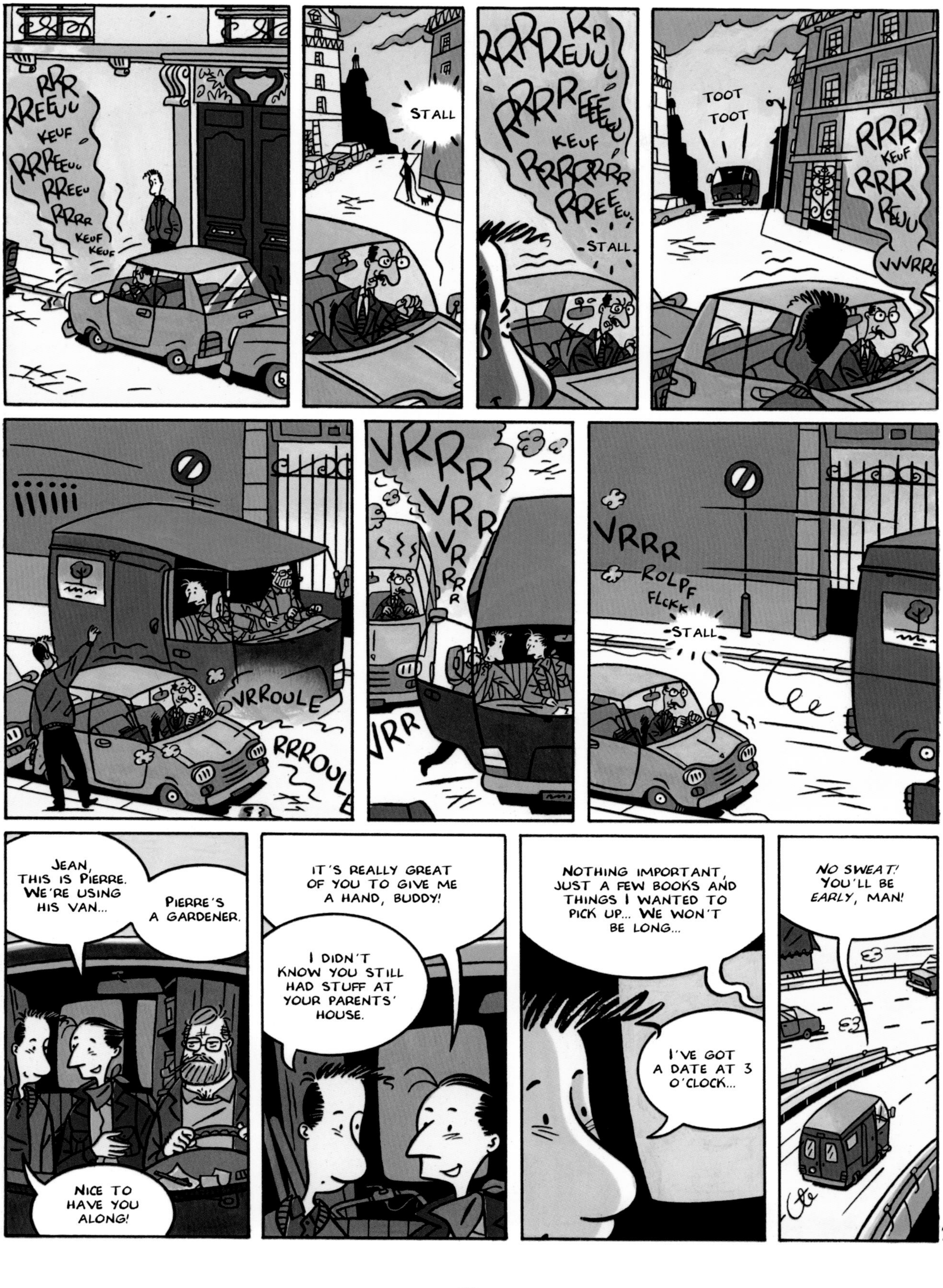
RRR RREEUU KEUF RRREEUU RREEU RRRR KEUF KEUF
STALL
RRRRREUU RRRREEEEU KEUF RRRRRRRR RREEEU
STALL
TOOT TOOT
RRR KEUF RRR REUU
VVVRR
VRROULE
RRROULE
VRRR VRR VRRR
VRR
VRRR
ROLPF
FLCKK
STALL
JEAN, THIS IS PIERRE. WE'RE USING HIS VAN...
PIERRE'S A GARDENER.
NICE TO HAVE YOU ALONG!
IT'S REALLY GREAT OF YOU TO GIVE ME A HAND, BUDDY!
I DIDN'T KNOW YOU STILL HAD STUFF AT YOUR PARENTS' HOUSE.
NOTHING IMPORTANT, JUST A FEW BOOKS AND THINGS I WANTED TO PICK UP... WE WON'T BE LONG...
I'VE GOT A DATE AT 3 O'CLOCK...
NO SWEAT! YOU'LL BE EARLY, MAN!
2

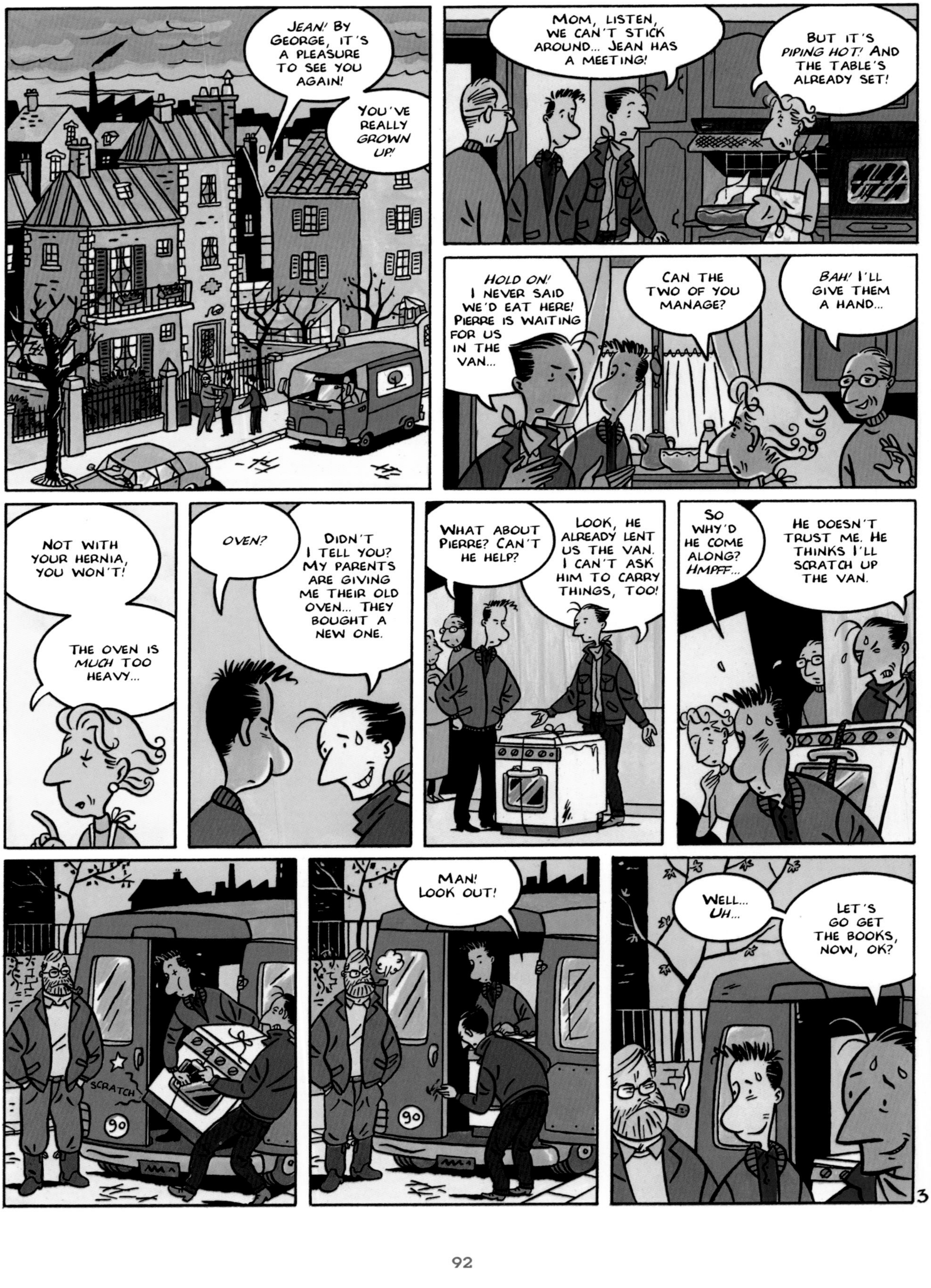
JEAN! BY GEORGE, IT'S A PLEASURE TO SEE YOU AGAIN!
YOU'VE REALLY GROWN UP!
MOM, LISTEN, WE CAN'T STICK AROUND... JEAN HAS A MEETING!
BUT IT'S PIPING HOT! AND THE TABLE'S ALREADY SET!
HOLD ON! I NEVER SAID WE'D EAT HERE! PIERRE IS WAITING FOR US IN THE VAN...
CAN THE TWO OF YOU MANAGE?
BAH! I'LL GIVE THEM A HAND...
NOT WITH YOUR HERNIA, YOU WON'T!
THE OVEN IS MUCH TOO HEAVY...
OVEN?
DIDN'T I TELL YOU? MY PARENTS ARE GIVING ME THEIR OLD OVEN... THEY BOUGHT A NEW ONE.
WHAT ABOUT PIERRE? CAN'T HE HELP?
LOOK, HE ALREADY LENT US THE VAN. I CAN'T ASK HIM TO CARRY THINGS, TOO!
SO WHY'D HE COME ALONG? HMPFF...
HE DOESN'T TRUST ME. HE THINKS I'LL SCRATCH UP THE VAN.
SCRATCH
MAN! LOOK OUT!
WELL... UH...
LET'S GO GET THE BOOKS, NOW, OK?
3

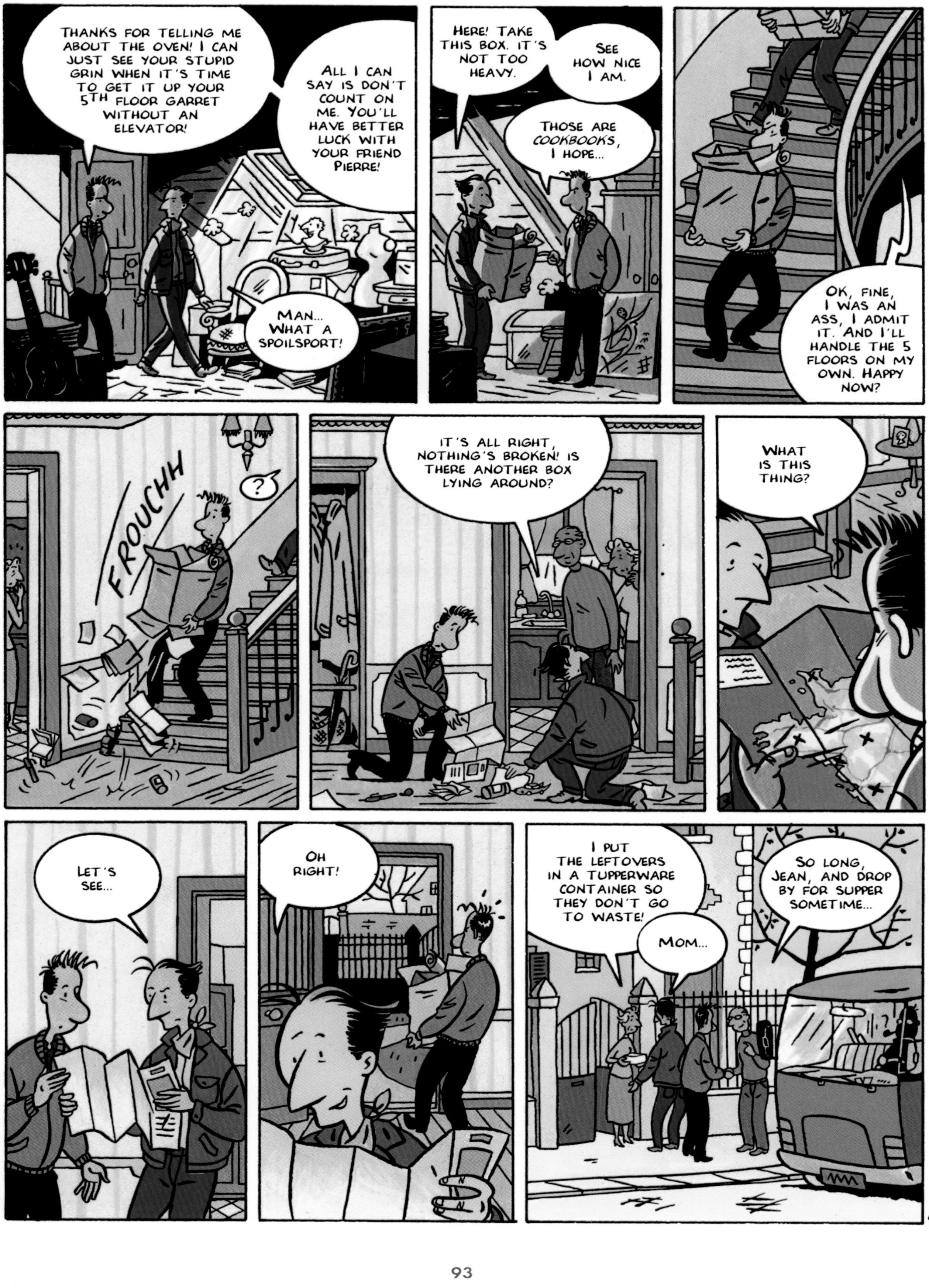
THANKS FOR TELLING ME ABOUT THE OVEN! I CAN JUST SEE YOUR STUPID GRIN WHEN IT'S TIME TO GET IT UP YOUR 5TH FLOOR GARRET WITHOUT AN ELEVATOR!
ALL I CAN SAY IS DON'T COUNT ON ME. YOU'LL HAVE BETTER LUCK WITH YOUR FRIEND PIERRE!
MAN... WHAT A SPOILSPORT!
HERE! TAKE THIS BOX. IT'S NOT TOO HEAVY.
SEE HOW NICE I AM.
THOSE ARE *COOKBOOKS*, I HOPE...
OK, FINE, I WAS AN ASS, I ADMIT IT. AND I'LL HANDLE THE 5 FLOORS ON MY OWN. HAPPY NOW?
FROUCHH
?
IT'S ALL RIGHT, NOTHING'S BROKEN! IS THERE ANOTHER BOX LYING AROUND?
WHAT IS THIS THING?
LET'S SEE...
OH RIGHT!
I PUT THE LEFTOVERS IN A TUPPERWARE CONTAINER SO THEY DON'T GO TO WASTE!
MOM...
SO LONG, JEAN, AND DROP BY FOR SUPPER SOMETIME...
4

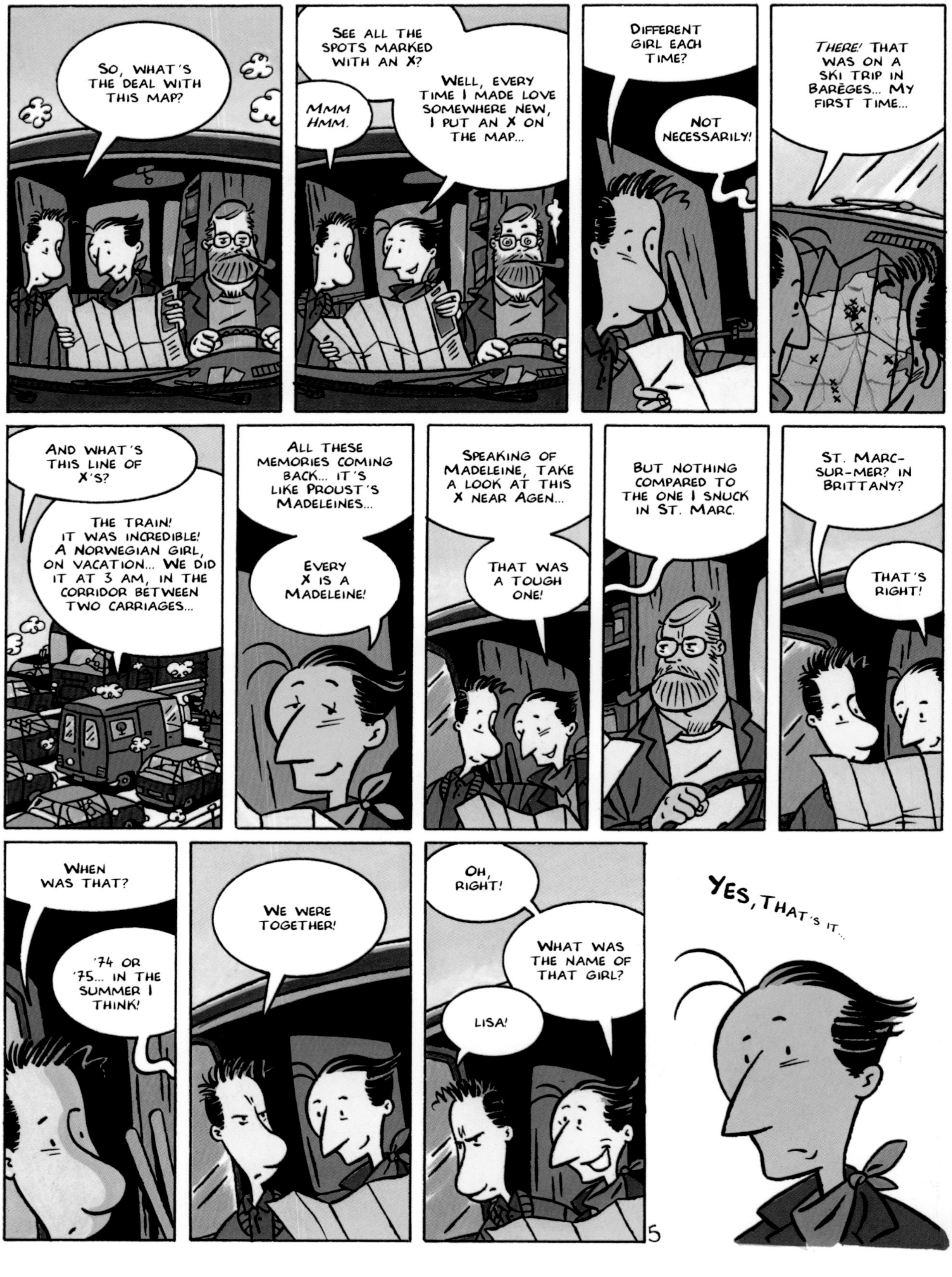
So, what's the deal with this map?
See all the spots marked with an X?
Mmm hmm.
Well, every time I made love somewhere new, I put an X on the map...
Different girl each time?
Not necessarily!
There! That was on a ski trip in Barèges... My first time...
And what's this line of X's?
The train! It was incredible! A Norwegian girl, on vacation... We did it at 3 AM, in the corridor between two carriages...
All these memories coming back... it's like Proust's Madeleines...
Every X is a Madeleine!
Speaking of Madeleine, take a look at this X near Agen...
That was a tough one!
But nothing compared to the one I snuck in St. Marc.
St. Marc-sur-mer? In Brittany?
That's right!
When was that?
'74 or '75... in the summer I think!
We were together!
Oh, right!
What was the name of that girl?
Lisa!
Yes, that's it...
5

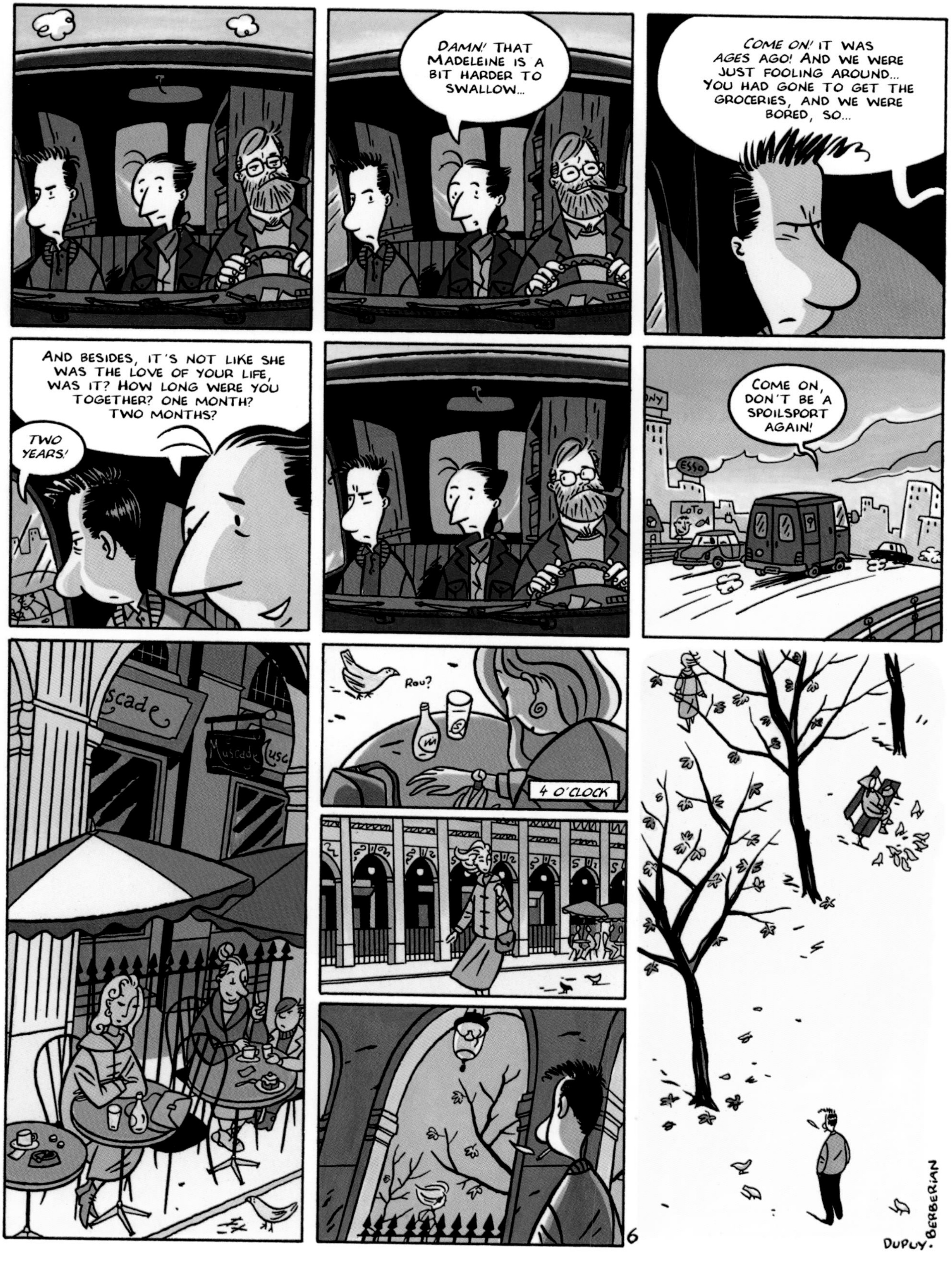
DAMN! THAT MADELEINE IS A BIT HARDER TO SWALLOW...
COME ON! IT WAS AGES AGO! AND WE WERE JUST FOOLING AROUND... YOU HAD GONE TO GET THE GROCERIES, AND WE WERE BORED, SO...
AND BESIDES, IT'S NOT LIKE SHE WAS THE LOVE OF YOUR LIFE, WAS IT? HOW LONG WERE YOU TOGETHER? ONE MONTH? TWO MONTHS?
TWO YEARS!
COME ON, DON'T BE A SPOILSPORT AGAIN!
ESSO
LOTO
Muscade
Rou?
4 O'CLOCK
6
DUPUY. BERBERIAN

INSOMNIA - FOURTH AND FINAL PART

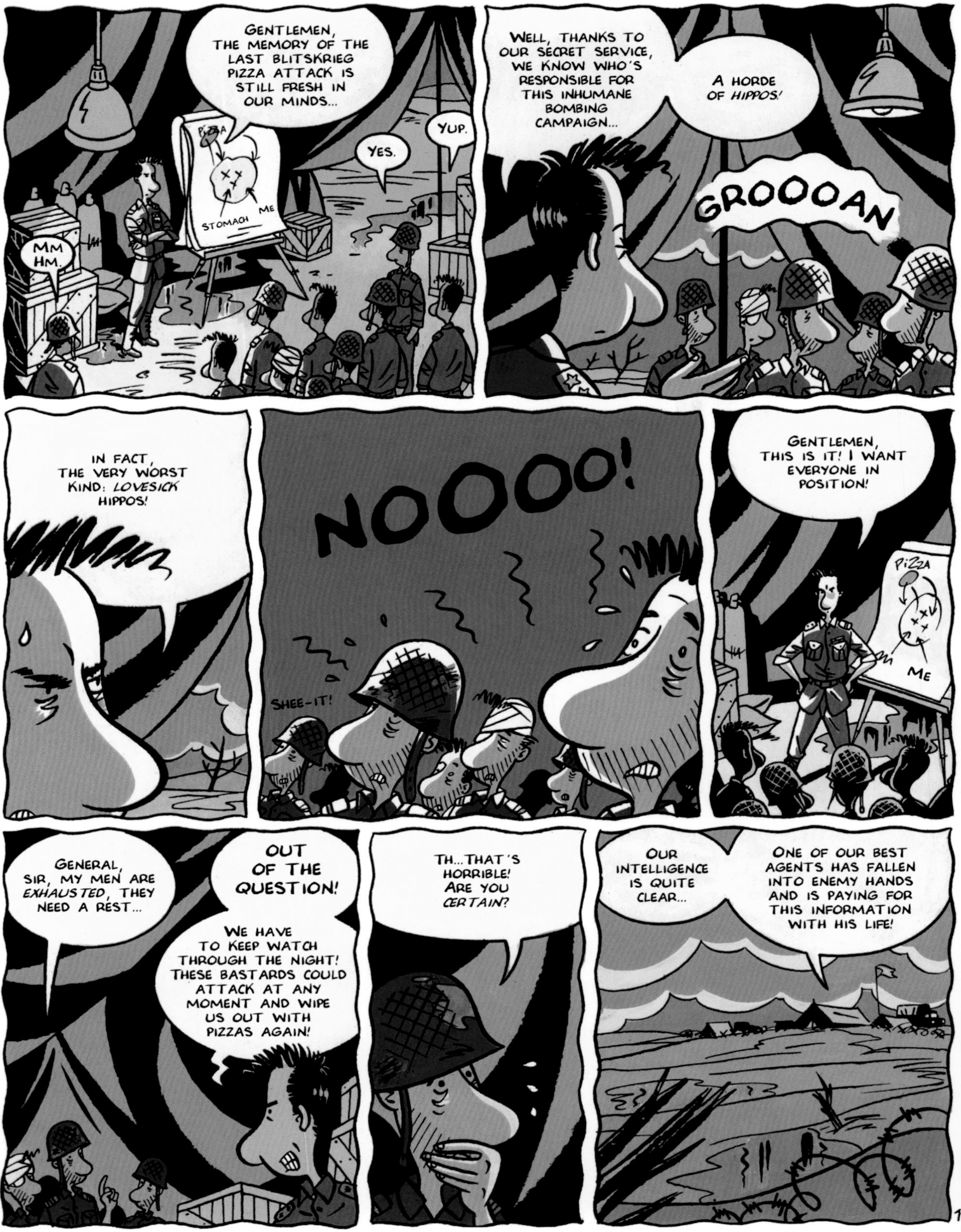
GENTLEMEN, THE MEMORY OF THE LAST BLITSKRIEG PIZZA ATTACK IS STILL FRESH IN OUR MINDS...
PIZZA
STOMACH
ME
YUP.
YES.
MM HM.
WELL, THANKS TO OUR SECRET SERVICE, WE KNOW WHO'S RESPONSIBLE FOR THIS INHUMANE BOMBING CAMPAIGN...
A HORDE OF HIPPOS!
GROOOAN
IN FACT, THE VERY WORST KIND: LOVESICK HIPPOS!
NOOOOO!
SHEE-IT!
GENTLEMEN, THIS IS IT! I WANT EVERYONE IN POSITION!
PIZZA
ME
GENERAL, SIR, MY MEN ARE EXHAUSTED, THEY NEED A REST...
OUT OF THE QUESTION!
WE HAVE TO KEEP WATCH THROUGH THE NIGHT! THESE BASTARDS COULD ATTACK AT ANY MOMENT AND WIPE US OUT WITH PIZZAS AGAIN!
TH...THAT'S HORRIBLE! ARE YOU CERTAIN?
OUR INTELLIGENCE IS QUITE CLEAR...
ONE OF OUR BEST AGENTS HAS FALLEN INTO ENEMY HANDS AND IS PAYING FOR THIS INFORMATION WITH HIS LIFE!
1

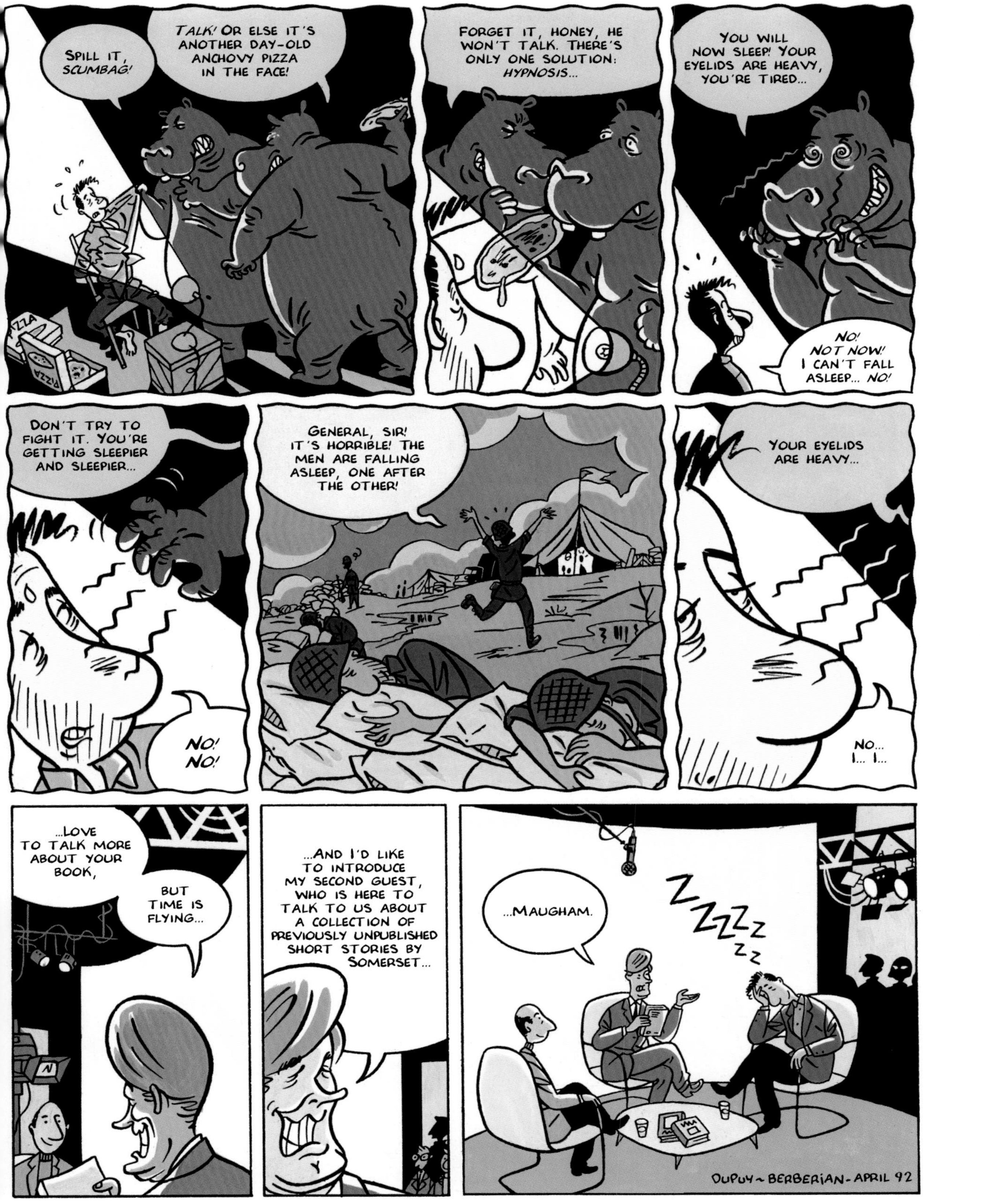

SPILL IT, SCUMBAG!
TALK! OR ELSE IT'S ANOTHER DAY-OLD ANCHOVY PIZZA IN THE FACE!
PIZZA
PIZZA
FORGET IT, HONEY, HE WON'T TALK. THERE'S ONLY ONE SOLUTION: HYPNOSIS...
YOU WILL NOW SLEEP! YOUR EYELIDS ARE HEAVY, YOU'RE TIRED...
NO! NOT NOW! I CAN'T FALL ASLEEP... NO!
DON'T TRY TO FIGHT IT. YOU'RE GETTING SLEEPIER AND SLEEPIER...
NO! NO!
GENERAL, SIR! IT'S HORRIBLE! THE MEN ARE FALLING ASLEEP, ONE AFTER THE OTHER!
YOUR EYELIDS ARE HEAVY...
NO... I... I...
...LOVE TO TALK MORE ABOUT YOUR BOOK,
BUT TIME IS FLYING...
...AND I'D LIKE TO INTRODUCE MY SECOND GUEST, WHO IS HERE TO TALK TO US ABOUT A COLLECTION OF PREVIOUSLY UNPUBLISHED SHORT STORIES BY SOMERSET...
...MAUGHAM.
ZZZZZ
ZZ
DUPUY ~ BERBERIAN - APRIL 92

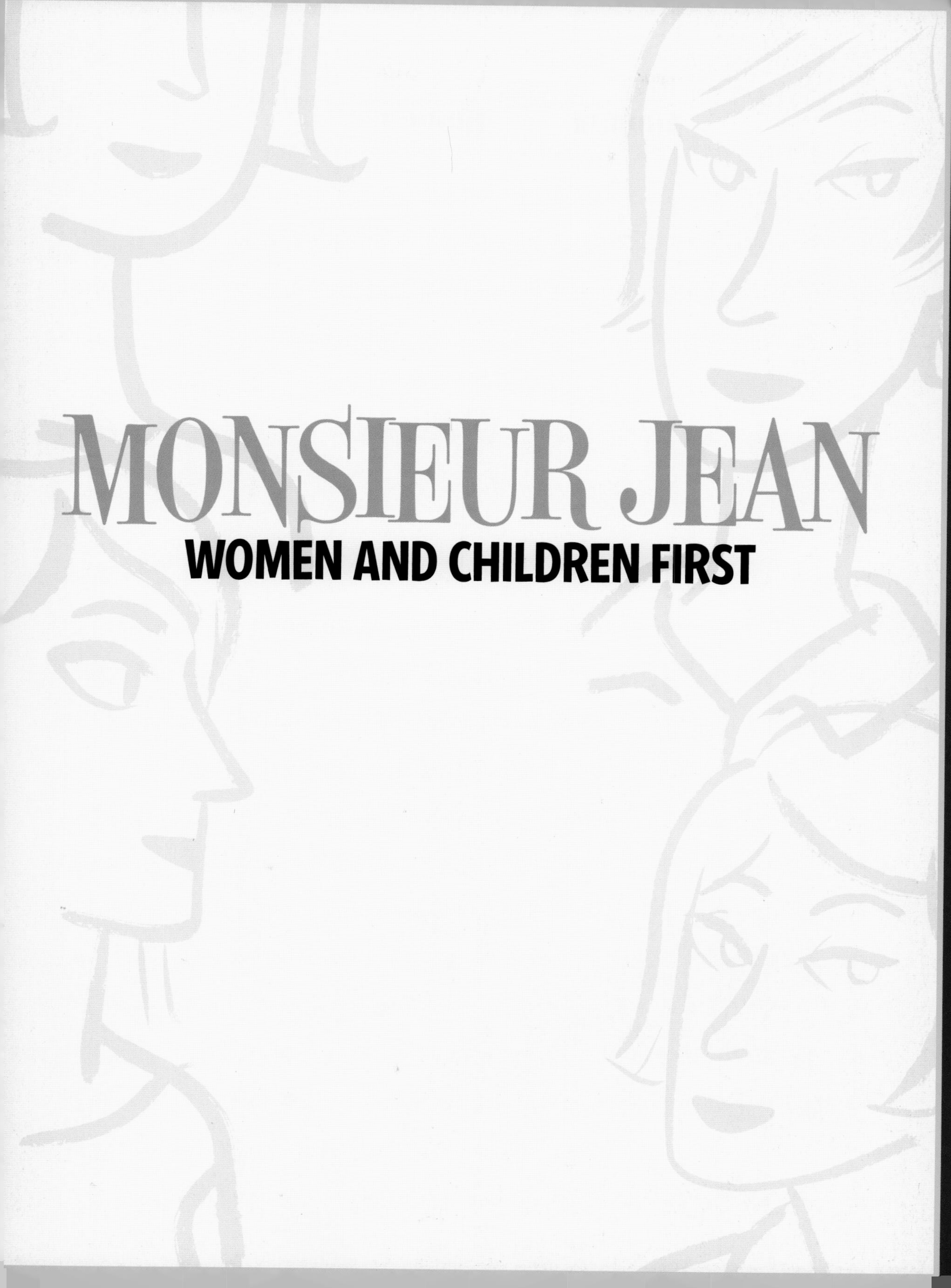

MONSIEUR JEAN

WOMEN AND CHILDREN FIRST

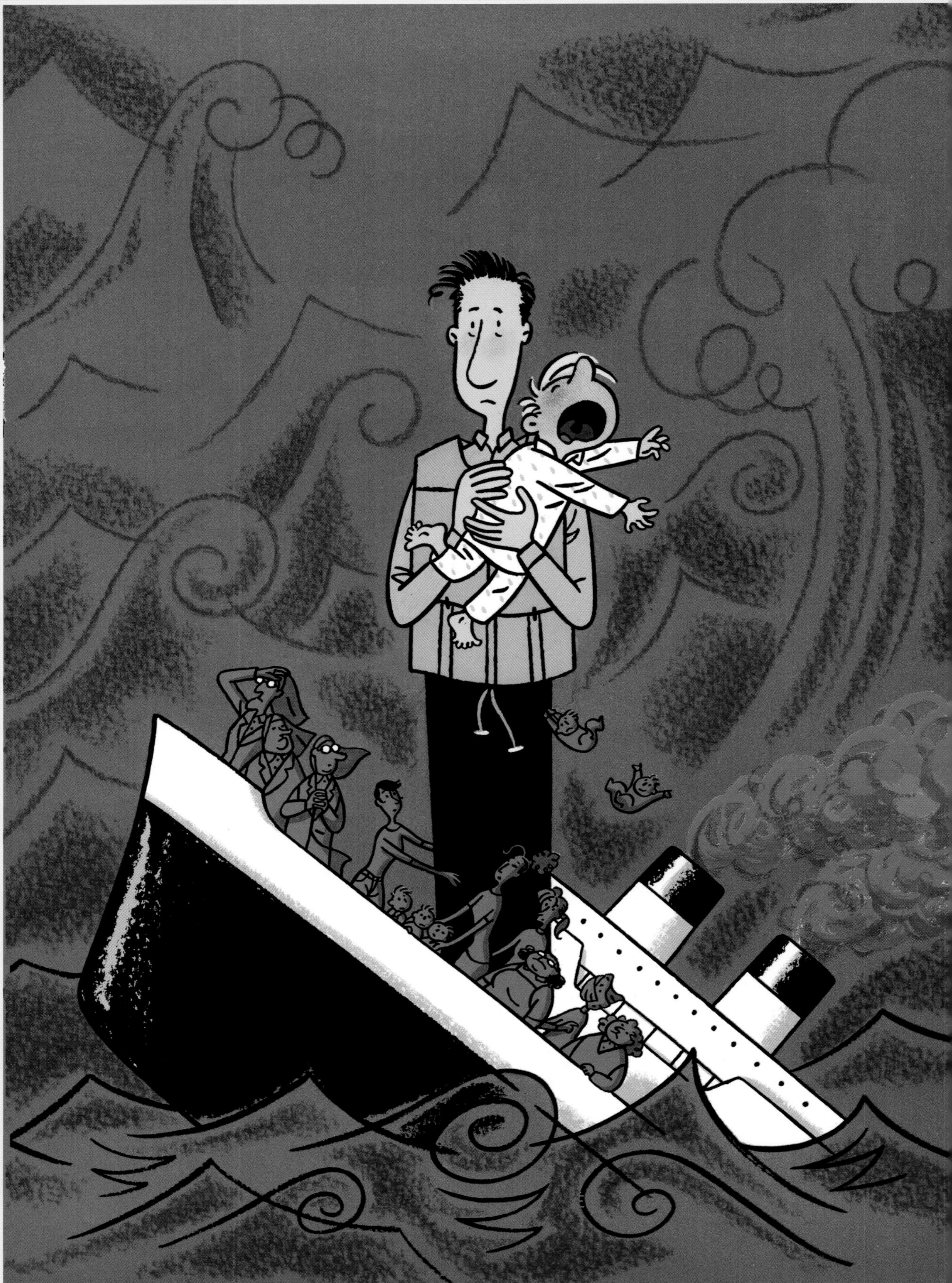

WOMEN AND CHILDREN FIRST

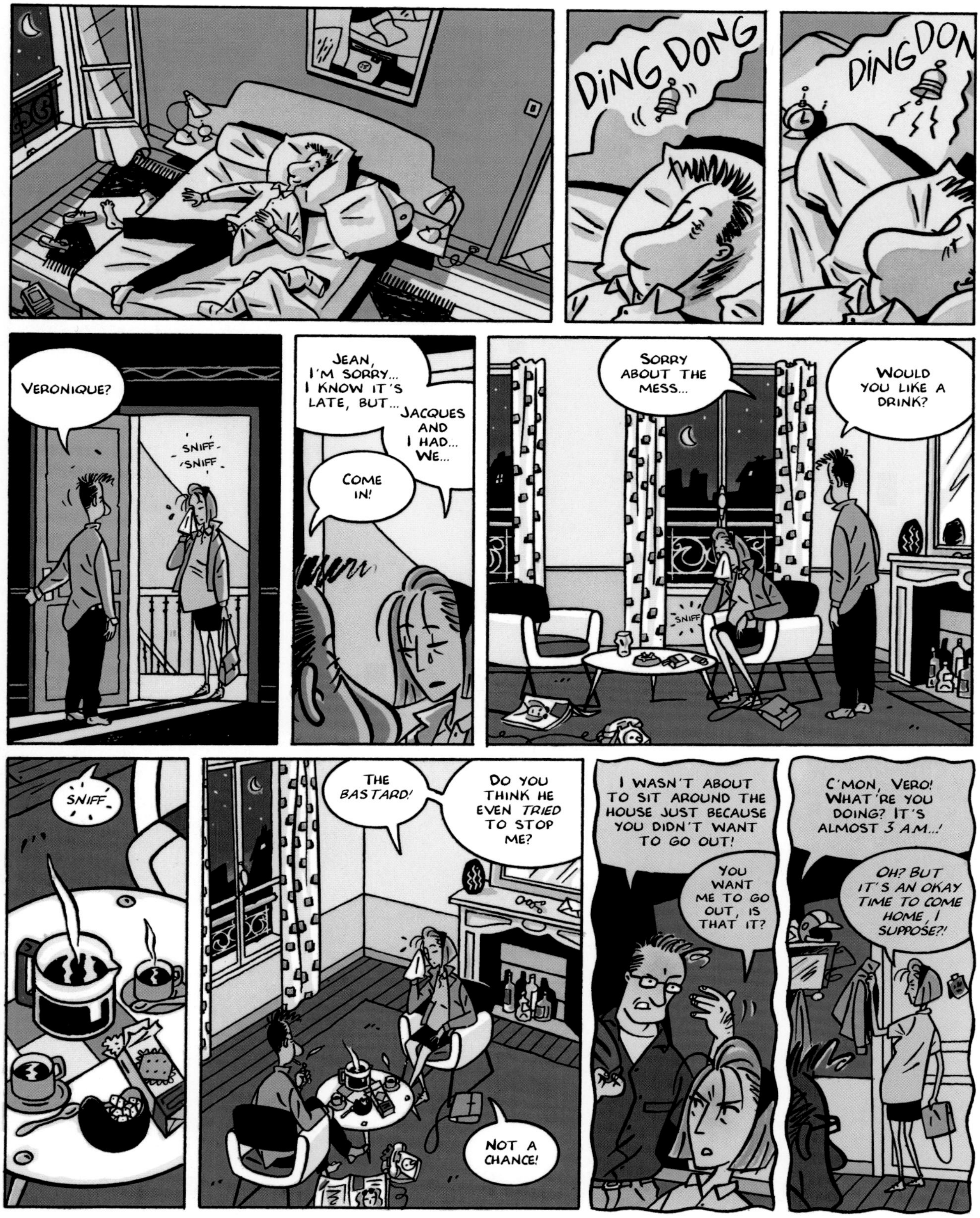
DING DONG
DING DON
VERONIQUE?
SNIFF SNIFF
JEAN, I'M SORRY... I KNOW IT'S LATE, BUT...
JACQUES AND I HAD... WE...
COME IN!
SORRY ABOUT THE MESS...
SNIFF
WOULD YOU LIKE A DRINK?
SNIFF
THE BASTARD!
DO YOU THINK HE EVEN TRIED TO STOP ME?
NOT A CHANCE!
I WASN'T ABOUT TO SIT AROUND THE HOUSE JUST BECAUSE YOU DIDN'T WANT TO GO OUT!
YOU WANT ME TO GO OUT, IS THAT IT?
C'MON, VERO! WHAT'RE YOU DOING? IT'S ALMOST 3 A.M...!
OH? BUT IT'S AN OKAY TIME TO COME HOME, I SUPPOSE?!

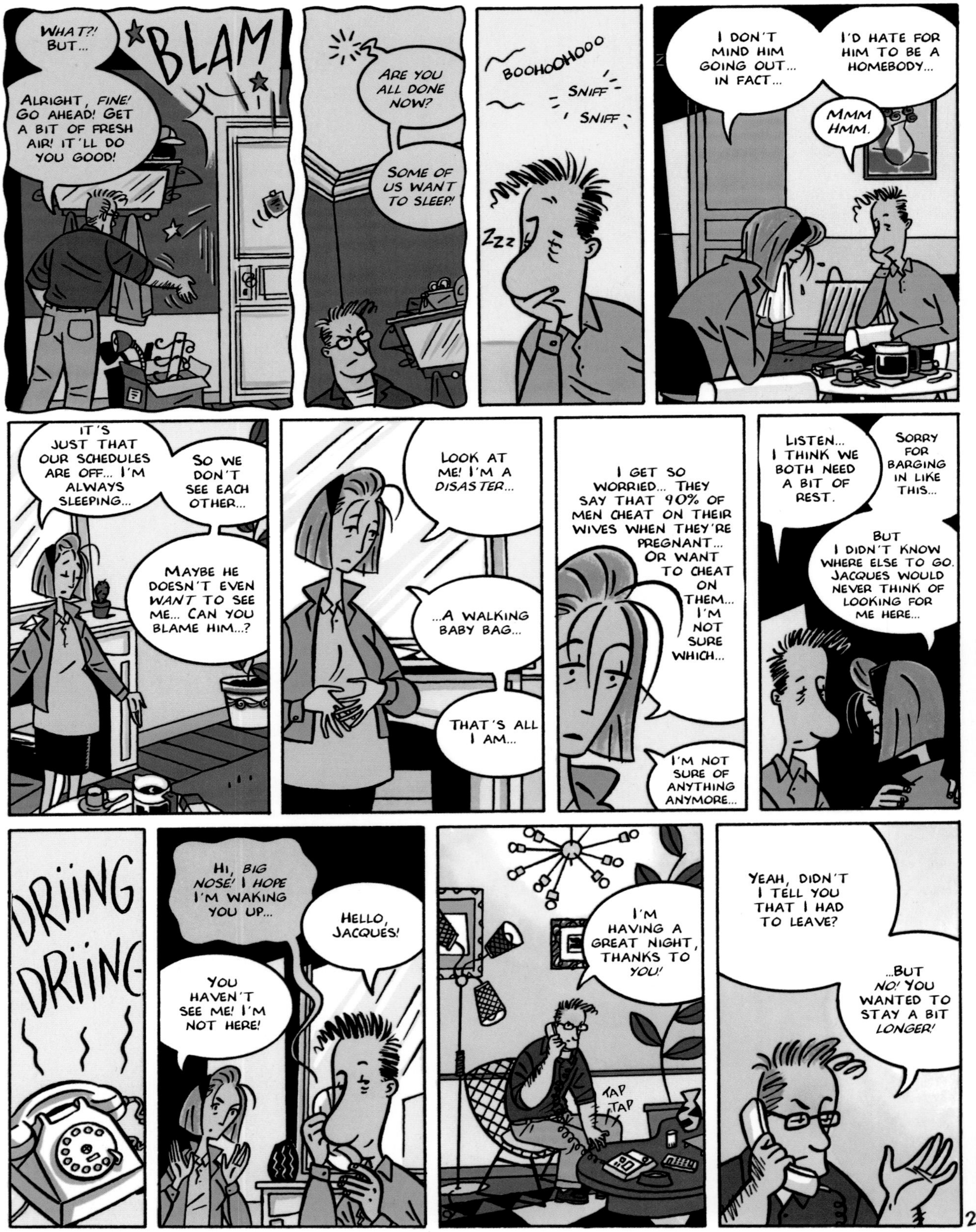
WHAT?! BUT...
BLAM
ALRIGHT, FINE! GO AHEAD! GET A BIT OF FRESH AIR! IT'LL DO YOU GOOD!
ARE YOU ALL DONE NOW?
SOME OF US WANT TO SLEEP!
BOOHOOHOOO
SNIFF
SNIFF
ZZZ
I DON'T MIND HIM GOING OUT... IN FACT...
I'D HATE FOR HIM TO BE A HOMEBODY...
MMM HMM.
IT'S JUST THAT OUR SCHEDULES ARE OFF... I'M ALWAYS SLEEPING...
SO WE DON'T SEE EACH OTHER...
MAYBE HE DOESN'T EVEN WANT TO SEE ME... CAN YOU BLAME HIM...?
LOOK AT ME! I'M A DISASTER...
...A WALKING BABY BAG...
THAT'S ALL I AM...
I GET SO WORRIED... THEY SAY THAT 90% OF MEN CHEAT ON THEIR WIVES WHEN THEY'RE PREGNANT... OR WANT TO CHEAT ON THEM... I'M NOT SURE WHICH...
I'M NOT SURE OF ANYTHING ANYMORE...
LISTEN... I THINK WE BOTH NEED A BIT OF REST.
SORRY FOR BARGING IN LIKE THIS...
BUT I DIDN'T KNOW WHERE ELSE TO GO. JACQUES WOULD NEVER THINK OF LOOKING FOR ME HERE...
DRIING
DRIING
HI, BIG NOSE! I HOPE I'M WAKING YOU UP...
HELLO, JACQUES!
YOU HAVEN'T SEE ME! I'M NOT HERE!
I'M HAVING A GREAT NIGHT, THANKS TO YOU!
TAP TAP
YEAH, DIDN'T I TELL YOU THAT I HAD TO LEAVE?
...BUT NO! YOU WANTED TO STAY A BIT LONGER!
2

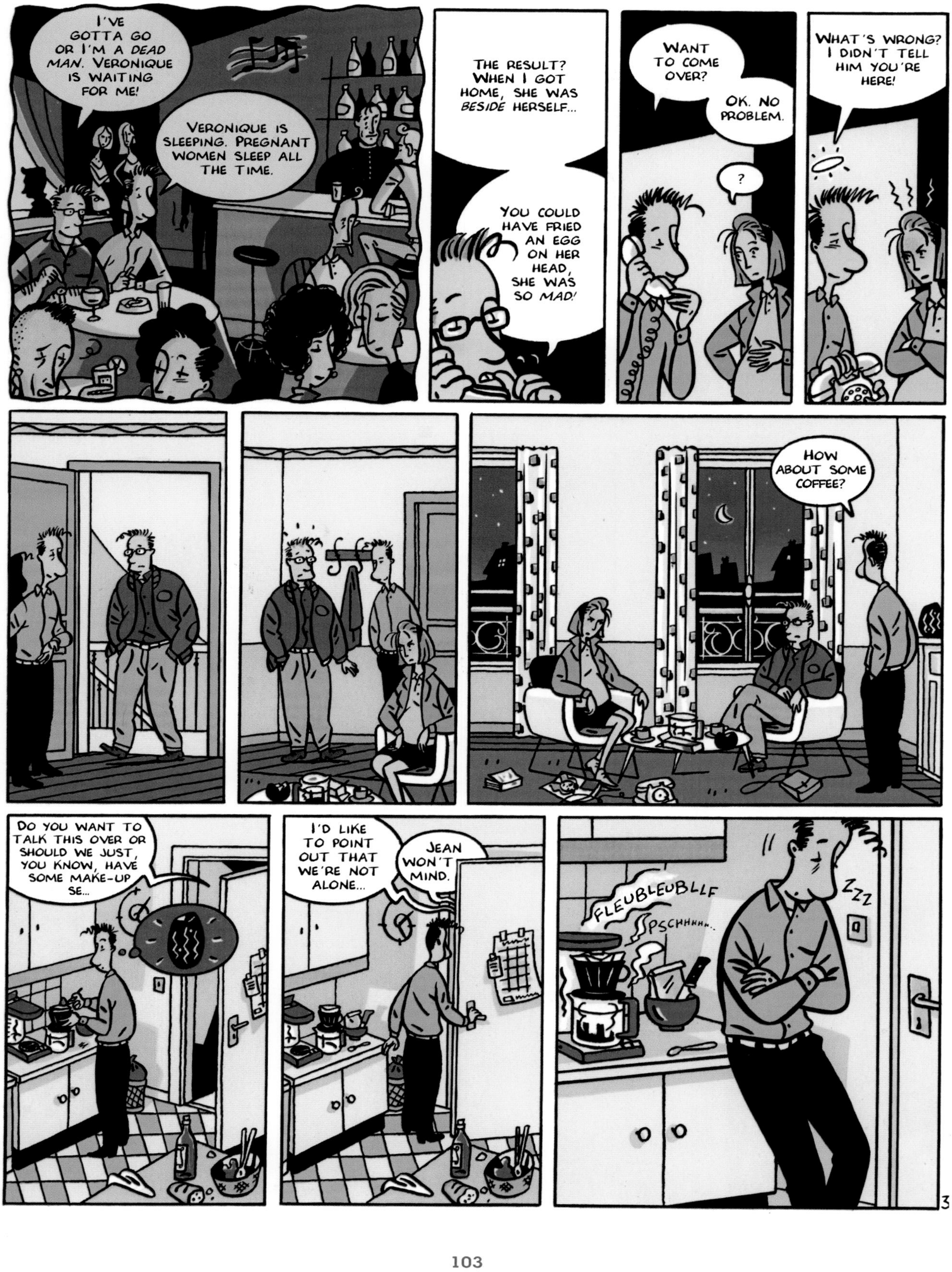

I'VE GOTTA GO OR I'M A DEAD MAN. VERONIQUE IS WAITING FOR ME!
VERONIQUE IS SLEEPING. PREGNANT WOMEN SLEEP ALL THE TIME.
THE RESULT? WHEN I GOT HOME, SHE WAS BESIDE HERSELF...
YOU COULD HAVE FRIED AN EGG ON HER HEAD, SHE WAS SO MAD!
WANT TO COME OVER?
OK. NO PROBLEM.
?
WHAT'S WRONG? I DIDN'T TELL HIM YOU'RE HERE!
HOW ABOUT SOME COFFEE?
DO YOU WANT TO TALK THIS OVER OR SHOULD WE JUST, YOU KNOW, HAVE SOME MAKE-UP SE...
I'D LIKE TO POINT OUT THAT WE'RE NOT ALONE...
JEAN WON'T MIND.
FLEUBLEUBLLF
PSCHHHHH...
ZZZ
3

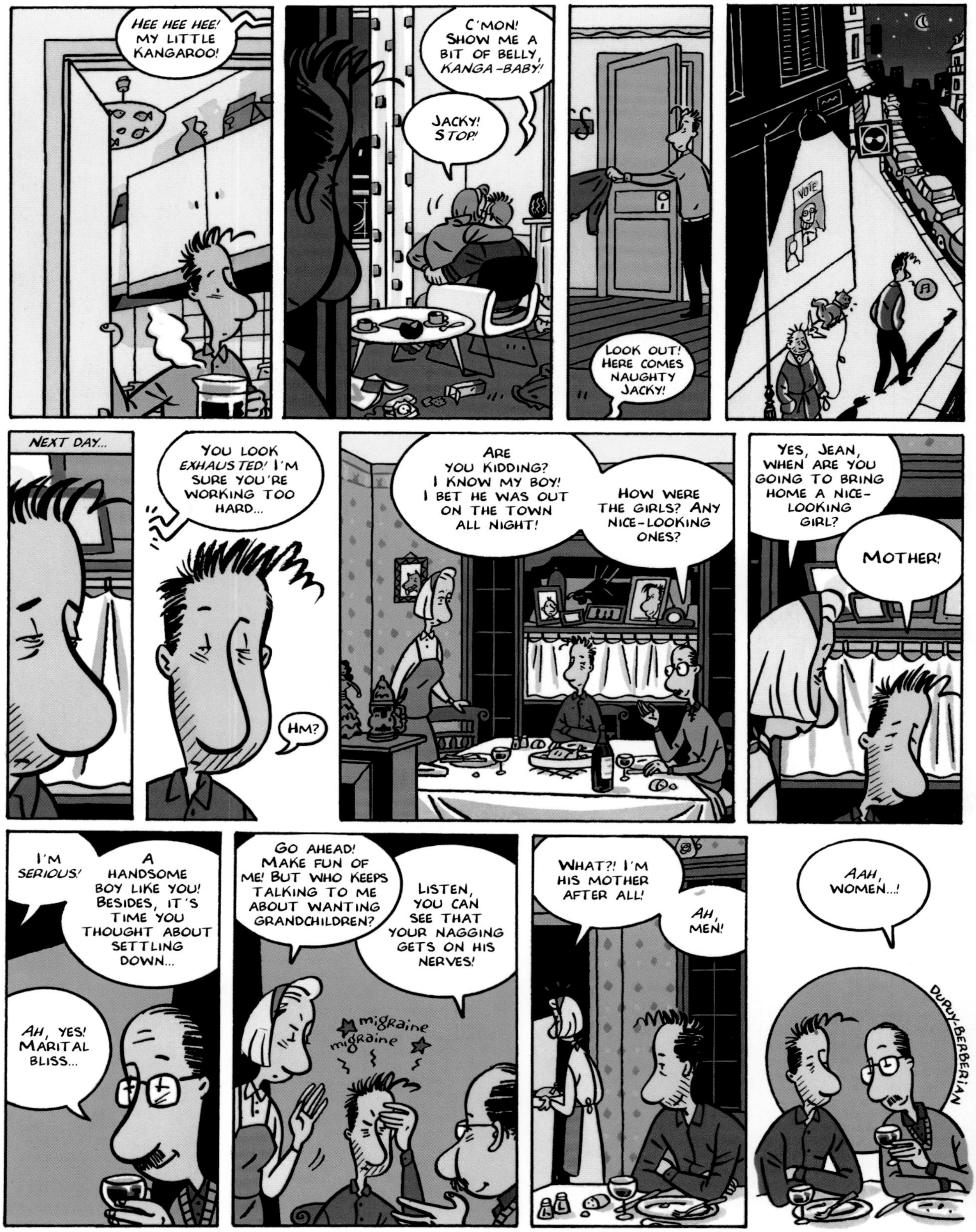
HEE HEE HEE! MY LITTLE KANGAROO!
C'MON! SHOW ME A BIT OF BELLY, KANGA-BABY!
JACKY! STOP!
LOOK OUT! HERE COMES NAUGHTY JACKY!
VOTE
NEXT DAY...
YOU LOOK EXHAUSTED! I'M SURE YOU'RE WORKING TOO HARD...
HM?
ARE YOU KIDDING? I KNOW MY BOY! I BET HE WAS OUT ON THE TOWN ALL NIGHT!
HOW WERE THE GIRLS? ANY NICE-LOOKING ONES?
YES, JEAN, WHEN ARE YOU GOING TO BRING HOME A NICE-LOOKING GIRL?
MOTHER!
I'M SERIOUS!
A HANDSOME BOY LIKE YOU! BESIDES, IT'S TIME YOU THOUGHT ABOUT SETTLING DOWN...
AH, YES! MARITAL BLISS...
GO AHEAD! MAKE FUN OF ME! BUT WHO KEEPS TALKING TO ME ABOUT WANTING GRANDCHILDREN?
LISTEN, YOU CAN SEE THAT YOUR NAGGING GETS ON HIS NERVES!
migraine
migraine
WHAT?! I'M HIS MOTHER AFTER ALL!
AH, MEN!
AAH, WOMEN...!
DUPUY-BERBERIAN

Manureva

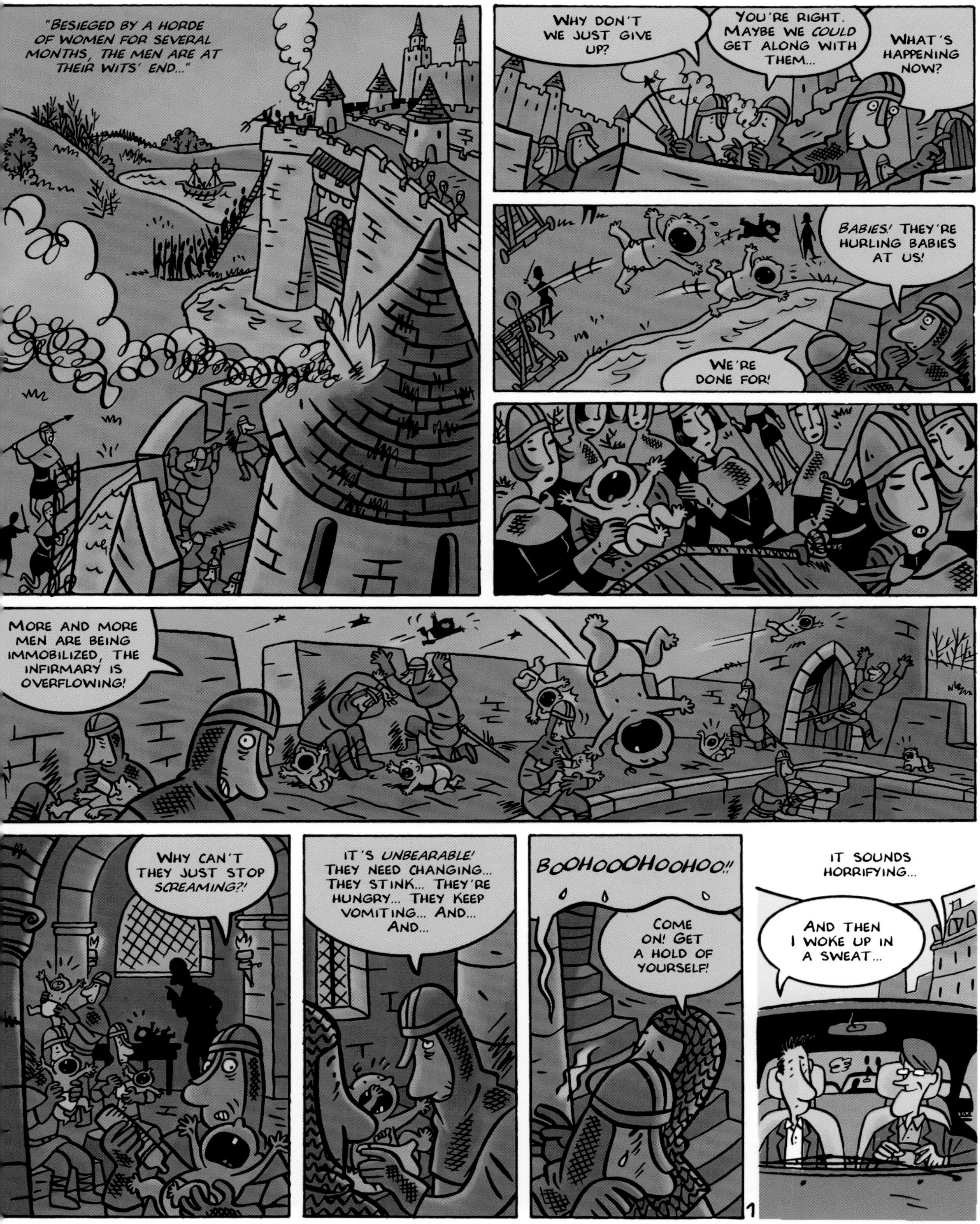

"Besieged by a horde of women for several months, the men are at their wits' end..."
Why don't we just give up?
You're right. Maybe we could get along with them...
What's happening now?
Babies! They're hurling babies at us!
We're done for!
More and more men are being immobilized, the infirmary is overflowing!
Why can't they just stop screaming?!
It's unbearable! They need changing... They stink... They're hungry... They keep vomiting... And... And...
BOOHOOOHOOHOO!!
Come on! Get a hold of yourself!
It sounds horrifying...
And then I woke up in a sweat...

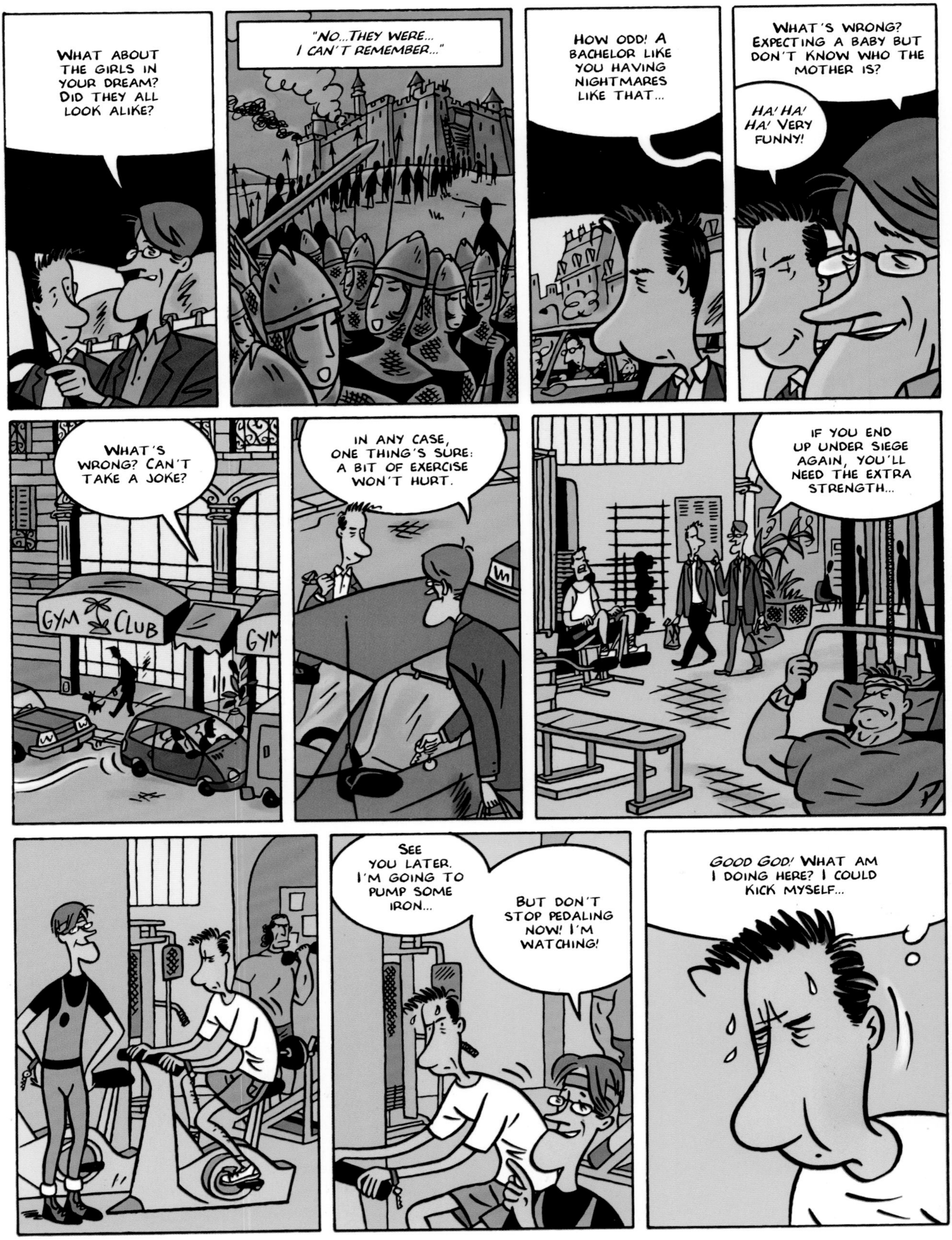
WHAT ABOUT THE GIRLS IN YOUR DREAM? DID THEY ALL LOOK ALIKE?
"NO...THEY WERE... I CAN'T REMEMBER..."
HOW ODD! A BACHELOR LIKE YOU HAVING NIGHTMARES LIKE THAT...
WHAT'S WRONG? EXPECTING A BABY BUT DON'T KNOW WHO THE MOTHER IS?
HA! HA! HA! VERY FUNNY!
WHAT'S WRONG? CAN'T TAKE A JOKE?
GYM CLUB
IN ANY CASE, ONE THING'S SURE: A BIT OF EXERCISE WON'T HURT.
IF YOU END UP UNDER SIEGE AGAIN, YOU'LL NEED THE EXTRA STRENGTH...
SEE YOU LATER. I'M GOING TO PUMP SOME IRON...
BUT DON'T STOP PEDALING NOW! I'M WATCHING!
GOOD GOD! WHAT AM I DOING HERE? I COULD KICK MYSELF...

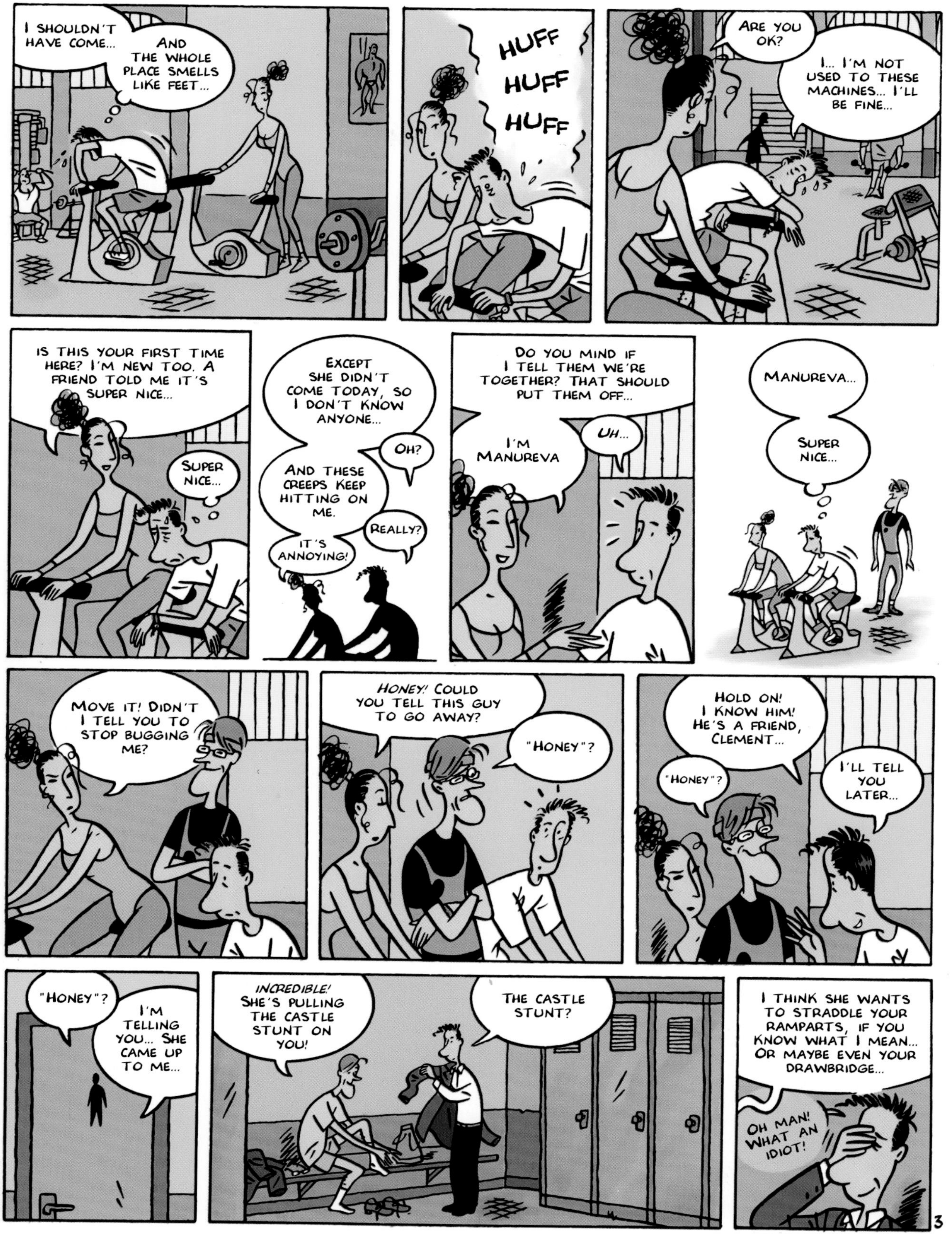
I SHOULDN'T HAVE COME...
AND THE WHOLE PLACE SMELLS LIKE FEET...
HUFF
HUFF
HUFF
ARE YOU OK?
I... I'M NOT USED TO THESE MACHINES... I'LL BE FINE...
IS THIS YOUR FIRST TIME HERE? I'M NEW TOO. A FRIEND TOLD ME IT'S SUPER NICE...
SUPER NICE...
EXCEPT SHE DIDN'T COME TODAY, SO I DON'T KNOW ANYONE...
OH?
AND THESE CREEPS KEEP HITTING ON ME.
REALLY?
IT'S ANNOYING!
DO YOU MIND IF I TELL THEM WE'RE TOGETHER? THAT SHOULD PUT THEM OFF...
UH...
I'M MANUREVA
MANUREVA...
SUPER NICE...
MOVE IT! DIDN'T I TELL YOU TO STOP BUGGING ME?
HONEY! COULD YOU TELL THIS GUY TO GO AWAY?
"HONEY"?
HOLD ON! I KNOW HIM! HE'S A FRIEND, CLEMENT...
"HONEY"?
I'LL TELL YOU LATER...
"HONEY"?
I'M TELLING YOU... SHE CAME UP TO ME...
INCREDIBLE! SHE'S PULLING THE CASTLE STUNT ON YOU!
THE CASTLE STUNT?
I THINK SHE WANTS TO STRADDLE YOUR RAMPARTS, IF YOU KNOW WHAT I MEAN... OR MAYBE EVEN YOUR DRAWBRIDGE...
OH MAN! WHAT AN IDIOT!
3

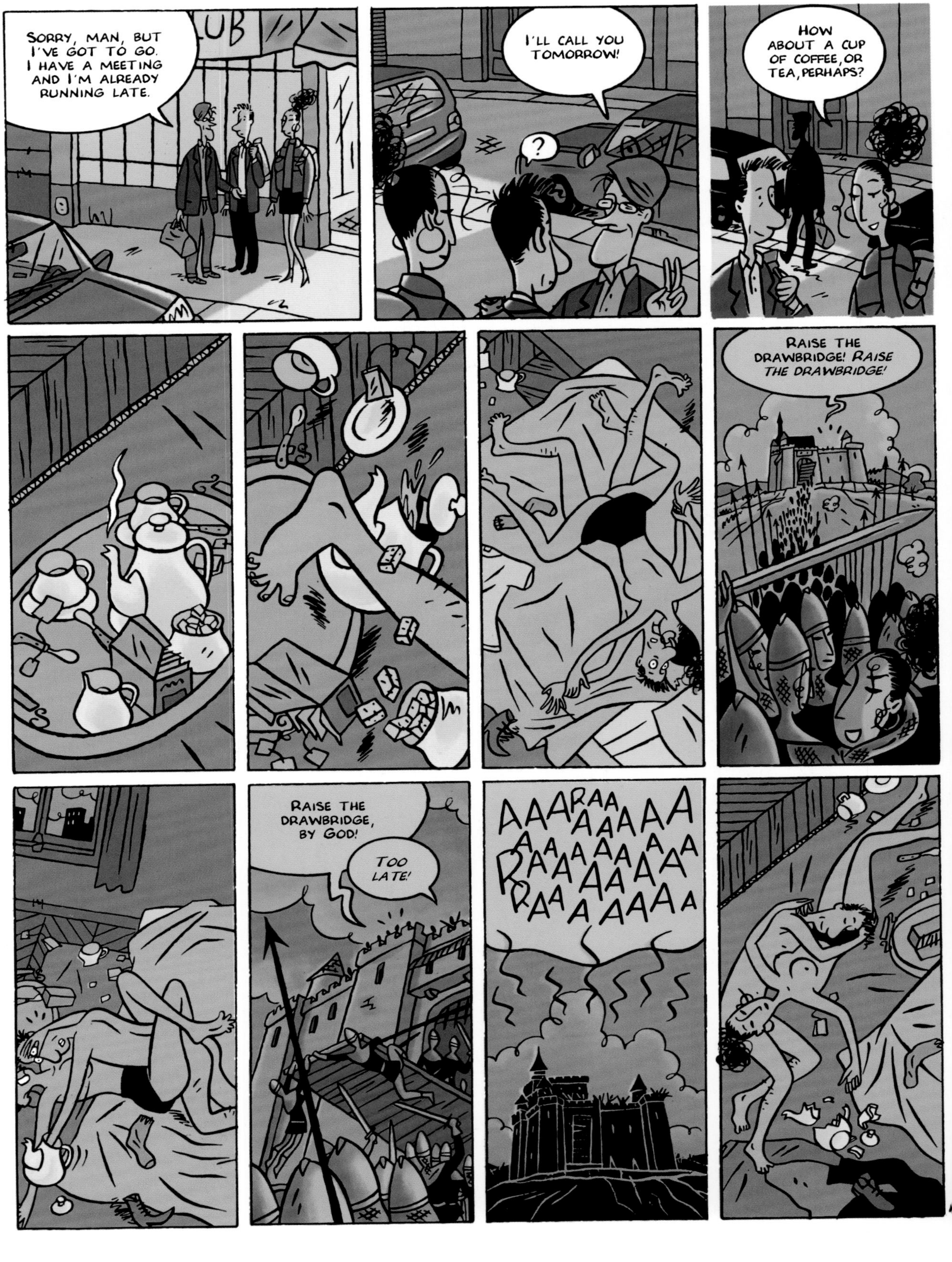
CLUB
SORRY, MAN, BUT I'VE GOT TO GO. I HAVE A MEETING AND I'M ALREADY RUNNING LATE.
I'LL CALL YOU TOMORROW!
?
HOW ABOUT A CUP OF COFFEE, OR TEA, PERHAPS?
RAISE THE DRAWBRIDGE! RAISE THE DRAWBRIDGE!
RAISE THE DRAWBRIDGE, BY GOD!
TOO LATE!
AAARAAAAAAA AAAAAAAAA RAAAAAAAAA RAAAAAAAA

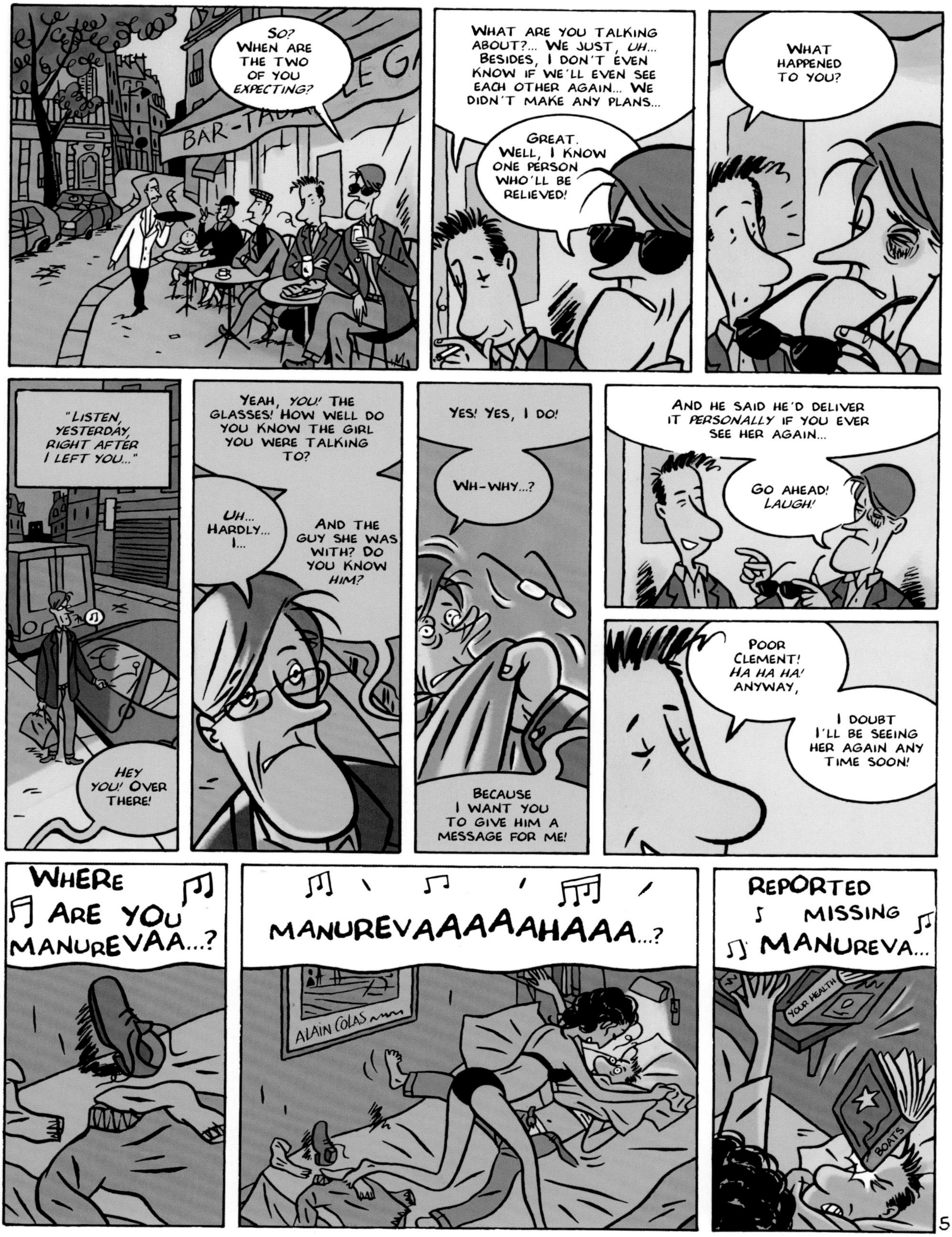
So? When are the two of you *expecting*?
What are you talking about?... We just, *uh*... Besides, I don't even know if we'll even see each other again... We didn't make any plans...
Great. Well, I know one person who'll be relieved!
What happened to you?
"Listen, yesterday, right after I left you..."
Hey you! Over there!
Yeah, *you!* The glasses! How well do you know the girl you were talking to?
Uh... hardly... I...
And the guy she was with? Do you know *him*?
Yes! Yes, I do!
Wh-why...?
Because I want you to give him a message for me!
And he said he'd deliver it *personally* if you ever see her again...
Go ahead! *Laugh!*
Poor Clement! *Ha ha ha!* Anyway,
I doubt I'll be seeing her again any time soon!
Where are you Manurevaa...?
Manurevaaaaahaaa...?
Alain Colas
Reported missing Manureva...
Your Health
Boats
5

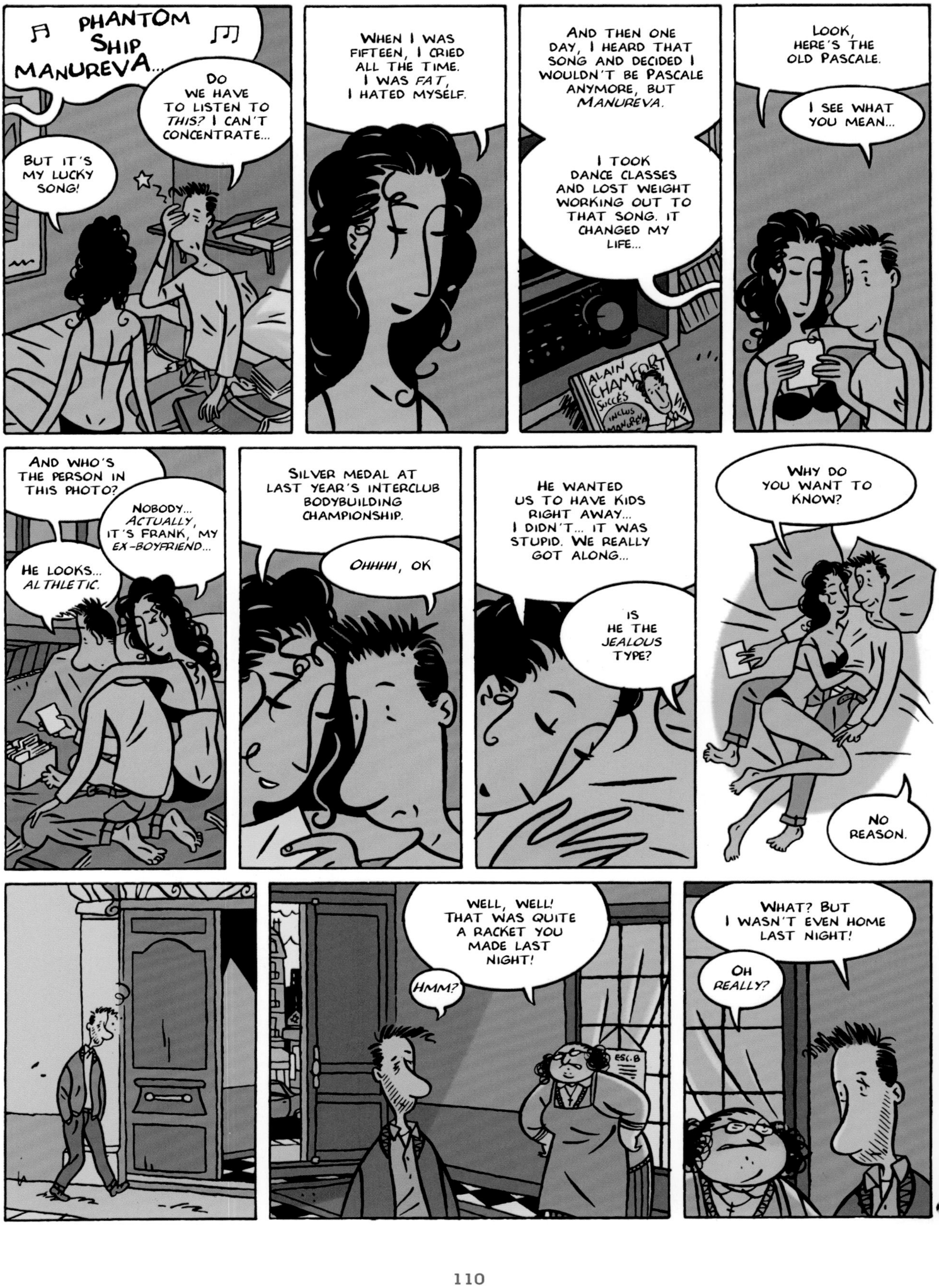
PHANTOM SHIP MANUREVA...
DO WE HAVE TO LISTEN TO THIS? I CAN'T CONCENTRATE...
BUT IT'S MY LUCKY SONG!
WHEN I WAS FIFTEEN, I CRIED ALL THE TIME. I WAS FAT, I HATED MYSELF.
AND THEN ONE DAY, I HEARD THAT SONG AND DECIDED I WOULDN'T BE PASCALE ANYMORE, BUT MANUREVA.
I TOOK DANCE CLASSES AND LOST WEIGHT WORKING OUT TO THAT SONG. IT CHANGED MY LIFE...
ALAIN CHAMFORT
SUCCÈS
INCLUS MANUREVA
LOOK, HERE'S THE OLD PASCALE.
I SEE WHAT YOU MEAN...
AND WHO'S THE PERSON IN THIS PHOTO?
NOBODY... ACTUALLY, IT'S FRANK, MY EX-BOYFRIEND...
HE LOOKS... ALTHLETIC.
SILVER MEDAL AT LAST YEAR'S INTERCLUB BODYBUILDING CHAMPIONSHIP.
OHHHH, OK
HE WANTED US TO HAVE KIDS RIGHT AWAY... I DIDN'T... IT WAS STUPID. WE REALLY GOT ALONG...
IS HE THE JEALOUS TYPE?
WHY DO YOU WANT TO KNOW?
NO REASON.
WELL, WELL! THAT WAS QUITE A RACKET YOU MADE LAST NIGHT!
HMM?
ESC. B
WHAT? BUT I WASN'T EVEN HOME LAST NIGHT!
OH REALLY?

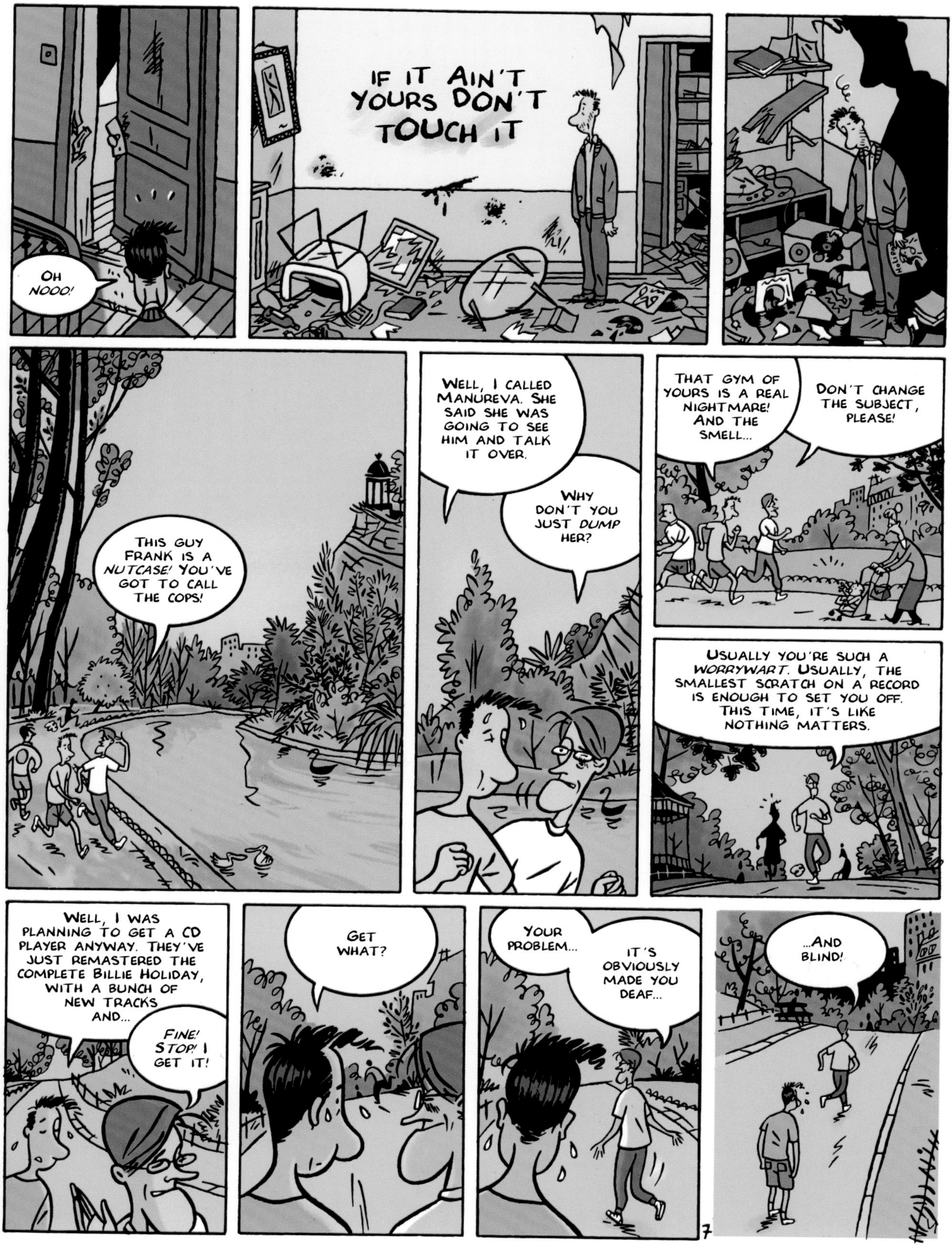

OH NOOO!
IF IT AIN'T YOURS DON'T TOUCH IT
THIS GUY FRANK IS A NUTCASE! YOU'VE GOT TO CALL THE COPS!
WELL, I CALLED MANUREVA. SHE SAID SHE WAS GOING TO SEE HIM AND TALK IT OVER.
WHY DON'T YOU JUST DUMP HER?
THAT GYM OF YOURS IS A REAL NIGHTMARE! AND THE SMELL...
DON'T CHANGE THE SUBJECT, PLEASE!
USUALLY YOU'RE SUCH A WORRYWART. USUALLY, THE SMALLEST SCRATCH ON A RECORD IS ENOUGH TO SET YOU OFF. THIS TIME, IT'S LIKE NOTHING MATTERS.
WELL, I WAS PLANNING TO GET A CD PLAYER ANYWAY. THEY'VE JUST REMASTERED THE COMPLETE BILLIE HOLIDAY, WITH A BUNCH OF NEW TRACKS AND...
FINE! STOP! I GET IT!
GET WHAT?
YOUR PROBLEM...
IT'S OBVIOUSLY MADE YOU DEAF...
...AND BLIND!
7

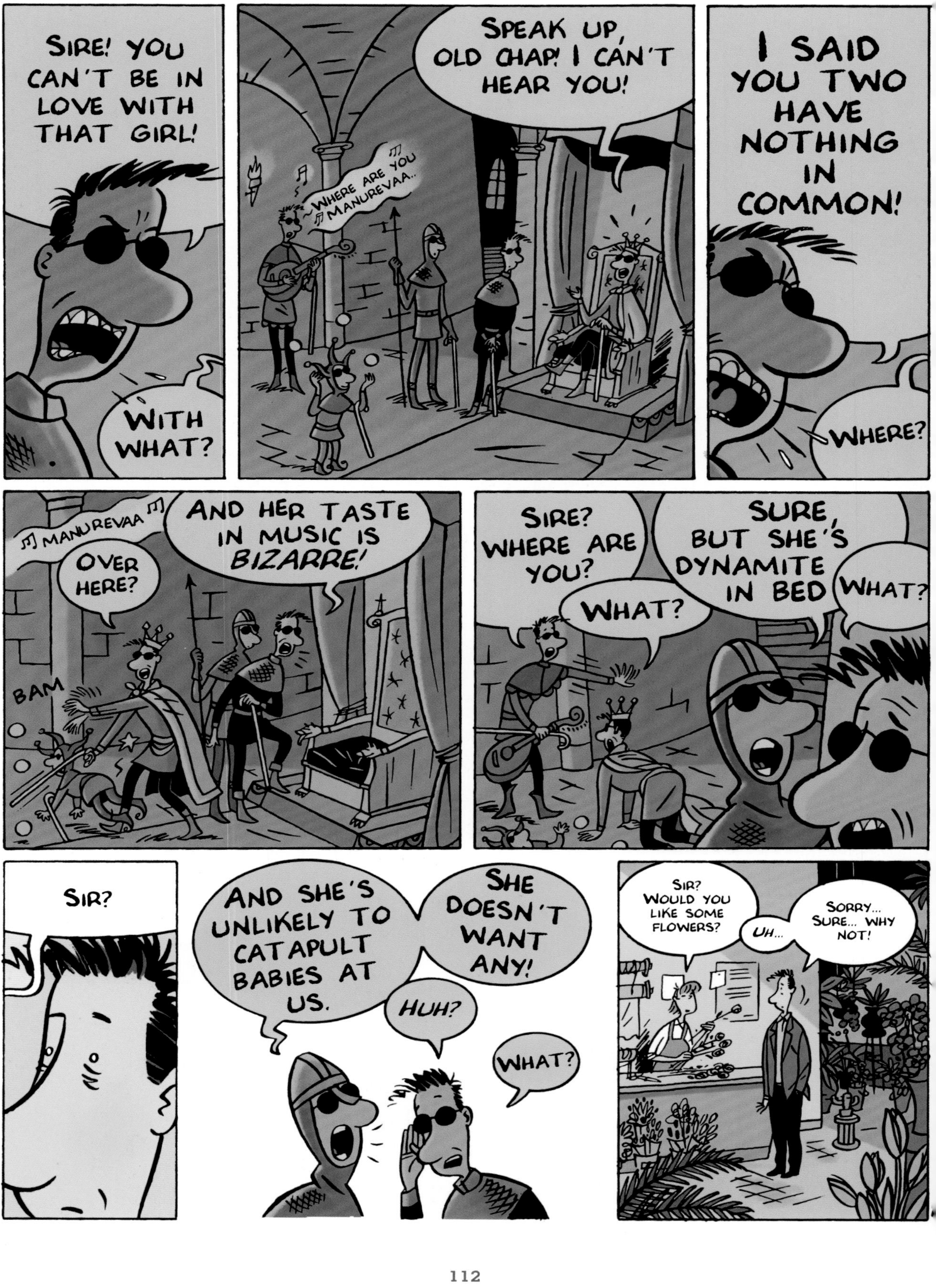
SIRE! YOU CAN'T BE IN LOVE WITH THAT GIRL!
WITH WHAT?
WHERE ARE YOU MANUREVAA..
SPEAK UP, OLD CHAP! I CAN'T HEAR YOU!
I SAID YOU TWO HAVE NOTHING IN COMMON!
WHERE?
MANUREVAA
OVER HERE?
AND HER TASTE IN MUSIC IS BIZARRE!
BAM
SIRE? WHERE ARE YOU?
WHAT?
SURE, BUT SHE'S DYNAMITE IN BED
WHAT?
SIR?
AND SHE'S UNLIKELY TO CATAPULT BABIES AT US.
SHE DOESN'T WANT ANY!
HUH?
WHAT?
SIR? WOULD YOU LIKE SOME FLOWERS?
UH...
SORRY... SURE... WHY NOT!

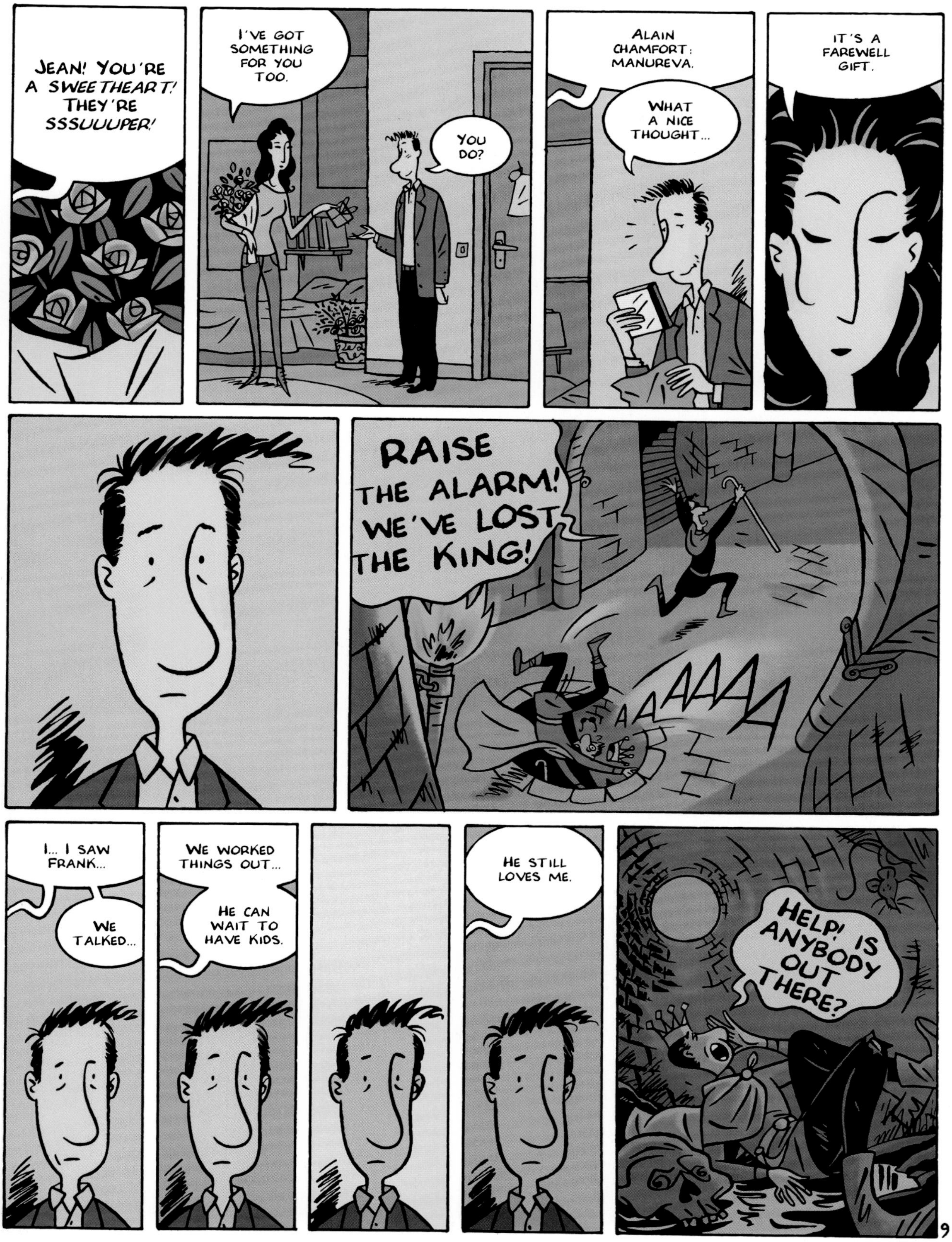
JEAN! YOU'RE A SWEETHEART! THEY'RE SSSUUUPER!
I'VE GOT SOMETHING FOR YOU TOO.
YOU DO?
ALAIN CHAMFORT: MANUREVA.
WHAT A NICE THOUGHT...
IT'S A FAREWELL GIFT.
RAISE THE ALARM! WE'VE LOST THE KING!
AAAAAAA
I... I SAW FRANK...
WE TALKED...
WE WORKED THINGS OUT...
HE CAN WAIT TO HAVE KIDS.
HE STILL LOVES ME.
HELP! IS ANYBODY OUT THERE?
9

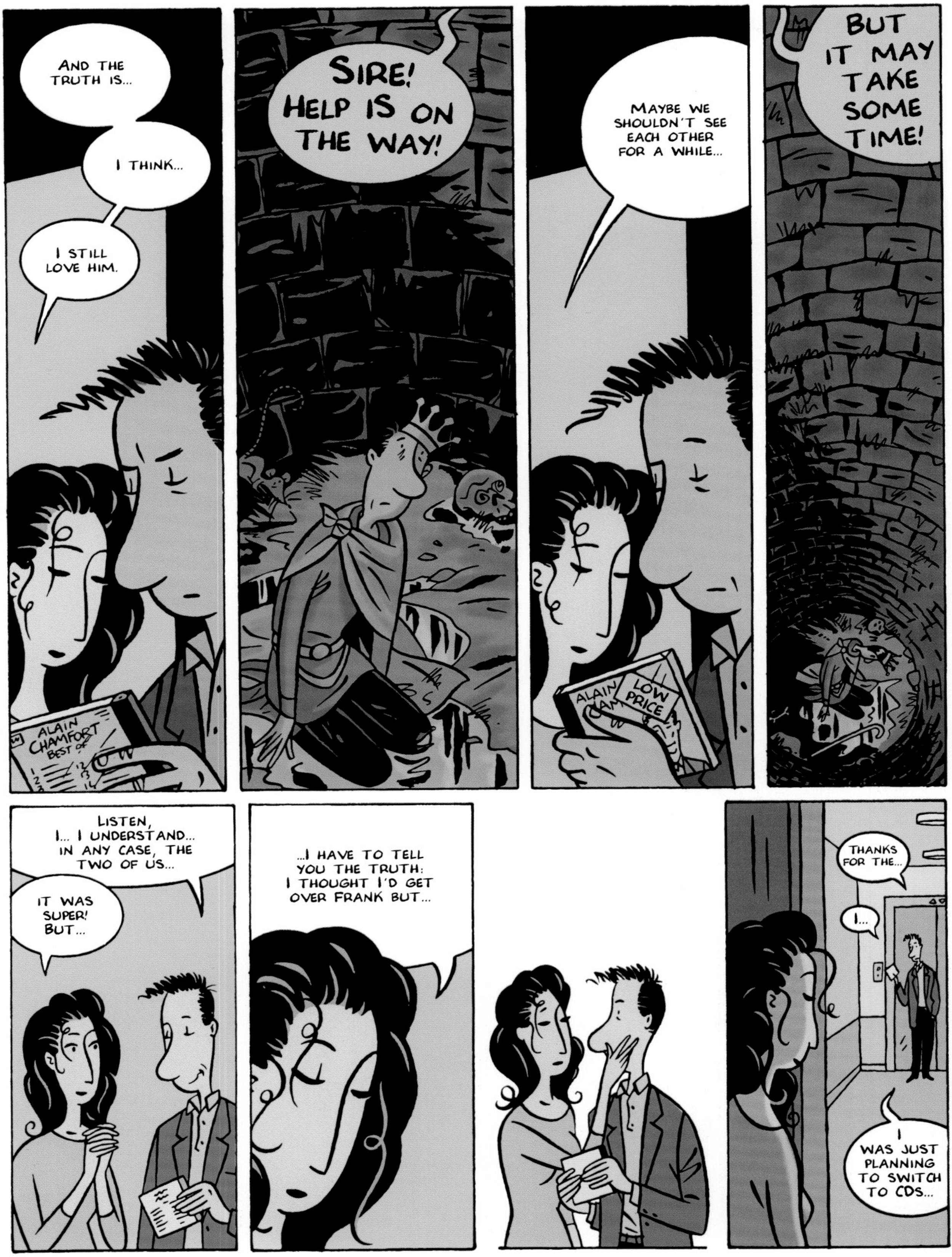
AND THE TRUTH IS...
I THINK...
I STILL LOVE HIM.
ALAIN CHAMFORT
BEST OF
SIRE! HELP IS ON THE WAY!
MAYBE WE SHOULDN'T SEE EACH OTHER FOR A WHILE...
LOW PRICE
BUT IT MAY TAKE SOME TIME!
LISTEN, I... I UNDERSTAND... IN ANY CASE, THE TWO OF US...
IT WAS SUPER! BUT...
...I HAVE TO TELL YOU THE TRUTH: I THOUGHT I'D GET OVER FRANK BUT...
THANKS FOR THE...
I...
I WAS JUST PLANNING TO SWITCH TO CDS...

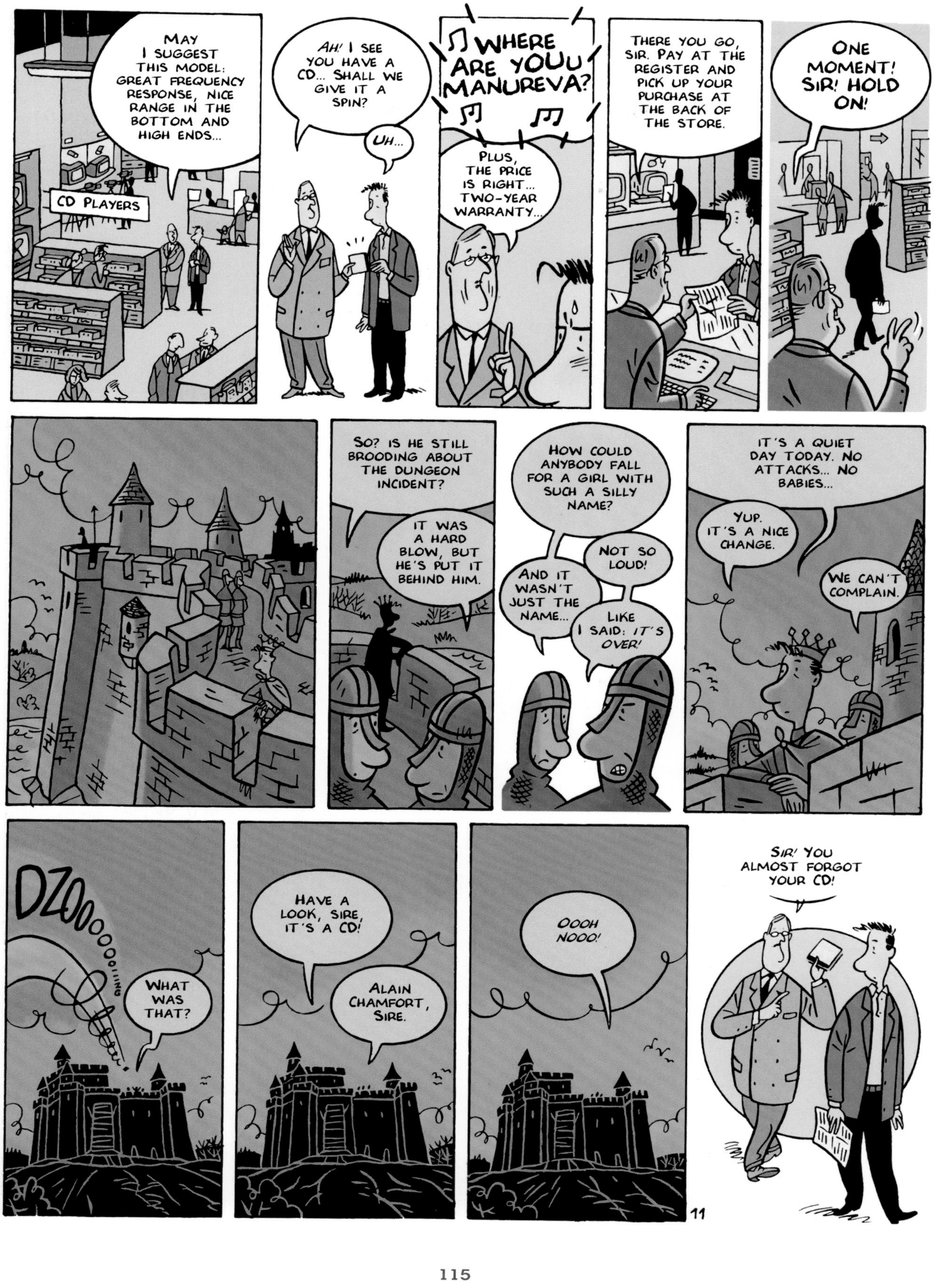

May I suggest this model: great frequency response, nice range in the bottom and high ends...
CD Players
Ah! I see you have a CD... Shall we give it a spin?
Uh...
Where are youu Manureva?
Plus, the price is right... Two-year warranty...
There you go, sir. Pay at the register and pick up your purchase at the back of the store.
One moment! Sir! Hold on!
So? Is he still brooding about the dungeon incident?
It was a hard blow, but he's put it behind him.
How could anybody fall for a girl with such a silly name?
Not so loud!
And it wasn't just the name...
Like I said: it's over!
It's a quiet day today. No attacks... No babies...
Yup. It's a nice change.
We can't complain.
DZOOooooiiing
What was that?
Have a look, sire, it's a CD!
Alain Chamfort, sire.
Oooh nooo!
Sir! You almost forgot your CD!
11

CATHY (NORWEGIAN WOOD)

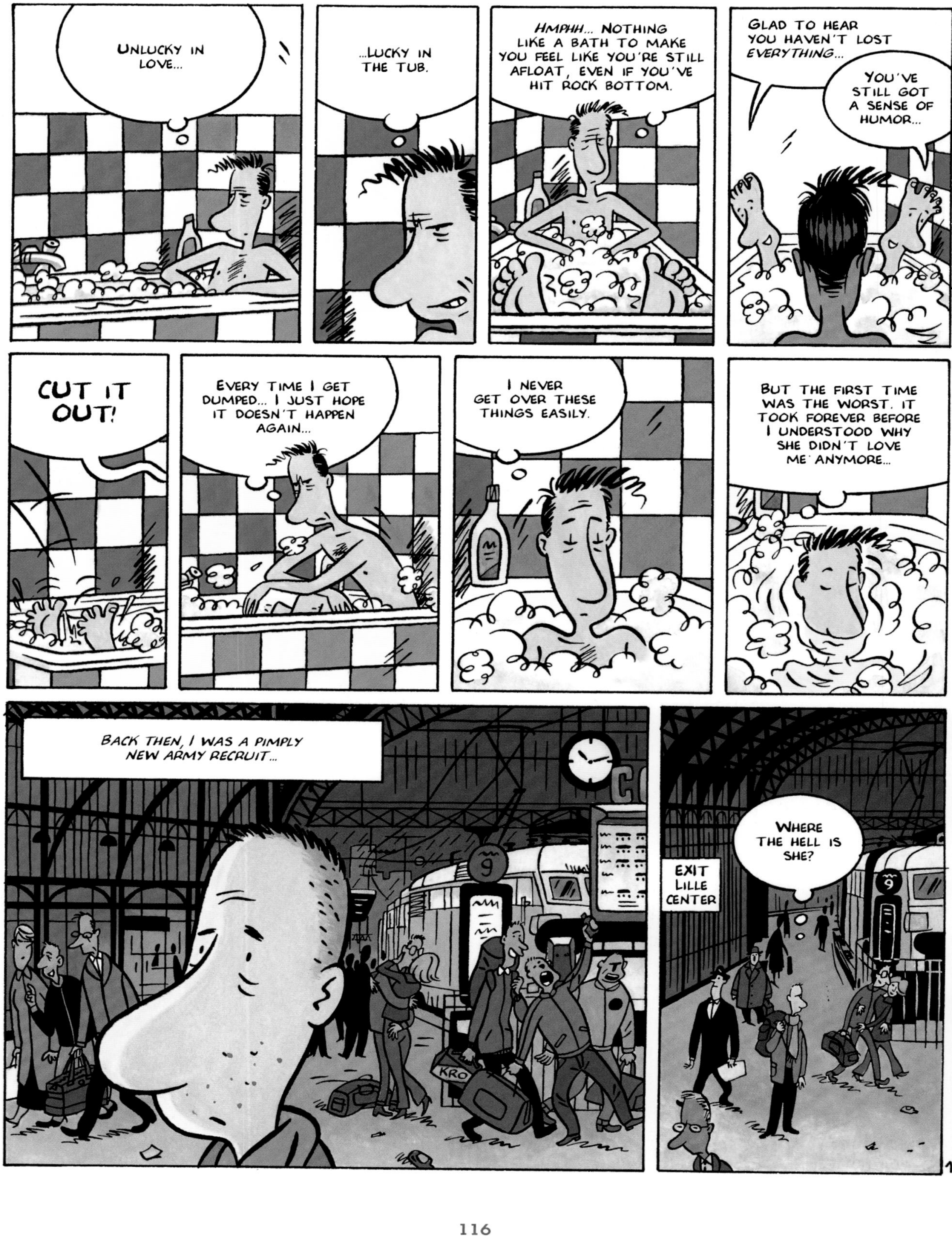
UNLUCKY IN LOVE...
...LUCKY IN THE TUB.
HMPHH... NOTHING LIKE A BATH TO MAKE YOU FEEL LIKE YOU'RE STILL AFLOAT, EVEN IF YOU'VE HIT ROCK BOTTOM.
GLAD TO HEAR YOU HAVEN'T LOST EVERYTHING...
YOU'VE STILL GOT A SENSE OF HUMOR...
CUT IT OUT!
EVERY TIME I GET DUMPED... I JUST HOPE IT DOESN'T HAPPEN AGAIN...
I NEVER GET OVER THESE THINGS EASILY.
BUT THE FIRST TIME WAS THE WORST. IT TOOK FOREVER BEFORE I UNDERSTOOD WHY SHE DIDN'T LOVE ME ANYMORE...
BACK THEN, I WAS A PIMPLY NEW ARMY RECRUIT...
EXIT LILLE CENTER
WHERE THE HELL IS SHE?

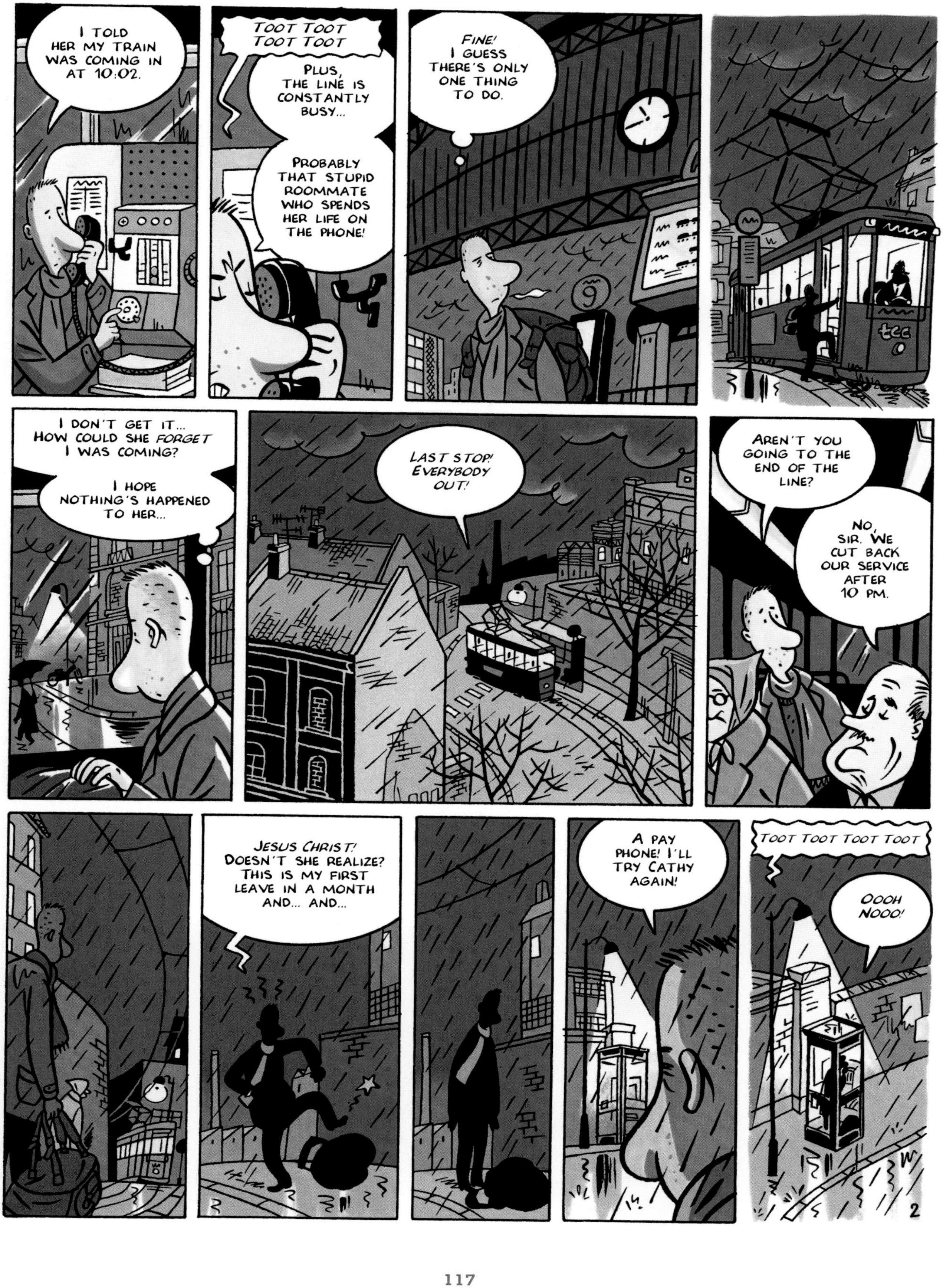
I TOLD HER MY TRAIN WAS COMING IN AT 10:02.
TOOT TOOT TOOT TOOT
PLUS, THE LINE IS CONSTANTLY BUSY...
PROBABLY THAT STUPID ROOMMATE WHO SPENDS HER LIFE ON THE PHONE!
FINE! I GUESS THERE'S ONLY ONE THING TO DO.
I DON'T GET IT... HOW COULD SHE FORGET I WAS COMING?
I HOPE NOTHING'S HAPPENED TO HER...
LAST STOP! EVERYBODY OUT!
AREN'T YOU GOING TO THE END OF THE LINE?
NO, SIR. WE CUT BACK OUR SERVICE AFTER 10 PM.
JESUS CHRIST! DOESN'T SHE REALIZE? THIS IS MY FIRST LEAVE IN A MONTH AND... AND...
A PAY PHONE! I'LL TRY CATHY AGAIN!
TOOT TOOT TOOT TOOT
OOOH NOOO!
2

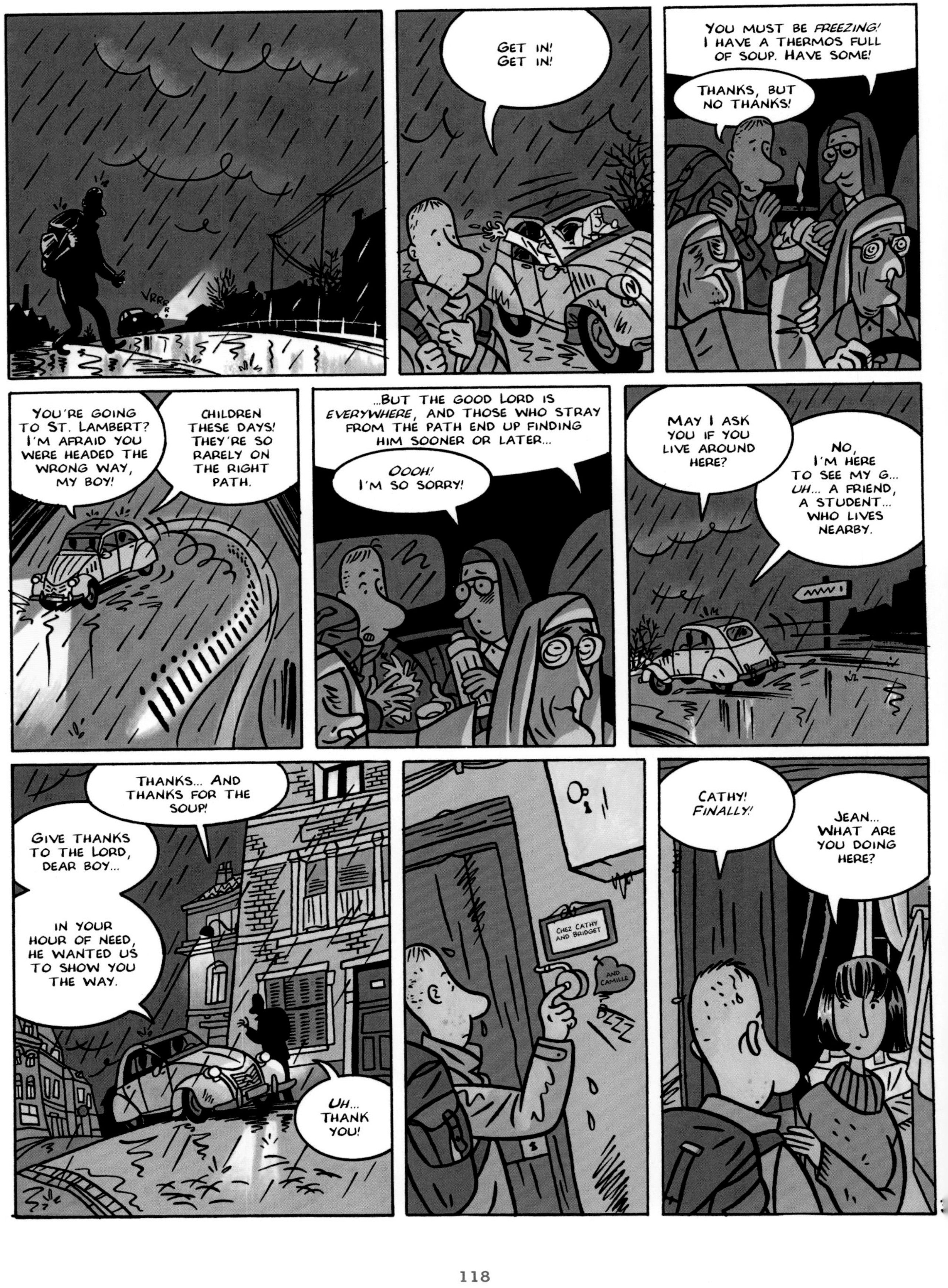
VRRR
GET IN! GET IN!
YOU MUST BE *FREEZING*! I HAVE A THERMOS FULL OF SOUP. HAVE SOME!
THANKS, BUT NO THANKS!
YOU'RE GOING TO ST. LAMBERT? I'M AFRAID YOU WERE HEADED THE WRONG WAY, MY BOY!
CHILDREN THESE DAYS! THEY'RE SO RARELY ON THE RIGHT PATH.
...BUT THE GOOD LORD IS *EVERYWHERE*, AND THOSE WHO STRAY FROM THE PATH END UP FINDING HIM SOONER OR LATER...
OOOH! I'M SO SORRY!
MAY I ASK YOU IF YOU LIVE AROUND HERE?
NO, I'M HERE TO SEE MY G... *UH*... A FRIEND, A STUDENT... WHO LIVES NEARBY.
THANKS... AND THANKS FOR THE SOUP!
GIVE THANKS TO THE LORD, DEAR BOY...
IN YOUR HOUR OF NEED, HE WANTED US TO SHOW YOU THE WAY.
UH... THANK YOU!
CHEZ CATHY AND BRIDGET
AND CAMILLE
BZZZ
CATHY! *FINALLY!*
JEAN... WHAT ARE YOU DOING HERE?

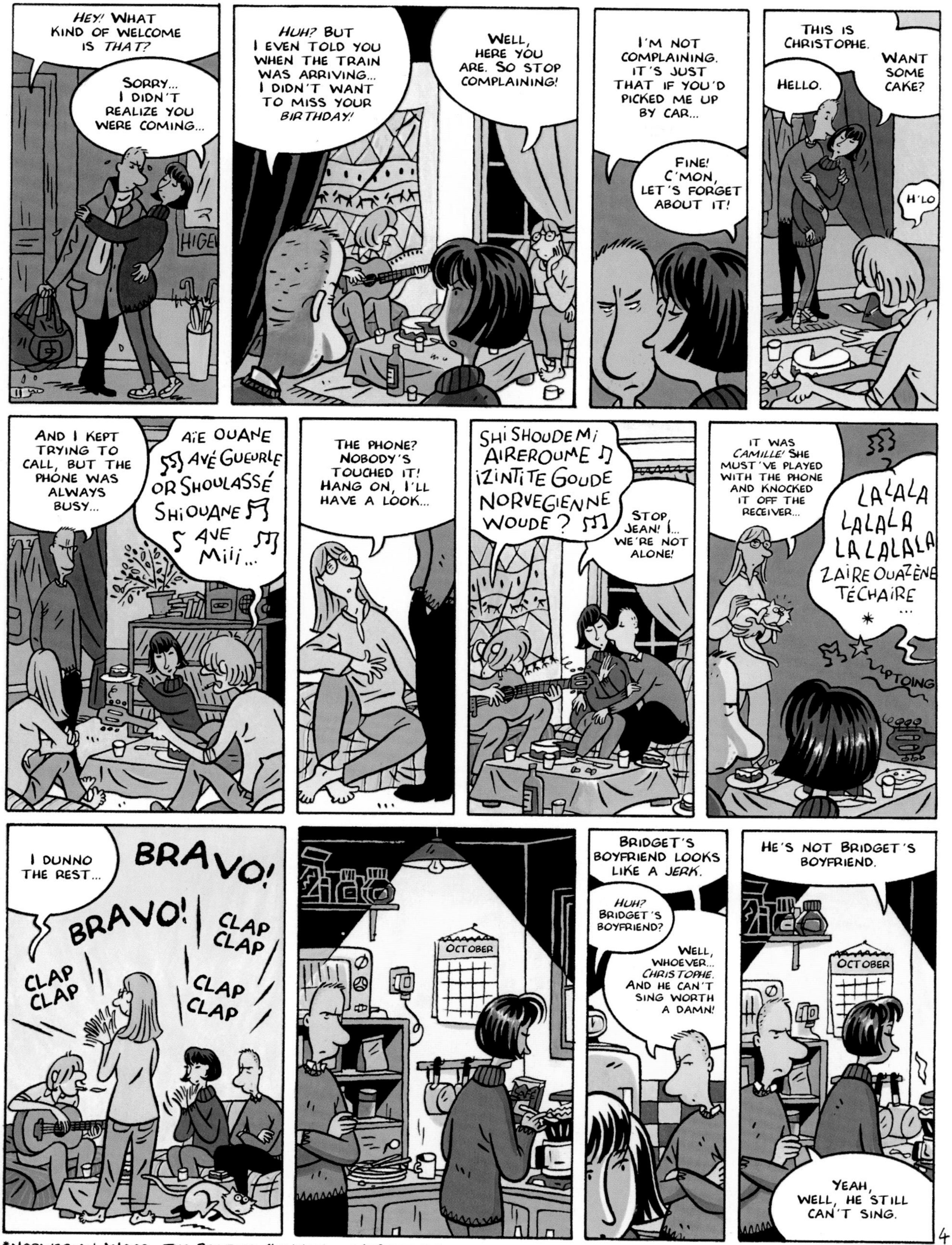
HEY! WHAT KIND OF WELCOME IS THAT?
SORRY... I DIDN'T REALIZE YOU WERE COMING...
HIGE
HUH? BUT I EVEN TOLD YOU WHEN THE TRAIN WAS ARRIVING... I DIDN'T WANT TO MISS YOUR BIRTHDAY!
WELL, HERE YOU ARE. SO STOP COMPLAINING!
I'M NOT COMPLAINING. IT'S JUST THAT IF YOU'D PICKED ME UP BY CAR...
FINE! C'MON, LET'S FORGET ABOUT IT!
THIS IS CHRISTOPHE.
HELLO.
WANT SOME CAKE?
H'LO
AND I KEPT TRYING TO CALL, BUT THE PHONE WAS ALWAYS BUSY...
AïE OUANE AVÉ GUEURLE OR SHOULASSÉ SHIOUANE AVE MIII...
THE PHONE? NOBODY'S TOUCHED IT! HANG ON, I'LL HAVE A LOOK...
SHI SHOUDE MI AIREROUME IZINTITE GOUDE NORVEGIENNE WOUDE?
STOP, JEAN! I... WE'RE NOT ALONE!
IT WAS CAMILLE! SHE MUST'VE PLAYED WITH THE PHONE AND KNOCKED IT OFF THE RECEIVER...
LALALA LALALA LALALALA ZAIRE OUAZÈNE TÉCHAIRE ... *
PTOING
I DUNNO THE REST...
BRAVO!
BRAVO!
CLAP CLAP
CLAP CLAP
CLAP CLAP
OCTOBER
BRIDGET'S BOYFRIEND LOOKS LIKE A JERK.
HUH? BRIDGET'S BOYFRIEND?
WELL, WHOEVER... CHRISTOPHE. AND HE CAN'T SING WORTH A DAMN!
HE'S NOT BRIDGET'S BOYFRIEND.
OCTOBER
YEAH, WELL, HE STILL CAN'T SING.
4

*NORWEGIAN WOOD: THE BEATLES (LENNON - MCCARTNEY)

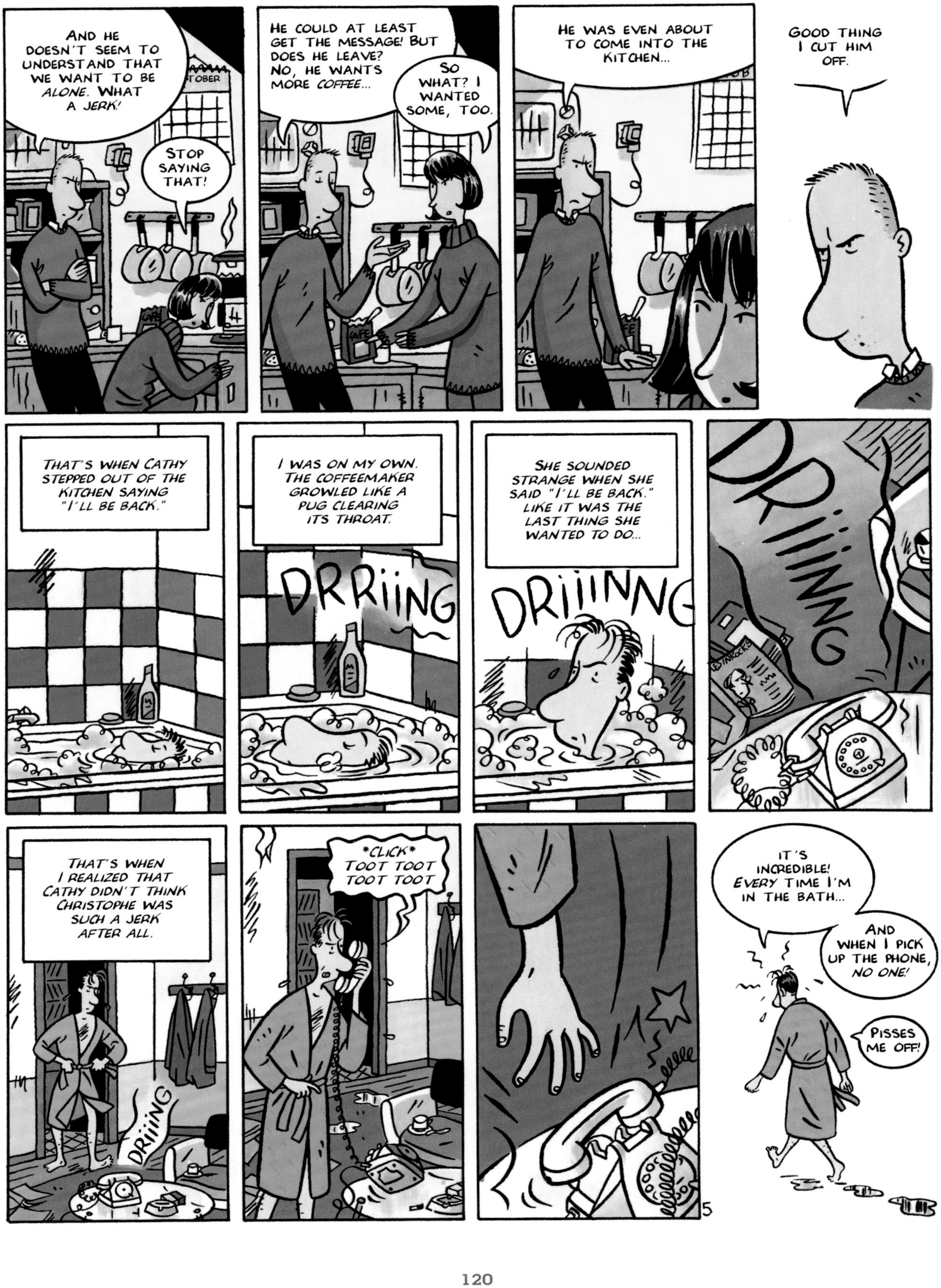
AND HE DOESN'T SEEM TO UNDERSTAND THAT WE WANT TO BE ALONE. WHAT A JERK!
STOP SAYING THAT!
HE COULD AT LEAST GET THE MESSAGE! BUT DOES HE LEAVE? NO, HE WANTS MORE COFFEE...
SO WHAT? I WANTED SOME, TOO.
HE WAS EVEN ABOUT TO COME INTO THE KITCHEN...
GOOD THING I CUT HIM OFF.
THAT'S WHEN CATHY STEPPED OUT OF THE KITCHEN SAYING "I'LL BE BACK."
I WAS ON MY OWN. THE COFFEEMAKER GROWLED LIKE A PUG CLEARING ITS THROAT.
DRRIING
SHE SOUNDED STRANGE WHEN SHE SAID "I'LL BE BACK." LIKE IT WAS THE LAST THING SHE WANTED TO DO...
DRIIINNG
DRIIIINNG
THAT'S WHEN I REALIZED THAT CATHY DIDN'T THINK CHRISTOPHE WAS SUCH A JERK AFTER ALL.
DRIIING
CLICK TOOT TOOT TOOT TOOT
IT'S INCREDIBLE! EVERY TIME I'M IN THE BATH...
AND WHEN I PICK UP THE PHONE, NO ONE!
PISSES ME OFF!
5

GRO
GROGL!
GGGR

OCTOBER

GRO
GROGL
GGGR

YES! I'LL TALK TO HIM TONIGHT. HE'LL BE GONE TOMORROW MORNING...

BUT YOU'VE GOT TO LEAVE NOW!

NO! DON'T KISS ME, THIS ISN'T THE RIGHT MOMENT!

IS CHRISTOPHE STILL HERE?

NO. HE WENT HOME.

I HOPE HE DIDN'T GO BECAUSE OF ME.

JEAN, THERE'S SOMETHING I HAVE TO TELL YOU...

NO, LET ME TALK FIRST.

CRUNCH
CRUNCH

CRUN
CR--

WELL... UH... I THINK I'LL GO TO BED NOW, TOO.

COME ON, CAMILLE...

GOOD NIGHT!

6

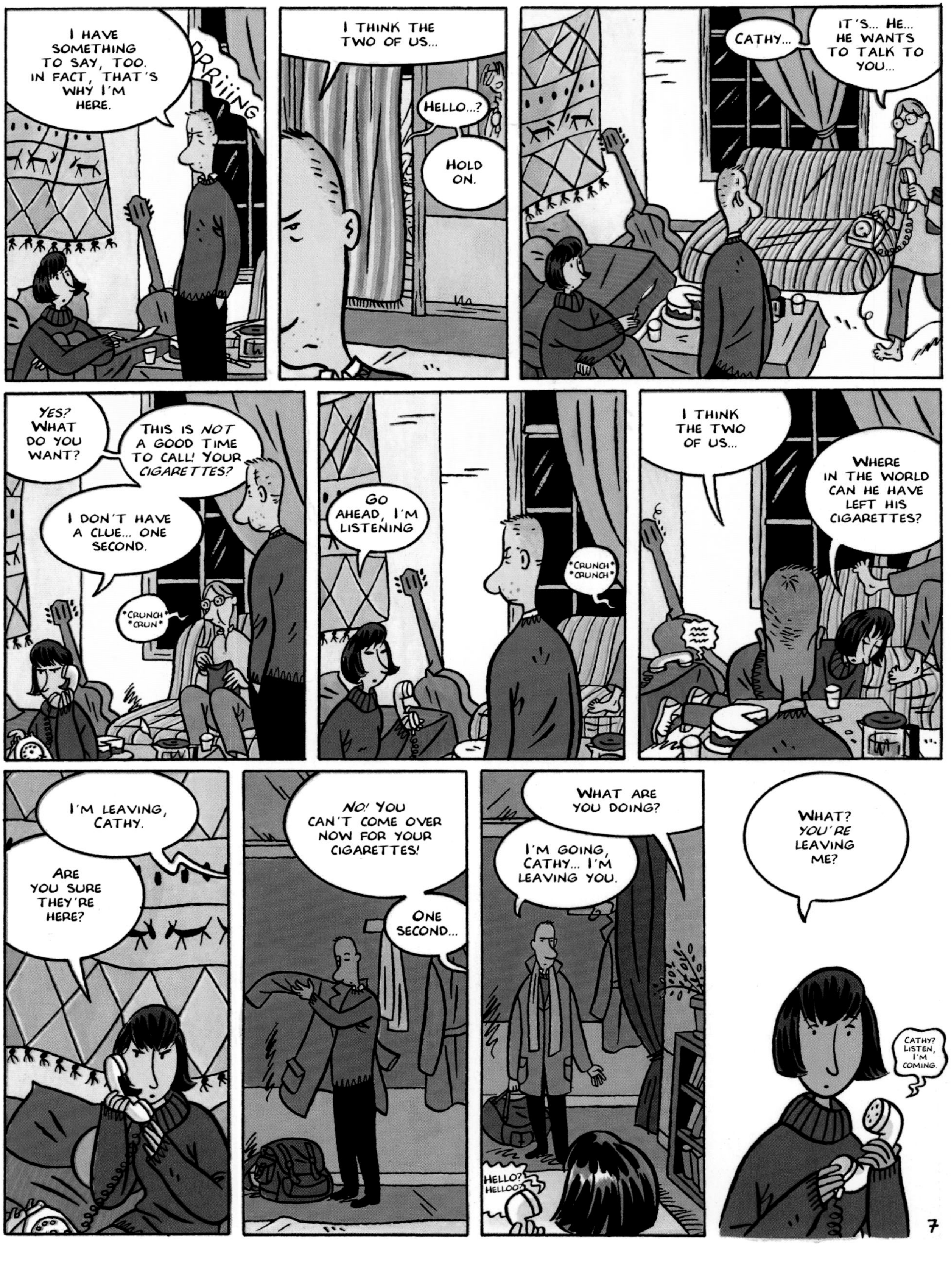
I HAVE SOMETHING TO SAY, TOO. IN FACT, THAT'S WHY I'M HERE.
DRRiiiNG
I THINK THE TWO OF US...
HELLO...?
HOLD ON.
CATHY...
IT'S... HE... HE WANTS TO TALK TO YOU...
YES? WHAT DO YOU WANT?
THIS IS NOT A GOOD TIME TO CALL! YOUR CIGARETTES?
I DON'T HAVE A CLUE... ONE SECOND.
CRUNCH *CRUN*
GO AHEAD, I'M LISTENING
CRUNCH *CRUNCH*
I THINK THE TWO OF US...
WHERE IN THE WORLD CAN HE HAVE LEFT HIS CIGARETTES?
I'M LEAVING, CATHY.
ARE YOU SURE THEY'RE HERE?
NO! YOU CAN'T COME OVER NOW FOR YOUR CIGARETTES!
ONE SECOND...
WHAT ARE YOU DOING?
I'M GOING, CATHY... I'M LEAVING YOU.
HELLO? HELLO?
WHAT? YOU'RE LEAVING ME?
CATHY? LISTEN, I'M COMING.
7

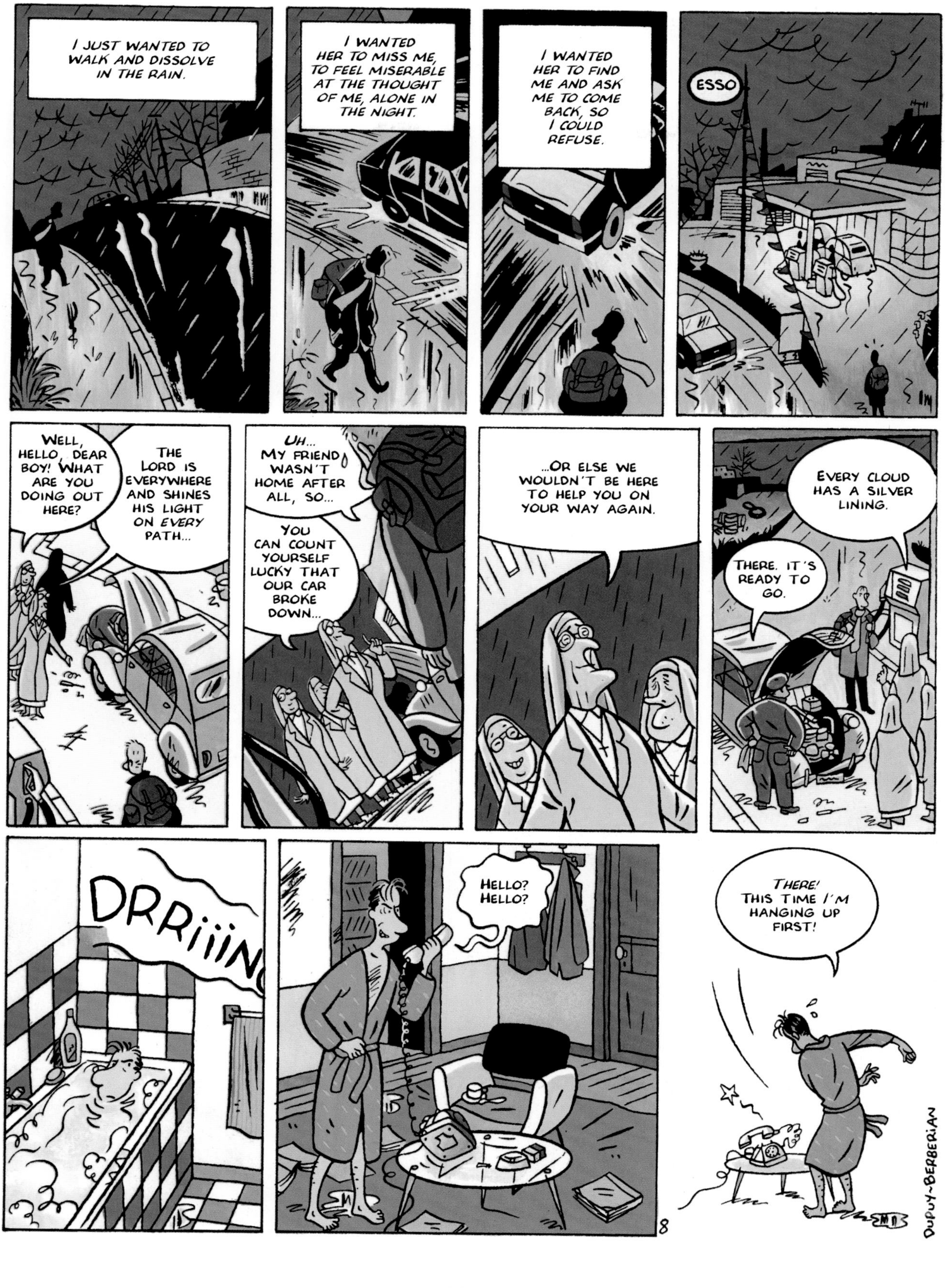

I JUST WANTED TO WALK AND DISSOLVE IN THE RAIN.
I WANTED HER TO MISS ME, TO FEEL MISERABLE AT THE THOUGHT OF ME, ALONE IN THE NIGHT.
I WANTED HER TO FIND ME AND ASK ME TO COME BACK, SO I COULD REFUSE.
ESSO
WELL, HELLO, DEAR BOY! WHAT ARE YOU DOING OUT HERE?
THE LORD IS EVERYWHERE AND SHINES HIS LIGHT ON EVERY PATH...
UH... MY FRIEND WASN'T HOME AFTER ALL, SO...
YOU CAN COUNT YOURSELF LUCKY THAT OUR CAR BROKE DOWN...
...OR ELSE WE WOULDN'T BE HERE TO HELP YOU ON YOUR WAY AGAIN.
EVERY CLOUD HAS A SILVER LINING.
THERE. IT'S READY TO GO.
DRRiiiN
HELLO? HELLO?
THERE! THIS TIME I'M HANGING UP FIRST!
8
DUPUY~BERBERIAN

WILD YOUTH

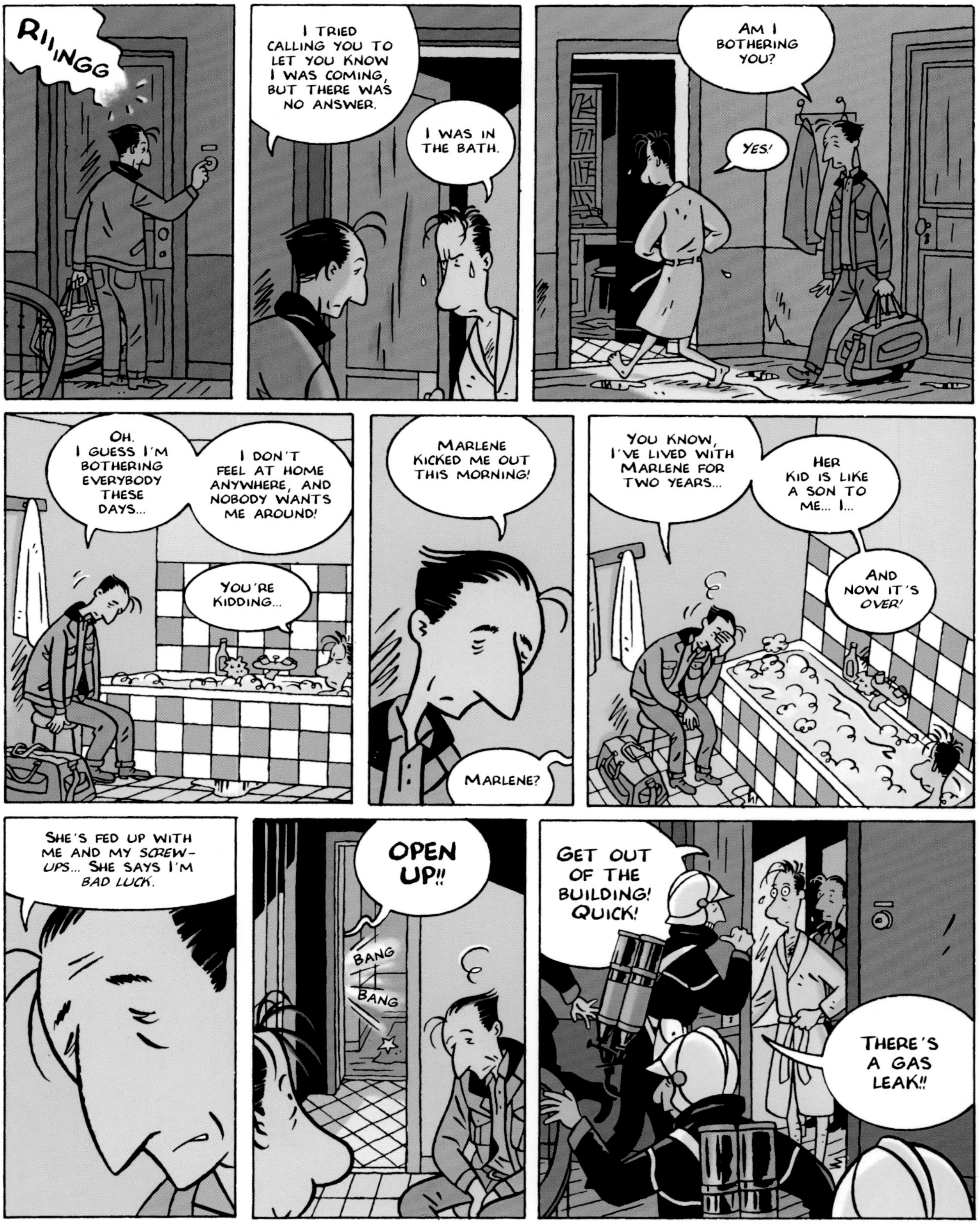
RIIINGG
I TRIED CALLING YOU TO LET YOU KNOW I WAS COMING, BUT THERE WAS NO ANSWER.
I WAS IN THE BATH.
AM I BOTHERING YOU?
YES!
OH. I GUESS I'M BOTHERING EVERYBODY THESE DAYS...
I DON'T FEEL AT HOME ANYWHERE, AND NOBODY WANTS ME AROUND!
YOU'RE KIDDING...
MARLENE KICKED ME OUT THIS MORNING!
MARLENE?
YOU KNOW, I'VE LIVED WITH MARLENE FOR TWO YEARS...
HER KID IS LIKE A SON TO ME... I...
AND NOW IT'S OVER!
SHE'S FED UP WITH ME AND MY SCREW-UPS... SHE SAYS I'M BAD LUCK.
OPEN UP!!
BANG
BANG
GET OUT OF THE BUILDING! QUICK!
THERE'S A GAS LEAK!!

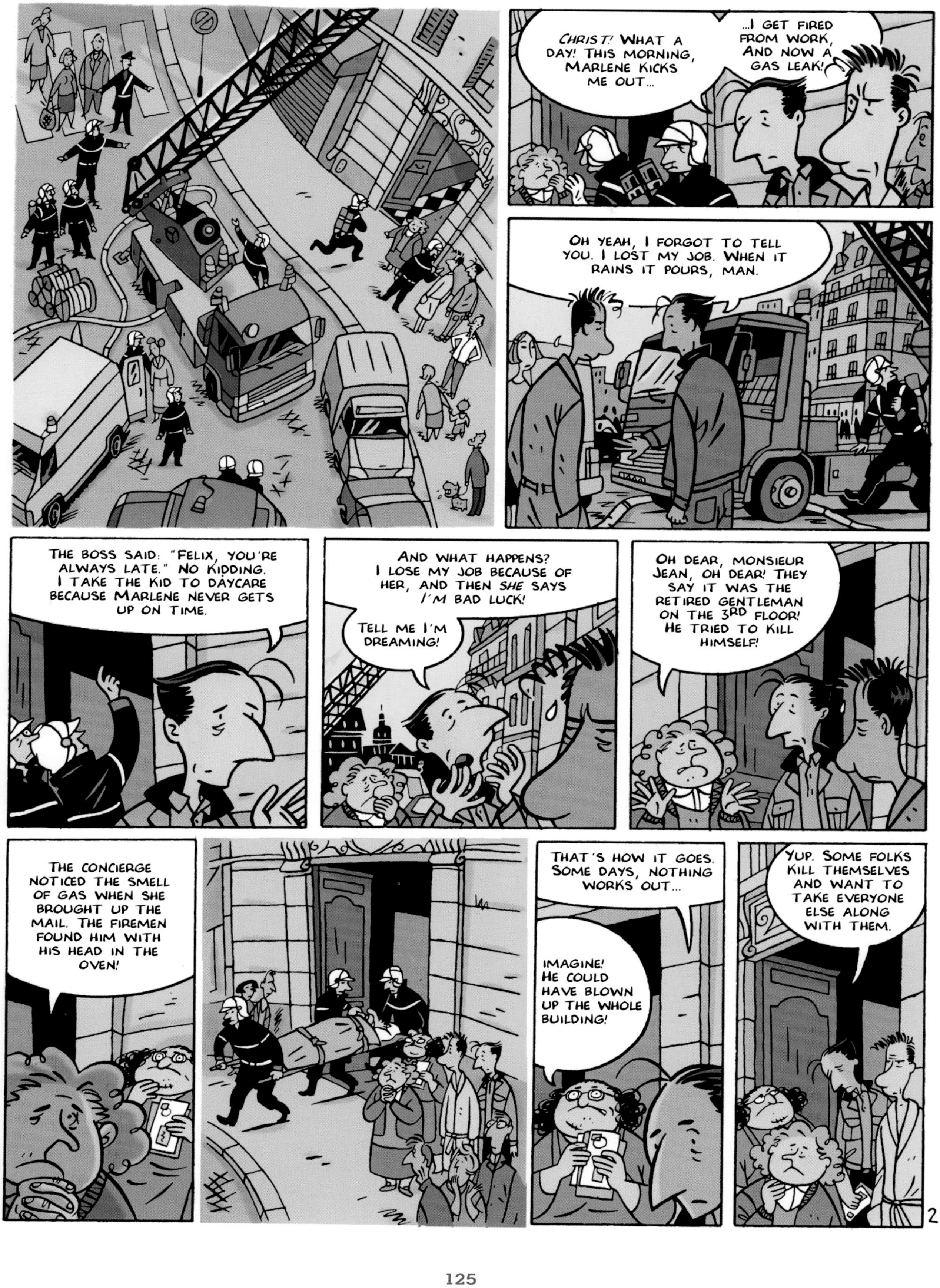
CHRIST! WHAT A DAY! THIS MORNING, MARLENE KICKS ME OUT...
...I GET FIRED FROM WORK, AND NOW A GAS LEAK!
OH YEAH, I FORGOT TO TELL YOU. I LOST MY JOB. WHEN IT RAINS IT POURS, MAN.
THE BOSS SAID: "FELIX, YOU'RE ALWAYS LATE." NO KIDDING. I TAKE THE KID TO DAYCARE BECAUSE MARLENE NEVER GETS UP ON TIME.
AND WHAT HAPPENS? I LOSE MY JOB BECAUSE OF HER, AND THEN SHE SAYS I'M BAD LUCK!
TELL ME I'M DREAMING!
OH DEAR, MONSIEUR JEAN, OH DEAR! THEY SAY IT WAS THE RETIRED GENTLEMAN ON THE 3RD FLOOR! HE TRIED TO KILL HIMSELF!
THE CONCIERGE NOTICED THE SMELL OF GAS WHEN SHE BROUGHT UP THE MAIL. THE FIREMEN FOUND HIM WITH HIS HEAD IN THE OVEN!
THAT'S HOW IT GOES. SOME DAYS, NOTHING WORKS OUT...
IMAGINE! HE COULD HAVE BLOWN UP THE WHOLE BUILDING!
YUP. SOME FOLKS KILL THEMSELVES AND WANT TO TAKE EVERYONE ELSE ALONG WITH THEM.
2

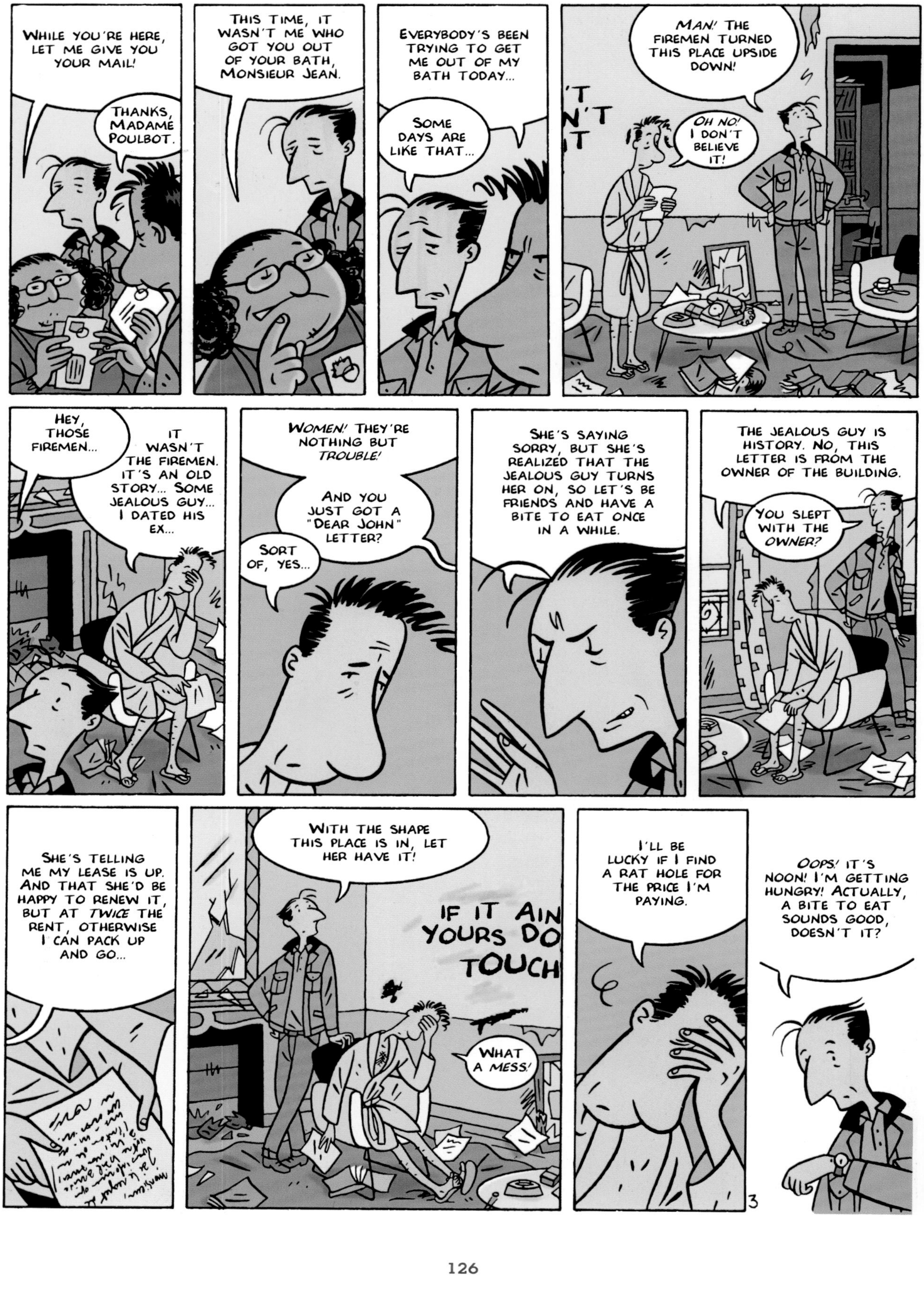

While you're here, let me give you your mail!
Thanks, Madame Poulbot.
This time, it wasn't me who got you out of your bath, Monsieur Jean.
Everybody's been trying to get me out of my bath today...
Some days are like that...
Man! The firemen turned this place upside down!
Oh no! I don't believe it!
Hey, those firemen...
It wasn't the firemen. It's an old story... Some jealous guy... I dated his ex...
Women! They're nothing but trouble!
And you just got a "Dear John" letter?
Sort of, yes...
She's saying sorry, but she's realized that the jealous guy turns her on, so let's be friends and have a bite to eat once in a while.
The jealous guy is history. No, this letter is from the owner of the building.
You slept with the owner?
She's telling me my lease is up. And that she'd be happy to renew it, but at twice the rent, otherwise I can pack up and go...
With the shape this place is in, let her have it!
If it ain yours do touch
What a mess!
I'll be lucky if I find a rat hole for the price I'm paying.
Oops! It's noon! I'm getting hungry! Actually, a bite to eat sounds good, doesn't it?
3

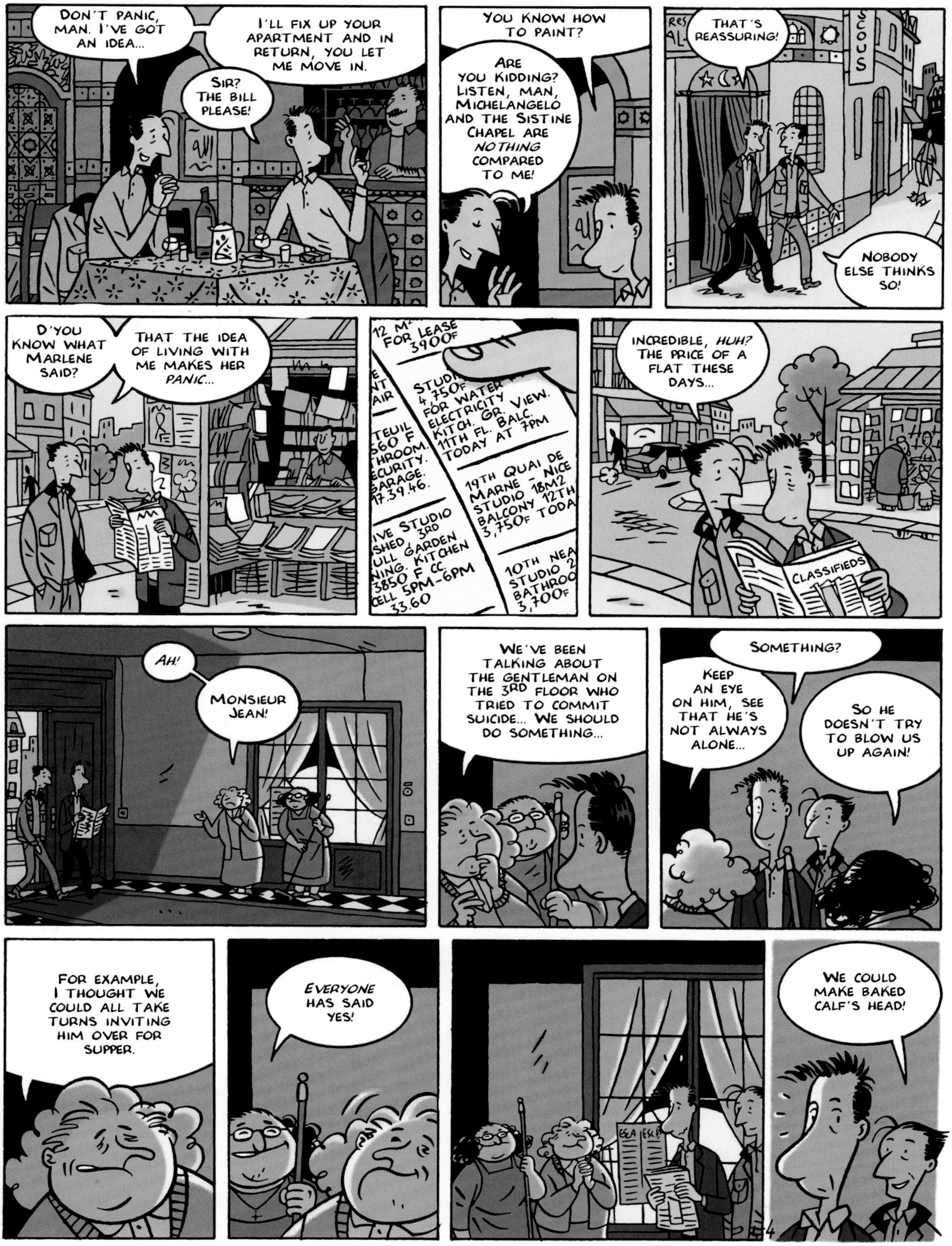
DON'T PANIC, MAN. I'VE GOT AN IDEA...
I'LL FIX UP YOUR APARTMENT AND IN RETURN, YOU LET ME MOVE IN.
SIR? THE BILL PLEASE!
YOU KNOW HOW TO PAINT?
ARE YOU KIDDING? LISTEN, MAN, MICHELANGELO AND THE SISTINE CHAPEL ARE NOTHING COMPARED TO ME!
SCOUS
THAT'S REASSURING!
NOBODY ELSE THINKS SO!
D'YOU KNOW WHAT MARLENE SAID?
THAT THE IDEA OF LIVING WITH ME MAKES HER PANIC...
12 M² FOR LEASE 3900F
4,750F FOR WATER
ELECTRICITY KITCH. GR. VIEW. 11TH FL. BALC. TODAY AT 7PM
19TH QUAI DE MARNE - NICE STUDIO 18M2
3850 F CC.
INCREDIBLE, HUH? THE PRICE OF A FLAT THESE DAYS...
CLASSIFIEDS
AH!
MONSIEUR JEAN!
WE'VE BEEN TALKING ABOUT THE GENTLEMAN ON THE 3RD FLOOR WHO TRIED TO COMMIT SUICIDE... WE SHOULD DO SOMETHING...
SOMETHING?
KEEP AN EYE ON HIM, SEE THAT HE'S NOT ALWAYS ALONE...
SO HE DOESN'T TRY TO BLOW US UP AGAIN!
FOR EXAMPLE, I THOUGHT WE COULD ALL TAKE TURNS INVITING HIM OVER FOR SUPPER.
EVERYONE HAS SAID YES!
WE COULD MAKE BAKED CALF'S HEAD!

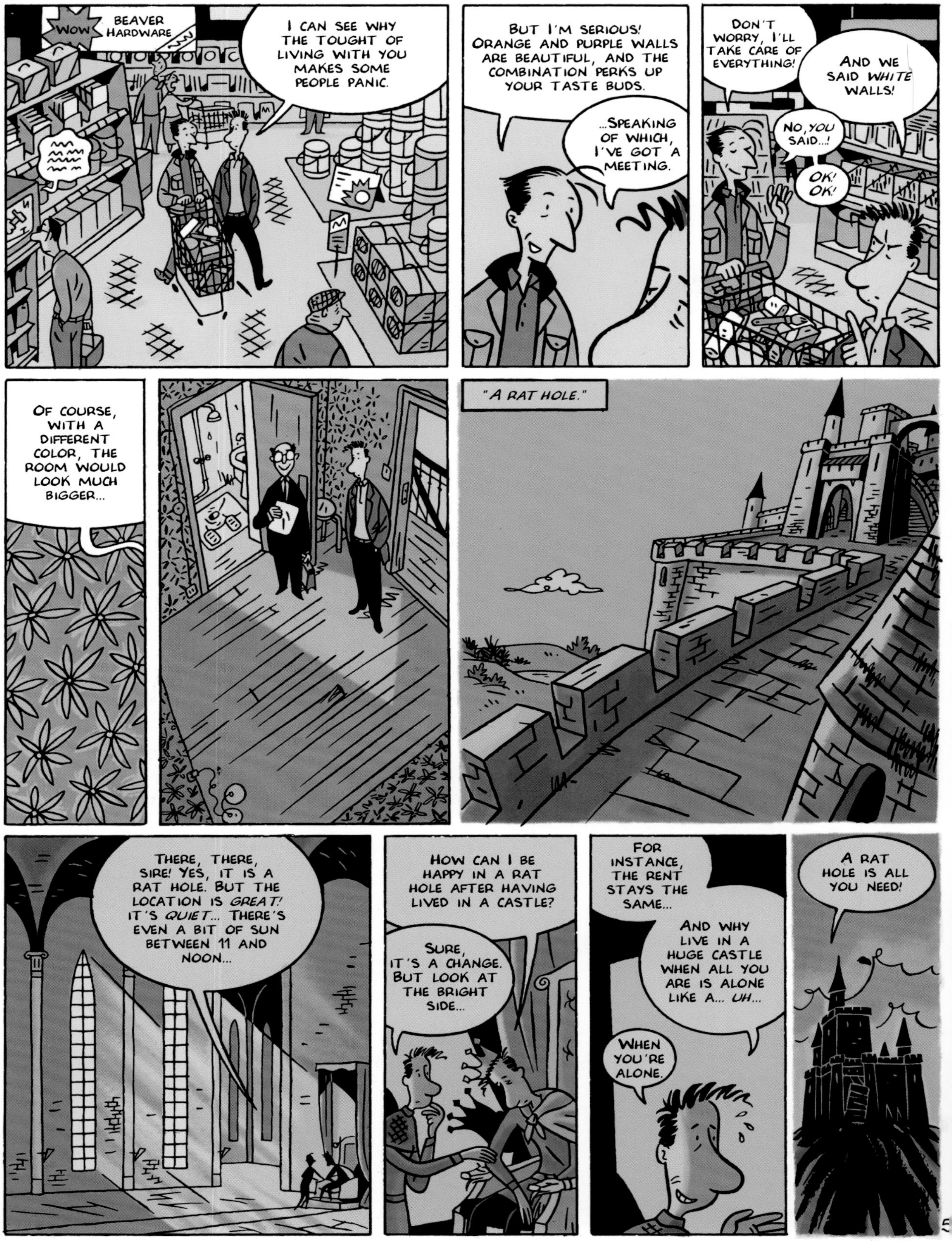
BEAVER HARDWARE
WOW
I CAN SEE WHY THE TOUGHT OF LIVING WITH YOU MAKES SOME PEOPLE PANIC.
BUT I'M SERIOUS! ORANGE AND PURPLE WALLS ARE BEAUTIFUL, AND THE COMBINATION PERKS UP YOUR TASTE BUDS.
...SPEAKING OF WHICH, I'VE GOT A MEETING.
DON'T WORRY, I'LL TAKE CARE OF EVERYTHING!
AND WE SAID WHITE WALLS!
NO, YOU SAID...!
OK! OK!
OF COURSE, WITH A DIFFERENT COLOR, THE ROOM WOULD LOOK MUCH BIGGER...
"A RAT HOLE."
THERE, THERE, SIRE! YES, IT IS A RAT HOLE. BUT THE LOCATION IS GREAT! IT'S QUIET... THERE'S EVEN A BIT OF SUN BETWEEN 11 AND NOON...
HOW CAN I BE HAPPY IN A RAT HOLE AFTER HAVING LIVED IN A CASTLE?
SURE, IT'S A CHANGE. BUT LOOK AT THE BRIGHT SIDE...
FOR INSTANCE, THE RENT STAYS THE SAME...
AND WHY LIVE IN A HUGE CASTLE WHEN ALL YOU ARE IS ALONE LIKE A... UH...
WHEN YOU'RE ALONE.
A RAT HOLE IS ALL YOU NEED!

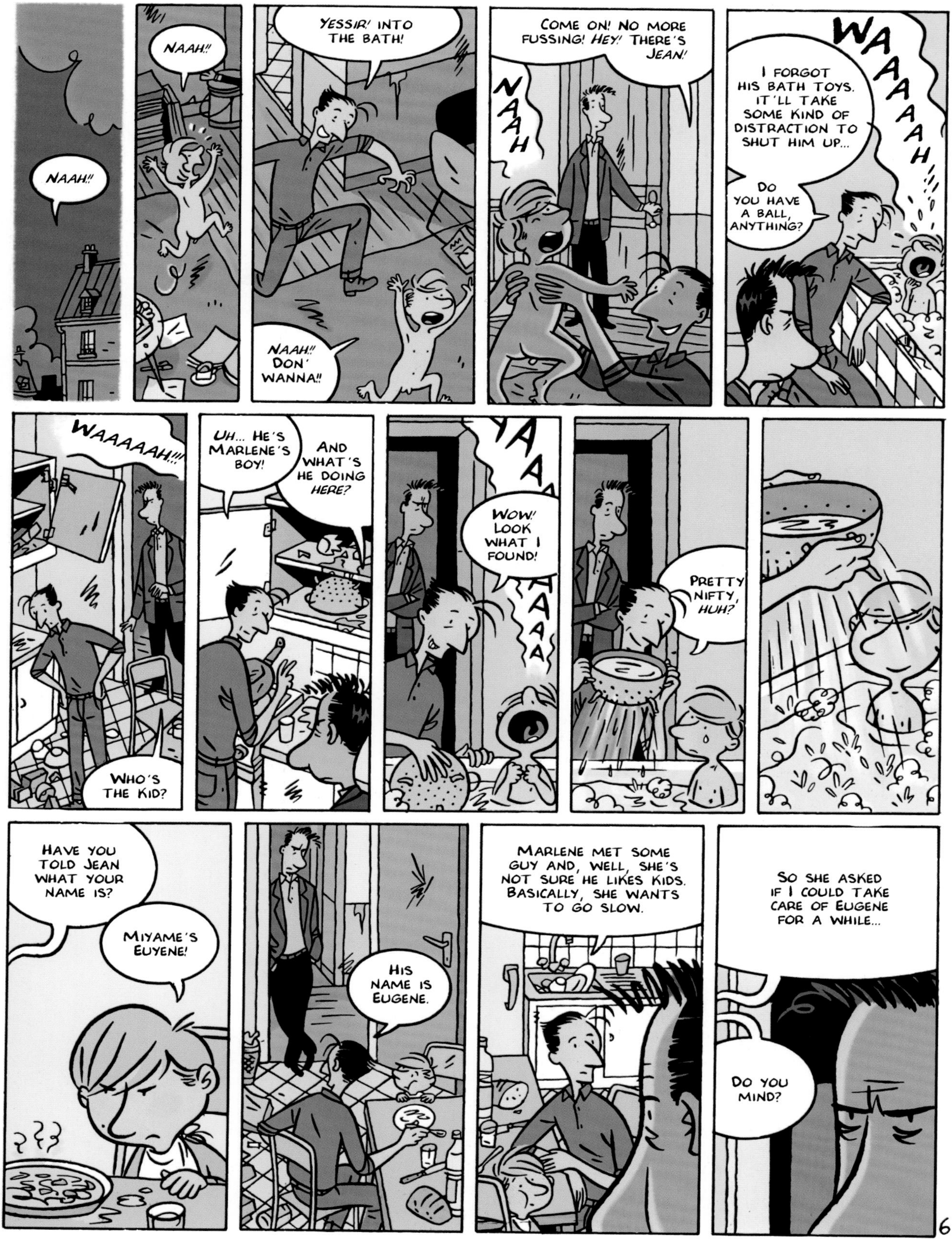
NAAH!!
NAAH!!
YESSIR! INTO THE BATH!
NAAH!! DON' WANNA!!
COME ON! NO MORE FUSSING! HEY! THERE'S JEAN!
NAAAH
WAAAAAAH
I FORGOT HIS BATH TOYS. IT'LL TAKE SOME KIND OF DISTRACTION TO SHUT HIM UP...
DO YOU HAVE A BALL, ANYTHING?
WAAAAAAH!!!
WHO'S THE KID?
UH... HE'S MARLENE'S BOY!
AND WHAT'S HE DOING HERE?
WOW! LOOK WHAT I FOUND!
PRETTY NIFTY, HUH?
HAVE YOU TOLD JEAN WHAT YOUR NAME IS?
MIYAME'S EUYENE!
HIS NAME IS EUGENE.
MARLENE MET SOME GUY AND, WELL, SHE'S NOT SURE HE LIKES KIDS. BASICALLY, SHE WANTS TO GO SLOW.
SO SHE ASKED IF I COULD TAKE CARE OF EUGENE FOR A WHILE...
DO YOU MIND?
6

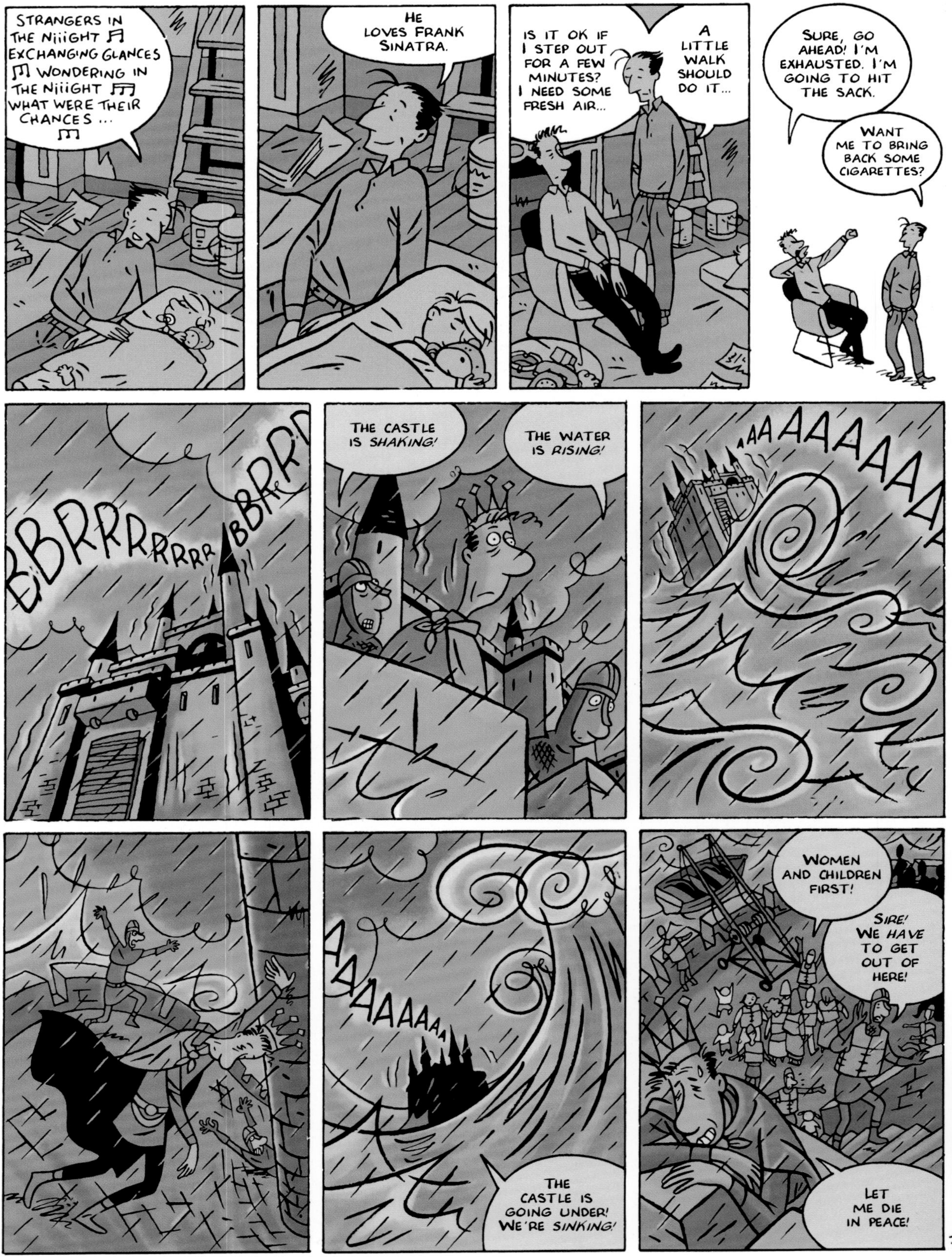

STRANGERS IN THE NiiiGHT ♫ EXCHANGING GLANCES ♫ WONDERING IN THE NiiiGHT ♫ WHAT WERE THEIR CHANCES ... ♫
HE LOVES FRANK SINATRA.
IS IT OK IF I STEP OUT FOR A FEW MINUTES? I NEED SOME FRESH AIR...
A LITTLE WALK SHOULD DO IT...
SURE, GO AHEAD! I'M EXHAUSTED. I'M GOING TO HIT THE SACK.
WANT ME TO BRING BACK SOME CIGARETTES?
BBRRRRRRRR BBRRR
THE CASTLE IS SHAKING!
THE WATER IS RISING!
AAAAAAAAAA
AAAAAAAAA
THE CASTLE IS GOING UNDER! WE'RE SINKING!
WOMEN AND CHILDREN FIRST!
SIRE! WE HAVE TO GET OUT OF HERE!
LET ME DIE IN PEACE!

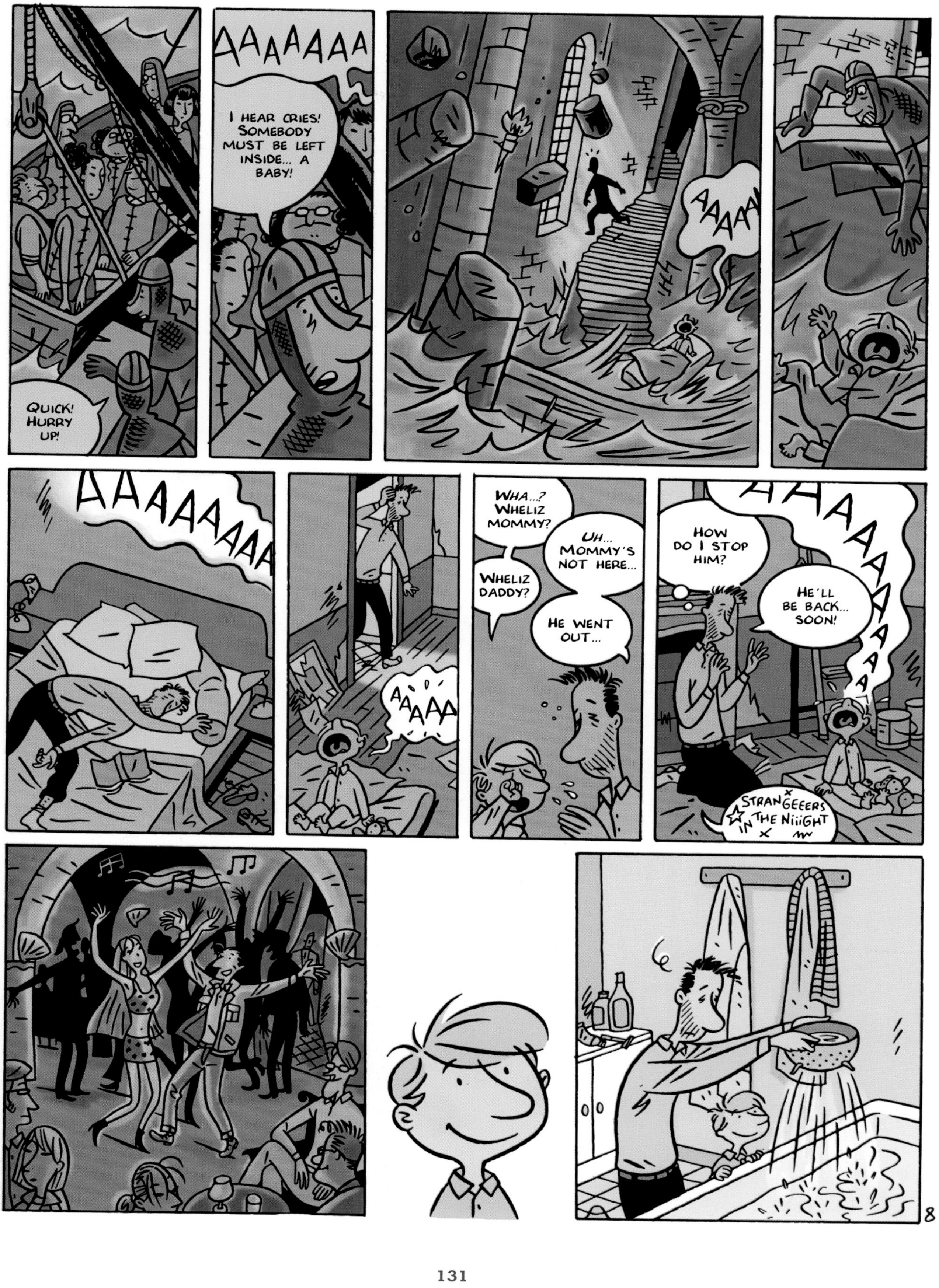
QUICK! HURRY UP!
AAAAAAA
I HEAR CRIES! SOMEBODY MUST BE LEFT INSIDE... A BABY!
AAAAA
AAAAAAAA
AAAAA
WHA...? WHELIZ MOMMY?
UH... MOMMY'S NOT HERE...
WHELIZ DADDY?
HE WENT OUT...
HOW DO I STOP HIM?
AAAAAAAAAAAA
HE'LL BE BACK... SOON!
STRANGEEERS IN THE NiiiGHT
8

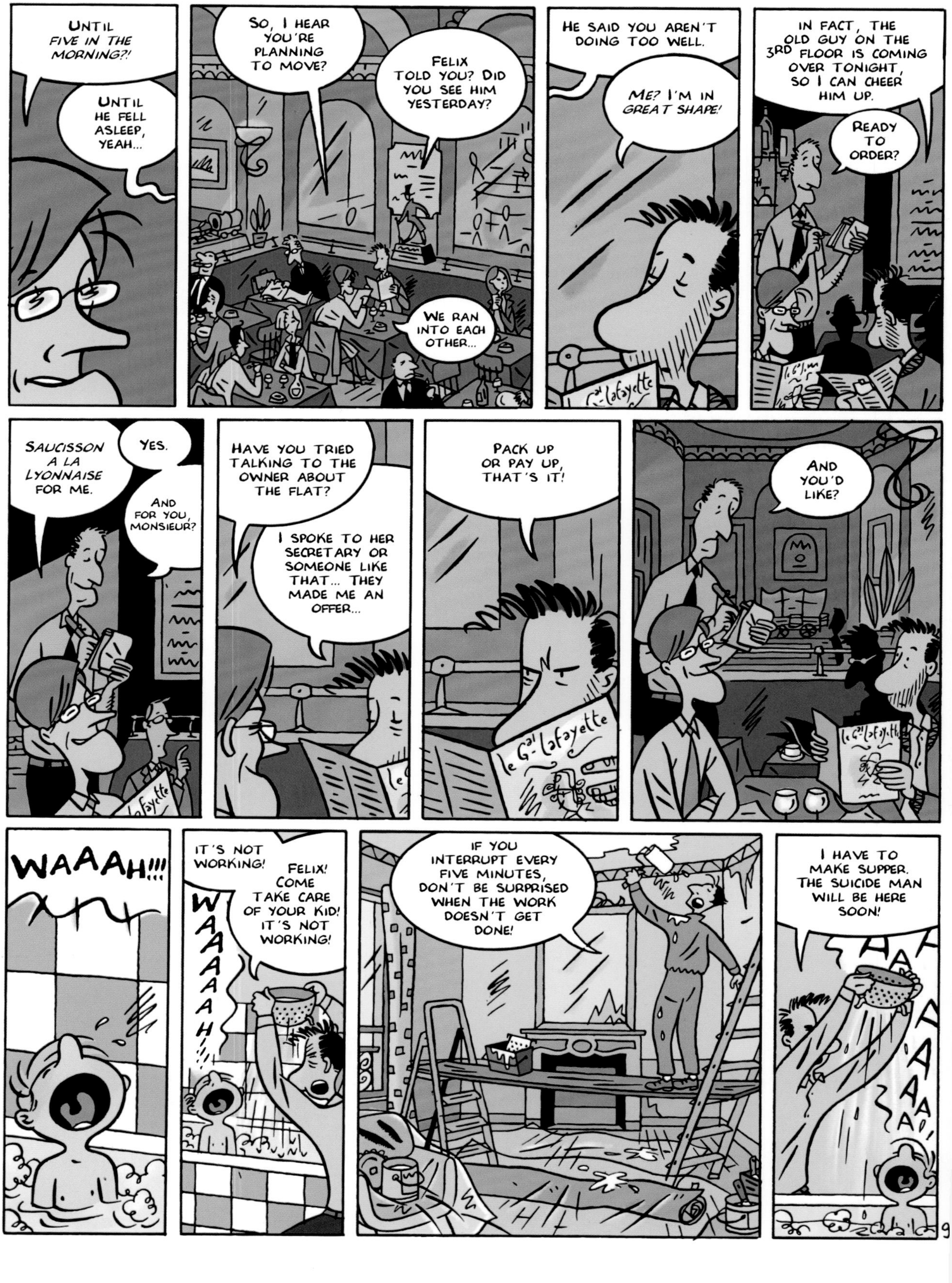
UNTIL FIVE IN THE MORNING?!
UNTIL HE FELL ASLEEP, YEAH...
SO, I HEAR YOU'RE PLANNING TO MOVE?
FELIX TOLD YOU? DID YOU SEE HIM YESTERDAY?
WE RAN INTO EACH OTHER...
HE SAID YOU AREN'T DOING TOO WELL.
ME? I'M IN GREAT SHAPE!
IN FACT, THE OLD GUY ON THE 3RD FLOOR IS COMING OVER TONIGHT, SO I CAN CHEER HIM UP.
READY TO ORDER?
SAUCISSON A LA LYONNAISE FOR ME.
YES.
AND FOR YOU, MONSIEUR?
HAVE YOU TRIED TALKING TO THE OWNER ABOUT THE FLAT?
I SPOKE TO HER SECRETARY OR SOMEONE LIKE THAT... THEY MADE ME AN OFFER...
PACK UP OR PAY UP, THAT'S IT!
AND YOU'D LIKE?
WAAAH!!!
IT'S NOT WORKING!
FELIX! COME TAKE CARE OF YOUR KID! IT'S NOT WORKING!
WAAAAAAAH!!!
IF YOU INTERRUPT EVERY FIVE MINUTES, DON'T BE SURPRISED WHEN THE WORK DOESN'T GET DONE!
I HAVE TO MAKE SUPPER. THE SUICIDE MAN WILL BE HERE SOON!

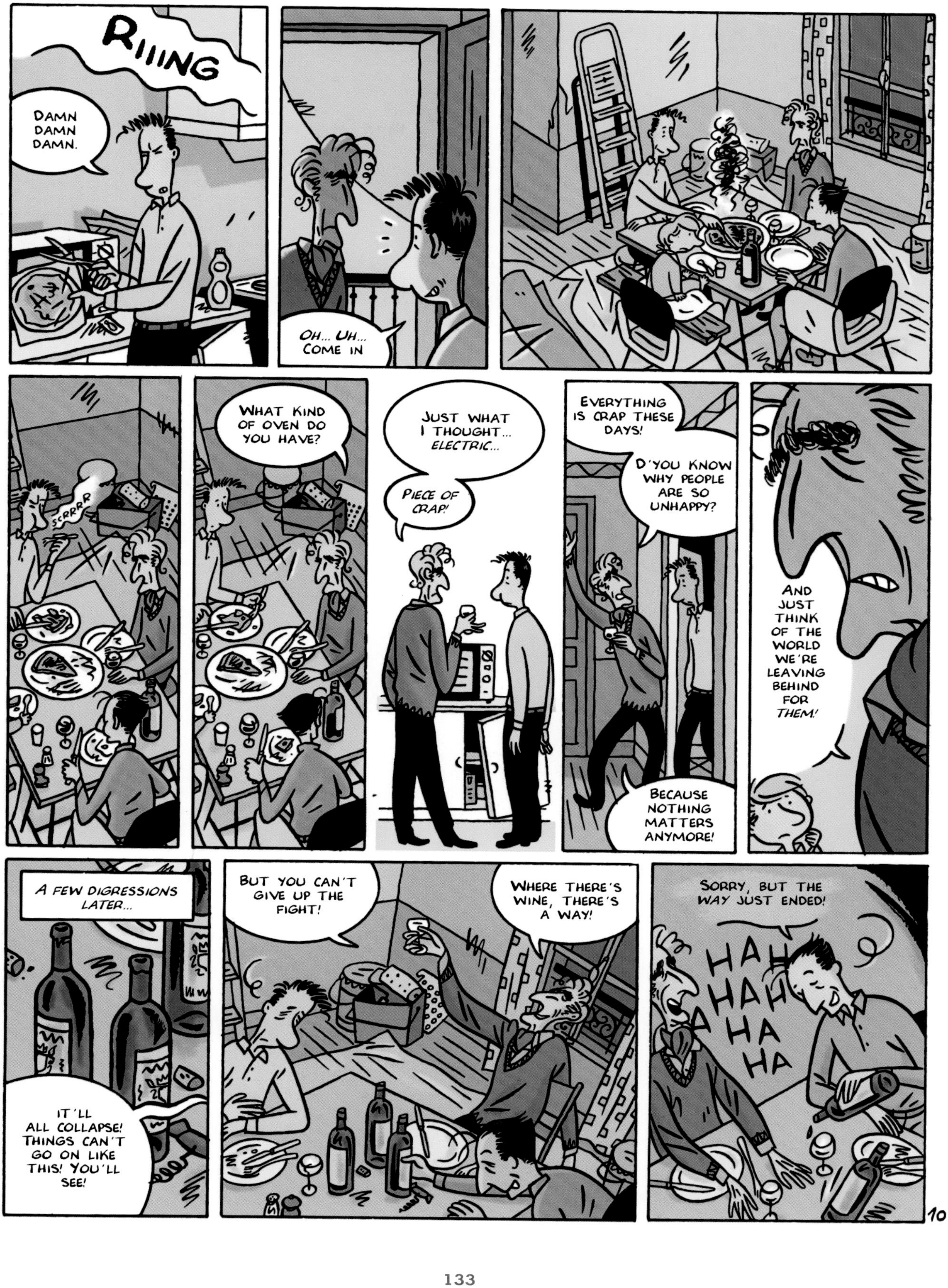
RIIING
DAMN DAMN DAMN.
OH... UH... COME IN
WHAT KIND OF OVEN DO YOU HAVE?
SCRRRR
JUST WHAT I THOUGHT... ELECTRIC...
PIECE OF CRAP!
EVERYTHING IS CRAP THESE DAYS!
D'YOU KNOW WHY PEOPLE ARE SO UNHAPPY?
BECAUSE NOTHING MATTERS ANYMORE!
AND JUST THINK OF THE WORLD WE'RE LEAVING BEHIND FOR THEM!
A FEW DIGRESSIONS LATER...
IT'LL ALL COLLAPSE! THINGS CAN'T GO ON LIKE THIS! YOU'LL SEE!
BUT YOU CAN'T GIVE UP THE FIGHT!
WHERE THERE'S WINE, THERE'S A WAY!
SORRY, BUT THE WAY JUST ENDED!
HAH HAH AHA HA HA
10

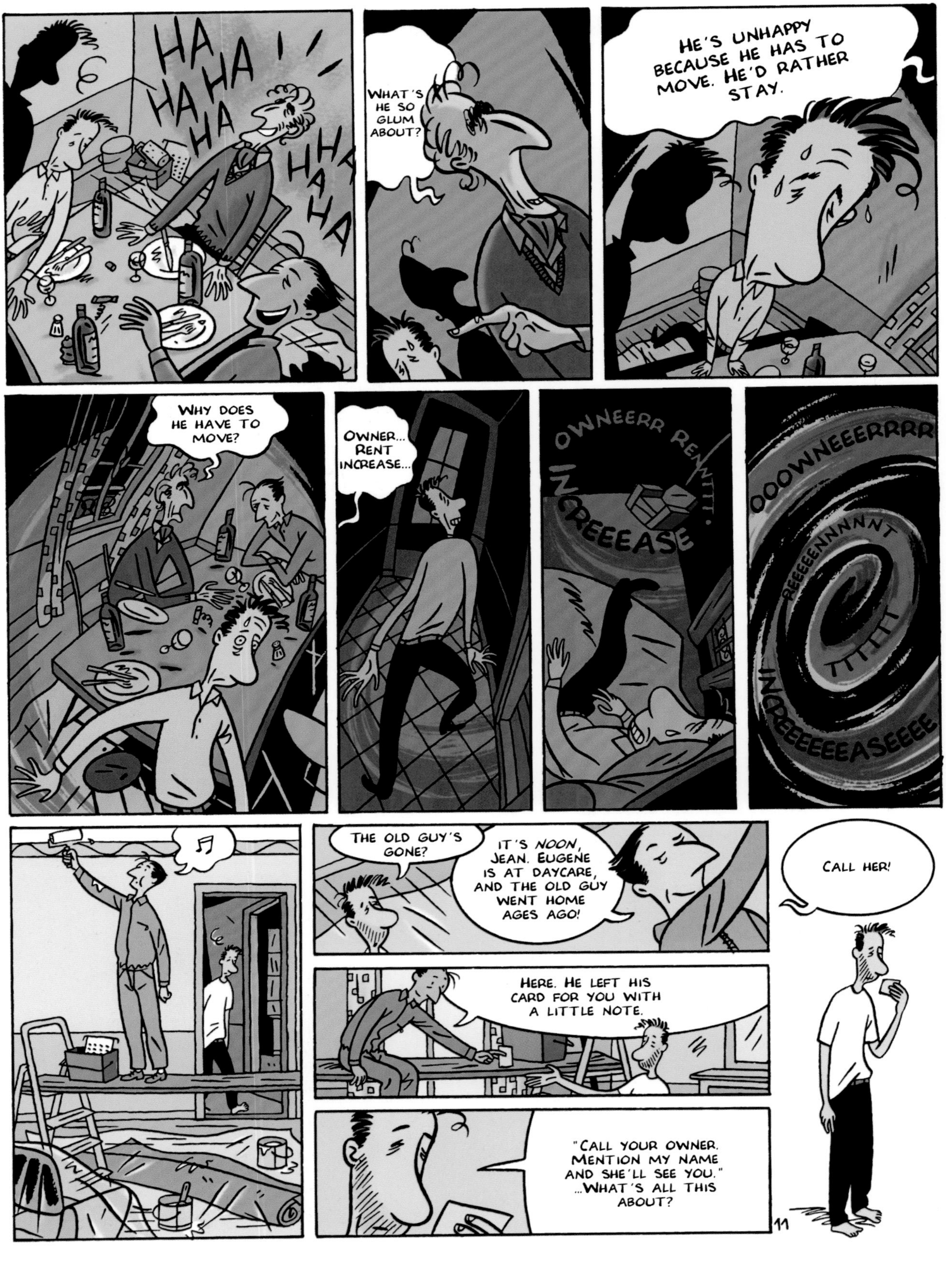
HA HA HA HA HA !
HA HA HA HA
WHAT'S HE SO GLUM ABOUT?
HE'S UNHAPPY BECAUSE HE HAS TO MOVE. HE'D RATHER STAY.
WHY DOES HE HAVE TO MOVE?
OWNER... RENT INCREASE...
OWNEERR RENTTT. INCREEEASE
OOOWNEEERRRR REEEENNNNNT INCREEEEEASEEEE
♪
THE OLD GUY'S GONE?
IT'S NOON, JEAN. EUGENE IS AT DAYCARE, AND THE OLD GUY WENT HOME AGES AGO!
CALL HER!
HERE. HE LEFT HIS CARD FOR YOU WITH A LITTLE NOTE.
"CALL YOUR OWNER. MENTION MY NAME AND SHE'LL SEE YOU." ...WHAT'S ALL THIS ABOUT?
11

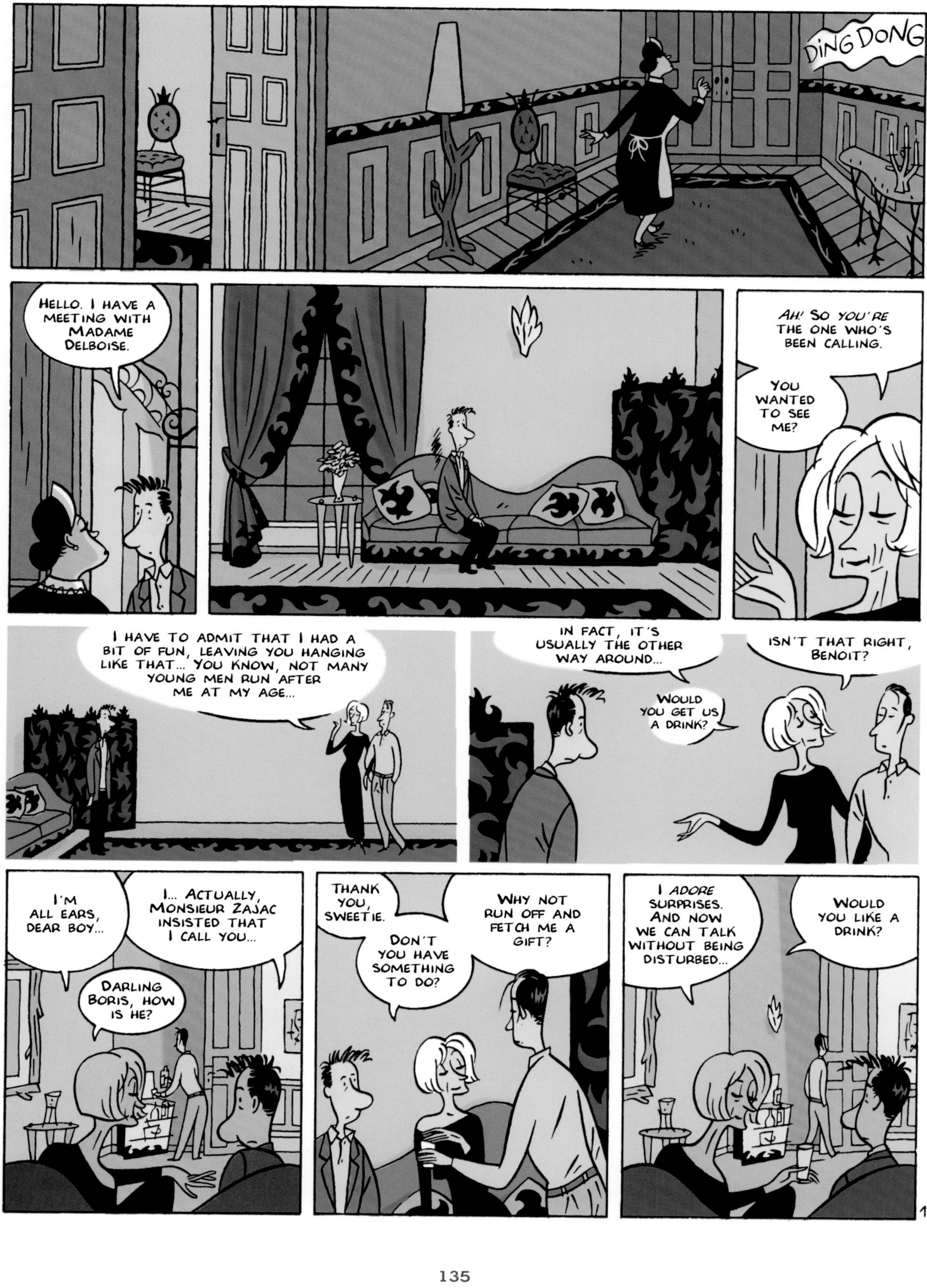
DING DONG
HELLO. I HAVE A MEETING WITH MADAME DELBOISE.
AH! SO YOU'RE THE ONE WHO'S BEEN CALLING.
YOU WANTED TO SEE ME?
I HAVE TO ADMIT THAT I HAD A BIT OF FUN, LEAVING YOU HANGING LIKE THAT... YOU KNOW, NOT MANY YOUNG MEN RUN AFTER ME AT MY AGE...
IN FACT, IT'S USUALLY THE OTHER WAY AROUND...
ISN'T THAT RIGHT, BENOIT?
WOULD YOU GET US A DRINK?
I'M ALL EARS, DEAR BOY...
I... ACTUALLY, MONSIEUR ZAJAC INSISTED THAT I CALL YOU...
DARLING BORIS, HOW IS HE?
THANK YOU, SWEETIE.
WHY NOT RUN OFF AND FETCH ME A GIFT?
DON'T YOU HAVE SOMETHING TO DO?
I ADORE SURPRISES. AND NOW WE CAN TALK WITHOUT BEING DISTURBED...
WOULD YOU LIKE A DRINK?
12

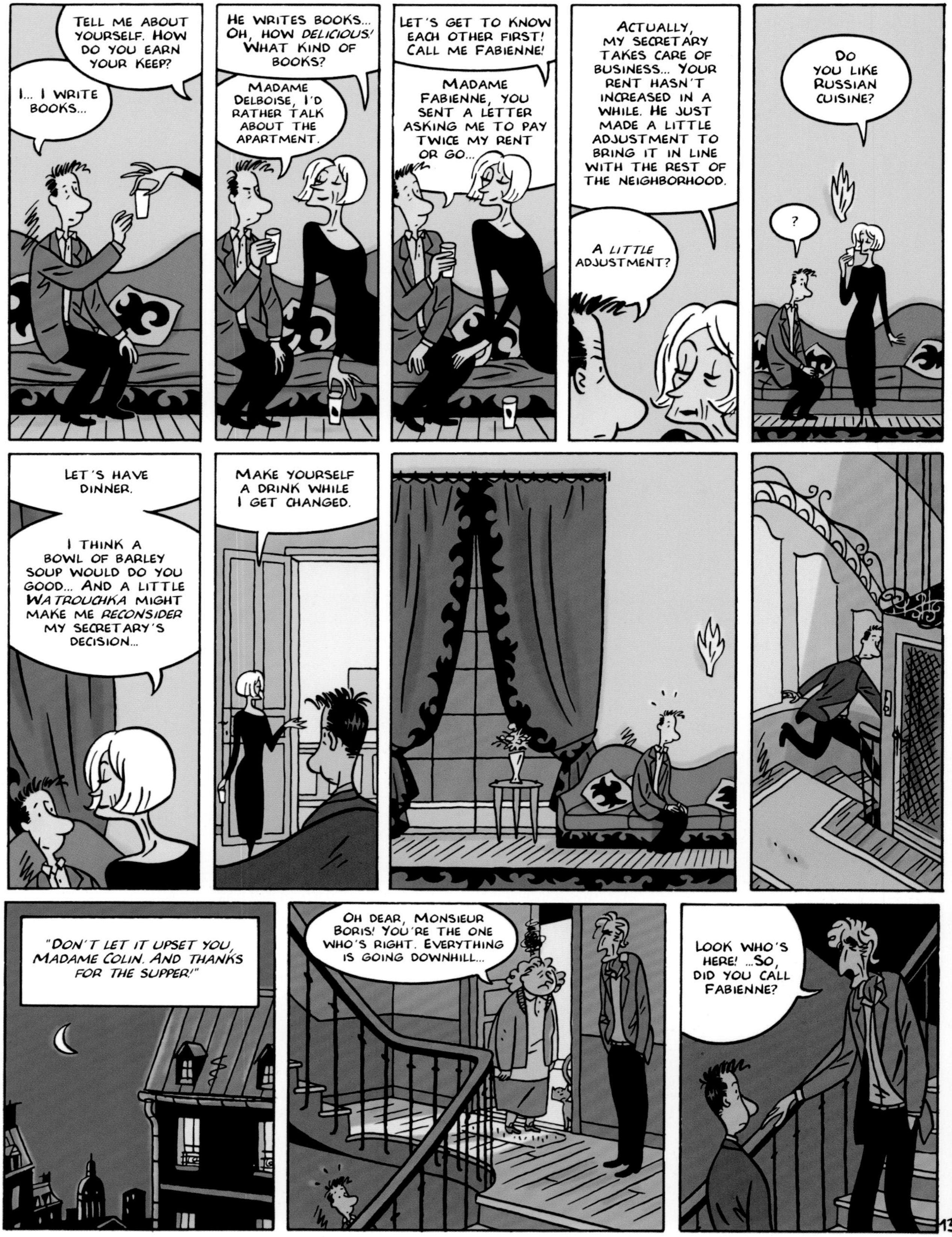

Tell me about yourself. How do you earn your keep?
I... I write books...
He writes books... Oh, how *delicious!* What kind of books?
Madame Delboise, I'd rather talk about the apartment.
Let's get to know each other first! Call me Fabienne!
Madame Fabienne, you sent a letter asking me to pay twice my rent or go...
Actually, my secretary takes care of business... Your rent hasn't increased in a while. He just made a little adjustment to bring it in line with the rest of the neighborhood.
A *little* adjustment?
?
Do you like Russian cuisine?
Let's have dinner.
I think a bowl of barley soup would do you good... And a little *Watrouchka* might make me *reconsider* my secretary's decision...
Make yourself a drink while I get changed.
"Don't let it upset you, Madame Colin. And thanks for the supper!"
Oh dear, Monsieur Boris! You're the one who's right. Everything is going downhill...
Look who's here! ...So, did you call Fabienne?

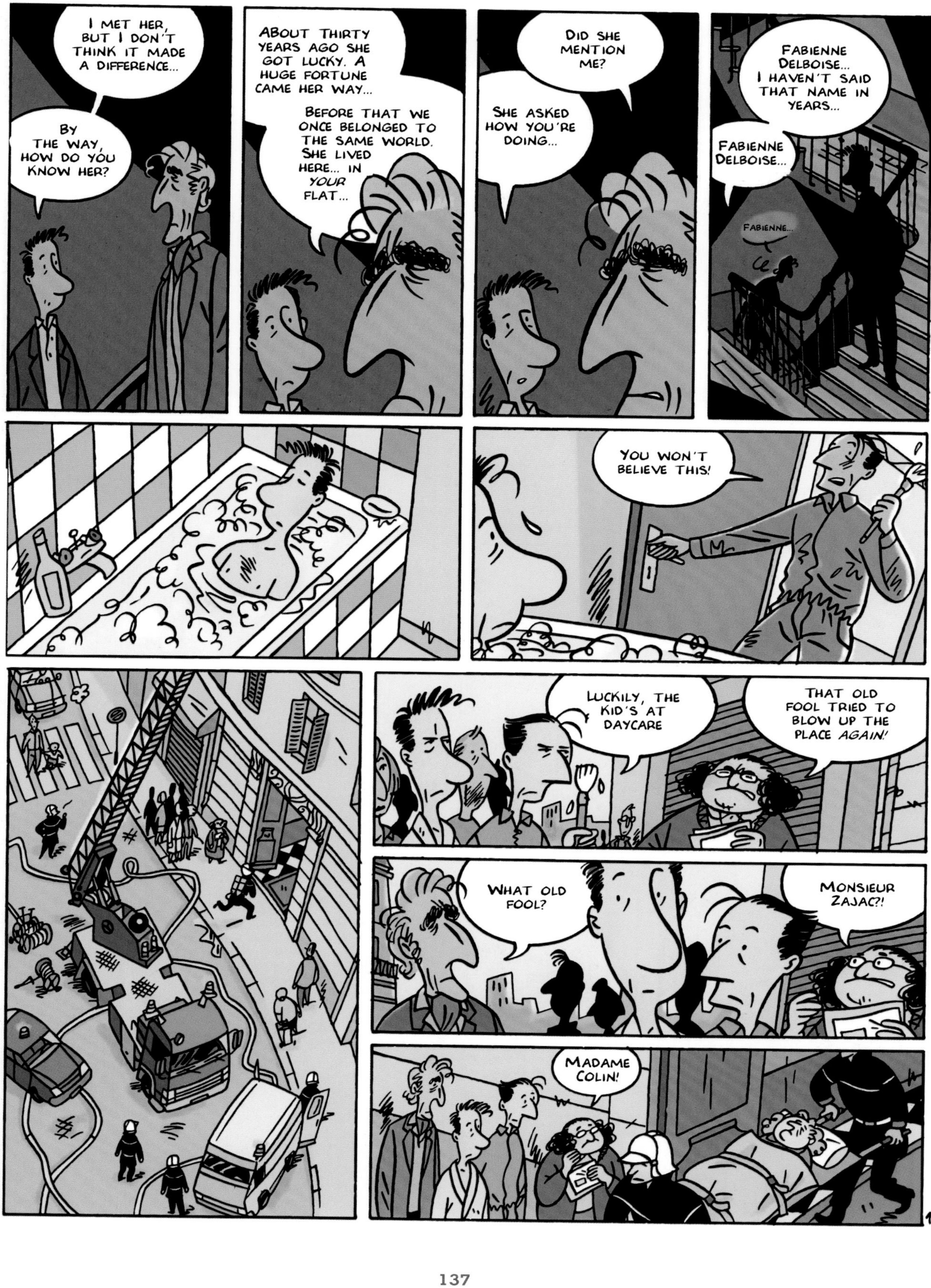

I MET HER, BUT I DON'T THINK IT MADE A DIFFERENCE...
BY THE WAY, HOW DO YOU KNOW HER?
ABOUT THIRTY YEARS AGO SHE GOT LUCKY. A HUGE FORTUNE CAME HER WAY...
BEFORE THAT WE ONCE BELONGED TO THE SAME WORLD. SHE LIVED HERE... IN *YOUR* FLAT...
DID SHE MENTION ME?
SHE ASKED HOW YOU'RE DOING...
FABIENNE DELBOISE... I HAVEN'T SAID THAT NAME IN YEARS...
FABIENNE DELBOISE...
FABIENNE...
YOU WON'T BELIEVE THIS!
LUCKILY, THE KID'S AT DAYCARE
THAT OLD FOOL TRIED TO BLOW UP THE PLACE *AGAIN*!
WHAT OLD FOOL?
MONSIEUR ZAJAC?!
MADAME COLIN!
14

THERE'LL BE A WAITING LIST FOR DINNER SOON...

WEEOOO WEEOOO

MONSIEUR JEAN, SOMEONE DROPPED THIS OFF FOR YOU.

THANKS.

"DEAR MONSIEUR, IT SEEMS YOU DON'T LIKE RUSSIAN CUISINE. PLEASE EXCUSE MY GAUCHE INVITATION..."

"AS FOR THE APARTMENT, I'VE SPOKEN WITH MY SECRETARY..."

THIS BUILDING HAS BAD KARMA...

ALL THESE SENIOR SUICIDES... MAYBE YOU'RE BETTER OFF MOVING AFTER ALL!

HOLD ON A SEC, I'M READING!

"I ASKED HIM TO EXTEND YOUR LEASE AND LEAVE YOU ALONE..."

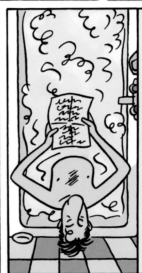

"Don't ask why... I'll just quote this song: 'Every day that comes around finds me feeling the same, drowning in sorrow, for nothing at all What will remain of the spring of our lives of our wild wild youth'"

Enjoy yours,

Fabienne Delboise

HEY JEAN! LISTEN...

I HAVE AN IDEA.

WHY DON'T WE GET A FLAT FOR THE TWO OF US - THREE, WITH EUGENE?

DUPUY-BERBERIAN JUIL. 94

"I'M NOT MOVING..."

"HUH?"

"AND NOW, IF YOU DON'T MIND, I'D LIKE A MOMENT TO ENJOY MY WILD YOUTH..."

"...AND HAVE A NICE BATH!"

"???"

Monsieur Jean's Vacation

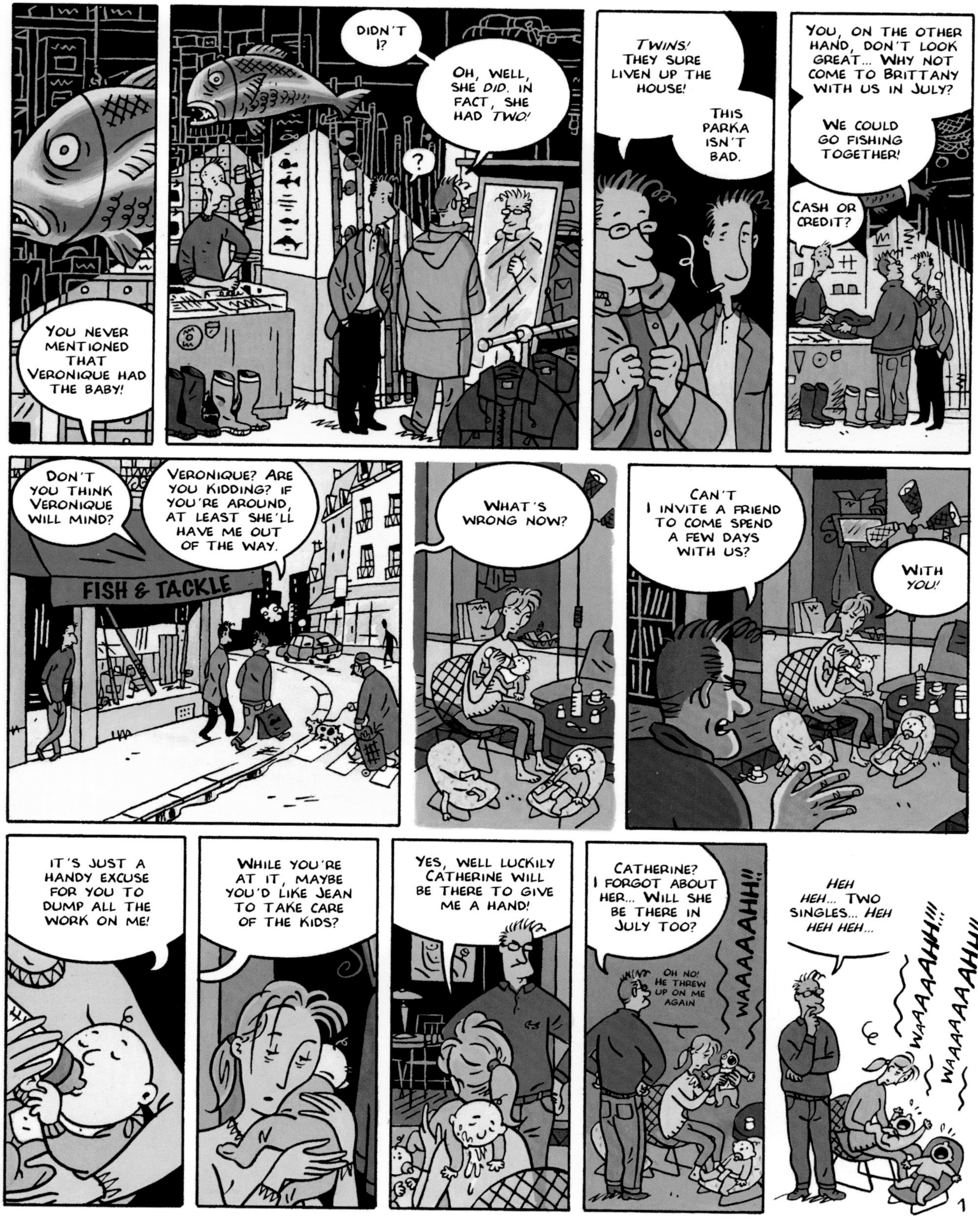

You never mentioned that Veronique had the baby!
Didn't I?
?
Oh, well, she *did*. In fact, she had *two*!
Twins! They sure liven up the house!
This parka isn't bad.
You, on the other hand, don't look great... Why not come to Brittany with us in July?
We could go fishing together!
Cash or credit?
Don't you think Veronique will mind?
Veronique? Are you kidding? If you're around, at least she'll have me out of the way.
FISH & TACKLE
What's wrong now?
Can't I invite a friend to come spend a few days with us?
With *you!*
It's just a handy excuse for you to dump all the work on me!
While you're at it, maybe you'd like Jean to take care of the kids?
Yes, well luckily Catherine will be there to give me a hand!
Catherine? I forgot about her... Will she be there in July too?
Oh no! He threw up on me again
WAAAAAAHH!!
Heh heh... Two singles... *Heh heh heh...*
WAAAAAAHH!!!
WAAAAAAAAHH!!
1

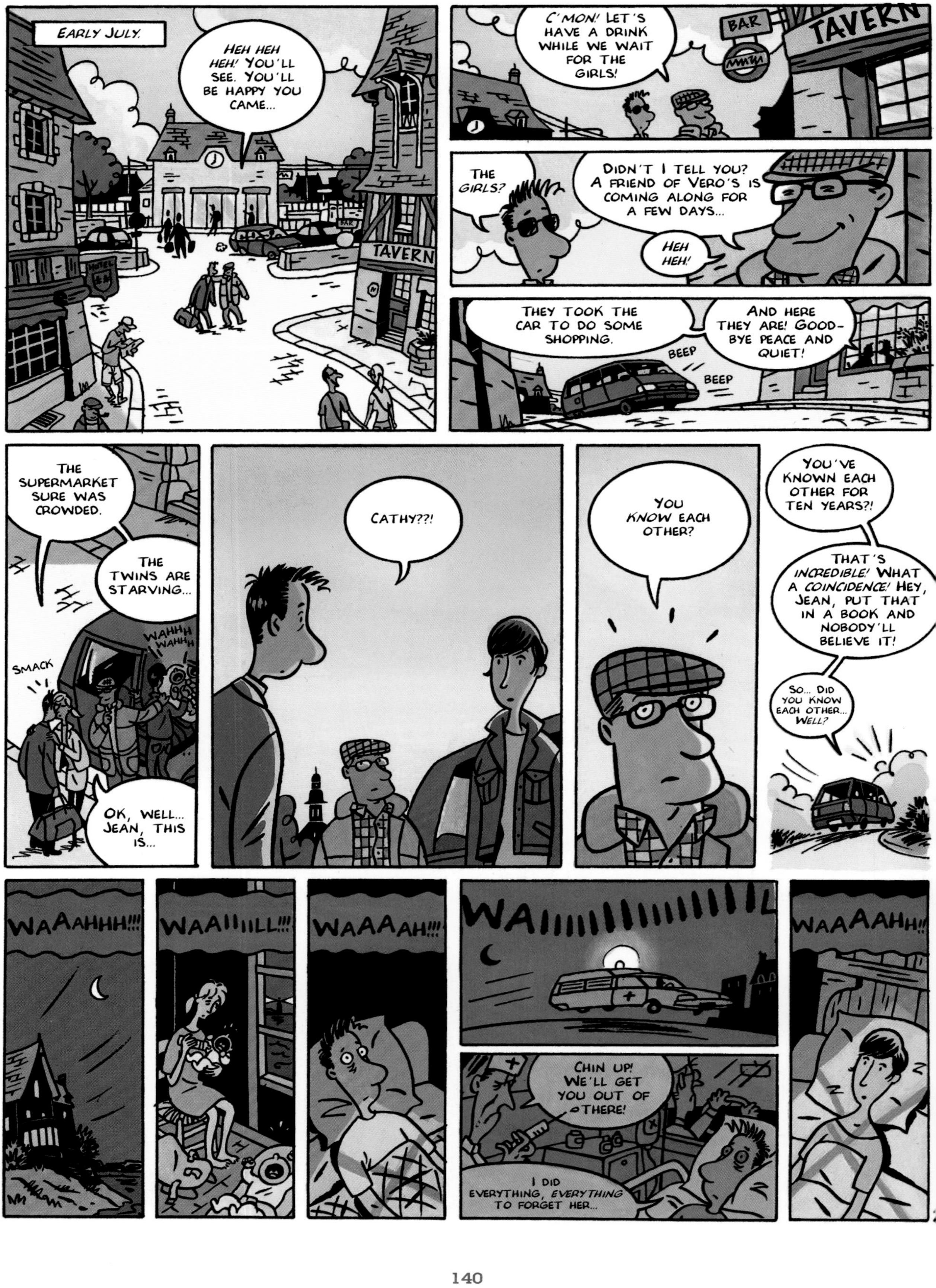
EARLY JULY.
HEH HEH HEH! YOU'LL SEE. YOU'LL BE HAPPY YOU CAME...
TAVERN
C'MON! LET'S HAVE A DRINK WHILE WE WAIT FOR THE GIRLS!
BAR
TAVERN
THE GIRLS?
DIDN'T I TELL YOU? A FRIEND OF VERO'S IS COMING ALONG FOR A FEW DAYS...
HEH HEH!
THEY TOOK THE CAR TO DO SOME SHOPPING.
AND HERE THEY ARE! GOOD-BYE PEACE AND QUIET!
BEEP
BEEP
THE SUPERMARKET SURE WAS CROWDED.
THE TWINS ARE STARVING...
WAHHH WAHHH
SMACK
OK, WELL... JEAN, THIS IS...
CATHY??!
YOU KNOW EACH OTHER?
YOU'VE KNOWN EACH OTHER FOR TEN YEARS?!
THAT'S INCREDIBLE! WHAT A COINCIDENCE! HEY, JEAN, PUT THAT IN A BOOK AND NOBODY'LL BELIEVE IT!
SO... DID YOU KNOW EACH OTHER... WELL?
WAAHHH!!!
WAAIIIILL!!!
WAAAAH!!!
WAIIIIIIIIIIIIIIL
WAAAAHH!!!
CHIN UP! WE'LL GET YOU OUT OF THERE!
I DID EVERYTHING, EVERYTHING TO FORGET HER...

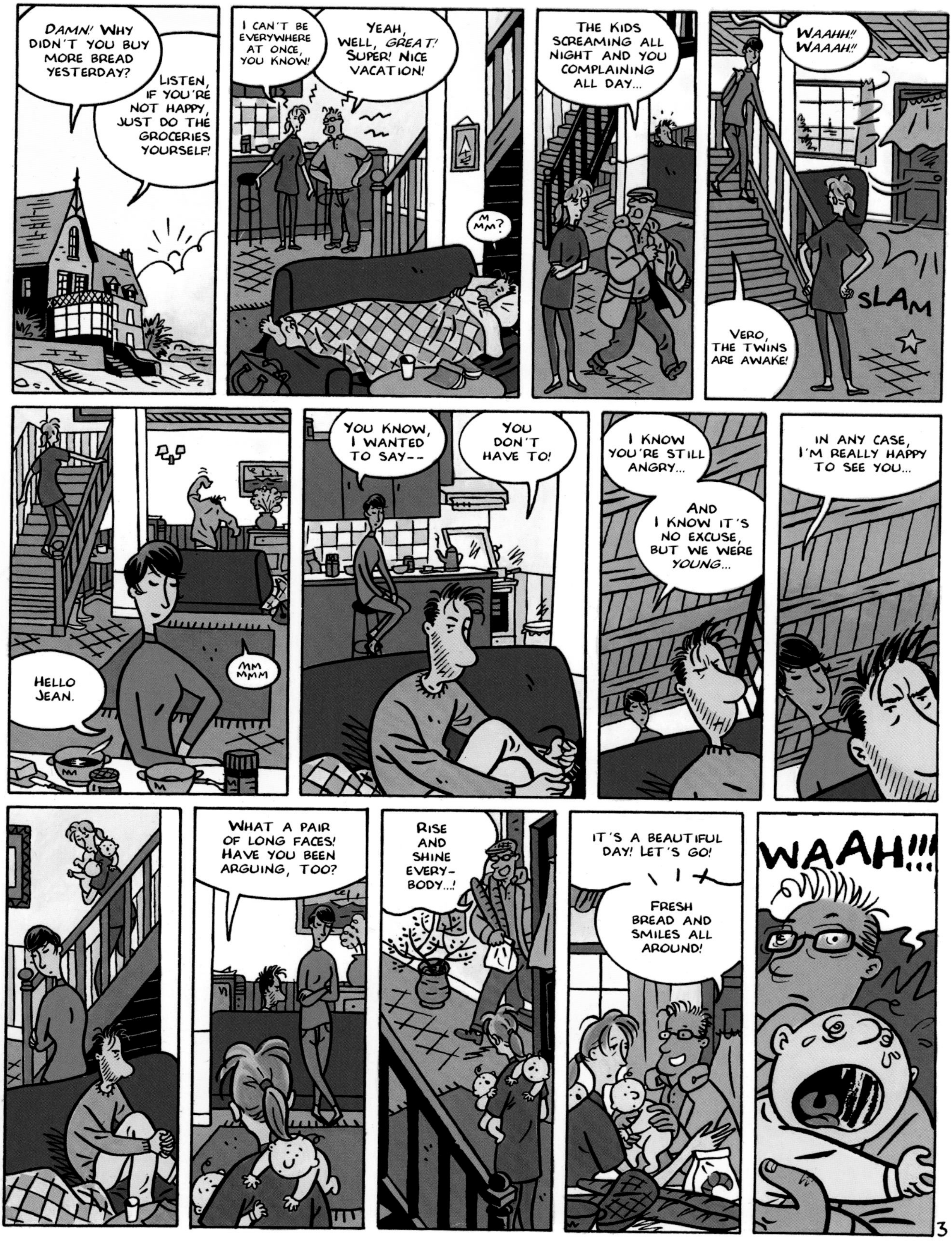
DAMN! WHY DIDN'T YOU BUY MORE BREAD YESTERDAY?
LISTEN, IF YOU'RE NOT HAPPY, JUST DO THE GROCERIES YOURSELF!
I CAN'T BE EVERYWHERE AT ONCE, YOU KNOW!
YEAH, WELL, GREAT! SUPER! NICE VACATION!
M MM?
THE KIDS SCREAMING ALL NIGHT AND YOU COMPLAINING ALL DAY...
WAAHH!! WAAAH!!
SLAM
VERO, THE TWINS ARE AWAKE!
HELLO JEAN.
MM MMM
YOU KNOW, I WANTED TO SAY--
YOU DON'T HAVE TO!
I KNOW YOU'RE STILL ANGRY...
AND I KNOW IT'S NO EXCUSE, BUT WE WERE YOUNG...
IN ANY CASE, I'M REALLY HAPPY TO SEE YOU...
WHAT A PAIR OF LONG FACES! HAVE YOU BEEN ARGUING, TOO?
RISE AND SHINE EVERY-BODY...!
IT'S A BEAUTIFUL DAY! LET'S GO!
FRESH BREAD AND SMILES ALL AROUND!
WAAH!!!
3

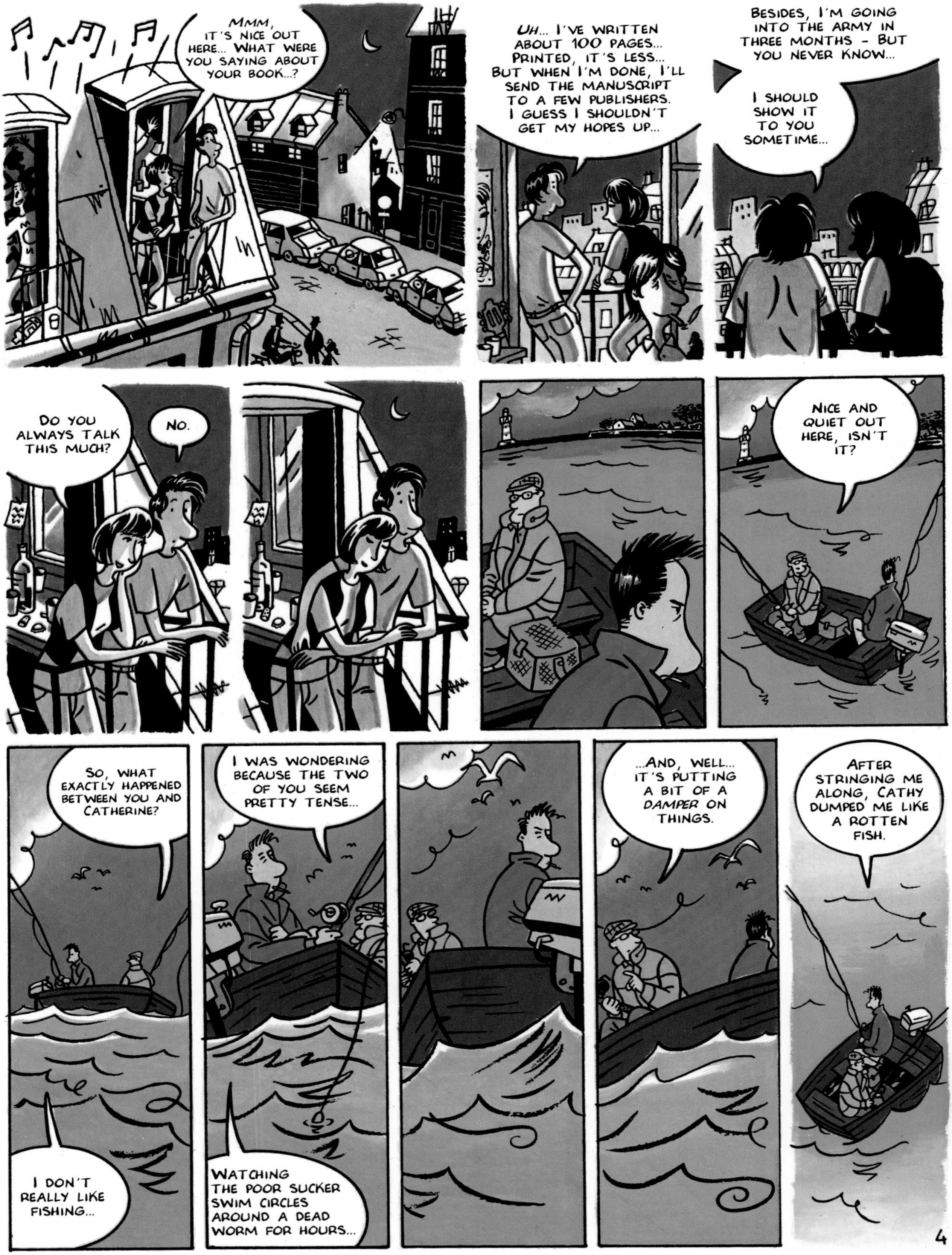
MMM, IT'S NICE OUT HERE... WHAT WERE YOU SAYING ABOUT YOUR BOOK...?
UH... I'VE WRITTEN ABOUT 100 PAGES... PRINTED, IT'S LESS... BUT WHEN I'M DONE, I'LL SEND THE MANUSCRIPT TO A FEW PUBLISHERS. I GUESS I SHOULDN'T GET MY HOPES UP...
BESIDES, I'M GOING INTO THE ARMY IN THREE MONTHS - BUT YOU NEVER KNOW...
I SHOULD SHOW IT TO YOU SOMETIME...
DO YOU ALWAYS TALK THIS MUCH?
NO.
NICE AND QUIET OUT HERE, ISN'T IT?
SO, WHAT EXACTLY HAPPENED BETWEEN YOU AND CATHERINE?
I DON'T REALLY LIKE FISHING...
I WAS WONDERING BECAUSE THE TWO OF YOU SEEM PRETTY TENSE...
WATCHING THE POOR SUCKER SWIM CIRCLES AROUND A DEAD WORM FOR HOURS...
...AND, WELL... IT'S PUTTING A BIT OF A DAMPER ON THINGS.
AFTER STRINGING ME ALONG, CATHY DUMPED ME LIKE A ROTTEN FISH.
4

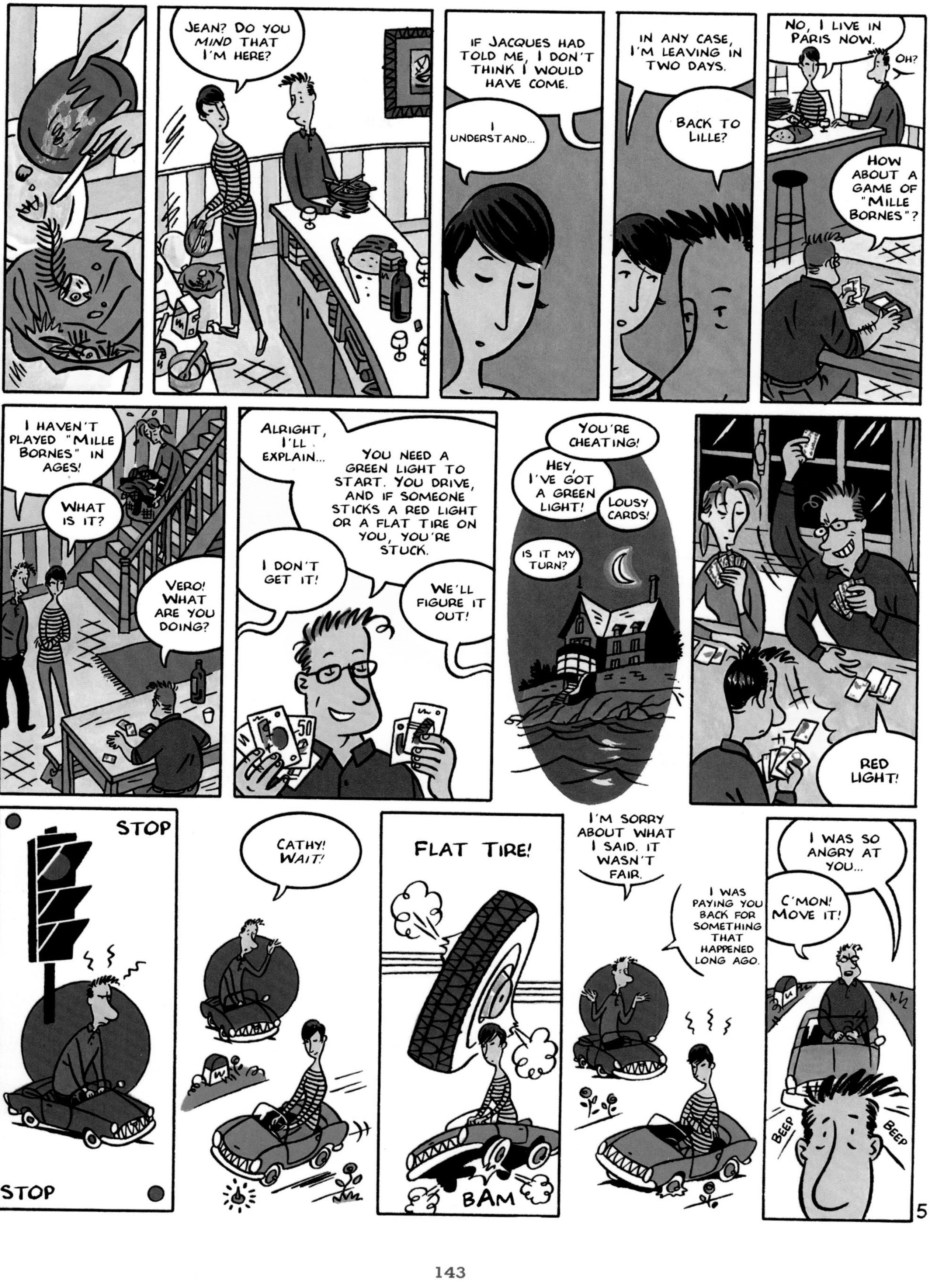
JEAN? DO YOU MIND THAT I'M HERE?
IF JACQUES HAD TOLD ME, I DON'T THINK I WOULD HAVE COME.
I UNDERSTAND...
IN ANY CASE, I'M LEAVING IN TWO DAYS.
BACK TO LILLE?
NO, I LIVE IN PARIS NOW.
OH?
HOW ABOUT A GAME OF "MILLE BORNES"?
I HAVEN'T PLAYED "MILLE BORNES" IN AGES!
WHAT IS IT?
VERO! WHAT ARE YOU DOING?
ALRIGHT, I'LL EXPLAIN...
YOU NEED A GREEN LIGHT TO START. YOU DRIVE, AND IF SOMEONE STICKS A RED LIGHT OR A FLAT TIRE ON YOU, YOU'RE STUCK.
I DON'T GET IT!
WE'LL FIGURE IT OUT!
YOU'RE CHEATING!
HEY, I'VE GOT A GREEN LIGHT!
LOUSY CARDS!
IS IT MY TURN?
RED LIGHT!
STOP
STOP
CATHY! WAIT!
FLAT TIRE!
BAM
I'M SORRY ABOUT WHAT I SAID. IT WASN'T FAIR.
I WAS PAYING YOU BACK FOR SOMETHING THAT HAPPENED LONG AGO.
I WAS SO ANGRY AT YOU...
C'MON! MOVE IT!
BEEP
BEEP
5

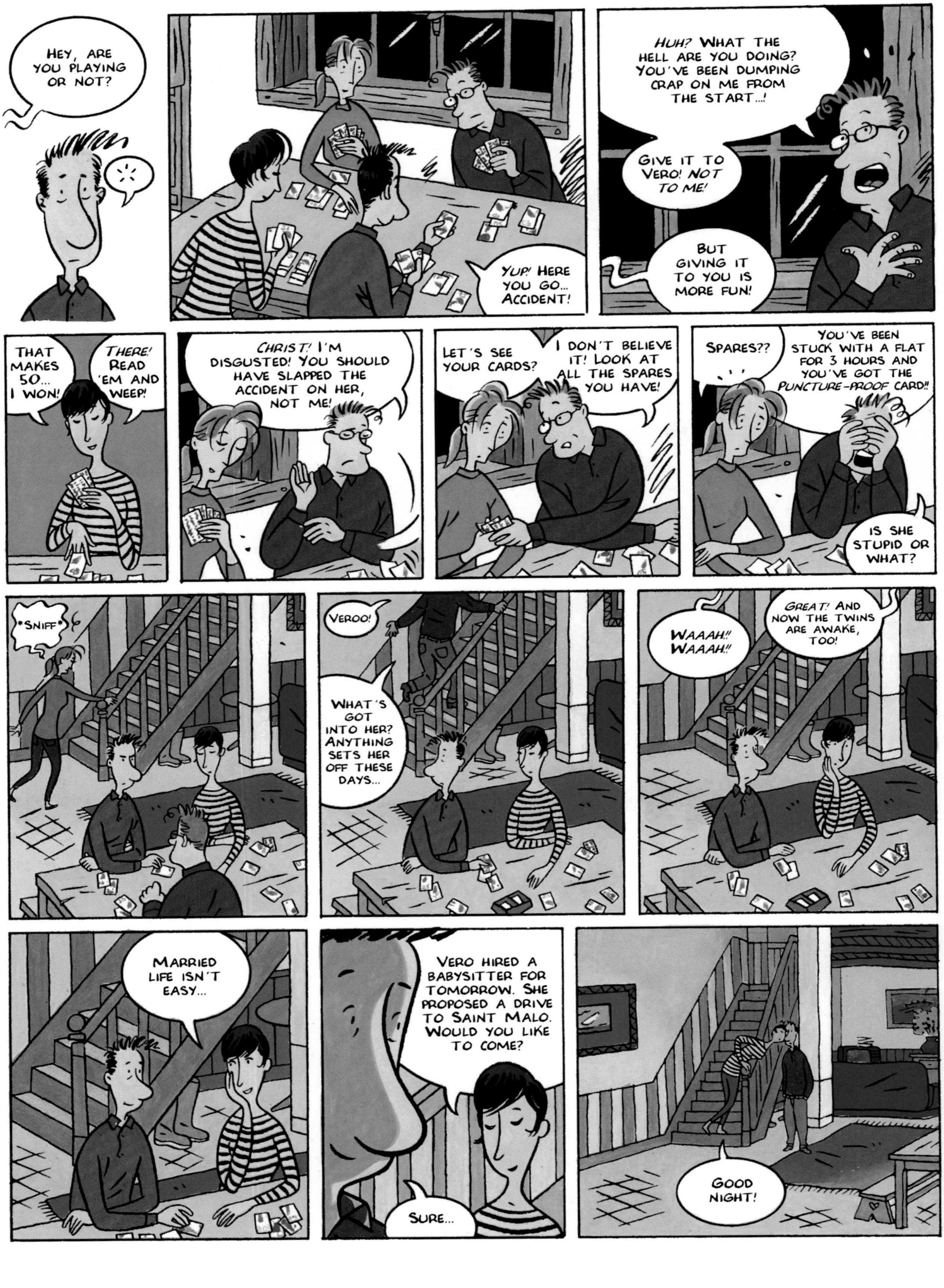
HEY, ARE YOU PLAYING OR NOT?
YUP! HERE YOU GO... ACCIDENT!
HUH? WHAT THE HELL ARE YOU DOING? YOU'VE BEEN DUMPING CRAP ON ME FROM THE START...!
GIVE IT TO VERO! NOT TO ME!
BUT GIVING IT TO YOU IS MORE FUN!
THAT MAKES 50... I WON!
THERE! READ 'EM AND WEEP!
CHRIST! I'M DISGUSTED! YOU SHOULD HAVE SLAPPED THE ACCIDENT ON HER, NOT ME!
LET'S SEE YOUR CARDS?
I DON'T BELIEVE IT! LOOK AT ALL THE SPARES YOU HAVE!
SPARES??
YOU'VE BEEN STUCK WITH A FLAT FOR 3 HOURS AND YOU'VE GOT THE PUNCTURE-PROOF CARD!!
IS SHE STUPID OR WHAT?
SNIFF
VEROO!
WHAT'S GOT INTO HER? ANYTHING SETS HER OFF THESE DAYS...
WAAAH!! WAAAH!!
GREAT! AND NOW THE TWINS ARE AWAKE, TOO!
MARRIED LIFE ISN'T EASY...
VERO HIRED A BABYSITTER FOR TOMORROW. SHE PROPOSED A DRIVE TO SAINT MALO. WOULD YOU LIKE TO COME?
SURE...
GOOD NIGHT!

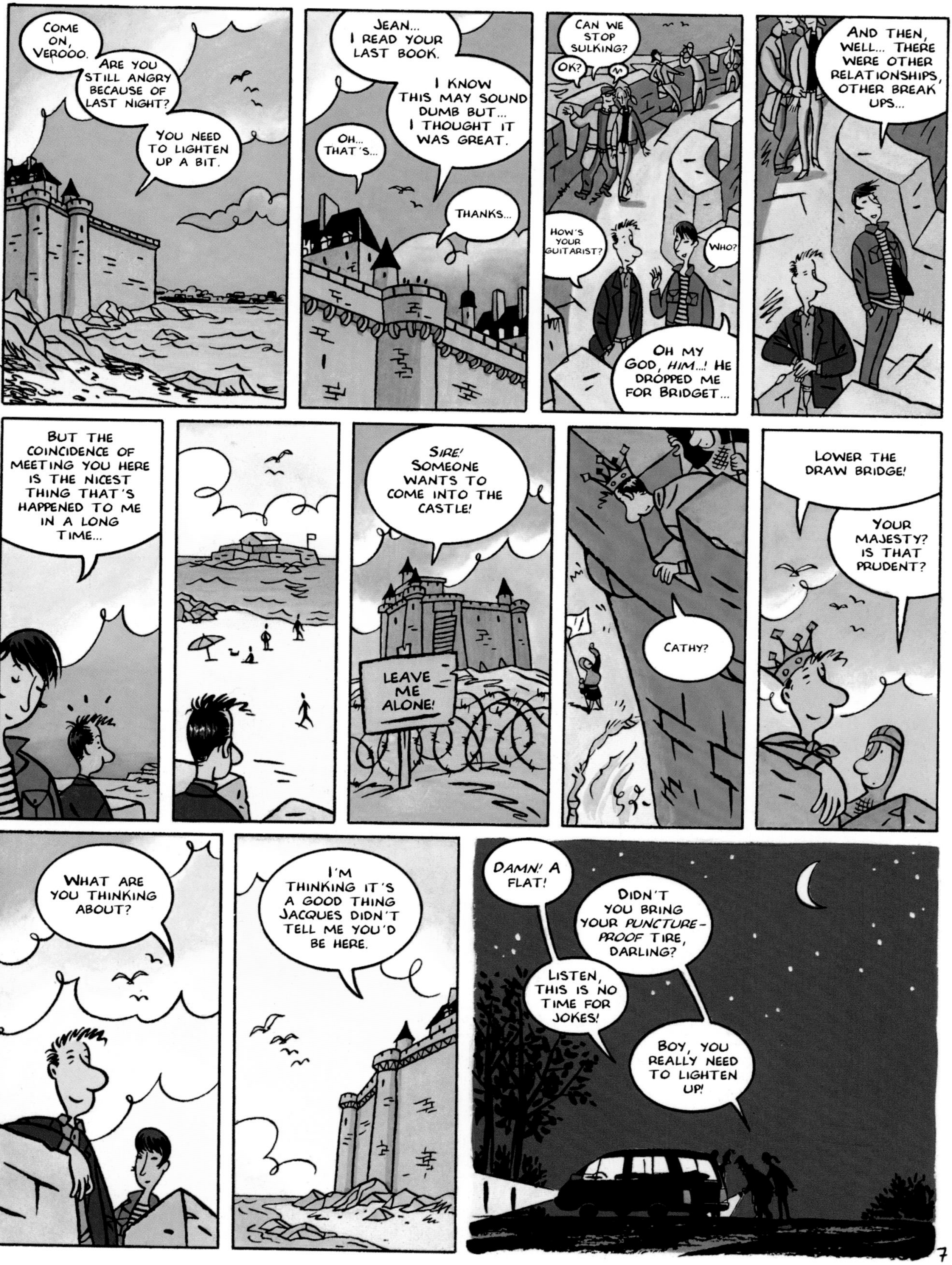
COME ON, VEROOO.
ARE YOU STILL ANGRY BECAUSE OF LAST NIGHT?
YOU NEED TO LIGHTEN UP A BIT.
JEAN... I READ YOUR LAST BOOK.
I KNOW THIS MAY SOUND DUMB BUT... I THOUGHT IT WAS GREAT.
OH... THAT'S...
THANKS...
CAN WE STOP SULKING?
OK?
HOW'S YOUR GUITARIST?
WHO?
OH MY GOD, HIM...! HE DROPPED ME FOR BRIDGET...
AND THEN, WELL... THERE WERE OTHER RELATIONSHIPS, OTHER BREAK UPS...
BUT THE COINCIDENCE OF MEETING YOU HERE IS THE NICEST THING THAT'S HAPPENED TO ME IN A LONG TIME...
SIRE! SOMEONE WANTS TO COME INTO THE CASTLE!
LEAVE ME ALONE!
CATHY?
LOWER THE DRAW BRIDGE!
YOUR MAJESTY? IS THAT PRUDENT?
WHAT ARE YOU THINKING ABOUT?
I'M THINKING IT'S A GOOD THING JACQUES DIDN'T TELL ME YOU'D BE HERE.
DAMN! A FLAT!
DIDN'T YOU BRING YOUR PUNCTURE-PROOF TIRE, DARLING?
LISTEN, THIS IS NO TIME FOR JOKES!
BOY, YOU REALLY NEED TO LIGHTEN UP!
7

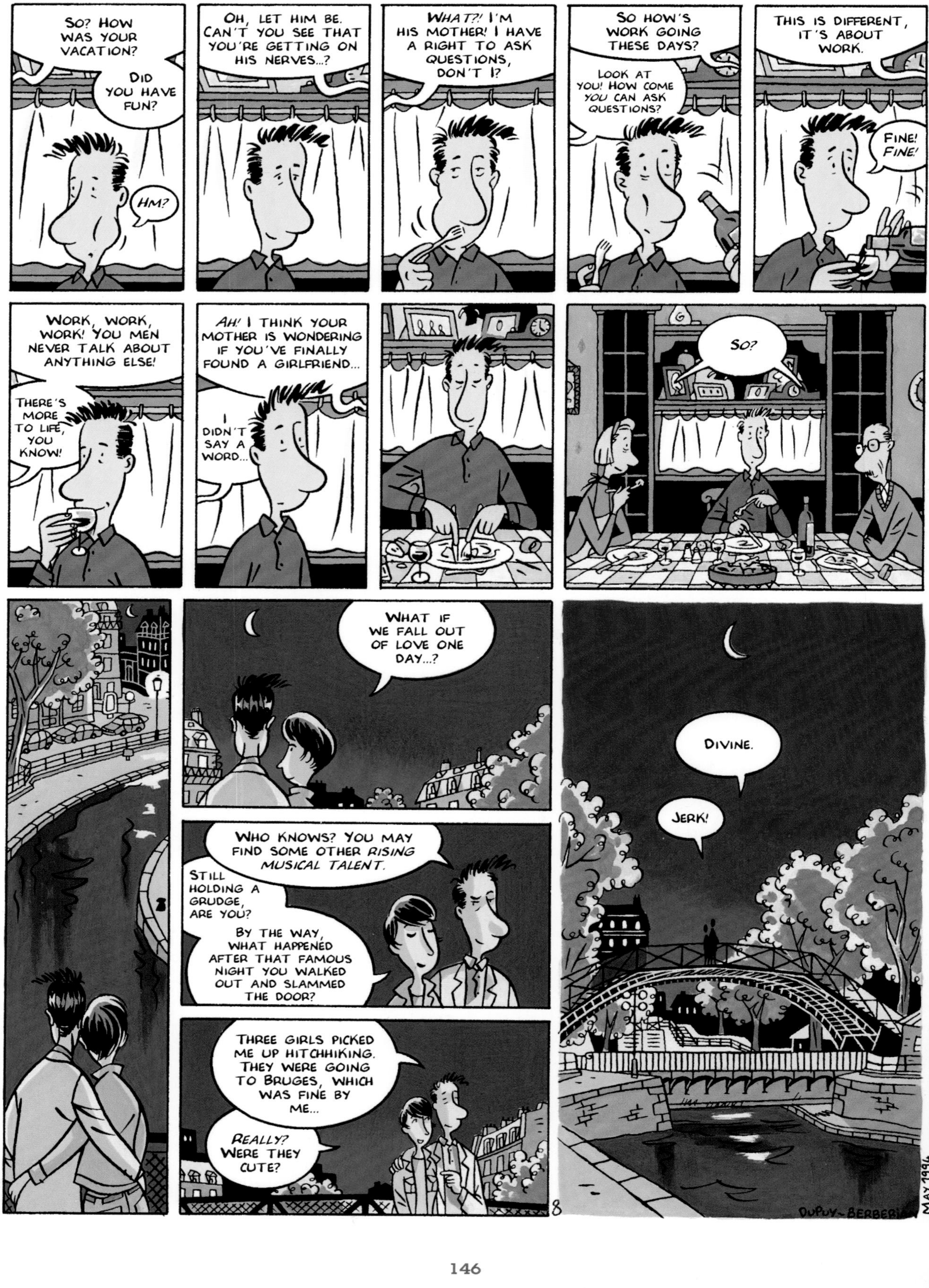
So? How was your vacation?
Did you have fun?
Hm?
Oh, let him be. Can't you see that you're getting on his nerves...?
What?! I'm his mother! I have a right to ask questions, don't I?
So how's work going these days?
Look at you! How come you can ask questions?
This is different, it's about work.
Fine! Fine!
Work, work, work! You men never talk about anything else!
There's more to life, you know!
Ah! I think your mother is wondering if you've finally found a girlfriend...
I didn't say a word...
So?
What if we fall out of love one day...?
Who knows? You may find some other rising musical talent.
Still holding a grudge, are you?
By the way, what happened after that famous night you walked out and slammed the door?
Three girls picked me up hitchhiking. They were going to Bruges, which was fine by me...
Really? Were they cute?
Divine.
Jerk!
8
Dupuy-Berberian
May 1994

MONSIEUR JEAN

LET'S BE HAPPY BUT NOT SHOW IT

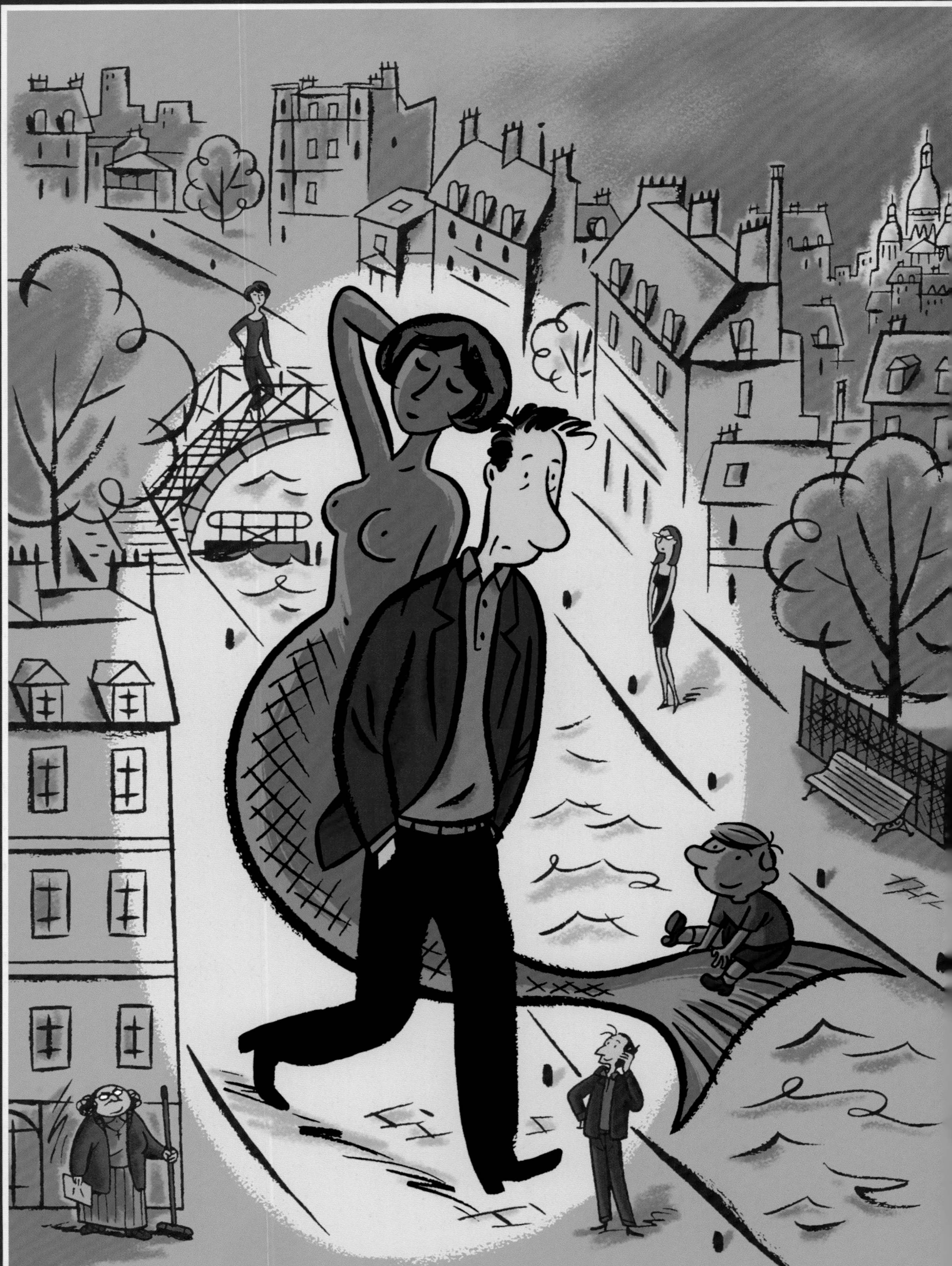

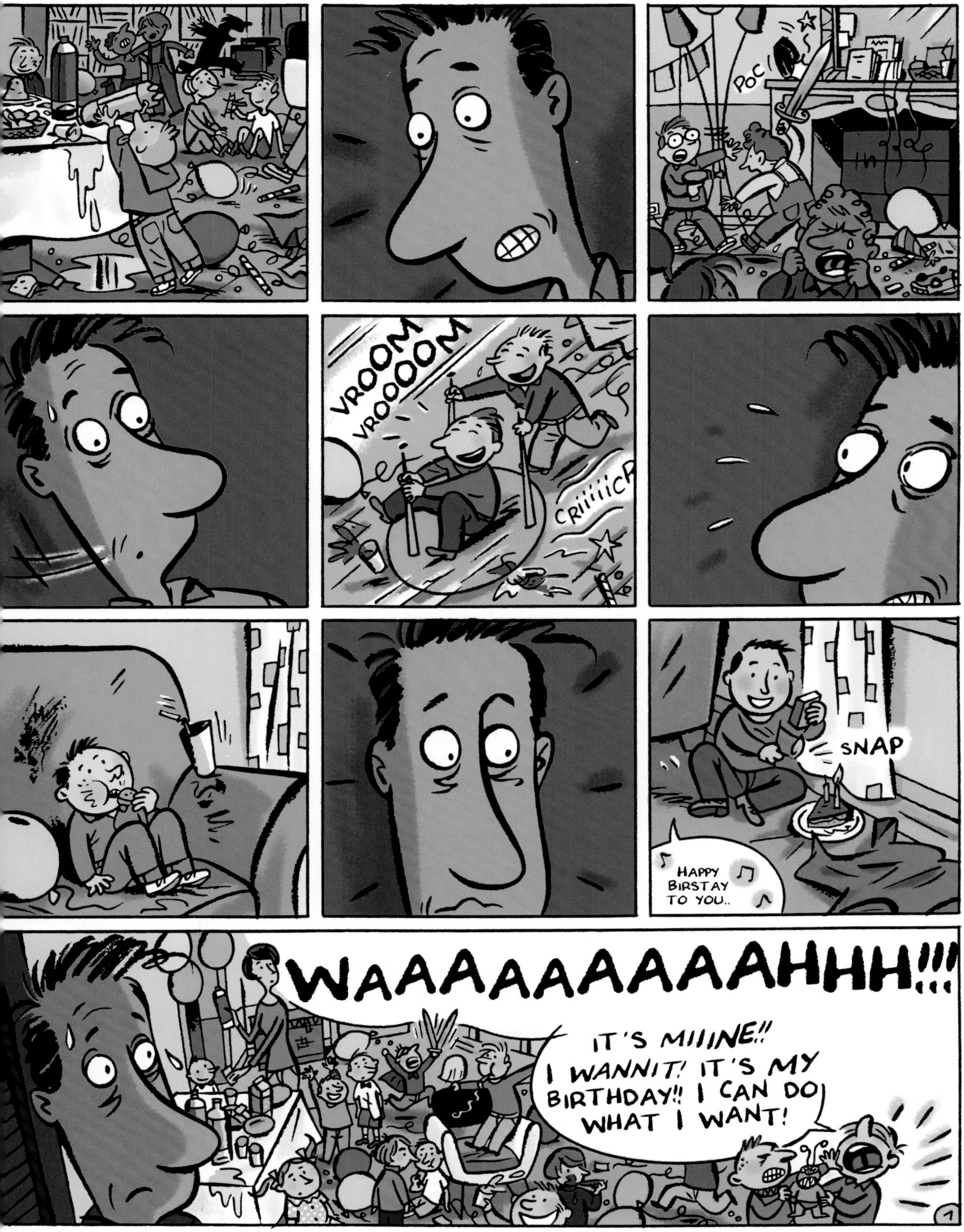
POC
VROOM
VROOOOOM
CRiiiiiCR
SNAP
HAPPY BIRSTAY TO YOU..
WAAAAAAAAAAHHH!!!
IT'S MIIINE!! I WANNIT! IT'S MY BIRTHDAY!! I CAN DO WHAT I WANT!

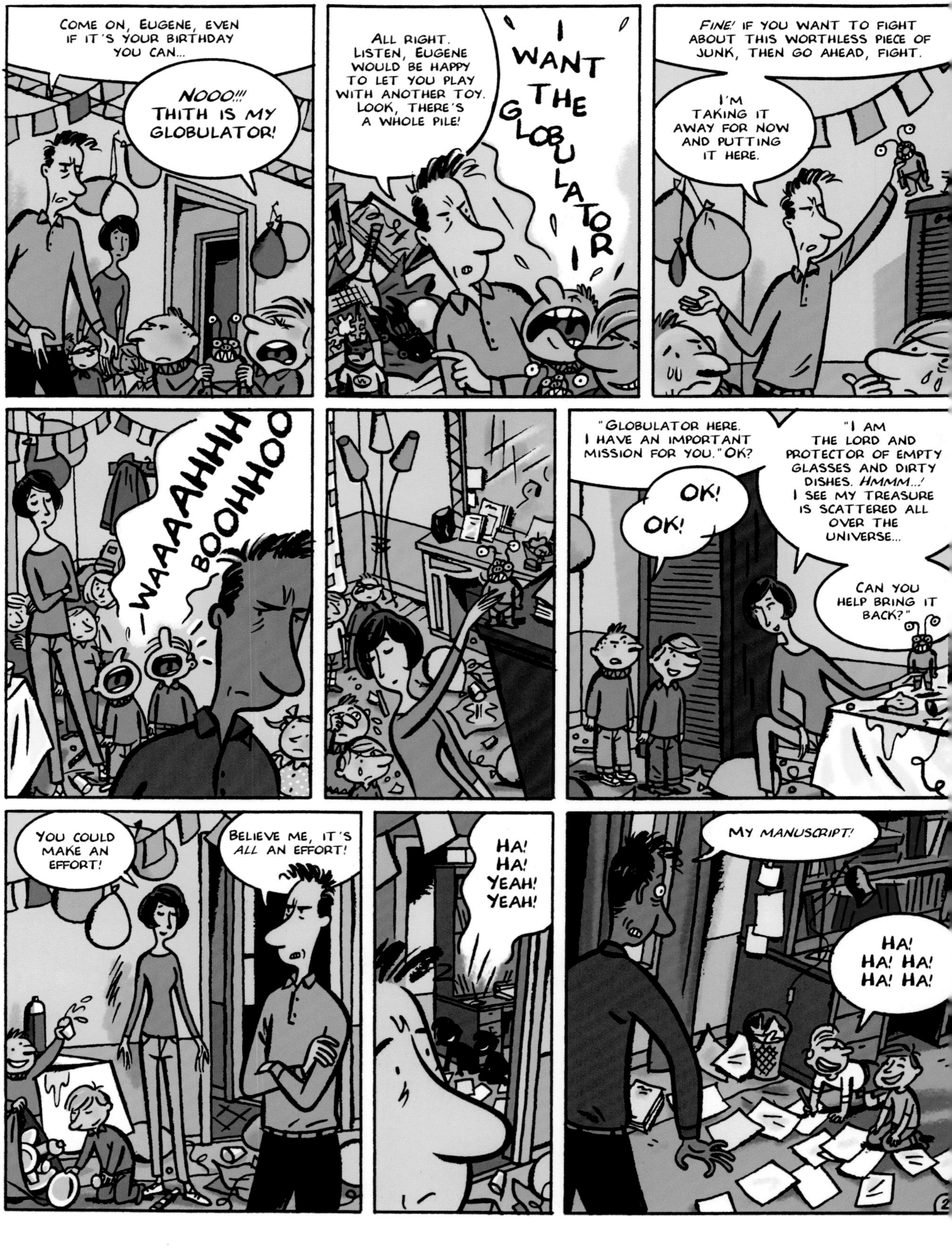
COME ON, EUGENE, EVEN IF IT'S YOUR BIRTHDAY YOU CAN...
NOOO!!! THITH IS MY GLOBULATOR!
ALL RIGHT. LISTEN, EUGENE WOULD BE HAPPY TO LET YOU PLAY WITH ANOTHER TOY. LOOK, THERE'S A WHOLE PILE!
I WANT THE GLOBULATOR
FINE! IF YOU WANT TO FIGHT ABOUT THIS WORTHLESS PIECE OF JUNK, THEN GO AHEAD, FIGHT.
I'M TAKING IT AWAY FOR NOW AND PUTTING IT HERE.
WAAAAHHH BOOHHOO
"GLOBULATOR HERE. I HAVE AN IMPORTANT MISSION FOR YOU." OK?
OK!
OK!
"I AM THE LORD AND PROTECTOR OF EMPTY GLASSES AND DIRTY DISHES. HMMM...! I SEE MY TREASURE IS SCATTERED ALL OVER THE UNIVERSE...
CAN YOU HELP BRING IT BACK?"
YOU COULD MAKE AN EFFORT!
BELIEVE ME, IT'S ALL AN EFFORT!
HA! HA! YEAH! YEAH!
MY MANUSCRIPT!
HA! HA! HA! HA! HA!

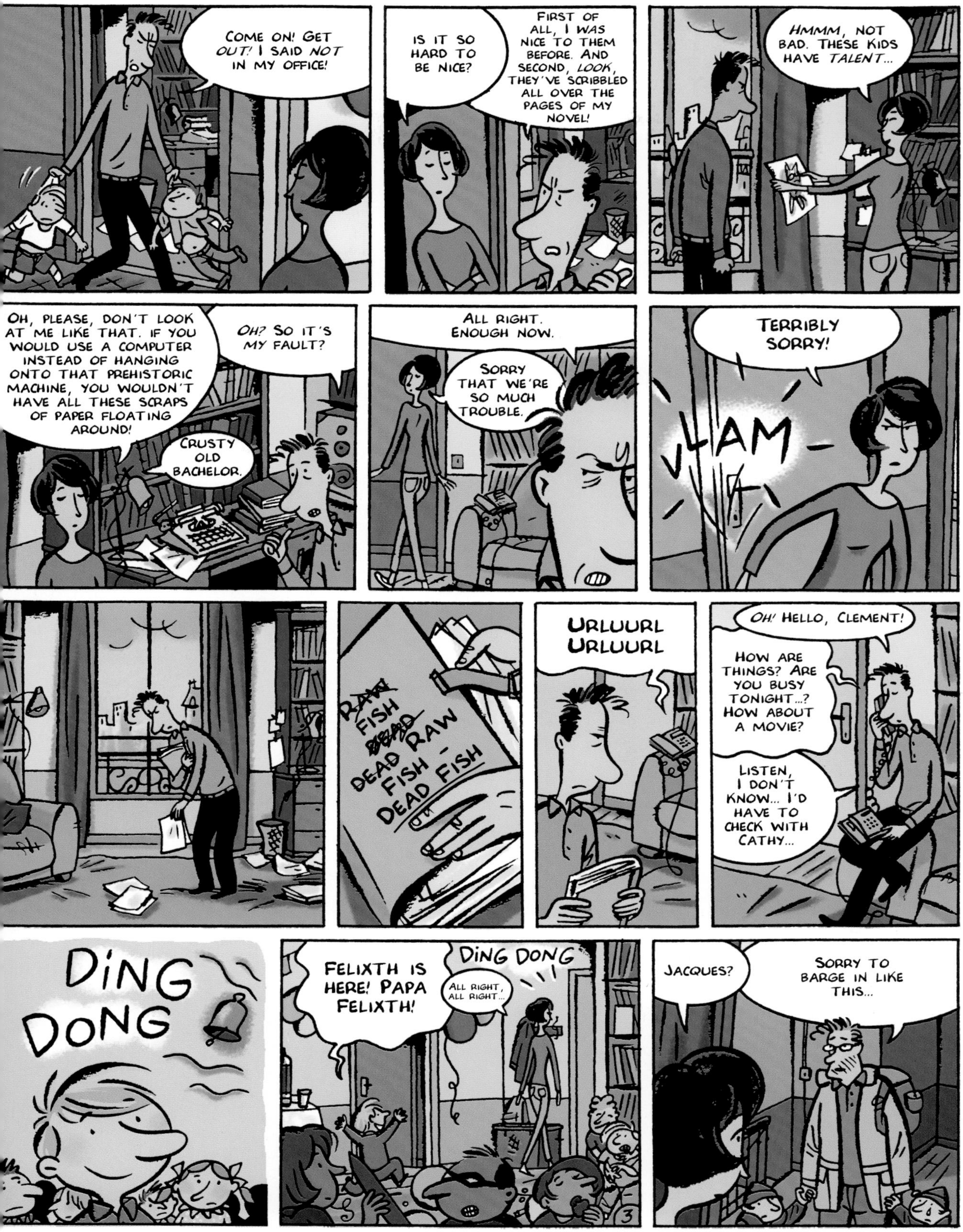

COME ON! GET OUT! I SAID NOT IN MY OFFICE!
IS IT SO HARD TO BE NICE?
FIRST OF ALL, I WAS NICE TO THEM BEFORE. AND SECOND, LOOK, THEY'VE SCRIBBLED ALL OVER THE PAGES OF MY NOVEL!
HMMM, NOT BAD. THESE KIDS HAVE TALENT...
OH, PLEASE, DON'T LOOK AT ME LIKE THAT. IF YOU WOULD USE A COMPUTER INSTEAD OF HANGING ONTO THAT PREHISTORIC MACHINE, YOU WOULDN'T HAVE ALL THESE SCRAPS OF PAPER FLOATING AROUND!
OH? SO IT'S MY FAULT?
CRUSTY OLD BACHELOR.
ALL RIGHT. ENOUGH NOW.
SORRY THAT WE'RE SO MUCH TROUBLE.
TERRIBLY SORRY!
VLAM
RAW FISH DEAD RAW FISH - DEAD FISH
URLUURL URLUURL
OH! HELLO, CLEMENT!
HOW ARE THINGS? ARE YOU BUSY TONIGHT...? HOW ABOUT A MOVIE?
LISTEN, I DON'T KNOW... I'D HAVE TO CHECK WITH CATHY...
DING DONG
FELIXTH IS HERE! PAPA FELIXTH!
DING DONG
ALL RIGHT, ALL RIGHT...
JACQUES?
SORRY TO BARGE IN LIKE THIS...

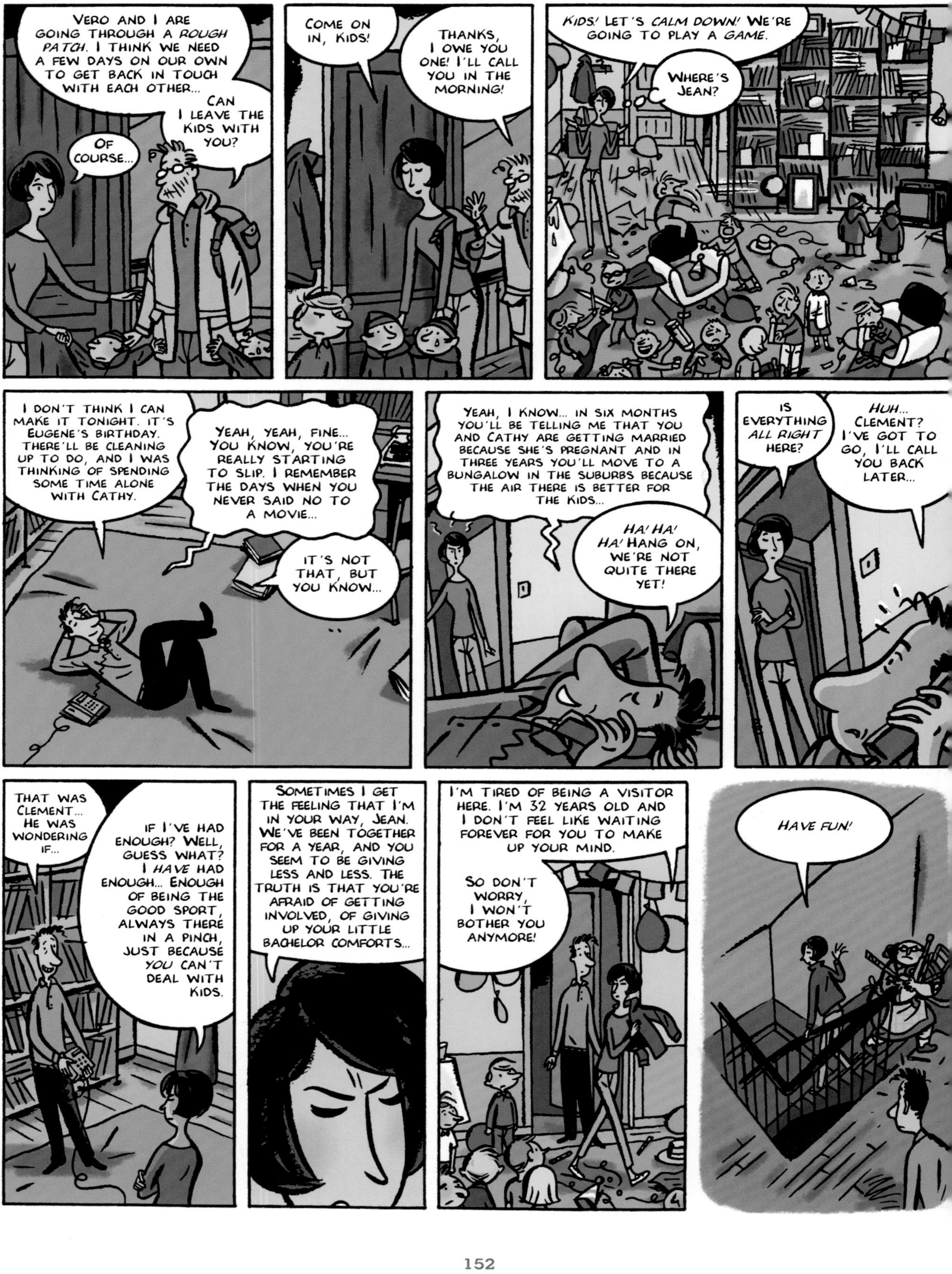
VERO AND I ARE GOING THROUGH A ROUGH PATCH. I THINK WE NEED A FEW DAYS ON OUR OWN TO GET BACK IN TOUCH WITH EACH OTHER...
CAN I LEAVE THE KIDS WITH YOU?
OF COURSE...
COME ON IN, KIDS!
THANKS, I OWE YOU ONE! I'LL CALL YOU IN THE MORNING!
KIDS! LET'S CALM DOWN! WE'RE GOING TO PLAY A GAME.
WHERE'S JEAN?
I DON'T THINK I CAN MAKE IT TONIGHT. IT'S EUGENE'S BIRTHDAY. THERE'LL BE CLEANING UP TO DO, AND I WAS THINKING OF SPENDING SOME TIME ALONE WITH CATHY.
YEAH, YEAH, FINE... YOU KNOW, YOU'RE REALLY STARTING TO SLIP. I REMEMBER THE DAYS WHEN YOU NEVER SAID NO TO A MOVIE...
IT'S NOT THAT, BUT YOU KNOW...
YEAH, I KNOW... IN SIX MONTHS YOU'LL BE TELLING ME THAT YOU AND CATHY ARE GETTING MARRIED BECAUSE SHE'S PREGNANT AND IN THREE YEARS YOU'LL MOVE TO A BUNGALOW IN THE SUBURBS BECAUSE THE AIR THERE IS BETTER FOR THE KIDS...
HA! HA! HA! HANG ON, WE'RE NOT QUITE THERE YET!
IS EVERYTHING ALL RIGHT HERE?
HUH... CLEMENT? I'VE GOT TO GO, I'LL CALL YOU BACK LATER...
THAT WAS CLEMENT... HE WAS WONDERING IF...
IF I'VE HAD ENOUGH? WELL, GUESS WHAT? I HAVE HAD ENOUGH... ENOUGH OF BEING THE GOOD SPORT, ALWAYS THERE IN A PINCH, JUST BECAUSE YOU CAN'T DEAL WITH KIDS.
SOMETIMES I GET THE FEELING THAT I'M IN YOUR WAY, JEAN. WE'VE BEEN TOGETHER FOR A YEAR, AND YOU SEEM TO BE GIVING LESS AND LESS. THE TRUTH IS THAT YOU'RE AFRAID OF GETTING INVOLVED, OF GIVING UP YOUR LITTLE BACHELOR COMFORTS...
I'M TIRED OF BEING A VISITOR HERE. I'M 32 YEARS OLD AND I DON'T FEEL LIKE WAITING FOREVER FOR YOU TO MAKE UP YOUR MIND.
SO DON'T WORRY, I WON'T BOTHER YOU ANYMORE!
HAVE FUN!

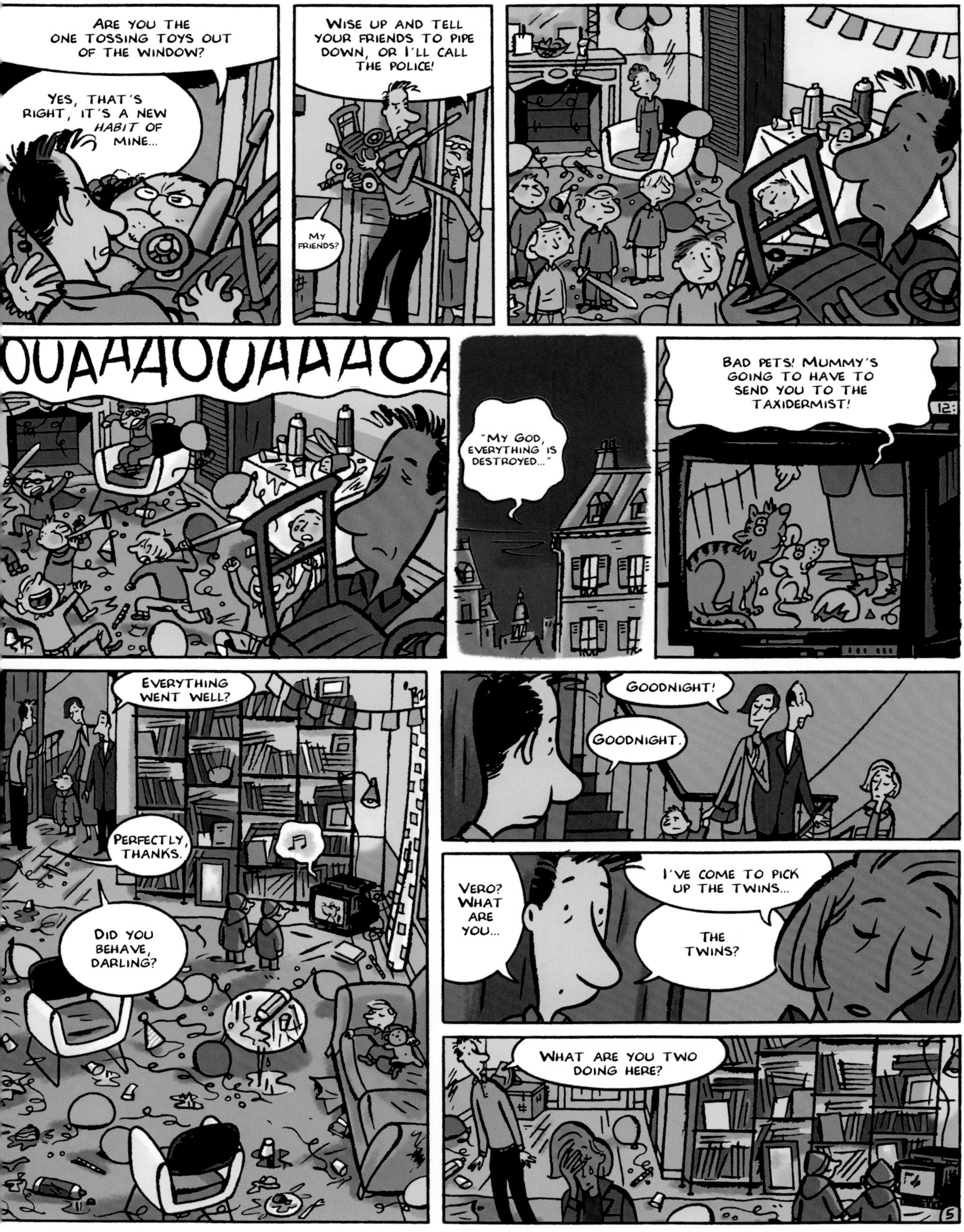
ARE YOU THE ONE TOSSING TOYS OUT OF THE WINDOW?
YES, THAT'S RIGHT, IT'S A NEW HABIT OF MINE...
WISE UP AND TELL YOUR FRIENDS TO PIPE DOWN, OR I'LL CALL THE POLICE!
MY FRIENDS?
OUAAAOUAAAAOA
"MY GOD, EVERYTHING IS DESTROYED..."
BAD PETS! MUMMY'S GOING TO HAVE TO SEND YOU TO THE TAXIDERMIST!
EVERYTHING WENT WELL?
PERFECTLY, THANKS.
DID YOU BEHAVE, DARLING?
GOODNIGHT!
GOODNIGHT.
VERO? WHAT ARE YOU...
I'VE COME TO PICK UP THE TWINS...
THE TWINS?
WHAT ARE YOU TWO DOING HERE?
5

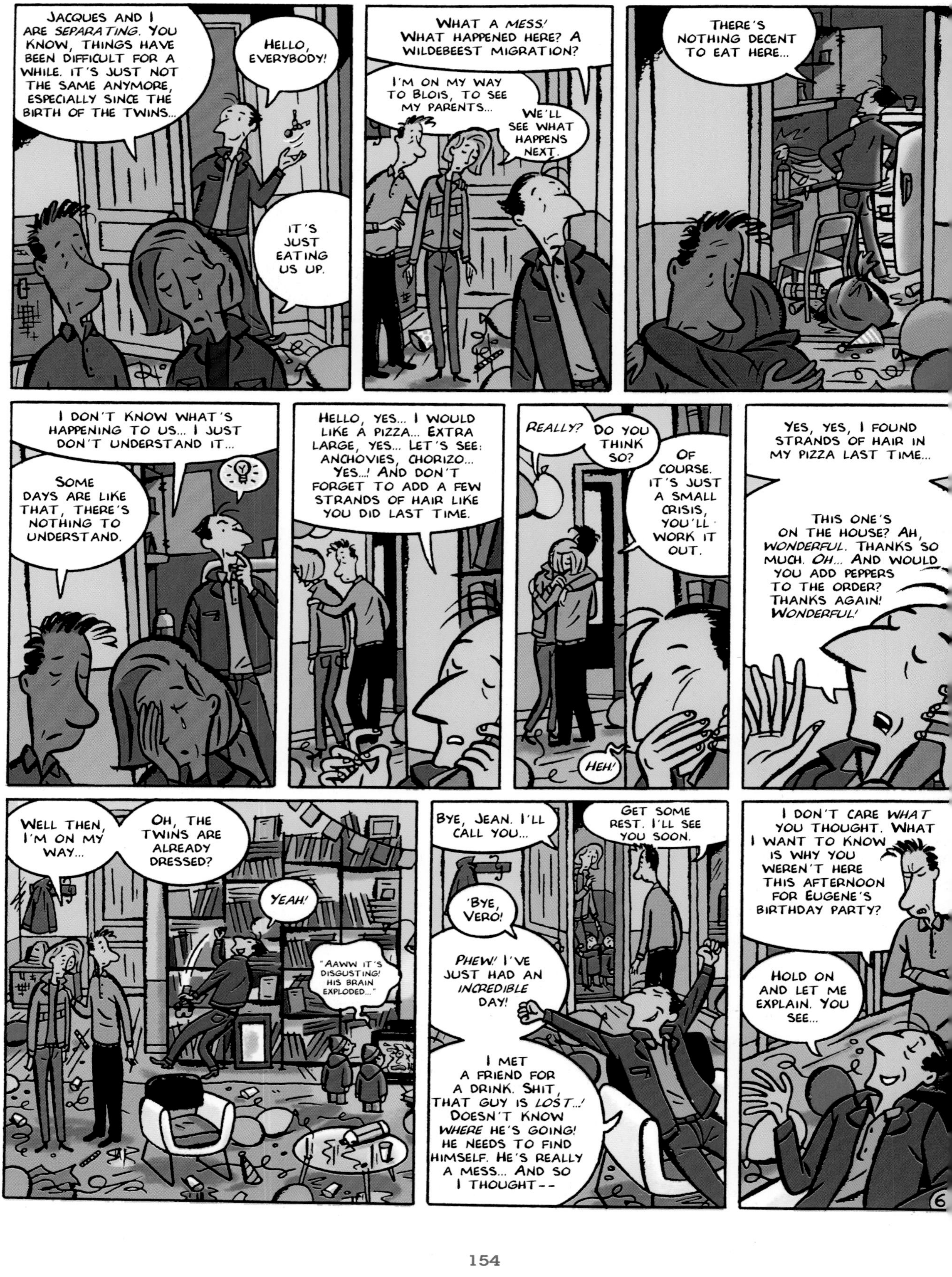
JACQUES AND I ARE *SEPARATING*. YOU KNOW, THINGS HAVE BEEN DIFFICULT FOR A WHILE. IT'S JUST NOT THE SAME ANYMORE, ESPECIALLY SINCE THE BIRTH OF THE TWINS...
HELLO, EVERYBODY!
IT'S JUST EATING US UP.
WHAT A *MESS!* WHAT HAPPENED HERE? A WILDEBEEST MIGRATION?
I'M ON MY WAY TO BLOIS, TO SEE MY PARENTS...
WE'LL SEE WHAT HAPPENS NEXT.
THERE'S NOTHING DECENT TO EAT HERE...
I DON'T KNOW WHAT'S HAPPENING TO US... I JUST DON'T UNDERSTAND IT...
SOME DAYS ARE LIKE THAT, THERE'S NOTHING TO UNDERSTAND.
HELLO, YES... I WOULD LIKE A PIZZA... EXTRA LARGE, YES... LET'S SEE: ANCHOVIES, CHORIZO... YES...! AND DON'T FORGET TO ADD A FEW STRANDS OF HAIR LIKE YOU DID LAST TIME.
REALLY?
DO YOU THINK SO?
OF COURSE. IT'S JUST A SMALL CRISIS, YOU'LL WORK IT OUT.
HEH!
YES, YES, I FOUND STRANDS OF HAIR IN MY PIZZA LAST TIME...
THIS ONE'S ON THE HOUSE? AH, *WONDERFUL*. THANKS SO MUCH. *OH*... AND WOULD YOU ADD PEPPERS TO THE ORDER? THANKS AGAIN! *WONDERFUL!*
WELL THEN, I'M ON MY WAY...
OH, THE TWINS ARE ALREADY DRESSED?
YEAH!
"AAWW IT'S DISGUSTING! HIS BRAIN EXPLODED..."
BYE, JEAN. I'LL CALL YOU...
GET SOME REST. I'LL SEE YOU SOON.
'BYE, VERO!
PHEW! I'VE JUST HAD AN *INCREDIBLE* DAY!
I MET A FRIEND FOR A DRINK. SHIT, THAT GUY IS *LOST*...! DOESN'T KNOW *WHERE* HE'S GOING! HE NEEDS TO FIND HIMSELF. HE'S REALLY A MESS... AND SO I THOUGHT--
I DON'T CARE *WHAT* YOU THOUGHT. WHAT I WANT TO KNOW IS WHY YOU WEREN'T HERE THIS AFTERNOON FOR EUGENE'S BIRTHDAY PARTY?
HOLD ON AND LET ME EXPLAIN. YOU SEE...
6

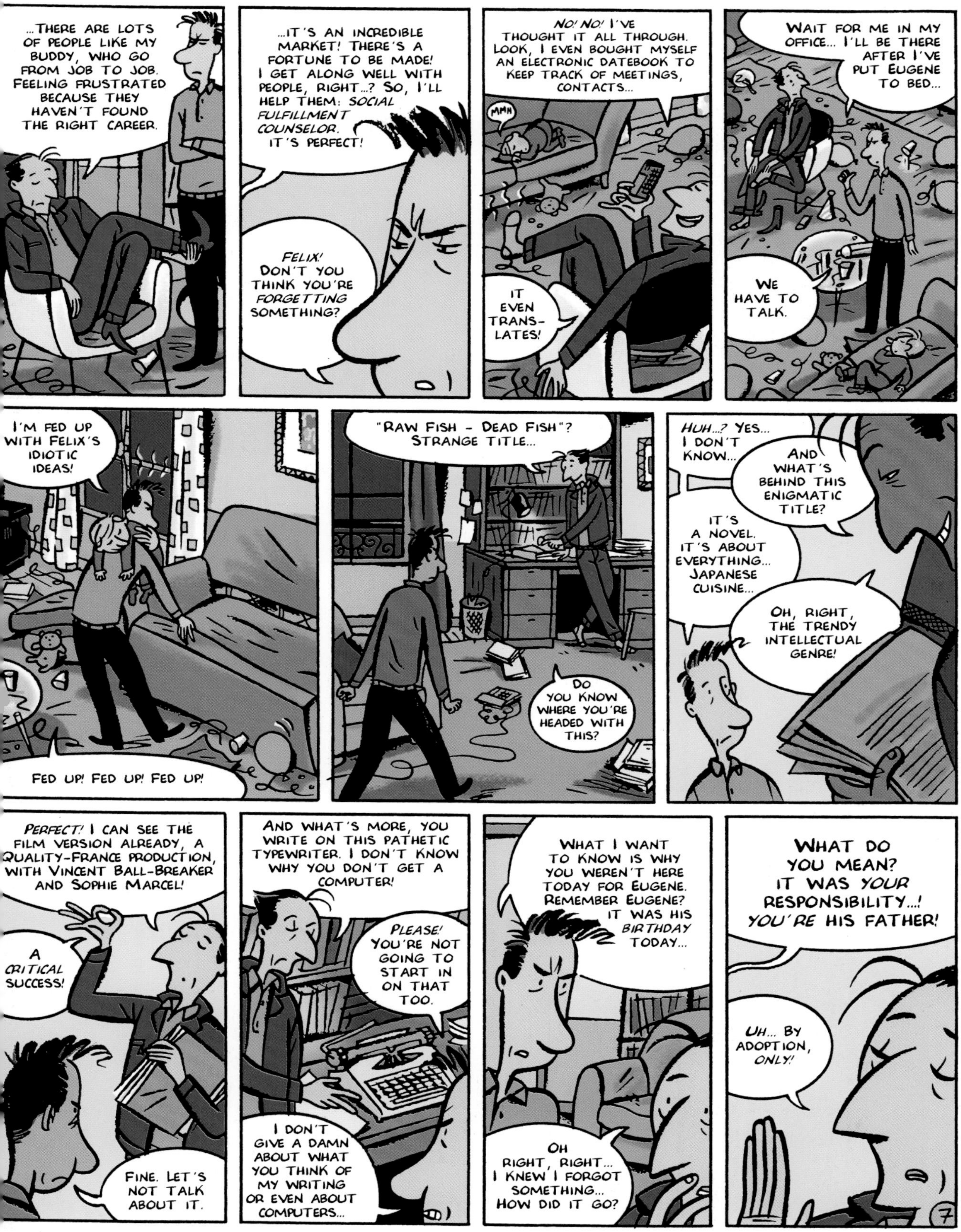
...THERE ARE LOTS OF PEOPLE LIKE MY BUDDY, WHO GO FROM JOB TO JOB. FEELING FRUSTRATED BECAUSE THEY HAVEN'T FOUND THE RIGHT CAREER.
...IT'S AN INCREDIBLE MARKET! THERE'S A FORTUNE TO BE MADE! I GET ALONG WELL WITH PEOPLE, RIGHT...? SO, I'LL HELP THEM: SOCIAL FULFILLMENT COUNSELOR. IT'S PERFECT!
FELIX! DON'T YOU THINK YOU'RE FORGETTING SOMETHING?
NO! NO! I'VE THOUGHT IT ALL THROUGH. LOOK, I EVEN BOUGHT MYSELF AN ELECTRONIC DATEBOOK TO KEEP TRACK OF MEETINGS, CONTACTS...
MMH
IT EVEN TRANS-LATES!
WAIT FOR ME IN MY OFFICE... I'LL BE THERE AFTER I'VE PUT EUGENE TO BED...
WE HAVE TO TALK.
I'M FED UP WITH FELIX'S IDIOTIC IDEAS!
FED UP! FED UP! FED UP!
"RAW FISH - DEAD FISH"? STRANGE TITLE...
DO YOU KNOW WHERE YOU'RE HEADED WITH THIS?
HUH...? YES... I DON'T KNOW...
AND WHAT'S BEHIND THIS ENIGMATIC TITLE?
IT'S A NOVEL. IT'S ABOUT EVERYTHING... JAPANESE CUISINE...
OH, RIGHT, THE TRENDY INTELLECTUAL GENRE!
PERFECT! I CAN SEE THE FILM VERSION ALREADY, A QUALITY-FRANCE PRODUCTION, WITH VINCENT BALL-BREAKER AND SOPHIE MARCEL!
A CRITICAL SUCCESS!
FINE. LET'S NOT TALK ABOUT IT.
AND WHAT'S MORE, YOU WRITE ON THIS PATHETIC TYPEWRITER. I DON'T KNOW WHY YOU DON'T GET A COMPUTER!
PLEASE! YOU'RE NOT GOING TO START IN ON THAT TOO.
I DON'T GIVE A DAMN ABOUT WHAT YOU THINK OF MY WRITING OR EVEN ABOUT COMPUTERS...
WHAT I WANT TO KNOW IS WHY YOU WEREN'T HERE TODAY FOR EUGENE. REMEMBER EUGENE? IT WAS HIS BIRTHDAY TODAY...
OH RIGHT, RIGHT... I KNEW I FORGOT SOMETHING... HOW DID IT GO?
WHAT DO YOU MEAN? IT WAS YOUR RESPONSIBILITY...! YOU'RE HIS FATHER!
UH... BY ADOPTION, ONLY!
7

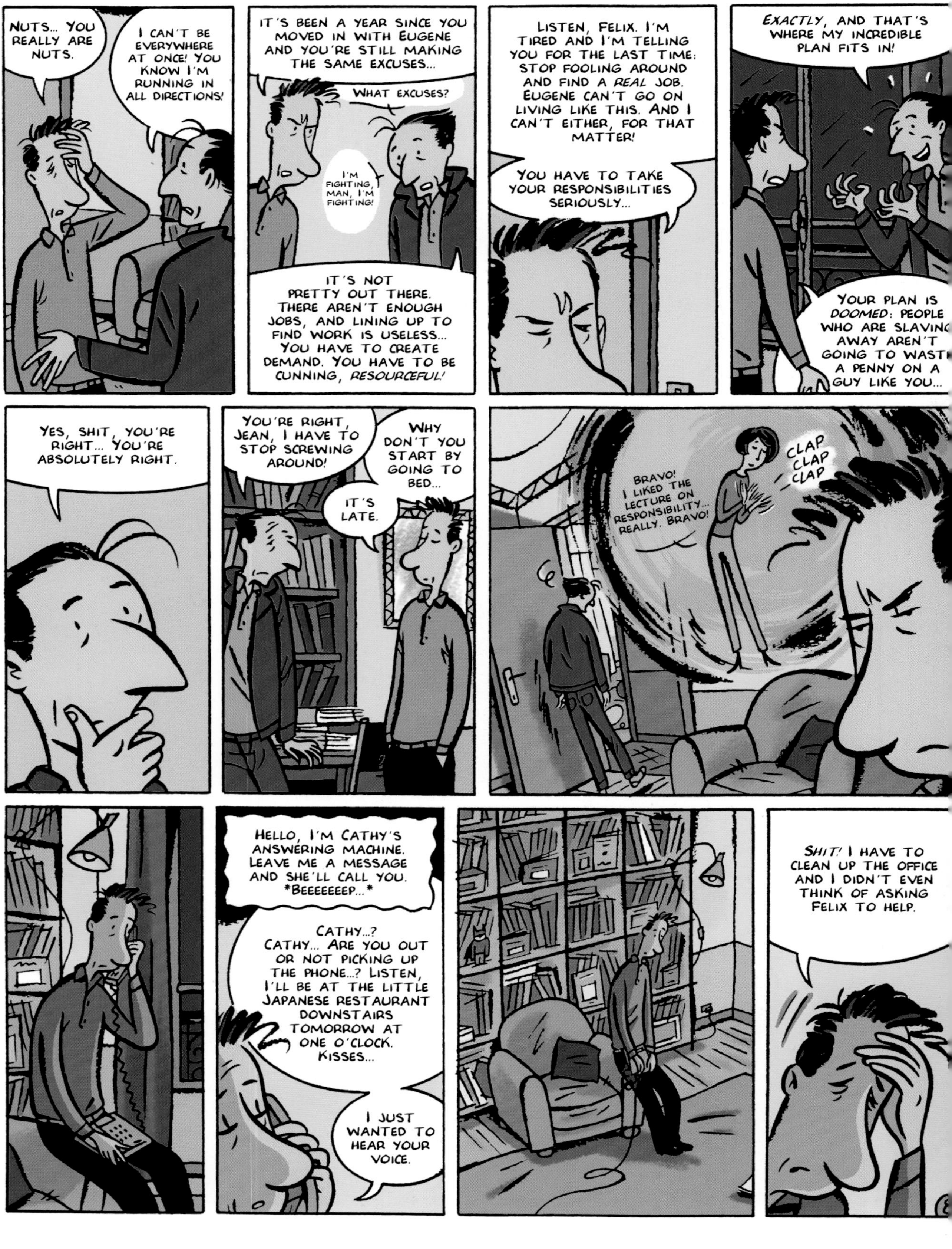
NUTS... YOU REALLY ARE NUTS.
I CAN'T BE EVERYWHERE AT ONCE! YOU KNOW I'M RUNNING IN ALL DIRECTIONS!
IT'S BEEN A YEAR SINCE YOU MOVED IN WITH EUGENE AND YOU'RE STILL MAKING THE SAME EXCUSES...
WHAT EXCUSES?
I'M FIGHTING, MAN, I'M FIGHTING!
IT'S NOT PRETTY OUT THERE. THERE AREN'T ENOUGH JOBS, AND LINING UP TO FIND WORK IS USELESS... YOU HAVE TO CREATE DEMAND. YOU HAVE TO BE CUNNING, RESOURCEFUL!
LISTEN, FELIX. I'M TIRED AND I'M TELLING YOU FOR THE LAST TIME: STOP FOOLING AROUND AND FIND A REAL JOB. EUGENE CAN'T GO ON LIVING LIKE THIS. AND I CAN'T EITHER, FOR THAT MATTER!
YOU HAVE TO TAKE YOUR RESPONSIBILITIES SERIOUSLY...
EXACTLY, AND THAT'S WHERE MY INCREDIBLE PLAN FITS IN!
YOUR PLAN IS DOOMED: PEOPLE WHO ARE SLAVING AWAY AREN'T GOING TO WASTE A PENNY ON A GUY LIKE YOU...
YES, SHIT, YOU'RE RIGHT... YOU'RE ABSOLUTELY RIGHT.
YOU'RE RIGHT, JEAN, I HAVE TO STOP SCREWING AROUND!
WHY DON'T YOU START BY GOING TO BED...
IT'S LATE.
BRAVO! I LIKED THE LECTURE ON RESPONSIBILITY... REALLY. BRAVO!
CLAP CLAP CLAP
HELLO, I'M CATHY'S ANSWERING MACHINE. LEAVE ME A MESSAGE AND SHE'LL CALL YOU. *BEEEEEEEP...*
CATHY...? CATHY... ARE YOU OUT OR NOT PICKING UP THE PHONE...? LISTEN, I'LL BE AT THE LITTLE JAPANESE RESTAURANT DOWNSTAIRS TOMORROW AT ONE O'CLOCK. KISSES...
I JUST WANTED TO HEAR YOUR VOICE.
SHIT! I HAVE TO CLEAN UP THE OFFICE AND I DIDN'T EVEN THINK OF ASKING FELIX TO HELP.

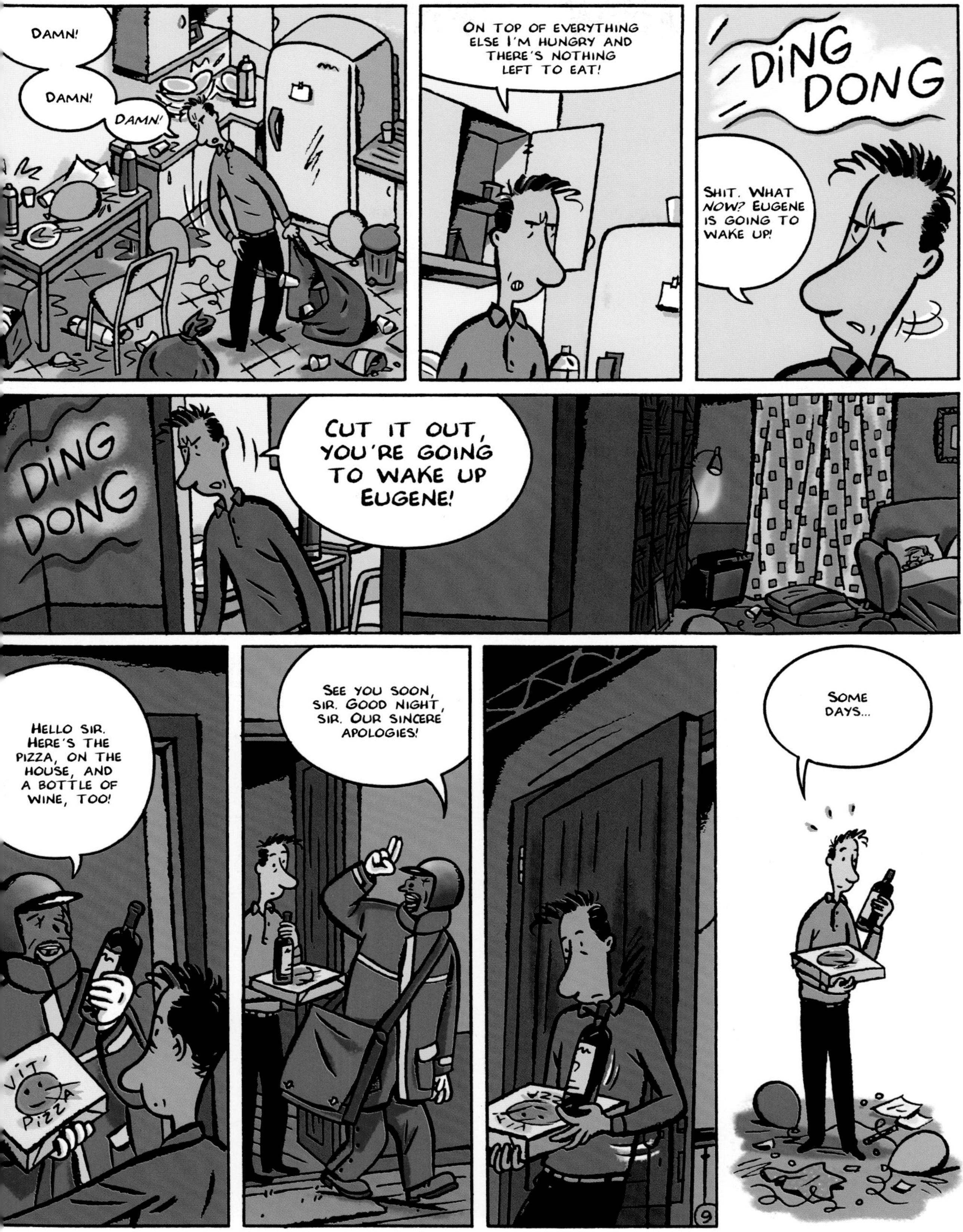
DAMN!
DAMN!
DAMN!
ON TOP OF EVERYTHING ELSE I'M HUNGRY AND THERE'S NOTHING LEFT TO EAT!
DING DONG
SHIT. WHAT NOW? EUGENE IS GOING TO WAKE UP!
DING DONG
CUT IT OUT, YOU'RE GOING TO WAKE UP EUGENE!
HELLO SIR. HERE'S THE PIZZA, ON THE HOUSE, AND A BOTTLE OF WINE, TOO!
VIT' PIZZA
SEE YOU SOON, SIR. GOOD NIGHT, SIR. OUR SINCERE APOLOGIES!
SOME DAYS...

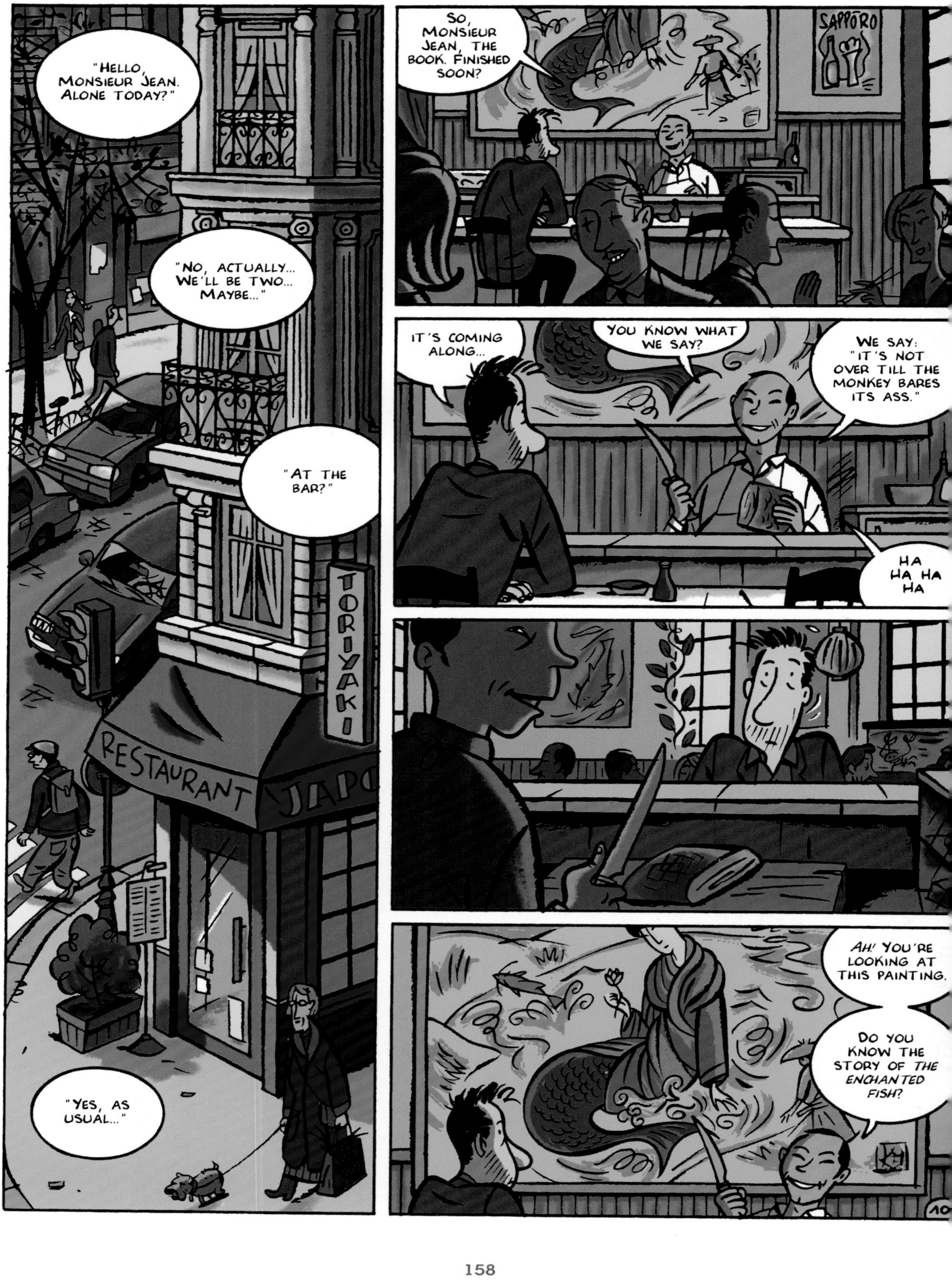
"Hello, Monsieur Jean. Alone today?"
"No, actually... We'll be two... Maybe..."
"At the bar?"
TORIYAKI
RESTAURANT JAPO
"Yes, as usual..."
SAPPORO
So, Monsieur Jean, the book. Finished soon?
It's coming along...
You know what we say?
We say: "It's not over till the monkey bares its ass."
HA HA HA HA
Ah! You're looking at this painting.
Do you know the story of *The Enchanted Fish*?
10

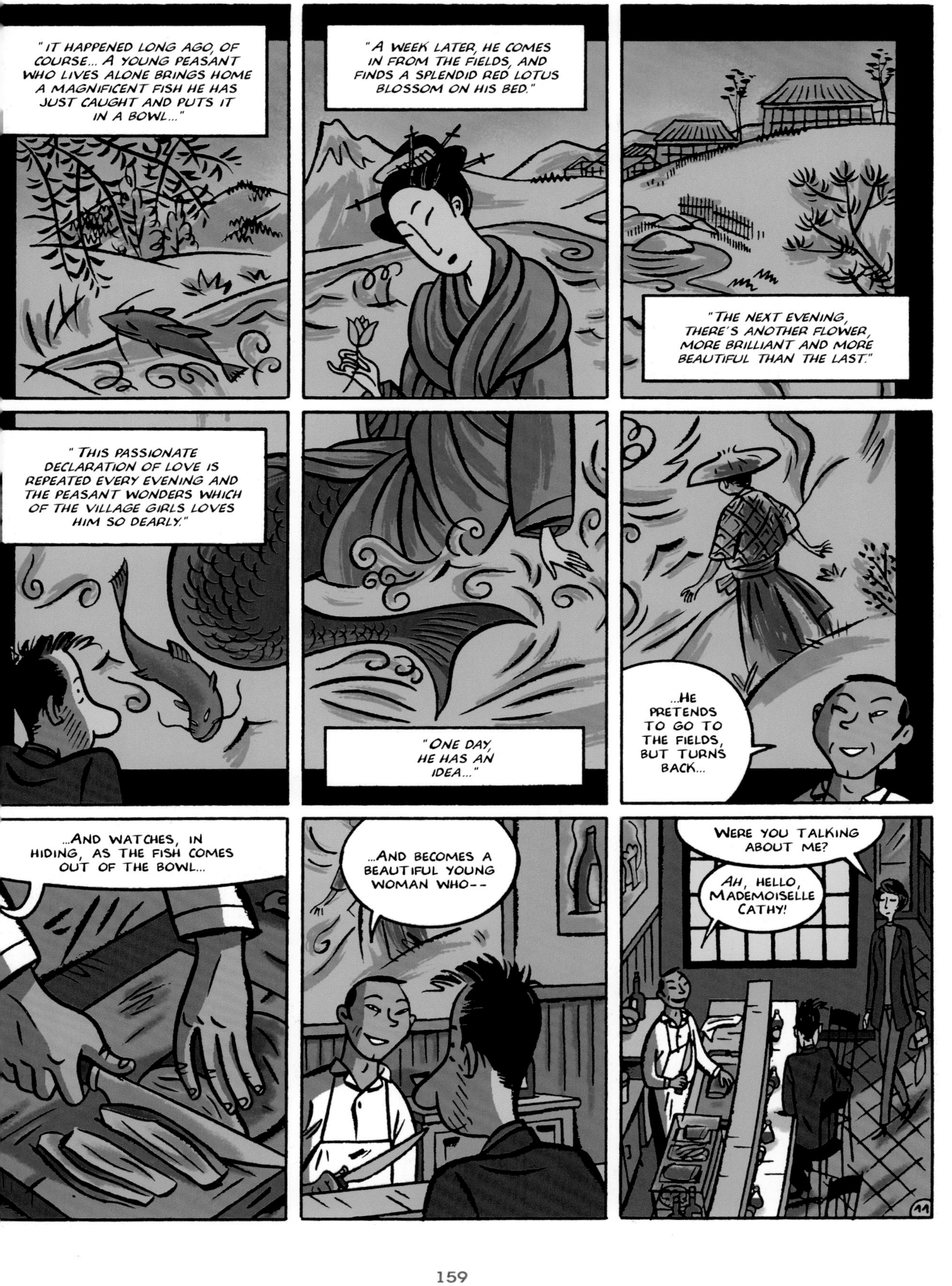
"IT HAPPENED LONG AGO, OF COURSE... A YOUNG PEASANT WHO LIVES ALONE BRINGS HOME A MAGNIFICENT FISH HE HAS JUST CAUGHT AND PUTS IT IN A BOWL..."
"A WEEK LATER, HE COMES IN FROM THE FIELDS, AND FINDS A SPLENDID RED LOTUS BLOSSOM ON HIS BED."
"THE NEXT EVENING, THERE'S ANOTHER FLOWER, MORE BRILLIANT AND MORE BEAUTIFUL THAN THE LAST."
"THIS PASSIONATE DECLARATION OF LOVE IS REPEATED EVERY EVENING AND THE PEASANT WONDERS WHICH OF THE VILLAGE GIRLS LOVES HIM SO DEARLY."
"ONE DAY, HE HAS AN IDEA..."
...HE PRETENDS TO GO TO THE FIELDS, BUT TURNS BACK...
...AND WATCHES, IN HIDING, AS THE FISH COMES OUT OF THE BOWL...
...AND BECOMES A BEAUTIFUL YOUNG WOMAN WHO--
WERE YOU TALKING ABOUT ME?
AH, HELLO, MADEMOISELLE CATHY!
11

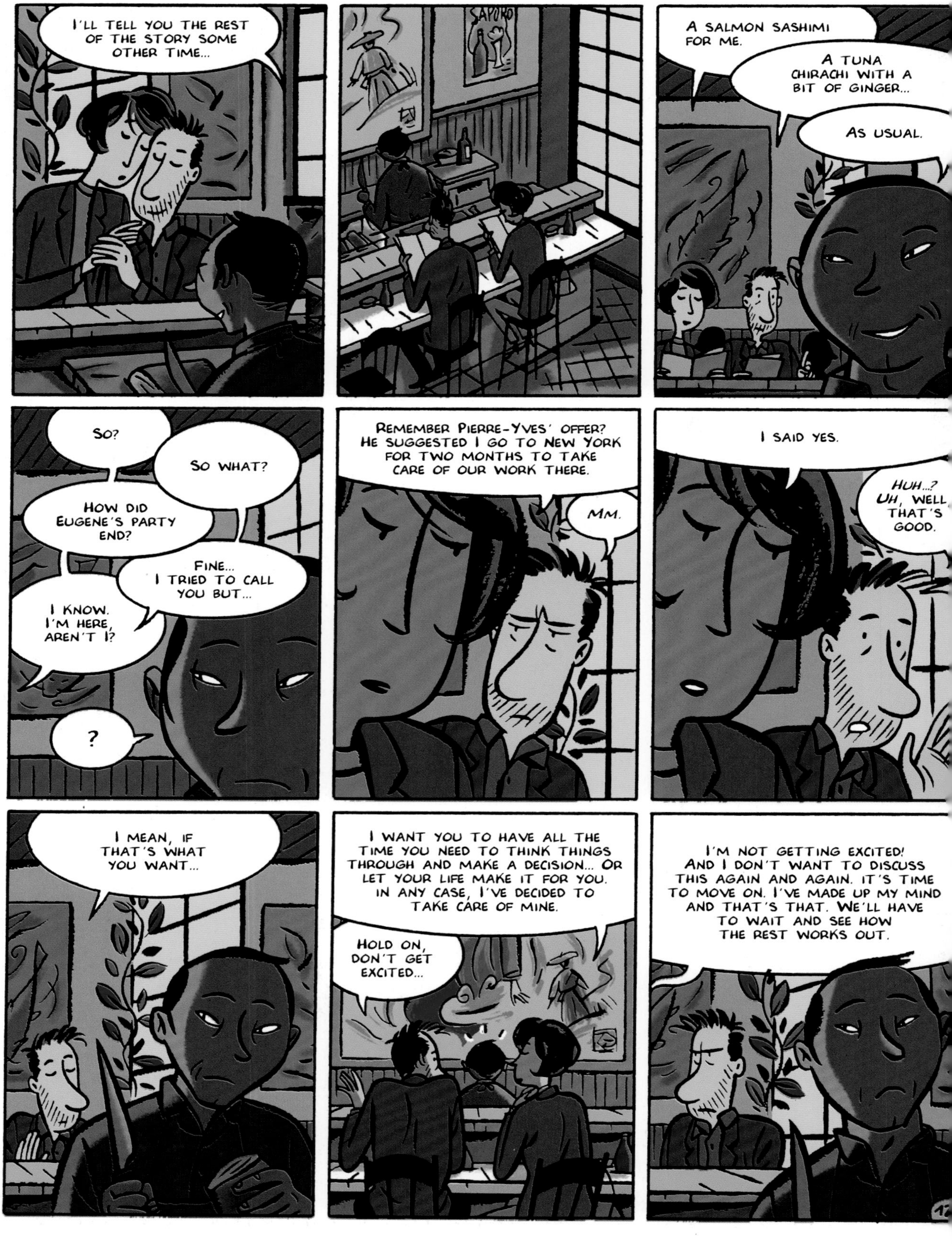
I'LL TELL YOU THE REST OF THE STORY SOME OTHER TIME...
A SALMON SASHIMI FOR ME.
A TUNA CHIRACHI WITH A BIT OF GINGER...
AS USUAL.
SO?
SO WHAT?
HOW DID EUGENE'S PARTY END?
FINE... I TRIED TO CALL YOU BUT...
I KNOW. I'M HERE, AREN'T I?
?
REMEMBER PIERRE-YVES' OFFER? HE SUGGESTED I GO TO NEW YORK FOR TWO MONTHS TO TAKE CARE OF OUR WORK THERE.
MM.
I SAID YES.
HUH...? UH, WELL, THAT'S GOOD.
I MEAN, IF THAT'S WHAT YOU WANT...
I WANT YOU TO HAVE ALL THE TIME YOU NEED TO THINK THINGS THROUGH AND MAKE A DECISION... OR LET YOUR LIFE MAKE IT FOR YOU. IN ANY CASE, I'VE DECIDED TO TAKE CARE OF MINE.
HOLD ON, DON'T GET EXCITED...
I'M NOT GETTING EXCITED! AND I DON'T WANT TO DISCUSS THIS AGAIN AND AGAIN. IT'S TIME TO MOVE ON. I'VE MADE UP MY MIND AND THAT'S THAT. WE'LL HAVE TO WAIT AND SEE HOW THE REST WORKS OUT.

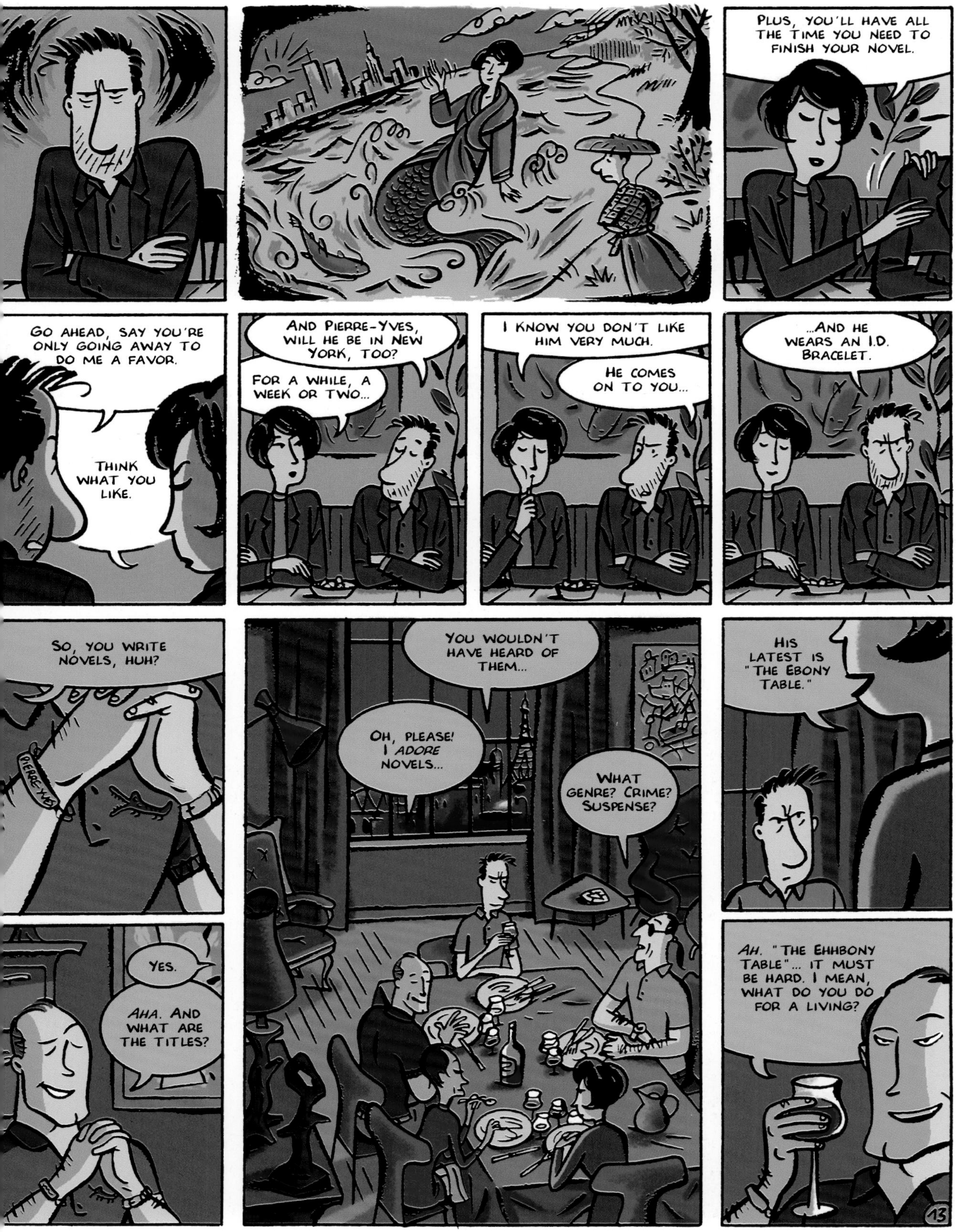
PLUS, YOU'LL HAVE ALL THE TIME YOU NEED TO FINISH YOUR NOVEL.
GO AHEAD, SAY YOU'RE ONLY GOING AWAY TO DO ME A FAVOR.
THINK WHAT YOU LIKE.
AND PIERRE-YVES, WILL HE BE IN NEW YORK, TOO?
FOR A WHILE, A WEEK OR TWO...
I KNOW YOU DON'T LIKE HIM VERY MUCH.
HE COMES ON TO YOU...
...AND HE WEARS AN I.D. BRACELET.
SO, YOU WRITE NOVELS, HUH?
PIERRE-YVES
YOU WOULDN'T HAVE HEARD OF THEM...
OH, PLEASE! I ADORE NOVELS...
WHAT GENRE? CRIME? SUSPENSE?
HIS LATEST IS "THE EBONY TABLE."
YES.
AHA. AND WHAT ARE THE TITLES?
AH. "THE EHHBONY TABLE"... IT MUST BE HARD. I MEAN, WHAT DO YOU DO FOR A LIVING?
13

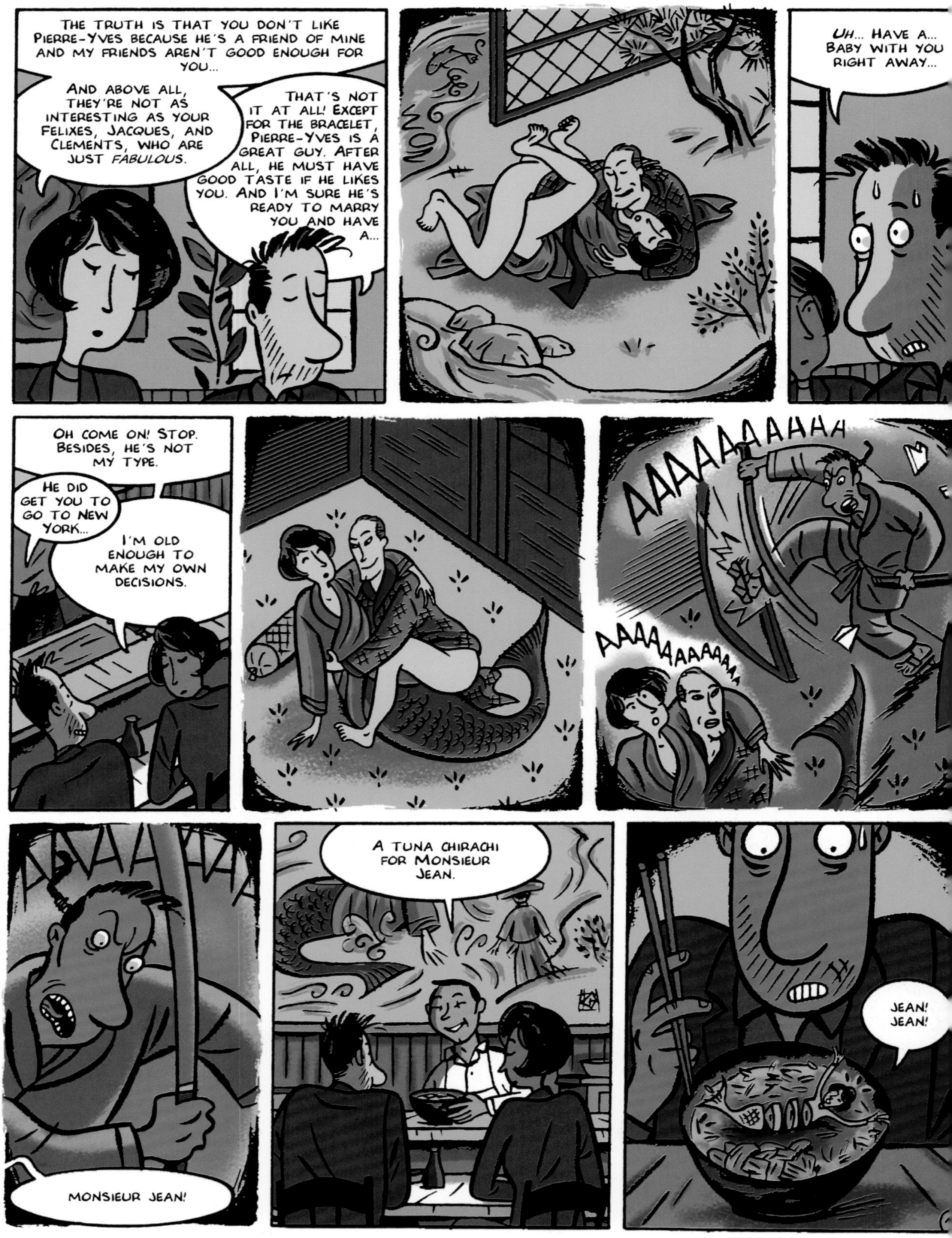
THE TRUTH IS THAT YOU DON'T LIKE PIERRE-YVES BECAUSE HE'S A FRIEND OF MINE AND MY FRIENDS AREN'T GOOD ENOUGH FOR YOU...
AND ABOVE ALL, THEY'RE NOT AS INTERESTING AS YOUR FELIXES, JACQUES, AND CLEMENTS, WHO ARE JUST *FABULOUS*.
THAT'S NOT IT AT ALL! EXCEPT FOR THE BRACELET, PIERRE-YVES IS A GREAT GUY. AFTER ALL, HE MUST HAVE GOOD TASTE IF HE LIKES YOU. AND I'M SURE HE'S READY TO MARRY YOU AND HAVE A...
UH... HAVE A... BABY WITH YOU RIGHT AWAY...
OH COME ON! STOP. BESIDES, HE'S NOT MY TYPE.
HE DID GET YOU TO GO TO NEW YORK...
I'M OLD ENOUGH TO MAKE MY OWN DECISIONS.
AAAAAAAAAAAA
AAAAAAAAAAAA
A TUNA CHIRACHI FOR MONSIEUR JEAN.
MONSIEUR JEAN!
JEAN! JEAN!

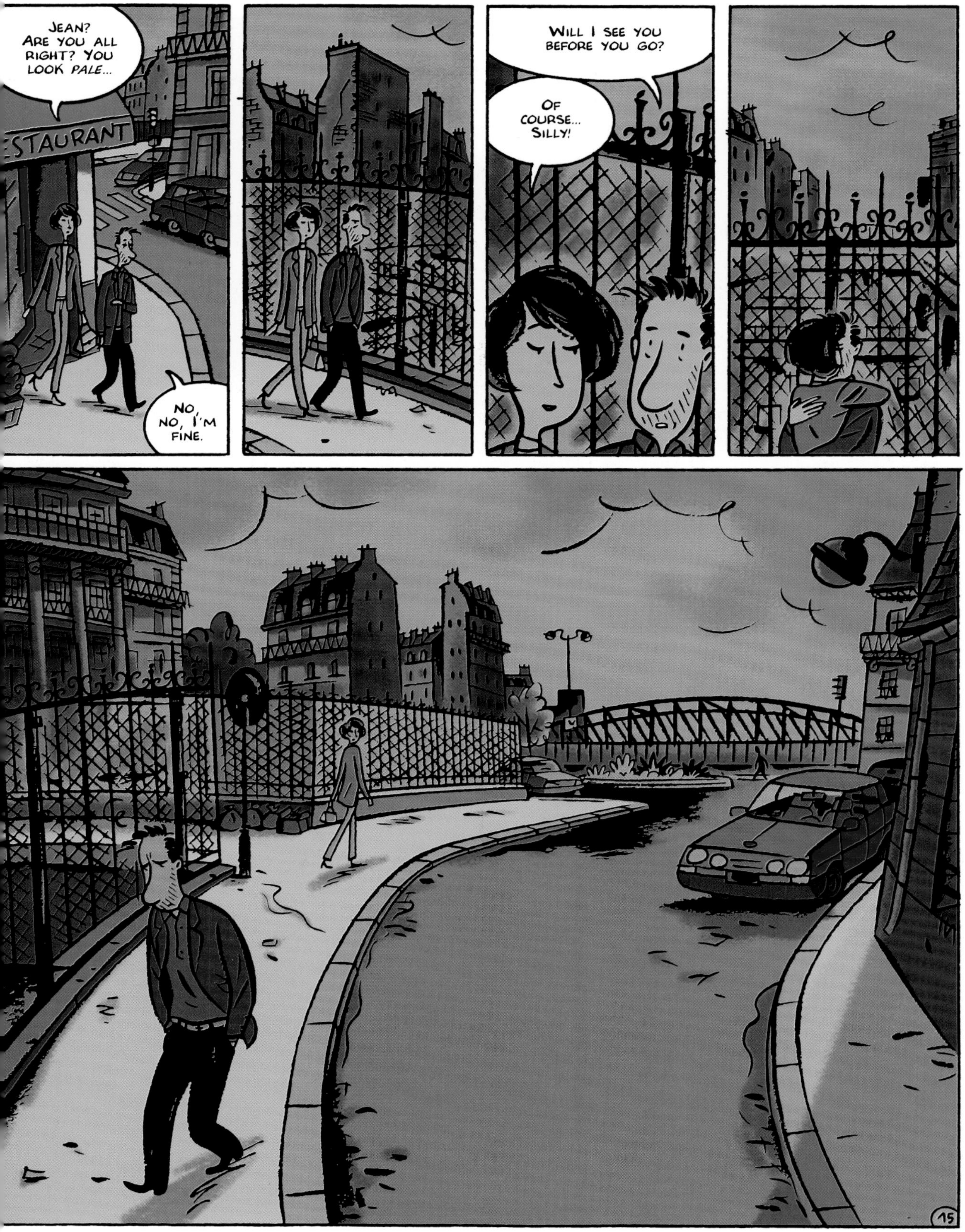

ESTAURANT
JEAN? ARE YOU ALL RIGHT? YOU LOOK *PALE*...
NO, NO, I'M FINE.
WILL I SEE YOU BEFORE YOU GO?
OF COURSE... SILLY!
15

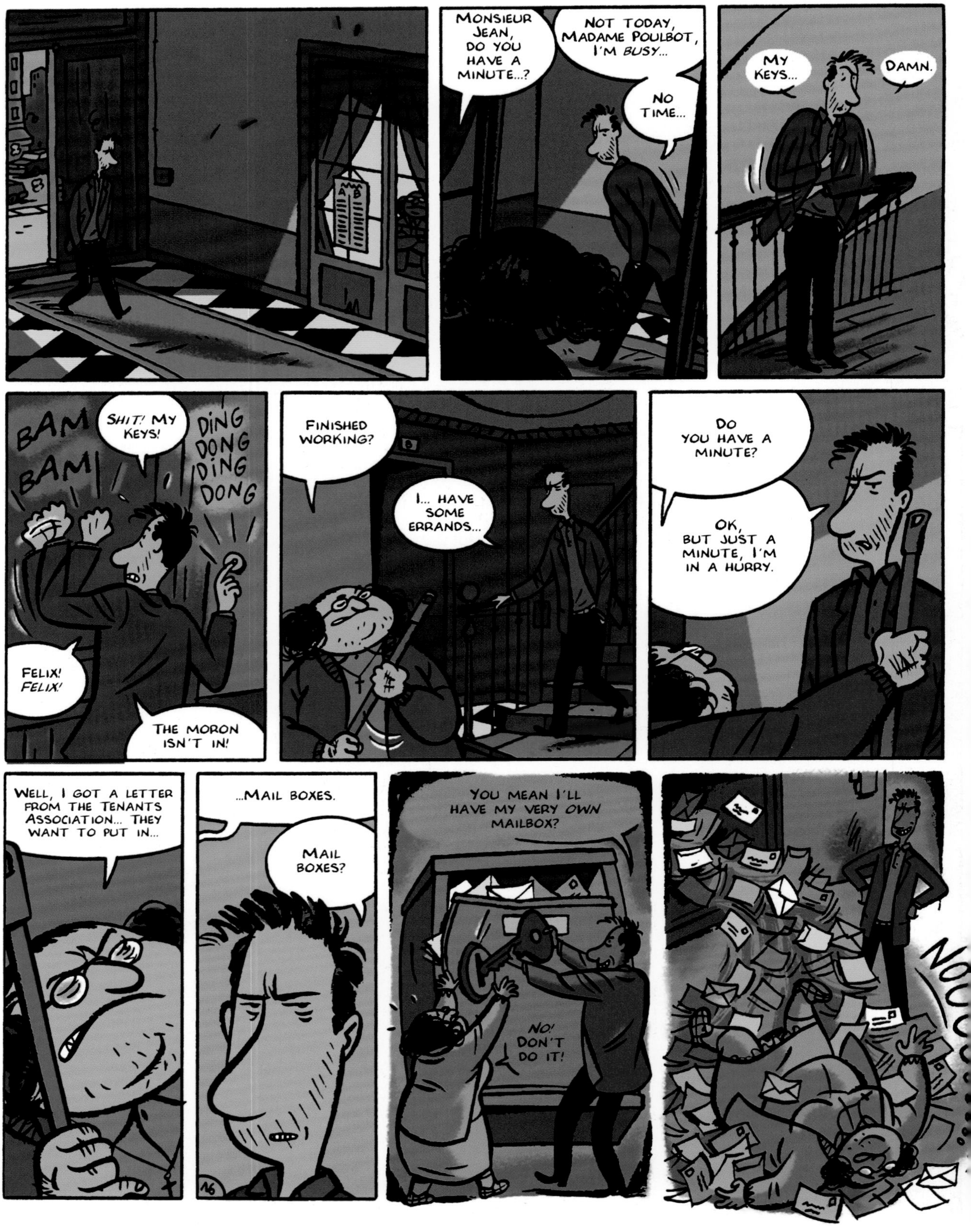
MONSIEUR JEAN, DO YOU HAVE A MINUTE...?
NOT TODAY, MADAME POULBOT, I'M *BUSY*...
NO TIME...
MY KEYS...
DAMN.
BAM BAM
SHIT! MY KEYS!
DING DONG DING DONG
FELIX! FELIX!
THE MORON ISN'T IN!
FINISHED WORKING?
I... HAVE SOME ERRANDS...
DO YOU HAVE A MINUTE?
OK, BUT JUST A MINUTE, I'M IN A *HURRY*.
WELL, I GOT A LETTER FROM THE TENANTS ASSOCIATION... THEY WANT TO PUT IN...
...MAIL BOXES.
MAIL BOXES?
YOU MEAN I'LL HAVE MY VERY *OWN* MAILBOX?
NO! DON'T DO IT!

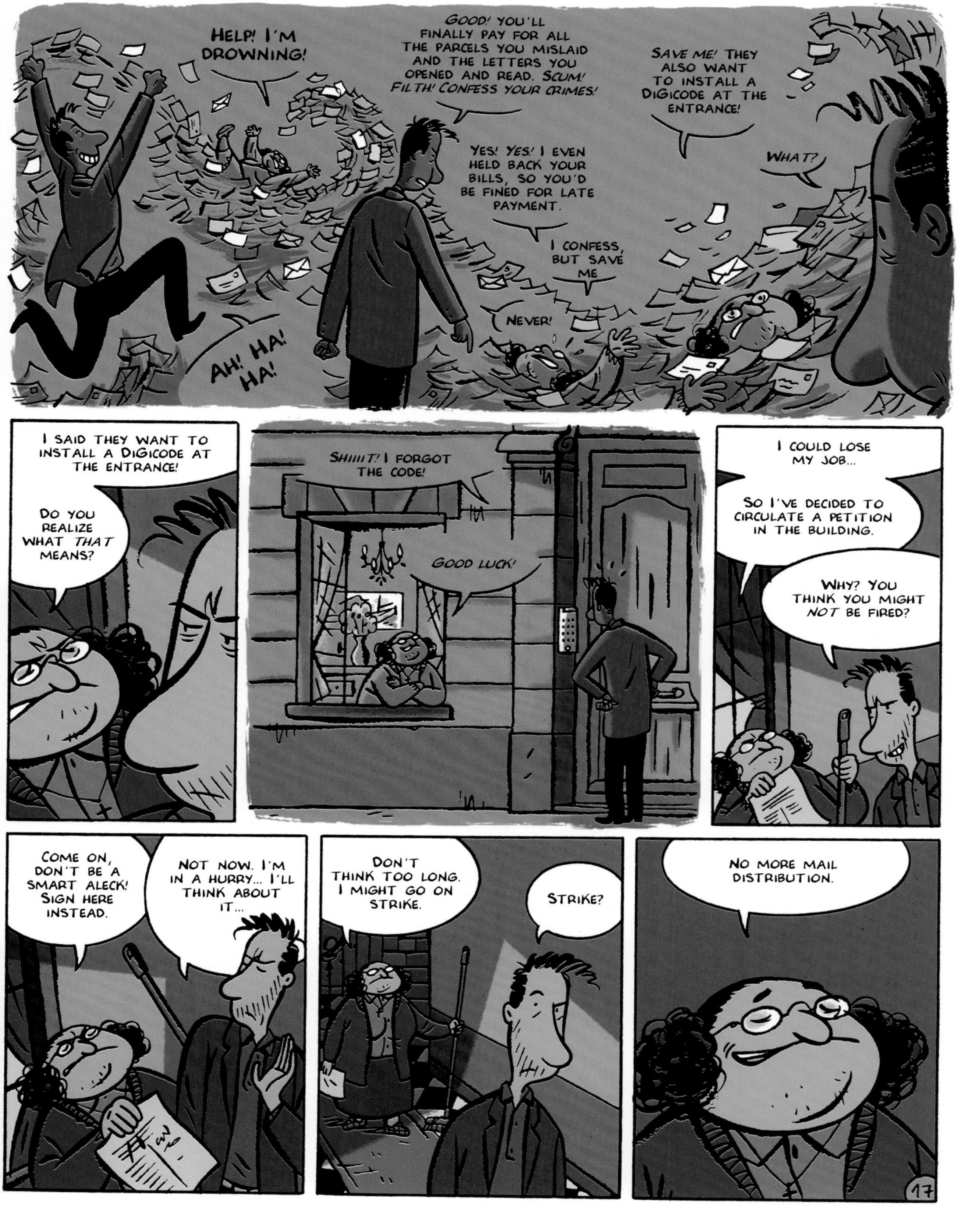
HELP! I'M DROWNING!
GOOD! YOU'LL FINALLY PAY FOR ALL THE PARCELS YOU MISLAID AND THE LETTERS YOU OPENED AND READ. SCUM! FILTH! CONFESS YOUR CRIMES!
YES! YES! I EVEN HELD BACK YOUR BILLS, SO YOU'D BE FINED FOR LATE PAYMENT.
I CONFESS, BUT SAVE ME
NEVER!
AH! HA! HA!
SAVE ME! THEY ALSO WANT TO INSTALL A DIGICODE AT THE ENTRANCE!
WHAT?
I SAID THEY WANT TO INSTALL A DIGICODE AT THE ENTRANCE!
DO YOU REALIZE WHAT THAT MEANS?
SHIIIT! I FORGOT THE CODE!
GOOD LUCK!
I COULD LOSE MY JOB...
SO I'VE DECIDED TO CIRCULATE A PETITION IN THE BUILDING.
WHY? YOU THINK YOU MIGHT NOT BE FIRED?
COME ON, DON'T BE A SMART ALECK! SIGN HERE INSTEAD.
NOT NOW. I'M IN A HURRY... I'LL THINK ABOUT IT...
DON'T THINK TOO LONG. I MIGHT GO ON STRIKE.
STRIKE?
NO MORE MAIL DISTRIBUTION.
17

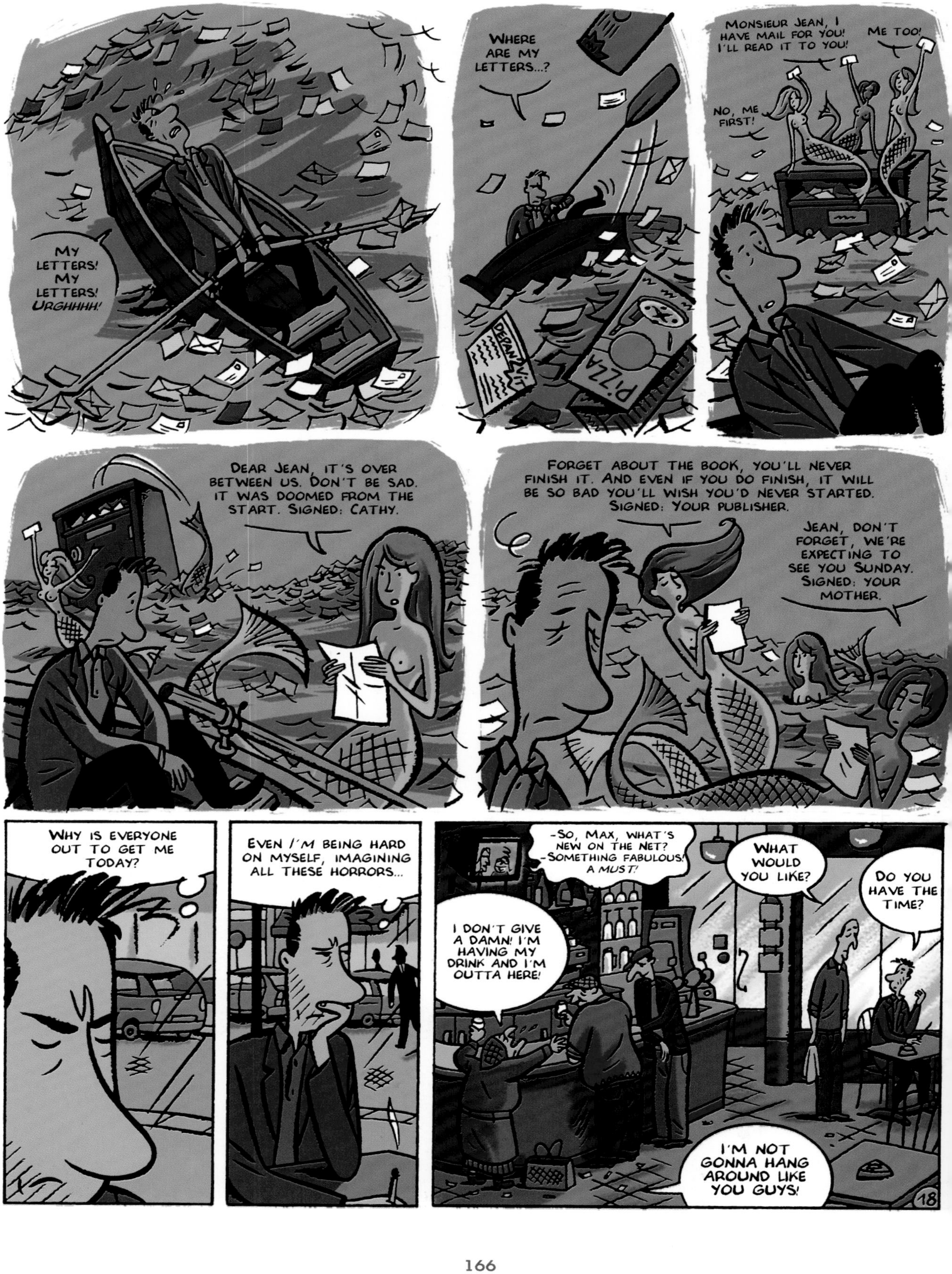
MY LETTERS! MY LETTERS! URGHHHH!
WHERE ARE MY LETTERS...?
PIZZA
MONSIEUR JEAN, I HAVE MAIL FOR YOU! I'LL READ IT TO YOU!
ME TOO!
NO, ME FIRST!
DEAR JEAN, IT'S OVER BETWEEN US. DON'T BE SAD. IT WAS DOOMED FROM THE START. SIGNED: CATHY.
FORGET ABOUT THE BOOK, YOU'LL NEVER FINISH IT. AND EVEN IF YOU DO FINISH, IT WILL BE SO BAD YOU'LL WISH YOU'D NEVER STARTED. SIGNED: YOUR PUBLISHER.
JEAN, DON'T FORGET, WE'RE EXPECTING TO SEE YOU SUNDAY. SIGNED: YOUR MOTHER.
WHY IS EVERYONE OUT TO GET ME TODAY?
EVEN I'M BEING HARD ON MYSELF, IMAGINING ALL THESE HORRORS...
-SO, MAX, WHAT'S NEW ON THE NET?
-SOMETHING FABULOUS! A MUST!
WHAT WOULD YOU LIKE?
DO YOU HAVE THE TIME?
I DON'T GIVE A DAMN! I'M HAVING MY DRINK AND I'M OUTTA HERE!
I'M NOT GONNA HANG AROUND LIKE YOU GUYS!
18

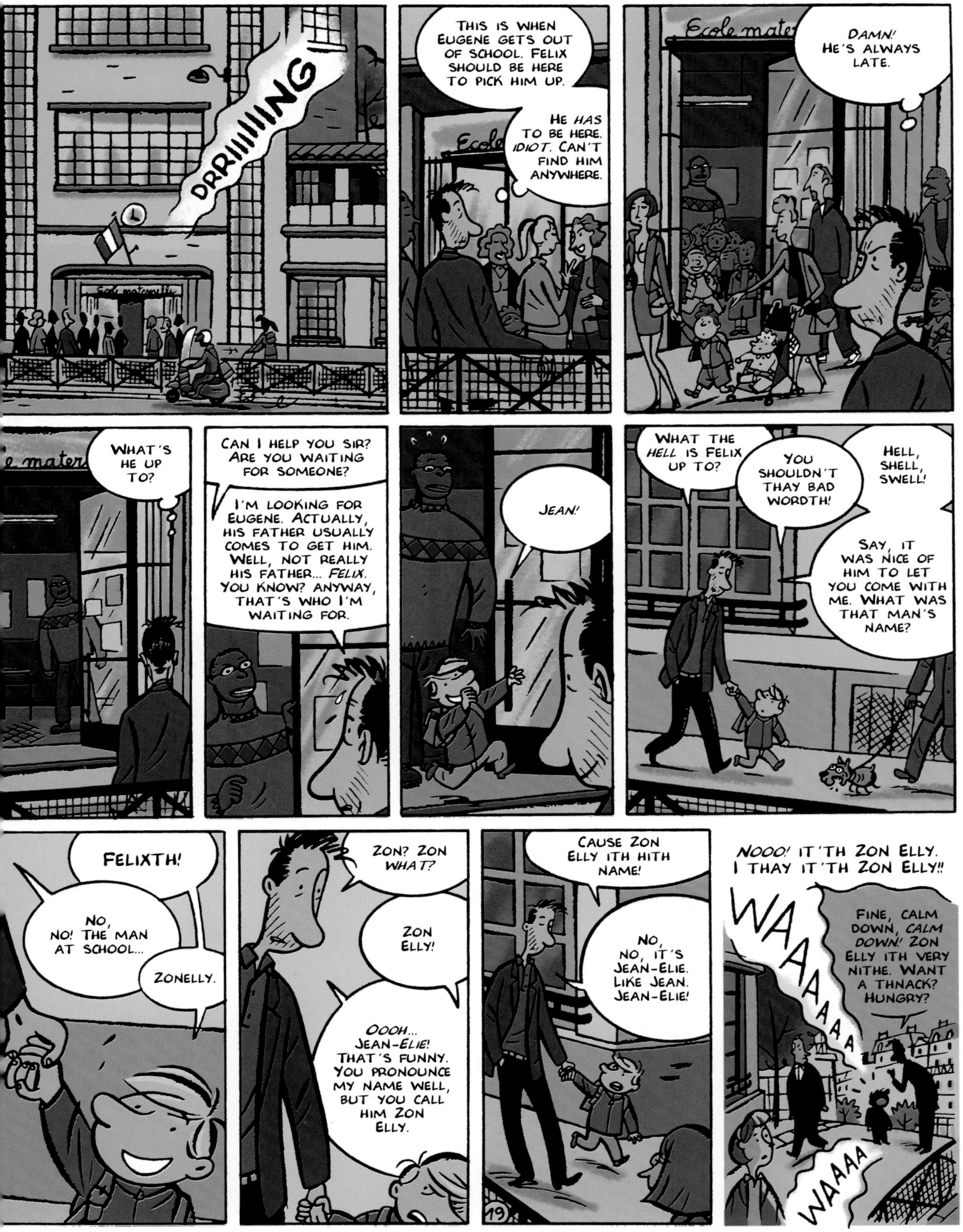
DRRIIIIIIING
THIS IS WHEN EUGENE GETS OUT OF SCHOOL. FELIX SHOULD BE HERE TO PICK HIM UP.
HE HAS TO BE HERE. IDIOT. CAN'T FIND HIM ANYWHERE.
DAMN! HE'S ALWAYS LATE.
WHAT'S HE UP TO?
CAN I HELP YOU SIR? ARE YOU WAITING FOR SOMEONE?
I'M LOOKING FOR EUGENE. ACTUALLY, HIS FATHER USUALLY COMES TO GET HIM. WELL, NOT REALLY HIS FATHER... FELIX. YOU KNOW? ANYWAY, THAT'S WHO I'M WAITING FOR.
JEAN!
WHAT THE HELL IS FELIX UP TO?
YOU SHOULDN'T THAY BAD WORDTH!
HELL, SHELL, SWELL!
SAY, IT WAS NICE OF HIM TO LET YOU COME WITH ME. WHAT WAS THAT MAN'S NAME?
FELIXTH!
NO, NO! THE MAN AT SCHOOL...
ZONELLY.
ZON? ZON WHAT?
ZON ELLY!
OOOH... JEAN-ELIE! THAT'S FUNNY. YOU PRONOUNCE MY NAME WELL, BUT YOU CALL HIM ZON ELLY.
CAUSE ZON ELLY ITH HITH NAME!
NO, NO, IT'S JEAN-ELIE. LIKE JEAN. JEAN-ELIE!
NOOO! IT'TH ZON ELLY. I THAY IT'TH ZON ELLY!!
WAAAAAAA
FINE, CALM DOWN, CALM DOWN! ZON ELLY ITH VERY NITHE. WANT A THNACK? HUNGRY?
WAAAA

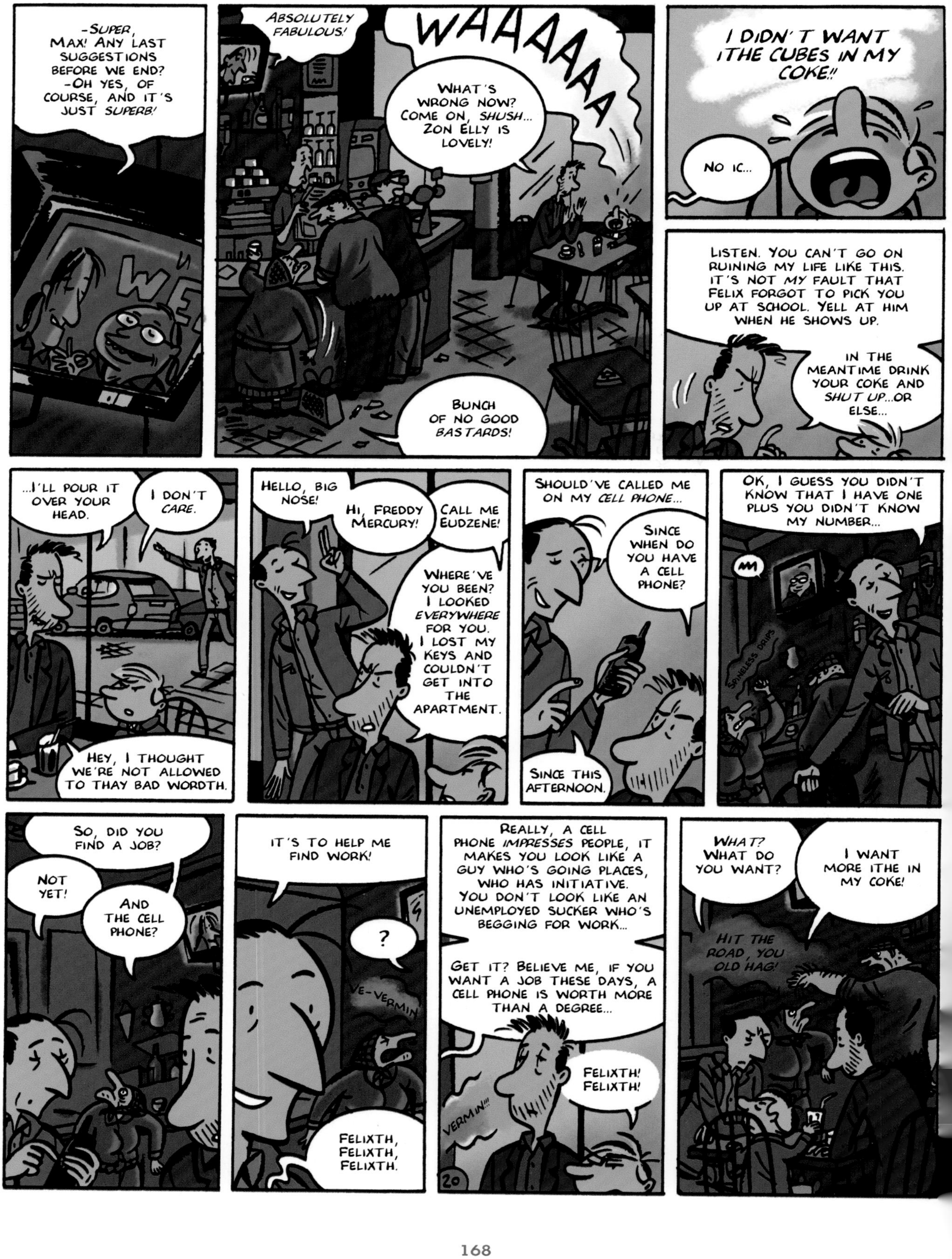
-SUPER, MAX! ANY LAST SUGGESTIONS BEFORE WE END? -OH YES, OF COURSE, AND IT'S JUST SUPERB!
WE
ABSOLUTELY FABULOUS!
WAAAAAA
WHAT'S WRONG NOW? COME ON, SHUSH... ZON ELLY IS LOVELY!
BUNCH OF NO GOOD BASTARDS!
I DIDN'T WANT ITHE CUBES IN MY COKE!!
NO IC...
LISTEN. YOU CAN'T GO ON RUINING MY LIFE LIKE THIS. IT'S NOT MY FAULT THAT FELIX FORGOT TO PICK YOU UP AT SCHOOL. YELL AT HIM WHEN HE SHOWS UP.
IN THE MEANTIME DRINK YOUR COKE AND SHUT UP...OR ELSE...
...I'LL POUR IT OVER YOUR HEAD.
I DON'T CARE.
HEY, I THOUGHT WE'RE NOT ALLOWED TO THAY BAD WORDTH.
HELLO, BIG NOSE!
HI, FREDDY MERCURY!
CALL ME EUDZENE!
WHERE'VE YOU BEEN? I LOOKED EVERYWHERE FOR YOU. I LOST MY KEYS AND COULDN'T GET INTO THE APARTMENT.
SHOULD'VE CALLED ME ON MY CELL PHONE...
SINCE WHEN DO YOU HAVE A CELL PHONE?
SINCE THIS AFTERNOON.
OK, I GUESS YOU DIDN'T KNOW THAT I HAVE ONE PLUS YOU DIDN'T KNOW MY NUMBER...
MM
SPINELESS DRIPS
SO, DID YOU FIND A JOB?
NOT YET!
AND THE CELL PHONE?
IT'S TO HELP ME FIND WORK!
?
VE-VERMIN
FELIXTH, FELIXTH, FELIXTH.
REALLY, A CELL PHONE IMPRESSES PEOPLE, IT MAKES YOU LOOK LIKE A GUY WHO'S GOING PLACES, WHO HAS INITIATIVE. YOU DON'T LOOK LIKE AN UNEMPLOYED SUCKER WHO'S BEGGING FOR WORK...
GET IT? BELIEVE ME, IF YOU WANT A JOB THESE DAYS, A CELL PHONE IS WORTH MORE THAN A DEGREE...
FELIXTH! FELIXTH!
VERMIN!!!
20
WHAT? WHAT DO YOU WANT?
I WANT MORE ITHE IN MY COKE!
HIT THE ROAD, YOU OLD HAG!

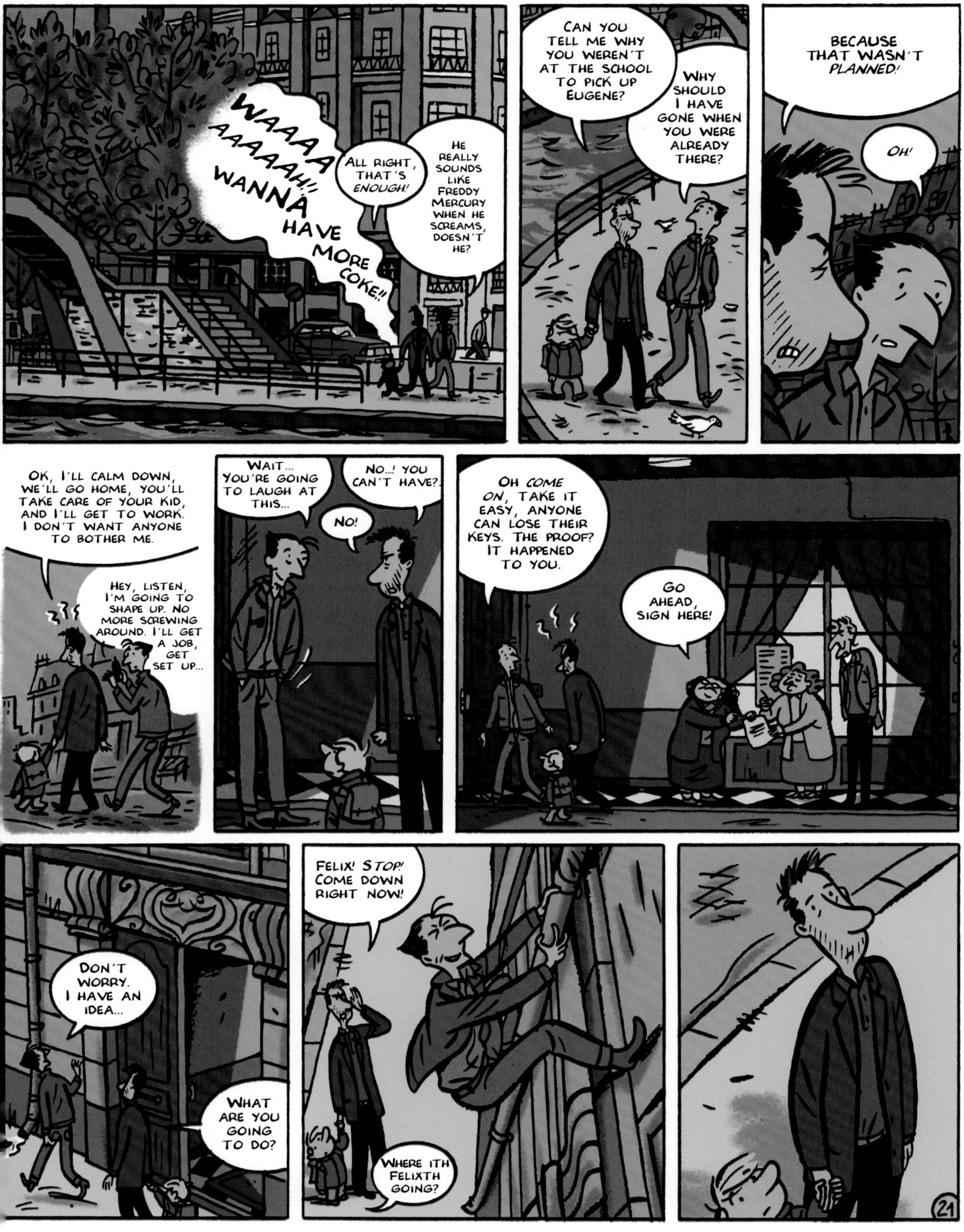
WAAAAAAAAAH!! WANNA HAVE MORE COKE!!
ALL RIGHT, THAT'S ENOUGH!
HE REALLY SOUNDS LIKE FREDDY MERCURY WHEN HE SCREAMS, DOESN'T HE?
CAN YOU TELL ME WHY YOU WEREN'T AT THE SCHOOL TO PICK UP EUGENE?
WHY SHOULD I HAVE GONE WHEN YOU WERE ALREADY THERE?
BECAUSE THAT WASN'T PLANNED!
OH!
OK, I'LL CALM DOWN, WE'LL GO HOME, YOU'LL TAKE CARE OF YOUR KID, AND I'LL GET TO WORK. I DON'T WANT ANYONE TO BOTHER ME.
HEY, LISTEN, I'M GOING TO SHAPE UP. NO MORE SCREWING AROUND. I'LL GET A JOB, GET SET UP...
WAIT... YOU'RE GOING TO LAUGH AT THIS...
NO...! YOU CAN'T HAVE?
NO!
OH COME ON, TAKE IT EASY, ANYONE CAN LOSE THEIR KEYS. THE PROOF? IT HAPPENED TO YOU.
GO AHEAD, SIGN HERE!
DON'T WORRY. I HAVE AN IDEA...
WHAT ARE YOU GOING TO DO?
FELIX! STOP! COME DOWN RIGHT NOW!
WHERE ITH FELIXTH GOING?
21

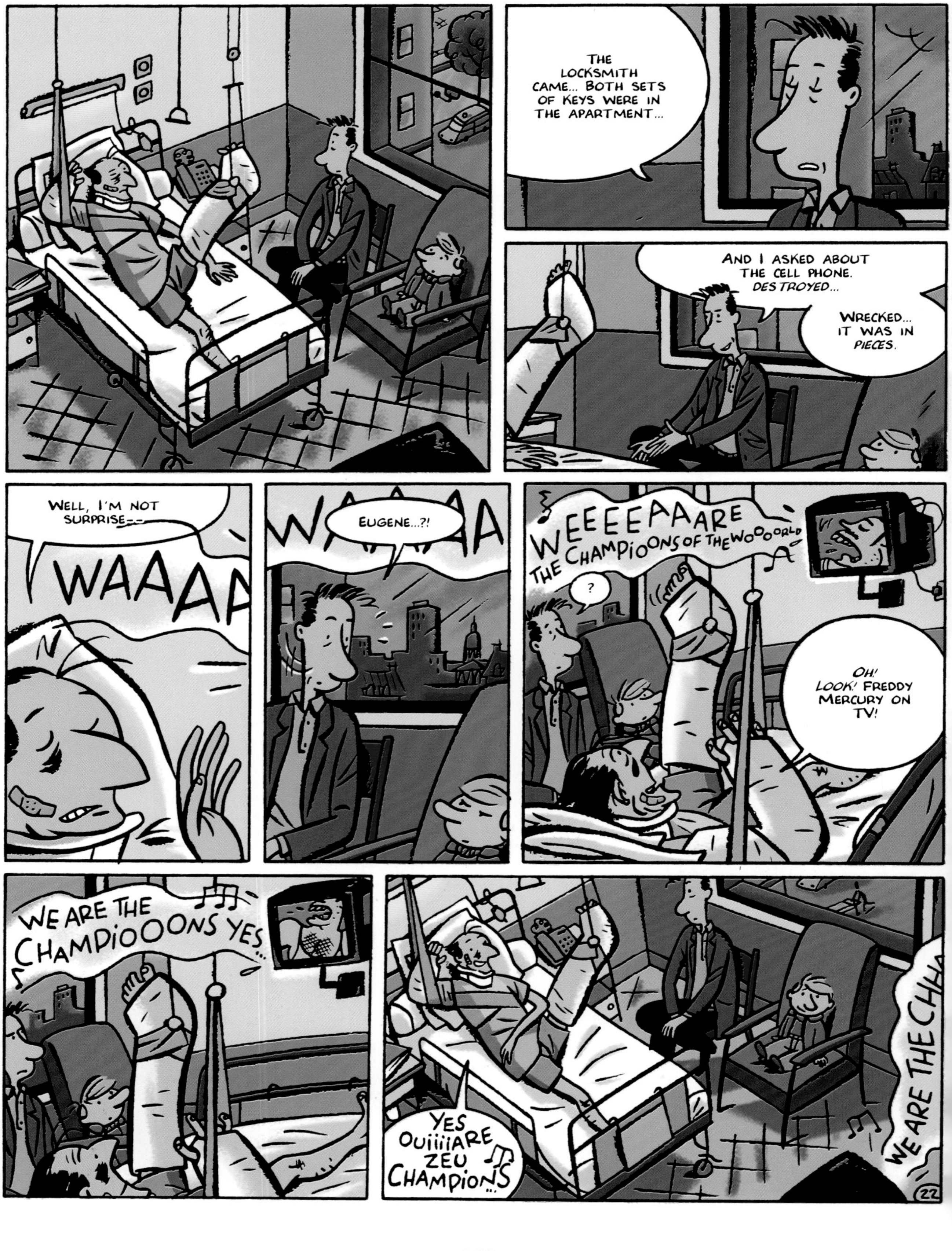
THE LOCKSMITH CAME... BOTH SETS OF KEYS WERE IN THE APARTMENT...
AND I ASKED ABOUT THE CELL PHONE. DESTROYED...
WRECKED... IT WAS IN PIECES.
WELL, I'M NOT SURPRISE--
WAAAA
WAAAAA
EUGENE...?!
WEEEEAAARE THE CHAMPIOONS OF THE WOOOORLD
?
OH! LOOK! FREDDY MERCURY ON TV!
WE ARE THE CHAMPIOOONS YES...
YES OUIIIIARE ZEU CHAMPIONS...
WE ARE THE CHA
22

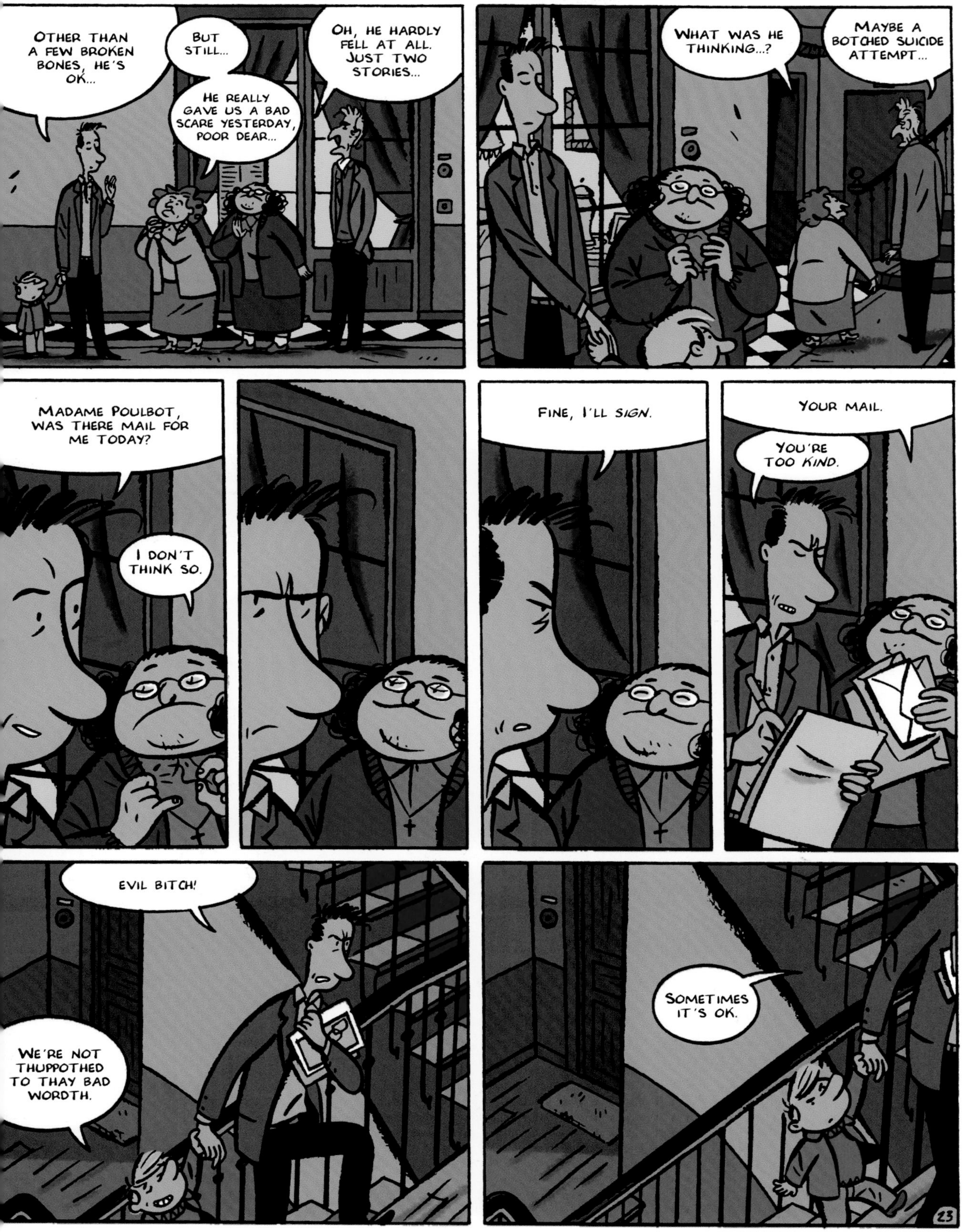
Other than a few broken bones, he's OK...
But still...
He really gave us a bad scare yesterday, poor dear...
Oh, he hardly fell at all. Just two stories...
What was he thinking...?
Maybe a botched suicide attempt...
Madame Poulbot, was there mail for me today?
I don't think so.
Fine, I'll *sign*.
Your mail.
You're too *kind*.
Evil bitch!
We're not thuppothed to thay bad wordth.
Sometimes it's OK.
23

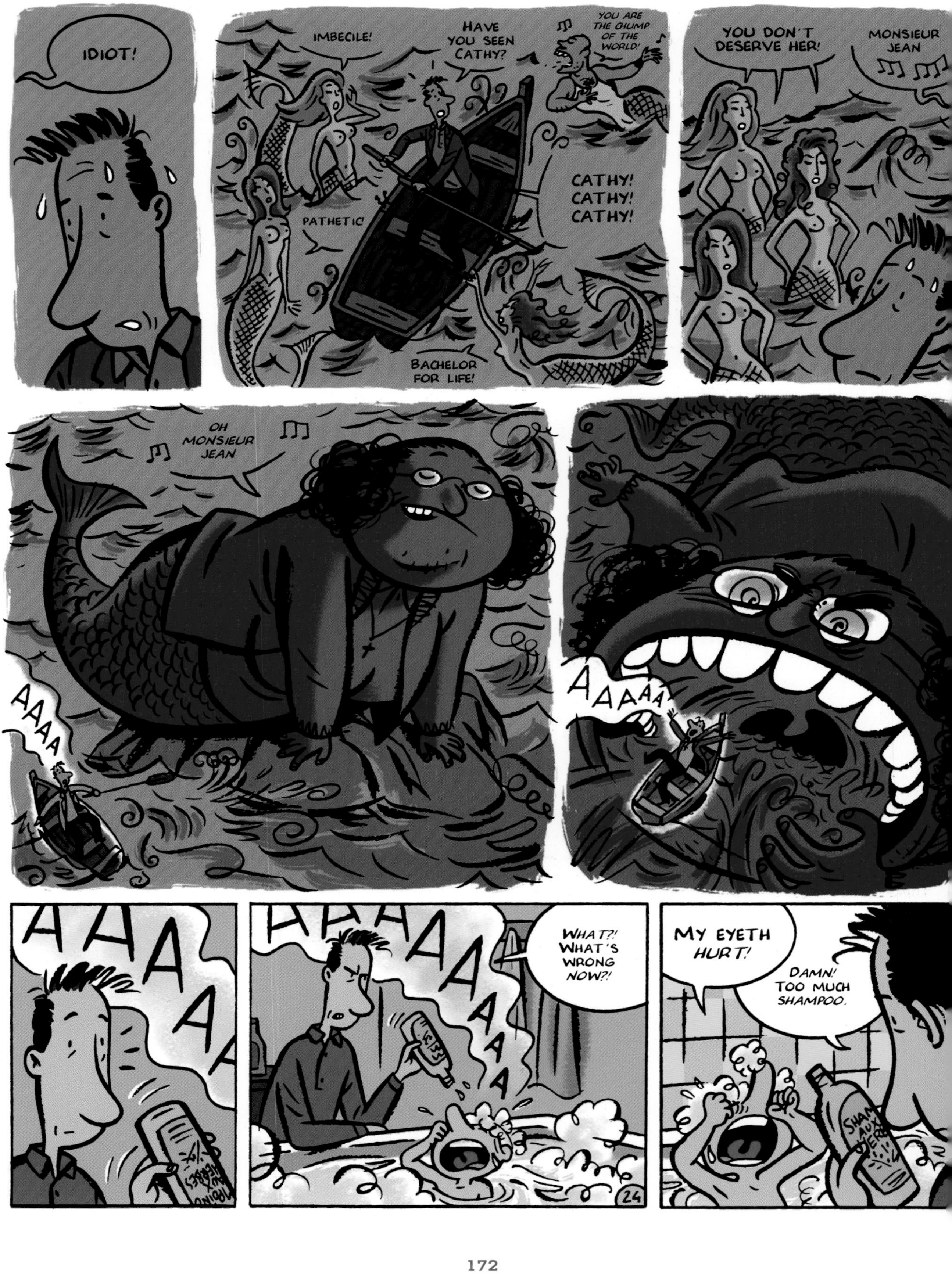
IDIOT!
IMBECILE!
HAVE YOU SEEN CATHY?
YOU ARE THE CHUMP OF THE WORLD!
PATHETIC!
CATHY! CATHY! CATHY!
BACHELOR FOR LIFE!
YOU DON'T DESERVE HER!
MONSIEUR JEAN
OH MONSIEUR JEAN
AAAA
AAAAA
AAAAA
AAAAAAAAA
WHAT?! WHAT'S WRONG NOW?!
MY EYETH HURT!
DAMN! TOO MUCH SHAMPOO.

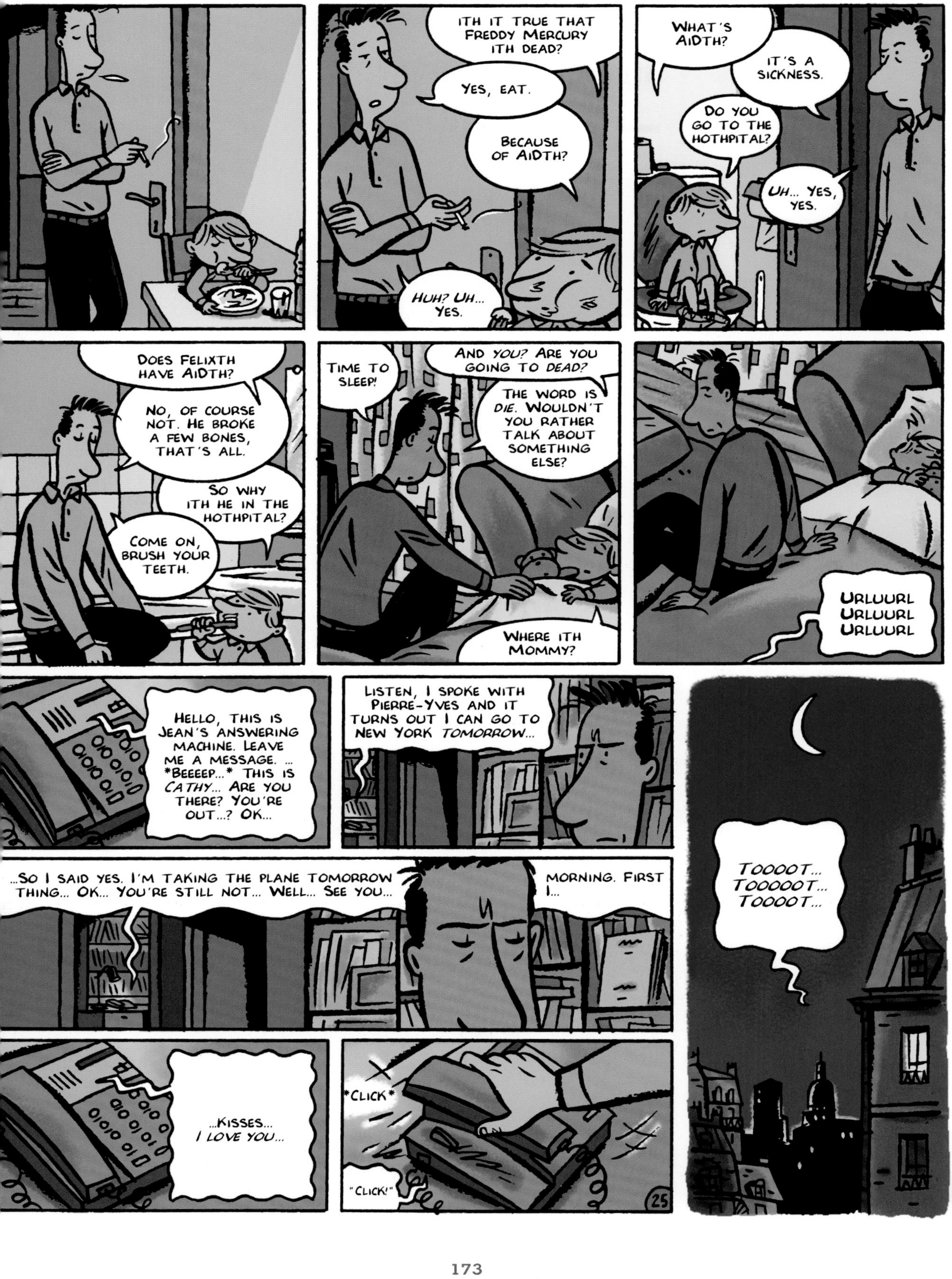

ITH IT TRUE THAT FREDDY MERCURY ITH DEAD?
YES, EAT.
BECAUSE OF AIDTH?
HUH? UH... YES.
WHAT'S AIDTH?
IT'S A SICKNESS.
DO YOU GO TO THE HOTHPITAL?
UH... YES, YES.
DOES FELIXTH HAVE AIDTH?
NO, OF COURSE NOT. HE BROKE A FEW BONES, THAT'S ALL.
SO WHY ITH HE IN THE HOTHPITAL?
COME ON, BRUSH YOUR TEETH.
TIME TO SLEEP!
AND YOU? ARE YOU GOING TO DEAD?
THE WORD IS DIE. WOULDN'T YOU RATHER TALK ABOUT SOMETHING ELSE?
WHERE ITH MOMMY?
URLUURL URLUURL URLUURL
HELLO, THIS IS JEAN'S ANSWERING MACHINE. LEAVE ME A MESSAGE. ... *BEEEEP...* THIS IS CATHY... ARE YOU THERE? YOU'RE OUT...? OK...
LISTEN, I SPOKE WITH PIERRE-YVES AND IT TURNS OUT I CAN GO TO NEW YORK TOMORROW...
...SO I SAID YES. I'M TAKING THE PLANE TOMORROW THING... OK... YOU'RE STILL NOT... WELL... SEE YOU...
MORNING. FIRST I...
...KISSES... I LOVE YOU...
CLICK
"CLICK!"
25
TOOOOT... TOOOOOT... TOOOOT...

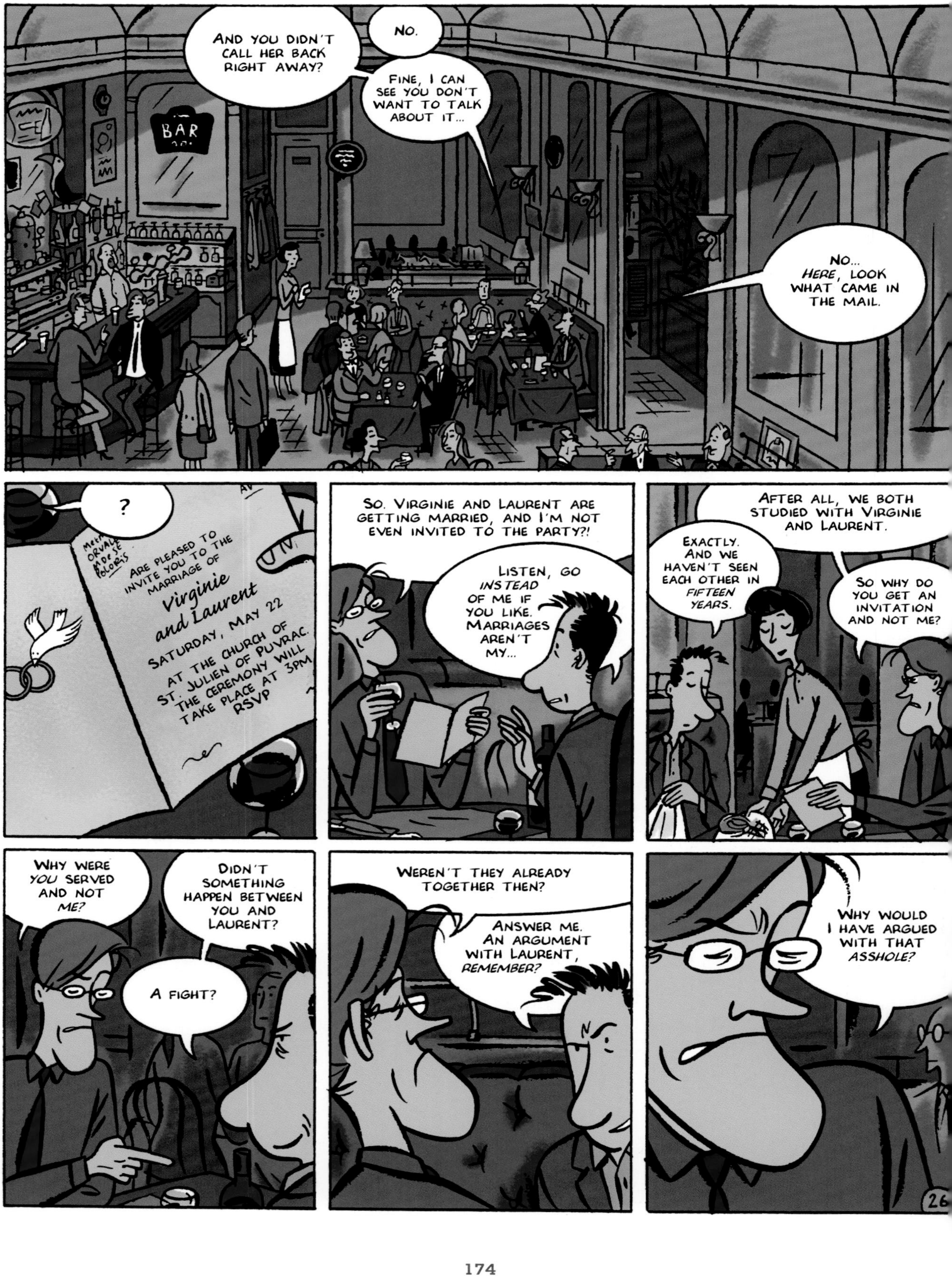
AND YOU DIDN'T CALL HER BACK RIGHT AWAY?
NO.
FINE, I CAN SEE YOU DON'T WANT TO TALK ABOUT IT...
BAR
NO... *HERE*, LOOK WHAT CAME IN THE MAIL.
?
ARE PLEASED TO INVITE YOU TO THE MARRIAGE OF
Virginie and Laurent
SATURDAY, MAY 22
AT THE CHURCH OF ST. JULIEN OF PUVRAC. THE CEREMONY WILL TAKE PLACE AT 3PM
RSVP
SO. VIRGINIE AND LAURENT ARE GETTING MARRIED, AND I'M NOT EVEN INVITED TO THE PARTY?!
LISTEN, GO *INSTEAD* OF ME IF YOU LIKE. MARRIAGES AREN'T MY...
AFTER ALL, WE BOTH STUDIED WITH VIRGINIE AND LAURENT.
EXACTLY. AND WE HAVEN'T SEEN EACH OTHER IN *FIFTEEN YEARS*.
SO WHY DO YOU GET AN INVITATION AND NOT ME?
WHY WERE *YOU* SERVED AND NOT *ME?*
DIDN'T SOMETHING HAPPEN BETWEEN YOU AND LAURENT?
A FIGHT?
WEREN'T THEY ALREADY TOGETHER THEN?
ANSWER ME. AN ARGUMENT WITH LAURENT, *REMEMBER?*
WHY WOULD I HAVE ARGUED WITH THAT *ASSHOLE?*
26

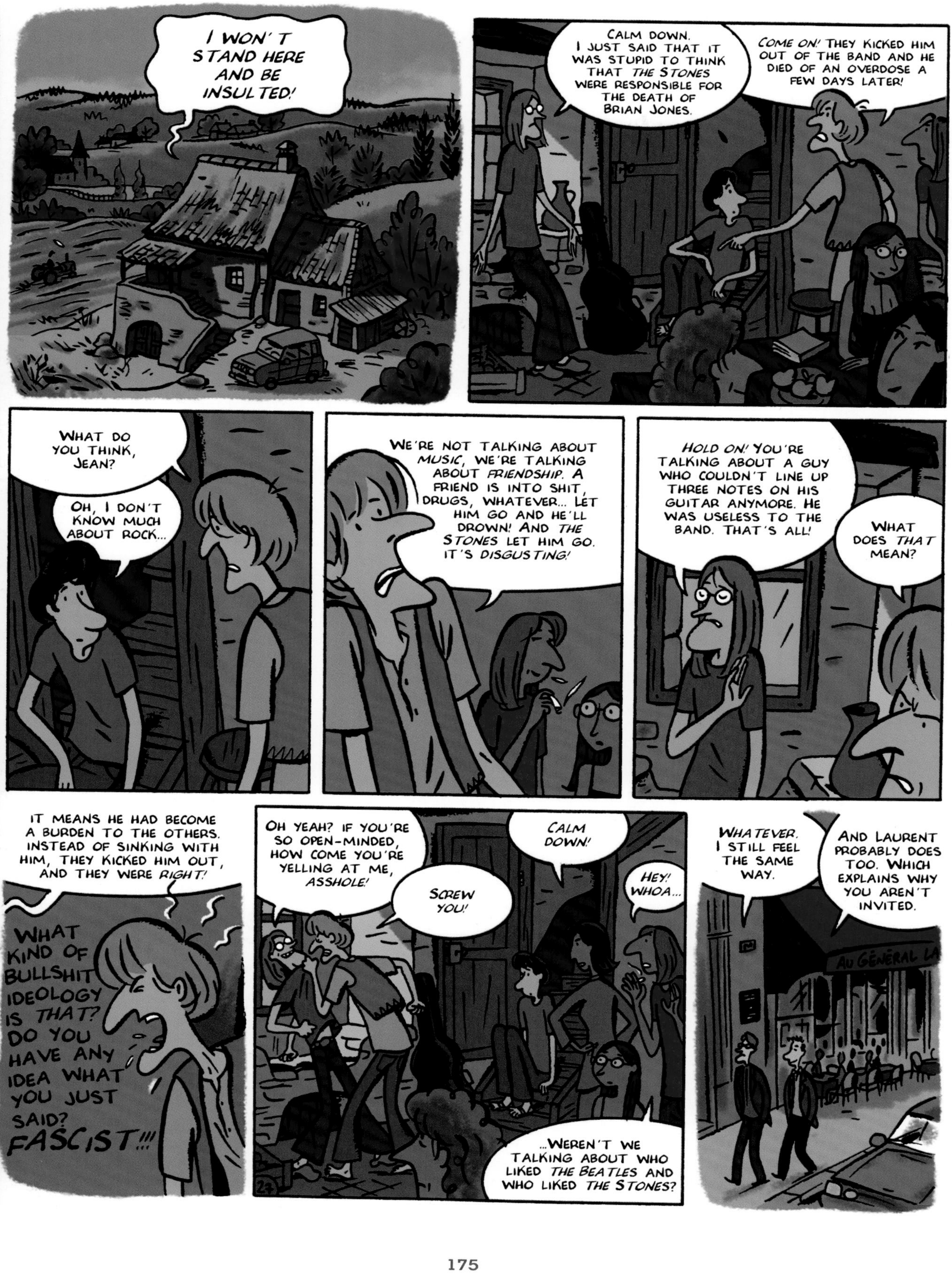
I WON'T STAND HERE AND BE INSULTED!
CALM DOWN. I JUST SAID THAT IT WAS STUPID TO THINK THAT THE STONES WERE RESPONSIBLE FOR THE DEATH OF BRIAN JONES.
COME ON! THEY KICKED HIM OUT OF THE BAND AND HE DIED OF AN OVERDOSE A FEW DAYS LATER!
WHAT DO YOU THINK, JEAN?
OH, I DON'T KNOW MUCH ABOUT ROCK...
WE'RE NOT TALKING ABOUT MUSIC, WE'RE TALKING ABOUT FRIENDSHIP. A FRIEND IS INTO SHIT, DRUGS, WHATEVER... LET HIM GO AND HE'LL DROWN! AND THE STONES LET HIM GO. IT'S DISGUSTING!
HOLD ON! YOU'RE TALKING ABOUT A GUY WHO COULDN'T LINE UP THREE NOTES ON HIS GUITAR ANYMORE. HE WAS USELESS TO THE BAND. THAT'S ALL!
WHAT DOES THAT MEAN?
IT MEANS HE HAD BECOME A BURDEN TO THE OTHERS. INSTEAD OF SINKING WITH HIM, THEY KICKED HIM OUT, AND THEY WERE RIGHT!
WHAT KIND OF BULLSHIT IDEOLOGY IS THAT? DO YOU HAVE ANY IDEA WHAT YOU JUST SAID? FASCIST!!!
OH YEAH? IF YOU'RE SO OPEN-MINDED, HOW COME YOU'RE YELLING AT ME, ASSHOLE!
SCREW YOU!
CALM DOWN!
HEY! WHOA...
...WEREN'T WE TALKING ABOUT WHO LIKED THE BEATLES AND WHO LIKED THE STONES?
WHATEVER. I STILL FEEL THE SAME WAY.
AND LAURENT PROBABLY DOES TOO. WHICH EXPLAINS WHY YOU AREN'T INVITED.
AU GÉNÉRAL LA

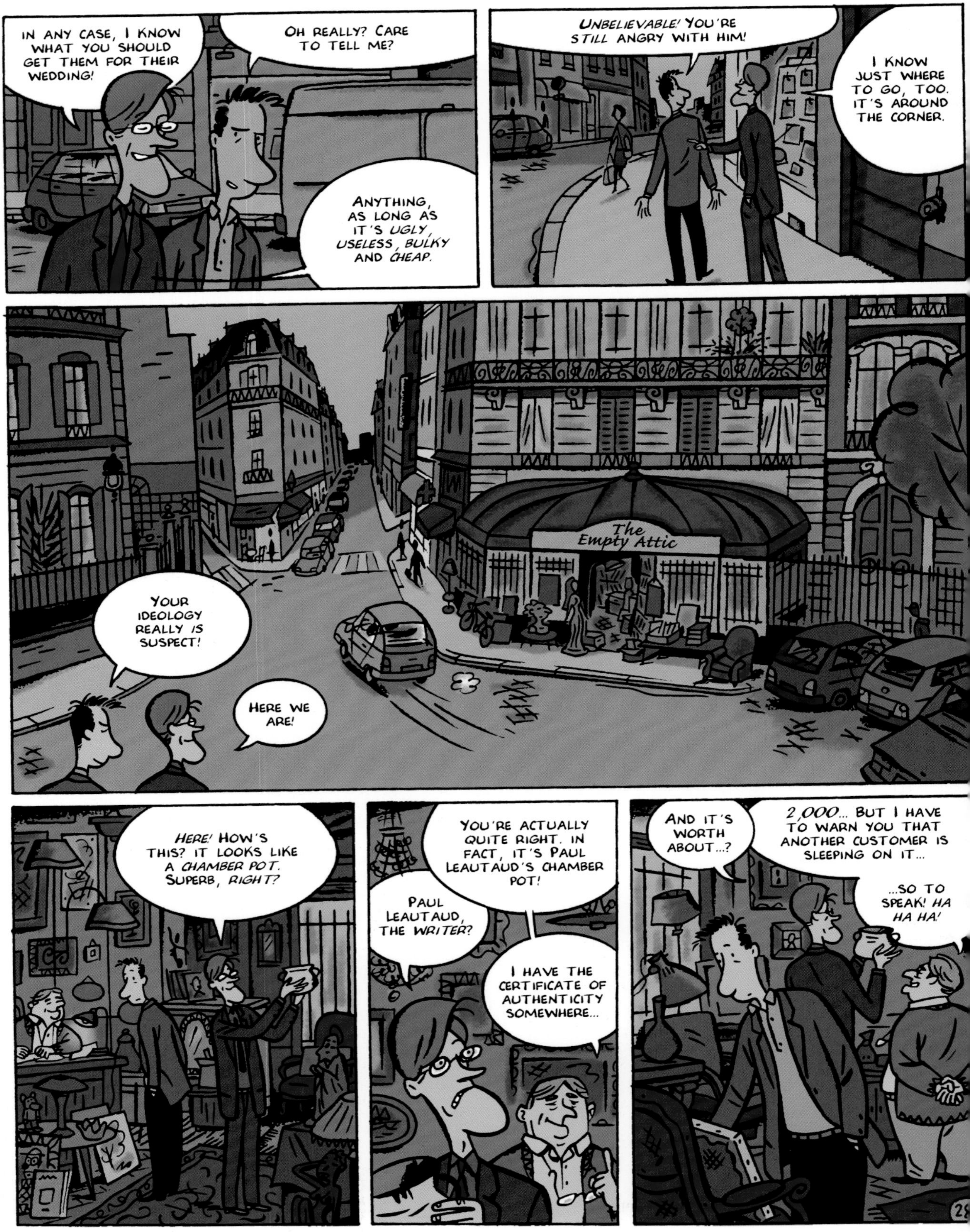
IN ANY CASE, I KNOW WHAT YOU SHOULD GET THEM FOR THEIR WEDDING!
OH REALLY? CARE TO TELL ME?
ANYTHING, AS LONG AS IT'S UGLY, USELESS, BULKY AND CHEAP.
UNBELIEVABLE! YOU'RE STILL ANGRY WITH HIM!
I KNOW JUST WHERE TO GO, TOO. IT'S AROUND THE CORNER.
The Empty Attic
YOUR IDEOLOGY REALLY IS SUSPECT!
HERE WE ARE!
HERE! HOW'S THIS? IT LOOKS LIKE A CHAMBER POT. SUPERB, RIGHT?
YOU'RE ACTUALLY QUITE RIGHT. IN FACT, IT'S PAUL LEAUTAUD'S CHAMBER POT!
PAUL LEAUTAUD, THE WRITER?
I HAVE THE CERTIFICATE OF AUTHENTICITY SOMEWHERE...
AND IT'S WORTH ABOUT...?
2,000... BUT I HAVE TO WARN YOU THAT ANOTHER CUSTOMER IS SLEEPING ON IT...
...SO TO SPEAK! HA HA HA!

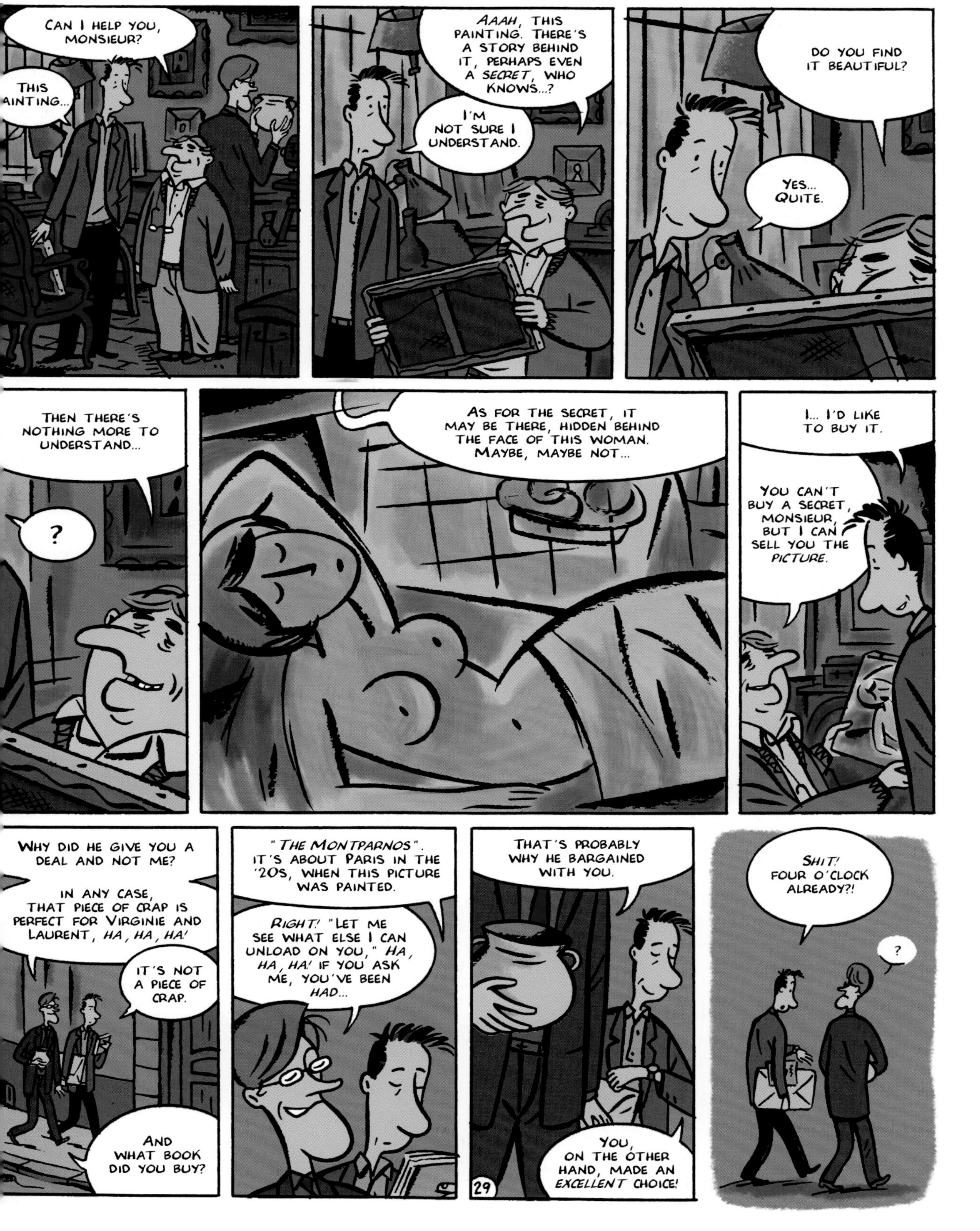
CAN I HELP YOU, MONSIEUR?
THIS PAINTING...
AAAH, THIS PAINTING. THERE'S A STORY BEHIND IT, PERHAPS EVEN A SECRET, WHO KNOWS...?
I'M NOT SURE I UNDERSTAND.
DO YOU FIND IT BEAUTIFUL?
YES... QUITE.
THEN THERE'S NOTHING MORE TO UNDERSTAND...
?
AS FOR THE SECRET, IT MAY BE THERE, HIDDEN BEHIND THE FACE OF THIS WOMAN. MAYBE, MAYBE NOT...
I... I'D LIKE TO BUY IT.
YOU CAN'T BUY A SECRET, MONSIEUR, BUT I CAN SELL YOU THE PICTURE.
WHY DID HE GIVE YOU A DEAL AND NOT ME?
IN ANY CASE, THAT PIECE OF CRAP IS PERFECT FOR VIRGINIE AND LAURENT, HA, HA, HA!
IT'S NOT A PIECE OF CRAP.
AND WHAT BOOK DID YOU BUY?
"THE MONTPARNOS". IT'S ABOUT PARIS IN THE '20S, WHEN THIS PICTURE WAS PAINTED.
RIGHT! "LET ME SEE WHAT ELSE I CAN UNLOAD ON YOU," HA, HA, HA! IF YOU ASK ME, YOU'VE BEEN HAD...
THAT'S PROBABLY WHY HE BARGAINED WITH YOU.
YOU, ON THE OTHER HAND, MADE AN EXCELLENT CHOICE!
29
SHIT! FOUR O'CLOCK ALREADY?!
?

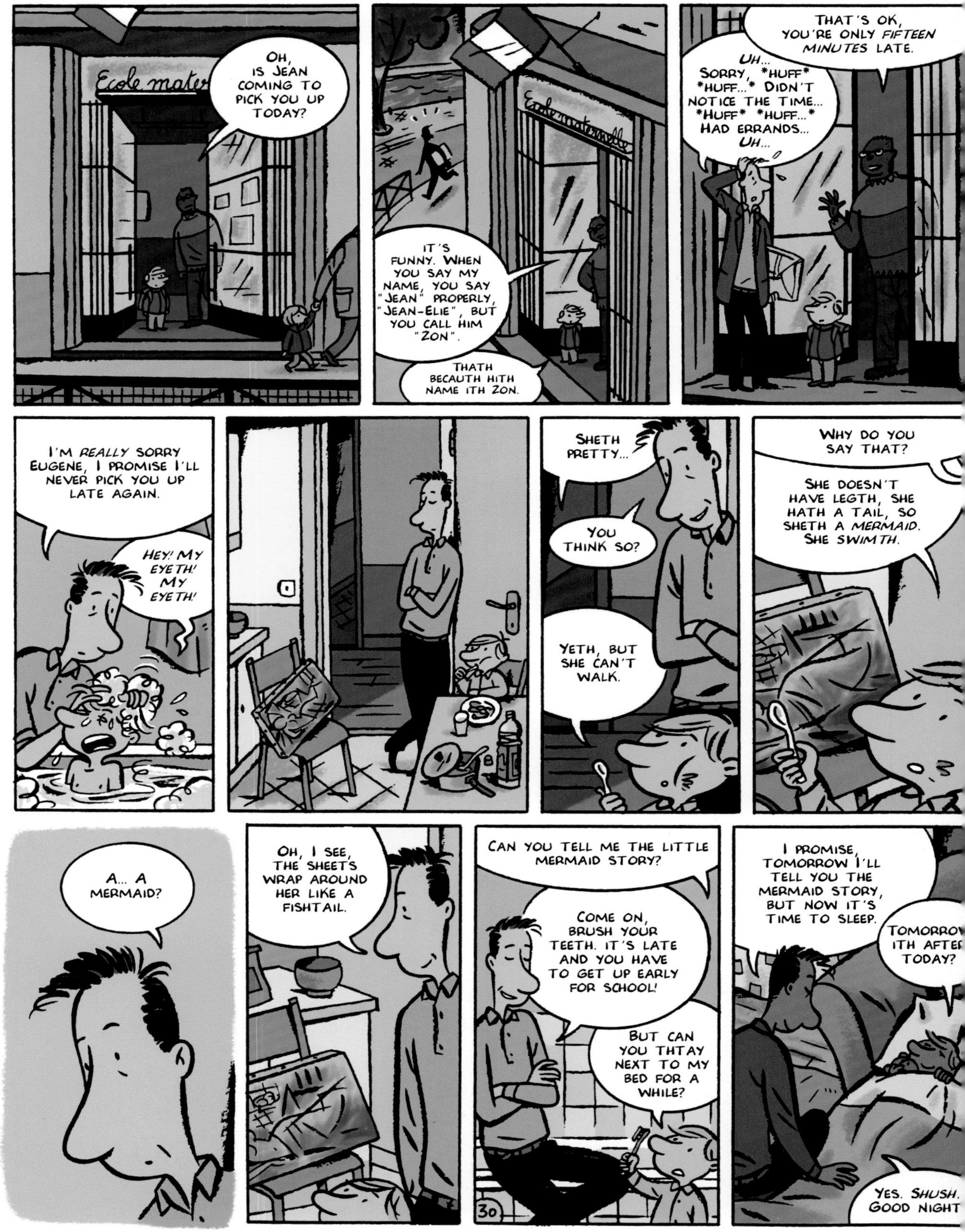
Ecole mater
OH, IS JEAN COMING TO PICK YOU UP TODAY?
Ecole maternelle
IT'S FUNNY. WHEN YOU SAY MY NAME, YOU SAY "JEAN" PROPERLY, "JEAN-ELIE", BUT YOU CALL HIM "ZON".
THATH BECAUTH HITH NAME ITH ZON.
THAT'S OK, YOU'RE ONLY FIFTEEN MINUTES LATE.
UH... SORRY, *HUFF* *HUFF...* DIDN'T NOTICE THE TIME... *HUFF* *HUFF...* HAD ERRANDS... UH...
I'M REALLY SORRY EUGENE, I PROMISE I'LL NEVER PICK YOU UP LATE AGAIN.
HEY! MY EYETH! MY EYETH!
SHETH PRETTY...
YOU THINK SO?
YETH, BUT SHE CAN'T WALK.
WHY DO YOU SAY THAT?
SHE DOESN'T HAVE LEGTH, SHE HATH A TAIL, SO SHETH A MERMAID. SHE SWIMTH.
A... A MERMAID?
OH, I SEE, THE SHEETS WRAP AROUND HER LIKE A FISHTAIL.
CAN YOU TELL ME THE LITTLE MERMAID STORY?
COME ON, BRUSH YOUR TEETH. IT'S LATE AND YOU HAVE TO GET UP EARLY FOR SCHOOL!
BUT CAN YOU THTAY NEXT TO MY BED FOR A WHILE?
30
I PROMISE, TOMORROW I'LL TELL YOU THE MERMAID STORY, BUT NOW IT'S TIME TO SLEEP.
TOMORROW ITH AFTER TODAY?
YES. SHUSH. GOOD NIGHT

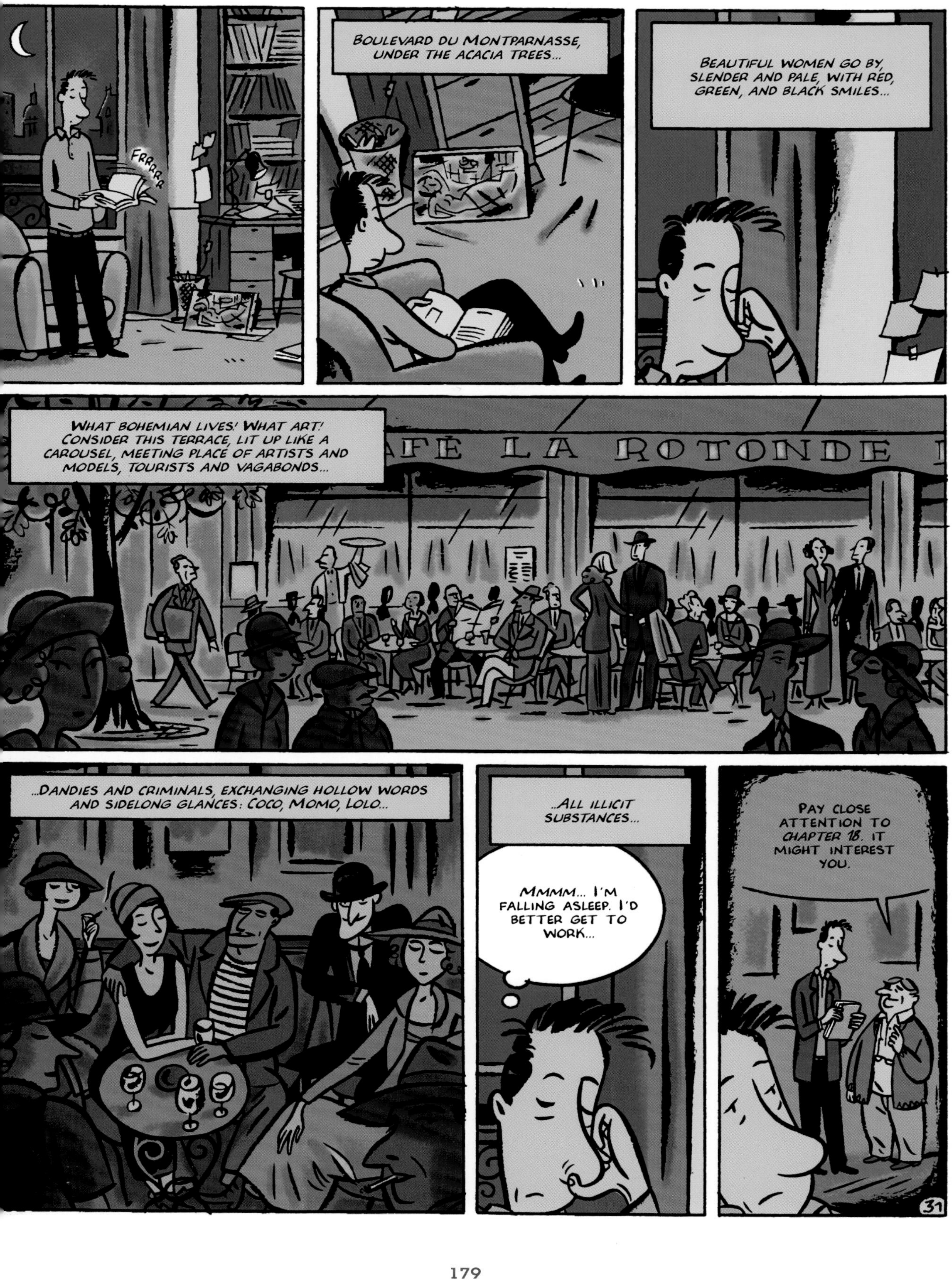
FRRRRRR
Boulevard du Montparnasse, under the acacia trees...
Beautiful women go by, slender and pale, with red, green, and black smiles...
What bohemian lives! What art! Consider this terrace, lit up like a carousel, meeting place of artists and models, tourists and vagabonds...
AFÉ LA ROTONDE
...Dandies and criminals, exchanging hollow words and sidelong glances: Coco, Momo, Lolo...
...All illicit substances...
Mmmm... I'm falling asleep. I'd better get to work...
Pay close attention to chapter 18. It might interest you.
31

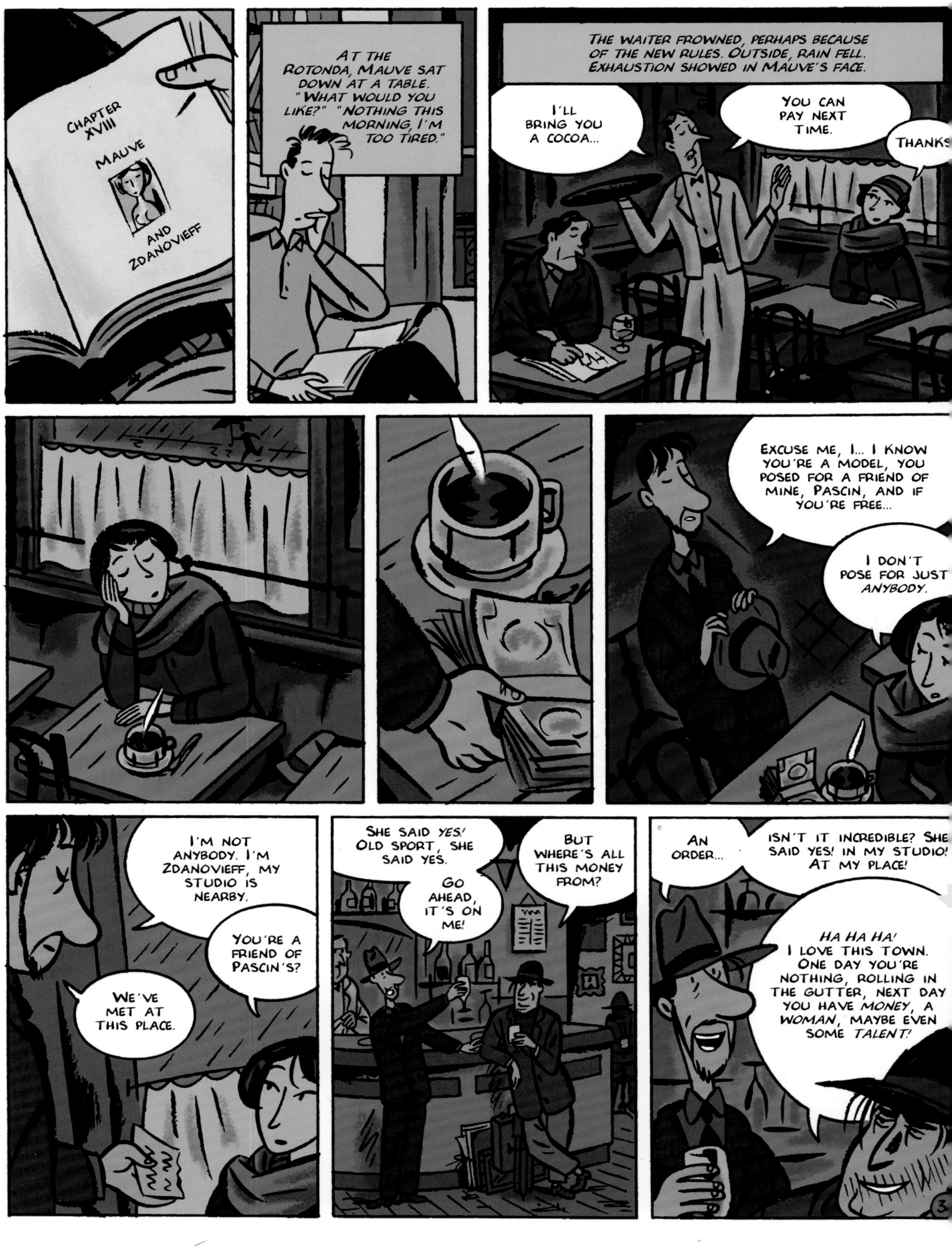
CHAPTER XVIII
MAUVE
AND ZDANOVIEFF
AT THE ROTONDA, MAUVE SAT DOWN AT A TABLE. "WHAT WOULD YOU LIKE?" "NOTHING THIS MORNING, I'M TOO TIRED."
THE WAITER FROWNED, PERHAPS BECAUSE OF THE NEW RULES. OUTSIDE, RAIN FELL. EXHAUSTION SHOWED IN MAUVE'S FACE.
I'LL BRING YOU A COCOA...
YOU CAN PAY NEXT TIME.
THANKS
EXCUSE ME, I... I KNOW YOU'RE A MODEL, YOU POSED FOR A FRIEND OF MINE, PASCIN, AND IF YOU'RE FREE...
I DON'T POSE FOR JUST *ANYBODY*.
I'M NOT ANYBODY. I'M ZDANOVIEFF, MY STUDIO IS NEARBY.
YOU'RE A FRIEND OF PASCIN'S?
WE'VE MET AT THIS PLACE.
SHE SAID *YES*! OLD SPORT, SHE SAID YES.
GO AHEAD, IT'S ON ME!
BUT WHERE'S ALL THIS MONEY FROM?
AN ORDER...
ISN'T IT INCREDIBLE? SHE SAID YES! IN MY STUDIO! AT MY PLACE!
HA HA HA! I LOVE THIS TOWN. ONE DAY YOU'RE NOTHING, ROLLING IN THE GUTTER, NEXT DAY YOU HAVE *MONEY*, A *WOMAN*, MAYBE EVEN SOME *TALENT*!

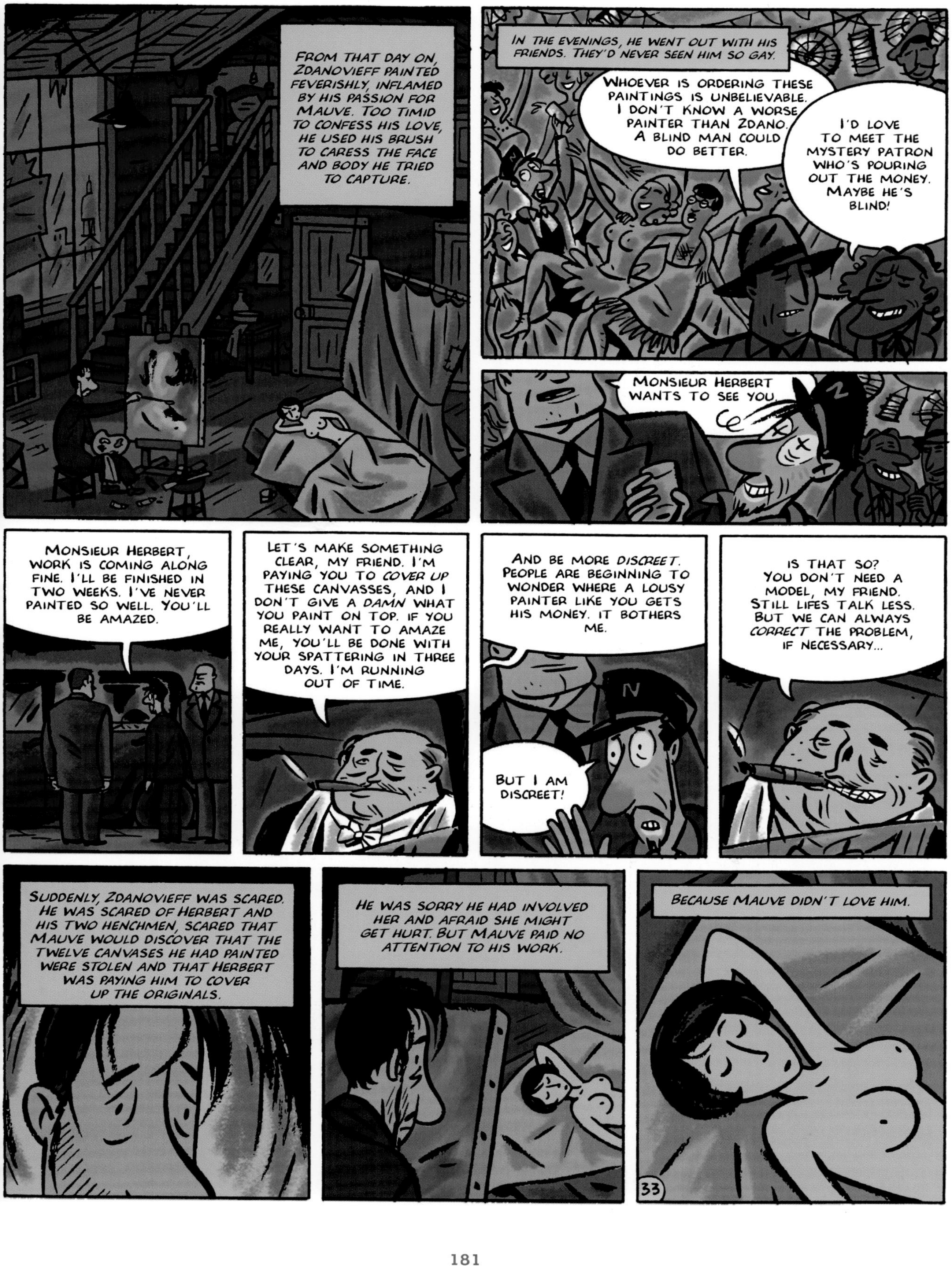
FROM THAT DAY ON, ZDANOVIEFF PAINTED FEVERISHLY, INFLAMED BY HIS PASSION FOR MAUVE. TOO TIMID TO CONFESS HIS LOVE, HE USED HIS BRUSH TO CARESS THE FACE AND BODY HE TRIED TO CAPTURE.
IN THE EVENINGS, HE WENT OUT WITH HIS FRIENDS. THEY'D NEVER SEEN HIM SO GAY.
WHOEVER IS ORDERING THESE PAINTINGS IS UNBELIEVABLE. I DON'T KNOW A WORSE PAINTER THAN ZDANO. A BLIND MAN COULD DO BETTER.
I'D LOVE TO MEET THE MYSTERY PATRON WHO'S POURING OUT THE MONEY. MAYBE HE'S BLIND!
MONSIEUR HERBERT WANTS TO SEE YOU.
MONSIEUR HERBERT, WORK IS COMING ALONG FINE. I'LL BE FINISHED IN TWO WEEKS. I'VE NEVER PAINTED SO WELL. YOU'LL BE AMAZED.
LET'S MAKE SOMETHING CLEAR, MY FRIEND. I'M PAYING YOU TO COVER UP THESE CANVASSES, AND I DON'T GIVE A DAMN WHAT YOU PAINT ON TOP. IF YOU REALLY WANT TO AMAZE ME, YOU'LL BE DONE WITH YOUR SPATTERING IN THREE DAYS. I'M RUNNING OUT OF TIME.
AND BE MORE DISCREET. PEOPLE ARE BEGINNING TO WONDER WHERE A LOUSY PAINTER LIKE YOU GETS HIS MONEY. IT BOTHERS ME.
BUT I AM DISCREET!
IS THAT SO? YOU DON'T NEED A MODEL, MY FRIEND. STILL LIFES TALK LESS. BUT WE CAN ALWAYS CORRECT THE PROBLEM, IF NECESSARY...
SUDDENLY, ZDANOVIEFF WAS SCARED. HE WAS SCARED OF HERBERT AND HIS TWO HENCHMEN, SCARED THAT MAUVE WOULD DISCOVER THAT THE TWELVE CANVASES HE HAD PAINTED WERE STOLEN AND THAT HERBERT WAS PAYING HIM TO COVER UP THE ORIGINALS.
HE WAS SORRY HE HAD INVOLVED HER AND AFRAID SHE MIGHT GET HURT. BUT MAUVE PAID NO ATTENTION TO HIS WORK.
BECAUSE MAUVE DIDN'T LOVE HIM.
33

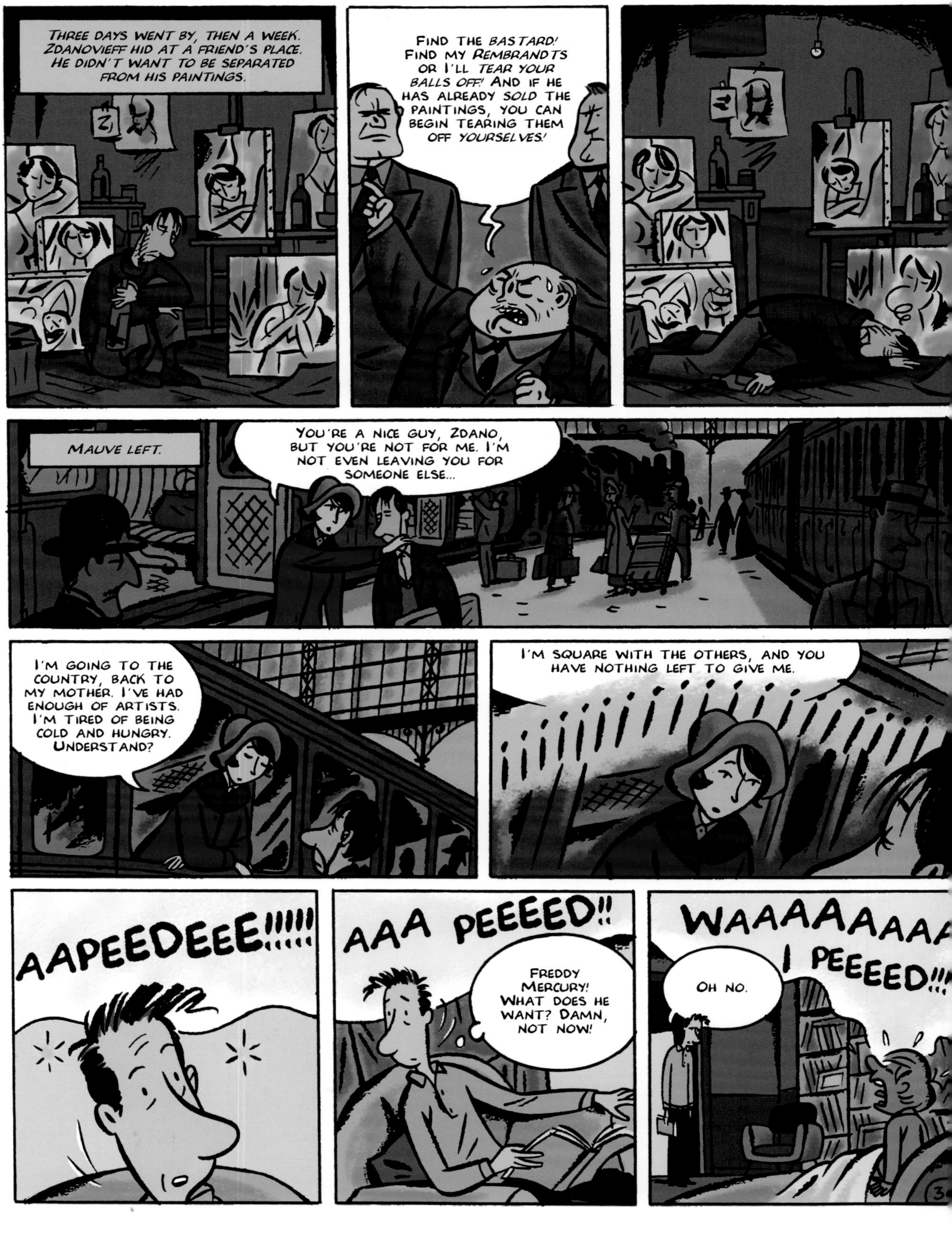
THREE DAYS WENT BY, THEN A WEEK. ZDANOVIEFF HID AT A FRIEND'S PLACE. HE DIDN'T WANT TO BE SEPARATED FROM HIS PAINTINGS.
FIND THE BASTARD! FIND MY REMBRANDTS OR I'LL TEAR YOUR BALLS OFF! AND IF HE HAS ALREADY SOLD THE PAINTINGS, YOU CAN BEGIN TEARING THEM OFF YOURSELVES!
MAUVE LEFT.
YOU'RE A NICE GUY, ZDANO, BUT YOU'RE NOT FOR ME. I'M NOT EVEN LEAVING YOU FOR SOMEONE ELSE...
I'M GOING TO THE COUNTRY, BACK TO MY MOTHER. I'VE HAD ENOUGH OF ARTISTS. I'M TIRED OF BEING COLD AND HUNGRY. UNDERSTAND?
I'M SQUARE WITH THE OTHERS, AND YOU HAVE NOTHING LEFT TO GIVE ME.
AAPEEDEEE!!!!!
AAA PEEEED!!
FREDDY MERCURY! WHAT DOES HE WANT? DAMN, NOT NOW!
WAAAAAAAA
I PEEEED!!!
OH NO.

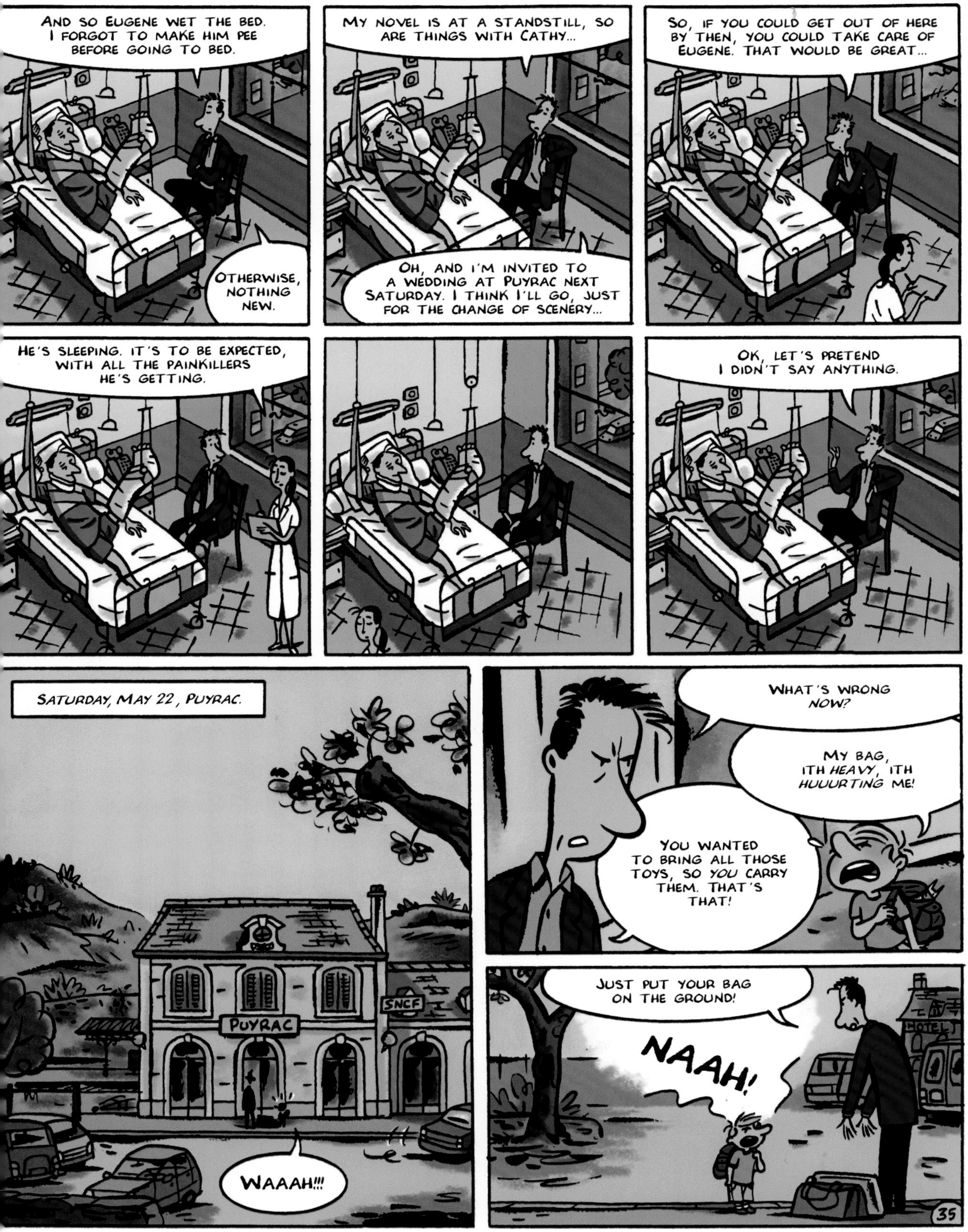

AND SO EUGENE WET THE BED. I FORGOT TO MAKE HIM PEE BEFORE GOING TO BED.
OTHERWISE, NOTHING NEW.
MY NOVEL IS AT A STANDSTILL, SO ARE THINGS WITH CATHY...
OH, AND I'M INVITED TO A WEDDING AT PUYRAC NEXT SATURDAY. I THINK I'LL GO, JUST FOR THE CHANGE OF SCENERY...
SO, IF YOU COULD GET OUT OF HERE BY THEN, YOU COULD TAKE CARE OF EUGENE. THAT WOULD BE GREAT...
HE'S SLEEPING. IT'S TO BE EXPECTED, WITH ALL THE PAINKILLERS HE'S GETTING.
OK, LET'S PRETEND I DIDN'T SAY ANYTHING.
SATURDAY, MAY 22, PUYRAC.
SNCF
PUYRAC
WAAAH!!!
WHAT'S WRONG NOW?
MY BAG, ITH HEAVY, ITH HUUURTING ME!
YOU WANTED TO BRING ALL THOSE TOYS, SO YOU CARRY THEM. THAT'S THAT!
JUST PUT YOUR BAG ON THE GROUND!
NAAH!
HOTEL
35

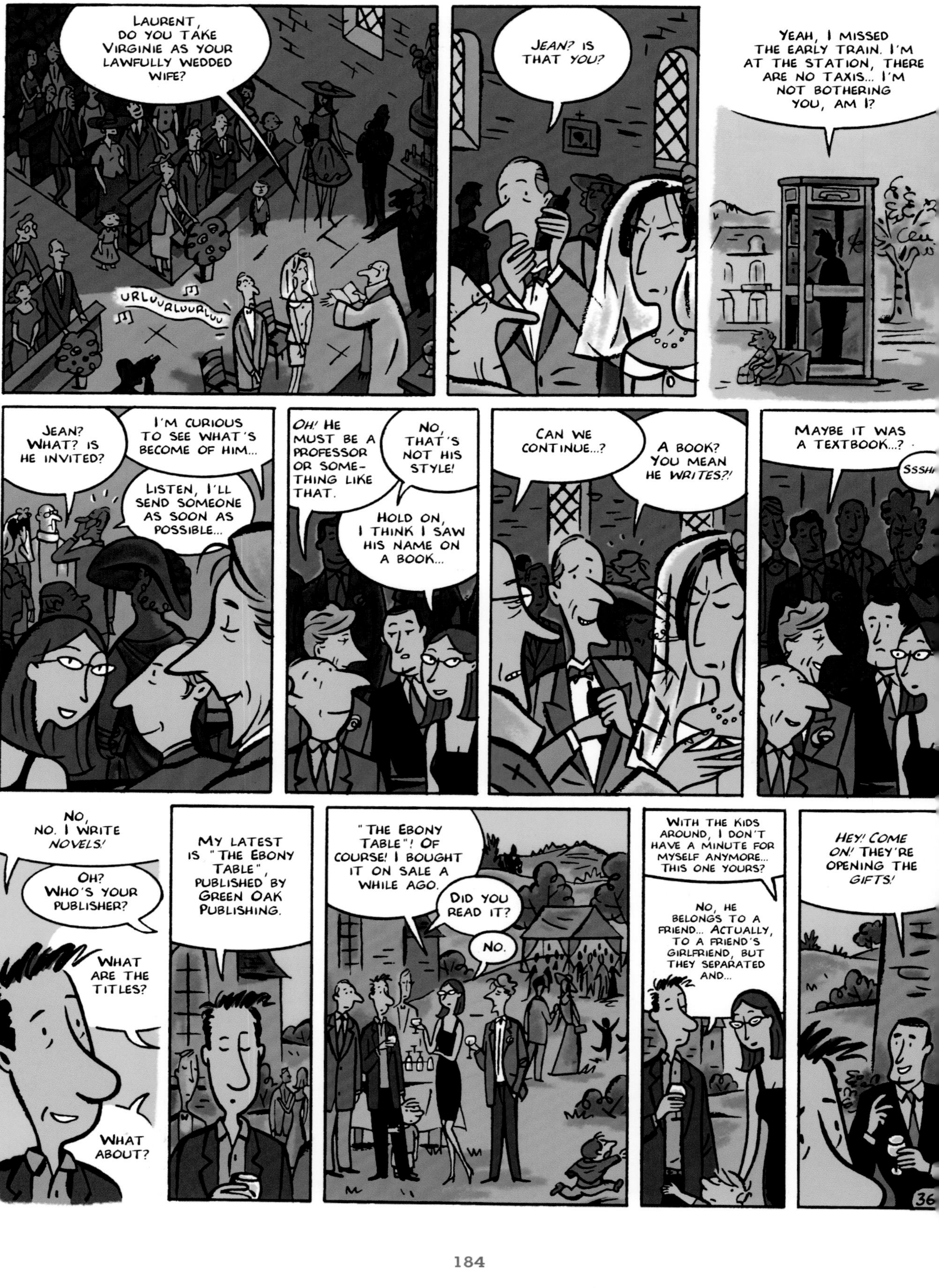
LAURENT, DO YOU TAKE VIRGINIE AS YOUR LAWFULLY WEDDED WIFE?
URLUURLUURLUU
JEAN? IS THAT YOU?
YEAH, I MISSED THE EARLY TRAIN. I'M AT THE STATION, THERE ARE NO TAXIS... I'M NOT BOTHERING YOU, AM I?
JEAN? WHAT? IS HE INVITED?
I'M CURIOUS TO SEE WHAT'S BECOME OF HIM...
LISTEN, I'LL SEND SOMEONE AS SOON AS POSSIBLE...
OH! HE MUST BE A PROFESSOR OR SOMETHING LIKE THAT.
NO, THAT'S NOT HIS STYLE!
HOLD ON, I THINK I SAW HIS NAME ON A BOOK...
CAN WE CONTINUE...?
A BOOK? YOU MEAN HE WRITES?!
MAYBE IT WAS A TEXTBOOK...?
SSSH
NO, NO. I WRITE NOVELS!
OH? WHO'S YOUR PUBLISHER?
WHAT ARE THE TITLES?
WHAT ABOUT?
MY LATEST IS "THE EBONY TABLE", PUBLISHED BY GREEN OAK PUBLISHING.
"THE EBONY TABLE"! OF COURSE! I BOUGHT IT ON SALE A WHILE AGO.
DID YOU READ IT?
NO.
WITH THE KIDS AROUND, I DON'T HAVE A MINUTE FOR MYSELF ANYMORE... THIS ONE YOURS?
NO, HE BELONGS TO A FRIEND... ACTUALLY, TO A FRIEND'S GIRLFRIEND, BUT THEY SEPARATED AND...
HEY! COME ON! THEY'RE OPENING THE GIFTS!
36

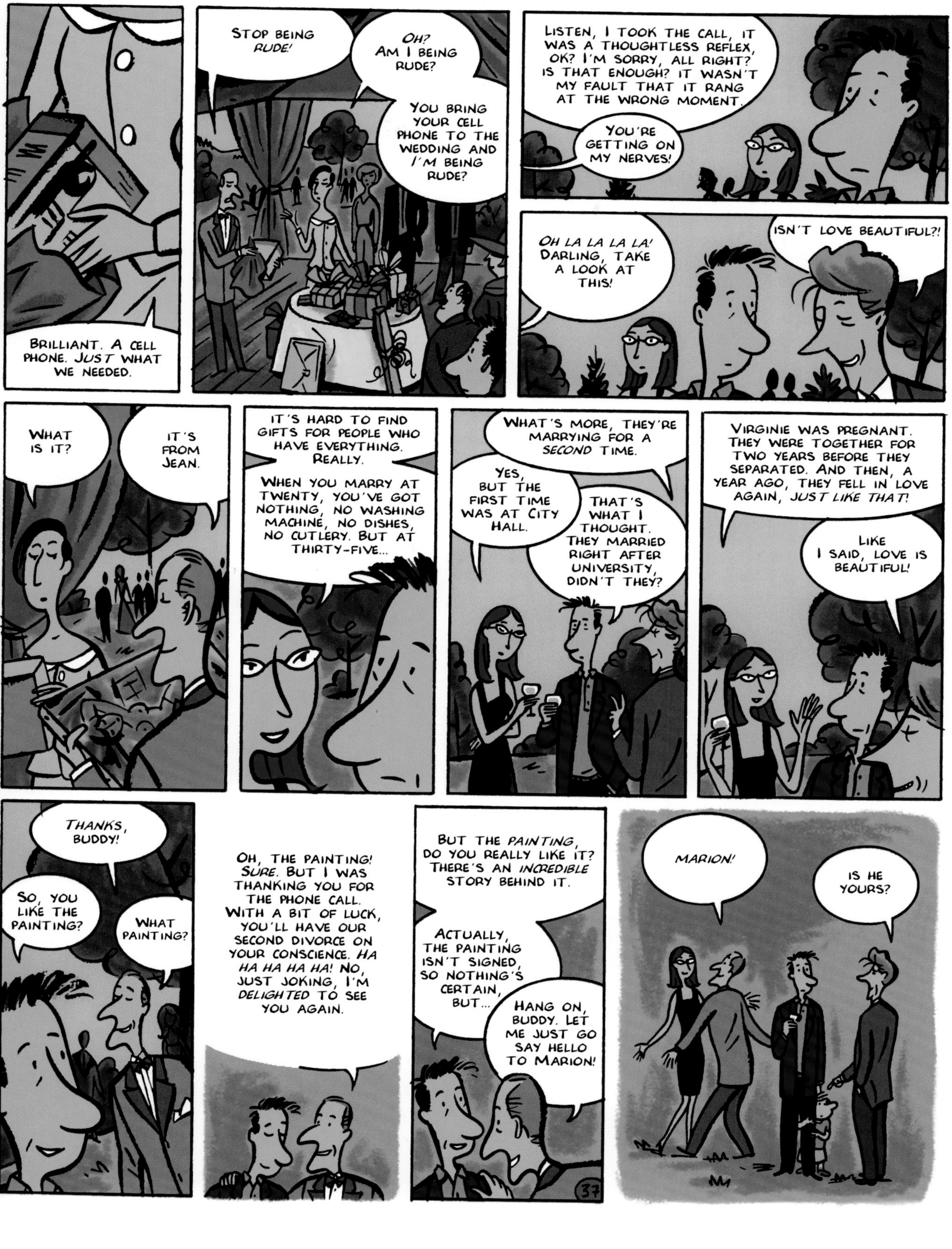
BRILLIANT. A CELL PHONE. JUST WHAT WE NEEDED.
STOP BEING RUDE!
OH? AM I BEING RUDE?
YOU BRING YOUR CELL PHONE TO THE WEDDING AND I'M BEING RUDE?
LISTEN, I TOOK THE CALL, IT WAS A THOUGHTLESS REFLEX, OK? I'M SORRY, ALL RIGHT? IS THAT ENOUGH? IT WASN'T MY FAULT THAT IT RANG AT THE WRONG MOMENT.
YOU'RE GETTING ON MY NERVES!
OH LA LA LA LA! DARLING, TAKE A LOOK AT THIS!
ISN'T LOVE BEAUTIFUL?!
WHAT IS IT?
IT'S FROM JEAN.
IT'S HARD TO FIND GIFTS FOR PEOPLE WHO HAVE EVERYTHING. REALLY.
WHEN YOU MARRY AT TWENTY, YOU'VE GOT NOTHING, NO WASHING MACHINE, NO DISHES, NO CUTLERY. BUT AT THIRTY-FIVE...
WHAT'S MORE, THEY'RE MARRYING FOR A SECOND TIME.
YES, BUT THE FIRST TIME WAS AT CITY HALL.
THAT'S WHAT I THOUGHT. THEY MARRIED RIGHT AFTER UNIVERSITY, DIDN'T THEY?
VIRGINIE WAS PREGNANT. THEY WERE TOGETHER FOR TWO YEARS BEFORE THEY SEPARATED. AND THEN, A YEAR AGO, THEY FELL IN LOVE AGAIN, JUST LIKE THAT!
LIKE I SAID, LOVE IS BEAUTIFUL!
THANKS, BUDDY!
SO, YOU LIKE THE PAINTING?
WHAT PAINTING?
OH, THE PAINTING! SURE. BUT I WAS THANKING YOU FOR THE PHONE CALL. WITH A BIT OF LUCK, YOU'LL HAVE OUR SECOND DIVORCE ON YOUR CONSCIENCE. HA HA HA HA HA! NO, JUST JOKING, I'M DELIGHTED TO SEE YOU AGAIN.
BUT THE PAINTING, DO YOU REALLY LIKE IT? THERE'S AN INCREDIBLE STORY BEHIND IT.
ACTUALLY, THE PAINTING ISN'T SIGNED, SO NOTHING'S CERTAIN, BUT...
HANG ON, BUDDY. LET ME JUST GO SAY HELLO TO MARION!
37
MARION!
IS HE YOURS?

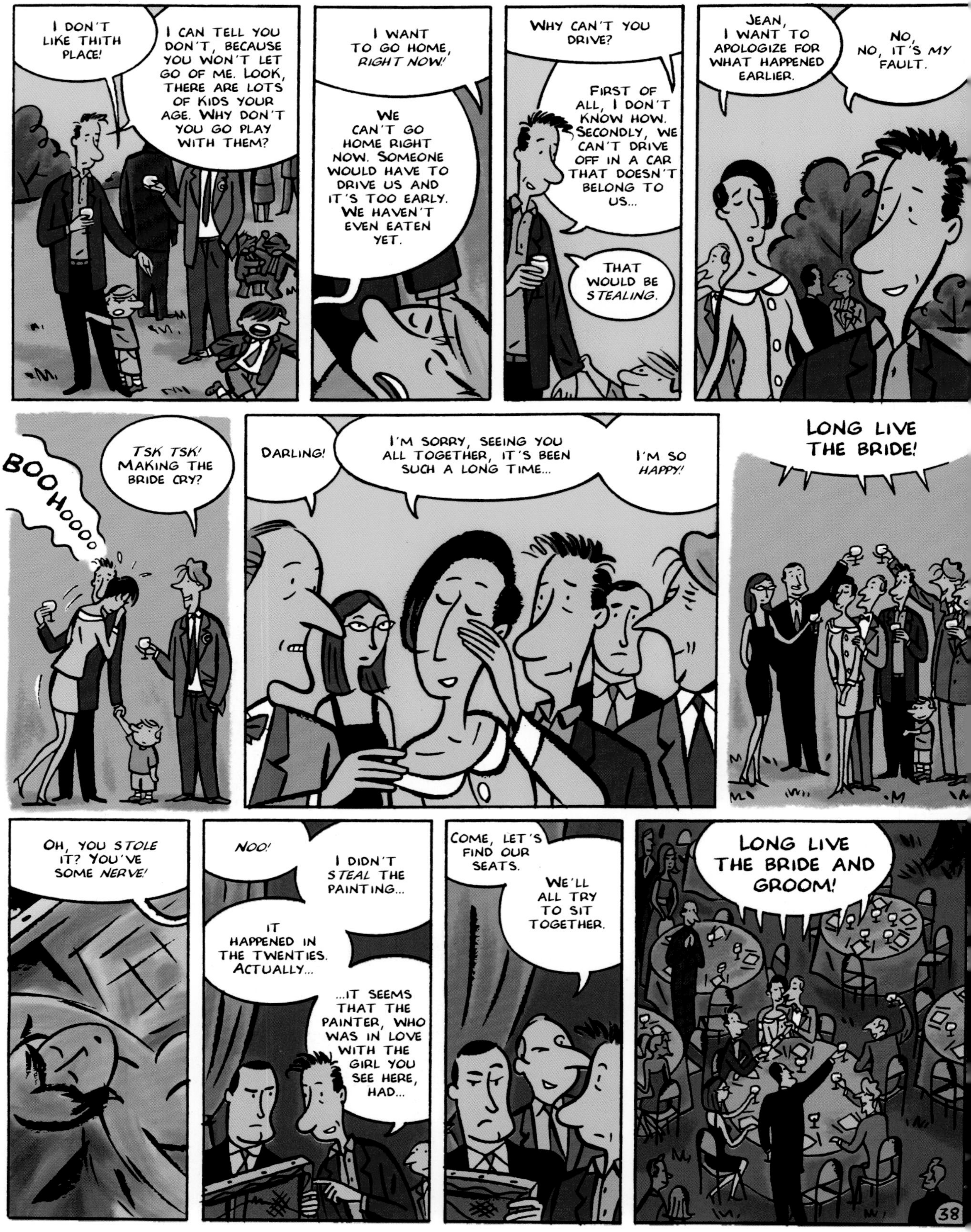
I DON'T LIKE THITH PLACE!
I CAN TELL YOU DON'T, BECAUSE YOU WON'T LET GO OF ME. LOOK, THERE ARE LOTS OF KIDS YOUR AGE. WHY DON'T YOU GO PLAY WITH THEM?
I WANT TO GO HOME, RIGHT NOW!
WE CAN'T GO HOME RIGHT NOW. SOMEONE WOULD HAVE TO DRIVE US AND IT'S TOO EARLY. WE HAVEN'T EVEN EATEN YET.
WHY CAN'T YOU DRIVE?
FIRST OF ALL, I DON'T KNOW HOW. SECONDLY, WE CAN'T DRIVE OFF IN A CAR THAT DOESN'T BELONG TO US...
THAT WOULD BE STEALING.
JEAN, I WANT TO APOLOGIZE FOR WHAT HAPPENED EARLIER.
NO, NO, IT'S MY FAULT.
BOOHoooo
TSK TSK! MAKING THE BRIDE CRY?
DARLING!
I'M SORRY, SEEING YOU ALL TOGETHER, IT'S BEEN SUCH A LONG TIME...
I'M SO HAPPY!
LONG LIVE THE BRIDE!
OH, YOU STOLE IT? YOU'VE SOME NERVE!
NOO!
I DIDN'T STEAL THE PAINTING...
IT HAPPENED IN THE TWENTIES. ACTUALLY...
...IT SEEMS THAT THE PAINTER, WHO WAS IN LOVE WITH THE GIRL YOU SEE HERE, HAD...
COME, LET'S FIND OUR SEATS.
WE'LL ALL TRY TO SIT TOGETHER.
LONG LIVE THE BRIDE AND GROOM!
38

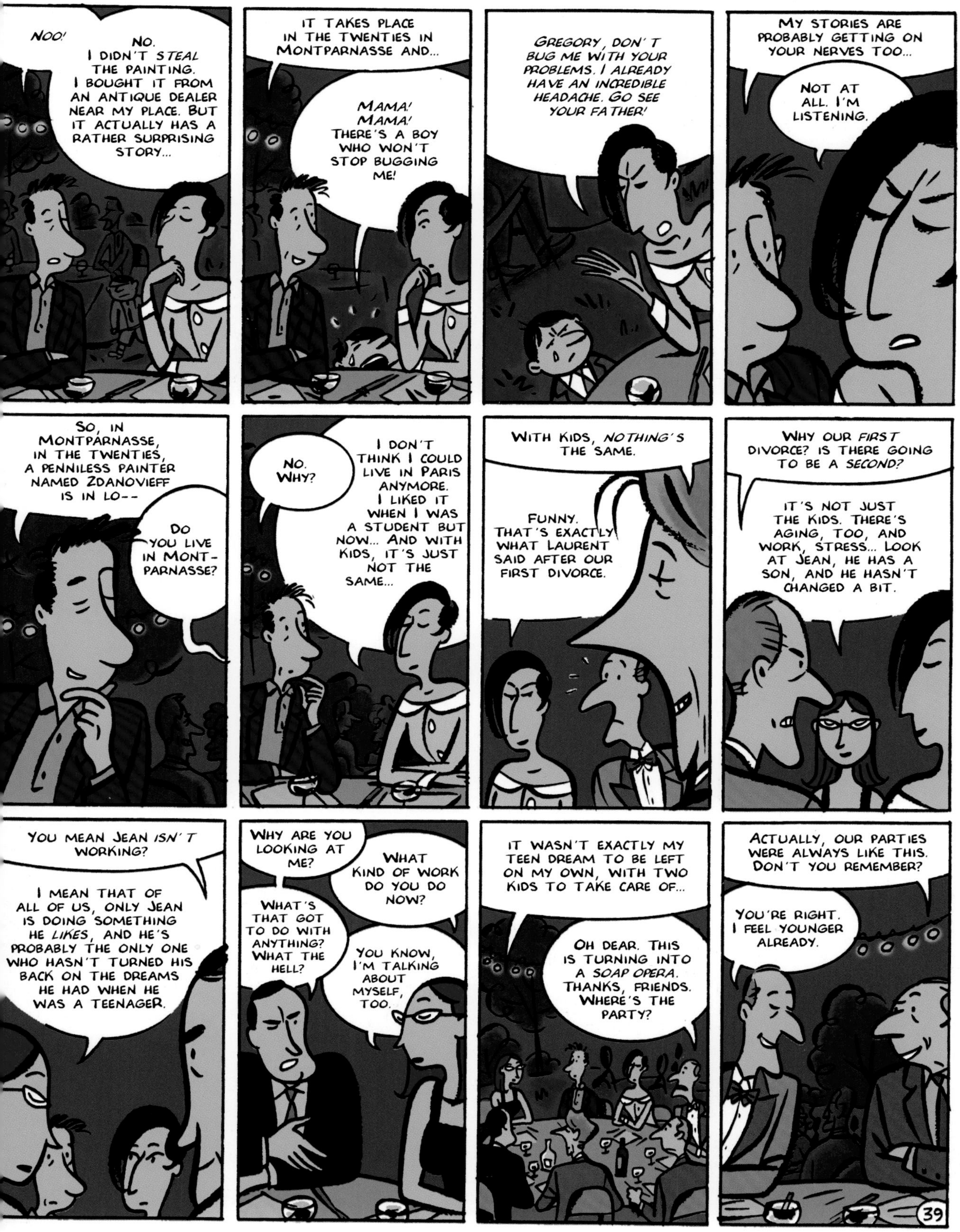
Noo!
No. I didn't *steal* the painting. I bought it from an antique dealer near my place. But it actually has a rather surprising story...
It takes place in the twenties in Montparnasse and...
Mama! Mama! There's a boy who won't stop bugging me!
Gregory, don't bug me with your problems. I already have an incredible headache. Go see your father!
My stories are probably getting on your nerves too...
Not at all. I'm listening.
So, in Montparnasse, in the twenties, a penniless painter named Zdanovieff is in lo--
Do you live in Mont-parnasse?
No. Why?
I don't think I could live in Paris anymore. I liked it when I was a student but now... And with kids, it's just not the same...
With kids, *nothing's* the same.
Funny. That's exactly what Laurent said after our first divorce.
Why our *first* divorce? Is there going to be a *second?*
It's not just the kids. There's aging, too, and work, stress... Look at Jean, he has a son, and he hasn't changed a bit.
You mean Jean *isn't* working?
I mean that of all of us, only Jean is doing something he *likes*, and he's probably the only one who hasn't turned his back on the dreams he had when he was a teenager.
Why are you looking at me?
What kind of work do you do now?
What's that got to do with anything? What the hell?
You know, I'm talking about myself, too.
It wasn't exactly my teen dream to be left on my own, with two kids to take care of...
Oh dear. This is turning into a *soap opera*. Thanks, friends. Where's the party?
Actually, our parties were always like this. Don't you remember?
You're right. I feel younger already.
39

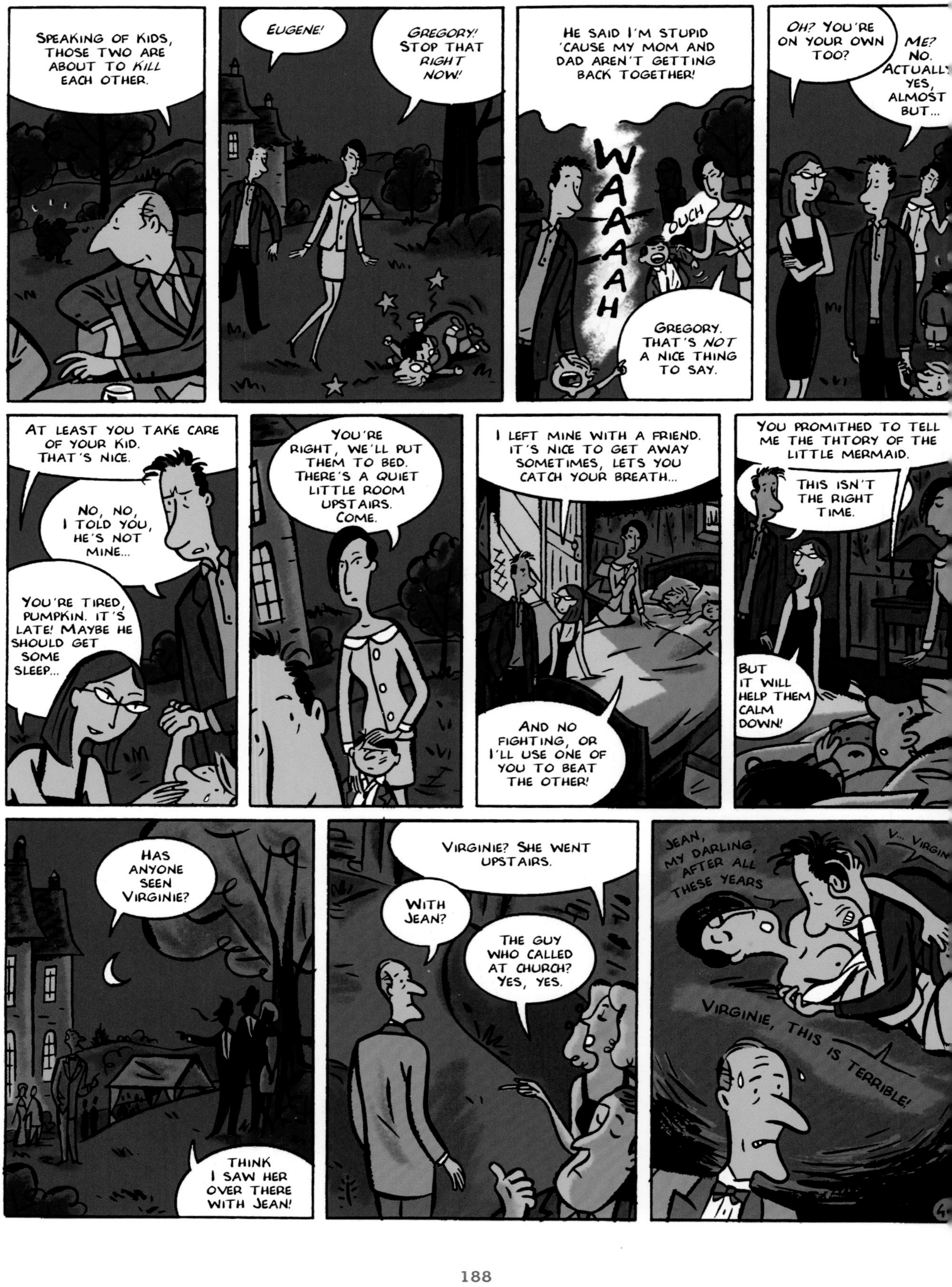

SPEAKING OF KIDS, THOSE TWO ARE ABOUT TO KILL EACH OTHER.
EUGENE!
GREGORY! STOP THAT RIGHT NOW!
HE SAID I'M STUPID 'CAUSE MY MOM AND DAD AREN'T GETTING BACK TOGETHER!
WAAAAAH
OUCH
GREGORY. THAT'S NOT A NICE THING TO SAY.
OH? YOU'RE ON YOUR OWN TOO?
ME? NO. ACTUALLY YES, ALMOST BUT...
AT LEAST YOU TAKE CARE OF YOUR KID. THAT'S NICE.
NO, NO, I TOLD YOU, HE'S NOT MINE...
YOU'RE TIRED, PUMPKIN. IT'S LATE! MAYBE HE SHOULD GET SOME SLEEP...
YOU'RE RIGHT, WE'LL PUT THEM TO BED. THERE'S A QUIET LITTLE ROOM UPSTAIRS. COME.
I LEFT MINE WITH A FRIEND. IT'S NICE TO GET AWAY SOMETIMES, LETS YOU CATCH YOUR BREATH...
AND NO FIGHTING, OR I'LL USE ONE OF YOU TO BEAT THE OTHER!
YOU PROMITHED TO TELL ME THE THTORY OF THE LITTLE MERMAID.
THIS ISN'T THE RIGHT TIME.
BUT IT WILL HELP THEM CALM DOWN!
HAS ANYONE SEEN VIRGINIE?
THINK I SAW HER OVER THERE WITH JEAN!
VIRGINIE? SHE WENT UPSTAIRS.
WITH JEAN?
THE GUY WHO CALLED AT CHURCH? YES, YES.
JEAN, MY DARLING, AFTER ALL THESE YEARS
V... VIRGIN
VIRGINIE, THIS IS TERRIBLE!

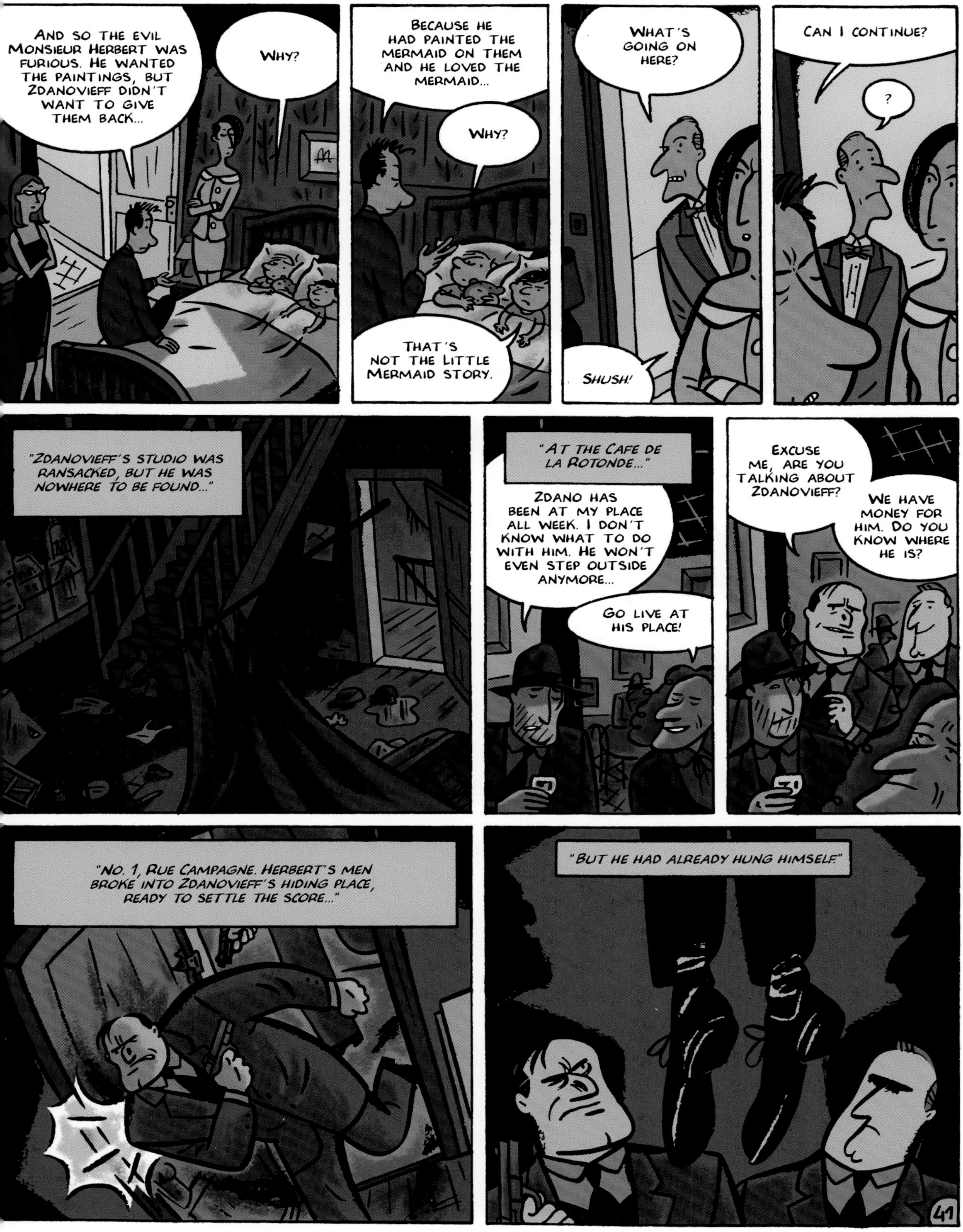

And so the evil Monsieur Herbert was furious. He wanted the paintings, but Zdanovieff didn't want to give them back...
Why?
Because he had painted the mermaid on them and he loved the mermaid...
Why?
That's not the little Mermaid story.
What's going on here?
Shush!
Can I continue?
?
"Zdanovieff's studio was ransacked, but he was nowhere to be found..."
"At the Cafe de la Rotonde..."
Zdano has been at my place all week. I don't know what to do with him. He won't even step outside anymore...
Go live at his place!
Excuse me, are you talking about Zdanovieff?
We have money for him. Do you know where he is?
"No. 1, Rue Campagne. Herbert's men broke into Zdanovieff's hiding place, ready to settle the score..."
"But he had already hung himself."
41

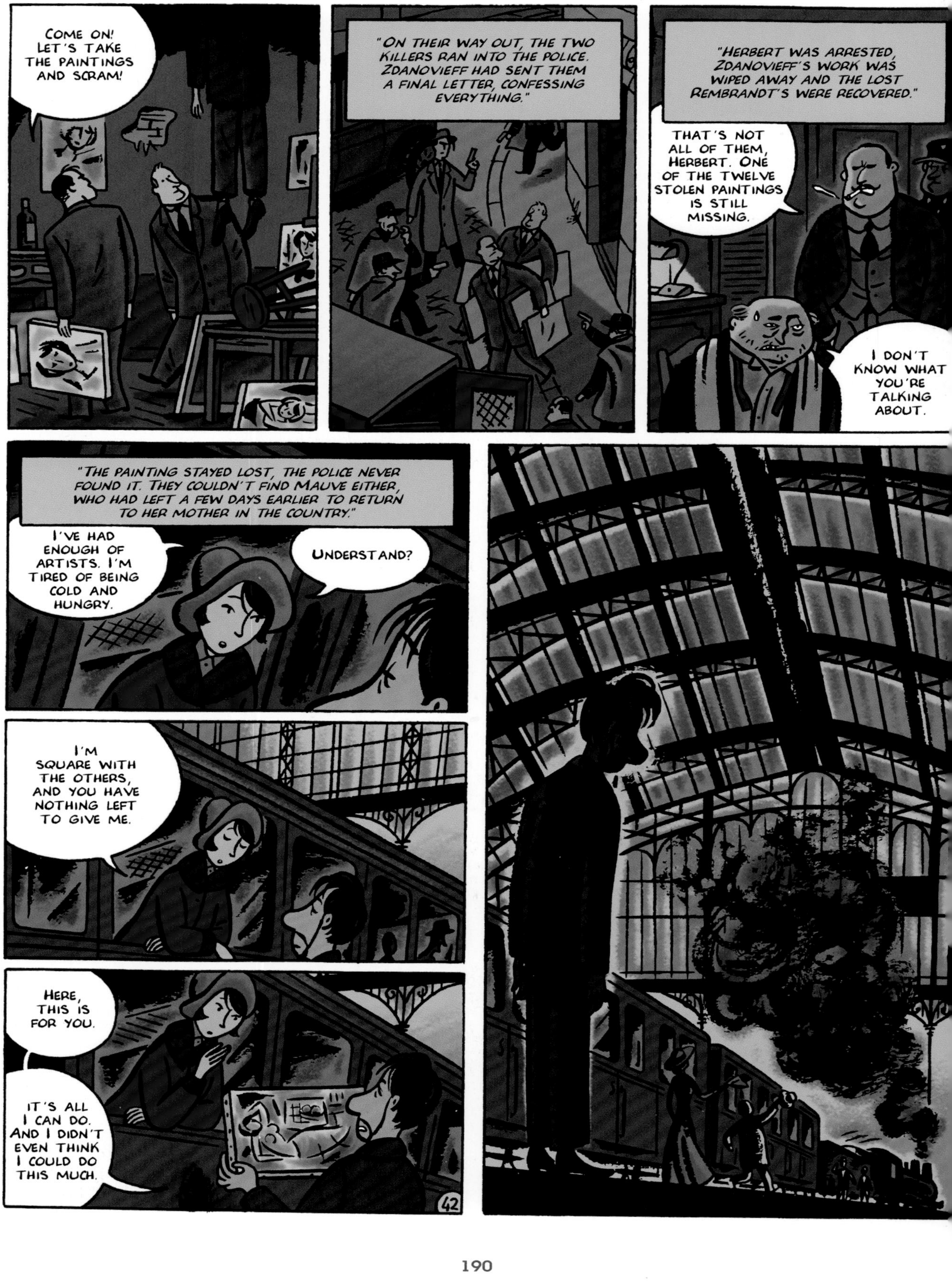
COME ON! LET'S TAKE THE PAINTINGS AND SCRAM!
"ON THEIR WAY OUT, THE TWO KILLERS RAN INTO THE POLICE. ZDANOVIEFF HAD SENT THEM A FINAL LETTER, CONFESSING EVERYTHING."
"HERBERT WAS ARRESTED, ZDANOVIEFF'S WORK WAS WIPED AWAY AND THE LOST REMBRANDT'S WERE RECOVERED."
THAT'S NOT ALL OF THEM, HERBERT. ONE OF THE TWELVE STOLEN PAINTINGS IS STILL MISSING.
I DON'T KNOW WHAT YOU'RE TALKING ABOUT.
"THE PAINTING STAYED LOST, THE POLICE NEVER FOUND IT. THEY COULDN'T FIND MAUVE EITHER, WHO HAD LEFT A FEW DAYS EARLIER TO RETURN TO HER MOTHER IN THE COUNTRY."
I'VE HAD ENOUGH OF ARTISTS. I'M TIRED OF BEING COLD AND HUNGRY.
UNDERSTAND?
I'M SQUARE WITH THE OTHERS, AND YOU HAVE NOTHING LEFT TO GIVE ME.
HERE, THIS IS FOR YOU.
IT'S ALL I CAN DO. AND I DIDN'T EVEN THINK I COULD DO THIS MUCH.
42

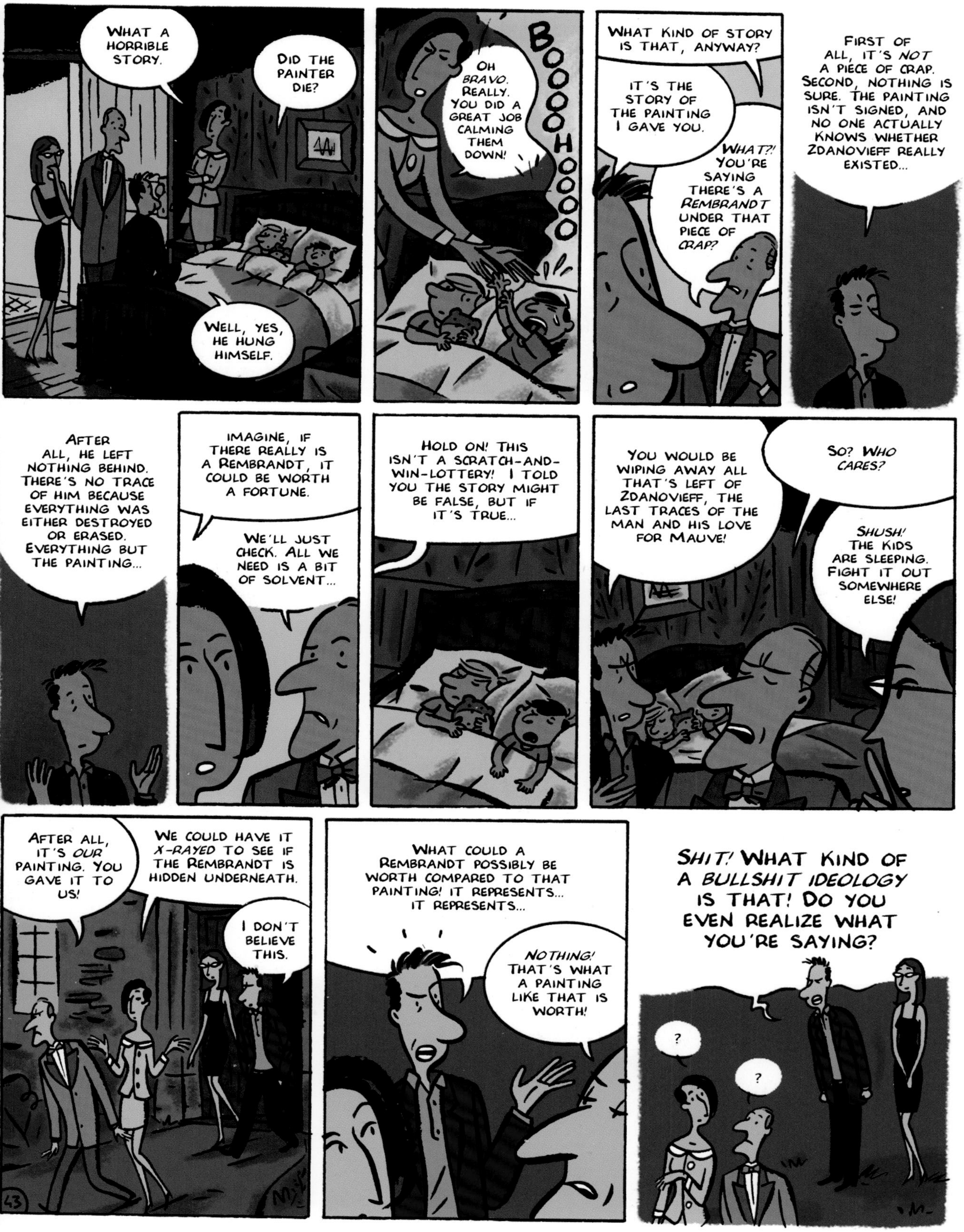

WHAT A HORRIBLE STORY.
DID THE PAINTER DIE?
WELL, YES, HE HUNG HIMSELF.
OH BRAVO. REALLY. YOU DID A GREAT JOB CALMING THEM DOWN!
BOOOOHOOOOO
WHAT KIND OF STORY IS THAT, ANYWAY?
IT'S THE STORY OF THE PAINTING I GAVE YOU.
WHAT?! YOU'RE SAYING THERE'S A REMBRANDT UNDER THAT PIECE OF CRAP?
FIRST OF ALL, IT'S NOT A PIECE OF CRAP. SECOND, NOTHING IS SURE. THE PAINTING ISN'T SIGNED, AND NO ONE ACTUALLY KNOWS WHETHER ZDANOVIEFF REALLY EXISTED...
AFTER ALL, HE LEFT NOTHING BEHIND. THERE'S NO TRACE OF HIM BECAUSE EVERYTHING WAS EITHER DESTROYED OR ERASED. EVERYTHING BUT THE PAINTING...
IMAGINE, IF THERE REALLY IS A REMBRANDT, IT COULD BE WORTH A FORTUNE.
WE'LL JUST CHECK. ALL WE NEED IS A BIT OF SOLVENT...
HOLD ON! THIS ISN'T A SCRATCH-AND-WIN-LOTTERY! I TOLD YOU THE STORY MIGHT BE FALSE, BUT IF IT'S TRUE...
YOU WOULD BE WIPING AWAY ALL THAT'S LEFT OF ZDANOVIEFF, THE LAST TRACES OF THE MAN AND HIS LOVE FOR MAUVE!
SO? WHO CARES?
SHUSH! THE KIDS ARE SLEEPING. FIGHT IT OUT SOMEWHERE ELSE!
AFTER ALL, IT'S OUR PAINTING. YOU GAVE IT TO US!
WE COULD HAVE IT X-RAYED TO SEE IF THE REMBRANDT IS HIDDEN UNDERNEATH.
I DON'T BELIEVE THIS.
43
WHAT COULD A REMBRANDT POSSIBLY BE WORTH COMPARED TO THAT PAINTING! IT REPRESENTS... IT REPRESENTS...
NOTHING! THAT'S WHAT A PAINTING LIKE THAT IS WORTH!
SHIT! WHAT KIND OF A BULLSHIT IDEOLOGY IS THAT! DO YOU EVEN REALIZE WHAT YOU'RE SAYING?
?
?

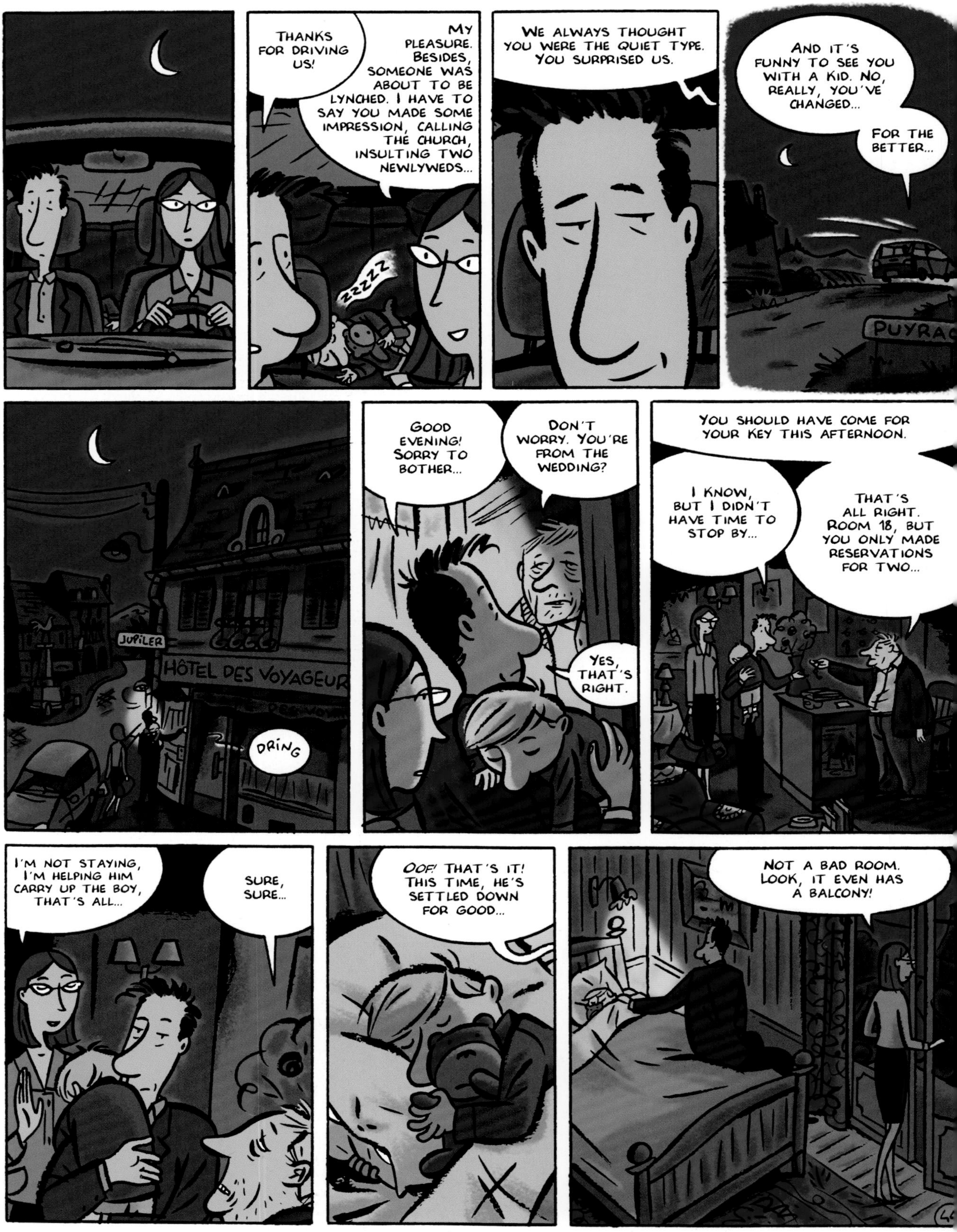
THANKS FOR DRIVING US!
MY PLEASURE. BESIDES, SOMEONE WAS ABOUT TO BE LYNCHED. I HAVE TO SAY YOU MADE SOME IMPRESSION, CALLING THE CHURCH, INSULTING TWO NEWLYWEDS...
ZZZZZ
WE ALWAYS THOUGHT YOU WERE THE QUIET TYPE. YOU SURPRISED US.
AND IT'S FUNNY TO SEE YOU WITH A KID. NO, REALLY, YOU'VE CHANGED...
FOR THE BETTER...
PUYRAC
JUPILER
HÔTEL DES VOYAGEUR
DRING
GOOD EVENING! SORRY TO BOTHER...
DON'T WORRY. YOU'RE FROM THE WEDDING?
YES, THAT'S RIGHT.
YOU SHOULD HAVE COME FOR YOUR KEY THIS AFTERNOON.
I KNOW, BUT I DIDN'T HAVE TIME TO STOP BY...
THAT'S ALL RIGHT. ROOM 18, BUT YOU ONLY MADE RESERVATIONS FOR TWO...
I'M NOT STAYING, I'M HELPING HIM CARRY UP THE BOY, THAT'S ALL...
SURE, SURE...
OOF! THAT'S IT! THIS TIME, HE'S SETTLED DOWN FOR GOOD...
NOT A BAD ROOM. LOOK, IT EVEN HAS A BALCONY!

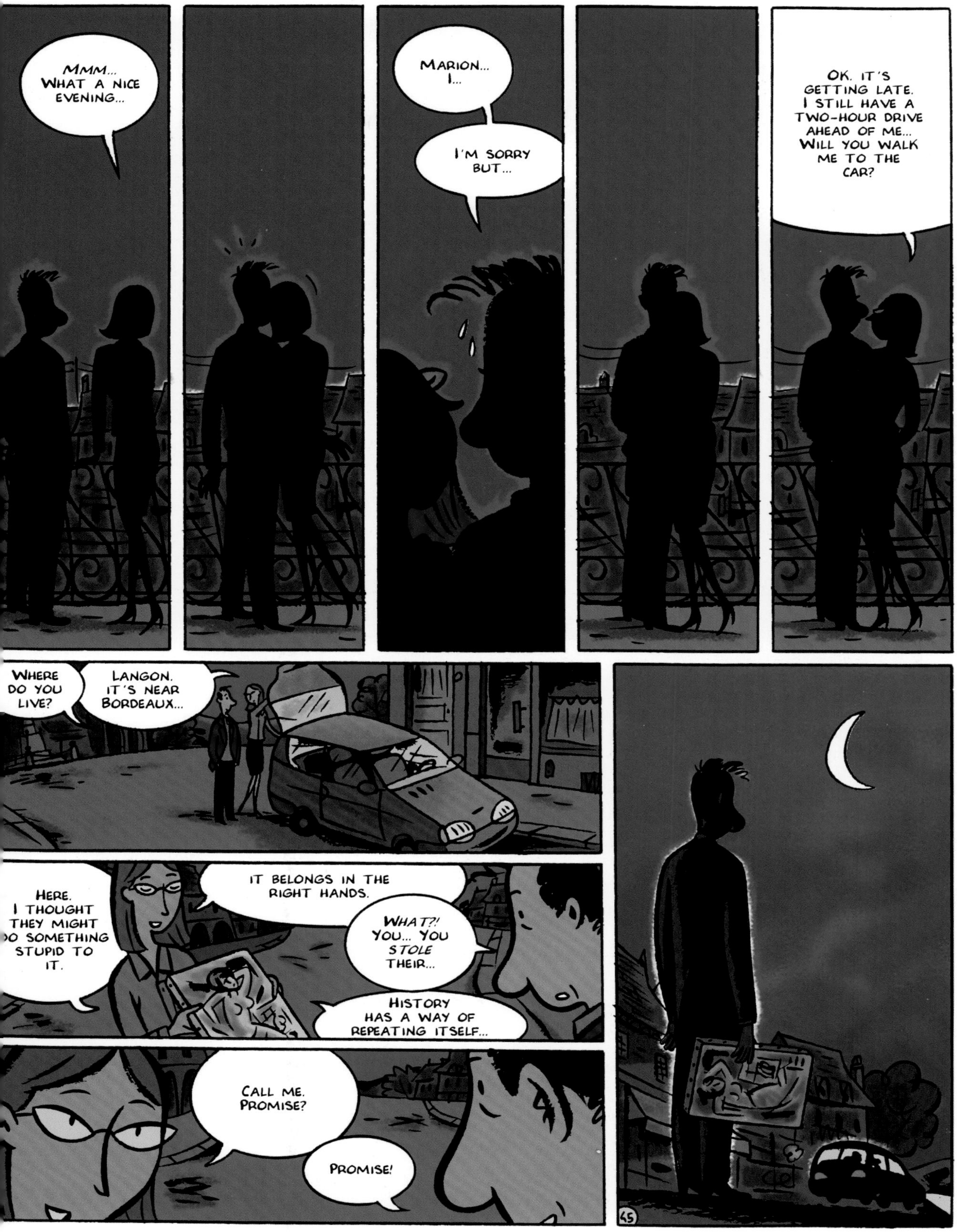
MMM... WHAT A NICE EVENING...
MARION... I...
I'M SORRY BUT...
OK. IT'S GETTING LATE. I STILL HAVE A TWO-HOUR DRIVE AHEAD OF ME... WILL YOU WALK ME TO THE CAR?
WHERE DO YOU LIVE?
LANGON. IT'S NEAR BORDEAUX...
HERE. I THOUGHT THEY MIGHT DO SOMETHING STUPID TO IT.
IT BELONGS IN THE RIGHT HANDS.
WHAT?! YOU... YOU STOLE THEIR...
HISTORY HAS A WAY OF REPEATING ITSELF...
CALL ME. PROMISE?
PROMISE!
45

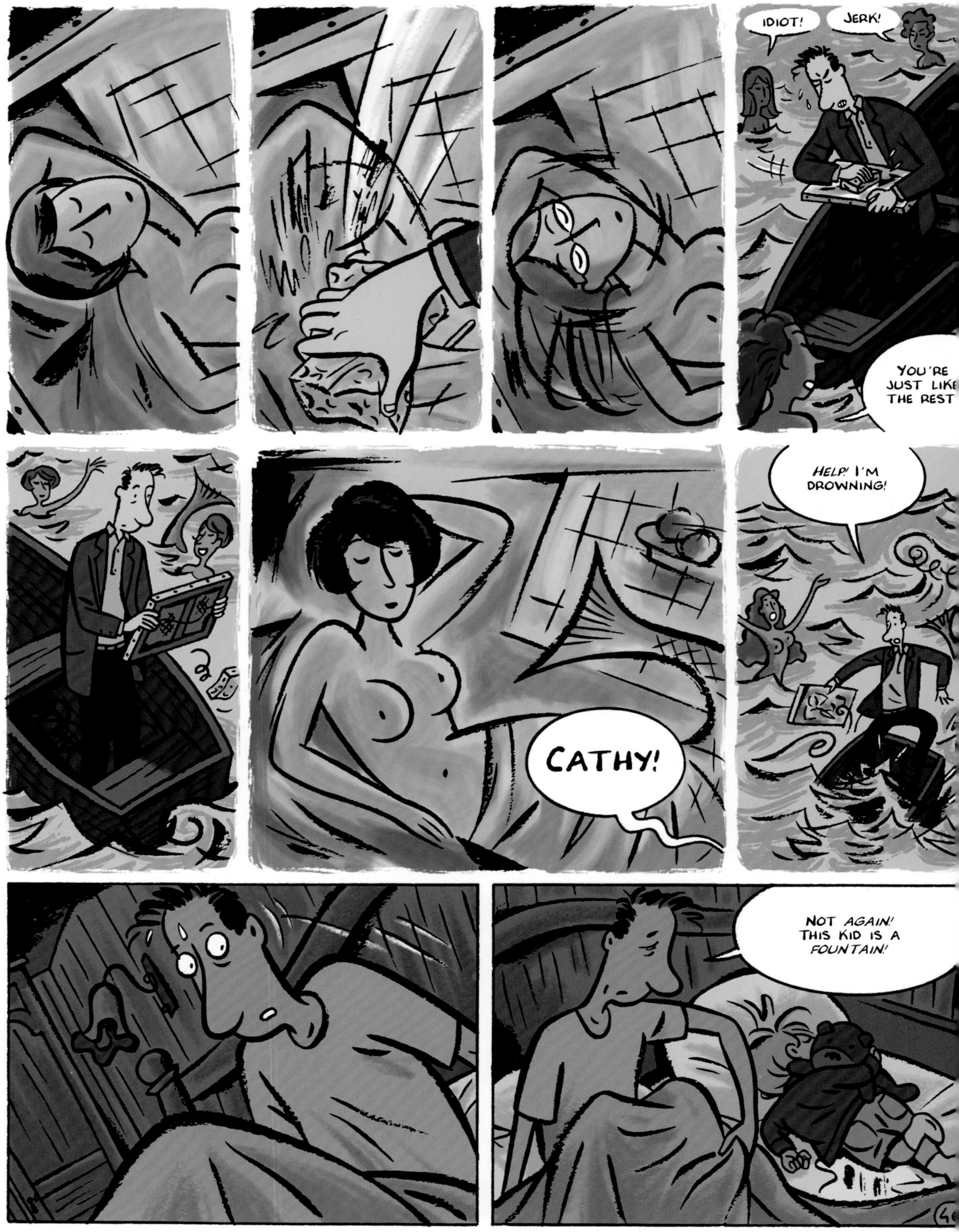
IDIOT!
JERK!
YOU'RE JUST LIKE THE REST
CATHY!
HELP! I'M DROWNING!
NOT AGAIN! THIS KID IS A FOUNTAIN!

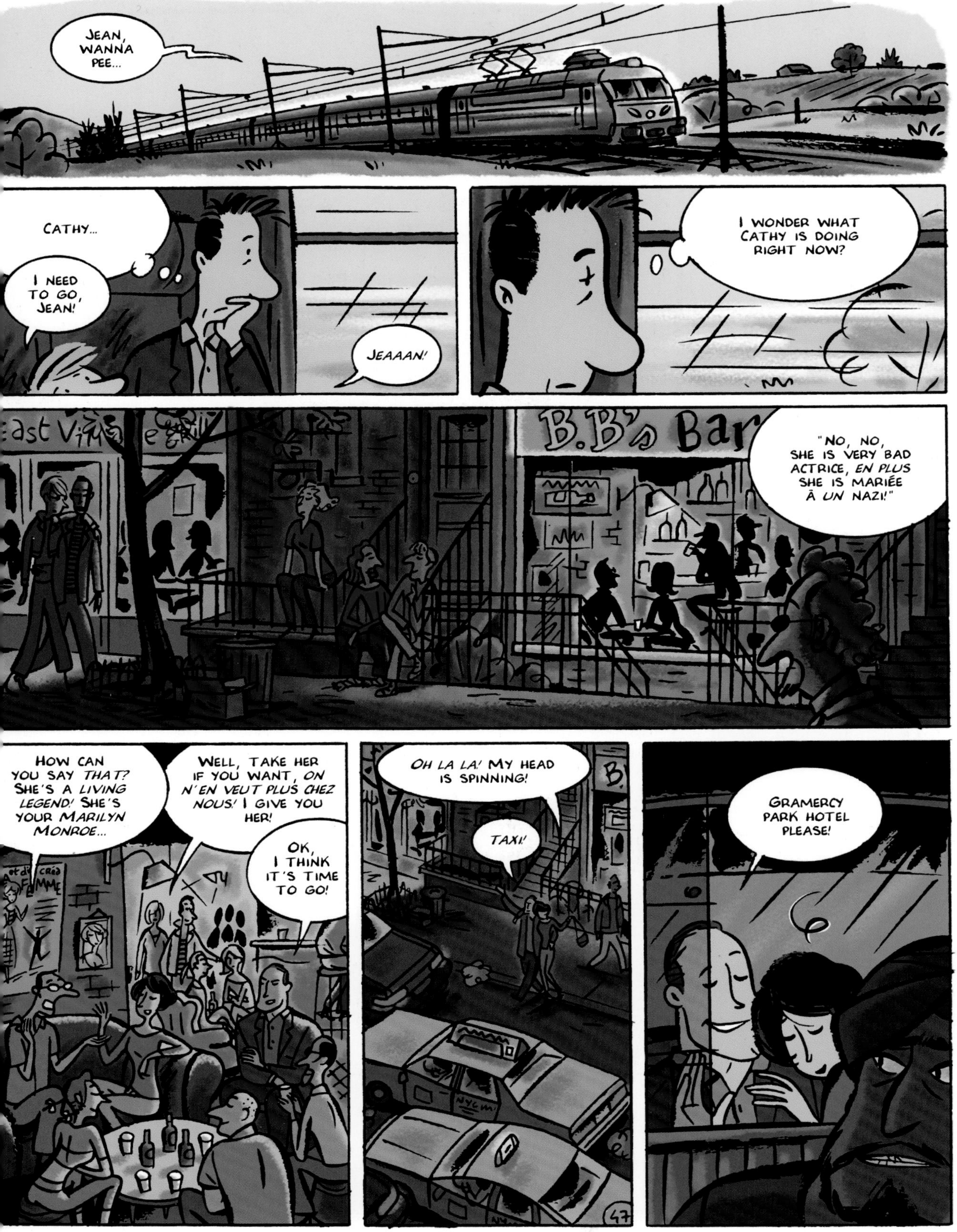
JEAN, WANNA PEE...
CATHY...
I NEED TO GO, JEAN!
JEAAAN!
I WONDER WHAT CATHY IS DOING RIGHT NOW?
B.B's Bar
"NO, NO, SHE IS VERY BAD ACTRICE, *EN PLUS* SHE IS MARIÉE À *UN* NAZI!"
HOW CAN YOU SAY *THAT*? SHE'S A *LIVING LEGEND*! SHE'S YOUR *MARILYN MONROE*...
WELL, TAKE HER IF YOU WANT, *ON N'EN VEUT PLUS CHEZ NOUS*! I GIVE YOU HER!
OK, I THINK IT'S TIME TO GO!
OH LA LA! MY HEAD IS SPINNING!
TAXI!
GRAMERCY PARK HOTEL PLEASE!

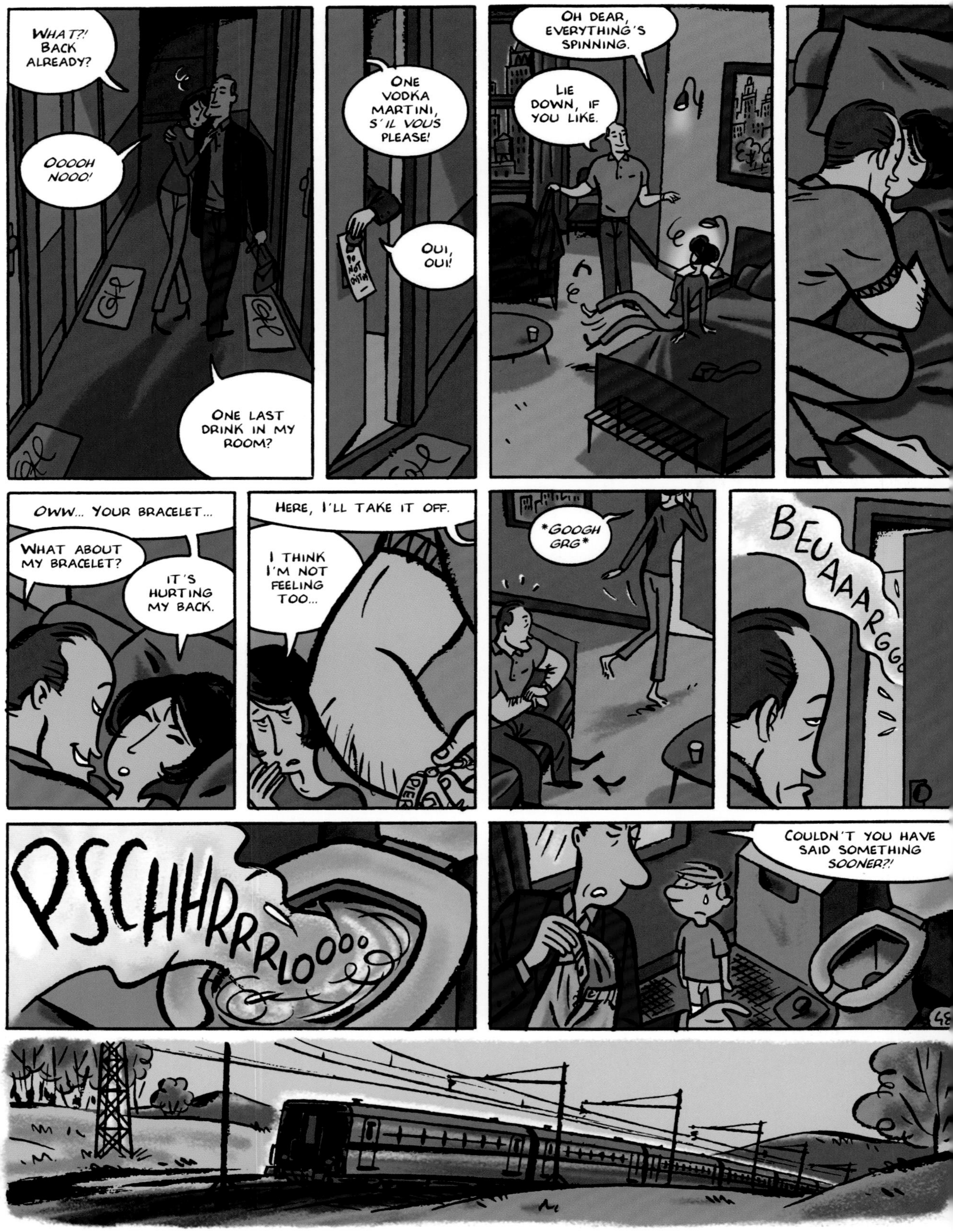

WHAT?! BACK ALREADY?
OOOOH NOOO!
ONE LAST DRINK IN MY ROOM?
ONE VODKA MARTINI, S'IL VOUS PLEASE!
OUI, OUI!
OH DEAR, EVERYTHING'S SPINNING.
LIE DOWN, IF YOU LIKE.
OWW... YOUR BRACELET...
WHAT ABOUT MY BRACELET?
IT'S HURTING MY BACK.
HERE, I'LL TAKE IT OFF.
I THINK I'M NOT FEELING TOO...
GOOGH GRG
BEUAAARGG
PSCHHRRRLOOOO
COULDN'T YOU HAVE SAID SOMETHING SOONER?!

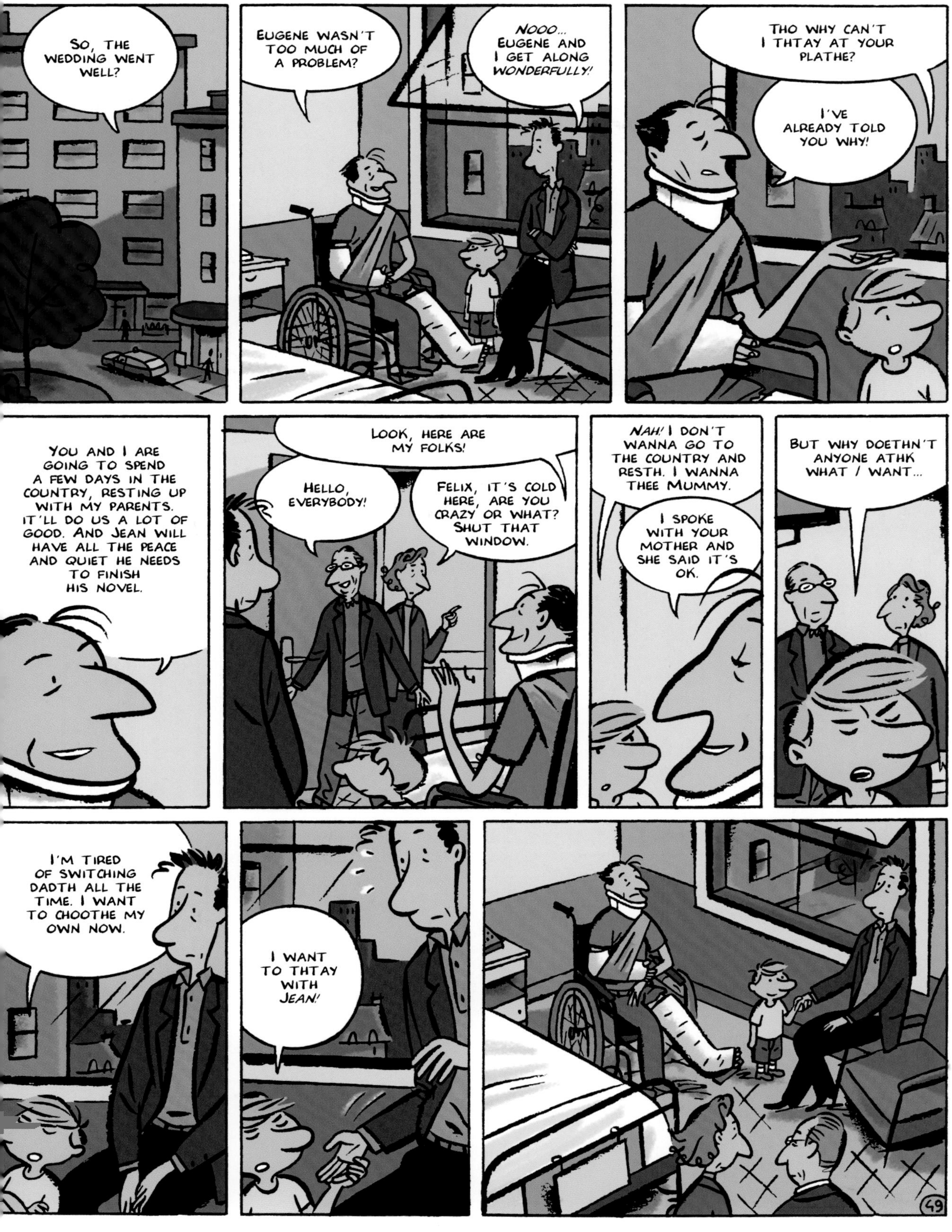

SO, THE WEDDING WENT WELL?
EUGENE WASN'T TOO MUCH OF A PROBLEM?
NOOO... EUGENE AND I GET ALONG WONDERFULLY!
THO WHY CAN'T I THTAY AT YOUR PLATHE?
I'VE ALREADY TOLD YOU WHY!
YOU AND I ARE GOING TO SPEND A FEW DAYS IN THE COUNTRY, RESTING UP WITH MY PARENTS. IT'LL DO US A LOT OF GOOD. AND JEAN WILL HAVE ALL THE PEACE AND QUIET HE NEEDS TO FINISH HIS NOVEL.
LOOK, HERE ARE MY FOLKS!
HELLO, EVERYBODY!
FELIX, IT'S COLD HERE, ARE YOU CRAZY OR WHAT? SHUT THAT WINDOW.
NAH! I DON'T WANNA GO TO THE COUNTRY AND RESTH. I WANNA THEE MUMMY.
I SPOKE WITH YOUR MOTHER AND SHE SAID IT'S OK.
BUT WHY DOETHN'T ANYONE ATHK WHAT / WANT...
I'M TIRED OF SWITCHING DADTH ALL THE TIME. I WANT TO CHOOTHE MY OWN NOW.
I WANT TO THTAY WITH JEAN!
49

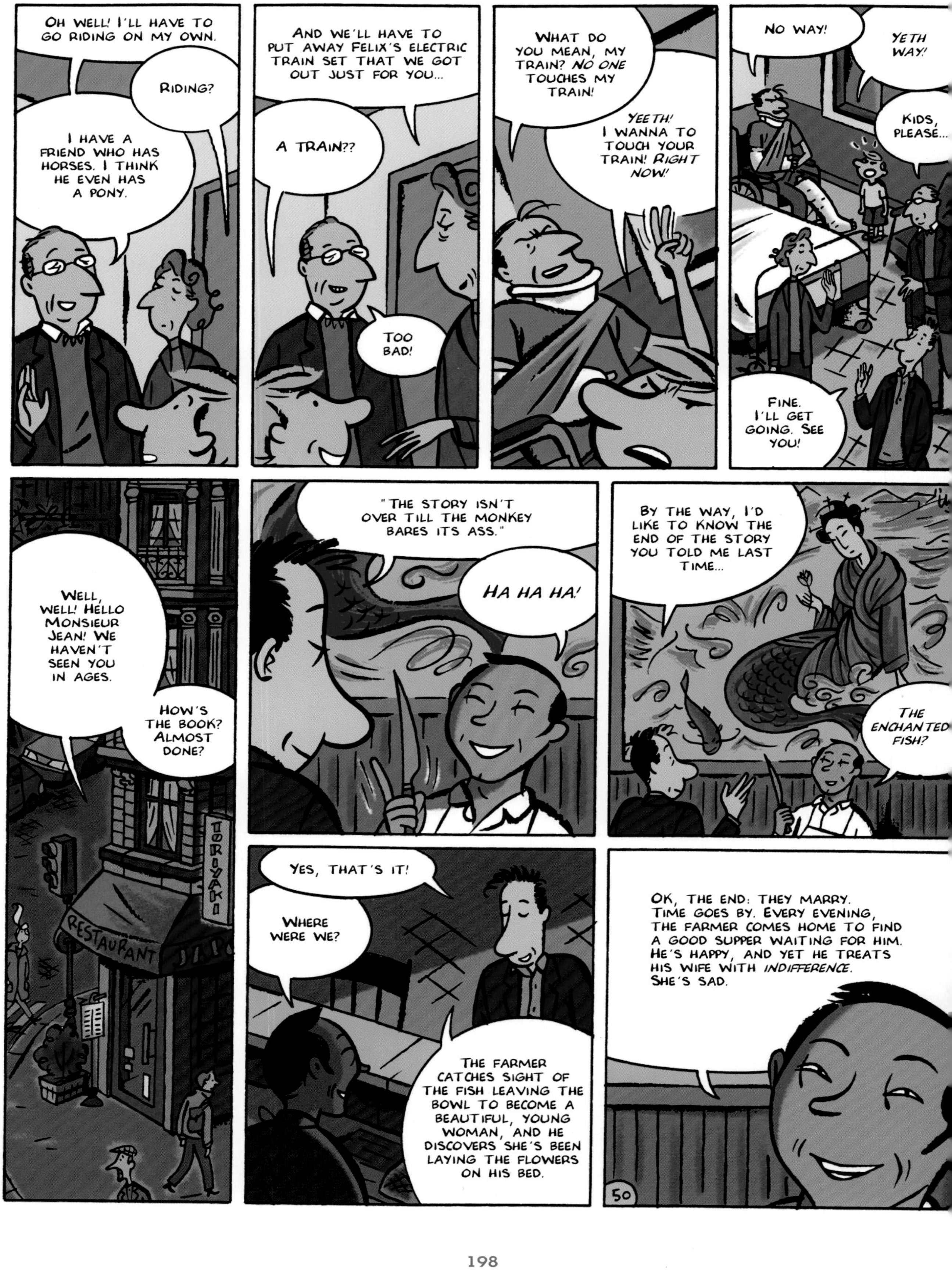
OH WELL! I'LL HAVE TO GO RIDING ON MY OWN.
RIDING?
I HAVE A FRIEND WHO HAS HORSES. I THINK HE EVEN HAS A PONY.
AND WE'LL HAVE TO PUT AWAY FELIX'S ELECTRIC TRAIN SET THAT WE GOT OUT JUST FOR YOU...
A TRAIN??
TOO BAD!
WHAT DO YOU MEAN, MY TRAIN? NO ONE TOUCHES MY TRAIN!
YEETH! I WANNA TO TOUCH YOUR TRAIN! RIGHT NOW!
NO WAY!
YETH WAY!
KIDS, PLEASE...
FINE. I'LL GET GOING. SEE YOU!
WELL, WELL! HELLO MONSIEUR JEAN! WE HAVEN'T SEEN YOU IN AGES.
HOW'S THE BOOK? ALMOST DONE?
TORIYAKI
RESTAURANT JAP
"THE STORY ISN'T OVER TILL THE MONKEY BARES ITS ASS."
HA HA HA!
BY THE WAY, I'D LIKE TO KNOW THE END OF THE STORY YOU TOLD ME LAST TIME...
THE ENCHANTED FISH?
YES, THAT'S IT!
WHERE WERE WE?
THE FARMER CATCHES SIGHT OF THE FISH LEAVING THE BOWL TO BECOME A BEAUTIFUL, YOUNG WOMAN, AND HE DISCOVERS SHE'S BEEN LAYING THE FLOWERS ON HIS BED.
OK, THE END: THEY MARRY. TIME GOES BY. EVERY EVENING, THE FARMER COMES HOME TO FIND A GOOD SUPPER WAITING FOR HIM. HE'S HAPPY, AND YET HE TREATS HIS WIFE WITH INDIFFERENCE. SHE'S SAD.
50

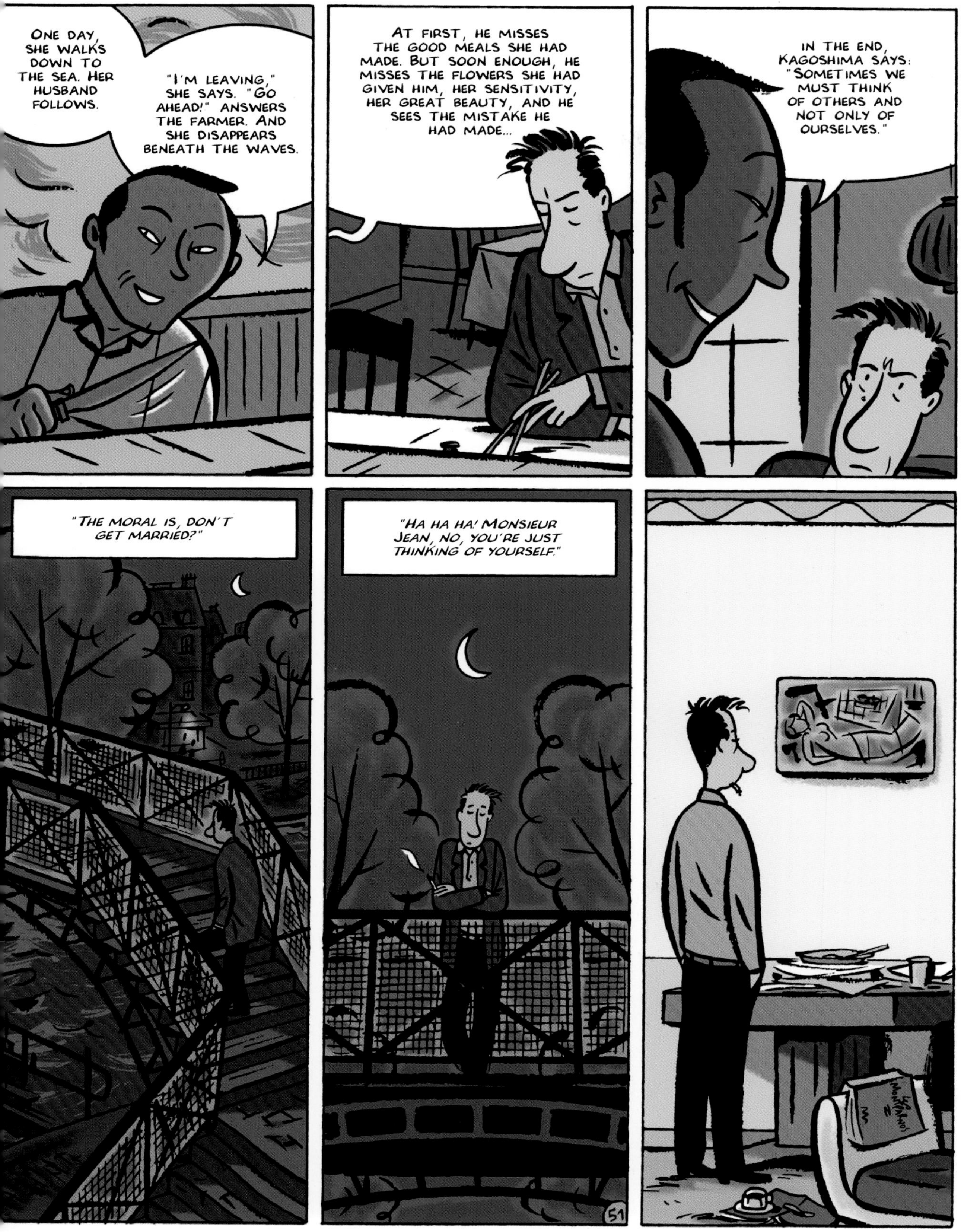
ONE DAY, SHE WALKS DOWN TO THE SEA. HER HUSBAND FOLLOWS.
"I'M LEAVING," SHE SAYS. "GO AHEAD!" ANSWERS THE FARMER. AND SHE DISAPPEARS BENEATH THE WAVES.
AT FIRST, HE MISSES THE GOOD MEALS SHE HAD MADE. BUT SOON ENOUGH, HE MISSES THE FLOWERS SHE HAD GIVEN HIM, HER SENSITIVITY, HER GREAT BEAUTY, AND HE SEES THE MISTAKE HE HAD MADE...
IN THE END, KAGOSHIMA SAYS: "SOMETIMES WE MUST THINK OF OTHERS AND NOT ONLY OF OURSELVES."
"THE MORAL IS, DON'T GET MARRIED?"
"HA HA HA! MONSIEUR JEAN, NO, YOU'RE JUST THINKING OF YOURSELF."
51

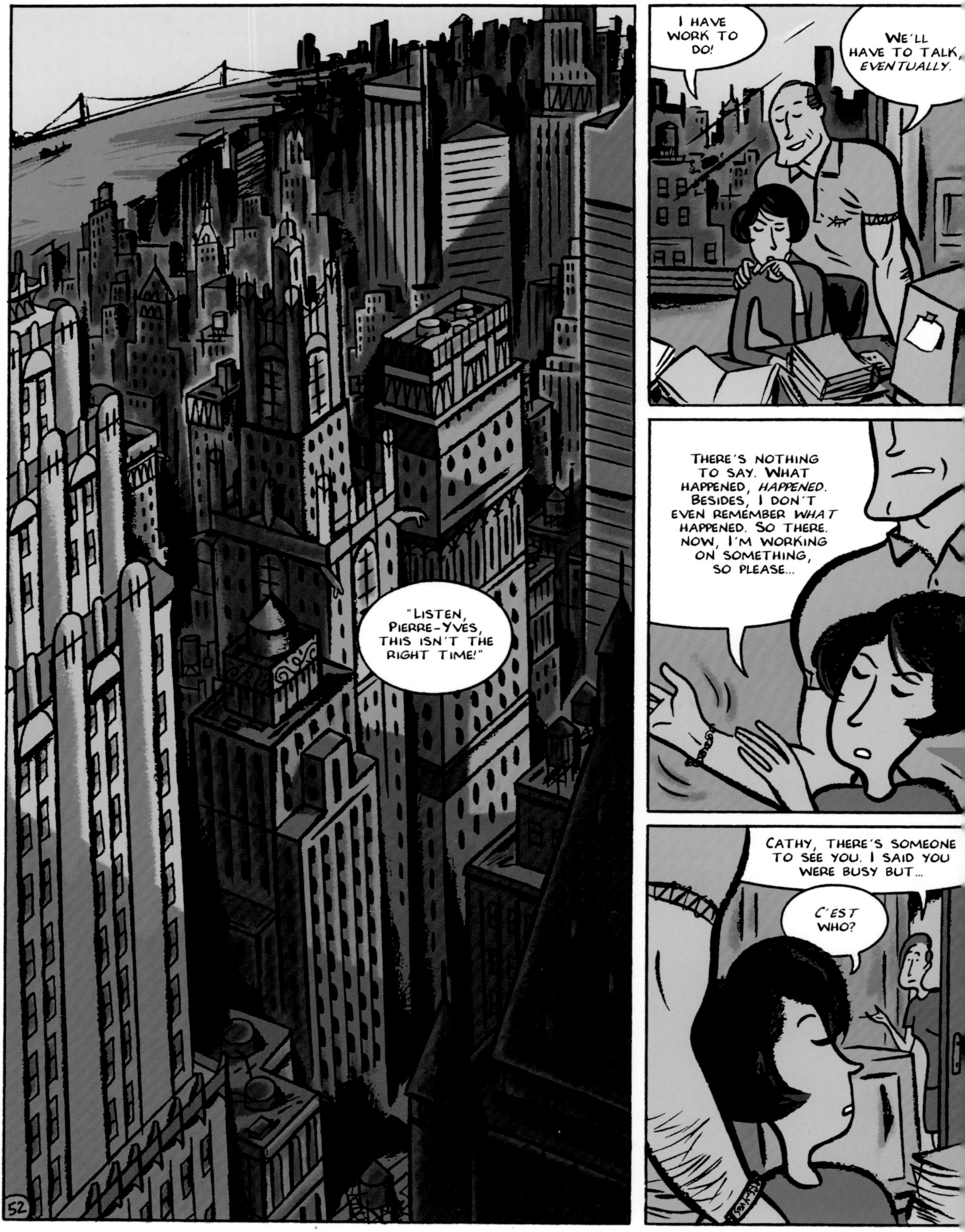
52
"Listen, Pierre-Yves, this isn't the right time!"
I have work to do!
We'll have to talk *eventually.*
There's nothing to say. What happened, *happened.* Besides, I don't even remember *what* happened. So there. Now, I'm working on something, so please...
Cathy, there's someone to see you. I said you were busy but...
C'est who?

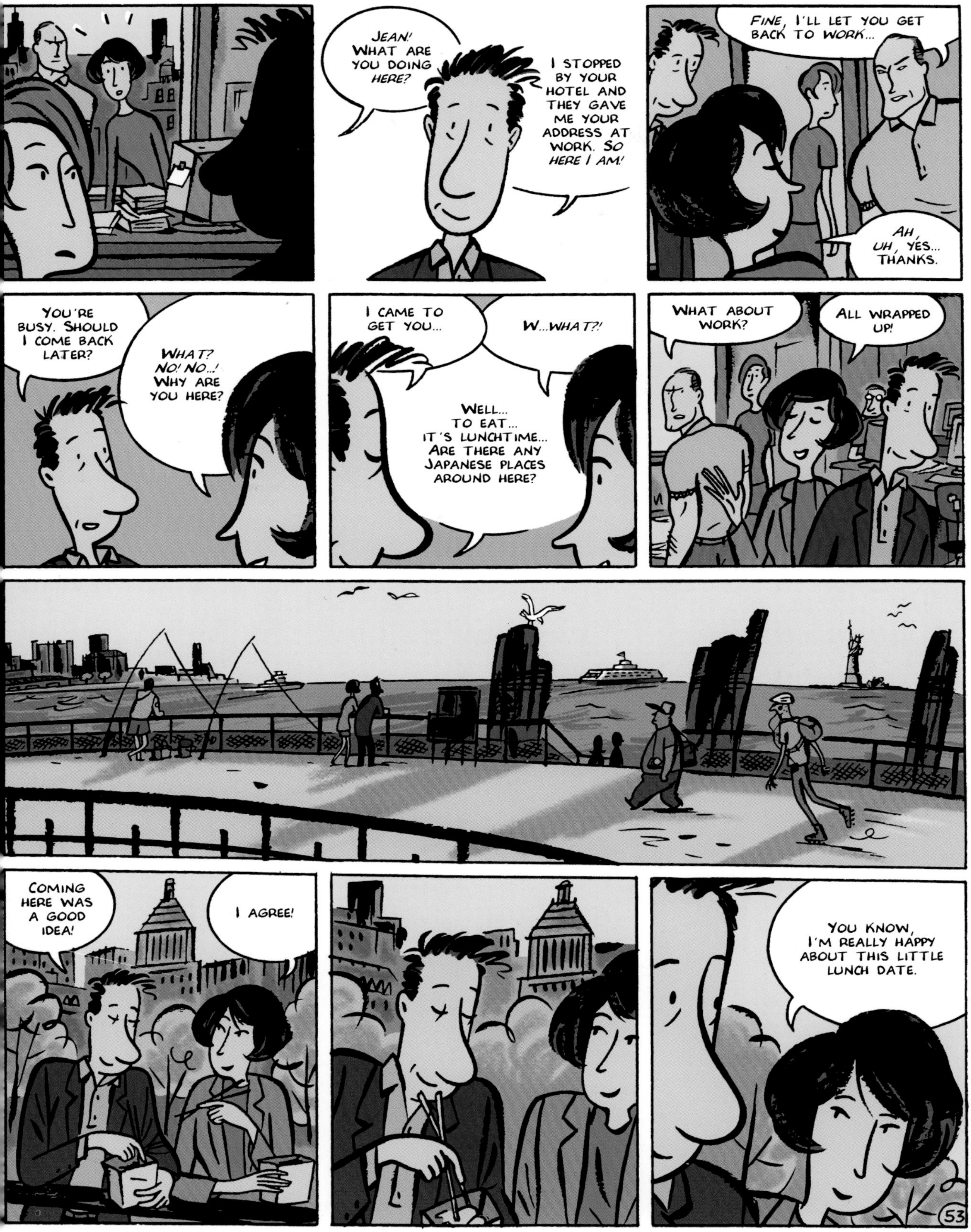
JEAN! WHAT ARE YOU DOING HERE?
I STOPPED BY YOUR HOTEL AND THEY GAVE ME YOUR ADDRESS AT WORK. SO HERE I AM!
FINE, I'LL LET YOU GET BACK TO WORK...
AH, UH, YES... THANKS.
YOU'RE BUSY. SHOULD I COME BACK LATER?
WHAT? NO! NO...! WHY ARE YOU HERE?
I CAME TO GET YOU...
W...WHAT?!
WELL... TO EAT... IT'S LUNCHTIME... ARE THERE ANY JAPANESE PLACES AROUND HERE?
WHAT ABOUT WORK?
ALL WRAPPED UP!
COMING HERE WAS A GOOD IDEA!
I AGREE!
YOU KNOW, I'M REALLY HAPPY ABOUT THIS LITTLE LUNCH DATE.
53

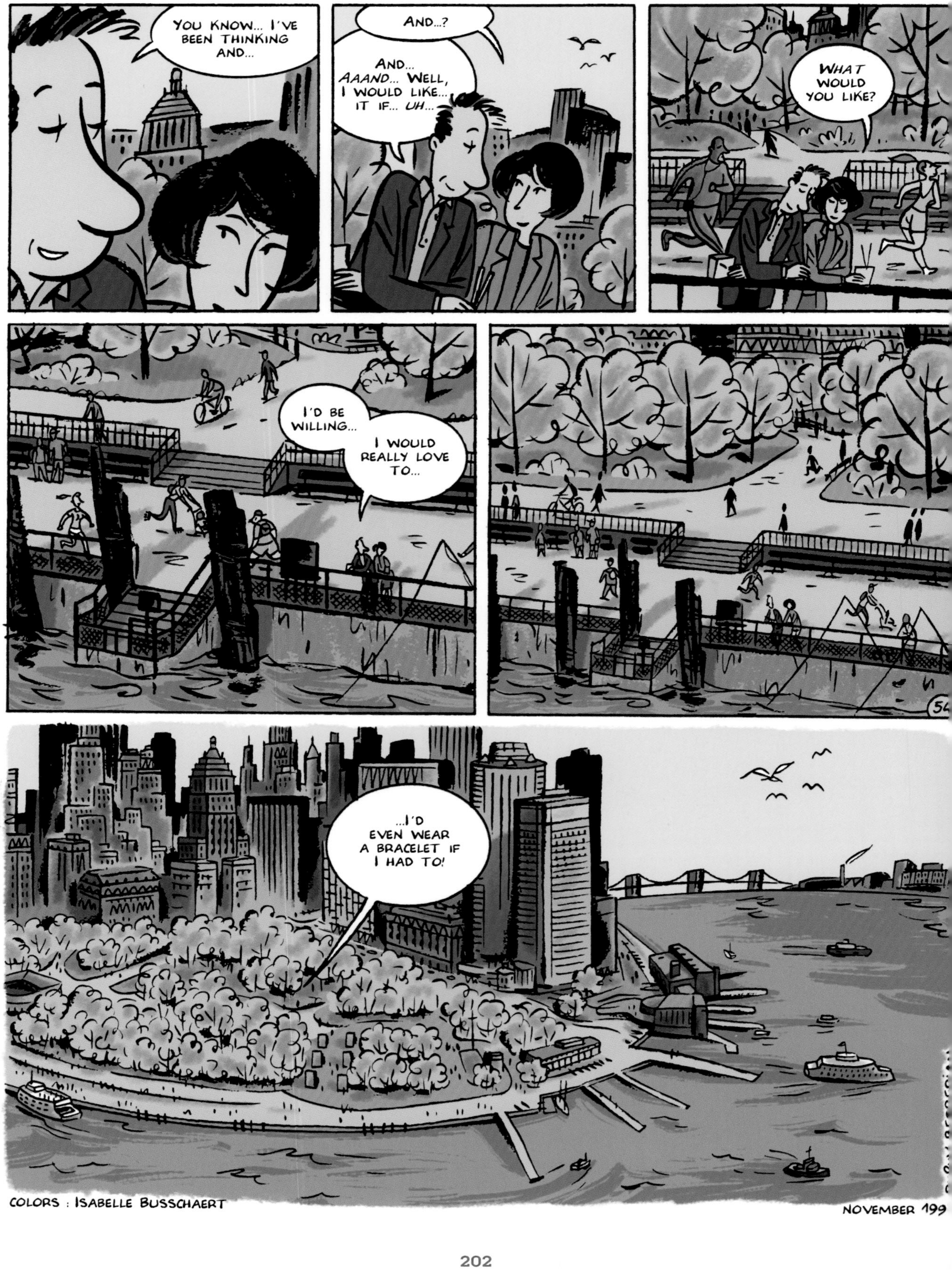
YOU KNOW... I'VE BEEN THINKING AND...
AND...?
AND... AAAND... WELL, I WOULD LIKE... IT IF... UH...
WHAT WOULD YOU LIKE?
I'D BE WILLING...
I WOULD REALLY LOVE TO...
54
...I'D EVEN WEAR A BRACELET IF I HAD TO!

COLORS : ISABELLE BUSSCHAERT

NOVEMBER 199

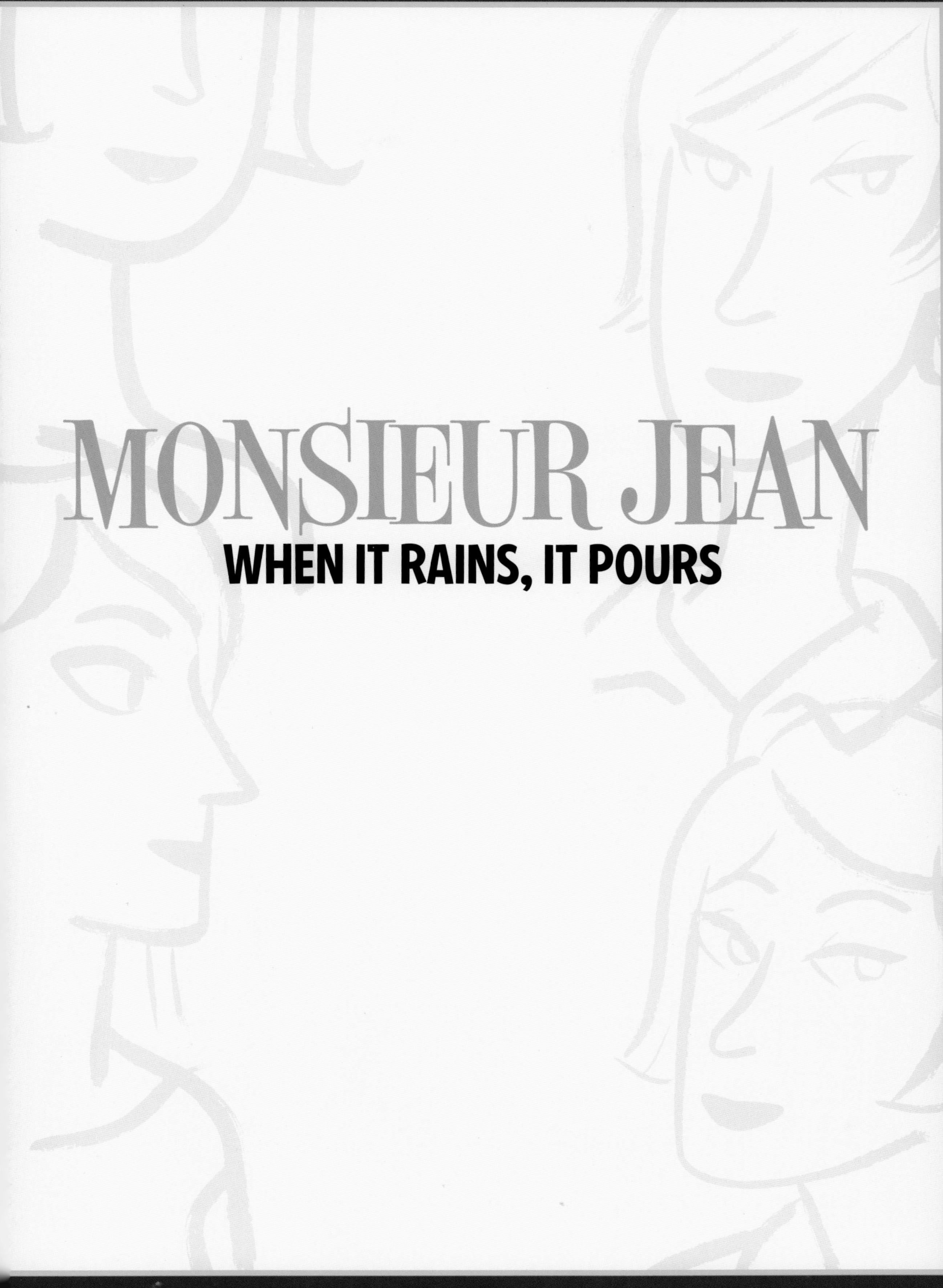

MONSIEUR JEAN

WHEN IT RAINS, IT POURS

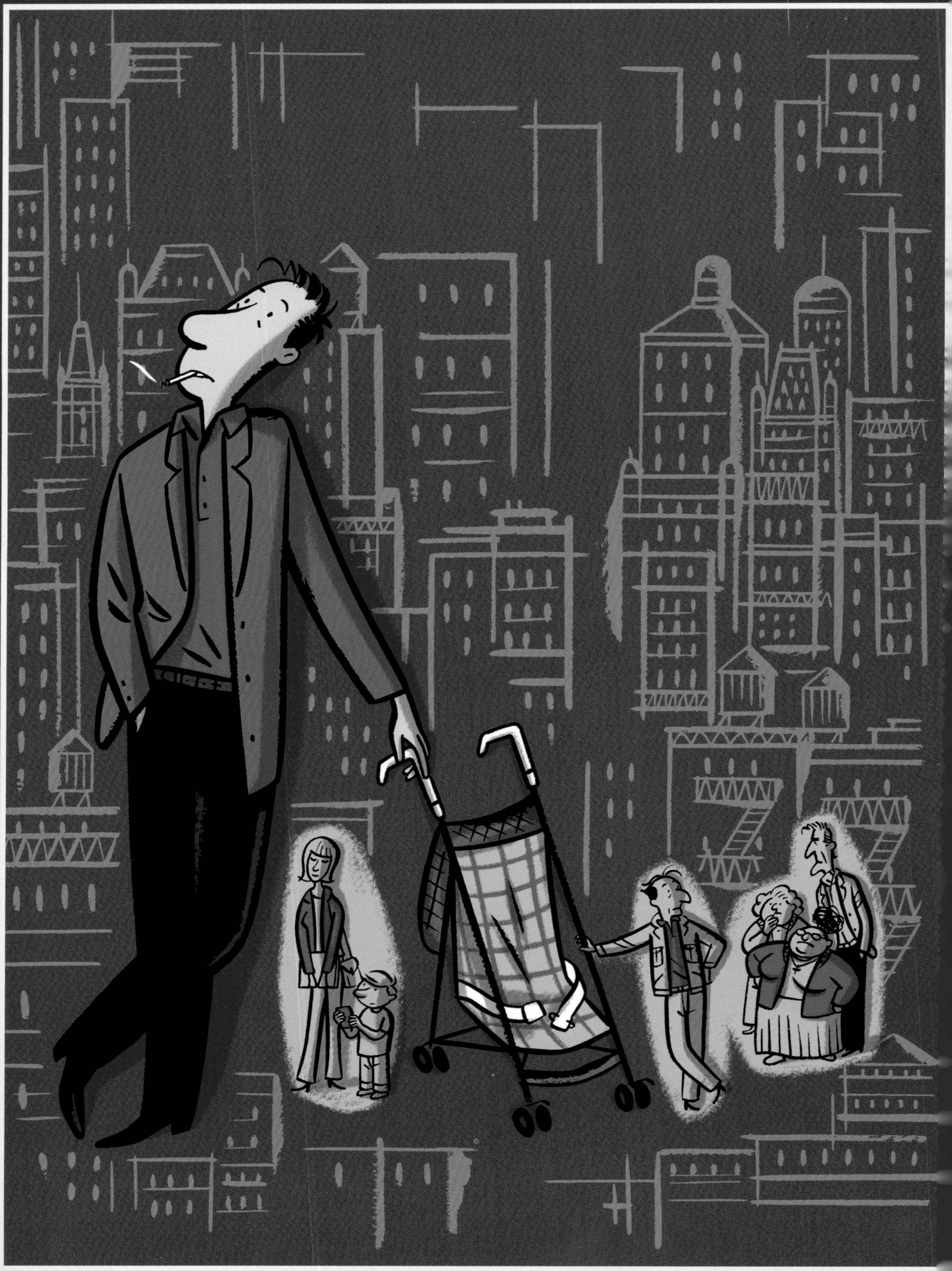

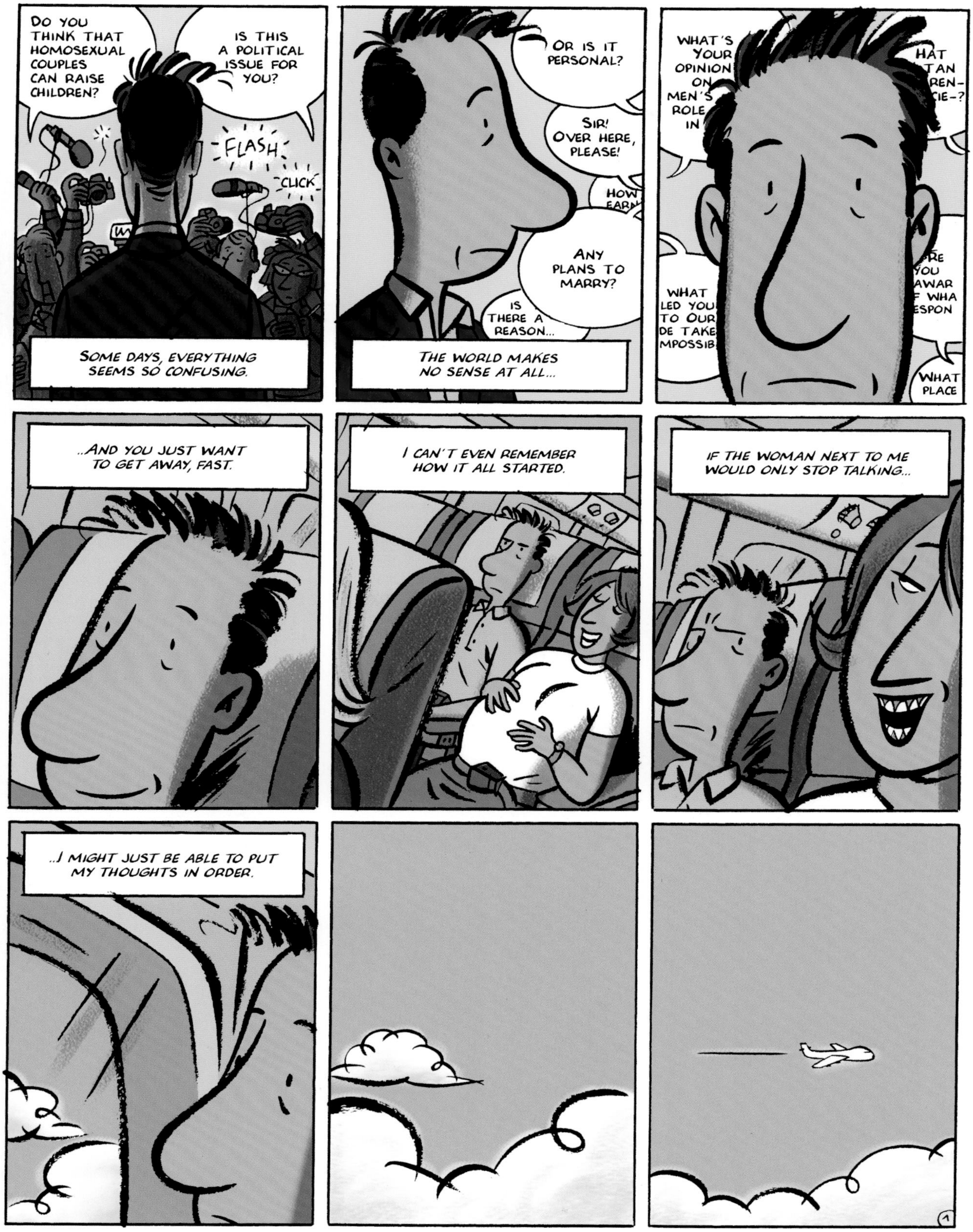

DO YOU THINK THAT HOMOSEXUAL COUPLES CAN RAISE CHILDREN?
IS THIS A POLITICAL ISSUE FOR YOU?
FLASH
CLICK
SOME DAYS, EVERYTHING SEEMS SO CONFUSING.
OR IS IT PERSONAL?
SIR! OVER HERE, PLEASE!
HOW EARN
ANY PLANS TO MARRY?
IS THERE A REASON...
THE WORLD MAKES NO SENSE AT ALL...
WHAT'S YOUR OPINION ON MEN'S ROLE IN
HAT TAN REN- CIE-?
WHAT LED YOU TO OUR DE TAKE MPOSSIB
RE YOU AWAR F WHA ESPON
WHAT PLACE
..AND YOU JUST WANT TO GET AWAY, FAST.
I CAN'T EVEN REMEMBER HOW IT ALL STARTED.
IF THE WOMAN NEXT TO ME WOULD ONLY STOP TALKING...
..I MIGHT JUST BE ABLE TO PUT MY THOUGHTS IN ORDER.

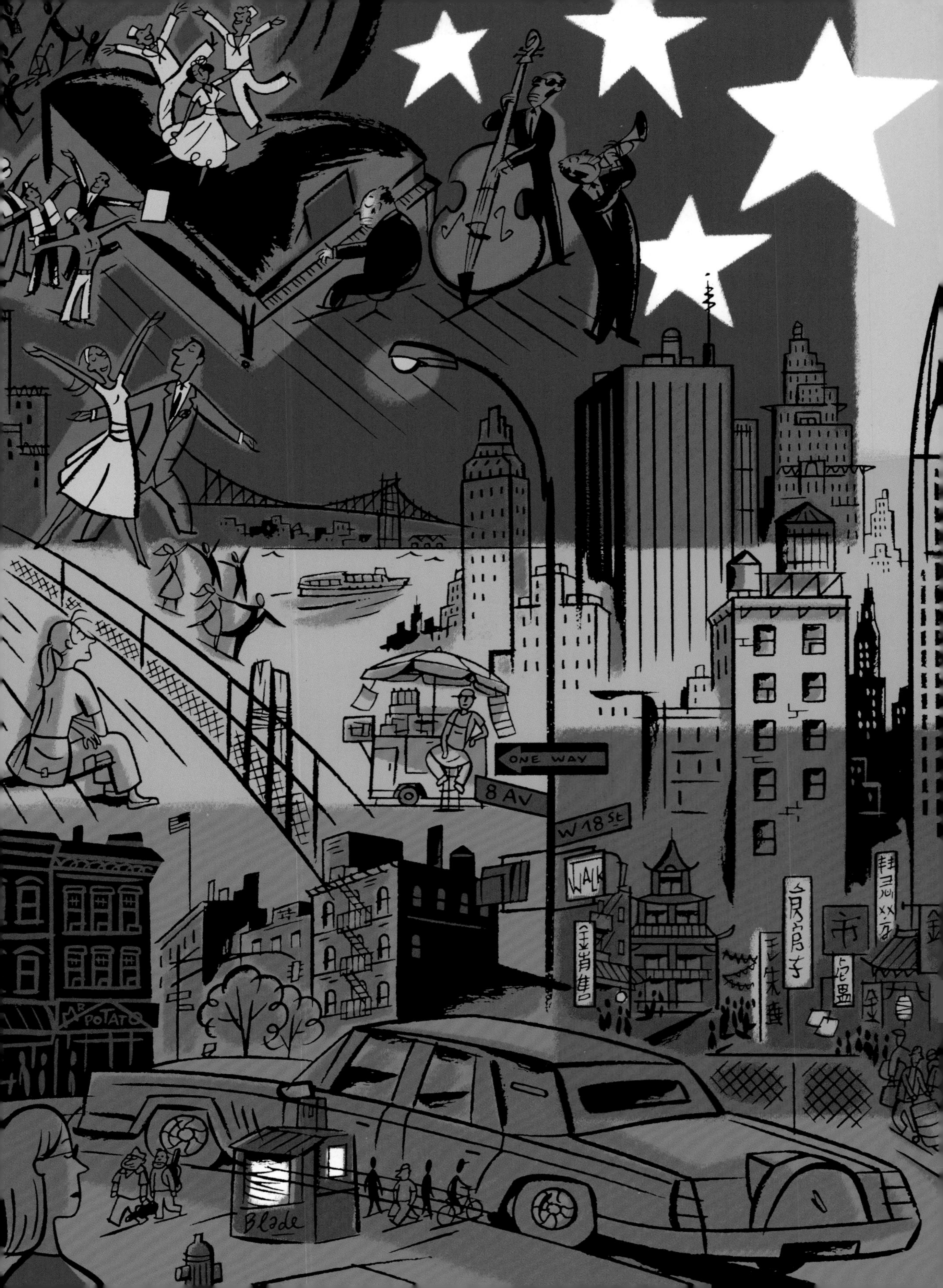
ONE WAY
8 AV
W 18 St
WALK
Blade

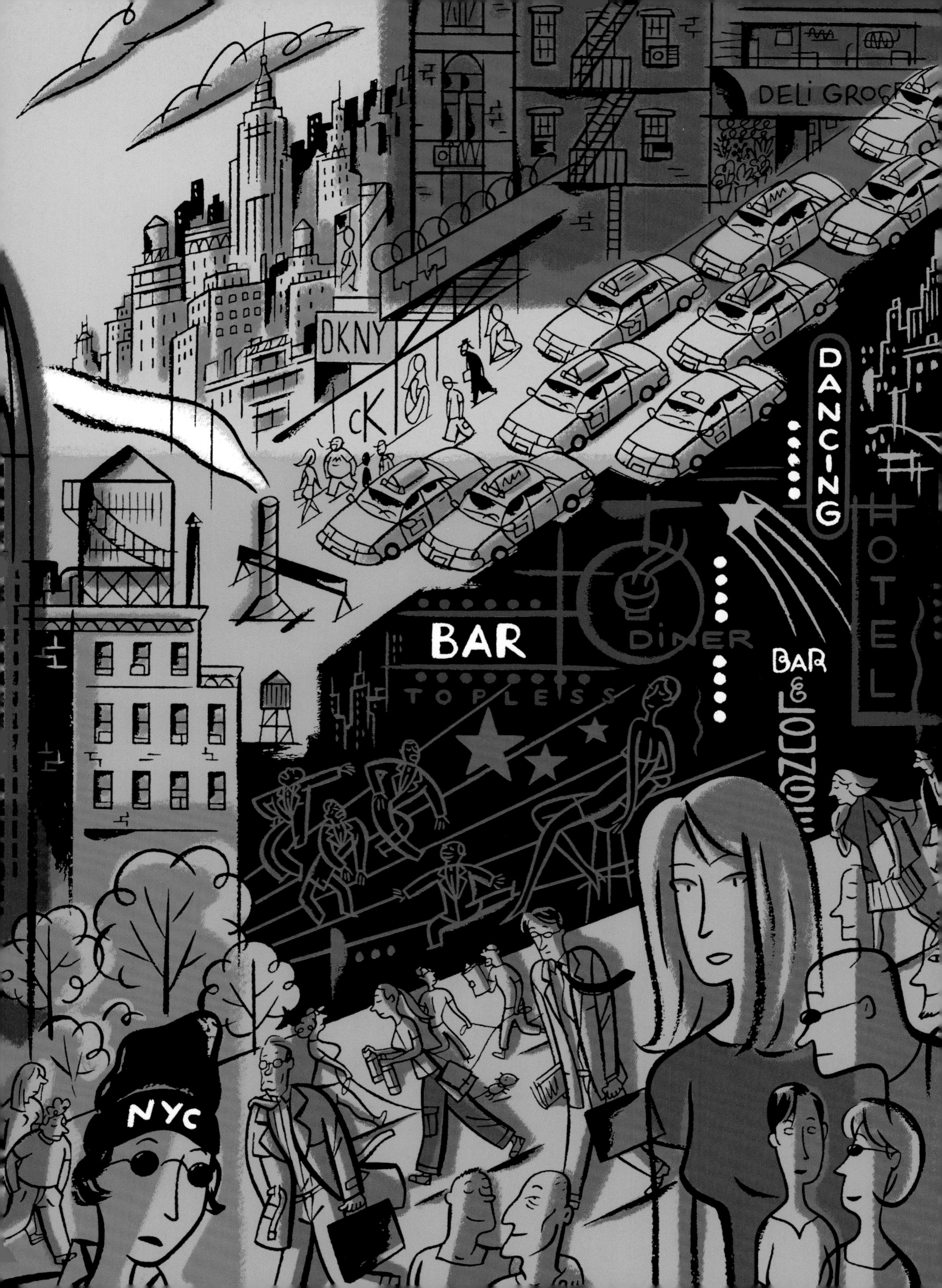
DELI GROC
DKNY
cK
DANCING
HOTEL
BAR
DINER
TOPLESS
BAR &
NYC

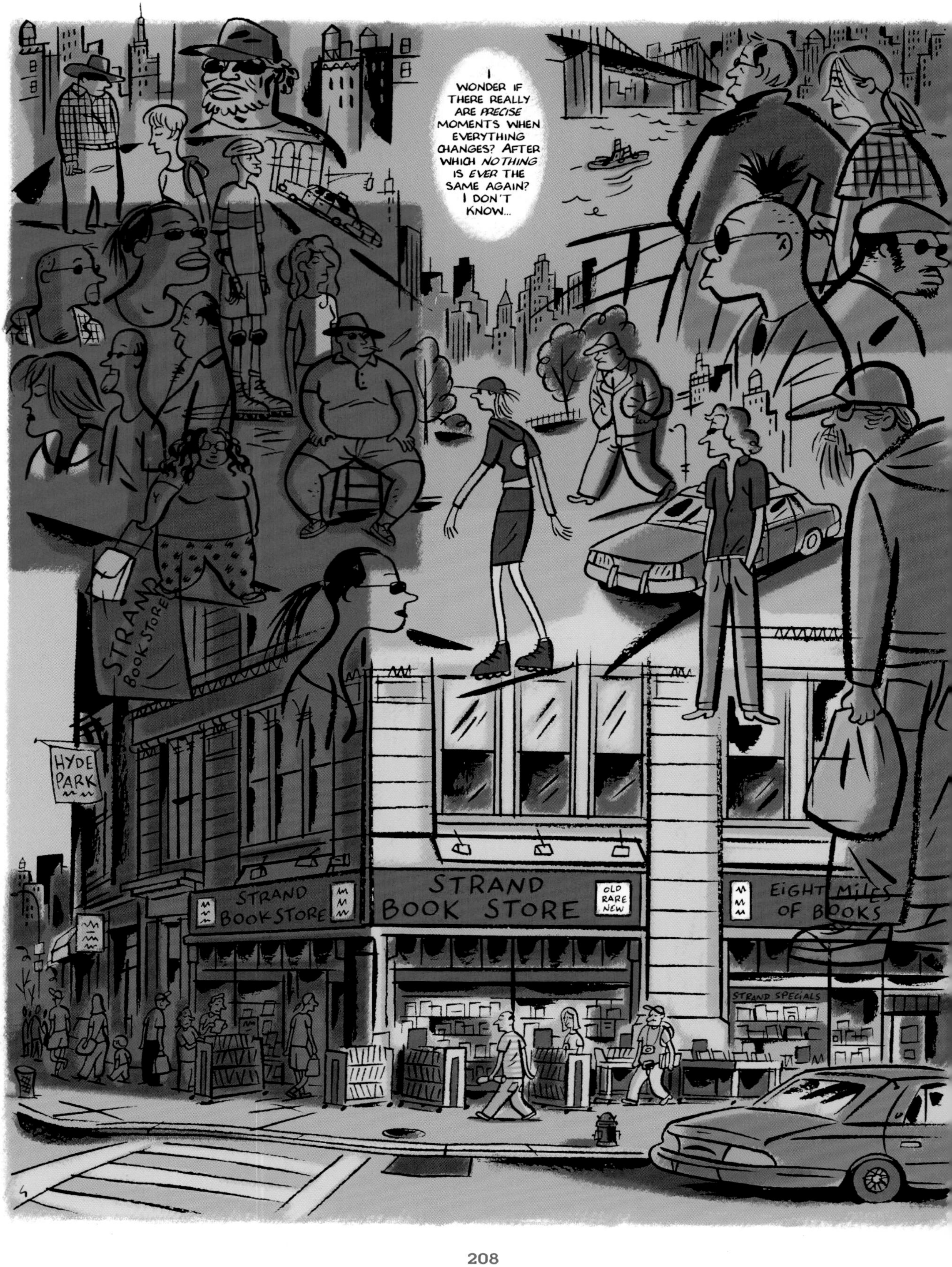
I WONDER IF THERE REALLY ARE PRECISE MOMENTS WHEN EVERYTHING CHANGES? AFTER WHICH NOTHING IS EVER THE SAME AGAIN? I DON'T KNOW...
STRAND BOOK STORE
HYDE PARK
STRAND BOOK STORE
STRAND BOOK STORE
OLD RARE NEW
EIGHT MILES OF BOOKS
STRAND SPECIALS

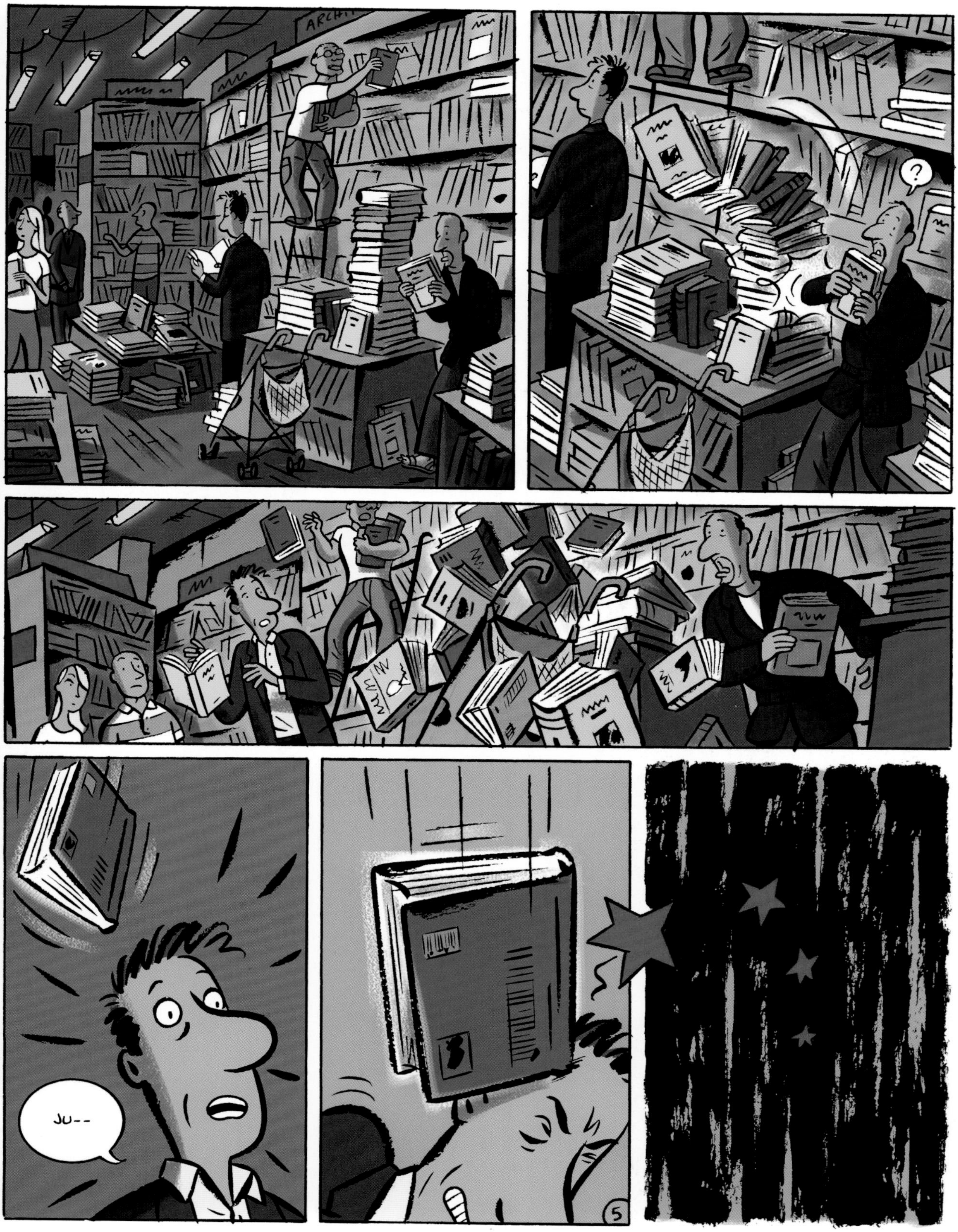
?
JU--

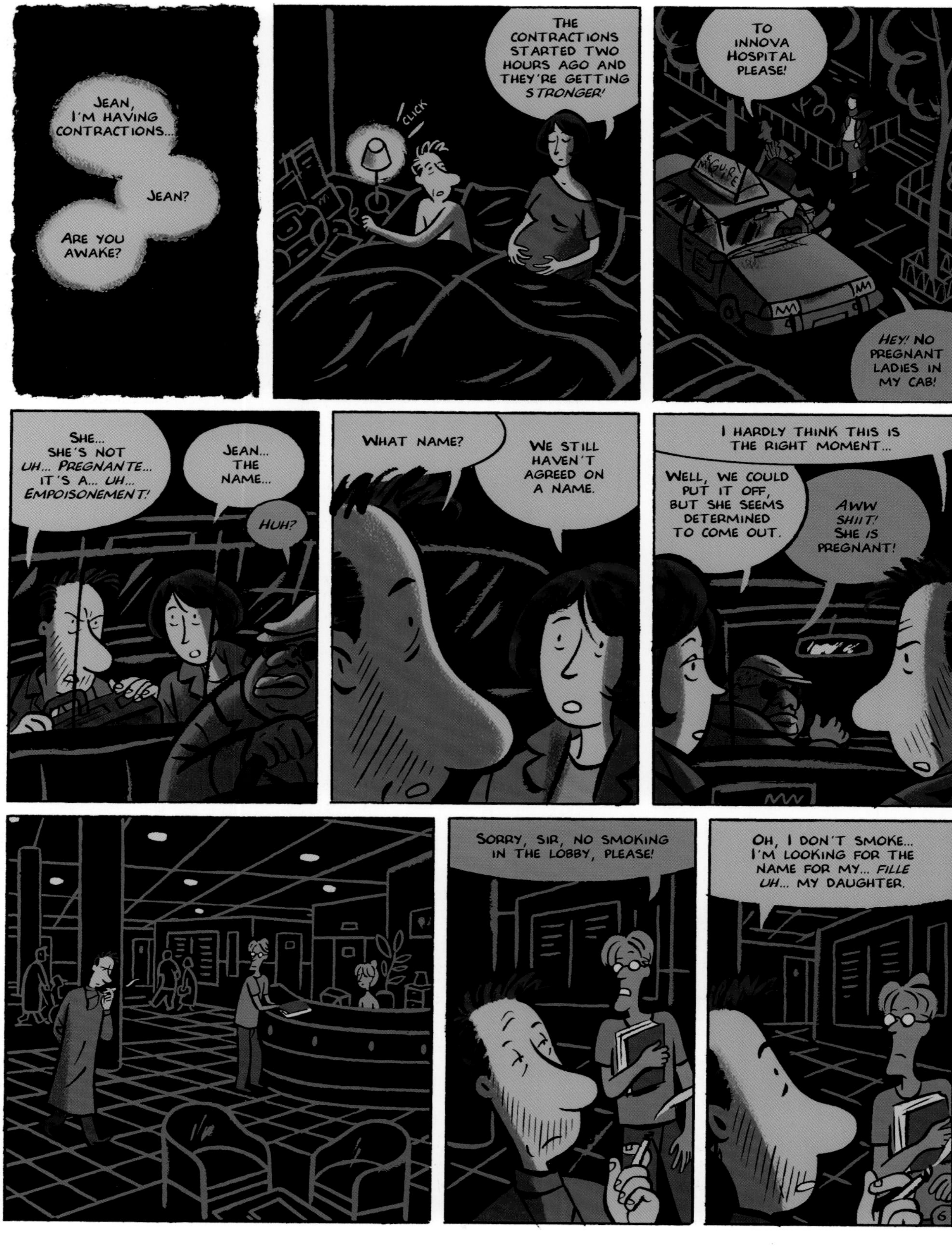

JEAN, I'M HAVING CONTRACTIONS...
JEAN?
ARE YOU AWAKE?
CLICK
THE CONTRACTIONS STARTED TWO HOURS AGO AND THEY'RE GETTING *STRONGER!*
TO INNOVA HOSPITAL PLEASE!
HEY! NO PREGNANT LADIES IN MY CAB!
SHE... SHE'S NOT *UH... PREGNANTE...* IT'S A... *UH... EMPOISONEMENT!*
JEAN... THE NAME...
HUH?
WHAT NAME?
WE STILL HAVEN'T AGREED ON A NAME.
I HARDLY THINK THIS IS THE RIGHT MOMENT...
WELL, WE COULD PUT IT OFF, BUT SHE SEEMS DETERMINED TO COME OUT.
AWW SHIIT! SHE IS PREGNANT!
SORRY, SIR, NO SMOKING IN THE LOBBY, PLEASE!
OH, I DON'T SMOKE... I'M LOOKING FOR THE NAME FOR MY... *FILLE UH...* MY DAUGHTER.
6

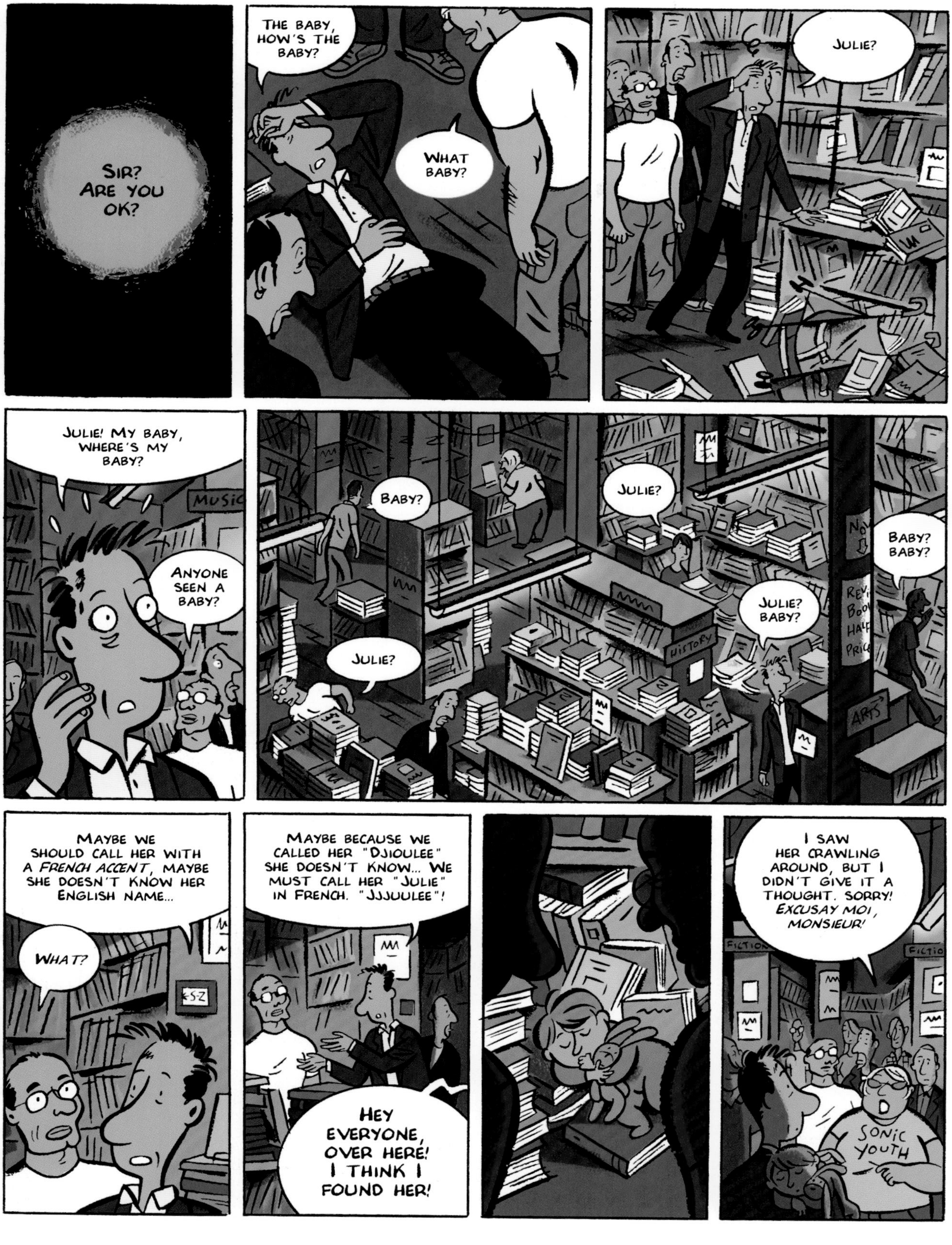
SIR? ARE YOU OK?
THE BABY, HOW'S THE BABY?
WHAT BABY?
JULIE?
JULIE! MY BABY, WHERE'S MY BABY?
MUSIC
ANYONE SEEN A BABY?
BABY?
JULIE?
BABY? BABY?
JULIE? BABY?
JULIE?
HISTORY
ARTS
MAYBE WE SHOULD CALL HER WITH A *FRENCH ACCENT*, MAYBE SHE DOESN'T KNOW HER ENGLISH NAME...
WHAT?
MAYBE BECAUSE WE CALLED HER "DJIOULEE" SHE DOESN'T KNOW... WE MUST CALL HER "JULIE" IN FRENCH. "JJJUULEE"!
HEY EVERYONE, OVER HERE! I THINK I FOUND HER!
I SAW HER CRAWLING AROUND, BUT I DIDN'T GIVE IT A THOUGHT. SORRY! *EXCUSAY MOI, MONSIEUR!*
FICTION
FICTION
SONIC YOUTH

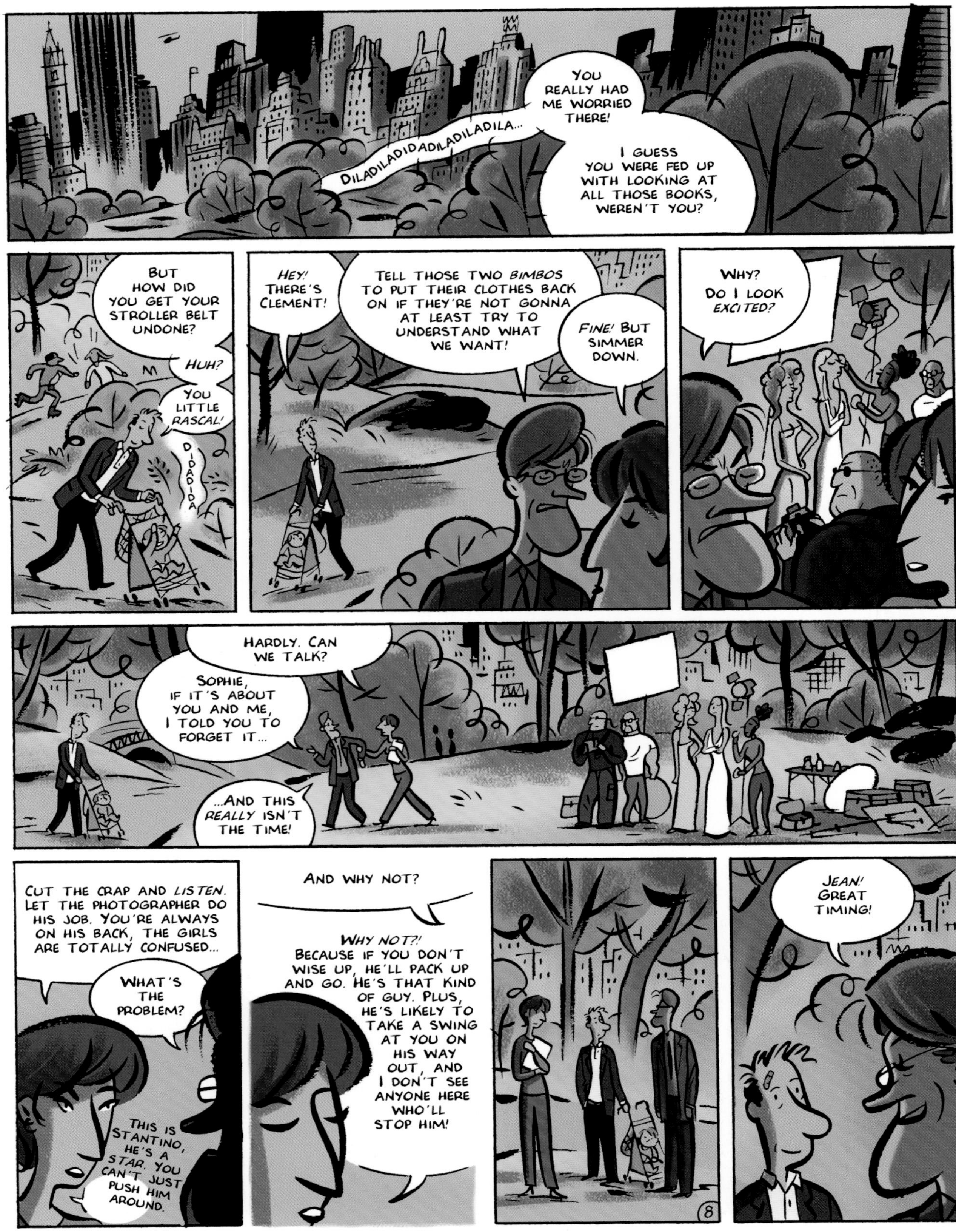
DILADILADIDADILADILADILA...
YOU REALLY HAD ME WORRIED THERE!
I GUESS YOU WERE FED UP WITH LOOKING AT ALL THOSE BOOKS, WEREN'T YOU?
BUT HOW DID YOU GET YOUR STROLLER BELT UNDONE?
HUH?
YOU LITTLE RASCAL!
DIDADIDA
HEY! THERE'S CLEMENT!
TELL THOSE TWO BIMBOS TO PUT THEIR CLOTHES BACK ON IF THEY'RE NOT GONNA AT LEAST TRY TO UNDERSTAND WHAT WE WANT!
FINE! BUT SIMMER DOWN.
WHY? DO I LOOK EXCITED?
HARDLY. CAN WE TALK?
SOPHIE, IF IT'S ABOUT YOU AND ME, I TOLD YOU TO FORGET IT...
...AND THIS REALLY ISN'T THE TIME!
CUT THE CRAP AND LISTEN. LET THE PHOTOGRAPHER DO HIS JOB. YOU'RE ALWAYS ON HIS BACK, THE GIRLS ARE TOTALLY CONFUSED...
WHAT'S THE PROBLEM?
THIS IS STANTINO, HE'S A STAR. YOU CAN'T JUST PUSH HIM AROUND.
AND WHY NOT?
WHY NOT?! BECAUSE IF YOU DON'T WISE UP, HE'LL PACK UP AND GO. HE'S THAT KIND OF GUY. PLUS, HE'S LIKELY TO TAKE A SWING AT YOU ON HIS WAY OUT, AND I DON'T SEE ANYONE HERE WHO'LL STOP HIM!
8
JEAN! GREAT TIMING!

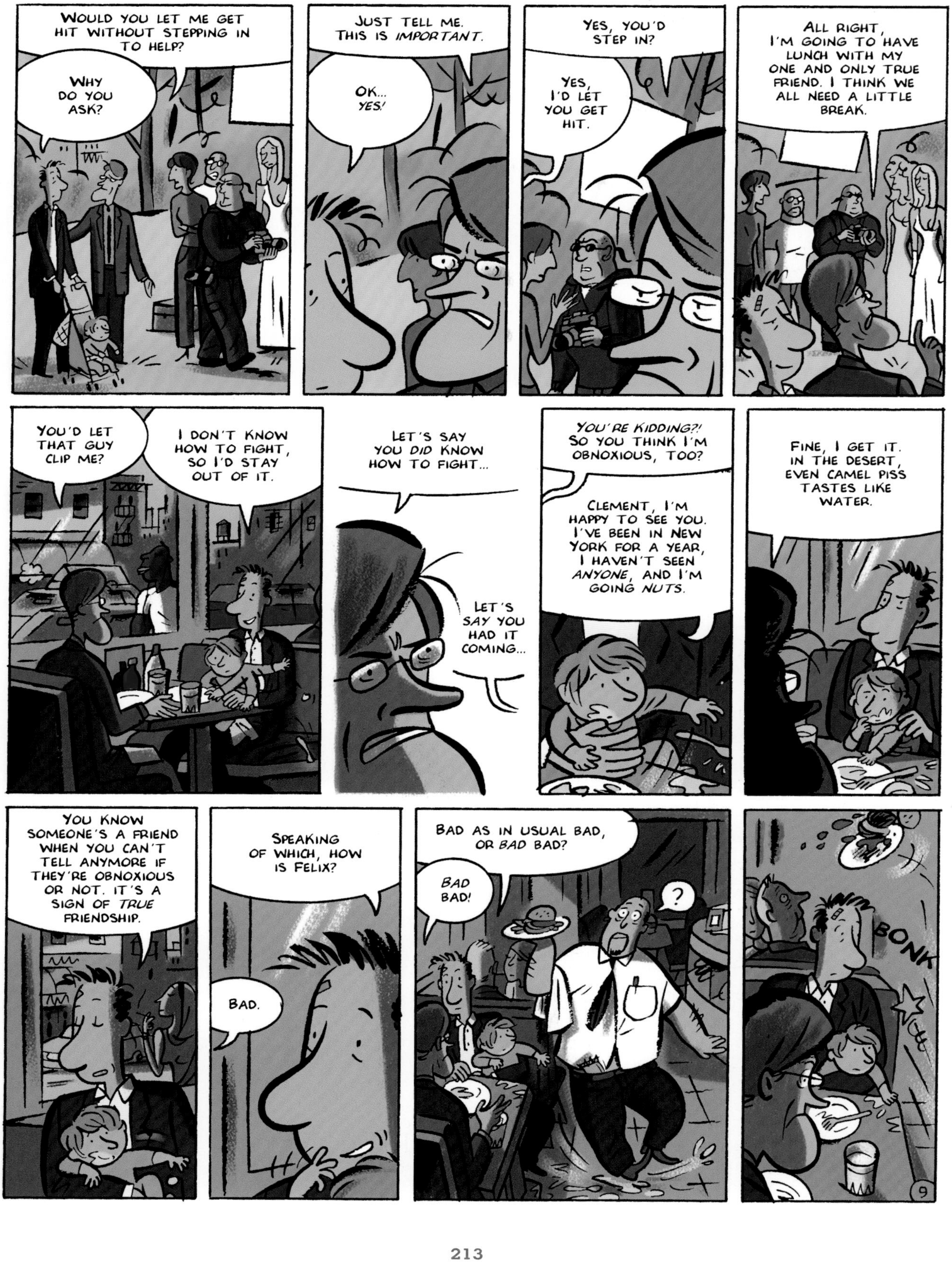
WOULD YOU LET ME GET HIT WITHOUT STEPPING IN TO HELP?
WHY DO YOU ASK?
JUST TELL ME. THIS IS *IMPORTANT*.
OK... *YES!*
YES, YOU'D STEP IN?
YES, I'D LET YOU GET HIT.
ALL RIGHT, I'M GOING TO HAVE LUNCH WITH MY ONE AND ONLY TRUE FRIEND. I THINK WE ALL NEED A LITTLE BREAK.
YOU'D LET THAT GUY CLIP ME?
I DON'T KNOW HOW TO FIGHT, SO I'D STAY OUT OF IT.
LET'S SAY YOU *DID* KNOW HOW TO FIGHT...
LET'S SAY YOU HAD IT COMING...
YOU'RE KIDDING?! SO YOU THINK I'M OBNOXIOUS, TOO?
CLEMENT, I'M HAPPY TO SEE YOU. I'VE BEEN IN NEW YORK FOR A YEAR, I HAVEN'T SEEN *ANYONE*, AND I'M GOING *NUTS*.
FINE, I GET IT. IN THE DESERT, EVEN CAMEL PISS TASTES LIKE WATER.
YOU KNOW SOMEONE'S A FRIEND WHEN YOU CAN'T TELL ANYMORE IF THEY'RE OBNOXIOUS OR NOT. IT'S A SIGN OF *TRUE* FRIENDSHIP.
SPEAKING OF WHICH, HOW IS FELIX?
BAD.
BAD AS IN USUAL BAD, OR *BAD* BAD?
BAD BAD!
?
BONK
9

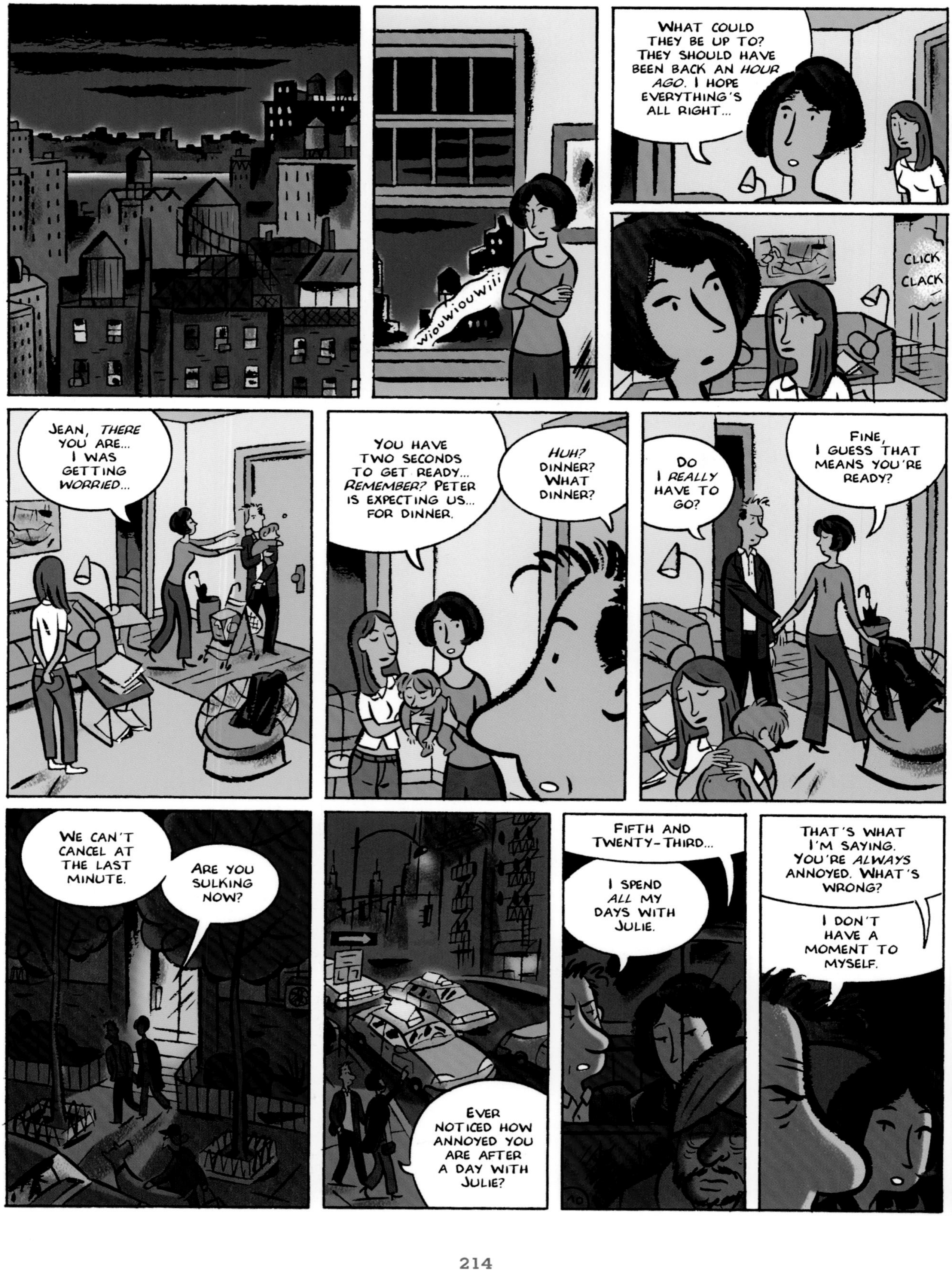
WIOUWIOUWIII
WHAT COULD THEY BE UP TO? THEY SHOULD HAVE BEEN BACK AN *HOUR* AGO. I HOPE EVERYTHING'S ALL RIGHT...
CLICK
CLACK
JEAN, *THERE* YOU ARE... I WAS GETTING *WORRIED*...
YOU HAVE TWO SECONDS TO GET READY... *REMEMBER?* PETER IS EXPECTING US... FOR DINNER.
HUH? DINNER? WHAT DINNER?
DO I *REALLY* HAVE TO GO?
FINE, I GUESS THAT MEANS YOU'RE READY?
WE CAN'T CANCEL AT THE LAST MINUTE.
ARE YOU SULKING NOW?
EVER NOTICED HOW ANNOYED YOU ARE AFTER A DAY WITH JULIE?
FIFTH AND TWENTY-THIRD...
I SPEND *ALL* MY DAYS WITH JULIE.
THAT'S WHAT I'M SAYING. YOU'RE *ALWAYS* ANNOYED. WHAT'S WRONG?
I DON'T HAVE A MOMENT TO MYSELF.

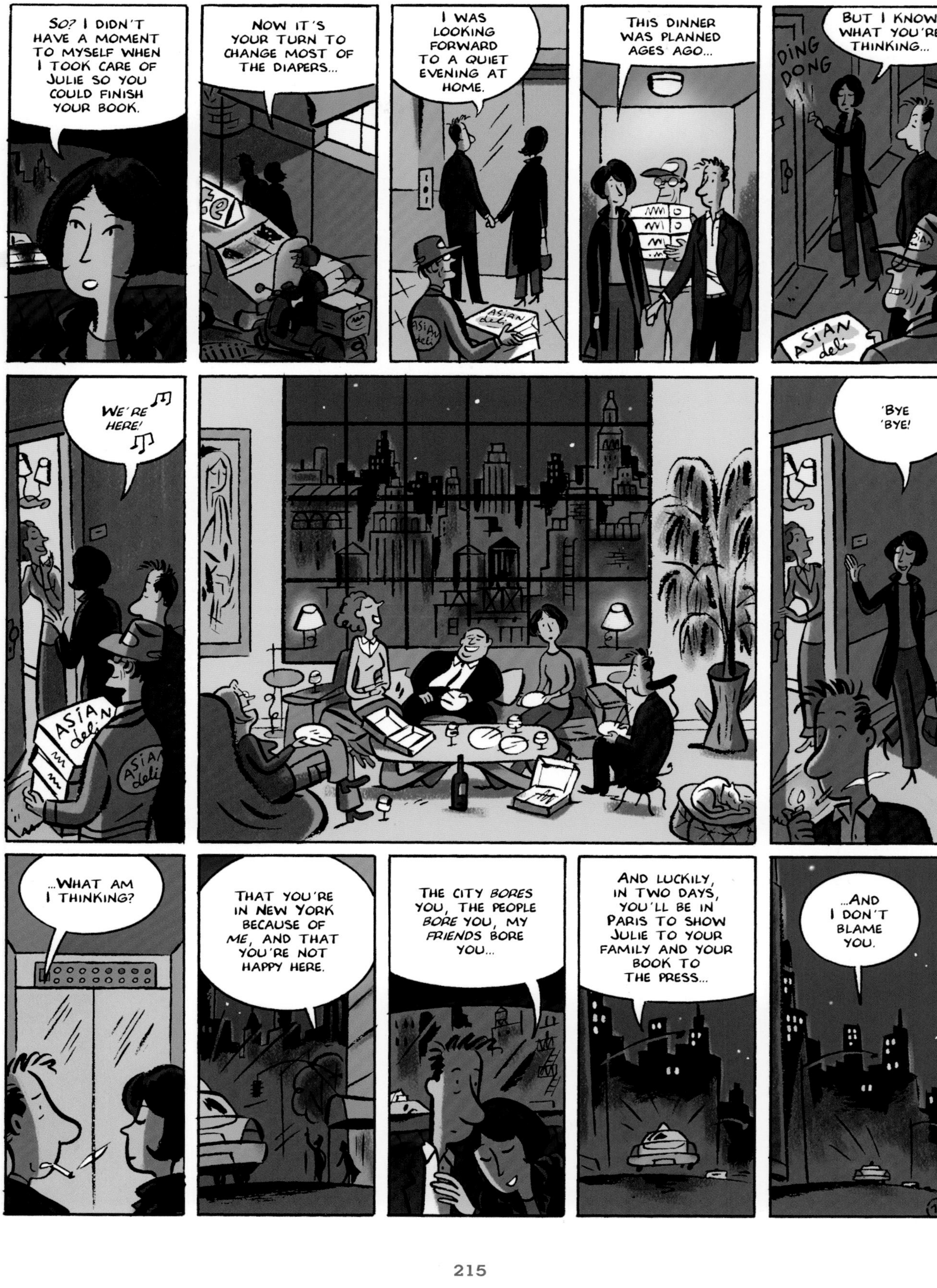

SO? I DIDN'T HAVE A MOMENT TO MYSELF WHEN I TOOK CARE OF JULIE SO YOU COULD FINISH YOUR BOOK.
NOW IT'S YOUR TURN TO CHANGE MOST OF THE DIAPERS...
I WAS LOOKING FORWARD TO A QUIET EVENING AT HOME.
ASIAN deli
THIS DINNER WAS PLANNED AGES AGO...
DING DONG
BUT I KNOW WHAT YOU'RE THINKING...
ASIAN deli
WE'RE HERE!
ASIAN deli
'BYE 'BYE!
...WHAT AM I THINKING?
THAT YOU'RE IN NEW YORK BECAUSE OF ME, AND THAT YOU'RE NOT HAPPY HERE.
THE CITY BORES YOU, THE PEOPLE BORE YOU, MY FRIENDS BORE YOU...
AND LUCKILY, IN TWO DAYS, YOU'LL BE IN PARIS TO SHOW JULIE TO YOUR FAMILY AND YOUR BOOK TO THE PRESS...
...AND I DON'T BLAME YOU.

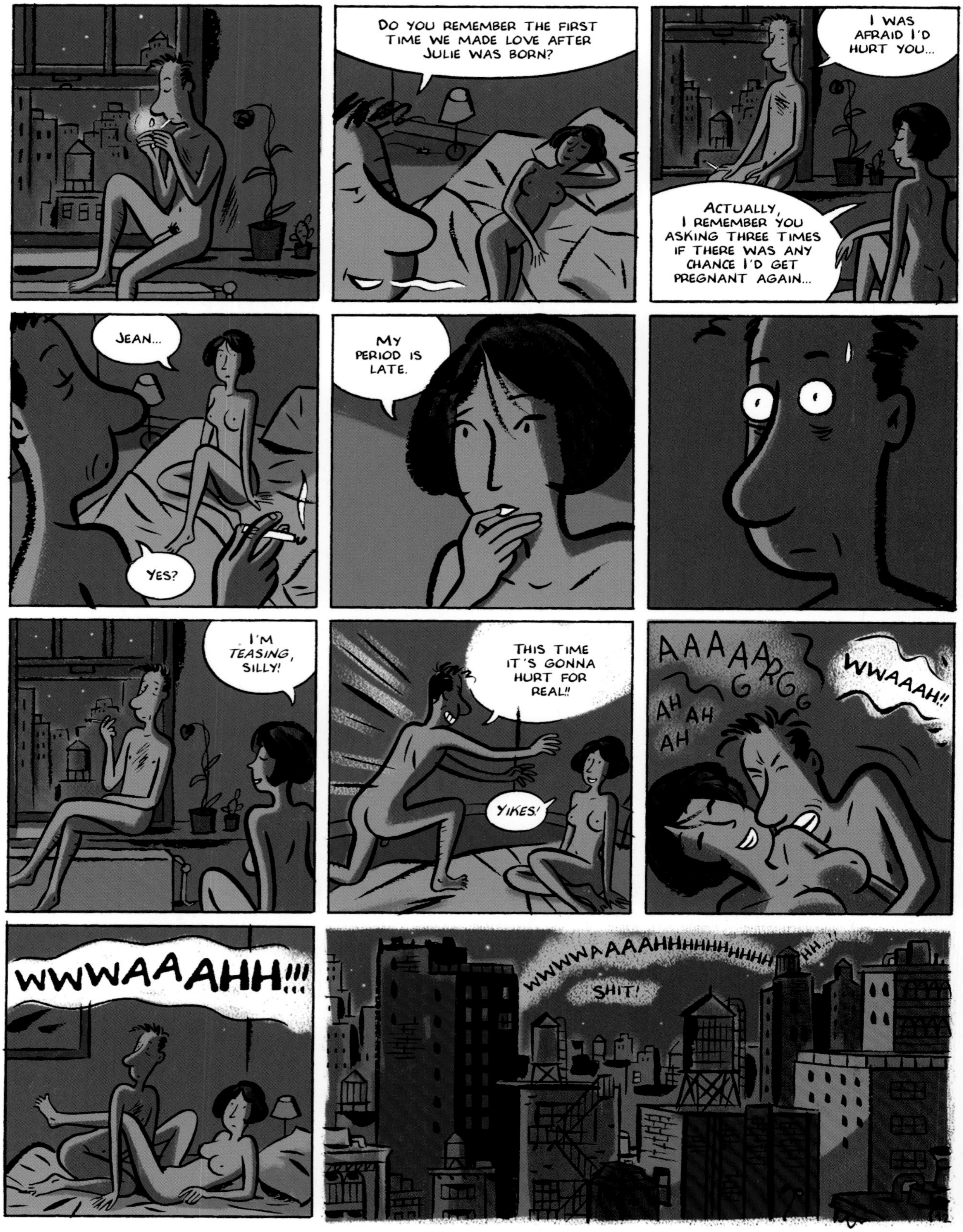

DO YOU REMEMBER THE FIRST TIME WE MADE LOVE AFTER JULIE WAS BORN?
I WAS AFRAID I'D HURT YOU...
ACTUALLY, I REMEMBER YOU ASKING THREE TIMES IF THERE WAS ANY CHANCE I'D GET PREGNANT AGAIN...
JEAN...
YES?
MY PERIOD IS LATE.
I'M TEASING, SILLY!
THIS TIME IT'S GONNA HURT FOR REAL!!
YIKES!
AAAAARGGG
AH AH AH
WWAAAH!!
WWWAAAAHH!!!
WWWWAAAAHHHHHHHHHHHHHHH...!!
SHIT!

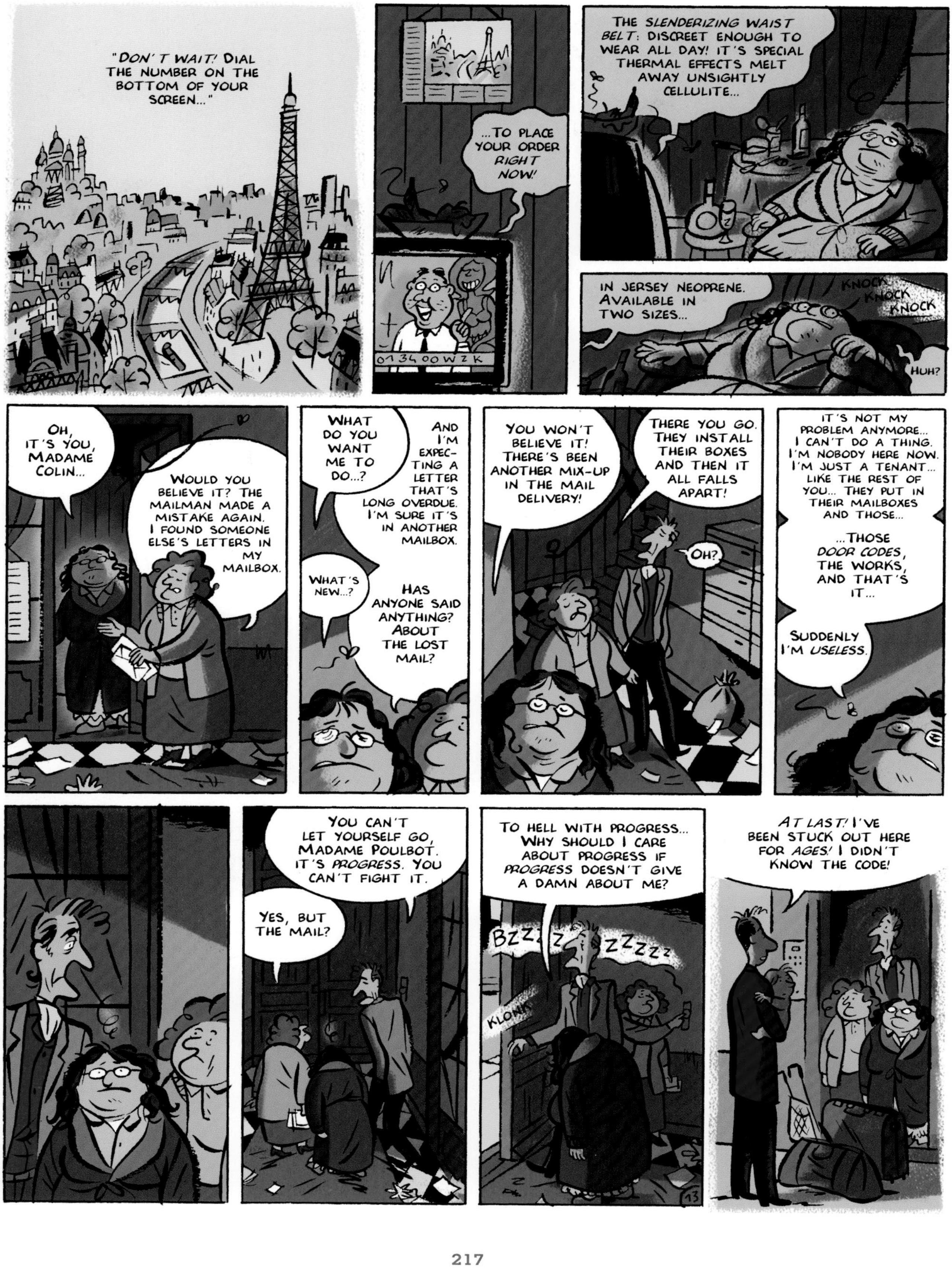
"DON'T WAIT! DIAL THE NUMBER ON THE BOTTOM OF YOUR SCREEN..."
...TO PLACE YOUR ORDER RIGHT NOW!
01 34 00 WZK
THE SLENDERIZING WAIST BELT: DISCREET ENOUGH TO WEAR ALL DAY! IT'S SPECIAL THERMAL EFFECTS MELT AWAY UNSIGHTLY CELLULITE...
IN JERSEY NEOPRENE. AVAILABLE IN TWO SIZES...
KNOCK KNOCK KNOCK
HUH?
OH, IT'S YOU, MADAME COLIN...
WOULD YOU BELIEVE IT? THE MAILMAN MADE A MISTAKE AGAIN. I FOUND SOMEONE ELSE'S LETTERS IN MY MAILBOX.
WHAT DO YOU WANT ME TO DO...?
AND I'M EXPECTING A LETTER THAT'S LONG OVERDUE. I'M SURE IT'S IN ANOTHER MAILBOX.
WHAT'S NEW...?
HAS ANYONE SAID ANYTHING? ABOUT THE LOST MAIL?
YOU WON'T BELIEVE IT! THERE'S BEEN ANOTHER MIX-UP IN THE MAIL DELIVERY!
THERE YOU GO. THEY INSTALL THEIR BOXES AND THEN IT ALL FALLS APART!
OH?
IT'S NOT MY PROBLEM ANYMORE... I CAN'T DO A THING. I'M NOBODY HERE NOW. I'M JUST A TENANT... LIKE THE REST OF YOU... THEY PUT IN THEIR MAILBOXES AND THOSE...
...THOSE DOOR CODES, THE WORKS, AND THAT'S IT...
SUDDENLY I'M USELESS.
YOU CAN'T LET YOURSELF GO, MADAME POULBOT. IT'S PROGRESS. YOU CAN'T FIGHT IT.
YES, BUT THE MAIL?
TO HELL WITH PROGRESS... WHY SHOULD I CARE ABOUT PROGRESS IF PROGRESS DOESN'T GIVE A DAMN ABOUT ME?
BZZZZZZZZZ
KLONK
13
AT LAST! I'VE BEEN STUCK OUT HERE FOR AGES! I DIDN'T KNOW THE CODE!

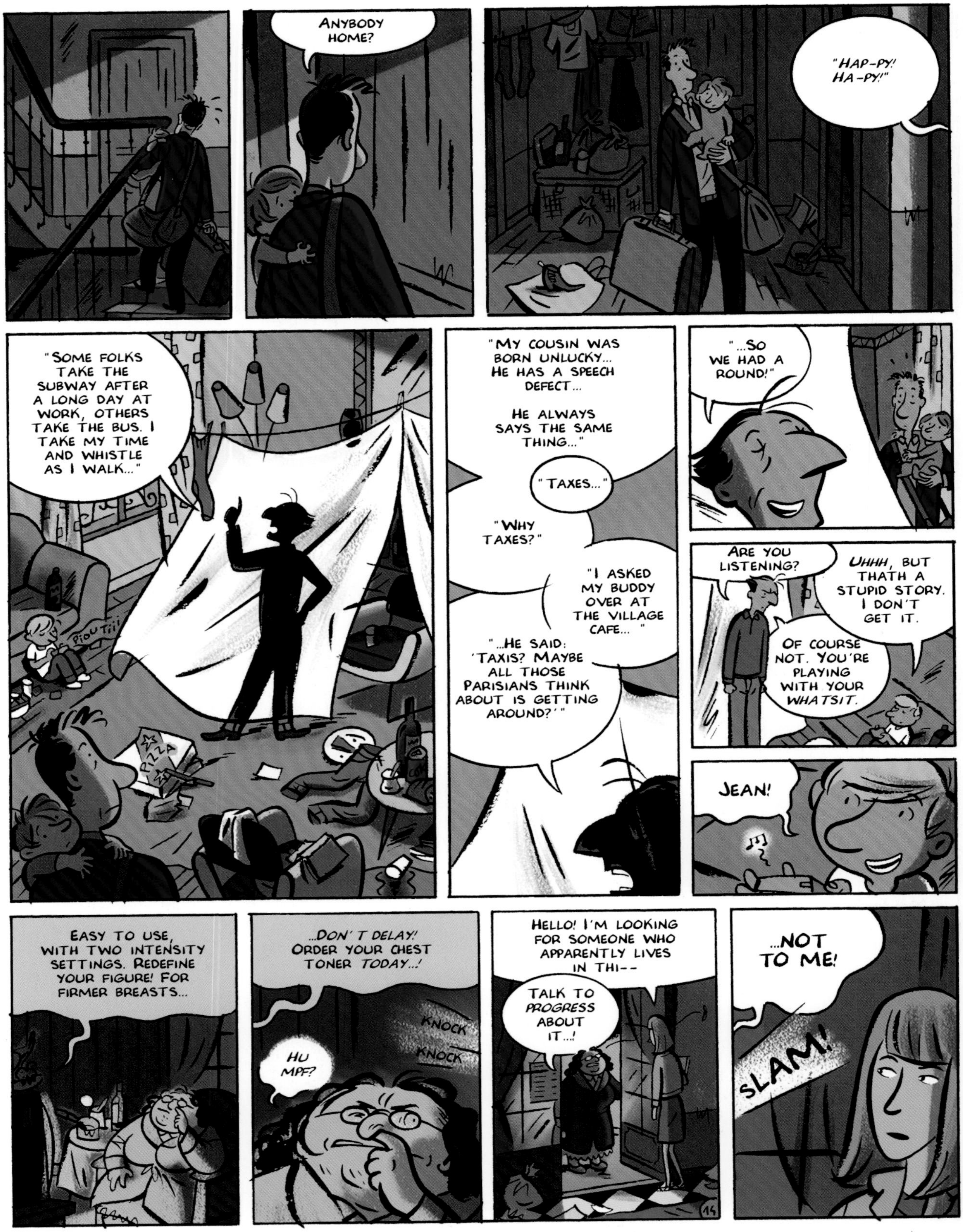

ANYBODY HOME?
"HAP-PY! HA-PY!"
"SOME FOLKS TAKE THE SUBWAY AFTER A LONG DAY AT WORK, OTHERS TAKE THE BUS. I TAKE MY TIME AND WHISTLE AS I WALK..."
PIOU TIII
"MY COUSIN WAS BORN UNLUCKY... HE HAS A SPEECH DEFECT...
HE ALWAYS SAYS THE SAME THING..."
"TAXES..."
"WHY TAXES?"
"I ASKED MY BUDDY OVER AT THE VILLAGE CAFE... "
"...HE SAID: 'TAXIS? MAYBE ALL THOSE PARISIANS THINK ABOUT IS GETTING AROUND?' "
"...SO WE HAD A ROUND!"
ARE YOU LISTENING?
UHHH, BUT THATH A STUPID STORY. I DON'T GET IT.
OF COURSE NOT. YOU'RE PLAYING WITH YOUR WHATSIT.
JEAN!
EASY TO USE, WITH TWO INTENSITY SETTINGS. REDEFINE YOUR FIGURE! FOR FIRMER BREASTS...
...DON'T DELAY! ORDER YOUR CHEST TONER TODAY...!
KNOCK
KNOCK
HU MPF?
HELLO! I'M LOOKING FOR SOMEONE WHO APPARENTLY LIVES IN THI--
TALK TO PROGRESS ABOUT IT...!
...NOT TO ME!
SLAM!

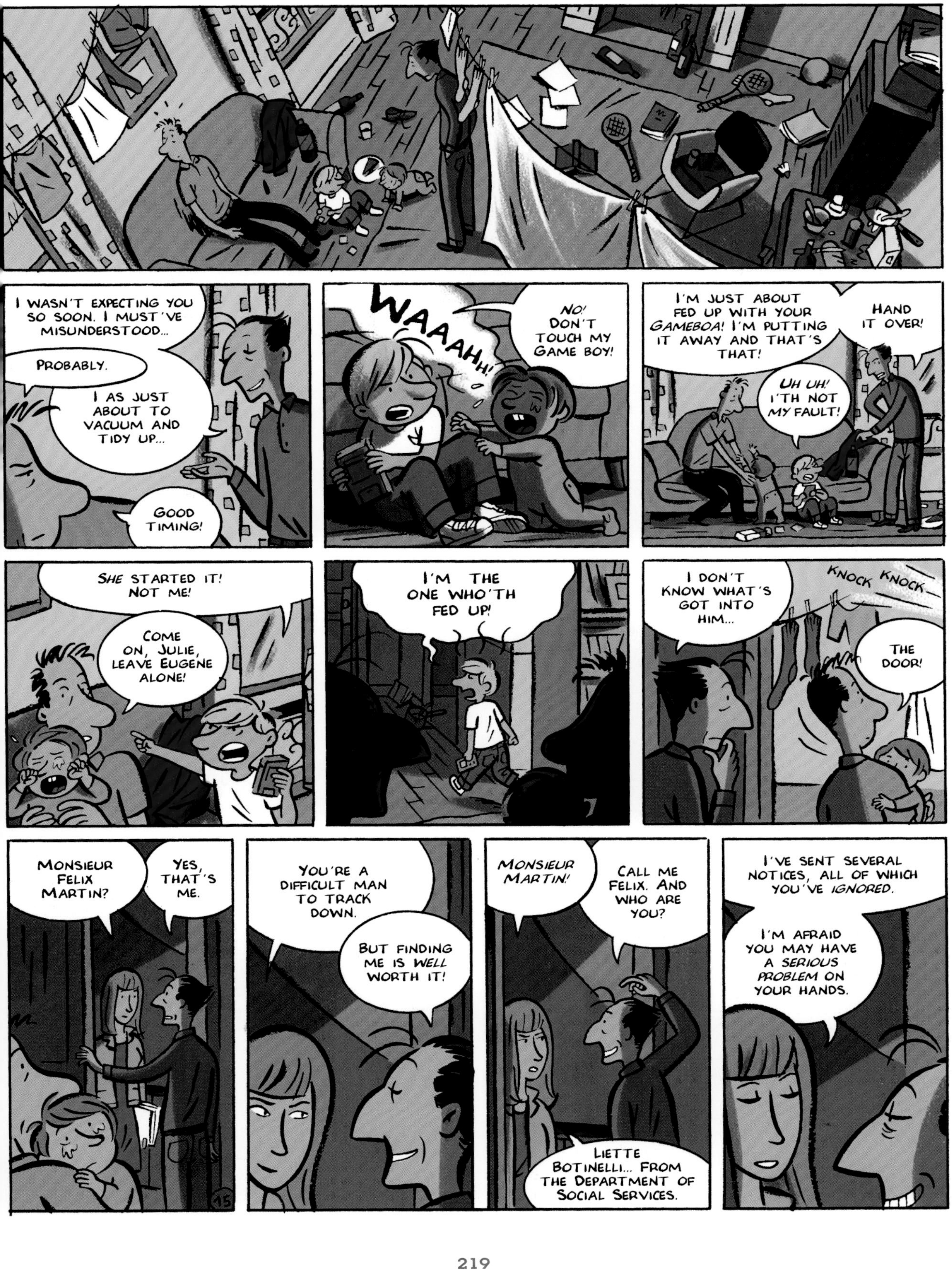

I WASN'T EXPECTING YOU SO SOON. I MUST'VE MISUNDERSTOOD...
PROBABLY.
I AS JUST ABOUT TO VACUUM AND TIDY UP...
GOOD TIMING!
WAAAHH!
NO! DON'T TOUCH MY GAME BOY!
I'M JUST ABOUT FED UP WITH YOUR GAMEBOA! I'M PUTTING IT AWAY AND THAT'S THAT!
HAND IT OVER!
UH UH! I'TH NOT MY FAULT!
SHE STARTED IT! NOT ME!
COME ON, JULIE, LEAVE EUGENE ALONE!
I'M THE ONE WHO'TH FED UP!
I DON'T KNOW WHAT'S GOT INTO HIM...
KNOCK KNOCK
THE DOOR!
MONSIEUR FELIX MARTIN?
YES, THAT'S ME.
15
YOU'RE A DIFFICULT MAN TO TRACK DOWN.
BUT FINDING ME IS WELL WORTH IT!
MONSIEUR MARTIN!
CALL ME FELIX. AND WHO ARE YOU?
LIETTE BOTINELLI... FROM THE DEPARTMENT OF SOCIAL SERVICES.
I'VE SENT SEVERAL NOTICES, ALL OF WHICH YOU'VE IGNORED.
I'M AFRAID YOU MAY HAVE A SERIOUS PROBLEM ON YOUR HANDS.

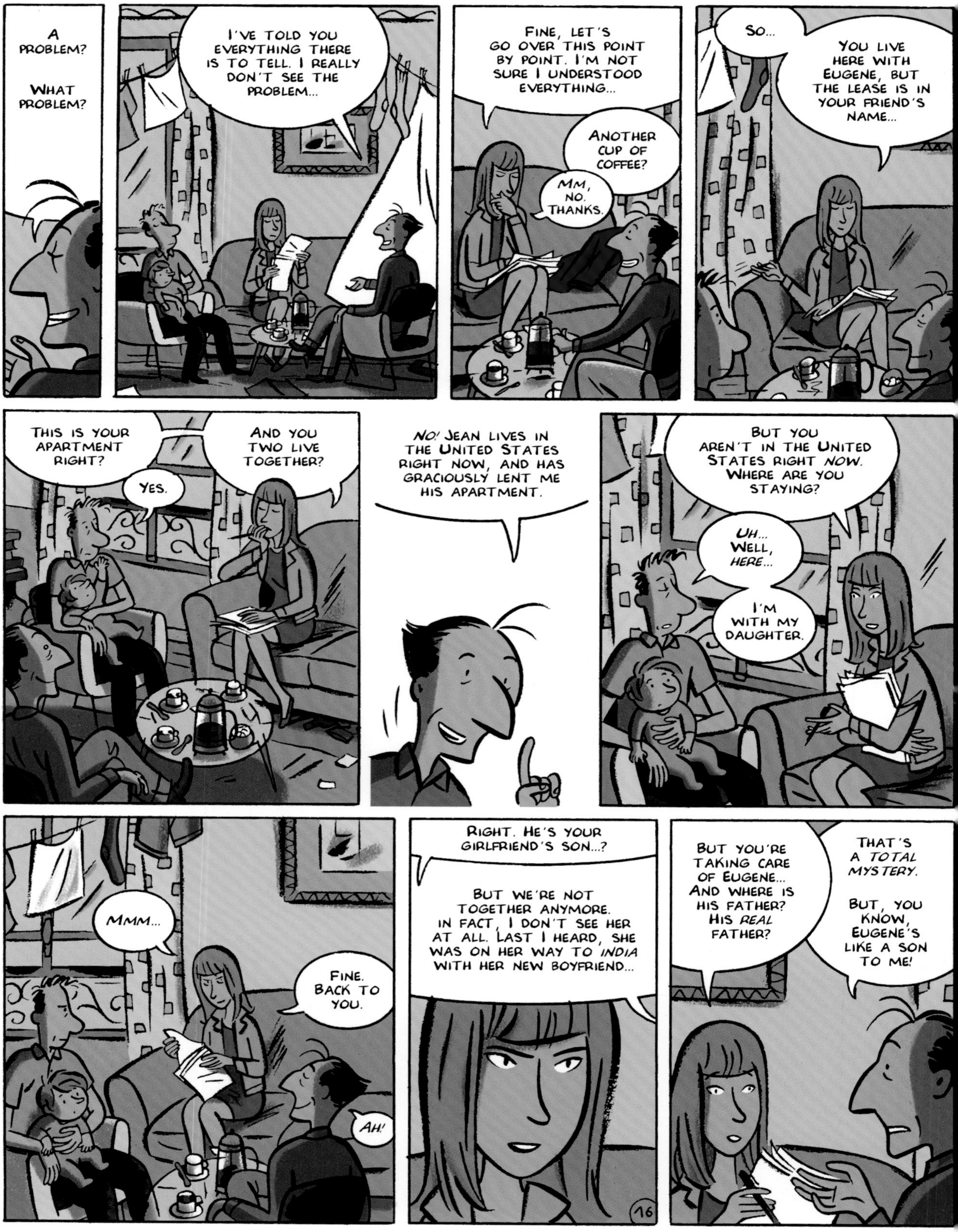
A PROBLEM?
WHAT PROBLEM?
I'VE TOLD YOU EVERYTHING THERE IS TO TELL. I REALLY DON'T SEE THE PROBLEM...
FINE, LET'S GO OVER THIS POINT BY POINT. I'M NOT SURE I UNDERSTOOD EVERYTHING...
ANOTHER CUP OF COFFEE?
MM, NO. THANKS.
SO...
YOU LIVE HERE WITH EUGENE, BUT THE LEASE IS IN YOUR FRIEND'S NAME...
THIS IS YOUR APARTMENT RIGHT?
YES.
AND YOU TWO LIVE TOGETHER?
NO! JEAN LIVES IN THE UNITED STATES RIGHT NOW, AND HAS GRACIOUSLY LENT ME HIS APARTMENT.
BUT YOU AREN'T IN THE UNITED STATES RIGHT NOW. WHERE ARE YOU STAYING?
UH... WELL, HERE...
I'M WITH MY DAUGHTER.
MMM...
FINE. BACK TO YOU.
AH!
RIGHT. HE'S YOUR GIRLFRIEND'S SON...?
BUT WE'RE NOT TOGETHER ANYMORE. IN FACT, I DON'T SEE HER AT ALL. LAST I HEARD, SHE WAS ON HER WAY TO INDIA WITH HER NEW BOYFRIEND...
16
BUT YOU'RE TAKING CARE OF EUGENE... AND WHERE IS HIS FATHER? HIS REAL FATHER?
THAT'S A TOTAL MYSTERY.
BUT, YOU KNOW, EUGENE'S LIKE A SON TO ME!

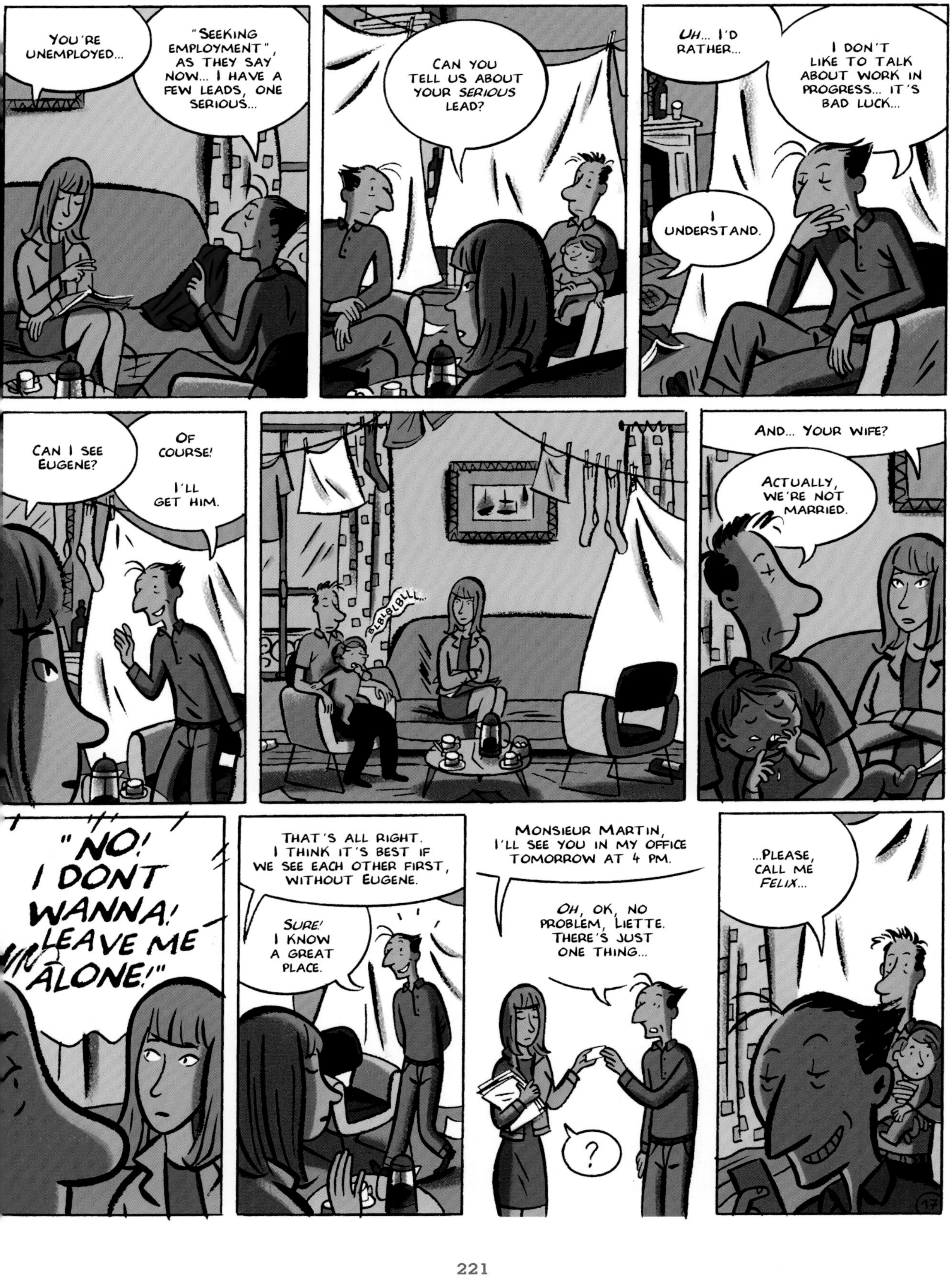
YOU'RE UNEMPLOYED...
"SEEKING EMPLOYMENT", AS THEY SAY NOW... I HAVE A FEW LEADS, ONE SERIOUS...
CAN YOU TELL US ABOUT YOUR SERIOUS LEAD?
UH... I'D RATHER...
I DON'T LIKE TO TALK ABOUT WORK IN PROGRESS... IT'S BAD LUCK...
I UNDERSTAND.
CAN I SEE EUGENE?
OF COURSE!
I'LL GET HIM.
BLBLBLBLL...
AND... YOUR WIFE?
ACTUALLY, WE'RE NOT MARRIED.
"NO! I DONT WANNA! LEAVE ME ALONE!"
THAT'S ALL RIGHT. I THINK IT'S BEST IF WE SEE EACH OTHER FIRST, WITHOUT EUGENE.
SURE! I KNOW A GREAT PLACE.
MONSIEUR MARTIN, I'LL SEE YOU IN MY OFFICE TOMORROW AT 4 PM.
OH, OK, NO PROBLEM, LIETTE. THERE'S JUST ONE THING...
?
...PLEASE, CALL ME FELIX...
17

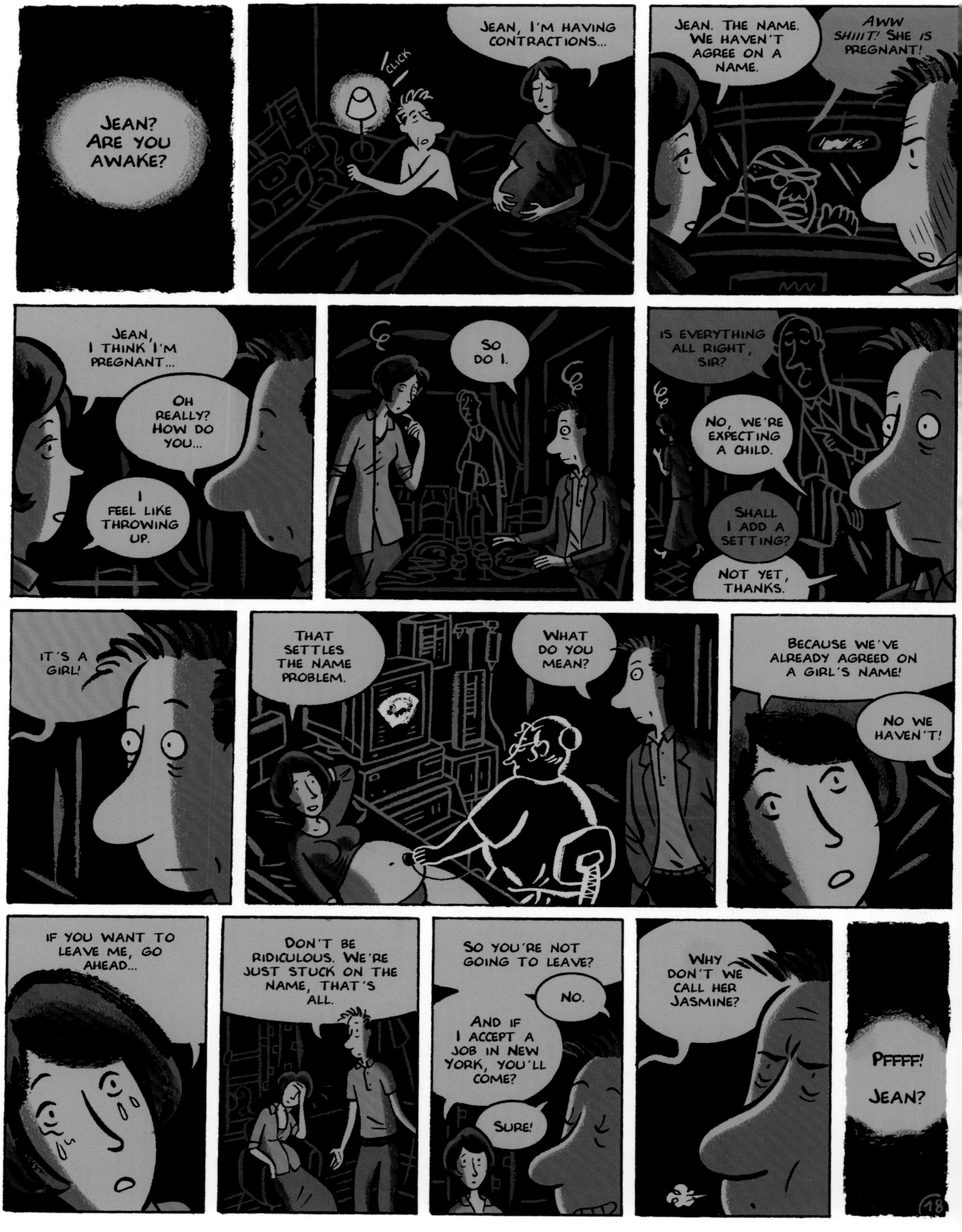
JEAN? ARE YOU AWAKE?
CLICK
JEAN, I'M HAVING CONTRACTIONS...
JEAN. THE NAME. WE HAVEN'T AGREE ON A NAME.
AWW SHIIIT! SHE IS PREGNANT!
JEAN, I THINK I'M PREGNANT...
OH REALLY? HOW DO YOU...
I FEEL LIKE THROWING UP.
SO DO I.
IS EVERYTHING ALL RIGHT, SIR?
NO, WE'RE EXPECTING A CHILD.
SHALL I ADD A SETTING?
NOT YET, THANKS.
IT'S A GIRL!
THAT SETTLES THE NAME PROBLEM.
WHAT DO YOU MEAN?
BECAUSE WE'VE ALREADY AGREED ON A GIRL'S NAME!
NO WE HAVEN'T!
IF YOU WANT TO LEAVE ME, GO AHEAD...
DON'T BE RIDICULOUS. WE'RE JUST STUCK ON THE NAME, THAT'S ALL.
SO YOU'RE NOT GOING TO LEAVE?
NO.
AND IF I ACCEPT A JOB IN NEW YORK, YOU'LL COME?
SURE!
WHY DON'T WE CALL HER JASMINE?
PFFFF!
JEAN?
78

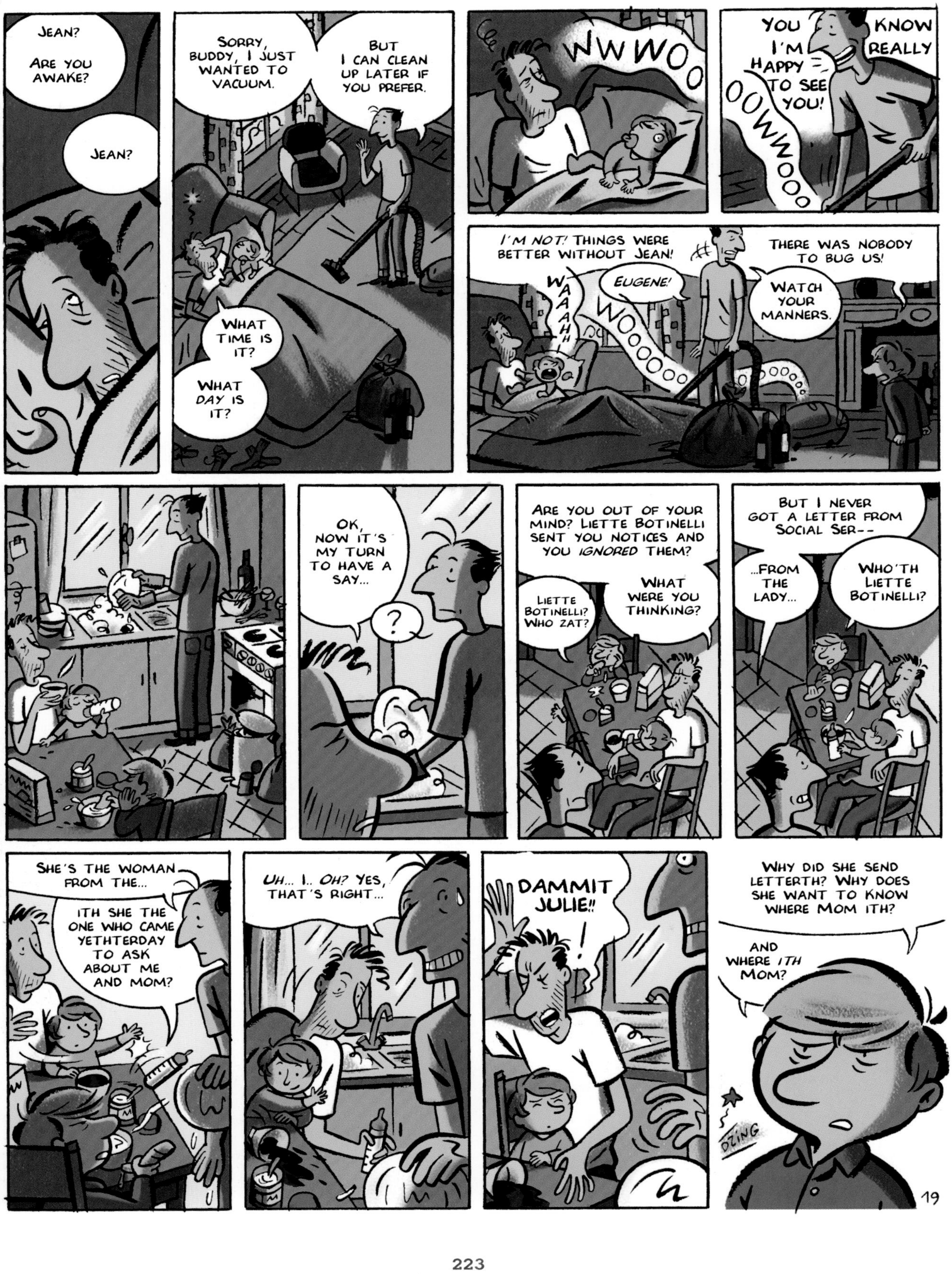
JEAN?
ARE YOU AWAKE?
JEAN?
SORRY, BUDDY, I JUST WANTED TO VACUUM.
BUT I CAN CLEAN UP LATER IF YOU PREFER.
WHAT TIME IS IT?
WHAT DAY IS IT?
WWWOOOOWWOOOO
YOU KNOW I'M REALLY HAPPY TO SEE YOU!
I'M NOT! THINGS WERE BETTER WITHOUT JEAN!
THERE WAS NOBODY TO BUG US!
WAAAAHH
EUGENE!
WOOOOOO
WATCH YOUR MANNERS.
OK, NOW IT'S MY TURN TO HAVE A SAY...
?
ARE YOU OUT OF YOUR MIND? LIETTE BOTINELLI SENT YOU NOTICES AND YOU IGNORED THEM?
LIETTE BOTINELLI? WHO ZAT?
WHAT WERE YOU THINKING?
BUT I NEVER GOT A LETTER FROM SOCIAL SER--
...FROM THE LADY...
WHO'TH LIETTE BOTINELLI?
SHE'S THE WOMAN FROM THE...
ITH SHE THE ONE WHO CAME YETHTERDAY TO ASK ABOUT ME AND MOM?
UH... I.. OH? YES, THAT'S RIGHT...
DAMMIT JULIE!!
WHY DID SHE SEND LETTERTH? WHY DOES SHE WANT TO KNOW WHERE MOM ITH?
AND WHERE ITH MOM?
DZING
19

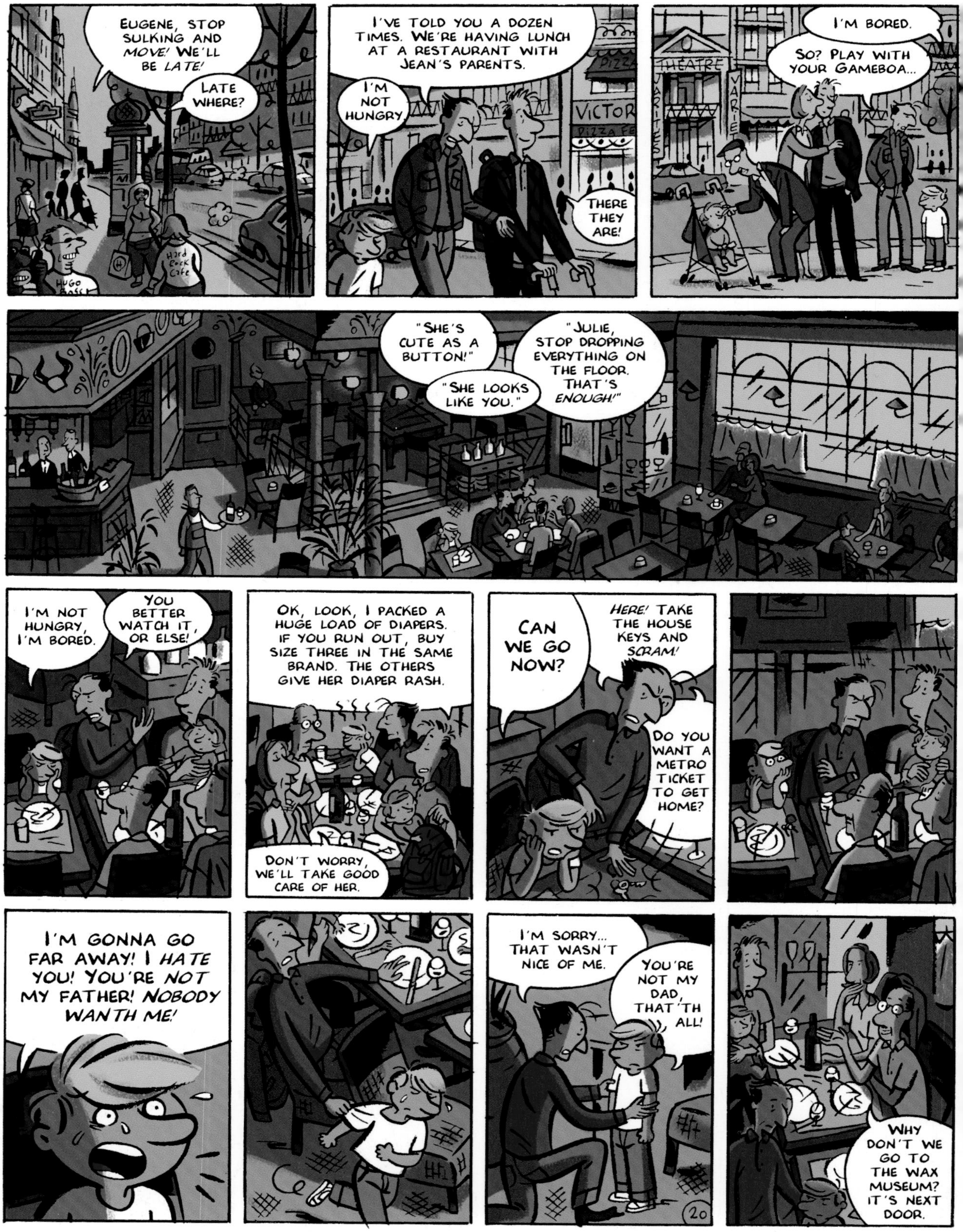
EUGENE, STOP SULKING AND MOVE! WE'LL BE LATE!
LATE WHERE?
HUGO BOSS
Hard Rock Cafe
I'VE TOLD YOU A DOZEN TIMES. WE'RE HAVING LUNCH AT A RESTAURANT WITH JEAN'S PARENTS.
I'M NOT HUNGRY.
THERE THEY ARE!
I'M BORED.
SO? PLAY WITH YOUR GAMEBOA...
THEATRE
VARIETES
"SHE'S CUTE AS A BUTTON!"
"SHE LOOKS LIKE YOU."
"JULIE, STOP DROPPING EVERYTHING ON THE FLOOR. THAT'S ENOUGH!"
I'M NOT HUNGRY, I'M BORED.
YOU BETTER WATCH IT, OR ELSE!
OK, LOOK, I PACKED A HUGE LOAD OF DIAPERS. IF YOU RUN OUT, BUY SIZE THREE IN THE SAME BRAND. THE OTHERS GIVE HER DIAPER RASH.
DON'T WORRY, WE'LL TAKE GOOD CARE OF HER.
CAN WE GO NOW?
HERE! TAKE THE HOUSE KEYS AND SCRAM!
DO YOU WANT A METRO TICKET TO GET HOME?
I'M GONNA GO FAR AWAY! I HATE YOU! YOU'RE NOT MY FATHER! NOBODY WANTH ME!
I'M SORRY... THAT WASN'T NICE OF ME.
YOU'RE NOT MY DAD, THAT'TH ALL!
WHY DON'T WE GO TO THE WAX MUSEUM? IT'S NEXT DOOR.

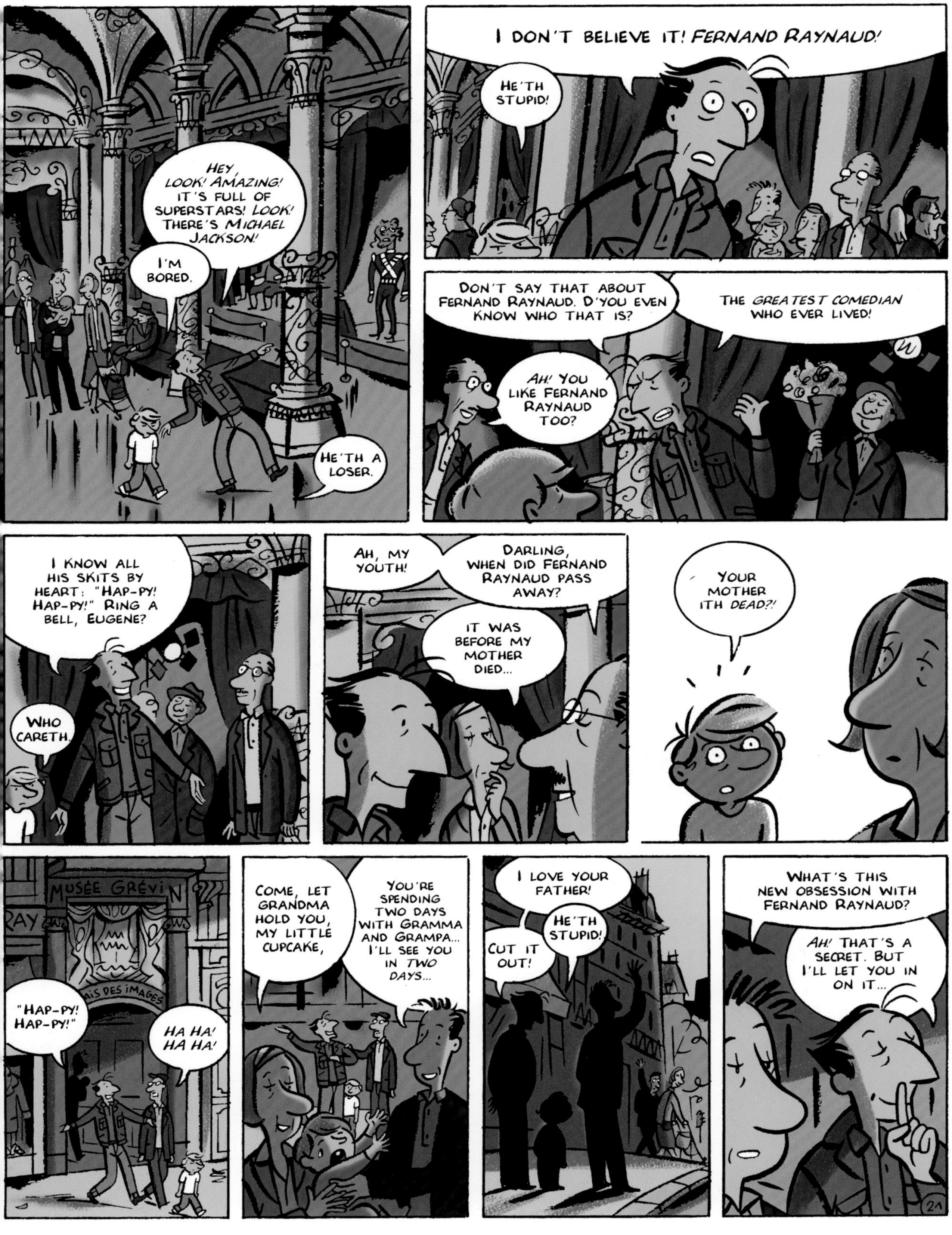

HEY, LOOK! AMAZING! IT'S FULL OF SUPERSTARS! LOOK! THERE'S MICHAEL JACKSON!
I'M BORED.
HE'TH A LOSER.
I DON'T BELIEVE IT! FERNAND RAYNAUD!
HE'TH STUPID!
DON'T SAY THAT ABOUT FERNAND RAYNAUD. D'YOU EVEN KNOW WHO THAT IS?
THE GREATEST COMEDIAN WHO EVER LIVED!
AH! YOU LIKE FERNAND RAYNAUD TOO?
I KNOW ALL HIS SKITS BY HEART: "HAP-PY! HAP-PY!" RING A BELL, EUGENE?
WHO CARETH.
AH, MY YOUTH!
DARLING, WHEN DID FERNAND RAYNAUD PASS AWAY?
IT WAS BEFORE MY MOTHER DIED...
YOUR MOTHER ITH DEAD?!
MUSÉE GRÉVIN
"HAP-PY! HAP-PY!"
HA HA! HA HA!
COME, LET GRANDMA HOLD YOU, MY LITTLE CUPCAKE,
YOU'RE SPENDING TWO DAYS WITH GRAMMA AND GRAMPA... I'LL SEE YOU IN TWO DAYS...
I LOVE YOUR FATHER!
HE'TH STUPID!
CUT IT OUT!
WHAT'S THIS NEW OBSESSION WITH FERNAND RAYNAUD?
AH! THAT'S A SECRET. BUT I'LL LET YOU IN ON IT...
21

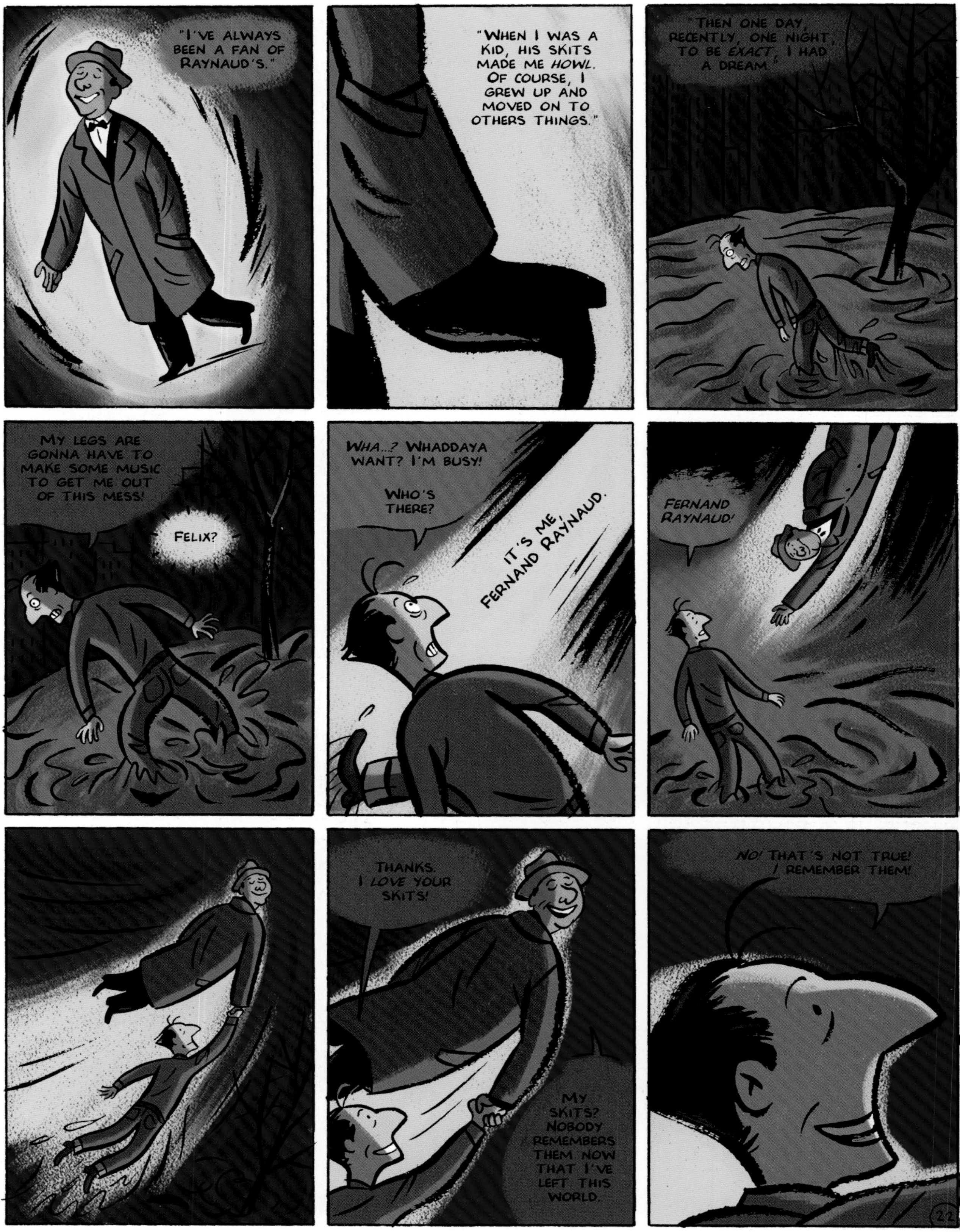
"I'VE ALWAYS BEEN A FAN OF RAYNAUD'S."
"WHEN I WAS A KID, HIS SKITS MADE ME HOWL. OF COURSE, I GREW UP AND MOVED ON TO OTHERS THINGS."
"THEN ONE DAY, RECENTLY, ONE NIGHT, TO BE EXACT, I HAD A DREAM."
MY LEGS ARE GONNA HAVE TO MAKE SOME MUSIC TO GET ME OUT OF THIS MESS!
FELIX?
WHA...? WHADDAYA WANT? I'M BUSY!
WHO'S THERE?
IT'S ME, FERNAND RAYNAUD.
FERNAND RAYNAUD!
THANKS. I LOVE YOUR SKITS!
MY SKITS? NOBODY REMEMBERS THEM NOW THAT I'VE LEFT THIS WORLD.
NO! THAT'S NOT TRUE! I REMEMBER THEM!
22

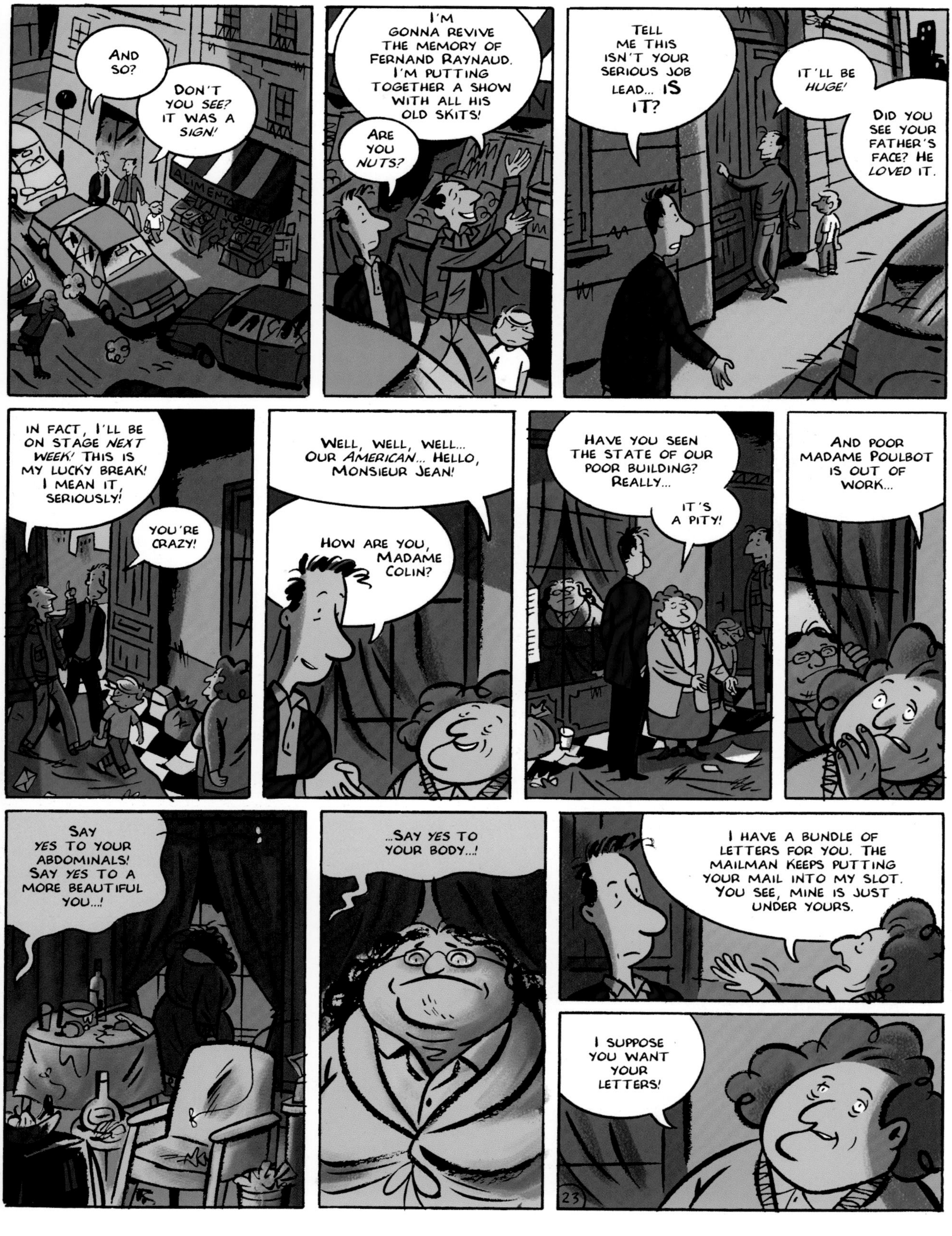
And so?
Don't you see? It was a sign!
Alimenta
I'm gonna revive the memory of Fernand Raynaud. I'm putting together a show with all his old skits!
Are you nuts?
Tell me this isn't your serious job lead... IS IT?
It'll be huge!
Did you see your father's face? He loved it.
In fact, I'll be on stage next week! This is my lucky break! I mean it, seriously!
You're crazy!
Well, well, well... Our American... Hello, Monsieur Jean!
How are you, Madame Colin?
Have you seen the state of our poor building? Really...
It's a pity!
And poor Madame Poulbot is out of work...
Say yes to your abdominals! Say yes to a more beautiful you...!
...Say yes to your body...!
I have a bundle of letters for you. The mailman keeps putting your mail into my slot. You see, mine is just under yours.
I suppose you want your letters!
23

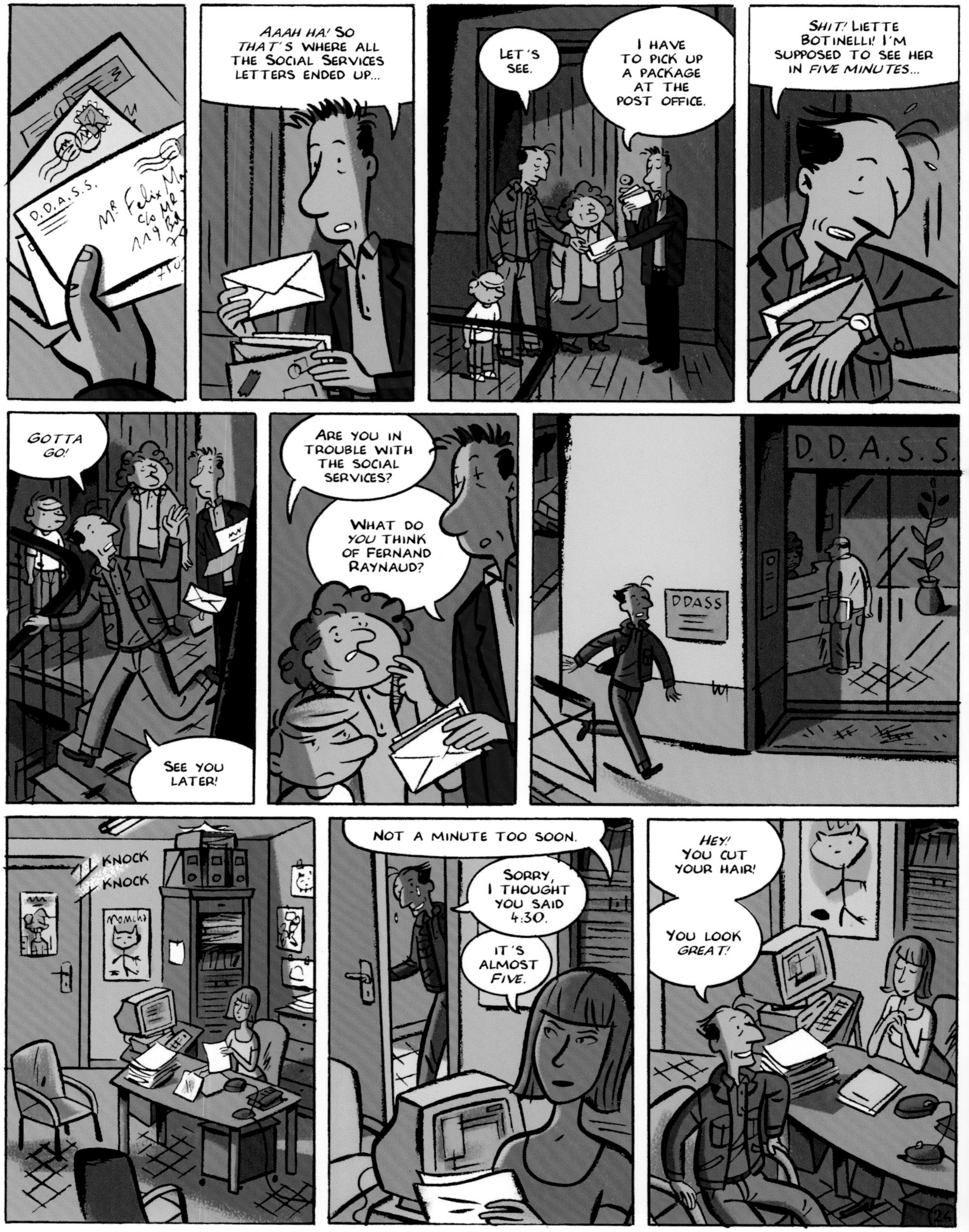
D.D.A.S.S.
Mr Felix M
AAAH HA! SO THAT'S WHERE ALL THE SOCIAL SERVICES LETTERS ENDED UP...
LET'S SEE.
I HAVE TO PICK UP A PACKAGE AT THE POST OFFICE.
SHIT! LIETTE BOTINELLI! I'M SUPPOSED TO SEE HER IN FIVE MINUTES...
GOTTA GO!
SEE YOU LATER!
ARE YOU IN TROUBLE WITH THE SOCIAL SERVICES?
WHAT DO YOU THINK OF FERNAND RAYNAUD?
D.D.A.S.S.
DDASS
KNOCK KNOCK
NOT A MINUTE TOO SOON.
SORRY, I THOUGHT YOU SAID 4:30.
IT'S ALMOST FIVE.
HEY! YOU CUT YOUR HAIR!
YOU LOOK GREAT!

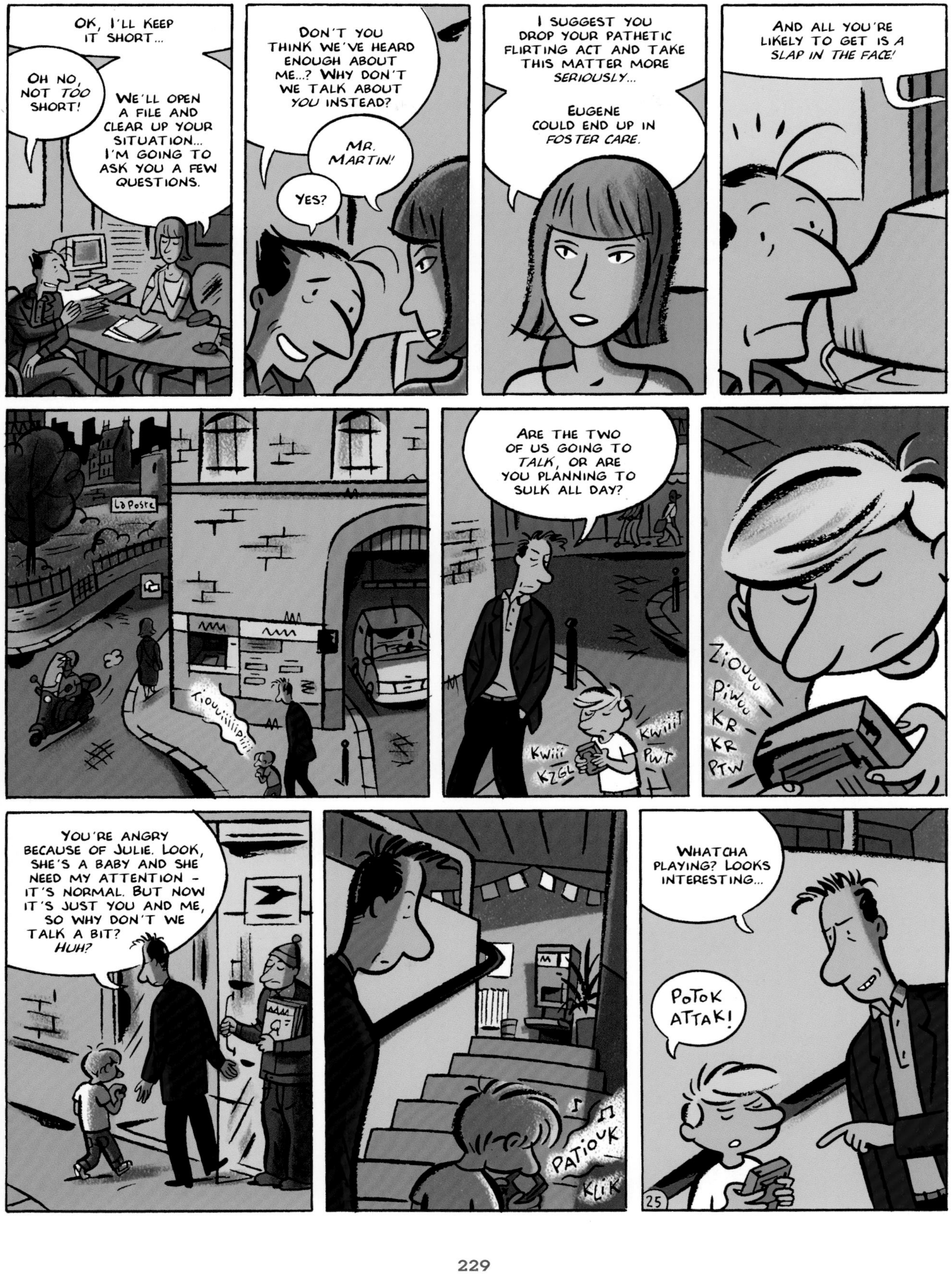
OK, I'LL KEEP IT SHORT...
OH NO, NOT *TOO* SHORT!
WE'LL OPEN A FILE AND CLEAR UP YOUR SITUATION... I'M GOING TO ASK YOU A FEW QUESTIONS.
DON'T YOU THINK WE'VE HEARD ENOUGH ABOUT ME...? WHY DON'T WE TALK ABOUT *YOU* INSTEAD?
MR. MARTIN!
YES?
I SUGGEST YOU DROP YOUR PATHETIC FLIRTING ACT AND TAKE THIS MATTER MORE *SERIOUSLY*...
EUGENE COULD END UP IN *FOSTER CARE.*
AND ALL YOU'RE LIKELY TO GET IS A *SLAP IN THE FACE!*
La Poste
Tiouuiiiiiipiiii
ARE THE TWO OF US GOING TO *TALK*, OR ARE YOU PLANNING TO SULK ALL DAY?
KWIII
KZGL
KWIIIT
PWT
ZIOUUU
PIWUU
KR
KR
PTW
YOU'RE ANGRY BECAUSE OF JULIE. LOOK, SHE'S A BABY AND SHE NEED MY ATTENTION - IT'S NORMAL. BUT NOW IT'S JUST YOU AND ME, SO WHY DON'T WE TALK A BIT? *HUH?*
PATIOUK
KLIK
WHATCHA PLAYING? LOOKS INTERESTING...
POTOK ATTAK!
25

YOU ACT LIKE IT'S ALL A GAME, BUT IT ISN'T. YOU HAVE *RESPONSIBILITIES* AND YOU'RE NOT TAKING THEM SERIOUSLY. I'M SORRY, BUT THE WAY THINGS STAND, YOU ARE CERTAINLY NOT THE PERSON BEST SUITED TO LOOK AFTER EUGENE'S EDUCATION...

YOU'RE RIGHT. RUB IT IN.

I DON'T WANT TO RUB IT IN, IT'S THE *TRUTH*...

IF IT ISN'T, *PROVE IT*. PUT UP A *FIGHT* IF YOU WANT TO KEEP EUGENE.

I DON'T KNOW...

MAYBE. MAYBE NOT...

YESTERDAY YOU MENTIONED A GREAT JOB LEAD.

WHAT SECTOR ARE YOU LOOKING AT?

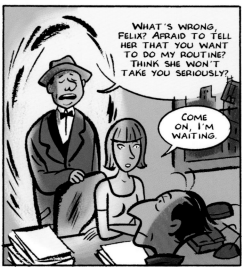

WHAT'S WRONG, FELIX? AFRAID TO TELL HER THAT YOU WANT TO DO MY ROUTINE? THINK SHE WON'T TAKE YOU SERIOUSLY?

COME ON, I'M WAITING.

GO AHEAD. TELL HER HOW YOU PLAN TO GET OUT OF THIS MESS.

WHEN YOU'VE GOT ENOUGH POWER POINTH, YOU CAN CHALLENGE OTHER POTOKTH TO A MATCH.

THE LOSER BECOMES KOTOP AND DOES EVERYTHING BACKWARDTH TILL HE GETH HITH POTOK POWER BACK.

AFTER THREE TIMETH, YOU DIE...

GET IT?

UH...

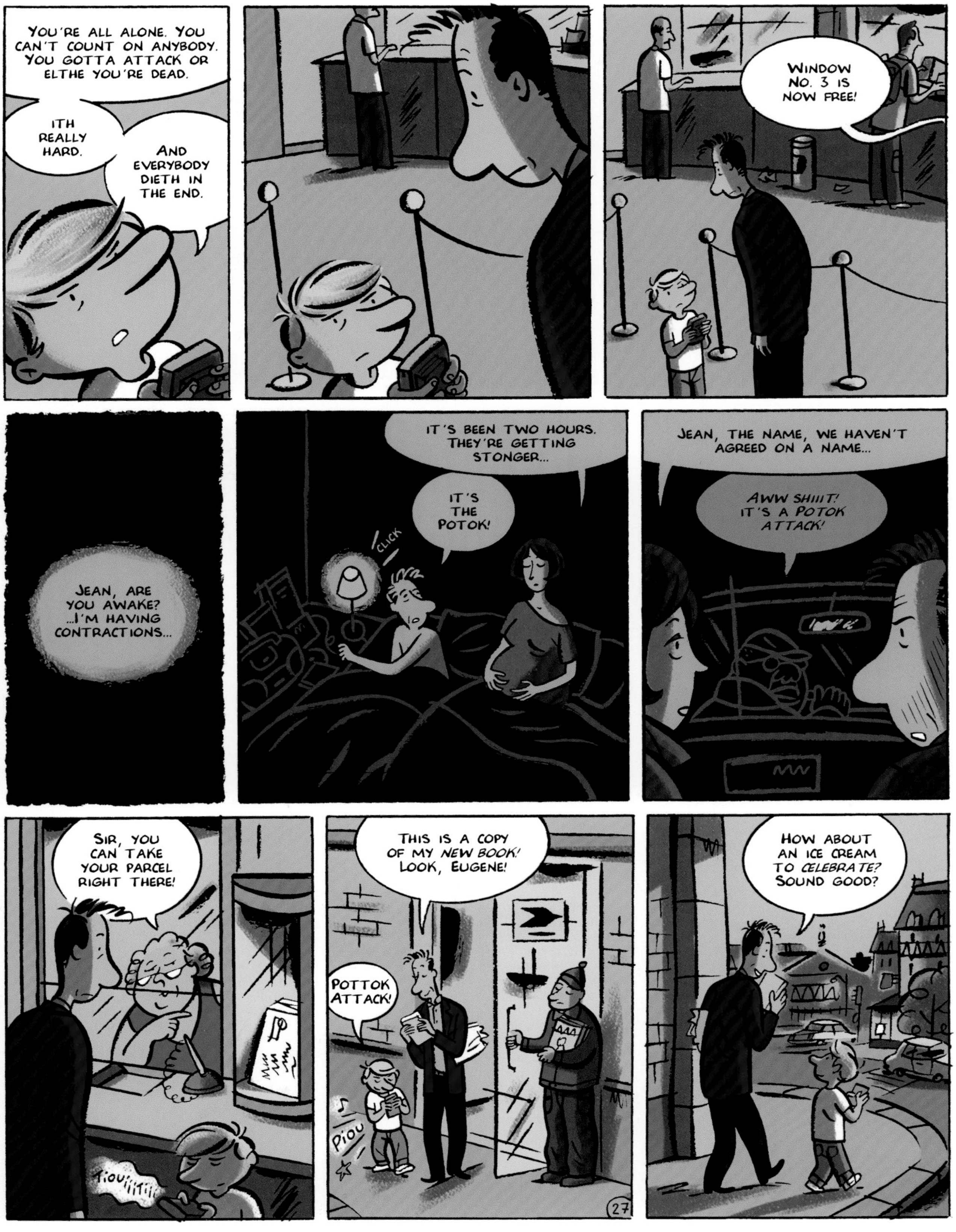
YOU'RE ALL ALONE. YOU CAN'T COUNT ON ANYBODY. YOU GOTTA ATTACK OR ELTHE YOU'RE DEAD.
ITH REALLY HARD.
AND EVERYBODY DIETH IN THE END.
WINDOW NO. 3 IS NOW FREE!
JEAN, ARE YOU AWAKE? ...I'M HAVING CONTRACTIONS...
IT'S BEEN TWO HOURS. THEY'RE GETTING STONGER...
CLICK
IT'S THE POTOK!
JEAN, THE NAME, WE HAVEN'T AGREED ON A NAME...
AWW SHIIIT! IT'S A POTOK ATTACK!
SIR, YOU CAN TAKE YOUR PARCEL RIGHT THERE!
TIOUIIIIII
THIS IS A COPY OF MY NEW BOOK! LOOK, EUGENE!
POTTOK ATTACK!
PIOU
27
HOW ABOUT AN ICE CREAM TO CELEBRATE? SOUND GOOD?

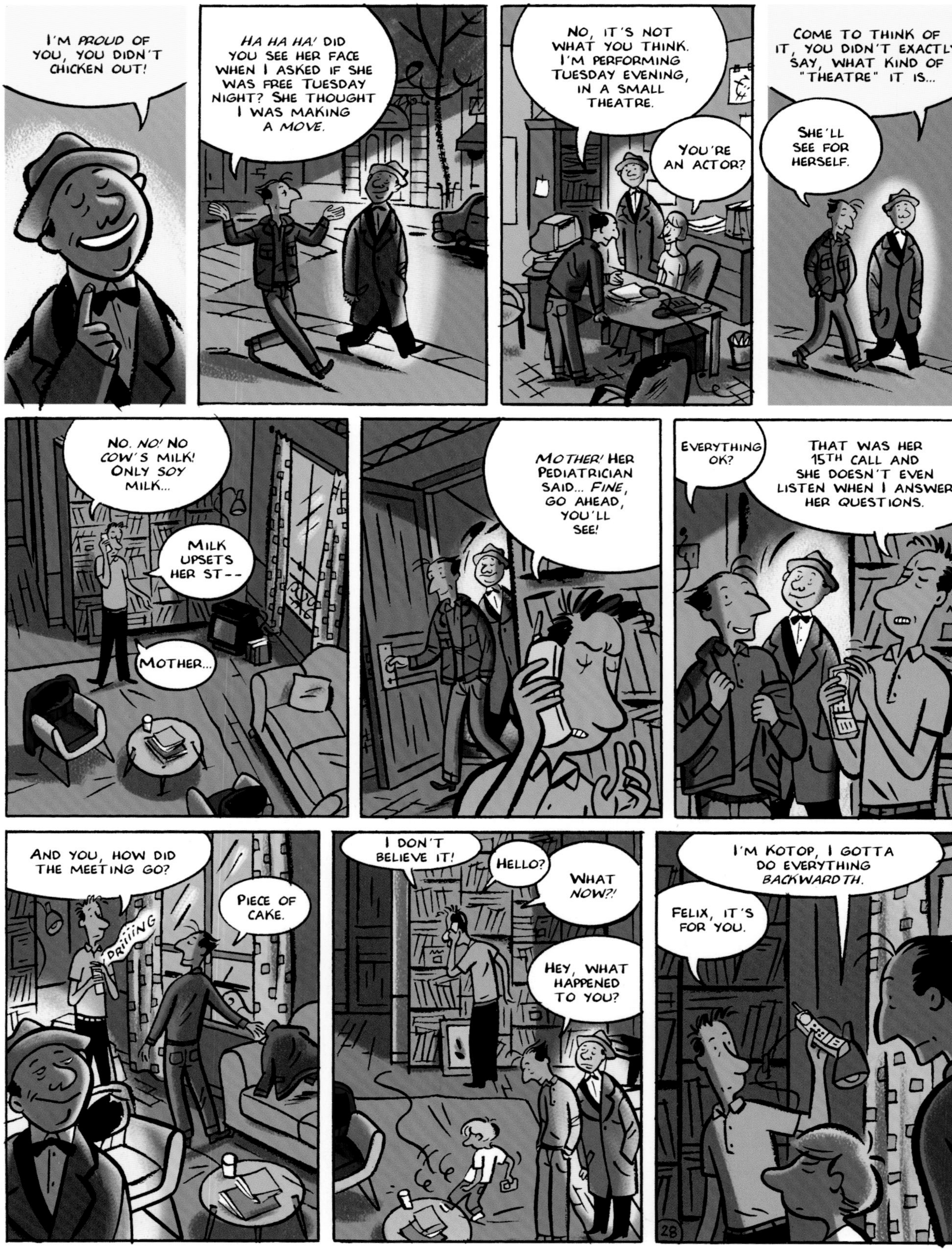
I'M PROUD OF YOU, YOU DIDN'T CHICKEN OUT!
HA HA HA! DID YOU SEE HER FACE WHEN I ASKED IF SHE WAS FREE TUESDAY NIGHT? SHE THOUGHT I WAS MAKING A MOVE.
NO, IT'S NOT WHAT YOU THINK. I'M PERFORMING TUESDAY EVENING, IN A SMALL THEATRE.
YOU'RE AN ACTOR?
COME TO THINK OF IT, YOU DIDN'T EXACTLY SAY, WHAT KIND OF "THEATRE" IT IS...
SHE'LL SEE FOR HERSELF.
NO. NO! NO COW'S MILK! ONLY SOY MILK...
MILK UPSETS HER ST--
MOTHER...
MOTHER! HER PEDIATRICIAN SAID... FINE, GO AHEAD, YOU'LL SEE!
EVERYTHING OK?
THAT WAS HER 15TH CALL AND SHE DOESN'T EVEN LISTEN WHEN I ANSWER HER QUESTIONS.
AND YOU, HOW DID THE MEETING GO?
DRIIIING
PIECE OF CAKE.
I DON'T BELIEVE IT!
HELLO?
WHAT NOW?!
HEY, WHAT HAPPENED TO YOU?
I'M KOTOP, I GOTTA DO EVERYTHING BACKWARDTH.
FELIX, IT'S FOR YOU.
28

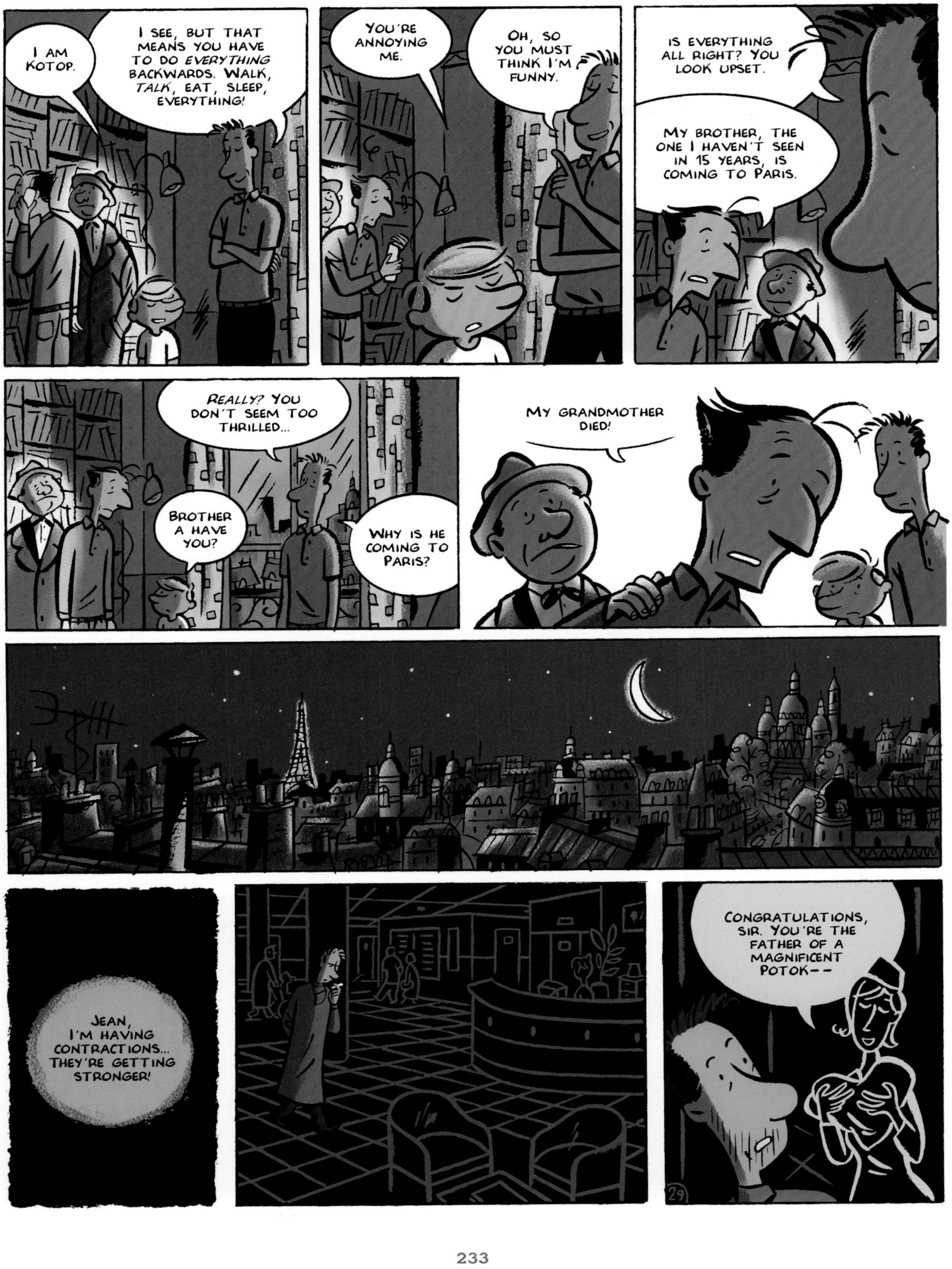
I AM KOTOP.
I SEE, BUT THAT MEANS YOU HAVE TO DO *EVERYTHING* BACKWARDS. WALK, *TALK*, EAT, SLEEP, EVERYTHING!
YOU'RE ANNOYING ME.
OH, SO YOU MUST THINK I'M FUNNY.
IS EVERYTHING ALL RIGHT? YOU LOOK UPSET.
MY BROTHER, THE ONE I HAVEN'T SEEN IN 15 YEARS, IS COMING TO PARIS.
REALLY? YOU DON'T SEEM TOO THRILLED...
BROTHER A HAVE YOU?
WHY IS HE COMING TO PARIS?
MY GRANDMOTHER DIED!
JEAN, I'M HAVING CONTRACTIONS... THEY'RE GETTING STRONGER!
CONGRATULATIONS, SIR. YOU'RE THE FATHER OF A MAGNIFICENT POTOK--
29

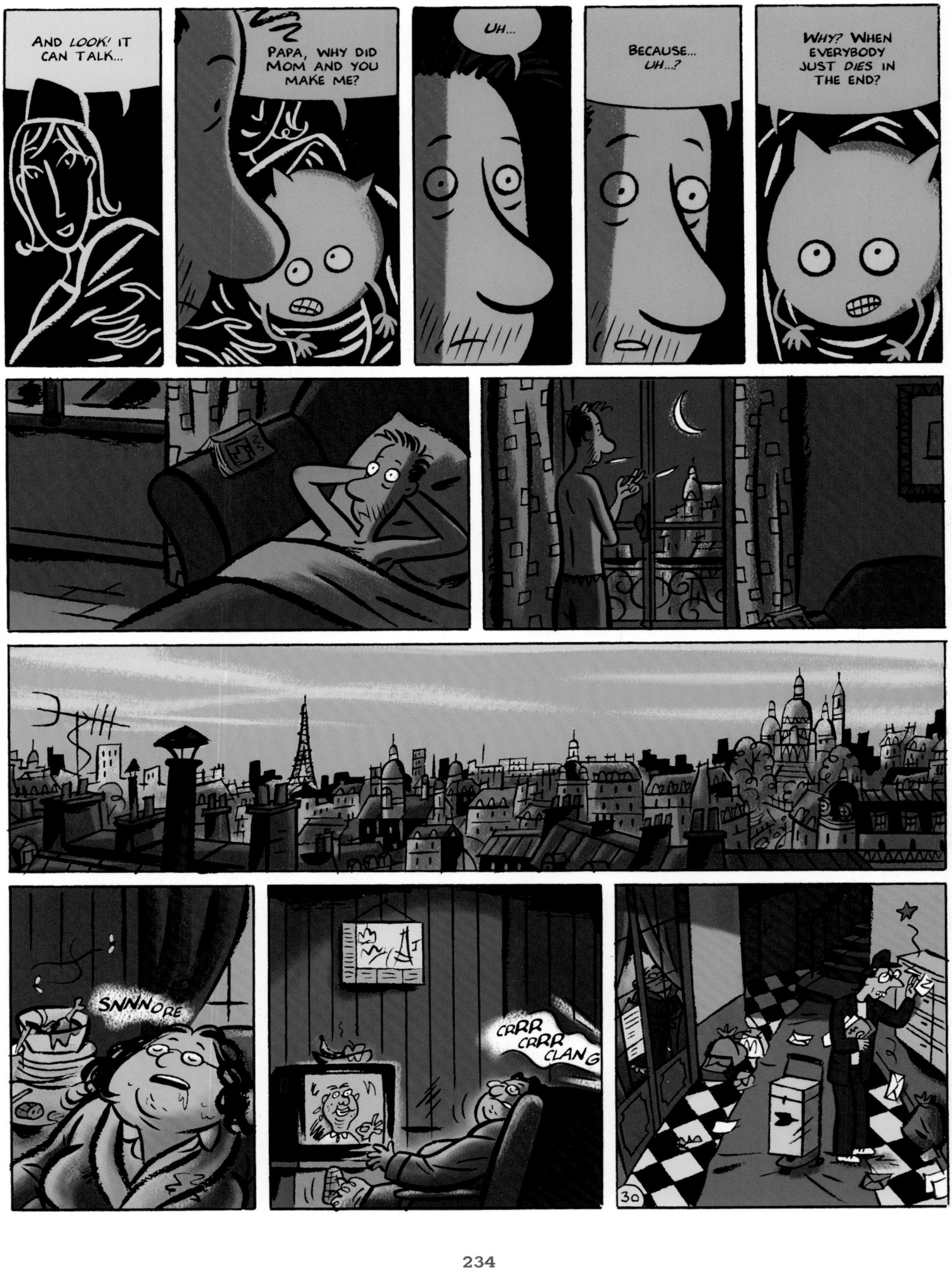

AND LOOK! IT CAN TALK...
PAPA, WHY DID MOM AND YOU MAKE ME?
UH...
BECAUSE... UH...?
WHY? WHEN EVERYBODY JUST DIES IN THE END?
SNNNORE
CRRR CRRR CLANG
30

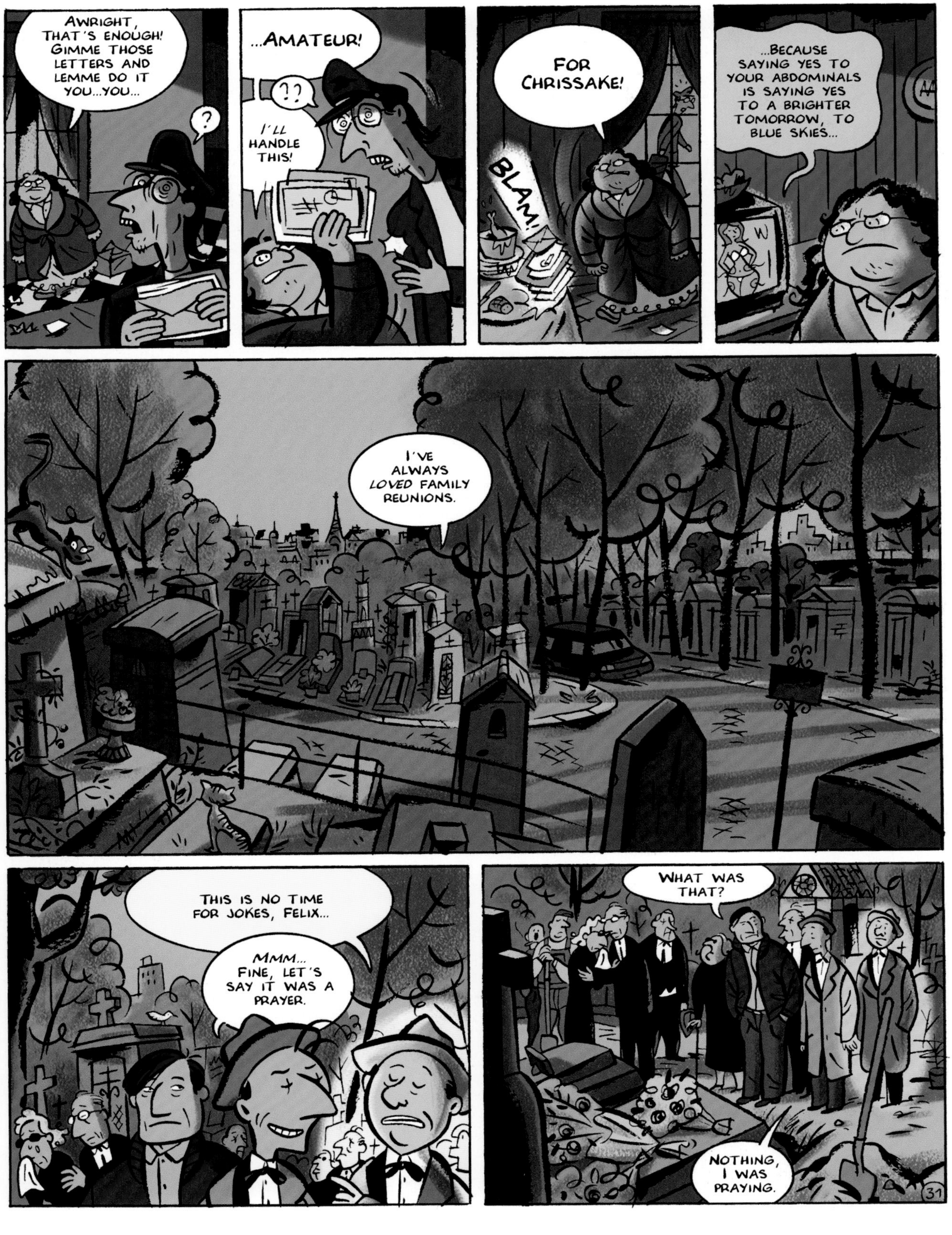
AWRIGHT, THAT'S ENOUGH! GIMME THOSE LETTERS AND LEMME DO IT YOU...YOU...
?
...AMATEUR!
??
I'LL HANDLE THIS!
FOR CHRISSAKE!
BLAM!
...BECAUSE SAYING YES TO YOUR ABDOMINALS IS SAYING YES TO A BRIGHTER TOMORROW, TO BLUE SKIES...
I'VE ALWAYS LOVED FAMILY REUNIONS.
THIS IS NO TIME FOR JOKES, FELIX...
MMM... FINE, LET'S SAY IT WAS A PRAYER.
WHAT WAS THAT?
NOTHING, I WAS PRAYING.
31

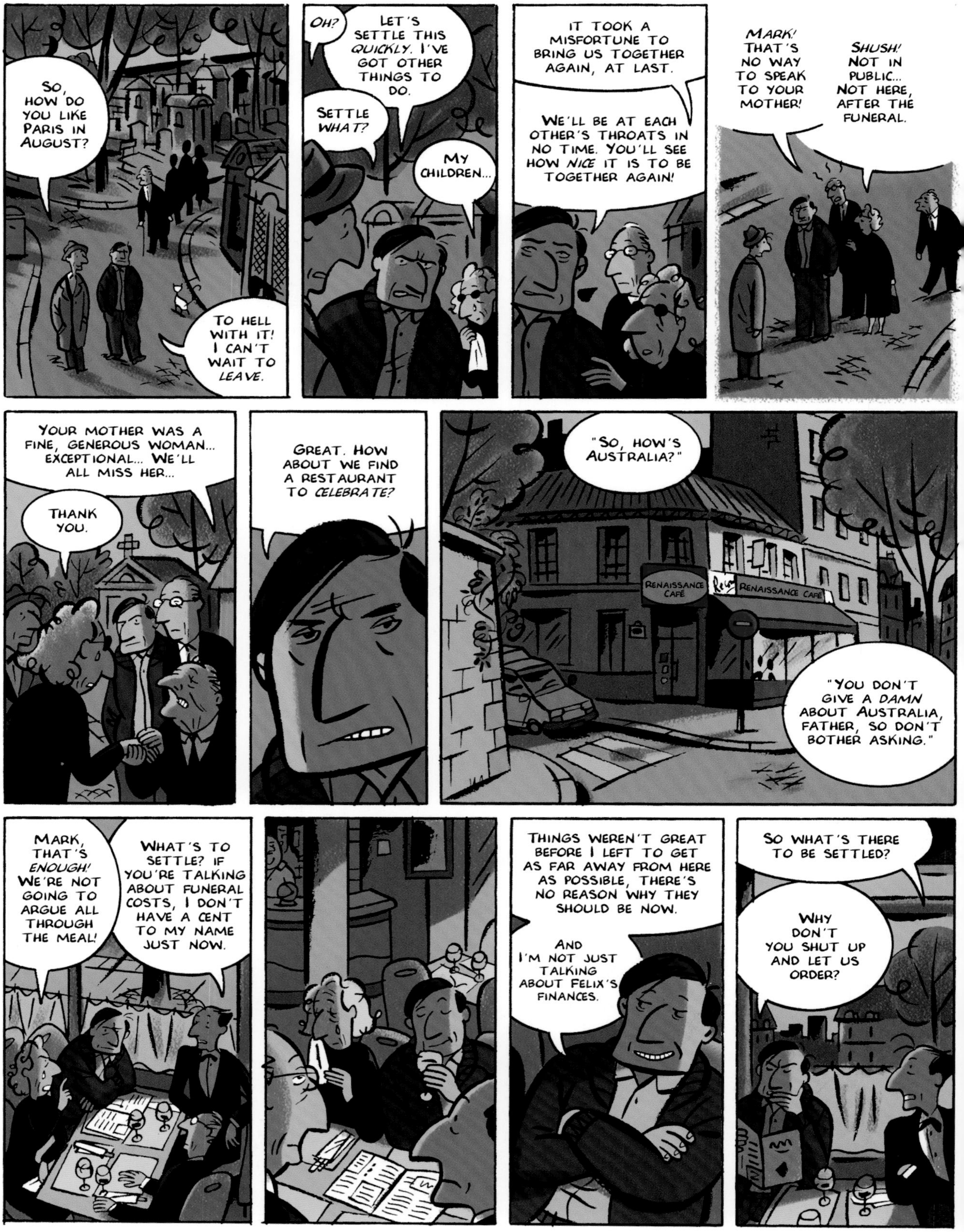

SO, HOW DO YOU LIKE PARIS IN AUGUST?
TO HELL WITH IT! I CAN'T WAIT TO LEAVE.
OH?
LET'S SETTLE THIS QUICKLY. I'VE GOT OTHER THINGS TO DO.
SETTLE WHAT?
MY CHILDREN...
IT TOOK A MISFORTUNE TO BRING US TOGETHER AGAIN, AT LAST.
WE'LL BE AT EACH OTHER'S THROATS IN NO TIME. YOU'LL SEE HOW NICE IT IS TO BE TOGETHER AGAIN!
MARK! THAT'S NO WAY TO SPEAK TO YOUR MOTHER!
SHUSH! NOT IN PUBLIC... NOT HERE, AFTER THE FUNERAL.
YOUR MOTHER WAS A FINE, GENEROUS WOMAN... EXCEPTIONAL... WE'LL ALL MISS HER...
THANK YOU.
GREAT. HOW ABOUT WE FIND A RESTAURANT TO CELEBRATE?
"SO, HOW'S AUSTRALIA?"
RENAISSANCE CAFÉ
RENAISSANCE CAFÉ
"YOU DON'T GIVE A DAMN ABOUT AUSTRALIA, FATHER, SO DON'T BOTHER ASKING."
MARK, THAT'S ENOUGH! WE'RE NOT GOING TO ARGUE ALL THROUGH THE MEAL!
WHAT'S TO SETTLE? IF YOU'RE TALKING ABOUT FUNERAL COSTS, I DON'T HAVE A CENT TO MY NAME JUST NOW.
THINGS WEREN'T GREAT BEFORE I LEFT TO GET AS FAR AWAY FROM HERE AS POSSIBLE, THERE'S NO REASON WHY THEY SHOULD BE NOW.
AND I'M NOT JUST TALKING ABOUT FELIX'S FINANCES.
SO WHAT'S THERE TO BE SETTLED?
WHY DON'T YOU SHUT UP AND LET US ORDER?

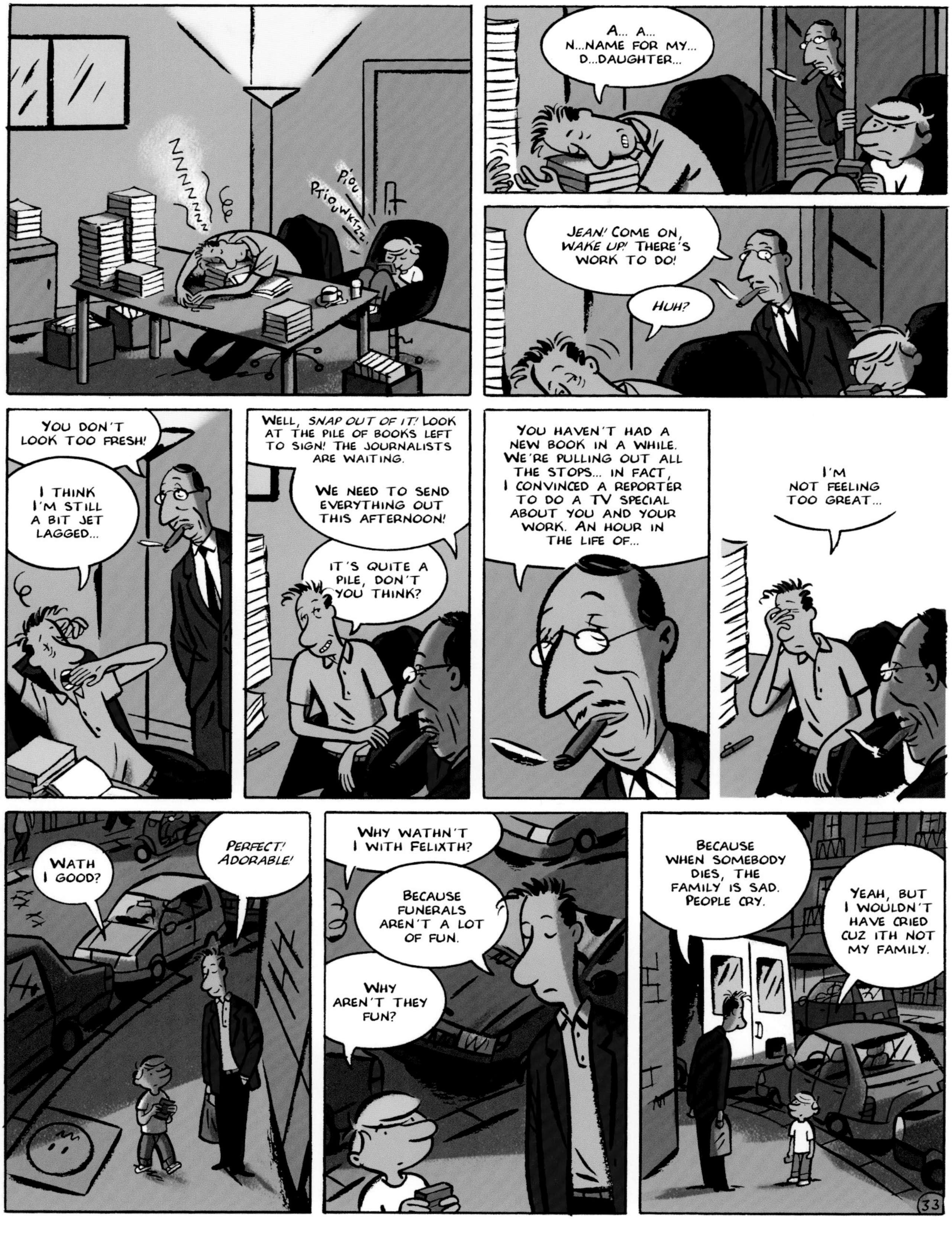
ZZZZZZZ
PTIOUWKTZZ PIOU
A... A... N...NAME FOR MY... D...DAUGHTER...
JEAN! COME ON, WAKE UP! THERE'S WORK TO DO!
HUH?
YOU DON'T LOOK TOO FRESH!
I THINK I'M STILL A BIT JET LAGGED...
WELL, SNAP OUT OF IT! LOOK AT THE PILE OF BOOKS LEFT TO SIGN! THE JOURNALISTS ARE WAITING.
WE NEED TO SEND EVERYTHING OUT THIS AFTERNOON!
IT'S QUITE A PILE, DON'T YOU THINK?
YOU HAVEN'T HAD A NEW BOOK IN A WHILE. WE'RE PULLING OUT ALL THE STOPS... IN FACT, I CONVINCED A REPORTER TO DO A TV SPECIAL ABOUT YOU AND YOUR WORK. AN HOUR IN THE LIFE OF...
I'M NOT FEELING TOO GREAT...
WATH I GOOD?
PERFECT! ADORABLE!
WHY WATHN'T I WITH FELIXTH?
BECAUSE FUNERALS AREN'T A LOT OF FUN.
WHY AREN'T THEY FUN?
BECAUSE WHEN SOMEBODY DIES, THE FAMILY IS SAD. PEOPLE CRY.
YEAH, BUT I WOULDN'T HAVE CRIED CUZ ITH NOT MY FAMILY.
33

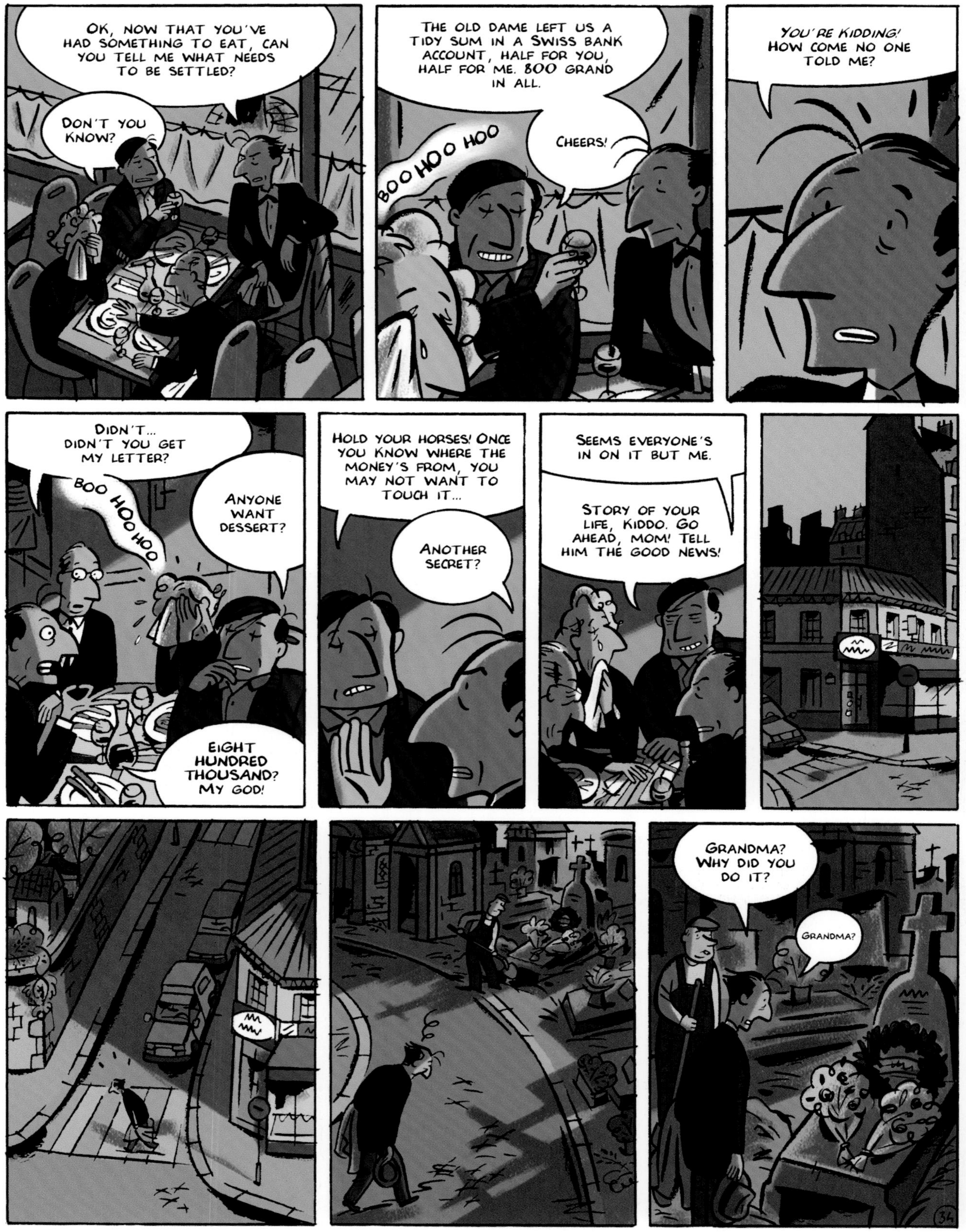
OK, NOW THAT YOU'VE HAD SOMETHING TO EAT, CAN YOU TELL ME WHAT NEEDS TO BE SETTLED?
DON'T YOU KNOW?
THE OLD DAME LEFT US A TIDY SUM IN A SWISS BANK ACCOUNT, HALF FOR YOU, HALF FOR ME. 800 GRAND IN ALL.
BOO HOO HOO
CHEERS!
YOU'RE KIDDING! HOW COME NO ONE TOLD ME?
DIDN'T... DIDN'T YOU GET MY LETTER?
BOO HOO HOO
ANYONE WANT DESSERT?
EIGHT HUNDRED THOUSAND? MY GOD!
HOLD YOUR HORSES! ONCE YOU KNOW WHERE THE MONEY'S FROM, YOU MAY NOT WANT TO TOUCH IT...
ANOTHER SECRET?
SEEMS EVERYONE'S IN ON IT BUT ME.
STORY OF YOUR LIFE, KIDDO. GO AHEAD, MOM! TELL HIM THE GOOD NEWS!
GRANDMA? WHY DID YOU DO IT?
GRANDMA?
34

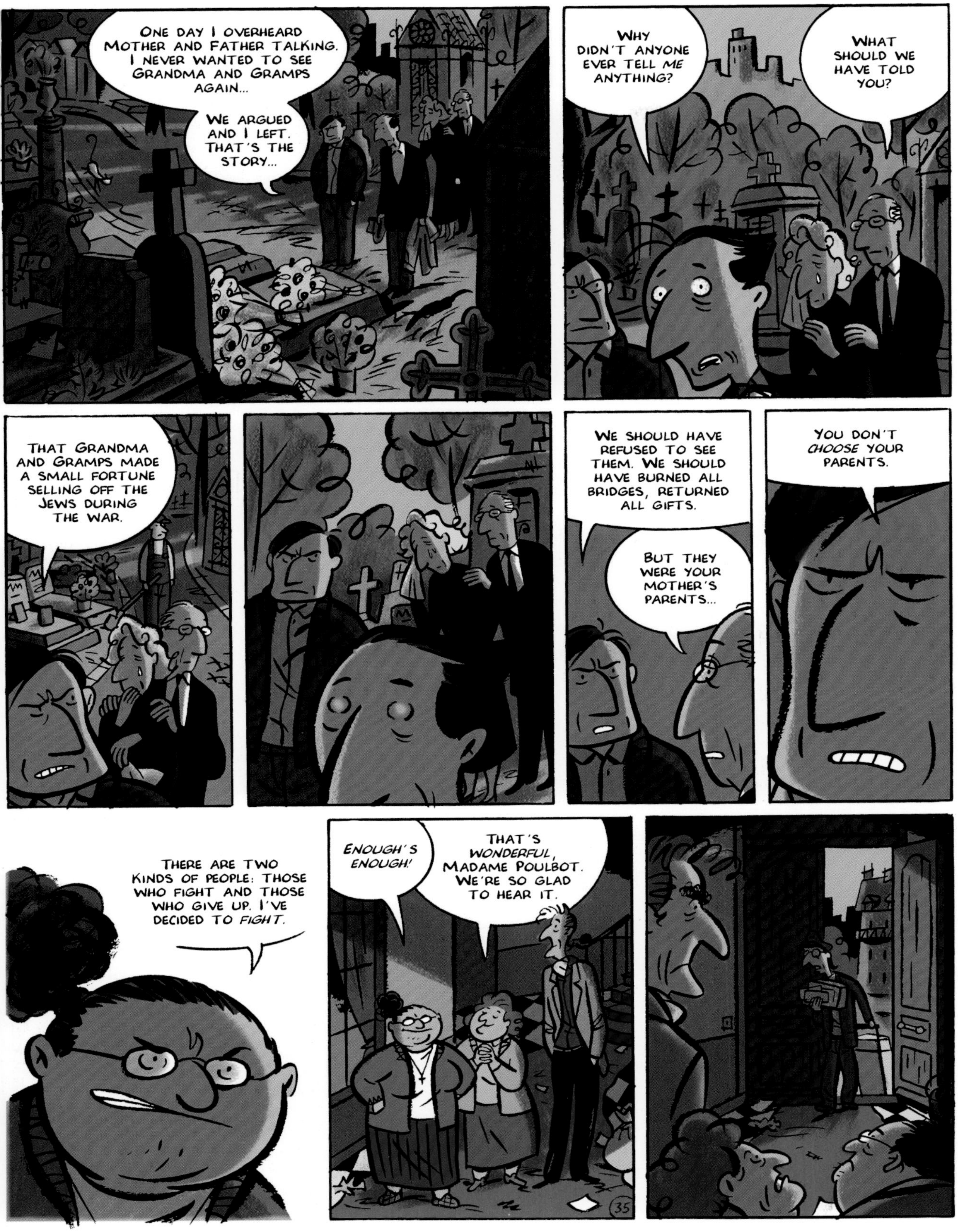

One day I overheard Mother and Father talking. I never wanted to see Grandma and Gramps again...
We argued and I left. That's the story...
Why didn't anyone ever tell *me* anything?
What should we have told you?
That Grandma and Gramps made a small fortune selling off the Jews during the war.
We should have refused to see them. We should have burned all bridges, returned all gifts.
But they were your mother's parents...
You don't *choose* your parents.
There are two kinds of people: those who fight and those who give up. I've decided to *fight*.
Enough's enough!
That's *wonderful*, Madame Poulbot. We're so glad to hear it.
35

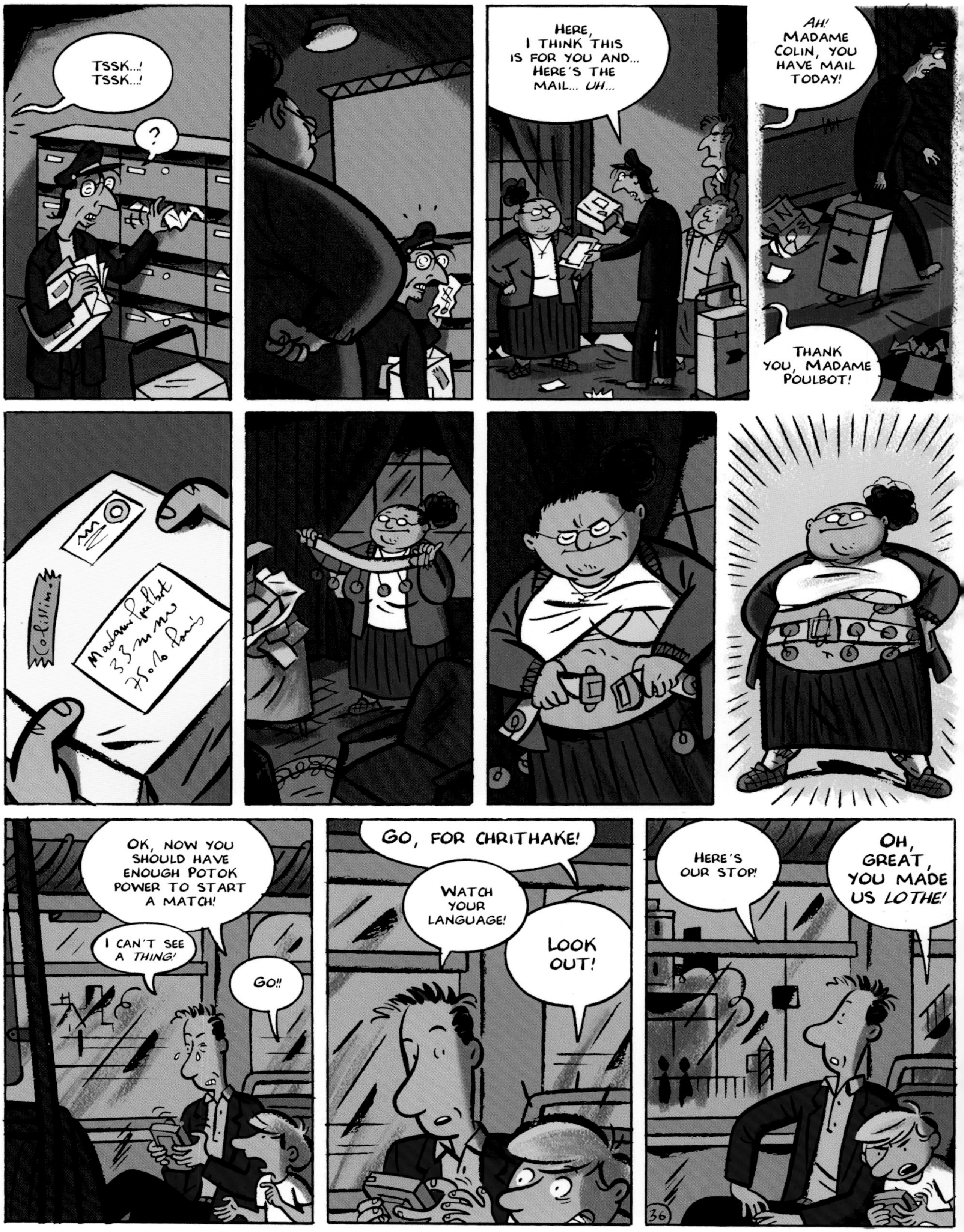
TSSK...! TSSK...!
?
HERE, I THINK THIS IS FOR YOU AND... HERE'S THE MAIL... UH...
AH! MADAME COLIN, YOU HAVE MAIL TODAY!
THANK YOU, MADAME POULBOT!
COLISSIMO
OK, NOW YOU SHOULD HAVE ENOUGH POTOK POWER TO START A MATCH!
I CAN'T SEE A THING!
GO!!
GO, FOR CHRITHAKE!
WATCH YOUR LANGUAGE!
LOOK OUT!
HERE'S OUR STOP!
OH, GREAT, YOU MADE US LOTHE!
36

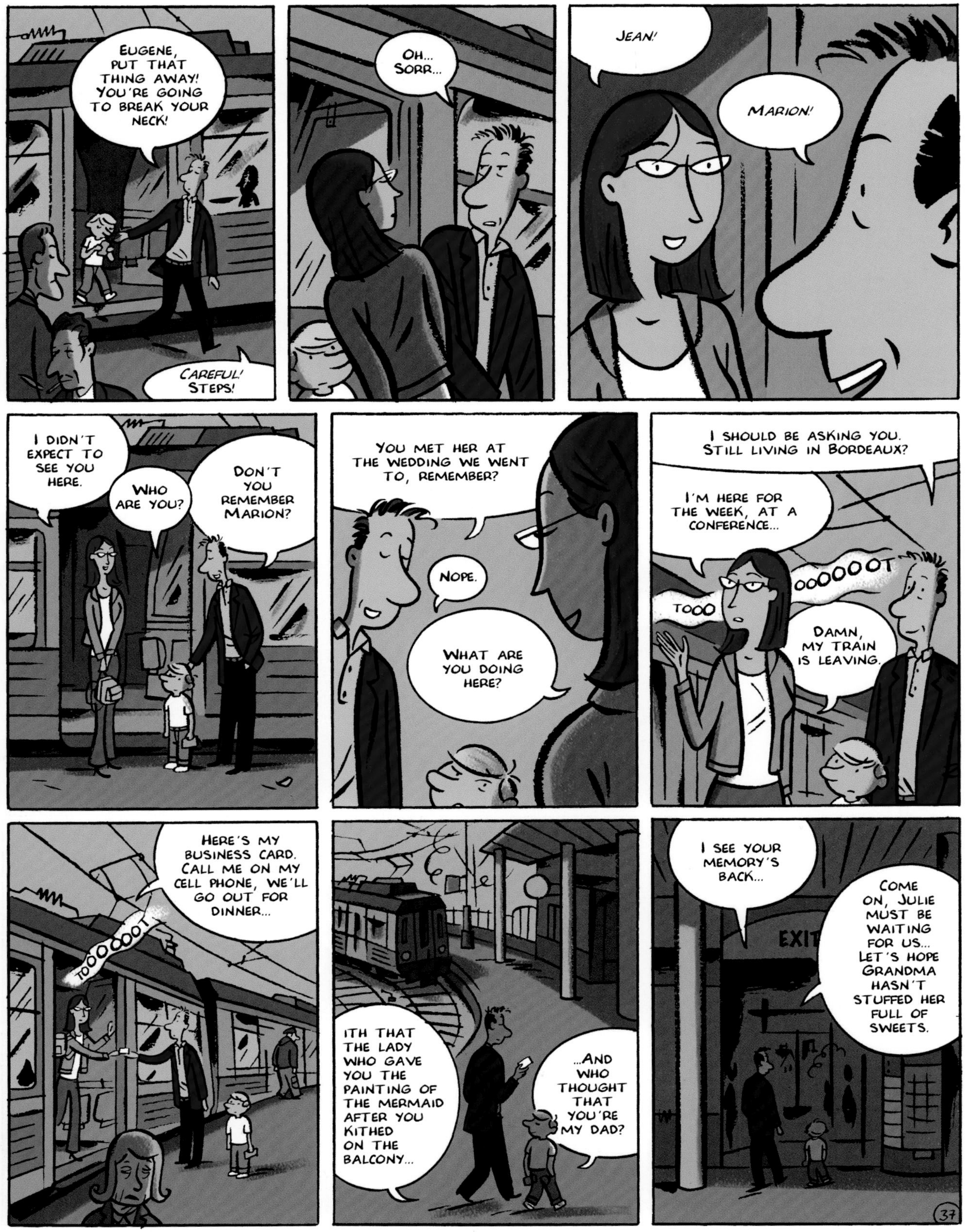
EUGENE, PUT THAT THING AWAY! YOU'RE GOING TO BREAK YOUR NECK!
CAREFUL! STEPS!
OH... SORR...
JEAN!
MARION!
I DIDN'T EXPECT TO SEE YOU HERE.
WHO ARE YOU?
DON'T YOU REMEMBER MARION?
YOU MET HER AT THE WEDDING WE WENT TO, REMEMBER?
NOPE.
WHAT ARE YOU DOING HERE?
I SHOULD BE ASKING YOU. STILL LIVING IN BORDEAUX?
I'M HERE FOR THE WEEK, AT A CONFERENCE...
TOOO
OOOOOOT
DAMN, MY TRAIN IS LEAVING.
HERE'S MY BUSINESS CARD. CALL ME ON MY CELL PHONE, WE'LL GO OUT FOR DINNER...
TOOOOOT
ITH THAT THE LADY WHO GAVE YOU THE PAINTING OF THE MERMAID AFTER YOU KITHED ON THE BALCONY...
...AND WHO THOUGHT THAT YOU'RE MY DAD?
I SEE YOUR MEMORY'S BACK...
COME ON, JULIE MUST BE WAITING FOR US... LET'S HOPE GRANDMA HASN'T STUFFED HER FULL OF SWEETS.
EXIT
37

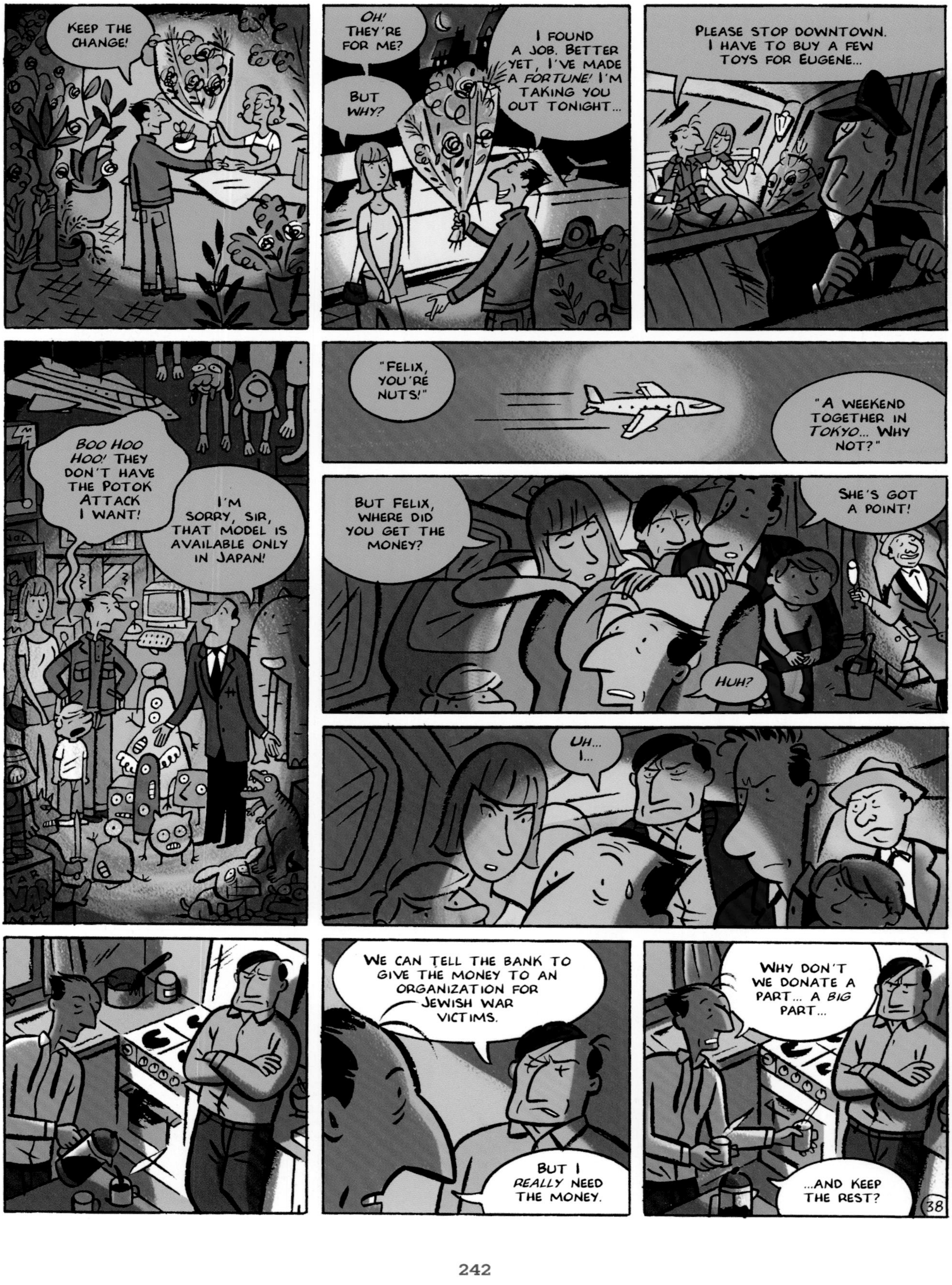
KEEP THE CHANGE!
OH! THEY'RE FOR ME?
BUT WHY?
I FOUND A JOB. BETTER YET, I'VE MADE A FORTUNE! I'M TAKING YOU OUT TONIGHT...
PLEASE STOP DOWNTOWN. I HAVE TO BUY A FEW TOYS FOR EUGENE...
BOO HOO HOO! THEY DON'T HAVE THE POTOK ATTACK I WANT!
I'M SORRY, SIR, THAT MODEL IS AVAILABLE ONLY IN JAPAN!
"FELIX, YOU'RE NUTS!"
"A WEEKEND TOGETHER IN TOKYO... WHY NOT?"
BUT FELIX, WHERE DID YOU GET THE MONEY?
SHE'S GOT A POINT!
HUH?
UH... I...
WE CAN TELL THE BANK TO GIVE THE MONEY TO AN ORGANIZATION FOR JEWISH WAR VICTIMS.
BUT I REALLY NEED THE MONEY.
WHY DON'T WE DONATE A PART... A BIG PART...
...AND KEEP THE REST?
38

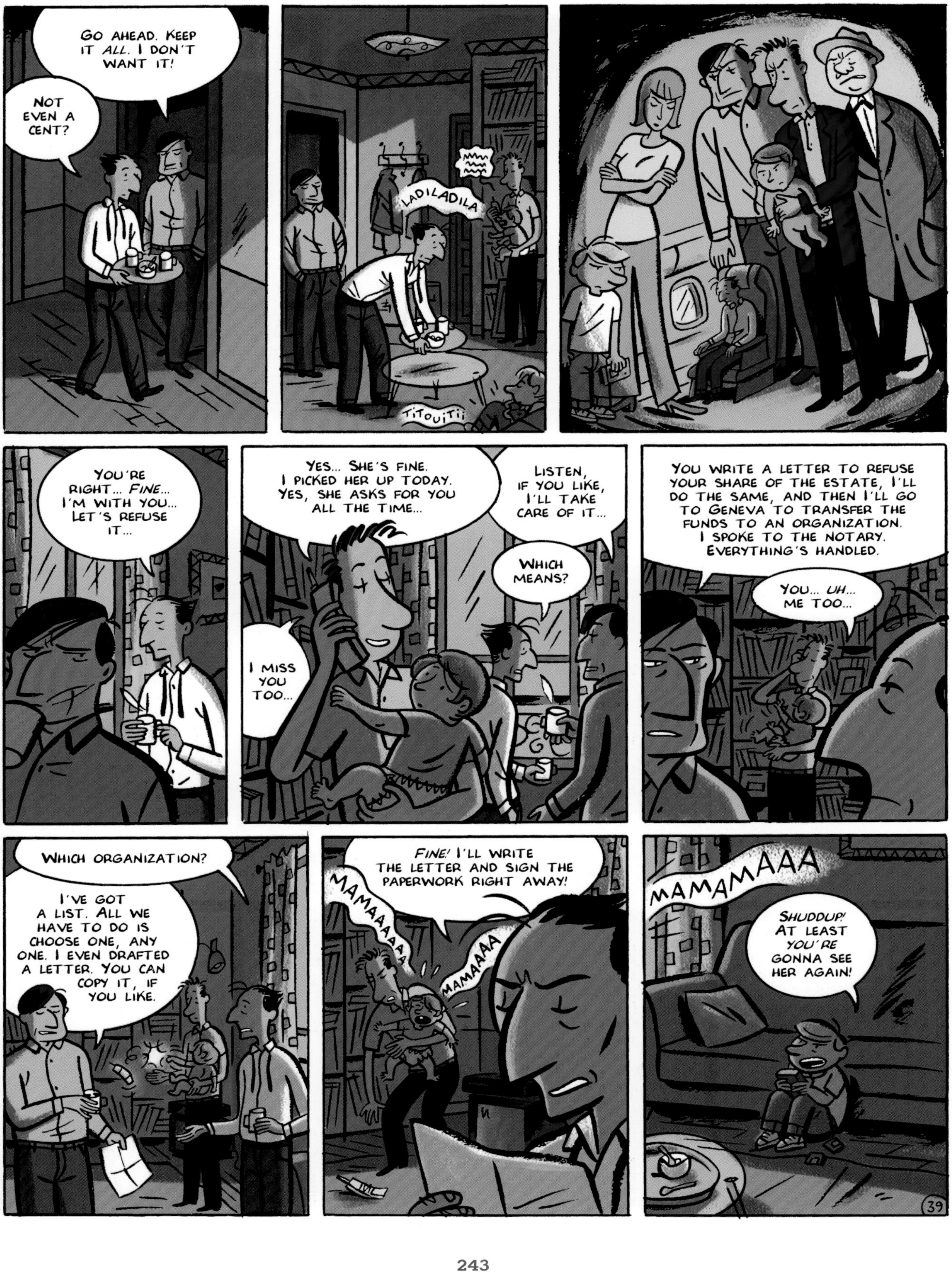
GO AHEAD. KEEP IT ALL. I DON'T WANT IT!
NOT EVEN A CENT?
LADILADILA
TITOUITI
YOU'RE RIGHT... FINE... I'M WITH YOU... LET'S REFUSE IT...
YES... SHE'S FINE. I PICKED HER UP TODAY. YES, SHE ASKS FOR YOU ALL THE TIME...
I MISS YOU TOO...
LISTEN, IF YOU LIKE, I'LL TAKE CARE OF IT...
WHICH MEANS?
YOU WRITE A LETTER TO REFUSE YOUR SHARE OF THE ESTATE, I'LL DO THE SAME, AND THEN I'LL GO TO GENEVA TO TRANSFER THE FUNDS TO AN ORGANIZATION. I SPOKE TO THE NOTARY. EVERYTHING'S HANDLED.
YOU... UH... ME TOO...
WHICH ORGANIZATION?
I'VE GOT A LIST. ALL WE HAVE TO DO IS CHOOSE ONE, ANY ONE. I EVEN DRAFTED A LETTER. YOU CAN COPY IT, IF YOU LIKE.
FINE! I'LL WRITE THE LETTER AND SIGN THE PAPERWORK RIGHT AWAY!
MAMAAAAAAA
MAMAAAA
MAMAMAAA
SHUDDUP! AT LEAST YOU'RE GONNA SEE HER AGAIN!
39

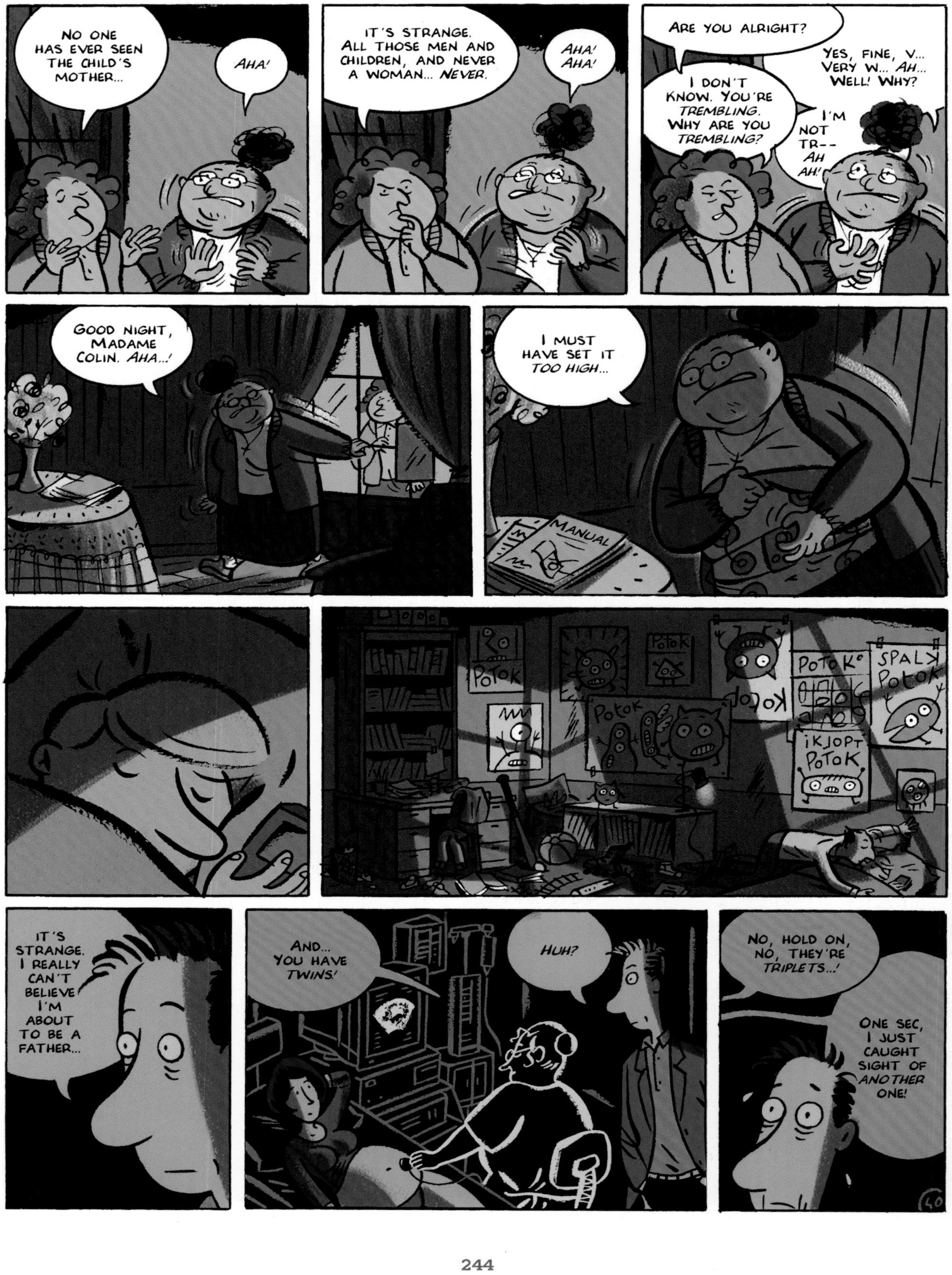
NO ONE HAS EVER SEEN THE CHILD'S MOTHER...
AHA!
IT'S STRANGE. ALL THOSE MEN AND CHILDREN, AND NEVER A WOMAN... NEVER.
AHA! AHA!
ARE YOU ALRIGHT?
YES, FINE, V... VERY W... AH... WELL! WHY?
I DON'T KNOW. YOU'RE TREMBLING. WHY ARE YOU TREMBLING?
I'M NOT TR-- AH AH!
GOOD NIGHT, MADAME COLIN. AHA...!
I MUST HAVE SET IT TOO HIGH...
MANUAL
POTOK
POTOK
POTOK
POTOK
POTOK
SPALK
POTOK
IKJOPT POTOK
IT'S STRANGE. I REALLY CAN'T BELIEVE I'M ABOUT TO BE A FATHER...
AND... YOU HAVE TWINS!
HUH?
NO, HOLD ON, NO, THEY'RE TRIPLETS...!
ONE SEC, I JUST CAUGHT SIGHT OF ANOTHER ONE!
40

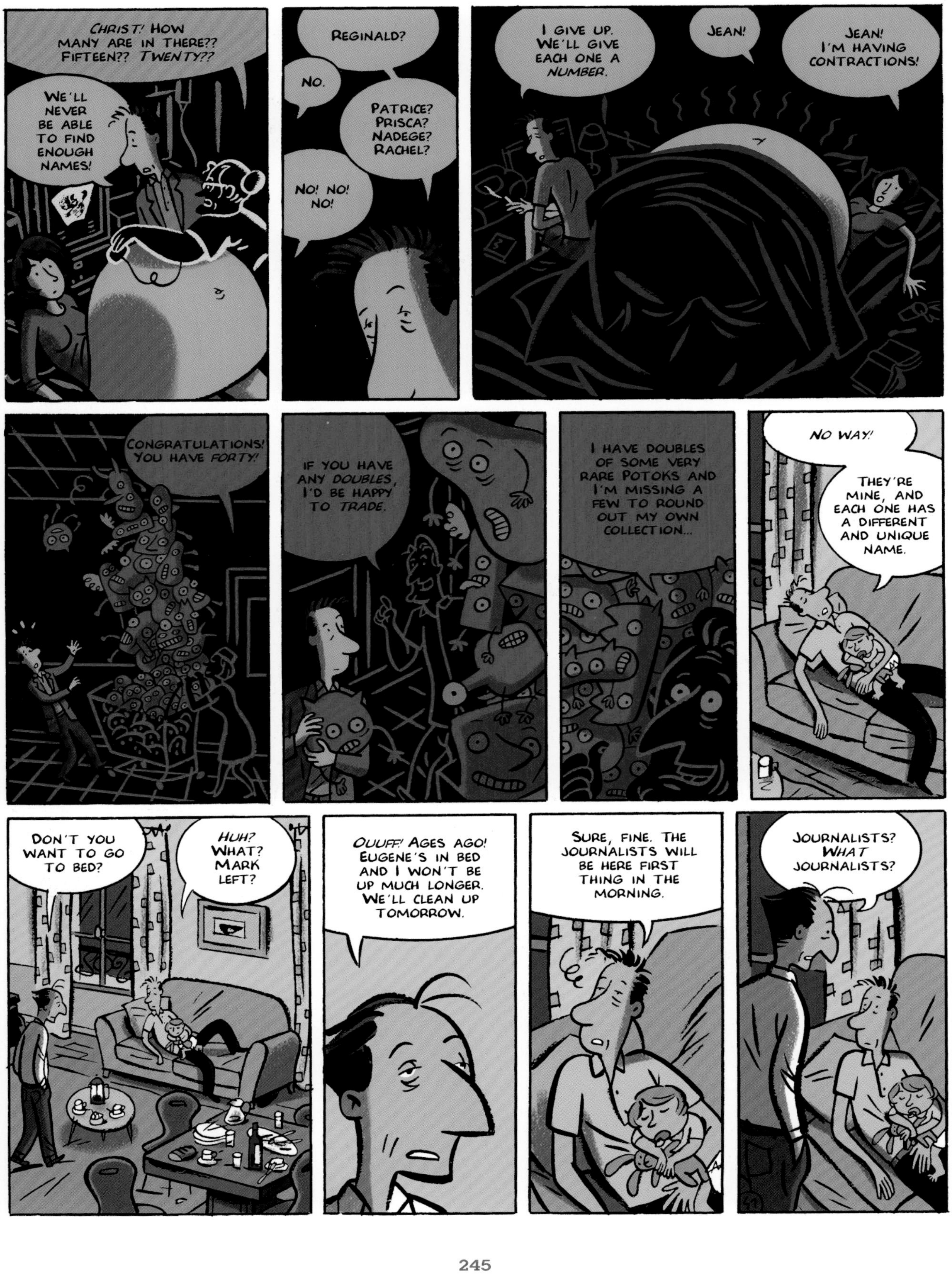
CHRIST! HOW MANY ARE IN THERE?? FIFTEEN?? TWENTY??
WE'LL NEVER BE ABLE TO FIND ENOUGH NAMES!
REGINALD?
NO.
PATRICE? PRISCA? NADEGE? RACHEL?
NO! NO! NO!
I GIVE UP. WE'LL GIVE EACH ONE A NUMBER.
JEAN!
JEAN! I'M HAVING CONTRACTIONS!
CONGRATULATIONS! YOU HAVE FORTY!
IF YOU HAVE ANY DOUBLES, I'D BE HAPPY TO TRADE.
I HAVE DOUBLES OF SOME VERY RARE POTOKS AND I'M MISSING A FEW TO ROUND OUT MY OWN COLLECTION...
NO WAY!
THEY'RE MINE, AND EACH ONE HAS A DIFFERENT AND UNIQUE NAME.
DON'T YOU WANT TO GO TO BED?
HUH? WHAT? MARK LEFT?
OUUFF! AGES AGO! EUGENE'S IN BED AND I WON'T BE UP MUCH LONGER. WE'LL CLEAN UP TOMORROW.
SURE, FINE. THE JOURNALISTS WILL BE HERE FIRST THING IN THE MORNING.
JOURNALISTS? WHAT JOURNALISTS?

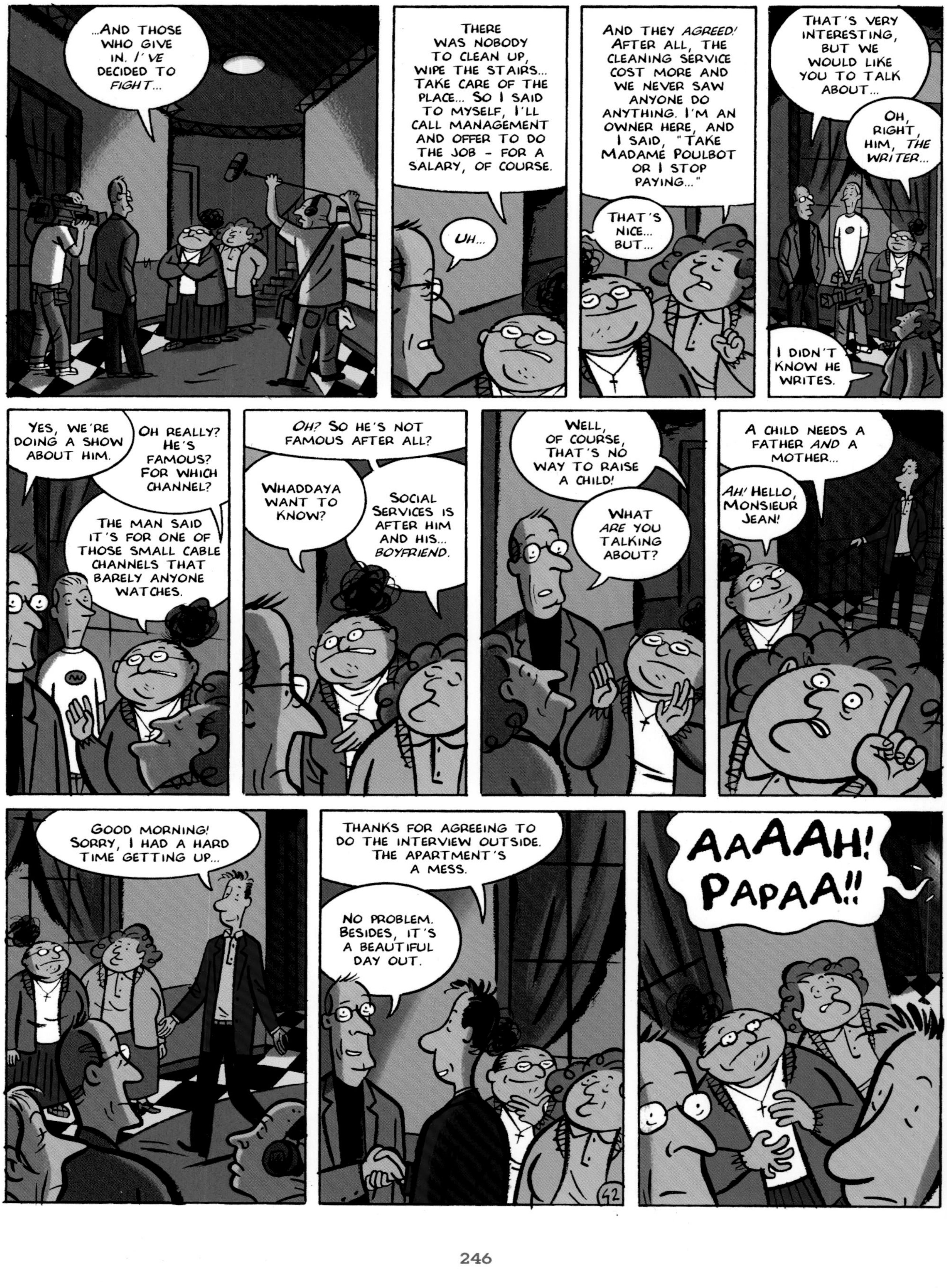
...AND THOSE WHO GIVE IN. I'VE DECIDED TO FIGHT...
THERE WAS NOBODY TO CLEAN UP, WIPE THE STAIRS... TAKE CARE OF THE PLACE... SO I SAID TO MYSELF, I'LL CALL MANAGEMENT AND OFFER TO DO THE JOB - FOR A SALARY, OF COURSE.
UH...
AND THEY AGREED! AFTER ALL, THE CLEANING SERVICE COST MORE AND WE NEVER SAW ANYONE DO ANYTHING. I'M AN OWNER HERE, AND I SAID, "TAKE MADAME POULBOT OR I STOP PAYING..."
THAT'S NICE... BUT...
THAT'S VERY INTERESTING, BUT WE WOULD LIKE YOU TO TALK ABOUT...
OH, RIGHT, HIM, THE WRITER...
I DIDN'T KNOW HE WRITES.
YES, WE'RE DOING A SHOW ABOUT HIM.
OH REALLY? HE'S FAMOUS? FOR WHICH CHANNEL?
THE MAN SAID IT'S FOR ONE OF THOSE SMALL CABLE CHANNELS THAT BARELY ANYONE WATCHES.
OH? SO HE'S NOT FAMOUS AFTER ALL?
WHADDAYA WANT TO KNOW?
SOCIAL SERVICES IS AFTER HIM AND HIS... BOYFRIEND.
WELL, OF COURSE, THAT'S NO WAY TO RAISE A CHILD!
WHAT ARE YOU TALKING ABOUT?
A CHILD NEEDS A FATHER AND A MOTHER...
AH! HELLO, MONSIEUR JEAN!
GOOD MORNING! SORRY, I HAD A HARD TIME GETTING UP...
THANKS FOR AGREEING TO DO THE INTERVIEW OUTSIDE. THE APARTMENT'S A MESS.
NO PROBLEM. BESIDES, IT'S A BEAUTIFUL DAY OUT.
42
AAAAH! PAPAA!!

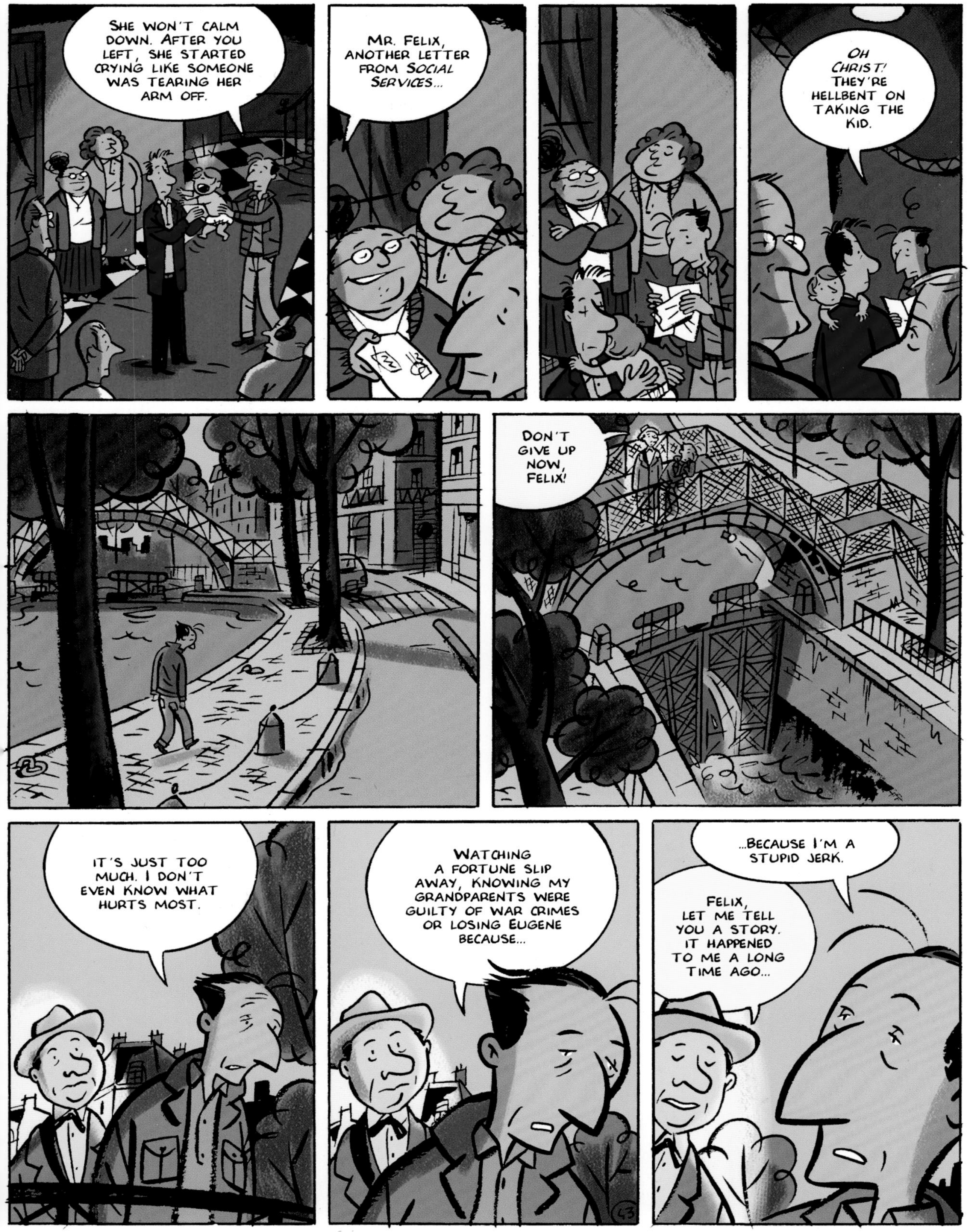
SHE WON'T CALM DOWN. AFTER YOU LEFT, SHE STARTED CRYING LIKE SOMEONE WAS TEARING HER ARM OFF.
MR. FELIX, ANOTHER LETTER FROM SOCIAL SERVICES...
OH CHRIST! THEY'RE HELLBENT ON TAKING THE KID.
DON'T GIVE UP NOW, FELIX!
IT'S JUST TOO MUCH. I DON'T EVEN KNOW WHAT HURTS MOST.
WATCHING A FORTUNE SLIP AWAY, KNOWING MY GRANDPARENTS WERE GUILTY OF WAR CRIMES OR LOSING EUGENE BECAUSE...
...BECAUSE I'M A STUPID JERK.
FELIX, LET ME TELL YOU A STORY. IT HAPPENED TO ME A LONG TIME AGO...
43

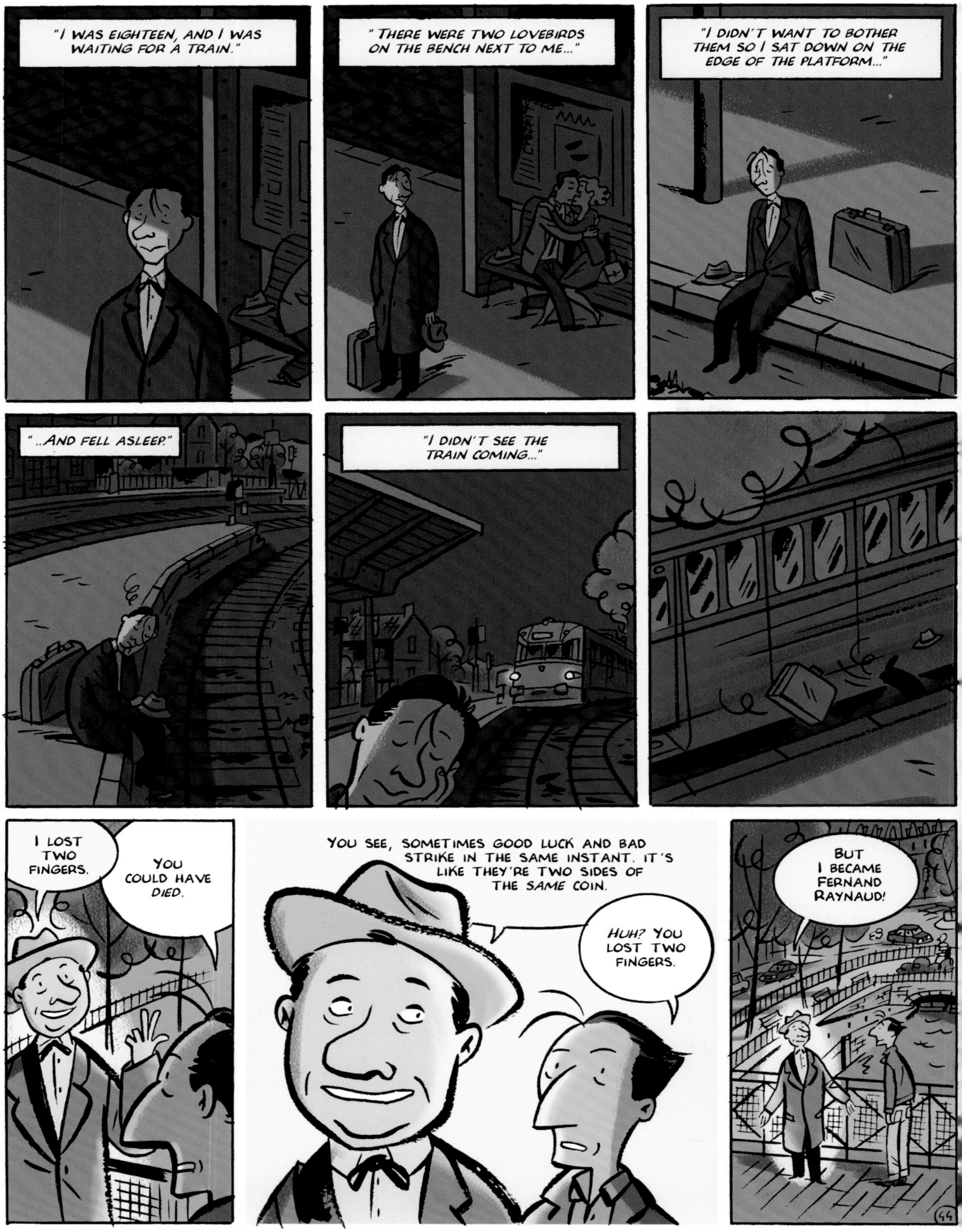
"I WAS EIGHTEEN, AND I WAS WAITING FOR A TRAIN."
"THERE WERE TWO LOVEBIRDS ON THE BENCH NEXT TO ME..."
"I DIDN'T WANT TO BOTHER THEM SO I SAT DOWN ON THE EDGE OF THE PLATFORM..."
"...AND FELL ASLEEP."
"I DIDN'T SEE THE TRAIN COMING..."
I LOST TWO FINGERS.
YOU COULD HAVE DIED.
YOU SEE, SOMETIMES GOOD LUCK AND BAD STRIKE IN THE SAME INSTANT. IT'S LIKE THEY'RE TWO SIDES OF THE SAME COIN.
HUH? YOU LOST TWO FINGERS.
BUT I BECAME FERNAND RAYNAUD!

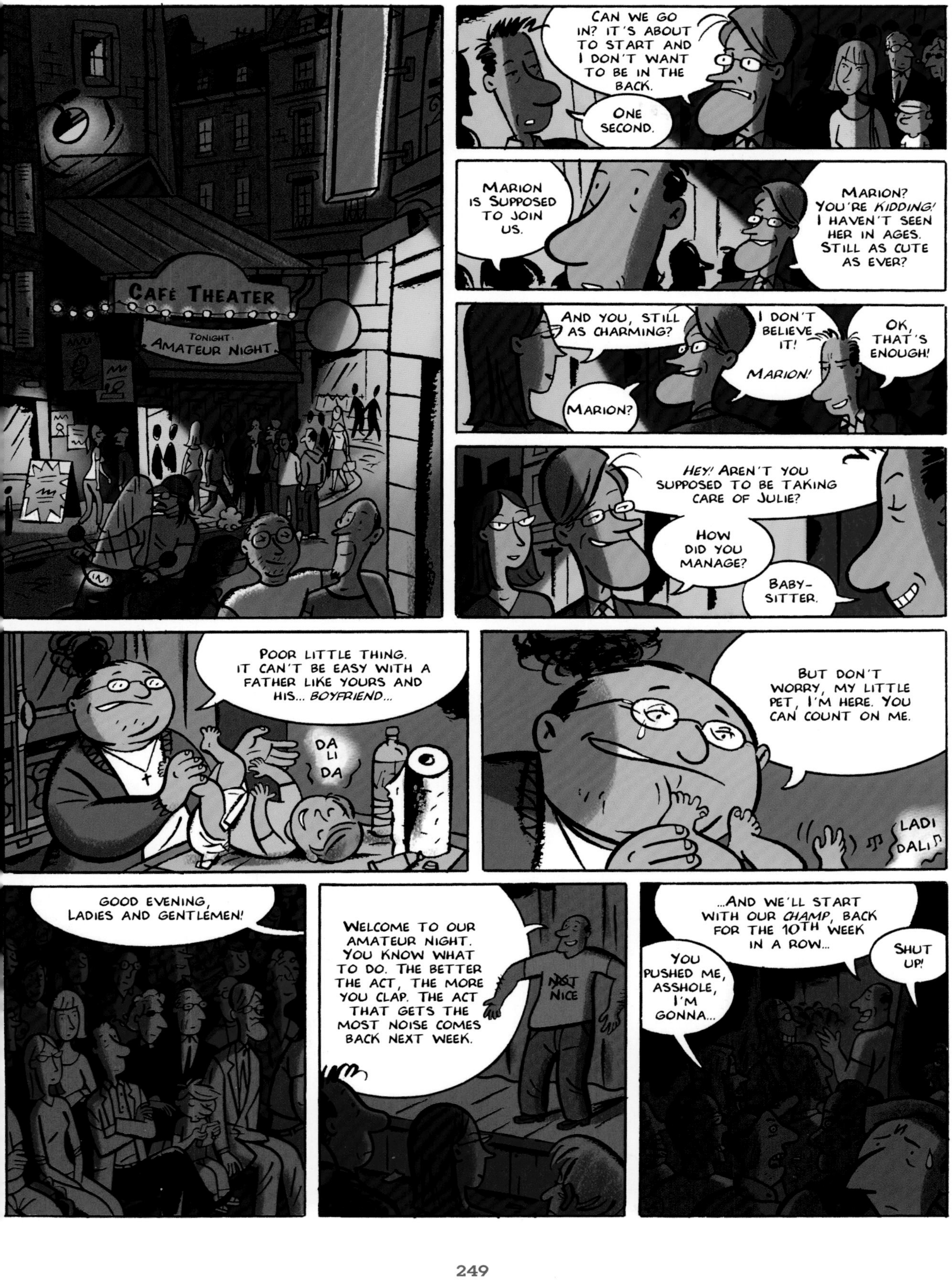
CAFÉ THEATER
TONIGHT: AMATEUR NIGHT
CAN WE GO IN? IT'S ABOUT TO START AND I DON'T WANT TO BE IN THE BACK.
ONE SECOND.
MARION IS SUPPOSED TO JOIN US.
MARION? YOU'RE KIDDING! I HAVEN'T SEEN HER IN AGES. STILL AS CUTE AS EVER?
AND YOU, STILL AS CHARMING?
MARION?
I DON'T BELIEVE IT!
MARION!
OK, THAT'S ENOUGH!
HEY! AREN'T YOU SUPPOSED TO BE TAKING CARE OF JULIE?
HOW DID YOU MANAGE?
BABY-SITTER.
POOR LITTLE THING. IT CAN'T BE EASY WITH A FATHER LIKE YOURS AND HIS... BOYFRIEND...
DA LI DA
BUT DON'T WORRY, MY LITTLE PET, I'M HERE. YOU CAN COUNT ON ME.
LADI DALI
GOOD EVENING, LADIES AND GENTLEMEN!
WELCOME TO OUR AMATEUR NIGHT. YOU KNOW WHAT TO DO. THE BETTER THE ACT, THE MORE YOU CLAP. THE ACT THAT GETS THE MOST NOISE COMES BACK NEXT WEEK.
NOT NICE
...AND WE'LL START WITH OUR CHAMP, BACK FOR THE 10TH WEEK IN A ROW...
YOU PUSHED ME, ASSHOLE, I'M GONNA...
SHUT UP!

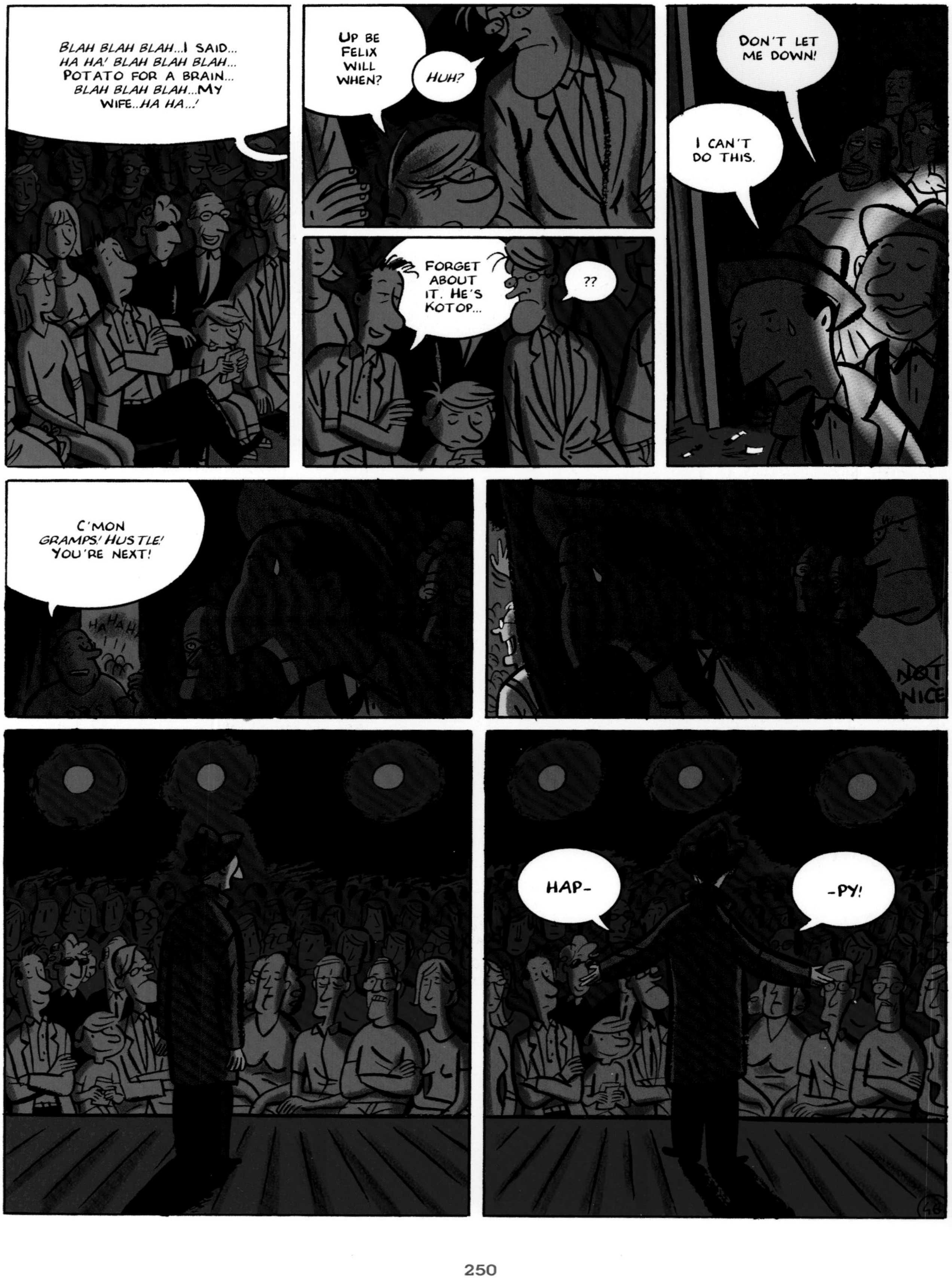
BLAH BLAH BLAH...I SAID... HA HA! BLAH BLAH BLAH... POTATO FOR A BRAIN... BLAH BLAH BLAH...MY WIFE...HA HA...!
UP BE FELIX WILL WHEN?
HUH?
DON'T LET ME DOWN!
I CAN'T DO THIS.
FORGET ABOUT IT. HE'S KOTOP...
??
C'MON GRAMPS! HUSTLE! YOU'RE NEXT!
NOT NICE
HAP-
-PY!

Oh, come on, you're not going to sulk all night!

You got thrown out, but it's not really your fault... Fernand Raynaud is a bit *passé*, that's all!

And if it cheers you up, I've got a plan... Jean told me about your run-in with those *assholes* at Social Services. Don't worry.

Drop by the agency and we'll say I'm "giving you a try." We put you on the payroll and *presto!* Problem solved... Thanks to Clement!

By the way, who's your girlfriend...?

Yes... People were *booing*. It almost turned into a *riot* when Felix started insulting the crowd...

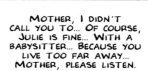

Mother, I didn't call you to... Of course, Julie is fine... With a babysitter... Because you live too far away... Mother, please listen.

...There's a show tonight. Can you tape it for me? ...Yes...it's an interview called "Photomaton" on Channel 5... Cable... in 10 minutes... *Great...!* Yes, me too...

Why isn't Mark here?

Three *Sabodets a la Lyonnaise!*

Mark? Mark left already!

He went to Geneva to claim the money and have it put in his account, since you turned down your share of the estate...

WHAT?!

47

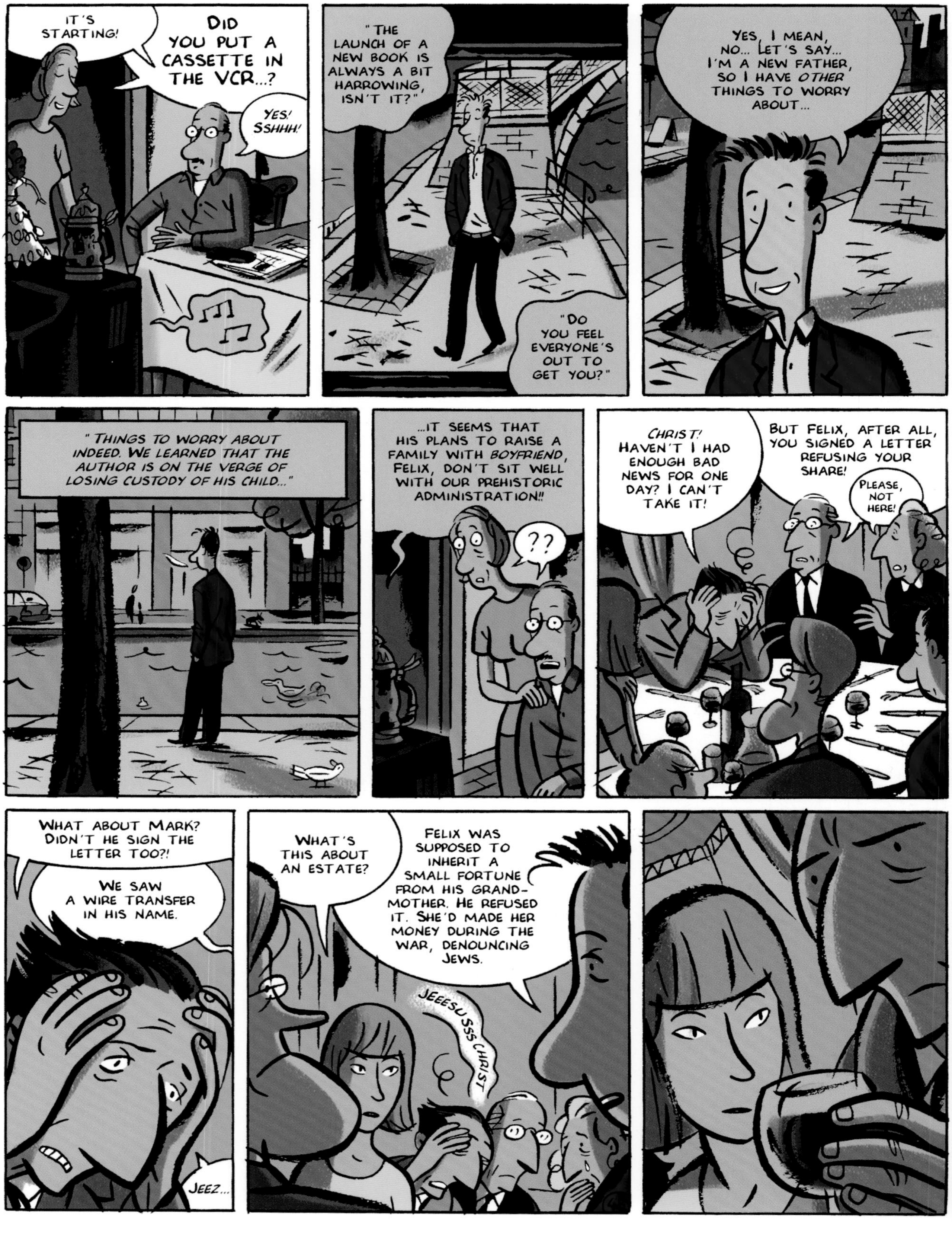
IT'S STARTING!
DID YOU PUT A CASSETTE IN THE VCR...?
YES! SSHHH!
"THE LAUNCH OF A NEW BOOK IS ALWAYS A BIT HARROWING, ISN'T IT?"
"DO YOU FEEL EVERYONE'S OUT TO GET YOU?"
YES, I MEAN, NO... LET'S SAY... I'M A NEW FATHER, SO I HAVE OTHER THINGS TO WORRY ABOUT...
"THINGS TO WORRY ABOUT INDEED. WE LEARNED THAT THE AUTHOR IS ON THE VERGE OF LOSING CUSTODY OF HIS CHILD..."
...IT SEEMS THAT HIS PLANS TO RAISE A FAMILY WITH BOYFRIEND, FELIX, DON'T SIT WELL WITH OUR PREHISTORIC ADMINISTRATION!!
??
CHRIST! HAVEN'T I HAD ENOUGH BAD NEWS FOR ONE DAY? I CAN'T TAKE IT!
BUT FELIX, AFTER ALL, YOU SIGNED A LETTER REFUSING YOUR SHARE!
PLEASE, NOT HERE!
WHAT ABOUT MARK? DIDN'T HE SIGN THE LETTER TOO?!
WE SAW A WIRE TRANSFER IN HIS NAME.
JEEZ...
WHAT'S THIS ABOUT AN ESTATE?
FELIX WAS SUPPOSED TO INHERIT A SMALL FORTUNE FROM HIS GRAND-MOTHER. HE REFUSED IT. SHE'D MADE HER MONEY DURING THE WAR, DENOUNCING JEWS.
JEEESUSSS CHRIST

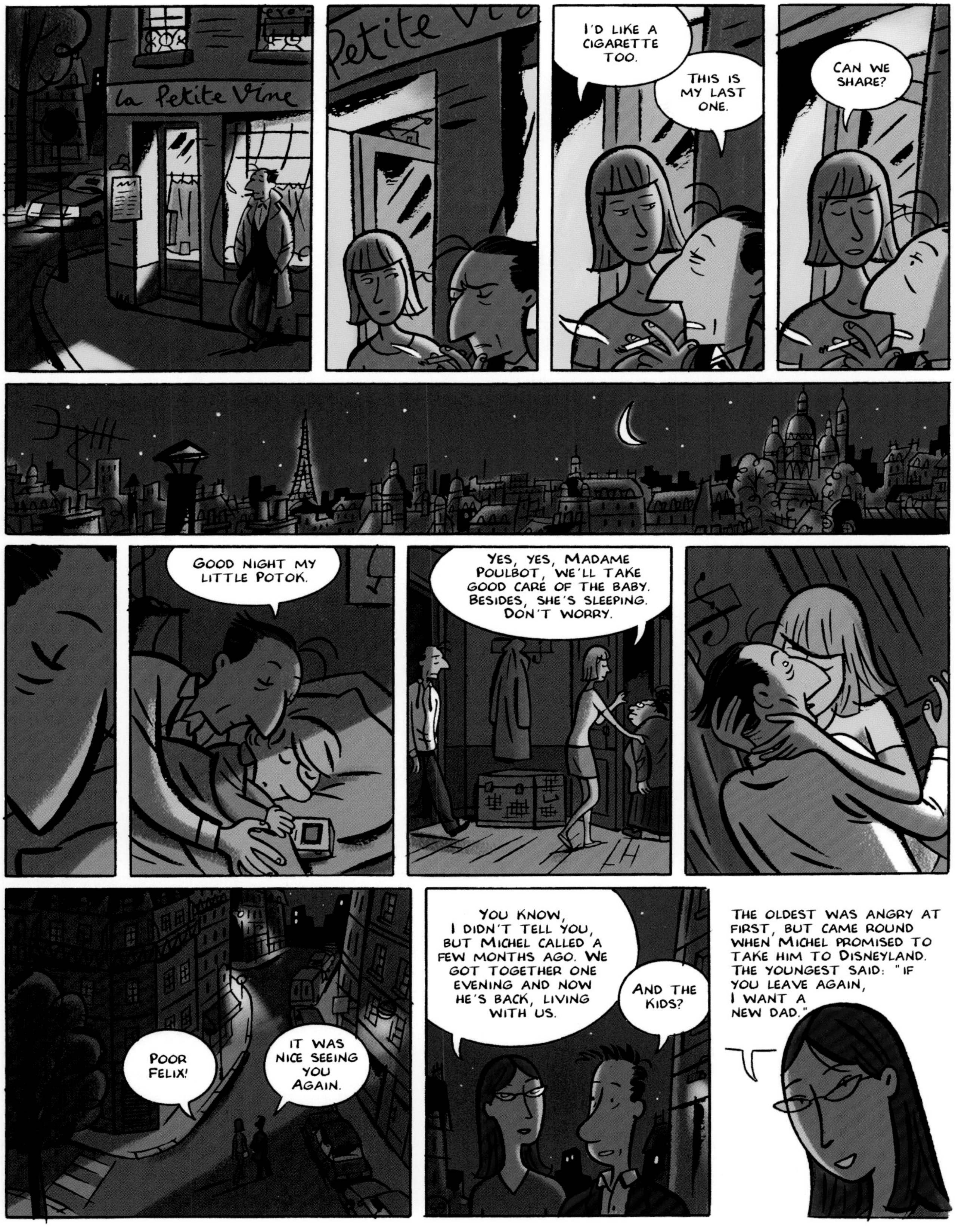
La Petite Vine
I'D LIKE A CIGARETTE TOO.
THIS IS MY LAST ONE.
CAN WE SHARE?
GOOD NIGHT MY LITTLE POTOK.
YES, YES, MADAME POULBOT, WE'LL TAKE GOOD CARE OF THE BABY. BESIDES, SHE'S SLEEPING. DON'T WORRY.
POOR FELIX!
IT WAS NICE SEEING YOU AGAIN.
YOU KNOW, I DIDN'T TELL YOU, BUT MICHEL CALLED A FEW MONTHS AGO. WE GOT TOGETHER ONE EVENING AND NOW HE'S BACK, LIVING WITH US.
AND THE KIDS?
THE OLDEST WAS ANGRY AT FIRST, BUT CAME ROUND WHEN MICHEL PROMISED TO TAKE HIM TO DISNEYLAND. THE YOUNGEST SAID: "IF YOU LEAVE AGAIN, I WANT A NEW DAD."

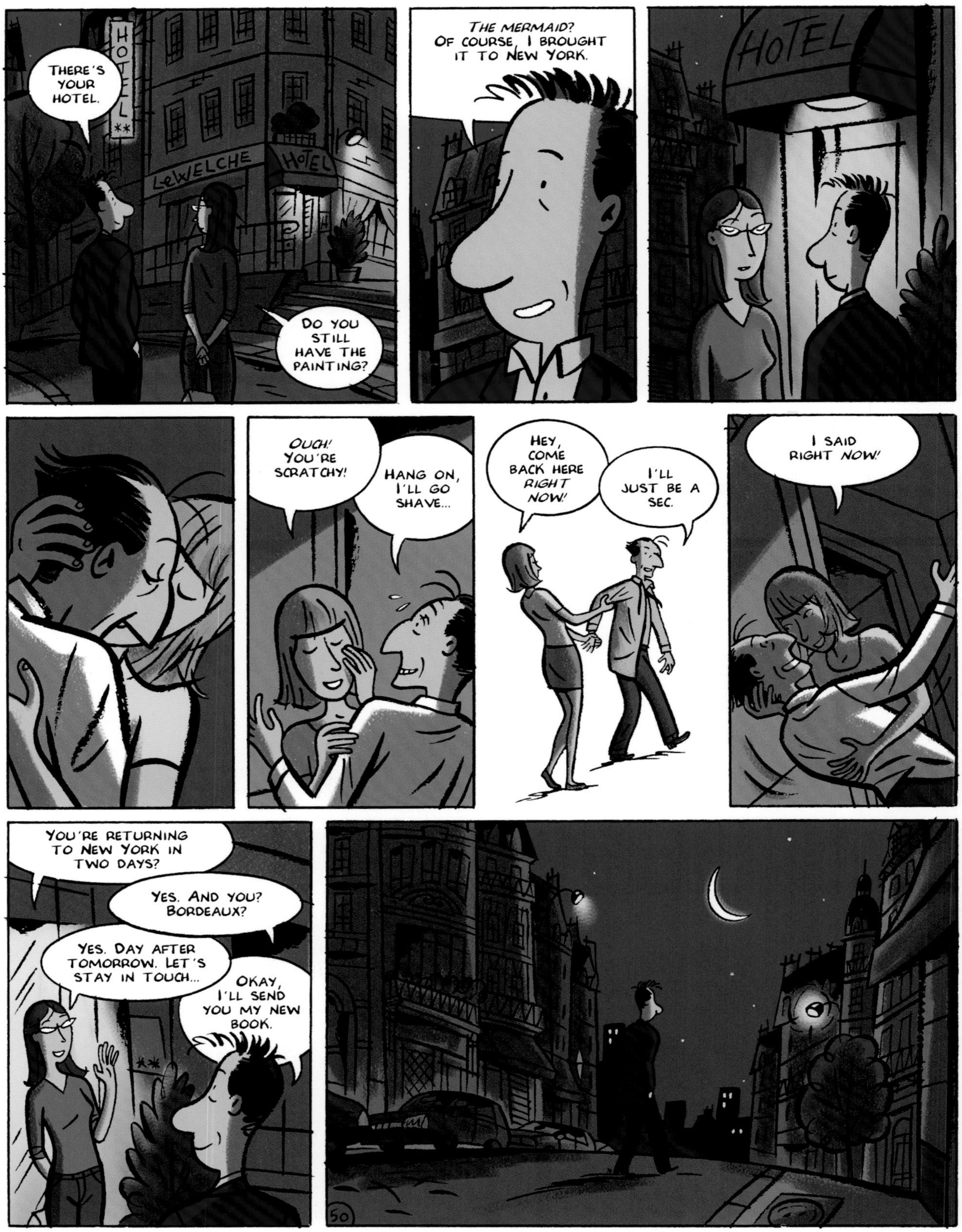
There's your hotel.
Do you still have the painting?
The mermaid? Of course, I brought it to New York.
Ouch! You're scratchy!
Hang on, I'll go shave...
Hey, come back here right now!
I'll just be a sec.
I said right now!
You're returning to New York in two days?
Yes. And you? Bordeaux?
Yes. Day after tomorrow. Let's stay in touch...
Okay, I'll send you my new book.
50

DRIIING DRIING DR

?

HELLO? OH, IT'S YOU...

YES, JUST A SEC...

WAAAAHHH

CAN YOU TAKE HER FOR A MOMENT?

NO PROBLEM.

WAAHH

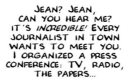

JEAN? JEAN, CAN YOU HEAR ME? IT'S *INCREDIBLE!* EVERY JOURNALIST IN TOWN WANTS TO MEET YOU. I ORGANIZED A PRESS CONFERENCE: TV, RADIO, THE PAPERS...

HELLO? JEAN?

DAMN, IT'S EVEN WORSE NOW! GIVE HER BACK TO ME!

WHO ARE YOU?

WAAAHH

WHAT'S GOING ON? THE NERVE OF WAKING PEOPLE UP SO EARLY!

CLICK

57

HUH?

TOOOOT TOOOOT TOOOOT

BUT IT'S *NOON!*

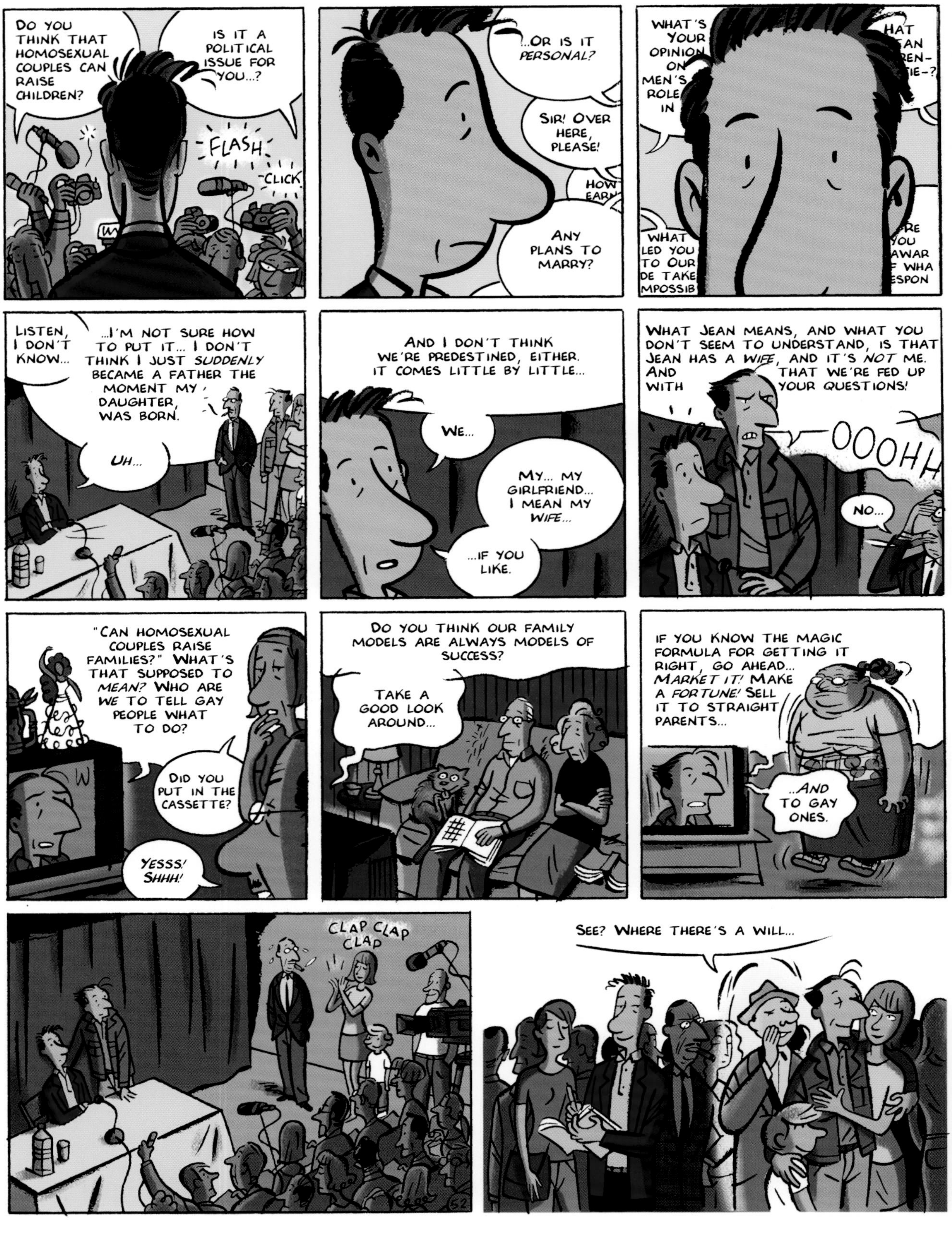
DO YOU THINK THAT HOMOSEXUAL COUPLES CAN RAISE CHILDREN?
IS IT A POLITICAL ISSUE FOR YOU...?
FLASH
CLICK
...OR IS IT *PERSONAL?*
SIR! OVER HERE, PLEASE!
HOW EARN
ANY PLANS TO MARRY?
WHAT'S YOUR OPINION ON MEN'S ROLE IN
HAT CAN REN- TIE-?
WHAT LED YOU TO OUR DE TAKE MPOSSIB
RE YOU AWAR F WHA ESPON
LISTEN, I DON'T KNOW...
...I'M NOT SURE HOW TO PUT IT... I DON'T THINK I JUST *SUDDENLY* BECAME A FATHER THE MOMENT MY DAUGHTER WAS BORN.
UH...
AND I DON'T THINK WE'RE PREDESTINED, EITHER. IT COMES LITTLE BY LITTLE...
WE...
MY... MY GIRLFRIEND... I MEAN MY *WIFE*...
...IF YOU LIKE.
WHAT JEAN MEANS, AND WHAT YOU DON'T SEEM TO UNDERSTAND, IS THAT JEAN HAS A *WIFE*, AND IT'S *NOT* ME. AND THAT WE'RE FED UP WITH YOUR QUESTIONS!
OOOHH
NO...
"CAN HOMOSEXUAL COUPLES RAISE FAMILIES?" WHAT'S THAT SUPPOSED TO *MEAN?* WHO ARE WE TO TELL GAY PEOPLE WHAT TO DO?
DID YOU PUT IN THE CASSETTE?
YESSS! SHHH!
DO YOU THINK OUR FAMILY MODELS ARE ALWAYS MODELS OF SUCCESS?
TAKE A GOOD LOOK AROUND...
IF YOU KNOW THE MAGIC FORMULA FOR GETTING IT RIGHT, GO AHEAD... *MARKET IT!* MAKE A *FORTUNE!* SELL IT TO STRAIGHT PARENTS...
...AND TO GAY ONES.
CLAP CLAP CLAP
SEE? WHERE THERE'S A WILL...

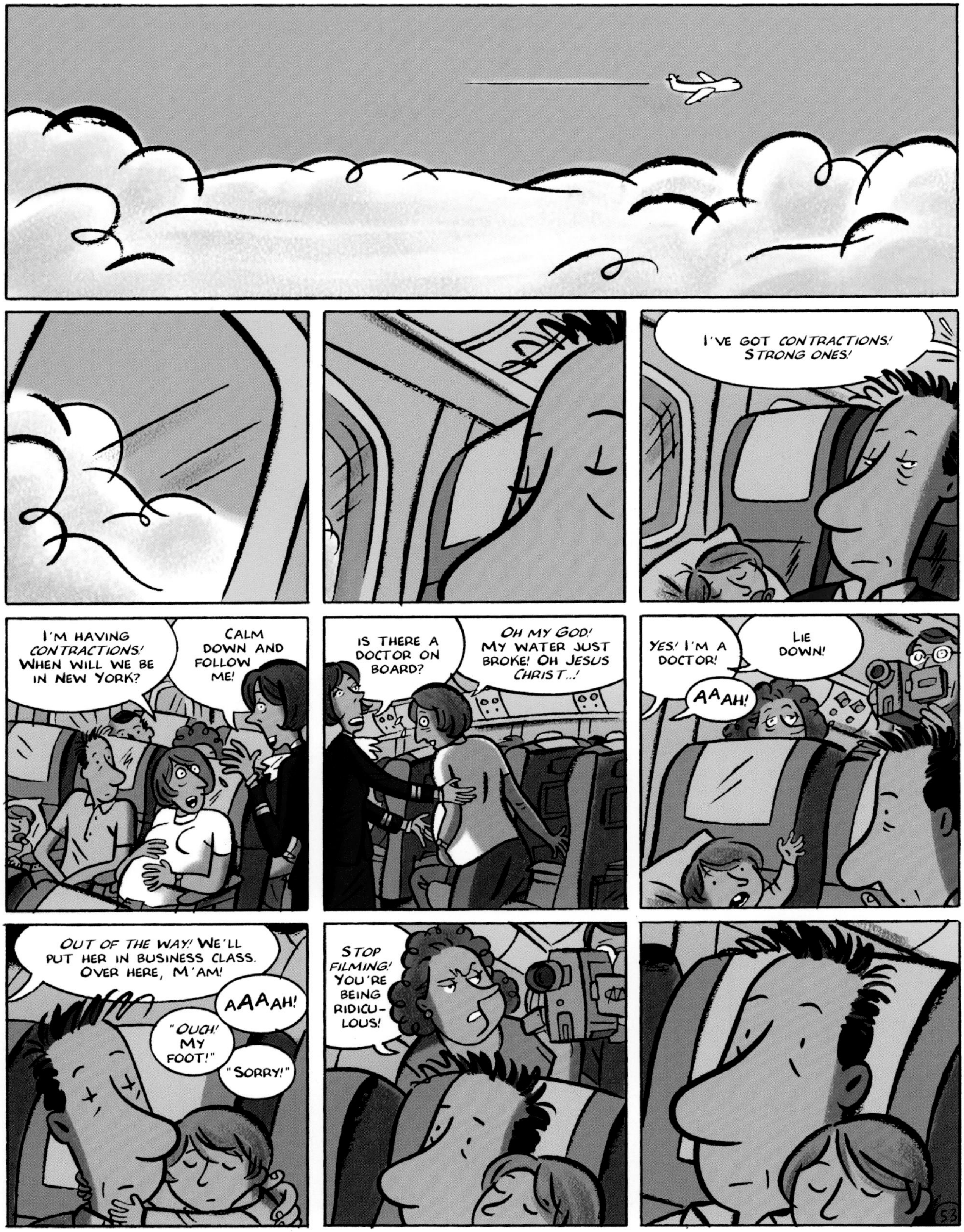
I'VE GOT CONTRACTIONS! STRONG ONES!
I'M HAVING CONTRACTIONS! WHEN WILL WE BE IN NEW YORK?
CALM DOWN AND FOLLOW ME!
IS THERE A DOCTOR ON BOARD?
OH MY GOD! MY WATER JUST BROKE! OH JESUS CHRIST...!
YES! I'M A DOCTOR!
LIE DOWN!
AAAH!
OUT OF THE WAY! WE'LL PUT HER IN BUSINESS CLASS. OVER HERE, M'AM!
AAAAH!
"OUCH! MY FOOT!"
"SORRY!"
STOP FILMING! YOU'RE BEING RIDICU-LOUS!
53

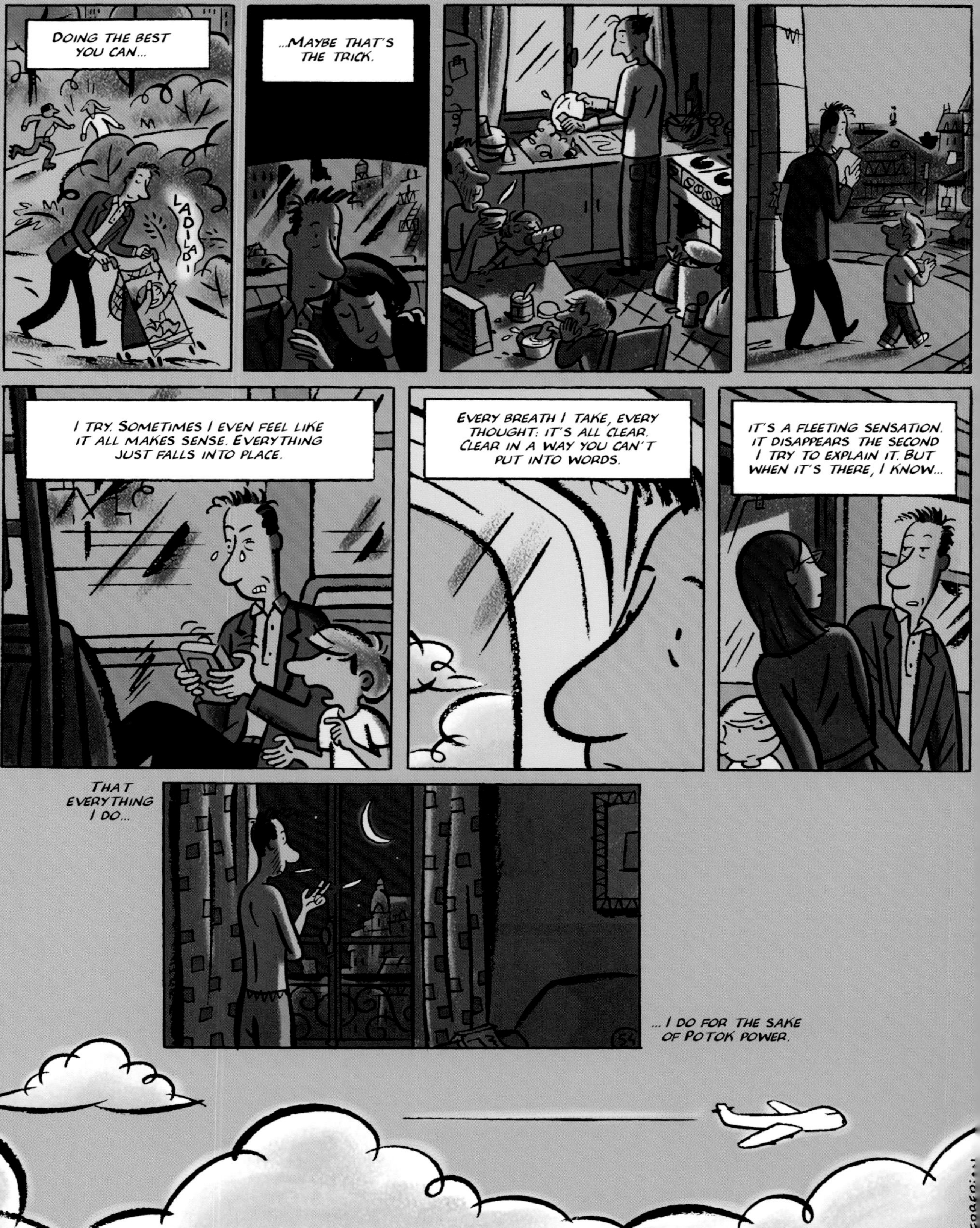
DOING THE BEST YOU CAN...
LADILADI
...MAYBE THAT'S THE TRICK.
I TRY. SOMETIMES I EVEN FEEL LIKE IT ALL MAKES SENSE. EVERYTHING JUST FALLS INTO PLACE.
EVERY BREATH I TAKE, EVERY THOUGHT: IT'S ALL CLEAR. CLEAR IN A WAY YOU CAN'T PUT INTO WORDS.
IT'S A FLEETING SENSATION. IT DISAPPEARS THE SECOND I TRY TO EXPLAIN IT. BUT WHEN IT'S THERE, I KNOW...
THAT EVERYTHING I DO...
...I DO FOR THE SAKE OF POTOK POWER.

COLORS : ISABELLE BUSSCHAËRT

FIN

APRIL 2001.

AFTERWORD

By Claude Ecken

Dupuy and Berberian probably first met Monsieur Jean in 1991 at a gallery opening or a cocktail party in Paris, or possibly at a soirée organized by a mutual friend, Clement, who worked in advertising. In fact, a party at Clement's is the most likely scenario, seeing as the two authors had always sought to express their visual talent on any medium possible, from the book to the canvas, from posters to newspaper illustrations, following the footsteps of artists they admired, notably Loustal and Tardi, and of many of their peers, such as François Avril, Philippe Petit-Roulet, and Jean-Claude Götting, to whom the first volume of *Monsieur Jean* is dedicated.

However, don't be fooled into thinking that these collaborators are any more enamored of high society than their principal character is. What interests them is the man *behind* the writer — probably because Monsieur Jean reflects their preoccupations as comic book creators, allowing them to muse on, and perhaps even analyze, their own lives through their characters.

They broach their topics lightheartedly because that's the only way they can. Both have always shared the belief that becoming a professional artist means living with certain constraints that limit the artist's capacity for spontaneity and sincerity, which in turn destroys the desire to create. And yet, enjoyment is the most fundamental reason for creation. That's why they left the French humor magazine *Fluide Glacial* — because the publishing schedule required them to produce work nonstop, something incompatible with their own artistic vision. That's also why *Monsieur Jean*'s publication has been so intermittent, with almost four years between Volumes 3 and 4. For Dupuy and Berberian, it's not about striking while the iron's hot, but rather, not serving the dish until everything is ready. That would also explain the series' high quality.

A Love Affair with the Everyday Life

Monsieur Jean is an accomplished author himself. From the very first pages, we know that he has published a successful novel, *The Ebony Table*, which has gotten him media coverage, but we know nothing about the plot, other than that the action takes place in Leningrad. He has found himself under the glare of fame's spotlight and a social position that we tend to associate with fabulous celebrity lifestyles. As weary of this association as he is annoyed at its utter disconnect from reality, Monsieur Jean doesn't hesitate to correct fellow conversationalists about it when they become unbearable. He learns quickly not to be too invested in his interactions with the press or the public, and to put his ego aside, once he figures out that paying too much attention to negative reviews could push him to bitterness and resentment.

But aside from that, this series isn't really about literature. True, in *Love and the Concierge*, Monsieur Jean is hired to improve a screenplay for a film that got off to a rocky start, and in *Insomnia*, he translates Somerset Maugham's short stories — or at least pretends to. But to dig any deeper into this theme would let loose a torrent of subtleties only accessible to people in the business, whereas depictions of procrastination, in the form of a distracting quest to find a misplaced CD in a collection, speak to everyone. The emphasis is less upon the author's specific actions and more upon the everyday framework surrounding them. We don't even learn about Jean's struggles with writer's block penning his follow-up novel until Volume 4. Above all, the narrative has ordinary life at its center: the everyday pleasure, misery, joy, and disappointment that everyone experiences. *Monsieur Jean*'s personality is depicted broadly enough to allow every reader to identify with him. He doesn't have a last name, and his first name is one of the most common in France. His life story is limited to famous settings and common places. He is middle-class, leaning perhaps towards slight refinement in his taste in painting, music, literature, and film. He has his group of friends, who we sometimes see at parties, the solid core composed of Felix, Clement, and Jacques. His indifferent friendliness makes him likeable; his elegant nonchalance charms and seduces. He's quick to fall for a pretty face, but never for more than a night. Monsieur Jean may live in Paris, but his creators see him more as a city dweller of any large metropolis, rather than a true Parisian, and they let us know that right away. He is a regular at all the nondescript places that you could find a version of in any other city: train stations, parks and bridges, plazas, bistros, corner stores, the local bookstore, the record store, the junk shop, and even the grocery store — after all, everyone needs to eat. He is thus depicted in all aspects as an ordinary man, comfortable with himself and his environment.

The misadventures in his life are the kind that could happen to anyone: babysitting a cat, helping a friend move. Only his particular and discerning gaze, observing everything without judgment, sets him apart. We often see him with his eyes half-closed, a smile on his lips, unsure of whether to be charmed by the predictability of whomever he is interacting with or weary of it. "I never could hide anything from you..." exclaims an ex-girlfriend Jean has run into, after he guesses that she's expecting a baby.

However, while Monsieur Jean does indeed standout and may be easy to get along with, he keeps his distance. At his core, he is solitary. He only likes company when he's in the mood to tolerate it; otherwise, it disturbs his peace of mind. Regardless, his friends frequently disrupt his tranquility. He's constantly interrupted by the telephone while he's in the bath, a comic device that seems emblematic of his situation, while being a simultaneous nod to *Tintin* creator Hergé, whose *ligne claire* style influenced both of the authors. But while irascible Captain Haddock broadcasts his contrariness to the world, Monsieur Jean, the perfect gentleman, conceals his annoyance behind outward indifference, creating dissonance between perception and reality. In fact, in the first few volumes, this kind of situation is the primary comedic device, like when Jean and his girlfriend are on the verge of breaking up and they get catcalled on the street — their actual situation totally incongruous with its outward perception. Jean's vivid imagination, projecting his fantasy onto the outside world, often brings him at odds with other people, places, and things: "What am I doing here?" he constantly asks himself, as he wanders through a museum, or waits for a friend who stood him up — situations he can't ever seem to escape.

Everything is laid out right at the start, with remarkable brevity. The first volume's title, *Love and the Concierge*, uses the juxtaposition of an inaccessible ideal and a trivial, conflict-laden reality to illustrate the interplay of oppositions that structure the narrative.

Towards Maturity

Dupuy and Berberian demonstrate the importance, to them, that the world of *Monsieur Jean* takes place in real time by dealing with Jean's anxiety as he approaches his thirties in Volume 2. This is a departure from the classic comic book, whose timeless, immortal hero can only develop within a fixed narrative timeframe. Showing the passage of time isn't limited to physically aging the characters with additional facial wrinkles, and then having them continue to have the same types of adventures. The points of reference established at the beginning of the series must evolve, too. Monsieur Jean cannot be a dilettante forever, savoring the carelessness of youth and casting an affectionately ironic glance upon the world. This newfound consciousness is manifested by more "mature" feelings or concerns, such as insomnia and attacks of nostalgia. His "early life crisis" doesn't push him to change, just to reassure himself. He even tests out his seduction skills during a stay in Portugal, which, in spite of everything, simply ends up putting things into perspective for him. Jean knows intuitively that he needs to get to a point where he can take stock of his youthful losses, memories, baggage, and inactivity, even with his gift for wasting all the time he's set aside to work.

His creators highlight this evolution with a more stylized drawing style, a visual innovation that sets it apart from the canon of Franco-Belgian comics. In Volume 3, *Women and Children First*, the crisis comes to a head. After getting dumped, Monsieur Jean flips through an album with sentimental photos of his life while he's listening to his friends talk about their relationship woes: Jacques and Veronique have been at odds since their twins were born; Felix and Marlene are separating, but he's keeping custody of Eugene, a child from a previous relationship. These situations allow the reader to understand Jean's fear of commitment: his refusal to be bothered, and thus his refusal to pursue a relationship, because one plus one sometimes equals three. Monsieur Jean imagines himself as a fortress besieged by women firing babies over his walls. He fears change, even though, as his circumstances force him to discover, he's pretty good with kids. However, his fears and refusal remain strong: in a dream sequence in Volume 5, Jean is in such an outrageous state of denial as he accompanies Cathy to the maternity ward that he tells the taxi driver that she has been poisoned. Later in the same volume he remarks that he doesn't have a moment to himself, and Cathy responds that that's true for everyone, reminding us in passing of one of his fundamental qualities: "The city bores you, the people bore you, my friends bore you..." The disengagement and independent spirit that were his charms have become his faults.

In spite of the humor, the series is frequently realistic and sincere. The sex scenes ring true, whether they are passionate, like with Manureva, or affectionate and funny, with Cathy. The carnal act isn't primitive, but full of personality. *Monsieur Jean* no longer naively falls in love with a pretty face: it's quickly apparent that his stormy relationship with Pascale, who, like him, absolutely refuses to have children, quickly reaches an impasse in spite of all the compromises they've made to stay together. The authors skillfully juggle the pieces of the puzzle, waiting patiently to put them together, like a painting in a Japanese restaurant whose motifs can be read just as well collectively or independently of each other. This is how the whole series works: gags are strung together into narratives, collected into a volume and given a spine. The authors can only organize these elements after having processed the independent existence of each episode, which could also serve to explain their relatively slow pace of production.

Correspondence and Corresponding

Throughout the narrative, the authors continually develop the comedic effect of correspondence and repetition, adding a deeper level of analysis to the series. The density created by these intensely layered connections brings the series together as a unified whole. Underneath the light humor of banal, everyday anecdotes, the series delves deeply into fundamental themes of the universal quest for happiness, giving it a profound sense of unity.

Just like a symphony, where the leitmotif is repeated with subtle variations, the other characters' arcs intersect and respond to Monsieur Jean's own fears, which in turn correspond with the lessons the authors have learned throughout their own lives.

Jean's commitment crisis, in Volumes 2 and 3, is a near-identical reflection of the authors'. At first glance, it could seem that no two people could be less alike. Philippe Dupuy, born in 1960 in Normandy, was an avid reader of the classic French kids magazine, *Le Journal de Mickey*, then moved directly to the weekly — and more grown-up — publication *Pilote*, which, in the 1960s and '70s, was part of the wave of works that eventually gave birth to modern French comics. He had the opportunity to be published early, before going back to making fanzines. Quite unlike Charles Berberian, who was born in Baghdad in 1959, and grew up in Lebanon, raised on superhero comics and *Tintin*. But he was also interested in graphic artists and poster designers like Tomi Ungerer and Ralph Steadman. Both Dupuy and Berberian were drawn to 1920s illustrators like Gus Bofa, Ralph Barton, Chas Laborde, Jen Bruller (aka Verors), and the elegant *Atomic style* linework of the new French comics scene, represented by Yves Chaland, Serge Clerc, and others, the successors of Hergé's *ligne claire*. And both wrote as well as drew, the scriptwriter indistinguishable from the artist. The duo is truly bicephalous. Their pride in their own output led them to create a single entity, even at risk of the disappearance of their individual identities. A casual mention of the Portuguese writer Pessoa during a stay in Lisbon isn't insignificant: this author, practically unknown during his lifetime, has been overshadowed by the 62 fictional identities that he used as pseudonyms in his writing. Volume 3's main conflict occurs when Felix stays at Jean's place, their duality reinforced when Felix gives his opinion on the décor, or when each of them takes turns taking care of Eugene. The necessity of knowing who's who and who does what led to the creation of *Maybe Later* (Drawn & Quarterly, 2006), a work of docu-fiction detailing the risks and misadventures that occur during the production of their opus, a mix of artistic activity and private life.

Maybe Later was therapeutic for the authors, but its emphasis on personal and epistolary writing is also of interest to the reader: when you speak about yourself, you end up speaking *to* yourself. One anecdote — Monsieur Jean searching for a letter that he wrote to his 30-year-old self when he was a child — actually happened to Berberian, who was himself in turn inspired by the legendary illustrator Mœbius. We never find out what's in the letter, just as we never learn the content of Jean's novels. The authors only remember that they wanted to make *The Ebony Table* a story told through letters, found in the false bottom of a dresser drawer, that are so fascinating that they inspire the person who discovered them to track down their author in Saint Petersburg.

Is this another facet of the story of the long-lost letter that demands, in a fit of nostalgia, the rediscovery of the author as an adolescent? From this point forward, we understand that Dupuy and Berberian were responsive to the works of Pessoa, discovered in a trunk, and attempted to integrate these literary anecdotes into their own narrative-in-progress.

A Catalogue of Nostalgia

All of the elements of one man's life are collected throughout these volumes, like a stack of boxes or journals full of anecdotes. Since these books are full of everyday events, readers can easily identifying with the characters, and personal recognition is accentuated by the fact that there are no references to specific current events, other than a headline from the newspaper *Libération* that speaks for itself: "Debts, Layoffs, Pollution, Disaster." History, after all, is irrelevant to real life.

But these volumes are an incredible catalogue of the minutiae of everyday life: microwaves; CD players striking vinyl a death blow; debit cards; cheap, compact, and easy to park city-made cars; cordless telephones, then cell phones; personal computers; camcorders... The VCR is the ultimate third-age accessory, even though kids don't even lift their eyes from their Game Boy. The distinctive signifiers of the period fill each panel: Freddie Mercury, fitness clubs, TV shopping, and new additions to the language. Modifications made to the urban environment are similarly chronicled: the Postal Service's new logo and overnight shipping services, protective walls built around schools, entry codes and apartment mailboxes making apartment concierges obsolete. Even the "new" homeless, who sell magazines on the street, have become incorporated into the landscape.

The tone becomes a bit more serious as the evolving society becomes less idyllic, filled with the professional, domestic, and existential difficulties we all encounter when we become adults. But each character's progression through life allows his convictions to be more clearly affirmed, even Felix, who ultimately prefers sincere feelings to a dishonorable legacy.

Visual innovation is at the forefront. Paintbrushes replace pens, lines become thinner and purer without losing any of their force or expressiveness, and artistic influences, namely the audacity of Fauvism, fill the final two albums. In the striking depictions of New York in the last volume, Matisse's art flies out from its frames to fill the page with colored rectangles. Everything comes full circle.

A series anchored so precisely in its own time does not age. As it loses modernity, it gains nostalgia, and its universality is never more apparent. From one decade to another, stories have a deeper meaning that doesn't change, as we can see from evocations of the past that came before: best exemplified by the appearance of French 1950s stand-up comic star Fernand Raynaud, whose humor is, at its core, not that different from Dupuy and Berberian's. He talks, essentially, about progress and social problems, all while hammering home his message of joy through simplicity: *Hap-py!* — as Felix passionately proclaims — shows us that everything has moved on, but nothing has changed.

Nostalgic types from the generations in question thank *Monsieur Jean* for being such a faithful mirror to them, but the universality of the character continues to attract an audience delighted to mature and age along with him.

We are all Monsieur Jean, learning, halfway between tears and laughter, how to move forward along the paths of our own existence in the best way possible. And it's certainly quite a trick to have fun while learning about the pursuit of happiness.

—May 2014

Born in 1954 in Alsace, France, Claude Ecken is a prolific and award-winning science fiction and crime novelist. He founded the Aix-en-Provence Comic Festival in 1981 and curated the National Convention of Science Fiction in Lodéve, in 1999. He has been a film critic for over 30 years at *L'Ecran Fantastique* magazine. He is also the writer of several comic book works, including the *Le Diable au Port* series with Benoit Lacou, as well as a frequent contributor to the *Cahiers de la BD* (the French literary comics journal published by French publishing house Glénat). He won the Masterton prize in 2013, and his recent children's novel, *Double ennemi*, was selected for 2014's Grand Prix de l'Imaginaire, one of France's biggest literary fiction awards.